Gone in Love Series

Gone Before

Chapter One

Audrey

SENIOR YEAR IS JUST a few weeks away. After that...freedom. No more being stuck in this small town. I'll move closer to Stella and we'll live our best lives. Well, as long as I have Justin with me, I will be. I know it's a long shot that we'll last considering we're high school sweethearts, but I have faith. What we have is so much more than puppy love. We have been each other's first everything. I'd like this to be our first adventure as well. Only one more year to make it through.

"Audrey, are you ready to go?" Stella is standing outside my bedroom door wearing a sundress and carrying a bag.

"Yeah, I guess." It's the one time of year we get together with our classmates and go to the local swimming area. It's part of the lake, but it's hidden away from the public. The only ones who know about it are the locals, and Stella.

She's practically grown up here during the summers and breaks. Mine and Tiffany's parents insisted on her coming here instead of the other way around. Maybe they feel like my uncle did Stella a disservice by not keeping her close to family, I don't know. They grew up here and he left as soon as he could. Not that I blame him. This town is stifling on the best of days. When drama pops up, it's downright suffocating.

"You don't sound too excited." She doesn't know what it's like to be here nonstop. To be stuck around the same people you've known since you were in diapers and see them every single day.

"That's because she doesn't want to go," Tiffany pipes up from behind Stella. When did she even get here? I didn't hear the front door open. Or close for that matter.

Stella tilts her head to the side as if she's a confused puppy. "Why not?"

I don't know if I can explain it. At least, not in a way that would make her understand. She went to a school where most of the people didn't even live in the same neighborhood. She didn't know her entire graduating class. She had her group of friends and didn't have to worry about someone knowing all of her business. Well, unless someone started spreading rumors, of course. "We don't have the same school experience here that you had in Austin."

"What's that supposed to mean?" She crosses her arms over her chest and scowls.

"That didn't come out right," I shake my head. "I've seen almost every single one of my classmates every day since we were in pre-k." When her expression doesn't change, I continue. "Think about it, Stella. Would you want to hang out with people you've known your entire life? All the time?"

"I've known both of you my entire life, and I happen to love hanging out with you." She points at both Tiffany and I to drive the point home. "I don't get what the issue is."

Tiffany sighs and passes by Stella to sit on my bed. "That's not exactly the same thing, though." She scoots back until she can lie down on my pillows. She makes herself entirely too comfortable on my bed, and it's super annoying how she treats my bedroom like her own. "We actually like you. A lot of the people in Audrey's class aren't all that great. Some even tease her."

"So...whose ass do I need to kick?" Stella pounds her fist against palm. "Nobody picks on my cousin but me."

"Calm down," Tiffany laughs. "She defends herself."

"I'm perfectly capable of taking care of myself," I murmur.

"Yep," Tiff nods. "And when she doesn't, Justin has zero issues taking care of it for her."

That catches Stella's attention. "Where is he, anyway? I figured we'd all ride over together."

I shrug, "I don't know. He said something about having to work this morning and he'd meet us over there." I wish he wasn't working so we could go together. It would make things so much easier and I wouldn't have to answer all the questions that are thrown at me about Stella. I could let Tiffany handle it and go on about my way. Hell, I'm not sure why these people even bother asking about her. She's here literally every summer and they should know her well enough by now. She would never give any of these guys the time of day either. Well, not long term anyway.

"Audrey," Stella is snapping her fingers. Dang it, I was in my own head again. I need to stop doing that when she's around. She begins to worry, and that's not why she's here.

"Yeah?"

"Do you know what time he gets off? We can hang around until then." This is what I love about my cousin. She's confident and assertive, but she's always able to tell when me and Tiff are feeling off. She really is the best, even when she annoys the hell out of me.

"It's fine," I sigh. "I know y'all are ready." I grab my bag with the towel and sunscreen in it and head toward the door. I can't forget it because without sunscreen Tiff will be as red as a tomato at the end of the day. "But…we can grab some food on the way over there. I'm starving."

"That might be the best, and most important thing, you've said in the last five minutes." Tiffany hops off my bed and rushes past me. "Shotgun," she shouts from down the hallway.

"Seriously." Glancing at Stella, I roll my eyes. "We should be mean and make her drive."

"Oh God no," Stella gasps in mock horror. "I know for a fact you've ridden with her. I wouldn't let my worst enemy in the car with her behind the wheel."

"Yeah," I nod. "You have a point. I'm not even sure how she passed driver's ed."

"Your guess is as good as mine." She motions toward the hallway. "I can ride in the backseat if you want to drive."

"Thanks." I pass her by and head in the same direction as Tiffany. It's a good thing she offered. Even though I've grown up on these roads, carsickness is my weakness. I'm just hoping Justin gets off earlier than he expects. I can't avoid the assholes of our school while also keeping a watchful eye on Tiff.

Chapter Two

Justin

HAVING to work when I was supposed to be off is bullshit. The bag of feed I toss on the shelf hits with a thunk. I swear my boss has favorites, and I'm clearly not it. The person who was supposed to be working is already at the swimming hole, no doubt having the time of their life. It doesn't help that he's related to the store owner. I always draw the short straw when others want to go live their best life. It makes getting out of this podunk town so much more appealing. I'm leaving and never coming back.

My name blares through the intercom system and I groan. Another person needs help loading whatever it is they bought. I would like to know how the hell they get it unloaded. If they have someone at home to get it out, why can't they bring that person to the store with them? The only reason I even have this shitty job is so I can have money to call my own. Something my dad can't dictate how I spend.

I place the bag of feed, back on the pallet, and head toward the front counter with my orders. I round the corner and want to head right back to where I was. "Mrs. Murphy," I fake a smile. "How are you today?"

"Oh, Justin," she waves her hand at me. "I'm just fine." Mrs. Murphy is a little old lady that runs the only animal rescue in town. She comes in at least once a week to pick up a massive amount of food for the animals she takes. I've always wondered how she pays for it all, but my dad says it's none of my business. The only thing he will say is that she's well off, especially after her husband passed. I also know for a fact that she has a perfectly healthy grandson that can help her with all the bags, but I'm guessing he's also at the swimming hole.

"That's good," I nod. "The usual amount of food?" Is it bad that I know what she gets every week? Maybe, but I'm somehow always the one that has to help her when she comes in. I turn toward the warehouse where she'll pull up in her truck.

"Yes, sir," she grins. "But I also need a couple of salt blocks."

That stops me in my tracks. "Okay," I draw out.

"We got a couple of cows that were found on one of the back roads. I had Andy help me get them loaded up and moved to the farm before they got hurt, or hurt anyone else."

"That's smart." I start back on my way to the warehouse, but call over my shoulder. "If you have any pictures, or a description, I'll put some flyers by the register asking if anyone is missing some cattle."

"You are such a sweetheart, Justin."

Yeah right. I roll my eyes and keep on going. I only have like an hour left until I get to leave. I will not be talked into working longer than I'm supposed to. Audrey is waiting for me, and I know she can't stand most of the people that will be there. The time needs to pass by quickly. My girl is waiting on me and there's no telling what craziness Tiffany is getting into.

I almost got roped into working longer, but I punched out before the boss could ask. Even though, I said I wouldn't, I'm a people pleaser, and would have done it anyway. I pull up to the swimming hole and try to find a place to park. I don't know how some of my classmates plan on getting out of here. So many cars are blocked in and there's no way in hell they can drive off without banging up another vehicle. I drive a little further until I'm in an area with no cars. I'm not a dumbass, and I won't have to ask anyone to move their car so I can leave.

Now I just need to find Audrey and her cousins. If she was on her own, she'd be easy to spot because she'd be on the fringes of the group. Not willing to let herself get too close to anyone. With Tiffany and Stella with her, there's no telling where she'll be. I pass by small groups of people, and they call out my name in acknowledgement. While I'm not one of the popular kids, I'm on decent terms with almost everyone. Except those assholes that like to pick on Audrey because she likes things a certain way and has backup plans for her backup plans. She's going to be a force to reckon with when we go to college.

"Tiffany, you're going to get hurt," I hear Audrey's voice just as I reach the edge of the lake. I'm not sure I want to keep going forward to see what shenanigans her cousin is up to. Tiffany laughs in response and I'm not sure I want to know what shenanigans she's getting into.

I push through the rest of the crowd and Audrey is glaring at her cousin with her hands on her hips, a spitting image of her mom when she's pissed. Tiffany is swaying back and forth on the tire swing, prepared to jump. It's too bad she's not out far enough to keep from hitting her ass on the floor of the lake. The rest of our classmates are cheering her on, and this isn't going to end well. Moving toward Audrey, I wrap my arms around her waist. "You know she's not going to listen to you, right?"

"You're finally here," she leans into my chest. "Maybe you can talk some sense into her."

A chuckle rumbles through my chest. "If you think that, I'm not sure you know your cousin all that well." It's hot as hell, but I'm not letting her go. I've waited all day to have her in my arms.

She shrugs and sighs. "I think I'll let Stella deal with her. I can't babysit her all the time. She's going to have to learn how to survive without me when we head off to college."

That seems so close and so far away at the same time. "So, you want to get away from everyone? We can go to the other side of the lake. And be alone for a bit."

She looks around at all the people around us and pulls herself from my hold. Grabbing my hand, she pulls me away from everyone else. "Stella and Tiff will figure out I'm not over here...eventually. I just want to get away from here."

Who am I to argue with her? I'll follow her anywhere.

Chapter Three

Audrey

We walk along the shore until the shouts and music from our classmates fade away. I probably should have stayed to make sure Tiffany isn't out of control, but she'll have to learn to handle herself after I graduate. Besides, I left her in Stella's capable hands. She'll get a taste of what I deal with all the time when she's not visiting us. Though, I'm sure those visits will become fewer and fewer since she's starting college soon. At least, until I move that direction. Both Justin and I plan on going to Hilltown University as fast as we can.

"You're awfully quiet," Justin bumps into me, breaking me from my thoughts.

"Sorry," I look up at him and get an eye full of sunshine. "Just wondering if leaving Tiffany was a wise decision."

He chuckles and shakes his head. "She's going to have to learn one day. She won't always have your conscience around to keep her out of trouble. I'm sure she'll be fine. It's not like anyone will do anything, or mess with her. She may be your younger cousin, but she's mean as hell when push comes to shove."

He would know. She's popped off at him on more than one occasion when he's done something to piss her off. "You're right." I lean into him despite it being hotter than hell. We've been dating for what seems like forever and he's my comfortable space when everything seems too much. "Do you think it'll be weird when we go off to college and we'll be around people we haven't known since they were in diapers?"

"Sure," he says and pulls us to a stop. "Even though the college isn't technically in a huge city, it's still a lot of people we don't know. I mean our town is the size of an ant hill. Anywhere would be an adventure compared to this. I did hear some whispers that some of our classmates are going there, too."

A shudder works its way through me. "I hope they are in completely different classes than me. I'm trying to escape this place. Not run straight back to the people who think I'm some mousy girl with no ambitions, or the ability to take care of myself."

Justin grabs my shoulders and turns me until I'm facing him. "Number one, you can take care of yourself just fine. Who cares if you don't like to party and get wasted like the rest of the people here. That doesn't make you mousy. It makes you smart. You don't get caught up in any of the gossip that happens in town. None of that is a bad thing. It means you're strong in your convictions, and if any of our classmates were smart, they'd respect that about you."

Wow. That wasn't what I was expecting. I never realized he felt that strongly about how others perceive me. "Do you like to do all the dumb things everyone else does?" We've always been together since we've been old enough to go to parties. I never thought to ask him before. Maybe I've been holding him back from all these things he's wanted to do and experience while we're in high school.

"I'm here with you, aren't I?" He responds as soon as the question is out of my mouth.

"True," I sit down on the almost muddy bank and put my feet in the water with my flipflops still on. "But that doesn't really answer the question."

"No, I don't like doing all that stuff." He takes his shoes off, tosses them aside, and sits down next to me. "That's one of the things that I love about you. You don't need all the drama that so many of the girls in our town crave. Everything isn't about you, and I love being where you are. I love you."

This boy. Even when I'm second guessing myself and worried about everyone else, he has a way of easing my mind. He still gives me butterflies even after these past few years we've been together. I feel like the luckiest girl in town knowing I have him in my corner. Knowing he has my back no matter what my mind tells me at times. "I love you, too."

He pulls me toward him and I try to pull away because I'm hot and sweaty. It's gross, but he's not having any of that. He only holds me tighter. "We're both gross," he mimics my thoughts. "Might as well be gross together." I look up at him and he's wearing his usual smirk when he thinks he's being funny.

"I guess," I try to pull away again, but it's half-hearted. The only place I ever want to be is wherever he is. It'll also be amazing when we're on our own and our parents aren't interfering. Mine love him and think he's the best thing since sliced bread. His dad isn't my biggest fan. I wish I knew what I did to make him hate me so much. Or at least that's what I tell myself. I don't think I really want to know. All it would do is drive a wedge between us.

"You better cheer up or I'll throw you in the lake."

"You wouldn't." In all actuality, I wouldn't put it past him.

"I guess you'll just have to wait and find out." He grabs my hand in his and puts them in his lap. "Have your parents said anything else about you going off to college?"

I'm about to answer him when I hear Tiffany's voice. "There you are," she screeches. "We've been looking all over for you."

I turn toward her, "I see you didn't hurt yourself."

"Yeah," Stella snorts. "She almost fell and it scared the shit out of her so she got down as fast as she could."

"I just didn't feel like jumping into the lake," Tiffany argues. It's not a good one, though.

Justin's shoulders sag when he realizes they are going to stay for a while. I know them being around all the time gets annoying, but he also knows when Stella is in town it's a package deal. He usually doesn't mind them, but when Tiffany has been drinking, she's grating. And we were in the middle of a conversation.

My cousins sit down next to me, and put their feet in the water. "What are y'all doing all the way out here away from the party?" Stella asks.

"You know I don't like large crowds of people." I lean back a little to bask in the sun. "We just wanted to get away for a bit."

"That makes sense," she nods in agreement. "Your classmates seem more unruly this year than they have in the past."

"It's their senior year," Tiffany laughs. "They are ready to get the hell out of here. I don't blame them at all. I'm sure my class will be the same way when we get to that level." She peers at both Justin and I, and squints her eyes. "But we can still have fun without them. How about a game of chicken?"

Justin looks at me and shrugs. "Let's do it. Y'all are going down." He knows as well as I do Tiff will keep nagging. Might as well get this over with. I have the power of sobriety on my side so this will be a quick game. Then I plan on spending some more quality alone time with my guy.

Chapter Four

Justin

"Best five out of seven?" It's the first question out of her mouth when she resurfaces from the water. You'd think she'd be tired after being taken down three times. "I can't let you and Audrey beat me. I'm queen at this game."

"Obviously not," Audrey snorts and slides off my shoulders, barely making a splash in the process. "If you were then we wouldn't be undefeated.

As much as it drives me crazy when her cousins are always around, I love seeing Audrey like this. Confident and unafraid to speak her mind. It's these glimpses that give me hope this will be the year she stops taking shit from some of our classmates and tells them off. I could keep speaking up on her behalf, but I know that bugs her, too. "Aren't y'all tired of being in the sun?" It should be setting in a couple of hours, and I don't really want to be out here when all these drunken idiots start leaving the lake.

"Oh crap," Audrey shrieks. "Tiffany, when is the last time you put sunscreen on? You're going to be hurting tomorrow."

"I'll be fine," she shrugs. "I don't burn as easily as I used to." She's looking at her shoulder to determine how sunburnt she is.

Stella laughs, "That's a load of shit. You are already getting red and you won't really be able to see how bad it is for a few hours."

"Maybe we should head out," Audrey points in the direction of the makeshift parking lot we've all created. "I'm pretty thirsty, anyway."

"You know what," Tiff nods in agreement. "That sounds like a great idea." She rushes out of the water and slips her coverup over her head. Not like it's much help now. That girl is going to be in a world of pain tomorrow if it doesn't hit her tonight.

The rest of us get out of the water and slip on our shoes. My tennis shoes are tight as I try to pull them over my wet feet. Next time I'll wear flip flops, but I don't like the way they feel. Especially when your feet are wet and the friction rubs your skin raw. At least it's a short walk to the car, and my extra pair of shoes.

"So," Stella breaks into the silence as we walk. "What's on the agenda for the rest of the day?"

I look to Audrey to see if she has plans for all of us. "What are you thinking? Bowling? Watching a movie?"

"Actually," she pauses and stares at the ground. "I was thinking y'all could take my car back and I could hang out with Justin for a bit." When she does look up, her eyes bounce around the scenery, doing everything to keep from looking at her cousins. "If that's okay with y'all?"

"Yeah, that's," Stella starts, but Tiffany is quick to cut her off. "But Audrey, Stella is only in town for a couple more days. You get to see Justin whenever you want for the most part."

"What if I promise to have her home early?" I try to calm down her outburst. "That will still leave plenty of time with y'all" I also plan on stopping to get ice cream, that will make sure Tiffany won't be too mad at me. I'm not sure about Stella, though. I've known her for a while, she's hard to read. "What do you say?"

"Fine," Tiffany stomps toward their car.

"Thanks Justin," Stella sighs. "I'll try to keep her in a good mood for a while."

"You're the best," Audrey rushes toward Stella and wraps her arms around her cousin. She digs in her still damp shorts picket and tosses keys at Stella. "If my parents ask where I'm at, tell them I'm with Justin."

Stella is pretty cool. She's a couple of years older than us, but you'd never be able to tell. She knows when to be serious and when to cut up. She'll definitely be someone awesome to have around when we head to Hilltown next year. For now, I need to figure out what exactly Audrey and I are going to do for the rest of the day.

"You realize we just went from one deserted area to another, right?" Audrey is sitting in the passenger seat digging through the fast-food bag for her curly fries and taco sauce. It's a weird combination, but I'm sure I do things she finds odd. I'd like to know how she even thought to try that combination.

"True," I nod, pulling down the makeshift dirt road by Mrs. Murphy's farm. "But here, we are alone." I waggle my eyebrows at her as I pull off the road and shift the car into park.

"Don't think you're getting car sex," she laughs. "That totally isn't happening. I'm not that type of person." Fluttering her eyelashes, she continues searching for the packets of taco sauce.

I gasp in mock surprise. "I, madame, am a gentleman." Turning the car off, I pop the trunk, open the door and head to the back of the car. I keep spare blankets and pillows back here for occasions such as these. I scoop them up in a bundle and bring them around to the hood of the car. Setting everything down, I try to straighten out the blanket without letting the pillows fall to the ground. I don't want to chance Audrey getting grass in her hair and her parents think something else happened.

"Justin, I already told you that isn't happening." She rolls her eyes and gets out of the car. I know she's giving me a hard time. The small smirk playing at the corner of her lips is all the proof I need. We've done this so many times before. The bag of food is still in her hand as she joins me at the front of the car. She's not letting that thing go no matter what happens. She sets the bag down and I help her get settled on the hood before I join her.

"Has anyone told you that you're a smartass lately?" She shakes her head in answer as she pulls a curly fry out of the bag and tosses it in her mouth. "Well, this is your reminder."

She slides her free hand into mine and we sit in silence, staring up at the stars. It's something we do when we want to get away from everything. She got the idea after watching a movie where two best friends sit outside an airport and talk about life while airplanes land. "Will you miss this when we go to college?"

"Miss what?" I look over at her and her eyes are still focused on the sky.

"Being able to see the stars without anything obstructing the view. Parking on a road like this and nobody thinking anything of it." She glances at me and scoots closer until her head is on my shoulder and her food is forgotten. "As much as I loathe living in this town, I think I'll miss these moments."

"We'll figure out a way to make it happen while we're at Hilltown." I pull my hand out of hers and wrap my arm around her shoulder. It may still be in the nineties, even though the sun has set, but I need to hold her close to me. "It may not be exactly the same, but we'll make due."

My phone buzzes in my pocket and vibrates against the hood of my car. There's only one person it can be, and I don't want to answer it. I don't want him to ruin our moment. It stops and there's silence for a whole ten seconds before it starts again.

Audrey winces at the noise. "I guess that's our cue to leave?" She pulls away from me and starts gathering the blankets in her arms.

While she rounds the car with the blankets, I shoot off a quick text letting my dad know I'll be home soon. This is the other thing I can't wait for. Not having to answer to him because I'll no longer be under his roof.

Chapter Five

Audrey

THE CAR IS silent aside from the road noise. The radio isn't even playing. Justin usually has some sort of music going, whether it's on the radio or the mixes I burned on CDs for him. The lack of…well, anything…tells me just how frustrated he is with this dad. I swear something crawled up his ass and died there. It's the only reason I can think of for why he hates me so much. I'm a very likeable person. Even though my classmates will tell you different, because I'm shy and don't deal with their level of insanity, I've never had a single adult despise me the way his dad does.

"Do you want to come in for a bit when you drop me off?" I reach across the console and place my hand in his. I know it's not much, but maybe it will calm him down some. "You can gather yourself before you have to go home and deal with your dad."

He gives my hand a squeeze, but his hand on the steering wheel is so tight his knuckles are turning white. "You know if I don't get home soon, he'll just lay into me more."

He's not wrong, but I hate that his dad is such a jerk. My parents can be strict, but it's nothing compared to his dad. Some days I'm surprised he still allows Justin to date me. It's like because he's had to raise Justin on his own, he doesn't want anyone else to be happy. Don't get me wrong, he's a decent dad, but overbearing. "Sidewalk drop off it is, then."

"Don't be upset." Another squeeze on my hand. Luckily his grip on the wheel has lessened. That's good. If he goes home as pissed as he was, it's sure to be another screaming match between them. And I won't be there to play referee. He may not like me, but he tries his best to not be an ass when I'm around.

"I'm not." I stare out the window. We pass by house after house until we get closer to mine. The only lights on are the living room and porch. My aunt and uncle's house, however, is lit up like a Christmas tree. Everyone must be over there. I breathe a sigh of relief. I'll get a few moments alone. Justin pulls up to my house and puts the car in park. "I guess I'll talk to you later."

My hand is on the handle. "Audrey, wait." He leans over the console and runs his fingers through my hair. He brings me closer to him, and his lips meet mine for the briefest moment. "We have one more year, then we are out of here."

Nodding my agreement, I open the car door. "Call me later. I love you."

"I love you, too." As soon as the door closes, he drives away. One year. That's all we have left to deal with his dad's control issues. Until then, we'll have to make the best of it.

I unlock the door and close it behind me. Leaning against the door, I sigh. This is not how I expected the night to end. Even with how crazy the lake party was in the beginning; I had gotten over it. Now, I have to sit with this frustration. Knowing that his father will do anything to make any time he spends with me miserable. It was never this bad when we first started dating, but it seems like the closer we get to adulthood the worse he gets. I mean, what the hell does he think is going to happen?

"Why didn't Justin stick around?" Tiffany's voice comes from the dark living room.

"Jesus, Tiff." I jump back, forgetting I'm already leaning against the door, and hit my head against it. "Why the hell are you sitting in the dark like some sort of creeper?"

There's a click before the lamp beside the sofa switches on. "Oh, did I scare you?" She asks as if she has zero clue that it is even a possibility.

Seriously? "Yes, you scared me. Why aren't you at your house?" I don't miss that she didn't answer my question. The only reason for that could be is that she's pissed at someone over there. My guess would be Stella. The both of them are overly competitive when it comes to game night.

She huffs and crosses her arms over her chest. "Mom told me to go somewhere and cool down. Apparently, I'm being a pain in the ass."

"What did you do?" I set my bag down and join her on the sofa. She's the baby in the family, and she's used to getting her way. When she doesn't, or doesn't win, she develops a pretty crappy attitude. I'm sure my aunt had a good reason for telling her to get herself under control.

Her cheeks are pink, but the evil grin is a sign that she regrets nothing. "I may have pulled Stella halfway across the table when we were playing spoons."

"That's it?" That's normal in our family. They've been doing it since we were kids, and honestly, we were more viscous then.

"I may have also pulled the chair out from under her when she was sitting down." She's still grinning. She's one of the most carefree and easy-going people I know, but when it comes to game nights…it's like she's possessed by some malevolent spirit. There's no in-between.

"So, you've basically been sent to time out." She nods. "We can watch a movie or something. I don't feel like going to game night."

"You know our parents will be mad if you don't make an appearance." She has a point, but right now I don't really care. I want to zone out and forget that Justin's dad hates me.

"They'll get over it." I get up and head to our DVD collection. "How about a cartoon? I could do with something that has nothing to do with real world problems."

"Like the reason Justin didn't stay to hang out, or walk you to the door?" She obviously didn't forget about that part.

"Yep." I grab a random movie and put it in the DVD player. "And it's the usual reason. The one person that manages to put my boyfriend in a foul mood."

"Ah." She rushes to the kitchen. "I'm making us some popcorn. Your night was significantly worse than mine."

Grabbing the blanket off the back of the sofa, I lie down and pull it over me. The opening credits are playing and the sound of tiny pops from the kitchen are the soundtrack to me falling asleep. I think I hear my phone ring, but I can't be sure I didn't imagine it. The sun must have gotten to me more than I thought because I cannot keep my eyes open.

Chapter Six

Justin

THERE ARE SO many other places I'd rather be than in my living room while Dad tells me all the ways I've disappointed him. I'm a straight A student, in the top ten of my class, and hold down a part time job. Compared to some people I go to school with, I happen to think I'm a huge fucking success. And the only person who has been there for me is Audrey. That's the real reason for this tongue lashing.

"Are you even listening to me, Son?" Dad's voice booms through the room. It's a wonder the neighbors can't hear him. If they can, I bet they're trying to guess what I've done to deserve this ire.

"Yes, Dad." My voice is devoid of all emotion. I could have been getting sloppy drunk with my classmates, acting like an ass, and he would have been fine with it. Why? Because I wouldn't have been with my longtime girlfriend. Tell me how that makes any kind of sense. If he gave me an actual reason besides the bullshit he's been spouting for the past year, it'd be different. I'd at least listen to what he has to say. But no, he acts like a toddler that hasn't gotten his way, and stomps his feet saying do what I want.

He's still talking and all I can think about is being at Audrey's house playing near deadly card games with her and her cousins. As annoying as it can be sharing my time with her, that would have been a walk in the park compared to this. "Damn it, Justin. I don't know why I even bother. It's not like you're going to listen to anything I have to say." That sounds like the scream fest is coming to an end. He's been going on for almost an hour. I honestly can't recall half of what he's said.

"I don't know why you do either." I spit out. I'm not usually one to talk back to him, but I'm getting tired of the same argument over and over. "You can't keep me away from Audrey." Though that's exactly what he did tonight by calling nonstop and basically forcing me to come home.

"You shouldn't be this serious with a girl at your age." He crosses his arms and glares down at me.

"Why, Dad?" I stand, forcing him to take a step back. "Give me one good reason and I'll stop spending all my free time with her."

"It's not healthy," he stammers. "And as long as you're under my roof, you'll do as I say."

"Maybe I won't be under your roof anymore." I set my shoulders back and stand at my full height, which is taller than my father. The idea has been brewing in the back of my mind for a while...since my birthday to be exact.

"You can't do that." A smug smile crosses his face. "You wouldn't make it a week. How exactly are you going to pay for anything?"

"I'm eighteen, Dad." His question isn't worth answering. He must have forgotten I have a damn job. I've worked at a fulltime capacity all summer. Aside from my insurance, gas, and phone bill, I don't have any other responsibilities. The extra money has been put away in case I need it. Right now, it sounds like I might.

"You're still my son." He's not going to let this go. It's time for me to go to my room before I say something, we both regret.

"Whatever...I'm going to bed." There's no use arguing with him any more tonight. He's not going to give me any valid reasons, and I'm not going to waste my breath. It's a losing battle no matter how you look at it, and it's not worth the energy and headache I feel coming on. I check my pocket for my phone and head down the hallway, half expecting him to call me back to the living room to be yelled at more.

I don't bother turning on the light when I get to my room. I wasn't lying when I said I was going to bed. The constant fighting with him over me dating Audrey is exhausting. My hopes of him dropping it one day are dwindling day by day. It seems it gets worse the closer I get to the school year. I'm not sure what he thinks is going to happen. It's not like I'm going to knock her up and ruin my future. We're careful when we have sex, and it's not like we've even done anything that many times. Both of us have big dreams of getting out of this shit hole town, and having a baby as teens is not part of that plan.

I'm halfway to my bed when I have a thought. I better close and lock my door. Otherwise, Dad may try to come in here and berate me more in another hour. He's done it before, and I have zero doubts he'll do it again. Especially after the moving out bombshell. I'm not saying it will happen for sure, but the option is there should I feel the need to get out of this house. It's times like these I wish he would have gotten remarried after my mom left. Hell, any kind of motherly influence would be nice. Maybe he wouldn't be such a controlling hardass if he was happy.

Pulling my phone out of my pocket, I lie down on my bed and call Audrey. If anyone can make this night better it's her. She has a way of talking me down after getting into it with Dad, and she's exactly what I need right now. Her phone rings a few times before rolling over to voicemail. She may not be able to hear it over whatever she's doing with her family. They are a boisterous bunch, but at least they have fun together. I'll try to call her one more time, and if she doesn't answer, I'll go to bed like I said I would.

The voicemail picks up again, and I leave a message this time. "Hey Audrey, I just wanted to hear your voice, but I guess you're busy. I hope you're kicking Tiffany's ass in whatever game y'all are playing. I have to open tomorrow so I'll come by when I get off work." There that doesn't sound too pathetic.

The cord to charge my phone is under the nightstand and I reach down to grab it before plugging it into my phone. I set it down on the very edge right next to my bed. Maybe she'll call me when she gets a chance. Or maybe she won't hear the message until tomorrow morning. Either way, it's way past time for me to call it a night. The boss likes for us to get to the store earlier than normal when we open and I have a feeling it's going to be a long day. Hopefully Dad chills out before I see him again. With my luck it's not likely to happen and he'll be up early to get on my ass about it, effectively ruining my day. I can't wait to get out of this town and away from him.

Chapter Seven

Audrey

THE SMELL of bacon pulls me out of my sleep and I stretch my body. My leg hits
something solid and I sit up, scanning the space around me. This isn't my bed
and Tiffany is curled up in a ball on the other side of the sofa. It takes me a few
moments, but I recall falling asleep before the movie even started last night.
Ugh, my body is going to be sore all day. This isn't the best place to sleep. It's
comfortable enough to lounge on while watching TV, but it sucks to sleep on.
It's even worse when there's another person taking up space.

Moving my head from left to right, I try to work out the tightness in my
neck. I stretch my legs again, out of habit, and end up kicking Tiffany. "Stop
Audrey," she mumbles in her sleep. The fact that she's still asleep is baffling.
She usually jumps right up at the smell of food. It doesn't matter what kind it
is, either. She is almost always hungry and usually beats everyone to the table.

I swing my legs over the edge of the sofa and there's a loud crunch when
my feet touch the floor. God, I hope it's not a junebug that found its way in
when my parents came in last night. It may be ridiculous, but I have an irrational fear of those things. I swear they dive bomb my hair and it takes forever
to get them out because of their stupid, sticky little legs. I don't even know
why they exist. They serve absolute zero purpose except to creep me out.
Luckily, when I look down, there is popcorn littering the floor. The bowl is
upside down on the floor in front of Tiffany. If I had to guess, she fell asleep
with it in her lap and knocked it off when she fell asleep. Leave it to her to
make such a huge mess when she's not even awake.

Bending down I scoop as much of it as I can into a bowl, but there are still kernels stuck in the carpet. I could be a jerk and pull out the vacuum. I can imagine the shock on Tiff's face when she wakes up with the loud noise right next to her head. It would serve her right for not going home or at least going to my bed. I know for a fact that she woke up at some point because the blanket that sits at the end of my bed is wrapped around her body. I'm almost certain she also ignored the mess she made knowing I would clean it up this morning. Yep, I'm doing it. Nothing can stop me and she'll get over it after she pouts for a bit about her sleep being interrupted.

My steps are quiet as I make my way from the living room to the kitchen. The laundry room is just on the other side and maybe I can sneak the vacuum without my mom noticing anything. I'm feet away from the laundry room when Mom's voice stops me in my tracks. "What are you doing?"

"Nothing." It comes out high pitched and squeaky. There's no way in hell she's going to believe me. She can tell when I'm lying a mile away.

"Don't you dare pester your cousin." It's like she's in my brain, and I'm not sure how I feel about it.

"Mom, I freaking stepped on popcorn." I cross my arms over my chest. "She didn't bother cleaning it up when she stole my blanket from my room. It would serve her right."

She points the tongs she's using to cook the bacon toward the table. "Sit. She can clean it up when she wakes up."

A part of me wants to defy her and do it anyway. The worst she would do is ground me, or lecture me to death about my cousins and I being forever bonded. How we shouldn't pick on each other. Blah, blah, blah, I've heard it all before and I don't really want to listen to it today after the night I had last night. "Fine." But I don't go straight to the table. I rush to the counter and swipe a couple of pieces of bacon faster than she attempt to swat at my hand. "But I'm eating these before I do."

She rolls her eyes and turns to flip the bacon. "Why didn't you come play games last night? We missed you. Maybe you could have kept that one," she points toward the living room, "under control."

"Please, Mom," it's my turn to roll my eyes. "You know there's no controlling her. She does whatever she feels like." I take a bite of the bacon and it's seriously the best way to wake up in the morning. "As for not playing games, Justin and I had to cut our date short last night."

"The usual reason?" I hate that she knows without me even saying a word. She has listened to me complain about Justin's dad on more than one occasion. She's given me advice when she can, but it doesn't always help. I can't force the man to like me.

"Yep." I take another bite. "Crap. He said he was going to call me last night but I fell asleep. I need to check my phone." I shove the rest of the bacon in my mouth and run to the living room. My phone is sitting on the coffee table, and I grab it looking for any sign that he called. There are two missed calls and a message. I listen to the message and my heart falls. Last night didn't go well for him at all.

My mom is still cooking bacon when I walk into the kitchen, but she must hear my footsteps. "Did he call?"

"Yeah, it went about as good as expected." Which means horrible if I know his dad as well as I think I do. He has to be at work in like thirty minutes. I wonder if I can beat him there with breakfast. It might at least make his day better. "Hey, Mom, can I steal some of the bacon?"

"You already did," she points at the crumbs on the table.

"I mean to take to Justin," I huff. She knows what I meant; she's just being difficult. "I'm also going to grab some donuts for him."

"I think that's a good idea." She's already heading toward the pantry to pull out a plastic baggie to hold the bacon. "Go get ready, and I'll have something ready for you."

It takes me less than ten minutes to brush my teeth and change my clothes. There's no time for a shower. It will have to wait until I get back. When I come back to the kitchen, my mom has a couple of bags on the counter. One holds more bacon than he has time to eat and three sausage biscuits. "Thanks, Mom. You're seriously the best."

"You're welcome," she shoos me away, "now hurry before he has to go into work. I'm sure he'll be happy to see you."

I wasn't lying when I said she's the best. Some of the girls at school gripe about how much they hate their mothers. I can't imagine feeling that way about mine. Even when she thinks I'm making a mistake; she lets me make it and learn from it. I always know she has my back no matter what happens in my life. Grabbing the keys, I rush out the door making sure to slam it as hard as I can. With any luck, Tiffany is now awake and Mom can deal with her.

Chapter Eight

Justin

I WAS RIGHT. He was sitting at the kitchen table when I went in there to grab some breakfast. He was poised, ready for an argument and I abandoned the search for food. There's no way in hell I'm going to give him the chance to pick up our argument again. I grab my keys off the hook and leave the house as soon as possible. I will not allow him to ruin my day. I'm going to go to work, do my job, and go see Audrey. That's all that's on my agenda today. And if he calls me while I'm at her house this evening…I'll put my phone on silent. Or turn it off.

My statement of moving out last night wasn't an idle threat. It's something I've thought about for a while. It's why I haven't really minded working these crazy hours over the summer. I'm saving up for that reason. But I don't want to do anything without talking to Audrey first.

I'm already sweating when I get in my car. It's going to be one of those days, and I hope like hell I'm not going to be in the warehouse all day. The plus side, it's likely to be peaceful. Not very many people my age willingly work the weekend hours. That's fine with me. I don't have time or energy to deal with stupid people. Case in point, my dad standing at the window as I back out of the driveway. Staying away from home as long as possible today is definitely my goal. Too bad Audrey's parents aren't cool enough to let me stay the night. I'd even sleep on the floor in the living room. Hell, I'd sleep in the driveway in my car if it meant not having to deal with my dad. I long for the relationships Audrey and Tiffany have with their parents. To be able to talk to

Dad about anything without him jumping down my throat would be a freaking miracle. One day I hope we can have that, but I don't know if it will ever happen.

It takes me less than ten minutes to get to work. My stomach growls as I pull into a parking spot. I should have stopped to get food. I had time, but my thoughts took over and I was in autopilot. Only eight hours until I get to see my girl. Only eight hours until she's my only focus. I want to make it special for her. I fire off a text to Tiffany to help me set something up. I'm not expecting a response any time soon. If I know her, she's still asleep, but I know she'll be willing to help.

My car door opens and I jump. Audrey's smiling face is in front of me holding two bags of food. "I freaking love you." It's the only thing I can say as my stomach growls again. I don't have to go inside for another ten minutes. "Get in."

She leans down and kisses me before running around to the other side of the car and slides into the passenger seat. "From the sound of your message it sounded like your night was hell, so I figured I'd do something to brighten up your day." How in the world did I find a girl who is genuinely good? And why can't anyone else see that past her shy personality?

"You being here did that. Food or no food." It's corny, I know, but it's also true. She's the bright spot in my day, always. She makes being around my dad bearable.

"Well, I'm happy I could do that." She opens one of the bags and hands me a sausage biscuit. "Mom made it this morning. I was going to bring you donuts, but you can see what she thought about that."

"I love your mom." The food is delicious and exactly what I needed.

"You better not love her more than me," she laughs. "She is pretty great, though." She grabs my free hand and slips her fingers between mine. "What time do you get off work today?"

"Four," I grimace around another bite. "I'm not even going home after I get off. I'm heading straight to your house."

"Things went that horribly?" She knows it did, but she's too sweet to say anything else.

"Yeah," I sigh. She hands me the bag of bacon. "I wish I understood what his problem is, but that's never going to happen. I did tell him I would move out if I had to."

"You did what?" She shrieks. "You can't move out."

"Why not?" Seriously, why does she think it's such a horrible idea. "I'm eighteen and can take care of myself. You can't tell me you wouldn't do the same thing if you were in my position."

"Maybe," she shrugs. "But it'll be hard keeping up an apartment, going to school, and working."

"I have money saved up." I still don't understand why she isn't on board with the idea. It's the perfect solution and it would provide us a place to hang out alone. A place for her to get away whenever she needs it.

"Yeah, but that should stay saved up. What if you need it when we leave for college?" She has a point. "I know Hilltown isn't in a huge city, but things are definitely more expensive there than they are here. Just think it over a little bit longer."

"Okay." She doesn't know I've been thinking about it for ages. It's fine though. It's not a decision to be made lightly. I glance at the clock on my radio, "oh shit. I need to go in before I'm late."

Before she gets out of the car, she pulls me closer and gives me a quick kiss. "I'll see you later, and don't make any hasty decisions."

"I won't." I kiss her this time. "I'll see you when I get off."

Without another word she's out of my car and heading toward her own. Even though she wasn't as excited about the prospect of me getting my own place as I thought she would be, her making the effort to make sure my day started out well speaks volumes.

"Where did Tiff and Stella go?" Audrey asks. She's leaning on my shoulder while we watch a movie. She somehow talked me into watching a cartoon movie. As much as I tried to protest it, I'm not to upset about it. There's something about watching movies from your childhood that transports you back to that time. That reminds you about the simpler times when you were carefree and enjoyed the little things.

"I don't know." I shrug and her head slips the tiniest bit. They've been gone longer than I anticipated. Hopefully they were able to get everything I needed. With all the bitching I do about splitting Audrey time with them, they pull through when I need them. They really do have our best interests at heart. And I secretly like having them around. It feels like a real family.

"Hopefully they're back soon. Mom will be done with dinner before they make it home at this rate."

"Why doesn't Tiffany ever eat at her house?" It's weird. She's always over here at dinner time.

Audrey snorts and laughs. "She does. Then she comes over here and eats again. I keep telling her it's going to catch up with her one day, but she doesn't listen." I can see it. Tiffany eats almost as much as I do.

My phone dings with a message, and since I'm with Audrey, there's only two people it could be. I glance over and see Tiffany's name on the screen. I'm just happy it's not my dad causing trouble again.

. . .

27

Tiffany: Ready

I don't respond. They have a plan to make themselves scarce. "Let's go watch the stars."

"Now?" She pulls her head back and scrunches her nose in confusion. "There are junebugs out there. You know they like to attack me the second I set foot out there."

"You'll be fine." I stand up and grab her hand, pulling her off the couch with me. I lead her toward the back door and she gasps as soon as I open it.

"What is all this?" Her free hand is covering her mouth and her eyes are glistening in the moonlight.

"A backyard date," I grin. "What else would it be?"

Tiffany and Stella made the backyard look amazing. Tiffany brought over this canopy net thing and they hung it from a branch on the tree. There's a table with a white cloth draped over it and two plates of spaghetti on opposite sides of the table. Christmas lights are wrapped around the tree and it's stunning. I'm going to have to buy the both of them something to show how much I appreciate their help.

"What about the dinner my mom is making?" She looks back toward the kitchen window while we make our way to our seats.

"She's taking it to your aunt's house. We have the backyard all to ourselves." I pull out one of the chairs and wait for her to sit down before I take my seat.

"Did you orchestrate this on your own?" She pulls a napkin into her lap and takes a drink of the lemonade already poured in a glass.

Tiffany and Stella are standing in the shadows on the side of the house. Both of them giving a thumbs up sign. "I had some help."

Audrey turns in the direction I'm looking. Her cousin's wave at her then run out of sight. "I can't believe you did all of this."

"It's the least I could do." Before we dig into our food, I take her hand in mine. "You brought me breakfast to make sure my day was great. You're constantly there for me even when my dad is being an ass. And you put things in perspective for me."

"I guess this means you aren't moving out of your house?" She raises an eyebrow and it's adorable. She tries to make it look intimidating, but there's nothing she could that would make her seem that way.

"No, I'm not." I sigh. It's the only thing I thought about all day. Even when I had to hear all the craziness our classmates got into last night. "You were right. It wouldn't be smart to move out. Not when we have a year left before leaving this town. And I wouldn't be able to do things like this for you if I had to pay rent."

She laughs and it's the best thing I've heard all day. "I'm glad you did the smart thing. I know your dad doesn't like me, but we'll get through it… together. Just like we've done everything else."

This girl never ceases to amaze me. She could have thrown an "I told you so" in my face, but she didn't. Dad will have to get over his misgivings. Audrey is it for me. I knew it right after we started dating. We only have to make through this year then we throw this small town behind us and begin living our lives without any complications. I can't wait for that day to come.

Gone Country

Chapter One

ALMOST JUMPING OUT MY SEAT, the shrill ring of my phone scares the hell out of me as I knock over my coffee right onto my keyboard. *Son of a bitch. I swear this shit only happens to me.* The IT department is not going to be happy with me in the morning.

My phone stops ringing for a whole two seconds before it starts again. I answer it without looking at the screen, "Hello?"

"Stella," Tiffany, my cousin, yells. "Come to the club with us tonight. It'll be fun." She sing-songs the last part because she knows it gets on my nerves.

"Sorry. I can't tonight. I need to get this report done for my boss."

"Don't tell me you're still at the office," Tiffany scolds. "I swear all you do is work. It's okay to take a break, you do know that, right?"

It's the same fight, over and over again. Both of my cousins think I work too much. But they don't understand. If I don't outperform everyone else, I won't get the promotion I've had my eye on for months.

"Yes," I huff, throwing paper towels over the liquid, hoping it will soak up because if not my keyboard's a goner. "I know that I can take a break, but he needs these reports first thing Monday morning."

"But it's Saturday," my cousin whines. "You should be out enjoying life, not holed up in your cubicle. You're only twenty-nine, come on *live a little.*"

"Tiff. I have a life. It may not be yours, but I have one." I scoop all the drenched paper towels into the trash can. "I'll be up and ready for brunch in the morning. You and Audrey will manage just fine without me tonight."

"I guess," she mutters, her voice no longer holding the excitement it had only moments ago. "We'll see you in the morning." She hangs up without telling me bye.

It's then that I know I've hurt her feelings. She always ends our calls with "bye, I love you." It started when we were kids and missing each other minutes after leaving the other's house. Audrey does it, too, just not as much. Audrey is the logical one of us, always thinking problems through. Tiffany, though…she's the free spirit and goes wherever the wind takes her.

We've always been thick as thieves. Summers at each other's houses, and always on the phone any chance we got. We knew at a very early age that we would always be more than cousins, we'd be best friends.

Hell, they moved to the same city I live in so we could be around each other. Others might see it as weird, but these two are my best friends. They are the ones who get me when most people don't. Well, that was true until I started this job. Now they say I work too hard and don't give myself any time off. If I didn't love what I do and have my eyes set on that coveted promotion, I could see where it might be a problem. However, I'm going after my goals and dream job. I only wish they could be more understanding. I think Audrey might, but not enough to keep from siding with Tiffany every time she brings it up.

There's no use dwelling on it. I need to finish up these reports, but I press the enter key on my sticky keyboard nothing happens. *Damn it, this is not good.* There's no way I'll finish compiling these if I can't get this to work. I write a quick note to the tech department to let them know about my keyboard. I'll have to drop it by there on my way out of the building and hope I don't trip over any of the five thousand wires they have everywhere. Seriously, they could clean it up some.

It looks like I'll be getting out of here early after all. But I'm not going to be clubbing with my cousins. I can access my work files from my laptop at home, thank God. Otherwise, I'd fail in my task. I can't let that happen.

Gathering my things and some paper from the printer, I make my way out of the office.

As I walk through my apartment door, the only thing that greets me is silence. I will admit that it's a little sad, but with all the hours I put in at the office, having a pet doesn't make sense. It wouldn't be fair for them to be cooped up in the house all day, and only getting my attention when I squeeze a bit of time away from my work duties.

Throwing my bag on the sofa, I glance at the end table. The normally green aloe vera plant is turning brown at the tips. *When did I last water this thing?* It's the only plant I've managed to keep alive. I've never claimed to have a green thumb, but I'm trying. If anything, my cousins will be happy to have a fresh supply of aloe to soothe their sunburns this summer.

Speaking of, I pull my phone out of my pocket, hoping to have a text from Tiffany. No such luck. She must still be angry with me. I don't blame her, not really. Yet, she knows how important this promotion is to me. I've been talking about it for months. I am always there to support her when she goes after everything she wants even when she gets burned from following ridiculous dreams. Right now, the only person I'm getting encouragement from is Audrey, and even she is giving me the cold shoulder. They'll get over it, though. Or, I hope they will. I can't imagine them being pissed at me for longer than a day.

My laptop sits on my coffee table, and I press the power button. While it's booting up, I tap on the Instagram app from my phone. I don't even have to scroll to find a picture of the girls at the bar. It's the first picture that pops up. I can barely see Audrey and Tiffany in the dark club, but the neon lights are illuminating their faces just enough for me to make out some of their features. Any other night, and I'd be in the picture with them. Instead, I'm at home, working.

A pang of jealousy rips through me, and I squash it down. I chose this. I could be out, dancing until my feet hurt, but this job is more important right now. This promotion is important. Once I get it, I'll be able to give myself a little more downtime. The need to bust my ass in order to prove my worth will not be a burden I have to bear for much longer. At least, that's what I keep telling myself, anyway. I double tap the image, and I hope they know I'm with them in spirit.

This stupid computer is still loading, so I change into a pair of sweatpants and a t-shirt. If I have to work, I'm going to be comfortable while doing it. It would be great if they'd allow me to work from home sometimes. I mean, I already do so much here that I never even get recognized, or compensated for. But, that's okay, once I finally get that promotion, I'll have a bit more freedom and can pass some minor things off to someone else. Though, that's not likely to happen too often. It's the same thing that's being done to me now, and it can be frustrating. Half the shit I do isn't even under my job description, but I keep doing it because I don't want to piss off my direct boss, Mr. Granger.

Settling on the sofa, I pull the laptop onto my legs and prop my feet on the coffee table. Having to redo everything that I've already done is going to suck, but I don't want them to have a reason to overlook me when they start announcing promotion candidates. That would be a punch in the gut after all the work, and time, I've put in.

The silence is overwhelming, so I turn on my TV for background noise. At the office silence is never an issue. There's always some sort of noise, whether it be someone walking past my desk, talking on the phone, or the whirring of the computers and copiers. Flipping through the channels, I settle on reruns of *Charmed* and turn the volume just loud enough to mask the stillness of my apartment. It's going to be a struggle not to watch.

Hours later my vision is blurring from shuffling between spreadsheets, and I desperately want to call it a night. The only thing pushing me forward is the desire to be offered what I want so much. I can see my dream job dangling on a string in front of me. There is nothing more important to me, except maybe my cousins, than earning that spot in the company.

Chapter Two

SOMETHING SLAMS INTO ME, and my eyes pop open. *What the actual fuck?*

Tiffany's face, framed by her long red hair, fills my view. "Good morning, Sunshine," she smirks.

"I'm really regretting giving you a key to my apartment," I groan. "Move so I can sit up."

Tiffany snorts, "I lost my copy months ago."

"What?" I shriek. She's just now telling me this?

She shrugs, and moves away from me. "We used Audrey's key to get in. She has it hidden in her purse to make sure she doesn't lose it."

I glare at her. "Maybe you should take a note from her book, and do the same."

I must have fallen asleep while working last night. Sitting up, I frantically search for my laptop. If that thing is broken from falling off my lap, I might as well quit my job and look for another one. "I moved it to the table," Audrey announces from the other side of the room. Thank God she had the good sense to move it before our youngest cousin attacked me.

"Thank you," I sigh. I'd lose it if something else happened to those reports. "Why are y'all here?" Glancing at the clock on the wall, the hands are at eight. It's way too early to be dealing with my cousins. "Brunch isn't for another few hours."

"Would you believe me if I said it's because we really missed you?" Tiffany fluttered her eyelashes. She's not fooling anyone with the sweet and innocent act.

"Nope," I shake my head. "Last night you were pissed at me for not going out. You are a grudge holder, and I know better. Why are you really here?"

"Whatever," she rolls her eyes and stomps toward the kitchen. My downstairs neighbors are not going to be happy about that.

Audrey walks across the room and sits on the sofa beside me, way too close for comfort. "She wanted to make sure you actually showed up for brunch, and this is the only way she could think of to do it."

I scoff. These two are too much, and are being absolutely ridiculous. "I have never missed our weekly brunch. And honestly, I'm a little hurt that y'all think so little of me." Audrey and Tiffany may be family, but they are also my best friends.

"Can you blame us?" Tiffany comes back into the living room with cups, orange juice, and the only bottle of vodka I have. "You have never turned down an offer to go out for a night on the town in the past. Hell, we've barely heard from you for the past few weeks. You are always shut away in your tiny office at work." She takes a second to nod toward my laptop. "You're even bringing work home."

I've tried to explain how important this position is to Tiffany but she doesn't get it. "The only reason I brought work home last night is because I spilled coffee all over my keyboard at the office when I answered your call." The sad thing is, I still have work to do since I fell asleep in the middle of it last night.

Audrey grabs the cups from Tiffany and sets them on the coffee table. "Why did you phrase it like that?" She eyes me while Tiffany fills the cups with orange juice. "How often are you bringing work home?"

Damn it. She would be the one to pick apart my sentences. I don't want to admit how often I bring stuff home. They would never stop giving me shit for it.

"From the silence," Tiffany says while adding more vodka than necessary to the cups. "She brings shit home a lot more often than she'd have us think." She picks up one of the cups and hands it to me. "Am I right?"

"Ugh," I groan. "Fine, you're right. Is that what you want to hear? I've been bringing a lot of work home." Tiffany opens her mouth to add her two cents, but I cut her off. I can't let more of her negativity fill the air. "I can't keep up with everything they are giving me, but I want to prove that I can handle anything, and that I'm ready for more responsibilities and deserve the promotion."

"Are they paying you for the hours you are working here?" Audrey purses her lips.

"Well," I draw the word out, stalling. "They don't know I've been doing it."

"That's the dumbest shit I've ever heard," Tiffany yells. "If you are busting your ass during your downtime, you should be compensated for it." She stands up and paces back and forth in front of my TV. "You work way to fucking much, Stella." She whirls around to face me, pointing her finger at me. "You can't enjoy life if you are cooped up in a building all day. How the hell are you going to meet someone, or fall in love? I mean, it's already affecting how much time you spend with us, your best friends." She stomps her foot. "No guy is going to put up with that, or want to come second to your job." She plops down on the floor. Her tantrum obviously over.

"Who said I was looking for a relationship?" I argue. "I'm focusing on me and getting my career underway. Men are the absolute last thing on my mind."

"Tiff has a point," Audrey says, barely above a whisper. "When is the last time you went on a date?"

"Does it matter?" I sigh. "When did this become the interrogate Stella show?"

"We only want to make sure you are doing what's best for you." Audrey grabs my hand and squeezes it. "We don't want you to lose yourself to this job and end up with regret."

"Fine," I relent. "I'll do my best to stop taking on more than I can handle." At least as far as they know. Nothing will stop me from achieving my goals. Pulling my hand from Audrey's, I stand up. "Now, let me get ready. I'm going to need food soon with the amount of vodka Tiffany put in those drinks."

After the strong drinks Tiffany poured us this morning, we Uber to brunch. There's no reason any of us need to drive. Traffic is busy for a Sunday morning and honking horns aren't helping the lingering bad moods. Most of the negative vibes are coming straight from Tiffany, still bitter about last night.

The driver pulls up to Trudy's, and puts the car in park. We step out into the warm and humid air. I really wish Fall or Winter would make their return. I'm over all this heat. One day I'll visit a place that experiences all four seasons, instead of this Texas heat. My cousins are ahead of me and walk into the restaurant without looking back to see if I am with them. I'm so caught up in my head, that I don't notice the door closing, and walk straight into it. When am I going to learn that I'm almost incapable of doing two things at once? However, it doesn't escape my notice that Tiffany didn't hold the door open for me. I hope karma is a real bitch, and they are out of her favorite drink.

"Thanks a lot, cuz," I smack her arm when I catch up to them.

"Oh, I'm sorry," she pitches her voice high. "I thought you were right behind me." She smirks before walking toward the hostess stand. She's such a liar. Her being mad is understandable, but she doesn't have to be a bitch about it.

The restaurant is packed, more than usual, and even though we are regulars, we have to wait for a table to open up. It's probably because we're here earlier than usual thanks to Tiffany and Audrey showing up at my apartment at the ass crack of dawn. This is one of the only places I'll actually wait for a table to open up. The food is that good. The drinks are too, and I weave around other patrons until I'm standing in front of the bar. I need more alcohol to deal with the animosity I'm feeling around my cousins. We've fought plenty of times, but this time feels different. As if it's hit Tiffany harder than usual. She has to be going through something she's not telling us about. The difference is, I won't pester her until she wants to beat me.

Since I'm a good cousin, and don't act like an ass when I'm frustrated, I save the first three seats that become available before ordering my drink. We are going to be here for a bit before our table is called, might as well get comfortable. I text both girls since they went to the restroom while I searched out seats for us.

Stella: Come to the bar. I've got us some seats until our table is ready.
Audrey: On our way
Tiffany: Did you also get us drinks? I'm thirsty.

Leave it to her to only think about herself. No thanks, or anything. Just a question in return. I don't respond to their texts. They will see as soon as they get over here. No matter how much they drive me crazy, I'm mature enough to make sure they are taken care of. I mean, I'm not a completely horrible person.

I'm eavesdropping on the conversation happening next to me when Audrey and Tiffany take their seats. The man and woman are arguing about not getting enough of the other's attention. That, right there, is one of the main reasons I'm glad to be single. There's no way in hell I'd be able to juggle both my job and a needy relationship.

Coming up behind me, I hear Tiffany's voice, "You are seriously the best," she reaches for her drink and wraps her lips around the straw of her Bloody Mary. I guess all is forgotten, at least for now. "Thank you, Stella." She puts her hand over mine and gives me a rueful smile. Finally, she's done being bitchy. I hate fighting with my two favorite people. It makes things weird, and while usually we're a handful when we're together…we can be assholes when we're fighting. Nobody likes being around us during those times.

"You're welcome," I answer. "A little pre-food drinking is better than waiting around, doing nothing. And it's the perfect pairing for chips and salsa."

They nod in agreement, grabbing a chip and dipping it in the salsa at the same time. If you didn't know better, you'd think they are sisters. Hell, everyone already does since they have names revolving around Audrey Hepburn. That's not the case though. Their moms are really close to each other and have had their names picked out since they thought about having children. They were obsessed with watching old Hepburn movies, and one chose Audrey while the other chose Tiffany after their favorite movie. Since Mom married into the family, she definitely wasn't prepared to follow the crowd on naming me after a Hepburn character. My aunts weren't thrilled about it, but they've become closer throughout the years. "How's everything going with y'all this week? With all the hours I'm working, I'm out of the loop. Give me all the details." Tiffany rolls her eyes at me. "You'd know that if you weren't at work all the time."

"Can we not go through this again?" The glass in my hand thuds against the bar top a little harsher than intended. It's just that I'm sick of going back to this every single time she opens her mouth. "We're here to have brunch and hang out. Not go over every single thing I'm doing that pisses you off."

"Fine," she shrugs. "Things have been going well. A new guy moved into the building over the week."

"He must be a looker if you've noticed him." As the free-spirit of the group, Tiffany goes wherever the wind blows her. She doesn't stick with relationships long and usually flutters off to the next guy whenever things start getting serious. I have to give her props, at least she's putting herself out there. She'll never be like me and practically married to her job.

"He's not really my type," she sighs. Yep, she's interested.

"I didn't realize you had a type," Audrey snorts.

"Shut up, asshole," she bumps our cousin's shoulder. "At least, I have the guts to talk to men. You sit over there all shy, and meek, expecting me to do all the work for you."

"I can't help it if I get nervous. Stupid shit comes out of my mouth every time I've attempted to approach someone." Audrey takes a sip of her drink and shrugs. "I can't help that I'm awkward."

I need to steer this conversation in another direction or else they are going to start fighting. "How's work going Audrey?"

"Same old, same old." She's been working at the same company for years, and nothing ever changes one way or the other. "Another year without a raise, but it's okay since nobody else is getting one either."

"Girl, I don't see how you are still working there." Breaking a chip in half, I dip it in the salsa. "You get more responsibilities added on, but don't get anything else in return."

"It's easy," she says. "I know what I'm doing, and I don't have to try too hard."

That is the lamest excuse I've ever heard. It fits her, though. She's always been the content one. I always want more, and Tiffany only wants to be able to do whatever she desires. We are completely different, and yet, somehow, we manage to click so well.

I'm dying to give her my opinion on the whole job thing when the buzzer on the bar for our table vibrates. Suddenly, my thoughts shift to what I'm going to order. I'm thinking enchiladas sound amazing right now. Weaving through the crowd toward the hostess stand isn't any easier. If anything, I think more people are here than before. After a quick glance at my phone, I sigh. We've already been here for almost an hour. If we decide to go shopping afterward, as is customary, I'm going to run out of time to get these reports finished.

Halfway through our meal, I jump when my cell phone vibrates against the table. The only people that would call me, besides my parents, are sitting directly in front of me. When the girls see who is calling, they groan in unison.

"Go ahead and answer it," Tiffany waves toward the phone. "I know your fingers are itching to hit the accept call button." She makes it sound like I'm having some secret affair.

My fingers creep toward the phone. The only thing keeping me from picking it up and answering is the scowl on Tiffany's face. If I answer, I'm drawing a line in the sand showing my cousins that I value my job more than I value my time with them. That's not the case, though. Instead of hurting their feelings, I press the button to mute it and let it go to voicemail. I can't believe I just did that. While this is a smart move in my relationship with Audrey and Tiffany, it could very well bite me in the ass at work. I have never ignored a call from my boss, even when I was down with the flu. Only time will tell what this disregard will cost me in the long run.

Tiffany's eyes widen, no doubt surprised by my behavior. It's definitely not normal, at least not for me. She doesn't acknowledge it any more than that and continues telling her story about her latest dating adventure. I swear, if this girl continues to go out with whoever direct messages her on all of those dating apps, she's going to wind up missing one day. She has exactly zero screening process when she agrees to go out with these men. It's a good thing her mama is none the wiser. She would throw a fit if she knew, and I won't be the one to fill her in any time soon.

My phone begins vibrating again, and it's Audrey that sighs this time. "You might as well answer it. Your boss isn't going to let up until you do."

She's right, even though I wish she wasn't. "Okay. Let me just see what he wants." I grab the phone and my finger hovers above the screen. "Maybe it's nothing and we can forget he ever called."

Swiping across the screen, I accept the call. "Hello?" Please be something I can answer now and not require me to put my cousins on the back burner once again.

"Stella, thank God you answered." My boss sounds frazzled, and that is never a good sign. At least, not for me. I swear this man can't do anything without me. It should be complementary, but hell, I'd love to be able to go a day without him acting as if everything is falling apart around him.

"Is everything okay?" I regret asking as soon as the words leave my mouth. Of course, something is wrong. He wouldn't be calling me otherwise.

"Have you finished those reports?" No, but I'm not going to tell him that. "I didn't see them in my email, and I need to go over them for tomorrow's meeting."

Of course, that's why he's blowing up my phone. I usually have the reports sent to him before I leave the office on Friday. The only bad thing is, they still aren't done, and I have absolutely nothing to send him. "I'm so sorry, sir. It must have slipped my mind." It didn't. Another thing he doesn't need to know.

"Can you get them sent to me today?" *Damn it.* His voice is strained and irritated. Not that I blame him. This is completely out of the norm for me. "I really need them tonight."

"N-no problem," I stutter. I hate letting people down. Especially, those that can affect my income. "I'm actually not home right now, but as soon as I get home, I will email them over."

"Thank you, Stella." His voice is cold, and I know I've disappointed him. The call is ended before I can utter another word.

"I'm guessing it wasn't a good call?" Audrey takes a bite of her enchiladas. Gee, I wonder how she guessed.

"Not even a little bit," I reply. "I'm going to have to skip out on shopping today, girls. Apparently, my boss needs this report right now, and after we're done eating, I'm going home to make sure I don't lose my job."

Tiffany mutters something under her breath, but I don't catch it. I'm not sure I want to know because it can't be good. And so begins round three of being pissed at Stella. It's frustrating, but some things are more important that shopping with the girls. Sometimes, it sucks being the oldest cousin in our little trio.

Chapter Three

THERE'S a shiny new keyboard sitting in front of my computer when I walk into my tiny office on Monday. Tiffany was wrong when she said I'm just another person in a cubicle. I've worked my ass off to get this small space of my own. I won't be satisfied until I have one of the big offices facing the city skyline. When I adjust my keyboard to precisely where I want it, I see there's a post it note hidden underneath with an annoyed message. *Try not to spill coffee all over this one. Keep it away from the keyboard.*

I swear the folks down in IT don't have any sort of empathy. It's not like I do it on purpose. Bad shit just happens to follow me wherever I go. It's a wonder I haven't broken something just walking and going about my day.

Searching around the room, I look for a wood surface to knock on. I don't need that vibe following me around for the rest of the day. The imitation wood my computer sits on will have to do. I give it three solid taps, and set my coffee down as far away from the keyboard as possible. The note could have been written slightly more tactfully, but I get it. They are replacing things in my office more often than not.

My boss, Mr. Granger, passes by my open door and nods. He's not overly talkative on a normal day, but today he didn't even say good morning. I guess he's still pissed about the reports being late. I knew there would be repercussions for not having them to him as early as I usually do.

A text message comes through on my phone.

Audrey: How much shit are you in with your boss?
Stella: Don't know yet. He just passed by my office and only nodded at me.

Audrey: Well, you can always crash at my house if you get fired and lose your apartment.

Her level of confidence in my situation is worrisome. It's my first somewhat major screw up, there's no way in hell they would fire me for that. Would they?

There's a soft knock on my office door. It opens slowly, and Ellen, the receptionist for our department, pokes her head inside. "Stella, Mr. Hart wants to see you in his office as soon as possible." She closes the door before I have a chance to respond, and scurries away to her desk. *Shit. I am going to be canned.* The big boss never calls anyone into his office without it being bad news. Granger just had to tell the owner about my screw up, and now I'm going to pay for my mistake. Next time, if there is a next time, I'm not leaving the building until everything is finished.

This is one of the things I loathe about working at this company. I have busted my ass to get this far, but I'm expected to drop everything to meet the demands of others. If I wasn't scared, I'd be fired, I wouldn't even bother going to see what Mr. Hart wants. Alas, here I am pushing my chair back and running off the moment he summons me. How am I supposed to do my job if I'm not at my desk?

My heels click clack against the hard floor, earning me curious glances from the customer service employees in the main area. There are usually only two reasons a person is called into the owner's office…you are either being promoted or let go. Worry gnaws at my gut at the prospect of being fired. I just got a bigger apartment and car after spending years saving, and I can't afford to no longer have a job.

Mr. Hart's personal secretary is seated at her desk in front of his office. "Hi Rosie, how are you doing today?"

"Oh, just fine." Her slightly wrinkled hand picks up the cup of coffee sitting in front of her and she takes a sip. She's much older than she looks. It must be all the beauty products she's had delivered here over the years have helped stop the aging process. I only hope to look as great as she does when I'm her age. That's a life goal, right there.

"That's great," I smile. "Um, Mr. Hart asked to speak with me?" Nerves are the only thing I can blame for making that statement come out as a question. Now is not the time for them to shake me up.

Rosie waves toward the door, "Go on in, Dear. He's waiting for you."

"Thanks Rosie," I give her desk a quick tap. Swallowing down my nerves, I knock on Mr. Hart's door twice even though it's open, and step inside. It's time to face whatever is awaiting me inside.

"Oh, Stella, you're here." Mr. Hart is looking at me through his thick wire-rimmed glasses. Honestly, glasses like that should have a plastic frame, but I'm not going to be the one to tell him that. "Come on in and have a seat." He doesn't seem mad, maybe I'm in the clear.

I hurry over to the chair closest to his desk. To most people the seat they choose to sit in wouldn't be a big deal, except it is to me. The chair closest to him shows that I'm not afraid of him, even though I'm terrified of what he could potentially say. "You asked to see me?"

He sets the pen and the paper pad he was writing on aside and meets my gaze. "Yes, I have an opportunity I would like to discuss with you."

A sigh of relief escapes my body without my permission, and I wish I could take it back. It shows a sign of weakness. "What did you have in mind, Sir?"

"We are opening up a new distribution center in Asheville. It's a small town outside the Dallas area." He leans closer as if readying himself to tell me a secret. "I want you to relocate there until the job is complete, and it's running smoothly."

The excitement I had at the word *opportunity* dies with the word *relocation*. I love living in Austin, and moving to a small town, even for a short amount of time, is not in my plan. "Are you sure I'm a right fit for this job? Shouldn't Mr. Granger be doing this since he's the head of operations?" Probably not the best question to follow up with, but I really don't want to move to a small town. I spent my entire life trying to get out of one. Also, Granger will most likely be pissed that I was asked and not him.

He must see that I'm not bouncing with joy to go. "Yes, you are. You aren't afraid to make the hard decisions and get things done. And I think this will be a great opportunity for you to show me that you're ready to lead your own team. You won't be stuck running production reports for people above you, or running errands for them. This will be your baby from the ground up. Making sure the building is ready to go, finding employees to fill it, and training them." He leans back in his chair, waiting for me to say something, and almost falls backwards. Correcting himself and placing his hand over his protruding stomach, he adds, "Did I mention we are also going to pay for the house you'll be staying in, and it comes with a healthy bonus?"

If it means more money in my bank account, and a possible promotion, then I'm one hundred percent in. I could finally give up apartment living and buy a house, maybe find a pet to greet me when I come home. My dislike of small towns is a small thing compared to a better lifestyle for myself. "How healthy are we talking?"

Chapter Four

Holy shit. I walk dazed to my office. That was not at all what I was expecting. Getting called to the boss's office is akin to getting called to the principal's office in grade school. I really don't want to relocate. I'm not even sure how I'd survive without my cousins. They may not support the amount of hours I put into my job, but they have always been there when I need them.

It's a good thing Mr. Hart gave me a few days to think it over. I need Audrey and Tiffany's input. I have a feeling Tiffany will not be happy about the job opportunity. She'll get over it, though. And she can always come visit me. Hell, I'm going to need their help moving all of my crap if I accept the offer.

Stella: I've got big news!!!!
Tiffany: You quit your over-demanding job and found a new one.
Audrey: Are you going to tell us?
Stella: No, Tiff. Yes, Audrey. Want to come over for dinner?
Audrey: See you there!
Tiffany: You're acting like she's going to make it home by dinner.

I swear Tiffany acts like a bitch because she knows it stings a little. Just because she flits from job to job, doing whatever she pleases, doesn't mean I can do the same thing. Her last text doesn't even deserve a response. This is a big deal. At least, it is to me, and I hope both of my cousins support it. I am sort of excited about this opportunity. Well, let's face it, it is really about the bonus, but still.

I look up to see that Mr. Granger is standing in my office door, lips pressed into a firm line. The high of being offered a possible promotion quickly dies. "Stella, can I speak with you?"

Why can't I catch a damn break? I knew he wouldn't be happy that Mr. Hart went around him to talk to me, but I didn't think he'd confront me about it. At least not quite so soon.

"Absolutely, Mr. Granger. What can I do for you?" My smile is plastic and fake. God, I hope I don't resemble some creepy clown.

He walks toward my desk and takes a seat in the only available chair in my office…mine. No excuse me or do you mind. A part of me wants to kick him out of it. The other part knows better than to push my luck. "I understand Mr. Hart gave you a big opportunity."

"Yes, sir," I lean against the window. Damn him for taking my chair. My coffee is inches from him, and I hope he swivels. His dress shirt would be stained brown, and I'd have to keep my laughter inside.

Alas, he doesn't turn. "You cannot screw this up. If you somehow fail in getting the center up and running, it's not only your job on the line."

Funny, Mr. Hart didn't give me that impression at all. "I'm not a hundred percent sure I'm going to take the offer. He gave me a few days to think it over."

A sly grin crosses Mr. Granger's lips. He obviously has no faith in my capabilities, and that only makes me want to march straight to Mr. Hart's office and accept his offer without a second thought. "You'd be crazy not to take him up on it. I wouldn't wait too long." Without another word, he stands up and walks out.

I love my job; I do, but dealing with asshole bosses is not something I enjoy. Why can't this man help his assistant move up in the company? There's no need for jealousy, or whatever crawled up his ass and died. His reaction to the news only makes me lean toward accepting the offer more than I was earlier. If only to prove him wrong.

I am running late. Tiffany is either going to be very pissed off, or happy because she gets to give me a big fat, I told you so. This time, it's not even because of work. It's all this stupid traffic blocking every direction that leads to my apartment.

For the first time in I don't know how long, I actually left work on time. Not only because I didn't want to hear crap from Tiffany, but also because I'm really excited to tell my cousins about this opportunity. I should have told them to meet me at my apartment later than six. Since I normally leave the office around seven, I never have to deal with this stuff. It was stupid of me to forget that everybody else also gets off at five and are just as anxious to get home as I am.

Seriously, it should not take me over an hour to get home. Hopefully, Audrey is already there and able to pay for food delivery. Though, I would feel better if she would answer her damn text messages. It's not that hard and literally takes two seconds. I could message Tiffany, but I don't feel like dealing with her right now.

Finally, I pull into the parking garage and find my allotted spot. It's a tight squeeze because the asshole parked beside me obviously does not know how to stay between the lines. All I know is there better not be a fucking dent in my car when I come out here in the morning. Grabbing my bag, I rush out of the car and toward the elevators. Thank God it's working. Otherwise, I'd be walking up six flights of stairs and I really don't want to do that. Truth be told, the elevator was a selling point for me picking this apartment. I can't imagine carrying groceries up that many floors without losing something along the way.

I'm not surprised when the door to my apartment is unlocked. I can hear Tiffany and Audrey through the door before I even open it fully. If it was quiet, I would be worried. "Hey guys, I'm finally here."

They are sitting on the couch, glasses of wine in hand. Tiffany sets her glass on the coffee table and crosses her arms, glaring at me beneath her lashes. "Do I get to say I told you so now?" Her age really shows sometimes. Or, maybe it's because I'm exhausted from the insane drive home, but I'm not in the mood for her crap.

"You would be a lot less bitchy if you didn't." I knew she was going to have an attitude when I got here. If there's anything you can count on in regards to my youngest cousin, it's that she has some crazy mood swings. "Besides, it wasn't work that made me come home late. I forgot how stupid traffic is during rush hour. It should not have taken me that long to get home, considering I'm like fifteen minutes from the office."

"You probably could have walked and gotten here faster," Tiffany shrugs. "Oh well," she sighs. "Guess that means I can't give you a hard time."

I snort and then start choking on my own spit. Instead of helping me, she starts laughing. "You act like that's going to stop you."

"You have a point." She picks up her wineglass and takes a sip, dropping the subject…for now.

"Has the delivery guy shown up yet?" I look around the room and don't see any take out bags. Shit, maybe he got here before they did.

"Yup," Audrey replies. "It's all in the kitchen, and I paid using the emergency card you have hidden in your room."

"Thank you so much." My shoulders sag in relief, and the stress of the day washes away. "I was worried we'd be here with no food and have to go out for the night." I toss my bag on the coffee table and sit down between them. "I'm way too wiped out to go anywhere."

Audrey taps her finger against her chin. "You should probably put your emergency card somewhere else. The top drawer of your nightstand is pretty obvious, and it wasn't very well hidden."

She's always the sensible one, and the only person I know that puts so much thought into something like that. I slip the glass of wine from her hand and take a small drink. "You're probably right, but if I had put it somewhere else, you wouldn't have been able to pay the delivery guy."

"I have money of my own," she grumbles and takes back her glass.

"Can we eat now?" Tiffany is already standing up and walking toward the kitchen. "The food is getting cold."

"Do you always think with your stomach?" Audrey and I follow behind her. I'm only a few years older than her and I swear I can feel the pounds jumping onto my body just by smelling food. "You realize it can be reheated, right?"

"Yep," she laughs. "But it's better when it's fresh from the restaurant, and my stomach has never steered me wrong." She's unpacking the foil tins from the bag and the aroma of tomatoes and basil fill the room. "So, what is this news you wanted to tell us?"

"Let's wait until after we eat." Grabbing the plates from the cabinet, I slide them next to the lasagna. "Can you grab the bottle of wine?"

"Sure thing, Cuz." She skips off to the living room to get the bottle they opened earlier.

"Is whatever you're going to tell us going to send her into one of her temper tantrums?" Audrey nudges me aside to grab some silverware out of the drawer. "I just want to prepare myself if that's the case."

I shrug. It's all I can do, since I have no idea how Tiffany will react. "She might."

"Damn it," Audrey mutters. Seconds later her eyes widen and she plasters a big smile on her face as Tiffany enters the kitchen. "This smells delicious." Her subject change is terrible, but Tiffany doesn't seem to notice.

It sucks that we always have to tiptoe around things with Tiff. She's the baby of the family and tends to always get whatever she wants. You'd think since she's such a free spirit she would be okay with change, but that's not the case. Honestly, I think she'd lose her direction if it wasn't for Audrey and me keeping her somewhat steady. I blame it on my aunt and uncle. They indulged her way too much as a child. Hell, they still do it now. If she needs help making her rent payments, they give her the money. No questions asked. One day that girl is going to have to grow up, and she's going to fight it tooth and nail.

"Can you tell us now?" Tiffany's bouncing in her seat. Her red hair shifting slightly with the movement. No more wine for her, she gets way too hyper. "The suspense is killing me." Let's hope that excitement sticks around after she hears my news.

"I was offered a promotion," I squeal and clap my hands together. They pull me up from my chair, at the same time, and wrap their arms around me. We're all jumping up and down, unable to reign in the happiness radiating off of me.

"So, it looks like all of those ridiculously late nights you've been putting in have paid off," Tiffany laughs. "When do you get that big corner office and fat check?"

I withdraw from the group hug and wrap my arms around my waist. This is the part I've been leery of telling them. The dirty dishes capture my attention, and I focus on those instead of them. "Well, there might be a caveat to the whole promotion thing."

Tiffany's eyebrow lifts in question. Audrey throws her hand on her hip and stares me down. "What exactly do you have to do get this promotion?" I can't tell if that's worry or accusation behind her question.

They are already defensive, but I hope they don't flip their shit after they hear the rest. "First off, it is an amazing opportunity for me. So, you can wipe those ugly scowls off your faces." I hold up my index finger letting them know that I'm not finished. "Second, it will require me to relocate for a short period of time."

"What do you mean relocate?" Tiffany shrieks. "You can't just move because your boss wants you to. That's ridiculous."

I don't think I'm going to get her on board to do what I need to do in order to move up at my company. "People move for their jobs all the time. It's not anything new. Besides, it's not like I will be gone forever. A few months max. You will barely even notice that I'm gone."

Audrey cuts into the conversation before our younger cousin has a chance to go into full tirade mode. "Where will you be moving if you accept this offer?"

It's a good thing I did a little bit of research before telling them about the promotion. "It's this little town about 45 minutes south of Dallas. I've already checked to see how far away it is from here, and it's only about four hours."

"Four hours is an eternity," Tiffany cuts in groaning. "Do you really have to move?" Her shoulders slump.

"You traveled further than that when you followed me and Audrey to Austin. It's not that bad," I roll my eyes. "And yes, I have to if I want the promotion. And that's only if I get the distribution center up and running without a hitch."

"What does your direct boss think about it?" Audrey sits down, in full on adulting mode.

"Nothing good. He's not happy that Mr. Hart went around him to ask me." I pour the last of the wine into my glass. "I think he wants me to fail so that I'll either be stuck where I am, or get canned."

"Your boss is an asshole," Tiffany deadpans. "I mean I'm not exactly happy about the prospect of you leaving for a few months, but I'm not hoping for you to fail. That would also make me an asshole."

"So, I have your support if I decide to take the offer?" Glancing at both of them, I take a drink of my wine. If they say no, I'm not sure what I'll do. They are my best friends, the ones I go to for everything. Even if I've been busy lately, I know despite their attitudes about it, they have my back. Tiffany paces back and forth in front of the kitchen sink, tapping her fingers on her thigh. "I mean, are you really worth a four-hour drive?" The dish towel from the table leaves my hand and sails through the air, hitting Tiff square in the face. "Damn, there's no need to be violent." She throws it back and knocks her glass over. Her aim is terrible. "Of course, we support you. I won't be jumping for joy when you aren't present for our weekly brunch, but I'm not so selfish that I would hold you back from your dream."

"That means a lot, Tiff. Thank you," I wrap my arms around her and give her a big squeeze. "Now, we should probably clean up the kitchen. I have to get some rest before I tell Mr. Hart my decision."

"Oh, man," Tiffany points to her wrist. "I have somewhere I need to be." She gives me a quick peck on the cheek, and rushes out of the apartment.

"You should have seen that coming," Audrey laughs. "I'll help you. And we'll come up with a game plan for when you move."

"Thanks," I mutter. "You know, your cousin really is an asshole."

"Last time I checked…she's your cousin, too."

She fills the sink with water as I gather the dishes off the table. "Yeah, I guess I'll claim her."

Chapter Five

My feet wobble in my heels as I make my way across the building to Mr. Hart's office. All of the other early birds stare at me. Their eyes wide, and whispers float through the mostly quiet room. I would be stupid to think it's not about me because I'm almost certain they've heard one version or another about my meeting yesterday. Maybe they've come up with their own speculations. Either way, I'm not a fan of being a part of the office gossip mill. It's never a good place to be, especially when it's typically fueled by jealousy.

I'm so focused on the jackholes I work with that I don't notice the small file box sitting on the floor. My shin crashes into the top, and I go sailing over the box. My hands slam against the floor, catching myself before my face eats tile. As if I wasn't already nervous, now we have my ungraceful fall in front of the entire office. Fuck my life. Honestly, I should come with a warning label-"will make an ass of herself at any given moment".

Slowly getting to my feet, I wipe my hands on my skirt. Tiny flecks of dirt and dust now cover my thighs. Proof that the office cleaning crew do not do a stellar job. Maybe I should bring that up with Mr. Hart while I'm in his office. Everyone should be disgusted at how dirty this floor is. Not to mention how nasty everything else must be.

I look up to see if anybody witnessed my epic crash. Of course, they saw me. Several of the guys have their hands over their mouths, attempting to hide their smirks and laughter. There were a few women just staring at me wearing shocked expressions. Not one of these jerks asked if I was okay. I swear, sometimes work is equivalent to being back in grade school. Except, people were a little more caring then.

"Don't worry everybody, I'm fine," I said feigning gratitude. Okay, so that was bitchy, but I don't really care.

Mr. Hart's office is mostly blocked by partitions, and today I am extremely grateful for that. His assistant, Rosie, is sitting behind her desk going through emails when I approach her. "Hey Rosie, is Mr. Hart in?"

"I'm sorry, Dear. He won't be in for another thirty minutes to an hour." She pauses in her scrolling, "What was that loud crash? Did somebody run into something? I swear some of the people out there are like bulls in a china shop."

My cheeks warm, and without looking in the mirror, I'm ninety percent sure they are bright red. "Actually," I sigh. "I'm the bull. I tripped over a stupid box and my face almost met the floor."

"Are you okay?" She rushes around her desk, puts her hands on my shoulders, checking me for injuries.

"I'm fine," I intend to nudge her away, but her mothering skills have taken over. There's no use trying to stop it. "The most I have is a nasty bruise on my leg where I hit the box."

Finally, she takes a step back looking at me with a questioning glance. "Well, if you're sure." Then, she walks around the desk to take a seat. "Do you want me to email you as soon as he comes into the office?"

Damn, I really wish he was here right now. I will have to deal with this nervous energy for at least another hour. "That would be great, Rosie. It's in regard to the meeting we had yesterday."

A sly smile takes over her face. "In that case, I'll push his other meetings back, and you will be the first person he speaks with." She winks at me, "This is a big opportunity for you, and I think you will do great." That woman knows everything that happens in this office. Hell, I'd be surprised if she didn't know everything that's going on in the entire building.

"Thanks." I give her a small wave, and head to my office. I guess I can work on whatever Mr. Granger emailed me late last night. As horrible as it is to say, I will definitely be happy not to be working so closely with him while I'm in Asheville.

There's a knock on my door and I stop filing. I've already gotten three paper cuts within a span of thirty minutes. Looking up, I gasp when I see who is standing in my doorway.

Why didn't Rosie let me know he was here? I would've gone to his office. It is weird seeing him on this side of the building, though. He must be impatient to hear my response.

"Did I startle you, Stella?" He takes a few steps toward my desk, and when he realizes there isn't an extra chair, he backs up and leans against the door-frame. He looks uncomfortable as his arms hang stiffly by his side.

"Sorry, Sir. I was expecting to meet you in your office." I glance around the room looking for something for him to sit on, but nothing magically appears in front of me. "Let me see if I can find an extra chair."

"Oh no, you don't have to go through all that trouble." He waves his hands in my direction. "I probably need to start taking more breaks to move around anyway."

It's weird having the head of the company standing without a place to sit. Finding an additional chair for my office has been bumped up on my list of priorities. "If you say so," I whisper. This is new territory for me, and I don't know how to navigate it.

"Rosie told me you were looking for me this morning. I take it you've made a decision about the relocation." He doesn't form it as a question so he has to know I've made a decision. I only hope it's the right one for me and my career. Only time will tell, I guess.

I clear my throat and place my hands on my desk to keep from fiddling with anything out of nerves. "Yes, Mr. Hart. I've decided I'd like to take the opportunity." I'm waiting for him to make a joke. To say he changed his mind, and he's sending Mr. Granger instead.

His hands smack together as he claps. "Excellent. I know you will do a fantastic job."

"I'm happy you have so much faith in me, and I will not let you down." His excitement is contagious, and I can't stop the wide grin from overtaking my lips. "When will I need to leave?" That's the one thing I forgot to ask when he first offered the possible promotion.

"Is two weeks enough time for you to get your affairs in order? If it is, I'll have Rosie call the rental property we found and let them know what your move-in date will be."

Damn, two weeks. I was expecting it to be more along the lines of a month, but the timeframe is doable. A mental list of everything that needs to happen forms in my mind. "Yes, two weeks is fine."

"Great," he taps the door frame with his knuckles. "I have a meeting in ten minutes, but I'll meet with you later this afternoon to discuss all of the arrangements." He turns to leave, and pauses with one foot out of the door. "You're going to go far in this company, Stella. This is only a stepping stone to get you where you want to be." He leaves without saying another word. My nerves are buzzing with excitement and nerves. *Can I do this?*

Two weeks. I'll be leaving the city that I love, and heading to a Podunk town. I hated going to these little towns in Nowheresville to visit family when I was a child. We were creative with how we spent our time, but Audrey and

Tiffany were the only people that made the trip bearable. I will make the best of it, though. The prize at the end is more than worth it.

"Do you really need all of this stuff?" Tiffany sighs and she tapes up the last few boxes. It's probably more than I actually need, but I have no idea what there is to do in Asheville. I want to be prepared.

They should be proud of me; I never have my shit together like this. I grabbed one of the throw pillows off of my sofa and toss it at her head. She ducks and it goes sailing over her. She sticks her tongue out at me and continues taping the box in front of her.

"Yes, I need all of this. The house comes completely furnished, but that doesn't mean it also comes with my clothes, makeup, and shoes. A girl has to have options."

"It's not like you're going there to impress anybody," Audrey rolls her eyes. "You are there for one thing. To set up this center without a hitch, get your promotion, and get your ass back here so that we aren't lonely."

These two are ridiculous. They act like they'll never see me again. "And I'm going to do all that. However, I am allowed to have some downtime. We can totally do Sunday brunch over video while I am gone."

"It's not the same, though." Audrey folds her arms over her chest and her bottom lip pokes out. *Dramatic much?*

Good gravy, she's starting to act like Tiffany. I guess I didn't realize she would be so upset with me leaving. She's usually the practical one. "We will figure something out. Y'all can come visit me, and I will come back down here when I can."

"I guess," Audrey sighs and picks up one of the boxes. "I'm bummed we don't get to go down with you."

"I know, me too." I scrunch up my nose. "But I'm excited to check it out before y'all get there. What if I show up and the house is a dumpster fire?"

I wanted them to make the trip with me more than anything, but they couldn't get off work for two days to do it. Luckily, they will be there bright and early on Friday morning. It's the only day they were able to take off, or at least I hope they will.

Tiffany snorts. "You work for one of the best project management companies in the city, there's no way they are going to put you in a crappy rental."

I hope she's right. I'm not sure what I would do if I walked up to my new temporary home and it was falling apart. Surely, Mr. Hart wouldn't do that. What am I saying? Mr. Hart most likely didn't set anything up. Most of that rests on Rosie's shoulders, and there's no way she would put me in a shady place. "We shall see." I grab one of the hair ties from the coffee table and throw my hair up in a ponytail. "Besides, I need to scope out some places we can hang out before y'all get there Friday morning."

"That's what I'm talking about," Tiffany laughs. "Finally! You have your priorities on the right path."

My apartment looks weird and bare. All the big stuff is still in place, but all the little touches that make the space my own are packed away so that I have a little bit of home with me while I'm gone. "Y'all are going to come check on the apartment while I'm gone, right? You don't have come over here daily, but once or twice a week to get the mail and make sure nobody realizes I'm not here would be amazing."

"We got you, sister." I love that she uses that term. It's something her mom has said since we were kids. It didn't matter which of us she was talking to, she always called us sister. And it works. These two, even though they are my cousins, feel like my sisters. They're the first to know anything and everything going on in my life. It's a bond that I hope never breaks. "Who knows, maybe I'll come stay here a couple of nights to get away from my crazy roommate. I really need a screening process the next time around." Tiffany has an evil grin on her face, and I don't trust it.

Pointing my finger at her, as if I'm scolding her, I shake my head. "No random dudes in my apartment. You can have whatever sexcapades you want in your own bed. Just don't do it here."

She gasps and covers her chest with her hand. "I would never do that."

Audrey crosses her arms over her chest. "Oh really? What about that time you practically had sex in front of me, or when you used my car and I found a condom wrapper in the backseat?" She pulls one arm away and points it at Tiffany. "You better get that agreement in writing. Or, do I need to count off all the other ways you have been irresponsible when it comes to men?"

"I was practically a kid when all that happened," she argues. "You can't hold what I did a million years ago against me forever. Besides, I'm not currently dating anyone right now. I'm only trying to avoid the roommate from hell."

"I'm trusting you, Tiff." This is going to bite me in the ass. I can already feel it. "Please don't let me down. Anyway, what's going on with your roommate?"

"I won't, I promise." She picks up the box holding all of my bathroom stuff. Deflection at its finest. I actually like her roommate, well as much as I can since I rarely see her. She keeps things tidy and organized. She's also the exact opposite of Tiffany. "Let's get some of the crap you're going to need loaded into your car. I'm sure you'll want to get an early start."

Each of us grabs a box. I can't believe I'm doing this. Tomorrow morning, I will begin a new adventure, and it terrifies me. My cousins better be there to catch me if this whole thing blows up in my face.

Chapter Six

Finally, a freaking gas station. I'm barely an hour out of Austin, and I already have to pee. Reason number one why I shouldn't drink a ton of water before a long drive. I'm shocked I haven't had to stop sooner. Tiffany and Audrey always make fun of me for my frequent stops. It got to the point where they wouldn't let me have anything to drink before a trip. They call me a time suck, and treat me like a child. At least, I stay hydrated and won't have a ton of wrinkles when I'm older. Point one for me.

I exit the highway and drive toward the gas station mentioned on the sign. Nothing has gone according to plan today. I woke up late after too many glasses of wine with the girls, completely missing the five alarms I had set. It may be overkill but I'm not a morning person and it takes some motivation to get my ass out of bed. Too bad it doesn't always work.

On top of that, Mr. Granger called and needed me in the office as soon as possible because he needed help with something. I won't even mention that it was something anyone in the office could've helped him with. My best guess is that he was doing everything he possibly could to delay my departure. I don't understand why this man wants me to fail so badly. I've never done something to disappoint him, at least I don't think I have. Each task he's set before me, I've completed on time and perfectly. Well, except that report fiasco a few weeks ago. That wasn't timely or perfect.

Let's just say this adventure is starting off rocky. Now I probably won't get to my destination until well after dark. I should have just waited and headed there with Audrey and Tiffany on Friday morning. Damn it, I shouldn't have drank with them last night. Peer pressure, man. It'll get me every time.

Now I'm sitting outside of this creepy ass gas station debating whether or not I have to pee that bad. The paint is peeling off the building. The front door has a thick coating of dust, and the open sign flickers on and off erratically. If I was with someone, I would suck it up and go inside. But I'm alone and the building gives me skeevy vibes. I'm going with my gut, and back out of the parking lot.

There is another gas station, that I know is amazing, a little further along the highway. At least there, I know the bathroom will be clean. It's what the gas station is known for, and they just so happen to be place strategically along the two major highways that run North to South. Well, that and being the size of a grocery store with a ton of cute things lining their shelves, and what seems like a million gas pumps. The other plus side…fountain Big Red, need I say more? The only problem I foresee is spending too much time, and money, in there while perusing all the stuff they have for sale. Maybe I will find something for Tiffany and Audrey to thank them for helping me. They didn't have to go out of their way, and take off work, to help me realize my goals. Even though they did their fair share of complaining about it.

Does everyone around here drive this slow on the highway? The worst part is it's only two lanes and I'm blocked in from all sides. It's going to take me forever to get used to this pace. Back in Austin, the motto is "go fast or get run over". This is one of the reasons I rarely visit my aunts and uncles. The slower pace feels like I'm moving at snail speed.

That isn't the only reason, though. The mere thought of staying in a tiny town for longer than necessary gives me hives. There's nothing to do except sit around at the kitchen table, or on the porch, and share the family gossip. I have to admit that it's not all bad. I've heard some crazy stories about my dad and aunts. It's just not my idea of a good time. All you do is sit and drink. There aren't any clubs or fun places to visit.

The British voice on my GPS blares through the speakers, and I jump, almost swerving off the road. They should really ease into the old voice so you have some warning. Something like those alarms that start off quietly and slowly build in volume until it's yelling at you to get out of bed. Maybe I need one of those alarms. My exit is in two miles, and I'm really hoping this car in front of me doesn't take the same one.

The Asheville city limits sign catches my eyes as I take the ramp on the service road. Lights fill the streets and cars are moving along at a steady pace. A coffee shop sits on the corner, and I feel my first moment of relief. A few of the stores I shop at back home can be seen dotting the busy road. Maybe it won't be so bad here after all. They have coffee and decent stores. I couldn't ask for much else.

The town lights are now only a reflection in my rearview mirror. I should have looked at the address to my rental house more closely. It appears I won't be staying in town, close to everything I could ever need. Nope. My phone is leading me straight to the middle of nowhere. *Damn it.* Next time I'm asked to relocate, I'm going to have to get with Rosie on the specifics. I assumed I would be in a nice apartment with a ton of pain in the ass neighbors. That's apparently not the case.

I haven't seen a house in over a mile, and forget about street lights. What in the world did I do to piss off Rosie so badly? There's no way she would have put me in the boonies without a reason. I'm going to call her first thing in the morning to see what the hell she was thinking when she picked this place.

My phone rings and the lit-up screen distracts me for a split second. It's Audrey, and I know she's expecting to talk to me tonight. I raise my hand to press the accept call button but jerk it away when a dark shape darts out into the road in front of me. I freak out and swerve, screaming, right into a ditch. The car groans and shakes as it comes to a jolting stop. I look back to see what kind of animal it was, but it's gone. As if it never existed. A loud hiss comes from the hood, and I groan. That doesn't sound promising. *Damn it.* I just bought this car.

Chapter Seven

No signal. I sigh in defeat as I will the service bars to show up on my phone. *Just freaking great.* Today officially wins for the suckiest day ever.

This relocation is already proving to be a huge mistake. I should have turned around the second my headlights met darkness. I bring the phone closer to my face, inspecting the map that is still on the screen. It doesn't look like there are any houses close to the one I'll be staying in. If I ever get there. It's completely isolated. I feel like I am in one of those eighties' horror movies. The ones where the dumb girl runs through the woods, barely dressed, and gets axed in the end.

Why did I say yes to this? I'm sitting here, in the ditch, completely stranded. *Son of a bitch.* Whatever it was that derailed my attempt to see my new temporary home was too small to be a dog, but too big to be a rabbit. I hope wherever it is, it's grateful that I didn't plow over it. Not that I would do anything intentionally, but I've seen my fair share of roadkill littering the road. Either way, there's no telling how much damage is now done to my car. My poor baby, she's barely two months old. I run my hand across the dashboard, trying to soothe the pain of an inanimate object, or maybe I am just trying to comfort myself. Either way, I feel a little bit better. If I don't get this car running, there's no way I'm going to be able to get back and forth from the distribution center now. What the fuck am I going to do?

Headlights shine in my rearview mirror. Finally, someone is coming down this stupid road. Maybe they will be the rescuer I desperately need right now. I have no idea how I'm going to get out of this predicament on my own since I can't get any cell reception in this spot. Otherwise, I would have called AAA.

Hopefully cell signal isn't an issue at the house. I need a way to talk to my best friends so they can talk me off the deep end when I want to throw in the towel.

If I can't get this person to stop, the only other option I have is to get out of my car and walk until I can find someone who will help me. In the dark, with the moon as my only source of light. On the plus side, the road doesn't look like it sees a ton of traffic. What am I even thinking about here? If I wouldn't pee at a gas station that looked creepy, there's no way in hell I'm going to willingly traipse off into the dark alone. Like I said before, that's just a bad horror movie waiting to happen.

Seconds pass as I watch the headlights get closer and a truck fly by me. Suddenly, the driver slam on the brakes. At least that means they saw me. Now, let's see if they decide to help or drive off like so many other drivers do in the city. The truck door swings open and a boot clad foot steps onto the ground. It seems as if they might be dressed to help me out of this sticky situation.

I can't really see who has come to my rescue since my headlights are facing the grassy hill at an awkward angle. But from the light glow of the moon, I can make out a tall figure with the frame of a man. I'm trying not to swoon and act like a damsel in distress, but his broad stature makes me want to see what he looks like up close.

I watch the man walk toward my car, trying to wipe images of serial killers out of my mind. His strides are long, steady, and confidence pours off of him. When his knuckles tap against the window, I roll it down. Thankful that at least this feature is still working. Even if he's here to help, I don't want to get out of the car until I know I'm not going to be chopped up into tiny pieces. Self-preservation is something I've learned after living in the city my entire life. Nobody has ever approached me, but that doesn't mean I shouldn't be prepared at all times.

He bends down until we are face to face. "Are you okay?" His voice is deep and holds a bit of a southern twang. His voice breaks the nighttime soundtrack of crickets and other creatures I can't identify. I need to know if his appearance matches the octave of his voice. It's a sound I could definitely get used to, and it doesn't sound like he could be a potential serial killer.

Lifting my hand over my head to the roof of my car, I search for the button to turn on the interior light, without losing eye contact with my rescuer. My finger hits the right button, and I squint my eyes as my car is illuminated. Going from dark to light is always a pain, and it takes a moment for my eyes adjust. My mouth falls open. The scruff on his face is hotter than it should be, and his dark brown eyes hold a spark in the dim car light. He is the exact opposite of anyone I have ever been interested in, and yet there is something about him. I have to remind myself that I'm only here for a small amount of time. I do not need to find the locals attractive.

"Miss?" A tinge of worry is laced in the question. "Are you alright?"

"Oh," I shake the lustful thoughts out of my head. "Yes, I'm fine. Well," I laugh nervously. "As fine as I can be, considering…" I wave my hand in a wide arc to include my predicament.

"Do you want me to look at your car and see if I can figure out what is wrong with it, or if it can be driven?" He seems genuine but then again so did Ted Bundy.

"Uh, sure." What else am I supposed to say? Calling anyone is out, and he's the first person I've seen come down this road in the past hour. "Can I help?" It's not like I'd be able to help with anything remotely car related. My dad wasn't one of those to teach me how to work on vehicles. We always took our cars to a mechanic. He said it was because he spent his entire teen years covered in grease, constantly fixing whatever happened to go awry in his old beat up truck. He didn't want that for me.

"No, I've got it. I just need to go back to my truck for a flashlight."

I turn toward the passenger seat for my purse, but the contents are scattered all over the floor. "I'm sure I have one in he—" When I face the window again, he's already gone, jogging to his truck. And I'm left talking to air. I didn't realize he meant right this second.

My mystery rescuer doesn't come back to the window. Instead, he clicks the flashlight on and begins inspecting my car. The deep frown on his face does not bode well for me. He goes a step further and gets down on the ground to look for damage underneath. The amount of time he's taking makes me nervous, and I wonder how I'm going to get to my destination if I can't drive the car. Maybe this is a sign that I need to get back to Austin as fast as I can. I am obviously not meant for country living.

His head pops above the hood of my car, and I jump. I need to lay off the scary movies. They're making me jump at every sudden movement, and if this place is as remote as it seems…I'll end up completely freaking myself out. He's back at my window and running his hands through his wavy locks. "Um, I don't think it's a good idea for you to drive it." He doesn't turn his flashlight off, and it shines right in my face. I squint my eyes from the brightness. When he notices, he points the light toward the ground. "I have a chain in the back of my truck, and I can tow it to your house tonight, if you want."

Leaving my new baby on the side of the road probably isn't a smart idea. There isn't anything in here that I'm worried about being stolen, it's just the car itself. I don't know anybody here, and I'm not sure what might happen if it is left unattended. "Yeah, that would be great." I hold my hand out of the window, "I'm Stella, by the way."

"I'm Johnny," he places his hand in mine. Calluses brush against my palm, and I'm a little surprised that I like the way it feels. Most of the guys I've held hands with work in offices and have no reason to have roughened hands. He pulls his hand away. "You're pretty trusting considering you're stuck in the middle of nowhere, and broken down. How do you know you can trust me?" He smirks, and leans back away from the window. His face now hidden in shadows, and I can't stop the shiver that runs through my body. This man is going to be trouble, I can already tell.

"I don't really have much of a choice," I shrug. "It's either sit out here in the dark by myself. Or, trust that you aren't some deranged serial killer." Even though he has definitely captured my attention, he hasn't set off my creep radar yet. It's so hard to find genuinely nice men these days. *Calm down, Stella. He's only being a good Samaritan.*

"Don't worry, I'm not a serial killer." He chuckles at my arched eyebrow. "Where do you live? I don't think I've seen you around here before, and I know everyone in this town." Damn, if he knows I'm an outsider, this town must be pea size.

I rattle off the address Rosie gave me. Johnny's nose scrunches at me in confusion. "I just moved here, and I was on my way to the house, when something ran out in the road and I ended up here. So, I'm not exactly sure where my house is." I feel like a complete dumbass for not knowing, but it's not my fault. This is why I wanted to get here during the day. But no, Mr. Granger had to ruin that for me.

"I know where it's at." He looks over my car and shakes his head. "It's the old Garnett place. Nobody has lived there in years, but it has a very narrow and twisty driveway, and I don't know if I can safely get your car down it in the dark."

Great, the news just gets better and better. The way he said the name of the house makes me think it's not even livable. I am seriously questioning what exactly I got myself into. Mr. Hart said my accommodations were nice and completely furnished. I hope that's true because I don't have anything with me, besides my clothes, shoes, and the essentials I'll need in the morning. Audrey and Tiffany won't be here with the rest of my crap until tomorrow. "Are there any other options that don't include me leaving my car on the side of the road?"

Johnny taps his chin, considering my question. "There is one, but I'm not sure how keen you are on going to a stranger's house. Other than that, it's leaving it here until you can get a tow truck."

Normally, it would be an automatic no if someone asked me to come to their house. Especially if I've just met them. But I'm sick of being in this car and feel gross from driving all day. Not to mention, I'm hungry. All of those points lead to me saying, "It depends on who the stranger is."

<h1 style="text-align:center">Chapter Eight</h1>

I'VE BEEN BANISHED to Johnny's truck. He wouldn't let me help with anything. I tried, and he sounded more frustrated than anything else. He even grabbed the few bags, and suitcases, I brought with me, and put them in the backseat. I mean, I'm not one of those people that thinks I need to do everything myself, but I'm fully capable of carrying my own stuff. Either he thinks I'm a nuisance, or he's a true gentleman. I'm not sure which, yet.

My hands reach forward, inches away from opening the glove compartment. The urge to go through his things to see what type of man he is over-powering me. I snatch them back before I go into spy mode. Here Johnny is, helping me out of a bind, and my first instinct is to snoop. I'm such a shitty human being.

The windows are rolled down, and a slight breeze comes through them. It doesn't help much. It's still crazy hot even though it's the middle of September. I hear grunts and groans coming from behind the truck, and I look in the side view mirror to see what the problem is. All I see is darkness. "Are you okay? Do you need any help?"

Johnny's head pokes out from behind the tailgate. "Nope. I'm good. I only need a couple more minutes and we'll be on the road."

"Suit yourself," I mutter under my breath. It would probably go a lot faster if I was out there helping him. Not sitting in the truck with nothing to do. Oh well, his loss.

I grab my phone from my purse and move it around in all directions. Still no service. I don't understand how this is possible with the amount of cell towers there are everywhere. It's a good thing I'm not in imminent danger. I'd be royally screwed. Luckily, I have a few games I can play without a connection. Seriously, anything to kill time is better than sitting in the cab of this truck, alone, with nothing to do.

The driver side door opens and Johnny slides in behind the wheel. Of course, the one game I'm trying to play needs an update. Can't do that without a damn signal. I throw the phone onto the seat beside me, and it hits with a dull thud. "Please tell me there is a signal somewhere in this town. I can't deal with being cut off from everything."

He shakes his head and smirks. "Yeah, there is. Most of the time you have to have a certain carrier in order for your phone to work flawlessly." He shrugs his shoulders and turns on the truck. "It's one of the downfalls of living out here."

"Well that's promising." I face the window and stare into the darkness. It's really going to suck if I can't talk to the girls on a daily basis. They are my only connection to my normal life. To home. I should have said no when Mr. Hart offered me the job. I have a sinking feeling that my stay here will be one big ball of suck.

Johnny taps his fingers against the steering wheel, adding a steady rhythm into the quiet stillness. It's soothing and annoying at the same time. I'm not sure how that's possible, but it's like my own personal hell right now. I just want to be home in my comfortable bed, listening to Audrey and Tiffany bicker over a video call. "So, what brings you this way?" His deep voice breaks the silence, and his fingers are no longer moving.

I eye him warily, unsure if I should answer. "A temporary relocation for my job. Though, I'm starting to regret the decision after the crappy night I've had." I continue staring outside, attempting to take in the scenery, and my surroundings, with only the light the moon is producing. Too bad there are so few out tonight. "Why? Are you trying to make sure I don't have anybody looking for me?"

He laughs so hard the truck swerves the tiniest bit. "I figured that would be the last of your concerns considering you got in the truck with me. But no, I'm just trying to make friendly conversation. Getting to know your neighbors is important in areas like this. We're all like family and look out for each other."

I look him up and down, deciphering the truth behind his words. Surely if he was going to do something horrible, he wouldn't have hooked my car up to his truck. "It's so different in the city. Most of the time when the people in my apartment building see each other they do their best to avoid each other at all costs. It's not exactly a super friendly environment."

I keep searching for store fronts, anything to make this place feel like something more than a forgotten space. "Wow, there really isn't anything out here is there?"

"Not really. We have a small convenience store, but that's about it." He has one hand on the wheel, and scratches the back of his neck with the other. Is he ashamed, or at a loss for words? "You will have to drive a good fifteen to twenty minutes to get to any big grocery stores, and an hour to get to Dallas." That's definitely not what I want to hear. Driving isn't an issue for me, but I'm used to the store being a couple of blocks away. I honestly don't even remember the last time I actually went to the grocery store. Most of the time I get them delivered, or eat out.

"Why in the hell would they choose to build a distribution center out here?" I mutter under my breath. Hopefully he can't hear me. I truly can't fathom the thought process behind corporate's decision, but who am I to question their decisions.

We pull off the road onto what I assume is a driveway. I can't really tell because there aren't any lights. He pulls to a stop in front of a small, older looking house. "I assume this is your house?"

"Yup," he shifts the truck into park. "If you want, you can hang out inside while I move your car to the garage. I can have the shop I work for pick it up in the morning."

I look from the house to him, and nod. "That would be great." Stretching my arms over my head, I sigh at the thought of being in a much bigger space. "Being in a car all day has my arms and legs so freaking stiff. Walking around, and stretching my muscles, is probably a good idea."

Before I even have a chance to pull the door handle, he's out of the truck, and opening the door for me. I flinch. Not out of fear or anything, but because this is not something I experience often. As soon as I'm out of the truck, he reaches into the backseat and pulls out a pizza and pack of beer. I didn't even know those were back there. Maybe that's why he wanted to put my bags in the truck. He didn't want to chance me ruining his dinner.

"I'll unlock the door for you. I have pizza." He lifts it up as if I didn't just see him pull it out of the truck. "And I'm sure there's something to drink in the refrigerator. I'm not sure if the beer is any good anymore. It's been sitting in the heat for longer than I anticipated." I follow him to the door, and walk in behind him. "Help yourself. It shouldn't take me too long to get your car unhooked from my truck."

"Thanks," I smile as he sets the pizza on the counter. "I really appreciate your help."

"No problem. I'll be right back." He walks quickly out of the house, like something is lighting his shoes on fire. Did I do something to offend him? I have no idea what is going on with him. I tried flirty banter, and he basically shut me down. Now he's acting like a teenager that doesn't know how to be in the same room as girl.

I'm beginning to think there's something wrong with me. I can't manage to capture a guy's attention long enough to do anything about it. Or...maybe it's him. He may not be all that great with women. I guess time will tell, not that I'm looking for someone to date. I have a job to do.

As he'll be occupied for a few minutes, it's time to do some snooping. The best place to accomplish that is the bathroom. What people keep in their cabinets is always a good indicator of what's going on in their life.

Chapter Nine

THIS CANNOT SERIOUSLY BE HAPPENING. First the car, then no phone signal, and
now this…what did I do to someone in a past life to deserve the shit storm my
day has been? Getting my foot out of the damn hole should not be this hard.
Johnny standing in the entryway laughing his ass off isn't helping. I thought
he was a gentleman. This isn't how people treat guests in their house.

"How did you manage to do that? I have all the plates and stuff on the
counter for the pizza." Johnny asks between gasps. I really don't think it's that
funny.

"I needed to wash my hands." It's a lie, but he doesn't need to know that. I
was snooping. How else was I going to establish once and for all that he didn't
have ill intentions? As far as I can tell, this guy is pretty clean. That's almost
unheard of in today's world. Everyone has dirt, including me. I'm sure there
are photos from high school somewhere online of me making a complete ass of
myself. I happen to think I'm perfectly normal, for the most part, anyway. I
guess I'll have to do more digging. There *has* to be some skeletons hiding in his
closet.

"Sure, you were," he mutters under his breath, and grabs my outstretched
hand. "You might want to turn your foot to the left, or it's going to get caught
on the wood. I'm sure that would hurt a hell of a lot more than your ego does
right now."

"Ugh," I roll my eyes. I listen to him, though. I shift my foot to the left and
point my toe. He pulls me up and I fall into his arms, completely unbalanced.
His fingers graze my back under my shirt, and linger for longer than necessary.
"Thank you," I pull away from him, and his smirk, and rub my hands down

my shirt, smoothing out fake wrinkles. My gaze falls on his mouth, still grin-ning at my stupidity. *Stop it.* I need to stop checking him out. He's hot as hell, but I do not have time in my life for men. Not today, tomorrow, or ever. I came to this Podunk town to do one thing, my job. As soon as it's done, I'll be driving my happy little ass right back to Austin. Johnny reaches around me and grabs the pizza box, flipping the lid open. "You didn't eat?" He looks from the pizza to me. "Do you not like pizza?"

"I like pizza just fine," I huff. "It's rude to eat when the person who bought it isn't eating at the same time." I hope that's a thing because right now I'm talking out of my ass. I spent the ten minutes it took him to unhook my car snooping through his bathroom and living room. I was just about to go through his kitchen cabinets when I heard a loud clang. The sound was loud, and scared the hell out of me. Hence, my foot falling into the hole. I stare the hole down as if it's wronged me somehow, and I guess it did. That's beside the point, though. "What's up with floor?" I nod toward it.

"It was weak," he picks up a slice of pizza and takes a bite. Cheese comes off in strands and covers his chin. It's kind of adorable. Stop it, brain. "I fell through it last night. I have all the stuff to fix it, and was actually going to do it tonight, until…" He waves his pizza in my direction, letting the sentence hang.

Until my driving mishap. I'm grateful for his help, but he doesn't have to rub it in. It's not like I sought out an animal running across the road.

Something in his pocket vibrates, and I look down. As much as I don't want to admit my attraction to him, a small part of me wonders who might be calling him, and my heart sinks a little at the thought of it being another woman. Wait a minute, that's my phone. "What are you doing with my phone?" I pluck it out of his pocket, but the Pop Socket on the back gets caught on the fabric and I accidentally pull him closer to me.

Johnny has enough foresight to set the pizza on the counter before helping me with my phone. His cheeks are a bright red, and knowing that I affect him makes me smile. At least I'm not the only one who is flustered. "Um, you left it in my truck when you got out, and it started ringing when I drove your car to the barn."

"Okay." My cousins have been blowing up my phone. There are so many notifications they don't all fit on the home screen preview. "But why did you have it in your pocket?"

He shrugs, and takes a step back. "I figured you might want it now that you have cell reception." Another step back. He's putting distance between us, and I can't tell if it's because he's scared of me and how I might react. Or, because he thinks I'm too much. It's not an inaccurate observation. I've been told many times that I'm high maintenance, even though I don't see it.

"Oh, well," my voice is shaky and breathless. Shit, he's really going to think I'm crazy if I keep going back and forth like this with my mood. It's not something I'm doing on purpose, but he's throwing me off my game. Add in the events of tonight, it's no wonder I'm flustered. "Thank you. I appreciate it."

My phone vibrates in my hand, and I almost drop it. "No problem." He nods toward my hand, "You might want to get that. It sounds like whoever is trying to call you won't give up until you answer." Is that a frown? Maybe he thinks I have a boyfriend badgering me and he's upset about it. A girl can wish.

Instead of answering, I decline the call and pull up my text messages.

Stella: I can't talk right now. I'll fill you in soon.
Audrey: What? Why not?
Tiffany: You aren't doing something stupid are you? And if you are…wait for me!
Stella: Don't worry about it. I will call y'all in less than two hours.

Pressing the button on the side of my phone, I turn it off. Otherwise, those two will keep texting and calling until I give them an answer they deem appropriate. They drive me insane sometimes.

"Is everything okay?" Johnny puts his hand on my shoulder. It's heavy, warm, and comforting. I didn't even notice him move closer to him. I have to stop zoning out, especially when I'm with someone I don't know.

"Yeah. It's just my cousins being worrywarts." My stomach growls, reminding me that I haven't eaten dinner. "Any chance I can get a slice of that pizza before you take me to my new house?"

He uses the hand that was on my shoulder to pick up the box, and I would almost rather him touch me than eat. There's a spark I've never felt before, even if he thinks I'm a moron for going off the road. "Of course. I told you to eat before I went outside."

"I was a bit distracted," I wave his statement off.

"I'm sure," he mumbles. Was I meant to hear that? I have a feeling he knows exactly what I was doing while he was outside. This is mortifying.

"On second thought," I grab a couple of slices of pizza and set them on a paper plate. "Can you take me now? I can eat on the way."

If I had to describe the driveway we pull into, it would be creepy as hell. Overgrown trees line the path on both sides, and it doesn't give me much hope for the condition of the house. It reminds me of those haunted houses they show on TV with the spooky landscapes overlaying the image of the house. Add in the fact that it's the middle of the night…and we have nailed the creep factor to a level ten.

"This driveway is extremely long," I say into the quiet cab. There has been zero talking since we got in. So, what if it's been less than five minutes? Some conversation is better than nothing. "Are we almost there?"

"Yes," he points into the darkness. "It's just around the next curve."

This driveway has way more curves than absolutely necessary. Who were these people that built this house? It's pretty far off the road, hidden behind a copse of trees, and a nightmare to get to. I'm only hoping that everything is functioning, and nothing is falling apart.

My eyes widened as soon as the house comes into view. It's not a worn down, shabby dwelling like I assumed it might be. No, it's everything a small-town girl could dream of. There are two floors, and I can't tell because it's dark, but I think the porch wraps all the way around. I'm bouncing in my seat, anxious to see what the inside looks like. "When you said old Garnett house, I assumed you meant it was going to be completely run down."

He laughs, "That's what you get for assuming." He pulls the truck right in front of the house, and puts it in park. "I'm not sure who's been taking care of it, but I think they've done some remodeling on the inside. This used to be the house where everyone in town would gather for cookouts and any sort of event. Mr. and Mrs. Garnett didn't have any kids, and I thought it was abandoned until a few years ago."

"Really?" My level of excitement has just gone up a few notches. If this house is as amazing on the inside as it is on the outside, it may not be so awful living here until the job is done.

Johnny nods, and unbuckles his seat belt. "Do you need help with your bags?"

I completely forgot about the duffel bags he set in the back seat before attaching my car to his truck with a chain. I won't even talk about how weird that looked. I could easily take them in myself, but I don't know that I want to go into this new place alone. What if the inside is a total shit show? Or worse… haunted. "Sure, I'll grab one and you grab the other?" Grabbing the door handle before he has a chance to come around, I swing the door open. I step down from the truck, and peer up at the house. This is either going to be awesome, or go up in flames. Either way, it's my home for the time being.

Chapter Ten

Sᴡᴇᴀᴛ ꜰᴏʀᴍꜱ between my hand and the bag I'm carrying, and my steps are clumsy as I walk up the stairs to the front door of my new home. Gently setting down my bag, I bend to pull the key out from under the mat. I breathe a sigh of relief when I feel the warm metal meet my fingertips. It was right where Rosie said it would be in the email she sent me with all the information. Deep breath in, and out. As I slip the key into the doorknob, I don't move my hand. This is a big moment. Not because I've never been on my own. It's just that I've never been this far away from my family. *How am I supposed to adult without them?*

"Do you need some help?" Johnny's voice behind scares the hell out of me. For a second, I forgot he was here. This man I don't even know has been a witness to the insanity of my life today. He must think I'm a moron.

I shake my head. I will not show weakness to this stranger. Even if he is attractive. "No, I'm sorry. I sort of spaced out for a second." There's no sense in delaying the inevitable. This is my life, for now, and I need to pull up my big girl panties and deal with it. I turn the key, pull it out and place it in my pocket. I'll need to put it on a keyring so I don't chance losing it in the future. Placing my hand back on the knob, I give it a small twist. The door opens, creaking with every inch. "Is it supposed to do that?"

"It's an old house," Johnny shrugs. "No matter how much remodeling has been done, it's likely to show its age in small ways."

Nodding, I pick up my bag and take a step inside. He follows right behind me. My hand finds the wall, feeling around for the light switch. There's no way I'm going a step further without a way to see what's around me. Finally, I find the switch, and the foyer is illuminated. My eyes adjust from the dark to the sudden brightness, and I gasp.

Johnny runs towards me. "Is everything okay? Is there something awful in here?" He's such a gentleman, and I can't wrap my head around why he'd be so kind to me. A woman he's never met before this night.

"No," I shake my head. "It's stunning." My eyes are tearing up at the sheer beauty of this house. He moves around me until his dark brown eyes meet mine. "Absolutely breathtaking." I'm not sure anymore if I'm talking about him, or the house. Either way, I'm in complete awe.

I clasp my hands together and turn in circles, taking in the entire room. "My cousins are never going to want to leave." Seeing this house has completely turned my day around. It's still a pretty shitty day, but this makes it absolutely worth it.

"I think I'm going to go," Johnny says quietly.

"Sorry," I cover my mouth. "I forgot you were here for a moment." Again… he doesn't need to know that, though. I'm such a horrible person for pushing him out of my mind so easily. It's not easy to do, considering he helped me out, and I keep checking him out every chance I get.

"It's all good," he says. "I'm glad your night seems to have turned around." He takes a couple of steps backward toward the door. "I'm going to find something to write my number on so you can call me in the morning. In case you need a ride, or help figuring out what to do about your car." He adds that last bit in a rush. I make him nervous, and I'm not sure how I feel about that. He seems like a genuinely nice guy, and someone I can see myself spending time with while I'm here. As friends only, I tell myself. You do not have time for any flings.

"Tiffany and Audrey should be here early in the morning, so I shouldn't need a ride anywhere. But I'll definitely call about the car. She's my brand-new baby." I practically run toward him, and wrap him in a hug. "Thank you for stopping tonight. I didn't think anyone was going to come to my rescue and I'd be left walking down a dark road to find help."

"You're welcome?" His voice goes up an octave, nowhere near the deep, sexy tone he had moments ago. Oh shit, did I make things weird? It wasn't my intention, but I felt like a hug was an appropriate gesture. And, I got to feel his body against mine. It's been so long since I've embraced someone other than my family.

I release my hold on him, giving him a slight chance of running away, frightened by the crazy blonde lady. He doesn't move. I pull my phone out of my back pocket and hold it toward him. "Here." Shoving it in his hands I back up, putting some distance between us. "Just put your number in my phone to make things easier. I never carry pen and paper with me. My entire life is in the palm of your hand right now. I'd be lost without it."

"Okay," he taps on my phone and hands it back to me. "I guess I'll talk to you tomorrow. If you need anything, don't hesitate to call. I'm less than five minutes away."

"Will do," I nod. "Goodnight Johnny. And really, thank you for everything." I walk him toward the door, and wave when his foot hits the bottom step. Watching him walk away isn't a bad view. His jeans hug him in all the right places, and I tamp down the little voice in my head telling him to come back. It's crazy to feel such a strong attraction to someone I've just met, right?

My phone is in my hand before he pulls out of the driveway, calling my cousins, as I'm making my way up the stairs to find my bedroom.

"It's about freaking time," Tiffany yells. "You were supposed to be there hours ago."

"I know," I sigh. "You wouldn't believe the day I've had. I had to stop to pee. And when I finally got here, something ran out in front of me, and I ended up in a ditch."

"Oh my gosh," Audrey whispers. "Are you okay?"

"Yeah, I'm fine. My car, not so much." I rub my forehead with my free hand, and plop onto the bed of what I assume is the master bedroom. It's definitely spacious with plenty of room to walk around. Hell, I could work out in here if I really wanted to. That's crazy talk, though. All I want to do right now is curl up in this blanket and pass out.

"This is why you need to go home with us more often. You have no idea how to drive on country roads." Tiffany chastises me. She's not normally the one who gripes me out about things like this. Maybe my absence is making her realize she needs to grow up. At least a little bit.

"If your car is messed up, how did you get to the house?" Audrey voice is full of suspicion.

"A guy stopped to help me. He fed me and gave me a ride. He even helped me get the car off the road."

"Are you insane?" Ah, my sensible cousin always ready to talk to me about the dangers of being out in the world alone. "He could have been a horrible person and hurt you."

"But he wasn't," I deadpan. "And I didn't want to sit around waiting for someone else to help. I didn't have any signal where it happened."

"That's why the call dropped when I was trying to call you," Tiffany says.

"Bingo." I move until my head finds the pillows. They are old and lumpy, but the thought of going back downstairs to get the bag holding my pillows is too much of a nuisance. "What time are y'all heading out in the morning?"

"We'll talk about this when we get there," Audrey whisper yells. She never raises her voice too much no matter how angry she is. "And we're leaving here around six thirty, and should be there around ten. Maybe sooner."

"You are lucky I love you," Tiffany pipes in. "That's entirely too early for me to wake up unless I have work."

"You'll be fine," I mutter. "Anyway, I'm pretty wiped out. I'm going to head to bed. I'll see y'all tomorrow. Love you."

"Love you, too," they chorus, and the line goes dead.

I set the alarm on my phone and place it on the table next to the bed. I'm not used to being surrounded by all this quiet. It'll be a miracle if I fall asleep at a decent time.

Chapter Eleven

I WAKE up minutes before my alarm goes off. There is absolutely no reason to be up before seven when my cousins are probably just now hitting the road. I know Audrey said they'd be leaving at six thirty, but let's be honest, there's no way they walked out of my apartment until probably right now. I know Tiffany too well.

First thing on the agenda, a shower. I feel gross from traveling yesterday, and after a rough night of sleep, I need to wash away my worries. I run downstairs to grab my bag that has my bathroom items in them. I may have slept on an old pillow last night, but I'm not trusting that this place has towels. I'd much rather use my own.

The climb up and down stairs is going to take some getting used to. It is one of the reasons why I'm not a huge fan of two-story houses, normally. However, this one might be an exception. The added bonus being I don't have to pay for it. I set my bag on the bed, and pull out my towel, and everything else I need. I'll probably need to shave just in case I see my sexy rescuer again today. I'm really hoping I do. *Stop it, Stella. The promotion is all that matters. Sexy man or no sexy man.*

The bathroom is attached to the bedroom so I undress as I walk into it. The curtains are open, though I doubt anyone can see me since I have absolutely no neighbors. I reach to turn on the water but something in the tub catches my eye. "What the hell is that?" I bend down to get a closer look, and hear the hiss coming from the snake hanging out beside the drain. I shriek, grab the towel I dropped on the floor, and wrap it around me.

Is this one of those times I can call Johnny? I'm hoping like hell it is because

I'm not touching that thing. I rush back into the room and grab my phone. Pressing his contact, I wait for the ringing and will him to answer. It's ringing for so long that I'm not sure he's going to answer. Just before it rolls over to voicemail, I hear his gruff voice over the line. "Hello?"

"Johnny?"

"Yeah. Stella? Is that you?"

"Yeah," I pant. "Can you come over here?"

"What's wrong?"

I don't have time to explain this to him. "I need you over as soon as possible." I'm breathing hard, and I can only imagine what I sound like to him. "Hurry, before this stupid thing tries to attack me." I hang up the phone and jump on my bed, sitting as close to the headboard as I can. There's no way I'm leaving this spot until he gets here to rescue me…once again.

All the joy and elation I felt when I walked into the house last night is gone. It went right out the window when a snake decided to slither its way up the drain into the shower. I'm not cut out for country life. Why couldn't Mr. Hart get me an apartment in town? A place that has less creepy crawlers' intent on scaring the shit out of me. I wish Johnny would hurry up and get here. I'm not prepared to deal with that thing in my bathroom. Hell, I don't know the first thing about wrangling a snake. I will just wait for Johnny to come.

I've never once needed a man to do anything for me, but I'm not too proud to admit that I'll gladly let one take care of this problem. He just needs to get his ass over here. I'm not sure why my first instinct was to call him. Maybe it was the way he helped me last night, or the fact that he told me to call him if I needed anything. I think this falls under the anything clause.

I'd be lying if I said I didn't want to see him again, though. When I fell into him last night, I felt a zing. One that I haven't felt in years. My sole focus has been on my career, and I haven't given myself time to date. The few times I've gone out, I've ended up with total assholes. It's possible my expectations are too high, and I have this weird notion that guys should be gentlemen and not obnoxious at all.

I hear footsteps pounding up the stairs to the porch, and seconds later the front door slams open. "Stella," Johnny calls. "Where are you?"

Wow, he got here faster than I thought he would. It hasn't even been a full five minutes and he's barging through my front door like some sort of superhero. "I'm upstairs," I yell to make sure he can hear me. Wait, how did he get inside. God, I'm such an idiot. I was so excited about the house last night that I didn't bother locking the door before coming upstairs. And I didn't think about it when I went downstairs earlier. *Shit.* I'm not telling Audrey about this mishap. She'll never let me live it down and I'll get an hour-long lecture from her. I'd rather do without that, thank you very much.

I hear his boots hit every single one of the steps leading from the front door to the landing. Each thud brings him closer to getting rid of the stupid snake in my bathroom. He skids to a stop when he sees me.

Holy shit. I am not prepared for what he is wearing. Or…maybe I should say a lack of what he's wearing. A simple white T-shirt covers his broad chest, but that's not where my eyes land. Their focus is on the loose-fitting boxers covering the top half of his legs. When you add in the boots, and disheveled hair, it has every part of me buzzing with energy. These hormones need to simmer down. Now is not the time.

My gaze slowly moves up to his face, and the smirk on his face lets me know he caught me gawking. "Are you done staring?" He crosses his arms over his chest and leans against the open door. "Why did you have me rush over here? You look perfectly fine to me."

I swallow past the lump in my throat. There has never been a man that can render me speechless, and yet here I am without a word to say. A noise from the bathroom brings me back to my senses. "There's a snake in my shower." My voice comes out barely above a whisper. He makes me nervous, especially when he looks as if he just rolled out of bed.

He quirks an eyebrow and stalks toward me. "Is that who I can thank for the view this morning?" His eyes travel up and down my body. I thought I freaked him out last night, and that's why he left so abruptly. But maybe he's been thinking about me as much as I've been thinking about him. Stop, Stella. You're imagining it. It's just adrenaline from rushing over here. It doesn't mean anything. Right?

Fuck. I look down and tighten the towel wrapped around my chest. How could I forget that I don't have any clothes on? It was the last thing on my mind when the slithering thing in my shower decided to make an appearance. I swear, since meeting Johnny last night, my brain doesn't function at normal capacity anymore. I can't stop thinking about him. Hell, I even dreamed about him. It was a rather nice dream, but that's beside the point. "That's not even important." I shriek. "Can you please just get it out of my house?"

"You seemed to have forgotten about the snake long enough to ogle me." He places both hands on the foot of my bed, and leans toward me. "From where I'm standing, the snake isn't a priority."

An image of him shifting his hands higher until they wrap around my thighs, flutters through my brain, and I scoot back as if that will make it go away. The distance is a good thing. Space, that's what I need.

"Well, it's a priority for me." I am doing all I can to give off my best stuck-up and high maintenance girl vibe. Then, hopefully, he'll back off. I'm here to do my job. That's it. I don't have time to be rolling around in the sack with the locals. "Can you just go deal with it?"

"Sure," he stands up to his full height, and towers over me. I'm not short by any means, but he would still be taller than me if I wore heels. "But I want to talk to you after." He doesn't wait for me to respond. Instead, he turns his back to me and marches straight toward the bathroom. What in the world could he want to talk to me about?

A few minutes pass by, and he walks out of the bathroom with the trashcan in his hand. "Is it in there?" I'm surprised he caught it so quickly. If it were up to me, I'd burn the house down and find a new place that isn't surrounded by nature.

"Yup," he nods his head. "Do you want to see what had you so terrified?"

He tilts the trashcan toward me, and I scramble to the top of the bed. My towel is slipping, and I'm doing my best to keep it secured. "Nope. I want it out of my house. All creepy crawly things are now officially banned."

He shakes his head and laughs. "That's not how it works, City Girl."

I feel like I should be insulted by the new nickname, except it's the truth. I'm city through and through. Even though I love the house, it would be much better if it was situated in an area that had more concrete than wildlife. Without another word, he leaves my bedroom. "Where are you going?"

"To get the snake out of your house." I follow him out, and he pauses on the stairs. "Unless you want me to put him back."

"No, I'm good," I wave him off, but I'm curious now. "What are you going to do with it?"

He's already at the front door, and walking onto the porch. "I'm going to release it back into the wild."

"Why?" My voice is louder than I intended, but I don't want that thing released anywhere. "It'll just come back inside, and we'll do this all over again."

"It's a grass snake," Johnny sighs. "They aren't venomous, and they'll help take care of any rodents you have out here. Besides, I'm fine with this being a recurring event." His eyes travel from my legs to wear the towel ends just under my ass.

"Rodents," I gasp. "You mean there are mice around here."

"Mice, possums," he shrugs. "There are things bigger, and worse, than this tiny snake out there." He points toward the woods to drive his point home. Now all I'm going to think about is four legged creatures trying to find their way into my home.

"I really didn't need that visual," I huff.

"Go take a shower, and I'll deal with the snake." He turns back toward me, "Maybe I'll even go grab something for breakfast and be back before you get out."

"And put some damn clothes on," I mutter under my breath before I walk back into my bedroom. He's entirely too distracting looking the way he does. He chuckles as he walks away from me. He wasn't supposed to hear that. One day what I think won't come out of my mouth. Today isn't that day.

Hearing the front door close, I decide to stay in the bedroom. As much as I want to follow him, if only to make sure he lets the snake loose far away from my house, it is time to jump in the shower. There's no way in hell I'm going to be known as the new girl who walks around the front yard in only a bath towel. What will the people in this tiny village think of me if word got out?

Chapter Twelve

It takes a lot of skill to wash your hair while keeping your eyes open. The only way I can ensure nothing else is going to come out of the drain is if I can see it at all times. I am not letting anything sneak up on me.

My thoughts drift to Johnny and I can't keep myself from wondering if he's back yet. I'm curious to see what he wants to talk about, and as much as I'm unwilling to have an actual relationship…I'm not opposed to a little bit of fun while I'm here. I know I said I'm here to do my job and go home, but that man is beyond delicious. Especially with this hero complex he has going on. He can save me any damn day of the week.

The sound of the squeaky bathroom door knob being turned sends heat through my body, settling between my thighs. Is Johnny walking in here? I mean, he felt comfortable enough to barge in to come to my rescue, yet again. He obviously wouldn't have any issue walking in after the way he was staring at my body earlier. He acted like a gentleman last night, but this morning, I got a glimpse of something entirely different. Today, he was much more playful, and I got the impression he is not afraid to go after what he wants. The only question is…should I make him work for it? Or, give in?

Sliding the shower curtain open, I manage to fall on my ass. My head a mere inch from smacking into the wall, and making this morning even more interesting. Tiffany and Audrey are standing on the other side of the shower giggling like they are twelve-years old. "We're here," they say in unison. Ugh, they sound like those creepy twins in the hallway from that horror movie. It's a good thing they don't look like each other, otherwise it would increase the freaky factor that much more.

"Sorry," Audrey winces. "We thought maybe you weren't in the shower yet."

"Because hearing running water wasn't a clue," I grab their outstretched hands. "Seriously, I could have busted my head open."

"But you didn't," Tiffany says with a smirk on her face.

"Do one of you assholes want to help me up?" My hands still have soap all over them and it's hard to get a grip on anything.

"By the way, who's the hunky half-dressed dude in your yard? Did you end up having a night of fun?" Tiffany asks as she give me a sly glance.

Do I really want to fill them in on this? They'll give me hell for days if I even give them the littlest bit of information about Johnny. But I guess if I do it now, I won't have to hear them nag me about it later. "Let me get this shampoo out of my hair, and I'll fill you in."

"Dude," Tiffany groans. "Why do you have so much stuff?"

Rolling my eyes, I ignore her and continue walking up the steps with the box in my hands. "I thought you were done complaining after we packed it all up."

"I was until I remembered that we have to unpack it." She pauses by the truck and looks around. "Where's Audrey?"

"Good question. I have no idea."

I set the box down inside the door, and search for my missing cousin. She's not downstairs, and I rush up to see where she's run off to. Lo and behold, she's in my room, putting my clothes into neat folded stacks on my bed. Except they aren't folded the same way I had them in the box. "What the hell are you doing?"

"Folding your clothes and putting them away. What does it look like?" She doesn't bother looking up, and moves to the next article of clothing.

"That is not folding. It looks like you're doing origami."

"I read this book about keeping everything tidy, and this is how that author folds her clothes."

I snort. "Well, I won't be folding them like that once you're gone so it's a waste of time." I snatch my pajama shorts out of her hand and toss them on the bed. "We have more boxes to unload."

"Do I have to?"

"Yep. Tiff might be complaining about it, but she didn't hide out to keep from helping." Honestly, I'm a little disappointed in Audrey. She's usually the one running full steam ahead.

"Fine," she pouts. "Let's get them all unloaded, then we can take a break."

Pfft. I shouldn't take one, but a break does sound nice. Anything to stop sweating in this stupid heat. Why can't Texas actually experience all the seasons? It would be great to feel Fall for longer than a few days. Other states get weeks, even months. Not Texas…we get Summer and Winter. There is no in-between.

Tiffany is struggling with two boxes piled on top of each other when we make it outside. "Here," I say. "Let me take one of those."

"Thanks," she breaths, and looks at Audrey. "Nice of you to join us."

"Shut up," Audrey bumps into her and the box in her hand wobbles the slightest bit.

"That better not have anything breakable in it."

Wrangling these two is going to be a pain in my ass, but at least they are here to help me. I could be doing this all alone. Although…I'm pretty sure Johnny would help me out if I needed him to. Seriously, I just met this guy. Why is he my go to person right now? Work, Stella. That is what you are here for.

We are all sitting on the front porch, bottles of water in hand when a truck rumbles down my driveway. There's only one person it can be…Johnny. I hate to admit that I've already memorized the way his truck sounds. It's an older model, but you wouldn't be able to tell with the shiny paint coating the metal. It's a deep red, almost maroon, and he looks damn fine sitting behind the wheel. I was wondering if he was actually going to come back. Luckily for him, he keeps his word. I'm starving, and I haven't had anything except coffee all day.

The truck comes to a slow stop, and he doesn't get out right away. He's staring at us as if we are insane. The second his truck door opens, the three of us stand up. Audrey is hiding behind one of the posts, and waves as he makes his way toward the porch. She's such a weirdo. I'm not sure how she even gets dates without Tiffany being the wing woman. She has no problem talking to us, but when it comes to men, it's like she loses her voice and confidence. Hopefully my time away will make her speak actual words to guys.

Before I can say hello, Tiffany speaks up. "I see you've found your clothes. What a shame," she shakes her head. Leave it to her to say exactly what she's thinking.

"Funny thing," he shrugs. "They were in my closet this whole time. Who knew?" His steps are long and measured as he walks up the porch stairs. He has a purpose for being here, and I'm terrified of what it might be. "Can I speak with you, Stella?" He waves the box of what I can now see are donuts as a bribe.

My eyes widen, and I nod. Deer meet headlights. What can I say, I'm a total sucker for a man with donuts. "Yeah, sure." I walk toward the open front door, but pause and wave my hand at my cousins. I'm horrible for not introducing the minute he got out of the truck. "I'd like you to meet my cousins, Audrey and Tiffany. This is Johnny."

I don't say anything else, or wait for them to respond. I don't miss one of them whispering, "Oh, they're going inside to talk." It has to be Tiffany because she snorts then laughs obnoxiously. She's also the only one who would even say something like that within hearing distance. I'm going to strangle her.

I walk into the kitchen and lean against the counter opposite of the island. Johnny sets the box down, and I'm grateful that he came back at all. The food is just icing on the cake. I cross my arms against my chest, hoping like hell it doesn't show all of my cleavage. Not that it matters after he saw almost my entire body this morning. "Ignore them, they are beyond ridiculous." My eyes search out anything but him.

"Eh, they're just having fun." I watch him study the kitchen out of the corner of my eye. He looks impressed, and I wonder what it looked like before I moved in. When his eyes meet mine, his breath hitches. He shoves his hands in his pockets and stands straighter. "Besides, I was half naked when they saw me for the first time. I'm pretty sure their thoughts went down the gutter right then and there."

"I've assured them that nothing happened between us, and that you were only here because of a stupid snake. They really need to learn to mind their own business instead of trying to get into mine." I reach for a donut, but he slides the box away.

He rushes around the island until he's standing directly in front of me. He's too close, and he smells really good. Nothing like the men in the city. It's woodsy, as if he spends a lot of time outdoors. "That can wait." I open my mouth to protest. Except he places a finger against my mouth, effectively cutting me off. Jerking my head back, I stare at him. He actually touched me. "I have a feeling you wouldn't have been too upset if something more did happen."

My cheeks burn, and I'm pretty sure I've given away what I was thinking. "You," I stutter. "You have no way of knowing that." I try to back away, but the stupid counter is behind me and I have nowhere to go.

He places his hands on the counter, boxing me in. Too close. Way too close. I can't think when he's right here, in my space. "Tell me that you aren't attracted to me in any way, and I will lay off. I'll talk to you about your car, and we can act as if we've never seen each other half naked." When I don't respond, he continues. "Or, I can talk to you about your car and we can have a little fun while you're here."

"What do you mean by fun?" My voice is husky, giving him the answer he wants.

"You know exactly what I mean." He leans closer, his lips a breath away from my ear. "No strings attached. You, me, and whatever we can think of to fill the time. Something to ease the stress of you missing home."

I duck under his arms, grab a donut, and back away from him. "That's pretty forward considering I don't even know you." I take a bite and continue walking backward until I run into the refrigerator. *Damn it.* I really need to learn the layout of this kitchen.

"That's the beauty of it," he says. "We're practically strangers. How long are you staying in town?" That probably would have been the better question for him to lead with. Not that I'm going to say yes, or anything.

"Two or three months, I think," I say around a mouthful of donut. Maybe that will be enough to ward him away.

"See," he argues, as if I've just cleared everything up. "That's not long enough for us to develop real feelings for each other. Hell, we don't even have to be exclusive with each other if it makes you feel better." He must see the disgusted look on my face because he corrects himself. "Or, we can. It's up to you." This man has lost his damn mind if he thinks I'm just going to jump into bed with him. It also makes me wonder what's wrong with him that he doesn't have a girlfriend already. "We don't have to see each other regularly. Whatever you decide is what will happen."

He sounds desperate now, and my defenses are up. "I'll have to think about it." I can't believe I'm actually considering this. "Until I decide, are you good with being friends seeing as you're the only person I know in this town."

"Sure." He smiles. Ugh, that smile is enough to make my panties drop straight to the floor. "If you change your mind, just let me know." He winks at me.

I move toward the box of donuts again, picking one up. "Now that whatever that was is out of the way, what did you want to discuss about my car?"

Chapter Thirteen

"So, are you going to take him up on his offer?" Tiffany and I are sitting at the kitchen table waiting for Audrey to return with the pizza. She didn't trust Tiffany to drive the rental truck to get food since it's in her name.

"I don't know," I bury my face in my hands. "I don't even know him. Besides, before we have any of these discussions, shouldn't we wait until Audrey gets back?"

Tiffany snorts. "Hell no. She is the voice of reason, and you listen to her way too much anyway." She pulls my hands from my face. "This is the perfect situation. He's not looking for anyone permanent, and neither are you. You can get your job done, and have a little fun on the side."

"But what if I catch feelings? Or my sexcapades with him interfere with my job? I can't afford for this project to go down in flames. I need this job." I scoot my chair back and stand up. "This could go wrong on so many levels." It's a good thing I'm wearing flipflops. Otherwise, my feet would be aching in the heels I typically wear with all the pacing I'm doing.

Now, it's Tiffany's turn to stand up. She rounds the table and grabs my shoulders. She's the baby out of the three of us, and almost four years younger than me. Taking her advice would be a lot easier if she had her shit in order and didn't move wherever the wind blows her. "Stop worrying so much. You have an amazing job that you've busted your ass for, and this distribution center is going to be up and running without a hitch. Go out and have fun. It's a win, win situation."

"Spoken like somebody who doesn't have any responsibilities," I sigh. She jerks her hands away from me, and hurt flashes across her face. "Sorry, I didn't mean it like that. I just don't know how to be like you."

She forces a smile onto her face and shrugs. "No biggie." She's playing it off, but I know my words hurt her more than she's willing to let on. "Just try not to overthink things. It's how I get through life; you don't see me stressing out over every little thing."

I'm choosing to let that last jab go because what I said was kind of bitchy. Maybe I should take her advice, though. Let loose and enjoy myself while I'm here.

"Dammit," Audrey's voice comes from the front of the house. "I am really missing the city right now. We could've had our food delivered to us within fifteen minutes. I wouldn't be struggling to open a door and carry three pizza boxes into a house I'm not familiar with." She grunts, and I hear a box slide. "A little help here would be nice."

Oh shit, Audrey is about to get pissed. She looks sweet and innocent, but when she loses her temper, it's not pretty. Instead of fighting over who is going to help her, we both run to the front door. Neither of us wants to frustrate her more than she already is. "Let me have those," I say grabbing the boxes out of her hands. "Thanks," she slips her shoes off before heading for the kitchen. "Tiff, can you go grab the wine out of the truck?"

"Sure thing," Tiffany salutes her. I can see why she decided to talk to me before Audrey came back. She didn't want me to get a "mom" lecture.

Audrey is pulling plates out of a box as I set the pizzas down. "You realize this place isn't even a town, right? Asheville reminds me of where you lived when we were kids. This…this is a village."

"I know," I groan. "It's not exactly what I was expecting, but I can't complain too much. I mean, it is free since the company is paying for it."

"Which is good," she agrees. "I just think living here is going to be hard for you without all the hustle and bustle of the city. You wanted to escape this life growing up, and you ended up in the small-town life again. Even if it's only for a short period of time."

"Who knows," I shrug. "It may not be all that bad."

"Please tell me you aren't considering getting involved with that guy," Audrey sighs.

Tiffany walks in with two bottles of wine, and stops in her tracks. Instead of putting in her two cents because it will get her nowhere with Audrey, she sets the bottles on the counter and begins searching for the wine glasses I packed. "I have a feeling we're going to need this," she whispers as she passes by me.

"Is it such a bad thing if I do?" I ask. "It's not like I'm staying here."

"He's a distraction, Stella," she stares at me, waiting for me to back down. For someone without kids, she sure does know how to use the scary mom voice. "You were the first one to tell us that your focus has to be your job. It's all about our promotion, remember?"

I roll my eyes. She's way too damn young to be giving me this speech. I've done nothing but focus on my career. I've pushed aside dates, and sacrificed having a life so I could work my way up the corporate ladder. Is it such a bad thing to veer off the path? "Let's not talk about it anymore tonight. Y'all are leaving in the morning, and we should make the most of tonight." Tiffany shoves a glass of wine in my hand before pouring one for her and Audrey. "I won't be in the same city as y'all for a few months."

"Lucky," Tiffany mumbles under her breath. It takes everything in me to hold back my laugh. This is exactly the type of escape she would welcome.

"Fine," Audrey agrees. "Here's to getting the distribution center up and running, and a future promotion."

As much as these two drive me crazy, I'm going to miss seeing them on a regular basis. Even though we can video each other, it's just not the same. They won't be here to tell me when to cover my eyes in scary movies, or drink with me when the job is getting to be too much. We clink our glasses together, and take a drink. I think they feel the same way.

Last night I didn't sleep well once Audrey and Tiffany left. I felt completely alone. Everything here is so quiet. There's no traffic noise, or sirens, to fill the background. All I can hear is the water hitting the bottom of the shower or the wind rustling leaves outside my window. I plan on downloading one of those white noise apps on my phone to make me feel more at home when I go to bed tonight.

One this is for sure, I will not be watching any horror movies while I'm here. This entire scenario is how they all start out. A girl alone in a house surrounded by a wooded area. No thank you, I choose life.

I sigh, as I pull out my clothes for my first day of work. I don't know anyone here, and I'm not sure how I'll be received. Small towns are known for being leery of outsiders, or at least in my experience. It's okay if I don't become chummy with the people here. It's not like I'll be here forever. Two months and I'm gone, back to the city where I belong.

My shower is quick. My eyes stay trained on bottom of the tub thanks to my new fear of snakes from a drain. Mondays are already hard enough. I don't need to be freaked out about one more thing. Of course, I could call Johnny to rescue me, but he's already supposed to be arranging something for me to get to work. I think he mentioned taking me in himself, if need be, until I can get a rental car. Being a burden to him isn't something I want to do, though. He has to have his own things he needs to get done. Chauffeuring me around shouldn't be one of them.

I almost slip on the tile floor as I get out of the shower. The box full of bathroom stuff is one of the few I haven't unpacked yet. I'm kicking myself for not doing that last night. This floor is slippery with condensation after my shower and I'm not a fan. My house in Austin would probably be the same way without my lush rug right in front of the shower entrance.

Getting dressed doesn't take me long, thanks to setting out my clothes beforehand. It always pays to be prepared, at least in this instance. Nerves creep along my spine, and I wish they would stop. This isn't something that's ever happened to me. Not even when I interviewed in front of Mr. Hart for the first time all those years ago.

This feels different, somehow. For the company, so much hinges on this center being up and running as fast as possible, and for me, I can't even think about how everything going smoothly could affect my position in the company. Success is the only option I have.

Up or down? That's the question that keeps running through my brain as I'm fixing my hair. I feel like down would make me seem more laid-back, but up will make me look professional. It's hard enough being a woman in management, and I don't want a new group of people to make any assumptions about me. I remember how judgmental some small-town communities can be. It seems so inconsequential to worry about how my hairstyle makes me look, but they need to know that I should be taken seriously.

In the end I decide to split it. My blonde hair is resting against my back, but the front is pulled back and held firmly in place with a barrette. Fingers crossed I made my first correct decision for the day.

The smell of coffee fills the house, and I inhale deeply. I will forever love Audrey for getting me a coffee pot, with a timer, for my birthday. I don't have to waste time in the mornings, going through the motions. All I have to do is add my cream and sugar, and I'm ready to go. It's the perfect solution to getting my ass in gear in the mornings. And if I oversleep, which has been known to happen, it will wake me up.

With my travel mug of caffeinated heaven, I step out onto the front porch looking for Johnny. He isn't here, but there is a car in my driveway. One I don't recognize. *What the hell?* Who would leave a car that obviously isn't mine in the driveway? A part of me is leery of walking toward it, but there is a square piece of paper tucked underneath the windshield wiper, and my curiosity gets the best of me as usual.

The handwriting is almost illegible. But I see Johnny's name at the bottom, and any uncertainty I had melts away.

Stella,

I had to go into work early this morning so I could order a few things for your car. This is my mom's old car, and she said it was okay for you to use it. Everything works great and it will get you where you need to go until you get a rental, or I get your car fixed.

Johnny

Wow, his mom must be very trusting. There's no way in hell I would let someone I don't know borrow my car. I don't even let Tiffany use my car, and she's my cousin. I'm tempted to leave it parked in my driveway and call an Uber to come pick me up, except I'm running late and I doubt they have that type of service out in the boonies. Reason number five hundred and sixty-five why I miss the city.

Chapter Fourteen

THE MAPS APP on my phone directs me to the distribution center. It doesn't take nearly as long as I thought it would, and it's only a few miles outside of Asheville. I hope Asheville has a decent bar so I can go to at the end of the day to unwind. The only thing that would make it better is if it was within walking distance from my place so I wouldn't have to drive like it is back at home.

Looking around the site where the new distribution center will be, the only person I come into contact with on my way into the building is one of the construction workers. "Can you tell me where the foreman is?"

"Sure thing," he sets down the tool bag he's carrying in his hand. "If you go through those doors," he points to the double metal doors in front of us. "And take a right, he should be putting the last touches on the office."

"Thanks." It's odd that he didn't even ask who I was. If a stranger walked onto a jobsite in a city, there's no doubt in my mind they would be asking who they were and what their business was. Way too damn trusting. Though that may work in my favor when I start hiring people. Unless of course, they are leery of "outsiders."

I am not sure if it is the tapping of my heels on the new floor or the sound of my heart thudding in my chest, but they are drowning out the sound of power tools all around me. My pesky nerves are back, and I need to dispel them before I meet with the foreman.

To my right is the office. The flickering fluorescent light giving the space a creepy feeling. I'm not looking forward to spending most of my time in there. Maybe I can bring a lamp in to keep the office illuminated and not have to turn those lights on.

"Can I help you?" A man with broad shoulders asks as I step inside. He doesn't look amused that a stranger is walking into his domain.

"Actually, you can," I nod my head and hold my hand out to shake his. "I'm Stella. Mr. Hart said you would be expecting me."

"Oh," he gives my hand a quick shake. "I'm Chance, and the foreman of this operation. I was just finishing up the desk. I can be out of your way in the next fifteen minutes."

"Thank you," I reply. "How much longer do you think it will take to finish the building?" Normally I would lead into this question with small talk, but I also have a Job Fair to plan, and I need to know when I can do that. The sooner I can get employees here and running things, the sooner I can go home.

He shrugs his shoulders, "Maybe a week. We didn't have any other jobs vying for our attention, so we were able to complete this faster than antici-pated. Right now, we're a month ahead of schedule."

"That's great," I exclaim. "It will work out perfectly with the rest of my plans."

"Glad we could help," he says. "I'm all done here. If you need anything, just holler. Myself or one of my guys will be able to help."

Left alone in the room, I can hear the sounds of drills down the hall. I have the distinct impression that these are going to be make up the soundtrack to next week as they finish up the building. Right now, there isn't much to work with, but that's okay. I can at least start getting everything organized. This way, it will all be ready to go when I hand this job over to whoever we hire. Hopefully, Mr. Hart has someone in mind, or else I'll have to start from scratch.

Taking a small break, I send Johnny a text.

Stella: Thanks for letting me borrow your mom's car. Is there anything she really likes I can give her to show my gratitude? Also, what's your address?

I wait a few moments for him to respond, but he doesn't. He must be busy at work. I'll probably grab a gift card of some sort, or wine, on my way home to give Johnny's mom. Hopefully, he'll give me his address and will be home when I decide to leave for the day. I need to see him, and consider this "friends with benefits" situation.

Looking at my phone one more time, I decide to stop waiting for a response and get my butt back in gear. I can do this. First, I will make this office a welcoming space for the new manager. After that, I can start planning the Job Fair.

Damn it, I should have paid more attention to where Johnny lived when he brought my car here the other night. He never replied to my message, and I feel like a dumbass for sending it. All I know is it's off the main road that cuts through town.

I slow down at every driveway entrance, searching for signs of my car. It's the only clue I have to finding his house. Fear of passing it sears through me. I'm getting closer to my house, and I still haven't spotted any possible candidates for his place. Maybe I should give up and go home. He'll text me when he gets the chance. I'm almost to the turnoff for my house when I spot my car outside a barn. That kind of matches the description Johnny gave of where he was leaving my car. Whipping into the driveway, I throw my hand in the air. Victory is mine. Holy shit, I can't believe I actually found it.

The butterflies in my stomach die at the realization as I notice his truck is nowhere in sight. I guess he's still at work. I can at least leave the gift I bought for his mom. No use wasting the trip, even if it is practically around the corner from me. I grab the bottle off the passenger seat, and search through the console for a scrap of paper. All I see is a couple of bank pens and some fast food napkins. That will have to work.

You weren't home when I stopped by. If you look to your right, there's a bottle of wine for your mom. I didn't know what to get her, but I wanted to do something to tell her thank you for letting me borrow her car. Hope she likes red. Can you take it to her for me? Also, call me so I know you got this.

Thanks,
Stella

My fingers are crossed that the wine doesn't get too hot before he gets home. Then I'll have to go buy something else. Not that it's a problem, but I don't know the woman, and I'm not certain she'll even like the wine.

Despite my claim of wanting to only be friends, the ball is now in his court. It's his turn to reach out to me. I'll know he's serious if he does. If he doesn't... I'm glad I didn't waste my time.

I hurry back to the car, escaping the heat the only other thing on my mind besides Johnny. There are still a few boxes of decorations I need to unpack. They are the last things that will make the house feel like it's truly my space for the duration of my stay.

~

My phone rings and I almost fall off the sofa. Ugh, this thing is not as comfortable as it looks. I wish they would have updated the furniture in here when they remodeled the rest of the house. I grab the ringing phone from the coffee table, and answer it before it goes to voicemail. "Hello." Good Lord is my voice really as deep as it sounds.

"Did I wake you?" I blink in confusion for a bit, then pull the screen back to see who's calling…Johnny.

I should have known it was him as soon as I answered. It's not like there are a ton of guys that call me at any given moment. "Damn. I must have dozed off," I sigh. "Did you get the bottle of wine I left for your mom?"

I take a second to wonder why he's calling before I remember that I asked him to. "Yep," he says. "I'll make sure to get it to her." Silence fills the receiver, and it's becoming awkward. "You should probably go back to sleep."

"It's okay. I need to stay awake." My mouth opens wide as I yawn. "Was there something else you needed?"

He doesn't miss a beat. "I was giving you a call per your note. But I also wanted to see if you've eaten yet."

My stomach growls, answering the question, but it's probably quiet enough that he doesn't hear it. "Actually, no." I stand up, needing to get off the couch before I'm stuck, or fall back to sleep.

"Do you want to come over for a late dinner?"

Should I or shouldn't I? I did say that it's his move, and he just made it. "Sure. What time do you want me there?"

"Anytime." His voice hitches, and it's adorable that I make him nervous. Especially after he came to my house and went all Alpha male on me. It only makes me want to figure him out even more.

"Okay, I'll be there in twenty." It's a good thing I know where he lives now. Downside, I have no clue what the hell I'm supposed to wear. Do I wear the leggings and t-shirt I have on now? Or, do I put something else? So many decisions.

"Sounds good. I'll see you then."

"Bye," I say and hang up before he can say anything else. Are we hanging out as friends, or is this a date? I mean friends hang out and eat dinner together. I need to see what other options I have for clothes. What I am wearing doesn't feel like it's right. It definitely sends the "friend zone" message loud and clear, but just because he's there now doesn't mean I want him to stay in that compartment until I leave.

Chapter Fifteen

Geez, he lives less than five minutes from my house, and I've still somehow managed to show up later than planned. In my defense, I had to make sure my makeup was on point without looking like I'm trying too hard. I don't know why I am trying to impress a man I barely know. I need to be focusing my attention, making sure this center opens with a bang, not on how handsome this man is. Yet, here I am, at his house for dinner.

The front door swings open before my foot touches the porch. "You scared the hell out of me."

"Sorry," he shrinks back. "I didn't want you to trip over anything since I haven't replaced the light out here, yet." He opens the door wider, inviting me in.

"Any chance you've fixed the floor in the kitchen. I don't want to fall through it again." I search for a wall peg to hold my bag to no avail. Instead, I set it on the small entryway table.

"Not yet," he shrugs. "It will have to wait until I have some free time since *someone*," he points his finger at me, "derailed my plans the other night. Besides, you wouldn't have fallen through it if you weren't being nosy."

"That wasn't my fault! I can't control things that run out in front of moving objects," I huff.

"I was just giving you a hard time." Johnny's shoulders shake with laughter he's trying to hide. "I'm glad you don't deny being nosy, though."

"Eh," I shrug my shoulders. "I needed to know what kind of person you were. And...to make sure you weren't a serial killer."

"You probably should have thought about that before you willingly got in my truck. What would you have done if I had no intention of bringing you to my house? Or actually helping you?"

"I guess it's a good thing we don't have to worry about that since you aren't *actually* dangerous. Besides, I'm sure I would have come up with something if my life was on the line." I wave his concern away, but he is eyeing me as if he wants to devour me whole. I've never been a huge fan of fairy tales, but I'd play the little red riding hood to his big bad wolf. He's obviously not as gentlemanly as I assumed. "Didn't you say you were cooking for me?" Talk about an abrupt subject change. Could I have made it anymore noticeable?

He laughs, walking around me and toward the oven. "You're lucky I didn't already eat. I thought you might stand me up when you didn't show up when you said you would." He's pulling pans out of the oven and sets them on the counter in front of him.

"There is no way I'd be a no show when food is involved. I very rarely get home-cooked meals." I watch his arms flex with every movement as he preps our plates. "I am sorry for getting here late. I had to figure out where Audrey put all the clothes she unpacked." Not entirely a lie.

"You must be busy if you never get a home cooked meal."

"I'm practically married to my job. No rest for the wicked and all that. My cousins wouldn't mind me taking more time off, though."

"Y'all seem pretty close." He adds macaroni and green beans to the pork chops on the plates.

"Yep. They are my best friends. We've been close since we were kids. Spent summers together, and called each other all the time. Our parents weren't fans of the phone bills, but I think they're happy we stayed in touch. When they graduated from high school, they left home and moved to Austin near me."

"Wow. I can't imagine moving across the state for anyone in my family." He grabs some silverware and motions me to follow him. "I hope it's okay with you if we eat in the living room seeing as how I don't have a kitchen table."

"That's fine with me." I take a seat on the sofa while he sets the plates on the coffee table. "I only eat at my table when Audrey and Tiffany come over. There's no sense going through the whole routine when it's only me."

"We might be more alike than you think. Let me grab us some drinks. Anything in particular that you want?"

"I'm good with water, thank you." Johnny turns toward the kitchen, and I'd be a liar if I said I wasn't checking out his ass. "Do you have any siblings?"

"Yeah," he hollers from the kitchen. "I have three brothers. After graduating, they left as soon as they could." He comes back and hands me one of two bottles of water. "They wanted to look for something bigger and better. I guess they seemed to have found it. I only see them a few times a year around the holidays."

"I can't imagine only seeing people I grew up with a handful of times a year. Hell, I'm not certain how I'm going to handle not seeing Audrey and Tiff every few days."

"I do believe I offered a way to distract you," he winks at me, and grabs his knife and fork. "Dig in before it's too cold to taste good."

I do as he says and moan as I bite into the pork chop. It's grilled with a hint of Italian seasoning. Anytime I've had chops on the grill they are sticky with barbecue sauce. These are perfection and I bypass using my fork and knife. Holding the meat between my fingers, I take another bite. It may not be lady-like, but he doesn't seem to mind.

"You need to stop making noises like that, or you're going to give me the wrong impression."

Maybe I want to give him that impression, even if I'm not doing it intentionally. This food is just *that* good. "I've never had chops cooked like this before. They're delicious."

"Stick around long enough and I'll show you how to make them. It's not hard."

His offer to be whatever I want flits through my mind. Would it be so bad to have a little fun while I'm here? Audrey is definitely not in my corner on this, but Tiffany has my back. What would it hurt? It's not like I'll be here long enough to catch feelings or anything. Having someone to do things with is totally reasonable, and if we end up in his bed, or mine, so be it.

The rest of the night goes by in a blur. He now knows all the horrible pranks my cousins and I played on each other as children, including the time Tiffany tried to make Audrey eat a dead frog. That didn't go over well with any of our parents. The shitty part was I got blamed for it. I'm the oldest and was supposed to set an example. Not let them act like the kids in *Lord of the Flies*.

I glance at the clock hanging above his television. Holy shit, it's midnight. I need to get home if I'm going to get enough sleep for work tomorrow. There's so much I need to do to prepare for the Job Fair.

"Why do I get the impression you're about to rush out the front door?" Johnny's voice breaks into my thoughts.

"Because I have to get to bed. I'm not a morning person, and I have so much to do tomorrow." I don't want to leave, but even if I'm planning on taking him up on his no strings offer, I don't put out on the first date. If that's what this is.

"You could always stay," he suggests.

"As tempting as the offer is, I really need to go. It's not like I live far away." If I did, my ass wouldn't be going anywhere. It would be the perfect excuse, but alas I'm minutes down the road.

"Okay, let me walk you to your car." He grabs my hand, and pulls me off the sofa. "You never know what wild animals lurk in the woods."

"Thank you for that frightening thought because living in the middle of nowhere by myself, isn't creepy enough." I pull the car key from my pocket, and notice that he still hasn't released my hand. I'm not going to say anything because it feels nice. Not only did this man cook for me, but he's the type of person to make sure I get to my car safely. Well, his mom's car.

He doesn't bother closing the front door as he leads me outside down the steps. I hope mosquitos don't invade his house. The ones I've seen could almost pass as small birds. He hesitates after opening the car door for me. "I had fun tonight."

"Me, too." It's shocking how easy it was to talk to him. All the past blind dates I've gone on have been dull, and quiet. Nothing like tonight. "Maybe next time I can cook you dinner."

"Sounds like a plan." He lets go of my hand, and takes a step backward. "Be careful on your way home."

The urge to kiss him is overwhelming. I may not jump in bed with someone on the first date, but I'm not opposed to kissing. I stand on my tiptoes, and press a quick peck on his lips. I begin sliding into the driver seat, but I don't make it far. Johnny pulls me toward him, wraps one arm around my waist, and uses his free hand to cup the back of my neck. His lips crash into mine, and I feel the electricity down to my toes. He kisses me like a man possessed, and I'm his way to freedom.

I pull back, unable to form words. He, on the other hand, grins. "Text me when you get home."

He doesn't say anything else. Just walks back to his porch and waits for me to get in the car. He doesn't go inside until I put the car in reverse. This man will be the death of any self-restraint I thought I had.

Chapter Sixteen

SHIT. Where the hell, did I leave my purse? I scour the car to see if maybe it slipped under one of the seats, and have zero luck. Running back up the porch stairs, I check the kitchen, the cabinets, and the refrigerator. The refrigerator thing is because of my aunts. Anytime they take a dish to whatever event they are attending they put their keys in the refrigerator so they don't forget their dishes. It's weird, and I have no clue why I would shove my purse in there, but it's worth a look. Too bad it's not in there.

I keep replaying my drive home last night. Did I even have it? I remember taking it inside Johnny's house and setting it on the table. *Damn it.* I never grabbed it on the way out. My mind was too focused on my hand in his, and then the kiss. Thank God I keep my phone in my pocket. Otherwise, I would have forgotten that, too. I grab it off the kitchen table and press Johnny's name.

Come on, come on, pick up the phone. "Hello?" His voice is gruff, and I can hear metal hitting metal in the background.

"Um, are you at work?" I feel horrible for bugging him if he is. That's totally unprofessional, and he seems to be extremely dedicated to his job. Almost as much as I am.

"Yeah, is something wrong?"

"Actually, yeah. Did I happen to leave my purse at your place last night?" Please say yes.

He laughs. This really isn't a laughing matter, but I guess I'm happy he's finding some humor in it. "Go check by your back door. I hid it behind the bush on the right side. I figured you might need it."

"You are a lifesaver. Thank you so much." I rush to the back door, and see the bush he mentioned. "Wait, nothing is going to attack me, right?"

"Grab a stick and wave it around in there first if you're scared."

"Are you mocking me?"

"Not at all." If it was possible to hear a smile, that's what it sounds like right now. "I just know you don't do country life."

Against my better judgement I stick my hand in the space between the wall and greenery. A sigh escapes me when my fingers brush the fabric of my purse. "Got it. I don't know how I would have gotten through today without this. I have to get things rolling for the Job Fair in a couple of weeks."

"No problem." He's quiet for a moment, and I hear someone call his name.

"You're busy. I'll talk to you later."

"Wait. What are you doing when you get off work?"

I walk back inside then my city girl instincts kick in as I close and lock the door behind me. There may not be any neighbors, but I'm not about to leave anyone easy access to get it. "Nothing. It's not like I know anyone here."

"Let's change that," he says. "Meet me after you get off and we can grab a drink."

Should I or shouldn't I? How are we supposed to keep it casual if we see each other on a daily basis?

He has to know I'm hesitating. "No pressure. We can go out as *friends*."

I don't miss the way he says friends. There's no way we can be just friends. Not after that kiss last night and how he set every part of me on fire. Screw it. If I'm going to do this, I might as well go all in. "Just give me the name and time. I'll be there."

"Great," he breathes. "I'll text you during my lunch break. See you later." Then he hangs up. He really needs to learn how to say "bye" or something. It annoys the hell out of me.

With my phone, and now my purse, in hand, it's time for this lady to get to work and kick some ass. It may only be my second day at the center, but I can already taste that promotion.

As I make preparations for the Job Fair I'll be holding, I am relieved that the all vendors accept email inquiries. If not...I'd be screwed. Well, not completely. I'd just have to make the calls from home and I don't want to do that here. The goal while I'm working in Asheville is to leave work at work. It's a lot easier since I don't have Mr. Granger's constant requests to bog me down. Maybe I'll even make some new friends with all this extra time I have. Or...maybe I'll spend a lot of time with Johnny. Right now, it could go either way.

I am anxious to meet him tonight. It's one thing to have dinner with him at his house, and quite another to be out in public with him. What if he leaves me alone at the bar? Being a shy wallflower is more Audrey's area of expertise, but I don't know *anyone* here. I'm terrified that the locals won't like me. This is why I love the city. Even if I make an ass of myself, the likelihood that I'll see any of those people again is slim. Here, though, I can tell it's a place where everyone knows everything.

Ugh, why did I decide this was a good idea? Next time Tiffany tells me I should go with the flow on something, I'm going to kick her in the ass. I'm not as uptight as Audrey, but I'm also nowhere near free spirited as Tiff. One day I'll learn my lesson, but today is not that day.

My phone rings, and I jump. My knee hits the underside of the desk, and pain shoots through my leg. Grabbing my phone, I check the screen to see who's calling. Damn, it's Mr. Hart. It's kind of odd that he's calling so soon after my arrival, but maybe not. Either way, I have to answer it.

"Hello." I pitch my voice an octave higher, and throw all the confidence I can muster into the greeting.

"Hello, Stella. How is everything going in Asheville?"

"Great," I squeak. He rivals Johnny when it comes to making me nervous, but in completely different ways. This man holds my future at the company in the palm of his hands. Johnny, on the other hand…well, I'm not entirely sure what he holds. I only know that he makes me want things I haven't wanted in a *very* long time.

"That's good." I imagine him nodding and tapping his fingers on his desk. It's something I've noticed him do during meetings. "Do you think we'll be able to open on the scheduled date?"

"If the construction crew keeps going at the rate they are right now, we may be able to open early." I clear my throat to tamp down my excitement at how easy this is going to be. "Unless, of course, you want to keep the original date."

"We will see how the Job Fair goes. Do you have any ideas on that, yet?"

"Yes, Sir. I'm working on that right now." I click my pen, anxious to get off the phone and back to work. "As soon as I finish emailing vendors about table and chair rentals, I'm going to check in and see what we need to stock the warehouse with before opening."

"Sounds good," he says. "Email me an update at the end of the week, please."

"I will. Have a great day Mr. Hart."

"You, too. Goodbye."

I tell him bye and hang up the phone. At least the big boss has manners, unlike some people I know. My phone dings with a text message. Speak of the devil.

Johnny: Meet me at Out of the Ashes at 6.

Stella: Someone is a bit demanding.

Johnny: You already agreed to go. :P I'm just giving you a place and time.

Stella: I guess. You could have said please.

Johnny: That's a no. If I formed it as a question, that gives you an opportunity to back out of our date.

Stella: Date? I thought we were going as "friends."

Johnny: I mean, if you want to look at it that way, and keep lying to yourself, that's your prerogative.

Stella: Fine. You might have a point. I'll see you there. Just know that I'll be hungry so they better have food.

Johnny: They have the best wings in town.

If I keep replying, I'll never get any work done. Putting my phone on airplane mode, I get back in gear. There's a lot to do, and while I have a couple of months to complete it, I'd rather not be scrambling at the last minute. That would only prove that I'm not ready to move up in the company, and Mr. Granger would be right. There's no way in hell I'm allowing that to happen.

Chapter Seventeen

Out of the Ashes is not at all what I was expecting. If a bar in Austin had a name like that, it would be a swanky hot spot. The place I've just pulled into looks like a dive bar with bathrooms that probably haven't been cleaned in ages. I know it's wrong of me to make that assumption, but for fucks sake. The paint on the sign is wearing off, and half the letters of the flashing "Open" sign are dull and barely visible.

Now would be the time to back out of this parking space and head home. There's a bottle of wine, and a frozen pizza, waiting for me. A totally balanced meal for a single woman.

Unfortunately, a shadow blocks the dying sunlight in front of my window. There's a knock on the glass, and Johnny peers down at me. I roll down the window and stare up at him, mouth gaping. He's in what I'm assuming is his work uniform, and I thought he looked hot as hell before. The stray grease marks and disheveled hair has me squeezing my legs together. "You weren't about to bail on me, were you?"

"Pfft," I snort. "No, why would you think that? Besides, how did you know this was the car I was in?"

"You had the car in reverse," he grins, knowing damn well he caught me in a lie. "And don't forget, you're in my mom's car. I spent enough time hiding from it when I was in my teens to know whose car it is."

I guess he has a point. And I'm the dumbass that totally forgot that I am, in fact, in his mom's car. "When do you think my car will be ready?"

"We can talk about that inside." He opens the door, and holds his hand out to me. I sigh, and turn the car off. "I promise it's not as sketchy as it looks." He nods toward the building in question. "I've been coming here for as long as I remember. I wouldn't take you somewhere shady for our first official date."

I roll my eyes at his use of the word *date*. "If you say so. But, if it sucks and I don't like it, you owe me a bottle of wine." Who the hell is this flirty version of me, and where did she come from? I don't know why, but Johnny, the guy I have known for *less* than a week, makes this girl come out.

"Deal." He holds my hand all the way to the entrance, only releasing it to hold the door open for me, and a few other people who are walking out. He's the best of both worlds from what I can tell—a gentleman in public and demanding in private. I believe this is something I can work with. As long as the stupid butterflies flitting around my stomach calm their shit. There are no emotions allowed. This is temporary. *Just keep telling yourself that.*

Looks can definitely be deceiving. From the outside this bar appears shady as hell. The inside though…it's as modern and sleek as the places I frequent in Austin.

"I take it you're surprised." A soft chuckle brushes against my neck. He wraps his arm around my waist and leads me toward a table by one of the few windows. "I told you I would never take you to a shithole on a date."

"So, you would take me to one if we weren't on one?" His raised eyebrow tells me I screwed up. "I mean," I stutter. "Not that this is a *date*. I still haven't completely agreed to anything."

"But you're considering it, and that's all that matters."

The smug grin on his face makes me want to smack him and kiss him. All of these contradicting emotions are driving me crazy. Johnny is so unlike the few men I've dated. He's just as over-confident, but he has a gentleness I've never experienced before. At least, not since my high school puppy love days. Ugh, stupid feelings need to go away. I don't have time for this.

"Stella," Johnny's voice interrupts my thoughts.

"Huh." He's staring at me and a waitress is standing at the edge of our booth. She is stunning. One of those women that will make everyone look twice with long curled blonde hair, sun-kissed skin, and shorts that are so short it's a wonder you can't see everything. There's no way in hell I'd ever be confident enough to wear anything like that unless I'm in the comfort of my own home. Maybe not even then.

"What do you want to drink?" He waves his hand toward the woman.

"Oh, sorry." My cheeks warm, and I wonder how long she's been there. Hopefully not long, or that would be embarrassing. "Whiskey sour, please."

"No problem." She taps the table, "I'll get those right out for you."

"Thanks, Angie." To his credit, he doesn't watch her walk away. That's surprising. Most guys at least glance at a beautiful woman. All the guys I dated would have, anyway. Proof that I have horrible taste in men, and maybe this isn't a good idea.

"A penny for your thoughts." He leans forward, forearms resting on the table. He's nuts if he thinks I'm going to tell him what's on my mind.

"Nothing. My mind just wandered off for a second." I pick up the menu Angie set down in front of me. "So, what's good to eat here?"

Johnny smirks and sits up, picking up his own menu. "Everything. I haven't had a bad dish in all the years I've been coming."

"Well, that narrows it down," I laugh. "What's with this place anyway? The outside looks like a decrepit building."

He shrugs and puts his menu down. I don't think he even looked at it. He was humoring me. "It's old."

"I don't mean anything bad by that. It's only that the inside and outside don't match at all. They could get some serious business if they updated and spruced it up. That's the first thing customers see, and likely turns them away."

"Everyone who lives in Asheville knows where it is. But, according to Angie, it's on her list of things to do."

"She owns this bar?" That makes me sound bitchy, but I fully expected some older man to own it.

"Yep," he crosses his arms over his chest, and his muscles bulge in the tight sleeves. I guess working on cars has some added benefits. "She inherited it from her father when he passed away. When he owned it, it was just another bar where the local drunks hung out. Then Angie took over and gutted the inside updating everything in here so she could open back up. She's actually the one who renamed it. Kind of like a caterpillar becoming a butterfly. She said she wanted to turn it from something ugly to a beautiful place where guys would be proud to take their dates." He winks at me then glances around the small bar. "I have to say, there have been fewer bar fights since she became the owner."

"Wow," I gasp. Seriously, I can't even imagine the state this room was in before she took over. "That's actually pretty amazing. If she ever wants to grow, I might know a few people that could make it happen. People in Austin would love this place." I tap my finger against my chin, my mind going a million miles an hour. "On second thought, she shouldn't fix the outside. It helps with the name. That is the old, and the inside is what came of it."

"Damn, Stella." Johnny shakes his head and laughs. "Are you sure you aren't in marketing? You kind of went off with that idea."

"Eh," I tilt my head. "It's not too far off from what I do now. Except my job is more of making sure shit gets done when it's supposed to."

"Well, I think you went down the wrong career path. But I'll introduce you and Angie when she comes back with our drinks."

"How long have you been working on cars?" I mean if we're talking jobs and day to day life, it's time I asked him.

"Since I was eighteen." Johnny rubs his chin, thinking. "Technically before that. I used to help my grandpa when he was alive. He always told me it was a good idea to know how to work on your own vehicle. Then I wouldn't have to depend on someone else to fix it."

"I feel like maybe that was directed at me."

"Not at all. Most people don't know where to locate the oil dipstick. Gramps made sure that I knew how to do at least the basics before I was even allowed to put the key in the ignition. Honestly, I can't think of anything else I'd do instead. I love working on cars. I feel like I'm doing something that helps others."

Angie approaches our table with a drink in each hand. "Here y'all go. Are you ready to order?"

"Yep," Johnny grabs the menu I set down. "But first, I'd like to introduce you to my *date*." His eyes gleam knowing that every reference to this being a date is getting under my skin. "Angie, this is Stella. She's here for a while to get the distribution center up and running. Stella, this is the owner of this fine establishment, Angie."

"It's nice to meet you," Angie holds her hand out to me.

I take it in mine, and I'm surprised to find that the palms of her hands are rough. She must do a lot of the work around here. Most people I know that own businesses sit around and let others do the grunt work. "It's nice to meet you, too. I love how you've decorated everything. It's completely unexpected."

"Thanks," she blushes. "I need to work on the outside, but it's all coming together."

"Actually," I interrupt. "I have a few ideas I want to run by you when you have a chance."

"I'd love that." Angie smiles. Someone calls her name, and she turns searching for the person. "I'll get you my number before you leave. What did y'all decided to eat?"

Johnny answers first, "Wings."

"And what about you Stella?"

"I'll have what he's having." I grin at Johnny. "He said they are the best in town."

"Alrighty, I'll get them out as soon as they are ready. I need to go see what this guy wants." She rushes in the direction of the man calling her name.

"Where's the rest of the staff?" I whisper.

"She doesn't usually have them all working during the week. She saves most of them for the weekend."

"I see."

"It hasn't been long since she re-opened the place. She doesn't want to jump all in just in case it folds."

"I'll help her get this place filled to the brim with patrons."

Johnny grabs my hand and squeezes it. "How are you going to have time to do your job, date me, *and* help Angie?"

"I have my ways." I pull my hand from his. "Besides, who said I was going to date you?"

"It's no use fighting the inevitable."

∼

"The wings were everything you promised them to be." We're walking out of the bar and to our cars. As skeptical as I was when I decided to meet Johnny here, I don't want the night to end.

"I told you. Maybe one day you'll listen to what I have to say." He bumps his shoulder into mine.

This is a bad idea. I know it is down to my core, but I can't fight my attraction to him. Besides, I can casually date. I'm a freaking adult. "What if I said, I'm leaning more into the yes column when it comes to dating you?"

"I would ask you to come over because I'm not ready to tell you goodnight." Hearing that makes me tingle. He's definitely been pushing for this and with all of his annoying comments that push all the right buttons. Even though it's terrifying that it's *me* he wants, I am starting to feel the same way. However, I'm not going to give in that easily. If I just give in, he'll come to expect it all the time. Though he may be bringing out a new side of me, I am not going to stop guarding my heart with the ferocity of a dog protecting its bone.

"I'll have to raincheck on tonight. But I'm not opposed to seeing you again." I grab the car keys from my pocket, and unlock the door. "Maybe I'll come over this weekend, and you can also show me the progress on my car."

"It's a date," he smirks and leans toward me. "But don't think you're getting out of here without me kissing you."

My back is against the car door, his fingers tangled in my long tresses, and his lips seared to my own. If he doesn't stop kissing me like this, I'll cave way too soon and go home with him right now.

His tongue sweeps across my lips before slipping into my mouth. My knees buckle and I wrap my arms around his waist to steady myself. Oh damn, he knows how to use his tongue, and I can only imagine what it would feel like pressed against my—.

My thoughts are interrupted as he pulls away. *Of course.* "Goodnight, Stella," he whispers into the night air. Talk about a complete shift in mood. "Text me when you get home so I know you made it."

I am left speechless and wanting more as he moves away from me. But I am not too stunned to miss the way he readjusts his pants as he takes a step back. Nodding, I open the car door and slide into the seat. "Goodnight Johnny," I mutter into the now vacant space where he was standing moments ago.

I'm going to need a cold shower, or two, and my trusty BOB.

Chapter Eighteen

I THOUGHT my office in Austin was quiet, it's nothing compared to this. I'll be happy when we fill this building with employees because right now...it's a little creepy. The construction workers are finished inside, and making the finishing touches that need to take place outside.

"Yes, Mr. Jones," I say into the receiver of my phone. "I'll need those tables here by the twentieth at four p.m.."

"Is there any way we can drop them off sooner?" He sounds impatient, but I told him the date and time in the email I originally sent on Monday.

I guess it wouldn't hurt anything to get them here earlier. It would give me extra time to set up for the Job Fair. "Yes, what time are you thinking?"

"Early morning, probably around nine."

"That sounds great. Just knock on the door for the dock when you get here."

"Yes ma'am. I'll see you then." Mr. Jones hangs up before I can say good-bye. Is it wrong that I pictured him tipping a cowboy hat when he said "yes, ma'am"? I know it's a stereotype, but I wouldn't be surprised to find that people around here actually do it. It's part of my vision of small towns. I remember being shocked that my aunts and uncles waved to everyone they passed on the road, even when they didn't know them. It's such a weird concept to me.

Pulling up the app on my phone that holds my checklist for the Job Fair I have to put on, I sigh. There's still so much shit I need to do, and I have no idea how I'm going to do it all on my own. I wonder if Mr. Hart would approve a request for an assistant while I'm down here. I add a line on the list to email

Rosie about it tomorrow. I would do it now, but talking with Mr. Jones wore me out. It took forever to get him on the topic of why *he* called me. I'm beginning to wonder if I am actually cut out for this job, or if I'm reaching too high with my goals of the promotion. Would it be the worst thing to be content with the position I have now? It could be worse. I could be like Tiffany and flit from job to job.

With my fingers on my temples, and my eyes closed, I attempt to rub away the stress starting to weigh on me. *You can do this, Stella. Don't let some grumpy old man break your spirit.* My phone ringing sounds like a siren in the silent building, and my knee bangs against the desk at the sound. *Son of a bitch.* I answer it without looking at who is calling. "Hello."

"What's up girl? How's small town life treating you?" Tiffany's voice comes through the receiver. Why is she calling me in the middle of the day?

"Shouldn't you be at work?"

"No," she draws out. "It's after six. Are *you* still at work?"

"Shit. I didn't even realize that much time has passed." Maybe that's why Mr. Jones was in a foul mood. He was ready to go home for the day. "How's everything back home? It's been over a week since I was there, and you assholes haven't filled me in on anything."

"Same old shit, different day." She pauses for a few seconds. "I *have* been staying at your apartment, though. My roommate is driving me crazy."

"Tiff, I don't think you've had one that doesn't annoy you. What did Bri do now?" I laugh. I can't help it. Tiffany approaches finding a roommate the same way she dates. Fast decisions without knowing anything about them.

"She threw out my fucking food." Her screeching is high enough to wake the dead.

"Was it old?"

"There may have been one or two things that needed to be thrown out," she concedes.

If I had to guess, it was more than that, but she's on a tirade. The last thing I feel like dealing with is getting bitched at for defending Bri. "Don't y'all have a rule about touching each other's food?"

"Yeah, but her neat freak self obviously doesn't know how to abide by it."

"Maybe it's time you found a new roommate."

"Already on it, Cuz." I can hear her smile through the phone and a pang of homesickness hits me in the gut. As much as I appreciate this opportunity, being away from my cousins has been terrible. "She's looking for a new place, and I've already put out an ad."

Oh Lord, this isn't going to go well unless Audrey helps with the process. "Do you want to send me a list of the applicants when they come in? I can check them out for you." Anything to keep her from finding someone that might hurt her in some way. She has zero self-preservation skills.

"Thanks, but no. I've got it under control."

"Oh yeah? How?"

"I'll see what my gut says when I meet them to tour the place. If I get bad vibes, they are an automatic no."

I snort. "One day that gut feeling is going to get your ass in serious trouble." I gather my things and shove them in my bag. I should stay to finalize more things for the Job Fair, but I promised myself I'd be out of here at five. No more work for today. It's nice being able set my own schedule without Mr. Granger breathing down my neck.

"Maybe, but I'm still alive." I imagine her shrugging as she says it. Sometimes, I wish I could be more like her and just take everything one day at a time. I mean I'm sort of doing that with Johnny, but it's terrifying.

"Shockingly," I mutter.

"Don't be bitter because you don't know how to have fun."

"I know how to have fun," I scoff as I walk out of the building and lock up. "I'm just careful about it."

"Prove it." Ugh, how am I supposed to do that? "Did you take the hot mechanic up on his offer?"

"Actually, yes."

"Seriously?" She laughs so loud I have to pull the phone away from my ear. "I didn't think you had it in you," she says between gasps. *Gee, thanks for the vote of confidence.*

"Whatever, asshole. He's fun to hang out with. I'm supposed to see him this weekend."

"Is 'hanging out' the new phrase for having all the sex?"

"No, we haven't done that…yet. But we've had dinner twice."

"Ugh," Tiffany groans. "You're such a goody two shoes. I'm going to start calling you Audrey before long."

"I don't have to screw every guy I come in contact with like someone else I know." I regret the words as soon as they leave my mouth. "I'm so sorry Tiff."

"It's all good. I'm confident in my sexy times." She pauses, "I need to get going anyway."

Fuck. "Okay. Love you."

"Love you, too." The line goes dead.

I need to figure out a way to apologize. I didn't mean to say it, but why was she on my ass about this whole Johnny thing? My fingers itch to call her back, but she needs time to cool off. I'll call tomorrow. If there's one thing I can count on with Tiffany, it's that she doesn't hold grudges.

I really need a drink after this insane day. It's a good thing I know the perfect bar.

Chapter Nineteen

Out of the Ashes is busier than it was when I came with Johnny. All the tables are filled with people chatting and enjoying a night out. Instead of waiting for a table to open up, I head straight to the bar. There's no use wasting an entire table on one person. Besides, maybe I'll be able to talk to Angie more about this place. It doesn't appear as if she needs help filling the seats but she could easily turn this into a must stop location for people coming through. Hell, she could help put Asheville on the map.

"Hi, Stella," Angie calls from the other side of the bar as I take my seat. It's loud and I can barely hear her over the music and chatter. "I didn't expect to see you back here so soon."

"It's been a long day," I sigh. "Any chance I can get a whiskey sour?"

"Absolutely. I'll bring it over in just a bit. Let me take care of this customer really quick." She finishes mixing a drink for someone directly in front of her. She's fast, I'll give her that. She barely has to watch what she's doing. If I were doing that, there'd be liquor all over the floor, and probably on me. I could never in a million years work behind a bar.

Angie walks toward me with my drink in hand. "Here you go, Hon. Do you want anything to eat?" She sets the glass down.

My stomach growls at the mention of food. I can't remember if I even took a lunch break today, but from the sound of it, I didn't. "Actually, yeah. Can I get an order of those wings I had the other day?"

"I'll get that in for you." She wipes the counter down before turning towards the kitchen. "I'll come chat as soon as it slows down. We're usually not this busy."

"It's a good thing, though. Lots of business means you can hire more people to take some of the burden off of yourself."

"That is so very true. I'll have those wings out soon." She rushes off to put in my order and wait on other people.

She's sweet and definitely someone I would be friends with if we lived in the same town. Why is it that a small part of me feels like I'm cheating on my cousins just thinking about this? Logically, I know we should stop being so codependent. Maybe then we could have lives instead of it revolving around each other. *Ugh.* Why am I being so maudlin tonight?

I'm not usually one to overthink things when it comes to them. Other parts of my life, yes. But the three of us have always been a given. I guess it has something to do with being alone for the first time in years that's giving me perspective. It's actually kind of nice not being with them all the time. Or dealing with one of Tiffany's tantrums on a daily basis.

It's like my own sort of vacation from my normal life, and figuring out who I am on my own. I lift my glass to my lips savoring the realization.

"Is this seat taken?" A deep voice whispers next to my ear. *His* deep voice. My glass almost slips from my grasp.

Amber liquid sloshes over the edge onto my fingers as I steady the glass. "You scared the hell out of me, Johnny. What are you doing here?"

"Probably the same thing as you. Getting a bite to eat, and having a few drinks." The smug grin on his face makes me roll my eyes. He's such a smart ass.

"Thank you for stating the obvious. How did you even know I was here? Are you stalking me?" I poke his chest. Hopefully by now he knows I'm only kidding. "You're making me rethink dating you if you're going to have serial killer behavior."

"Don't worry," he chuckles. "I'm not going to hack you into tiny pieces." He leans against the bar, forearms holding him up. "I'm here with a guy from work. Reaf and his wife trade nights when they hang out with friends. She gets one night a week for book club, and he gets one night."

"Wait, there's a book club that meets here?" I take a drink of my whiskey. "I love reading. Though, I can't remember the last time I actually had a chance to pick up a book."

"Hold your horses, Stella. I'm not sure how much they actually talk about books." He nods his head toward the front door. A guy who looks like he's barely out of high school is talking to the young woman at the hosts stand. "He says they mostly get together at a coffee shop and gossip about what's going on in their lives while drinking an insane amount of caffeine."

"Is he even old enough to drink?" I glance over Johnny's shoulder at the guy walking toward us. "He looks like a baby."

"If he wasn't, he wouldn't be here. I was actually supposed to hang out with him the night I found you stranded on the side of the road. His little girl was sick, and he had to cancel."

"I guess it's a good thing your plans changed. Otherwise, we wouldn't have met." I drop my voice a few octaves trying to sound sexy. His answering smirk tells me just how ridiculous I sound.

Reaf reaches us and holds out his hand. "You must be Stella." I place my hand in his and turn a questioning gaze toward Johnny. "He talks about you… a lot. He also said he got rid of a snake for you."

My cheeks warm. I hope he didn't tell him *everything* about that morning. Like the fact that we were both almost naked, and eyeing each other like people who've spent ages circling their feelings rather than two people that have barely met. "Yep," I try to hide my embarrassment. "I never had that issue before. At least, not where I live."

"Welcome to the country," Reaf laughs. "You never know what's going to show up." Johnny's eyes haven't left my face since Reaf started talking. Reaf notices, and backs away. "I'll let you catch up. Johnny, I'll text you when our table is ready."

"Thanks man." Johnny doesn't spare his friend a glance. "What are you doing tomorrow night?"

"Nothing that I know of. Why?"

"A few of us are going to a bonfire. Do you want to go with me?"

Bonfires really aren't my thing. Not that I've ever been to one. I just know what I've seen on TV and in the movies. It doesn't look like something I'd enjoy. On the other hand, I told Tiff I was capable of having unplanned fun. Turning this down would be the exact opposite. "Is it okay that I'm being invited last minute? I don't want to step on any toes."

"It's fine." He leans closer. "It's not a formal event. Just a few old friends getting together, drinking a few beers, and relaxing."

"Oh, okay. Sure, I'm game." I want to tell him it's my first one, but he'll think I'm crazy. "What time do I need to show up? And what's the address?"

"Meet me at my house around seven. Is that good with you?"

Reaf waves his arms to get Johnny's attention, in lieu of texting. "It looks like our table is ready. I'll see you tomorrow night. Text me when you get home."

"Okay." He leans in and gives me a soft kiss on my cheek. "I'll see you then."

Angie shows up with my wings as Johnny walks away. "He's got it bad for you. In all the years I've known him, he's never paid so much attention to a woman."

"Why not?" That's shocking to me, I figured he'd be a ladies' man.

"I don't know. I haven't seen him in any sort of relationship since high school."

That's interesting. I wipe the sticky spot where my whiskey spilled over, and lean my arms on the bar. "What happened to make that his last real relationship?"

She glances at me and then back at him. "That's not really my story to tell." Her knuckles tap on the bartop. "Do you need another drink?"

"Um, yes. Thank you." I watch her walk away to mix me another drink. She didn't take the opportunity to spill all the juicy details about Johnny. I remember my cousins telling me about how much shit people talked about each other in their small town. Angie definitely has my respect for keeping her lips sealed.

My thoughts are all over the place, and I don't notice the drink now in front until Angie speaks. "Let me know if you need anything else. We can talk business after I close if you're still here."

"Thanks." I look behind me in the direction Johnny and Reaf walked. He definitely piqued my interest more than he did before. Maybe he has more layers than I originally thought. And maybe my heart is getting a lot more than it bargained for.

Chapter Twenty

Nope. These aren't nerves racing through my body. It's just exhaustion from
the day. That's why I can't decide what to wear to the bonfire. I should call Tiff
and ask for her opinion, but I'm not going to. She still hasn't texted me after
what I said to her yesterday. Not that I blame her. I definitely put my foot in
my mouth. Maybe I'll drive down there and see her. There has to be something
I can do to get her to forgive me. Or, at least talk to me.

My phone vibrates across the dresser and I rush to it, hoping my thoughts
conjured a call from Tiffany. It's not her, though. Johnny's name flashes across
the screen. "Hello."

"Hey, Stella." Loud music is playing in the background. "Are you still
coming?"

"Yeah," I look around my room at the piles of clothes littering the floor and
bed. "I'm getting dressed. Why?"

"It's almost eight, and I was getting worried." He pauses and sucks in a
breath before letting it out. "But if you're not dressed, it sounds like your
house may be more fun."

"Very funny. I didn't realize the time. I'll be over in fifteen minutes."

Johnny chuckles, and the sound sends a shiver down my body. Just his
voice sends me into a tailspin. "Slow down. There's no rush. I was only
checking in."

"I feel horrible." Dammit. How did I lose track of time? I grab a few clothes
from the pile on my bed, not bothering to see what they are. "I'll be there
soon." I don't give him a chance to say anything else before hanging up. I have
ten minutes to get dressed and do something with my hair.

Dressed and hair in a high ponytail, I walk out of the house, locking the door behind me. It's a good thing he lives so close.

Johnny's truck is parked outside of his house when I pull up, but the house is dark. Maybe someone picked him up. He must have gotten tired of waiting. I'd meet him there, but I don't know where this bonfire is happening. He only told me to meet him at his house. Why is it so eerie? He really needs to get his porch light fixed because sitting in complete darkness makes me uneasy.

I grab my purse and dig around for my phone. I know it's in here somewhere. There's a possibility that he's not too far away and can turn around to come get me. My finger is hovering over his name when there's a knock on my window, and I jump. The phone flies out of my hand, landing somewhere in the backseat.

I'm scrambling to get my seatbelt off as someone begins to open the door. All I can think is that I need a weapon, and the only thing I have is a travel coffee mug. This is not how I imagined my night turning out. "Stella?" His voice stops me in my tracks, and I face the now open car door. "Are you okay?"

"Does it look like I'm okay?" I huff. "You scared the hell out of me. I was about to call you. I didn't expect you to sneak up on me like a crazy person."

He winces. "Sorry, I thought you saw me walking toward your car."

"In the dark?" I shake my head. "You could have been a deranged killer for all I know."

"You might want to lay off the horror movies," he laughs. "This is a small town and we know everyone here."

"Why aren't any of your lights on?"

"I was waiting in the truck. It seemed easier to meet you out here rather than invite you in only to leave again."

I guess that makes sense. It does nothing to quell my racing heart, though. He is right in one aspect. I need to stop watching scary movies period. Even better, Hollywood needs to stop setting horror movies in rural areas. Rather than let him know just how badly he's scared me; I steer the conversation in a different direction. "How far away is the bonfire?"

"Not far. It's actually on the back end of my property."

"How much land do you freaking have?"

"More than enough. My grandpa used to let the high school kids from Asheville go out there to hang out so at least they had somewhere safe to do whatever teenagers do." He shrugs and takes a step back, giving me space to get out of the car. "It's the perfect place. There aren't any buildings, or neighbors, and if anyone drinks more than they should, they are able to stay the night out there."

"What?" I shriek. "People actually do that?"

"Yep. We *are* in the country. Most people out here grew up camping. It's nothing they aren't used to."

"Y'all are weird."

"What do you do when you go out and drink too much? Surely you don't drive after that."

"I'm not a moron. I usually Uber wherever I need to go to avoid driving at all costs. Or if the place is close, I walk."

He nods his head, deep in thought. "That doesn't sound any safer to me."

"It's why I usually go places with Audrey and Tiffany. People tend to leave you alone if you're in a group."

"So, safety in numbers?"

"Exactly." I get out of the car and the heel of my boot sinks into the dirt. I groan. These boots were obviously a bad choice. I just wanted to give myself some height. I feel tiny compared to Johnny, and if I'm taller…it makes kissing him that much easier.

"Are you ready to head to the fire?" Johnny holds his hand out, waiting for me to grab it.

I slip my hand into his, and move to close the car door. "Lead the way." He walks me to the passenger side of his truck, opens the door, and helps me inside. "We're driving?"

"It's faster than walking." He glances down at my boots. "And I have a feeling your feet will thank me in the end."

I have no idea how I didn't hear the music from Johnny's house. The bass is pounding through the windows before we've even gotten to the other cars parked in the pasture. I can see outlines of people milling around a fire blazing at its full glory. My palms are beginning to sweat as fear seeps in. I don't know anyone here aside from Johnny. Meeting new people is something that's always been hard for me. I'm not necessarily shy, but Audrey and Tiffany are my people. They are the ones I do everything with. There's never been a need to find other people with them always around.

"Is it too late to do something else tonight?" I ask as Johnny parks the truck and faces me.

"Don't be nervous. These are good people. You'll have no problem fitting in. But, if you really want to go back to the house, or go home, I can take you back." With this, he begins to calm my nerves. He barely even knows me, yet he knows how to deal with my crazy.

I stare out the window, watching his friends, and trying so hard to tamp down the fear that they won't like me. The need to bail almost has me asking him to go back, but I need to do this. I need to stop being so wrapped up in my cousins lives that it stifles the chance to forge new friendships. "It's okay. I can do this."

He leans closer to me, placing his hand on my cheek. "If you feel uncomfortable at any time, just say the word and we'll go back to my place." His lips touch mine in soft and reassuring kiss.

"Let's do this." The words are more for me than him. The same thing I repeat to myself when I have a gigantic task ahead of me that needs to be tackled. Johnny gets out of the truck and comes around the front to open the door for me. His eyes never leaving mine, and some of the fear I had about being here melts away.

We walk hand in hand, toward the fire. All at once everyone stops their conversations and stares at us. I feel like a science experiment on display, waiting for the teacher to tell everyone what went wrong. "Everyone, this is Stella. Stella, this is everyone." He waves his hand across the expanse of open field.

Some wave awkwardly, but one person runs up and wraps her arms around me. "I'm so glad you made it."

"I didn't know you were going to be here, Angie." Relief spreads through my body. At least, I know two people here.

"Yep," she nods. "I had one of the guys I can rely on handle the bar tonight. Sometimes we all need a little time to take a break from adulting."

"Honestly, adulting is overrated," I laugh. "We spend our entire lives wanting to grow up, and realize when we're older that we want those simpler things."

"Girl, you're not telling me anything I don't already know." She walks us toward an ice chest, and Johnny goes over to a group of guys. "Want a beer?"

Beer isn't usually my drink of choice, but it's not like there's a stocked bar with liquor in the middle of a field. "Sure, whatever you have is fine." She grabs a bottle and opens it, handing it off to me. "Thanks." But before I can bring the bottle to my lips, she shoves a wedge of lime into the bottle.

"It helps with the taste," she grins.

I take a sip, and I'm surprised to find I like it. It's not like I've never had beer before, I've just never acquired the taste for it. I much prefer wine or whiskey. "It's good."

"I knew you'd like it." She rests her hand on my arm, and nods toward two camp chairs sitting by the fire. "Johnny set up some chairs for y'all, but since he's not using them, let's go chat."

"Sounds good to me. I'm just happy I know someone besides Johnny."

"These folks are harmless. You have nothing to worry about," she laughs. "We all grew up together, and a lot of them stayed close to home. It's one of the amazing things about living in a small town. We're all like family."

"That's pretty awesome. I didn't have a ton of friends in high school. I mostly talked to my cousins when we'd get out or on the weekends. I'd visit them every summer and during any breaks I had from school." Looking back, it's kind of sad just how much I relied on Audrey and Tiffany. I was in a ton of clubs during school with every opportunity to make friends, but I didn't. The one friend I thought I had turned out to be a horrible person and gossiped about me behind my back. Thus, began my lack of trust in people in general. If they weren't family, they didn't really matter to me.

"I love that you're so close with your cousins." She takes the chair closest to the fire and I sit in the one next to her. It's insanely hot, and I'm wondering why people have bonfires when it's still relatively warm outside. "I don't have many cousins, but the ones I do have…we don't get along at all."

"That sucks." And it does. I've gone a full twenty-four hours without knowing if Tiffany is still mad at me, and it's messing with me head. "I can't imagine not talking to my cousins. We are pretty much inseparable. In fact, when they heard about my temporary relocation for this job, they were not as happy as I would have liked."

"Oh," her face falls. "You aren't here permanently?"

"No. I work in management for a property firm in Austin. They are the ones opening the distribution center outside of Asheville. I'm here to make sure everything is good to go. Then I'll be going back home."

"Oh. That's good. I assumed most companies would hire that out."

"Most do, but the CEO of ours said I'd get a promotion if it opens without hitch. It's one I've been eyeing for a year, so here I am."

"I have no doubt you'll get it done." She smiles. I feel like she really means it. It's not a backhanded compliment, and she's not saying it just to make me feel better.

"Thanks. It's a lot more work than I thought it would be, though."

"It seems like everything in life is a lot harder than we think."

"So true." I raise my bottle, and tap it against hers. "To kicking ass and taking names in whatever we choose to do." Both of us take a drink and fall into easy conversation about nothing important.

I've lost track of Johnny, and that doesn't bother me in the slightest. I'm making a friend, and hopefully it will be a relationship that lasts long after I head back to Austin when this job is over.

I'm in the middle of telling her what I think she should do with marketing for the bar when her eyes widen. "Oh, shit. This isn't going to be good."

I follow her gaze toward the shiny black car making its way onto the pasture. "Who is it?"

She looks at me, then back at the car, now parking. "The girl who broke Johnny's heart."

Chapter Twenty-One

NOT GOOD, not good. Why wouldn't Johnny tell me that his ex was going to be here? A tall brunette woman steps out of the sleek car, and walks toward the fire. There is a confidence in her stride made easier by the fact she didn't wear boots with heels to a bonfire. Her clothes are so tight they cling to her skin. Her very demeanor reminds me of Tiffany when she's looking to hook up, and I know right then and there that I'm screwed.

I watch as she walks up to Johnny from behind and wraps her arms around him. When he realizes it's not me, his body stiffens. He breaks away from the woman behind him, and turns to face her. I have no idea what his expression is, but his hands are balled into fists. "What the fuck are you doing here?" His voice isn't loud, but the anger wrapped around the words stops all conversation.

"I heard there was a bonfire tonight, and I knew it could only be happening here." Her tone is sugary sweet as she hungrily eyes Johnny up and down.

"I'm guessing she's not supposed to be here?" I whisper, hoping Angie can hear me.

I catch her shaking her head out of the corner of my eye. "Nope. Hell, I didn't even know she was back in town."

"Any chance she'll leave?" Please say yes. I am fighting with the urge to march over and claim Johnny as mine so she'll back off. But I stop myself. We've only been on a couple of dates, and I know I don't have the right to make a claim over him. Or do I?

"I'm sure he'll ask her to, but Sarah will just sweet talk her way into staying."

Fuck. This is not good. Before I realize what I'm doing, I'm standing and making my way toward Johnny. I slip my arm into his and lean my head on his shoulder. I hold my free hand out, trying to defuse the situation. "Hi, I'm Stella."

She doesn't even glance my way. Instead she focuses on Johnny. "I hope it's okay if I hang out for a while. There's nothing to do at my parents' house, and it's so good to see old friends."

I don't like the way she says friends. Hell, I don't like the way she didn't even acknowledge my existence. I glance up at Johnny, waiting to see what he'll say. "Do whatever you want, Sarah," he spits out. "I'm not going to cause a scene. Just stay away from me."

He doesn't say anything else. He shifts his arm until it's wrapped around my side, and turns us until we're facing the other direction, leading us toward the chairs I was just occupying which Angie has conveniently left open.

The silence is getting to me. He's angry, and if the vibe I'm getting off of him is any indication, he has every right to be. His ex just crashed the small party he's having on his own property. "I'm guessing you two know each other?" I do my best to make it sound lighthearted, but I know he can hear the fear and tension in my voice.

"Yep." He grabs my unfinished beer and takes a swig, making a face. It has to be hot by now. Angie and I were so wrapped up in our conversation that I completely forgot about it. "She's my ex, and makes my life hell anytime she comes into town."

"I'm sorry." I glance toward the people talking now that the awkwardness has ended. Sarah is glaring at me, and a ball of unease settles in my stomach. I have a feeling she's going to make my life hell, too. This whole thing with Johnny is supposed to be easy, something we can both walk away from. Now, it's getting complicated.

I shiver despite the warmth. "Want to get out of here?"

His shoulders sag in relief. "Yes. My place, or yours?"

"Your house is closer." Right now, I only want away from the scary lady. I have a feeling he needs to be away from her, too.

"Let's go, then." He helps me up, and we start walking toward the truck. He's quiet until we run into Angie. "We're gonna head out. Feel free to shut this down whenever you want."

"We'll clear out of here soon." Her eyes shift to the vicinity Sarah is in. "I don't know who told her we were all out here, but I'll find out." Her eyes are on me, and she smiles.

"Thanks, Ang. We'll stop by the bar tomorrow." I guess he's already lining up our next date. I'm not upset about it, but I definitely need to find out what the hell went on with him and Sarah before anything else happens.

Johnny's house is now a beacon in the dark night. I swear he turned on every single light. He even grabbed a lightbulb and replaced the one on the porch. "Are you trying to protect yourself from the things that go bump in the night?"

"What?" He looks at me, confused. I point to all the light spilling into every room. "Oh, she just makes me uneasy."

"What happened with the two of you?" I don't want to know all the details but I need to know what might be coming at me when I'm not paying attention.

"Oh, you know, the same thing that makes up all tragic small-town love stories." He sits down on the sofa beside me, absentmindedly running his fingertips along my leg. "We were high school sweethearts. She wanted bigger and better things. I wanted to stay here. There was no in-between for her. I either went with her or I was going to lose her forever. I lost her. Then after she left, I found out she was screwing around on me. Any regret on following her was gone after I knew the truth."

"Why is she here now?" That must be why he doesn't want anything with strings attached. I totally respect him for that. He knows what he's capable of, and it sounds like trusting people is an issue we both have in common.

"I honestly have no clue." He turns until his back is up against the arm rest, and pulls me until I'm laying halfway on him and the couch. The steady thump of his heart is calming. "She doesn't visit very often, but when she does, I swear her only goal in life is to make mine miserable and try to screw with my head."

At least I know he doesn't want anything to do with her. If I would have heard any doubt in his words, I would have to end whatever we are. I don't need, nor want, that kind of drama in my life. "Was she always like that?"

"Honestly, yeah. I was just too stupid in love to realize it. No matter how many times my friends tried to warn me," he looks down at me and smiles. "I should listen to them more often, though. Angie really likes you."

"I like her too. She kept me company until shit hit the fan. It was nice to not feel like a tagalong or outsider. It honestly felt like we'd been friends for years."

"I'm happy for that. She's one of my closest friends. Our moms are best friends so we've known each other since we were in diapers."

"I got that feeling about her. She's very protective of you."

"Only because she doesn't want someone coming around and fucking me over the way Sarah did." The room falls silent after that. She is to him what my cousins are to me. He picks the remote off of the coffee table. "Want to watch a movie? I feel like maybe I need to turn this date around from the shit show it was back there."

"Sounds good to me." Just then a thought hits me, and I'm worried his bitchy ex will show up unannounced. "Will everyone be passing through your driveway when they leave?" I really don't want anything to interrupt our night more than it already has.

"Nah, Angie will make everyone leave through the gate that leads to a small access road." He starts scrolling through the guide menu on the tv. "Is there anything in particular you want to watch?"

"Nope, I'm good with anything that isn't sappy." He pauses on a sci-fi movie.

While I'm a huge fan of vampires, witches, and all that other stuff, science fiction has never been my thing. I don't say anything, though. I choose to snuggle as close to him as possible and watch the movie. With each minute that passes, all the uncertainty from Sarah showing up slips away. I let myself be held by this man that makes me feel everything I shouldn't. The only thing that would make it better is a bowl of popcorn.

My arm between us is falling asleep. I shift my body until I'm lying on my side in front of him and his back is against the sofa. His arm wraps around me to pull me closer to him until my back is touching him. His fingers rub gently along my waist where my shirt has shifted, exposing a tiny slip of skin, and heat races through my body.

His rough fingers are creating the perfect friction against my smooth skin. I shift my legs trying to ease the tension pooling below. All it does is turn me on even more than I am. He slides his other arm underneath me and his hand cups my breast. Gently squeezing until I'm all but panting.

As impossible as it seems, he pulls me even closer to him, and his hardness presses into my lower back. That's all the confirmation I need to know that he wants me as badly as I want him. I wiggle my ass, and he groans. The surge of glee I feel boosts my confidence. My hand slides past his until it reaches my pants button. I undo the button and slide my zipper down giving him permission to go lower. To make me come alive. Anticipation building. Waiting for him to make the next move.

Johnny's hand slides down. His fingertips brushing the top of my panties, and I shiver, before he pauses. "Not like this."

I suck in a breath. "What?"

"We aren't going to have sex for the first time on this ratty couch like a couple of horny teenagers." He slides out from behind me and grabs my hand. "Come one. My bed is much more comfortable."

I allow him to pull me up when he pulls me in for a deep toe-curling kiss.

Not wanting to waste any time, I head in the direction of his bedroom. I guess that is one benefit of my snooping the first night I was here.

With each step we take another layer of clothing off as it hits the floor. The look in his eyes is pure lust, and it is better than any foreplay I could imagine. I've never been as bold as I am right now, showing him what I want. Pulling him toward what I know is going to be an amazing end to the night. As my legs hit the edge of his bed, I fall backward. My bra and panties the only clothing I have left. He lifts himself on top of me, kissing every bare inch of my skin he can—any doubts I had about what we were going to do or be to each other melt away.

Chapter Twenty-Two

I squint as morning sunshine slips between the blinds. Ugh, why is the sun up? For a minute, I forget where I am, but quickly I take stock of my surroundings. *Dammit.* I was supposed to go home last night, not shack up with the hot mechanic. Not that I'm complaining. Last night was the best sex I think I've ever had.

Rolling over, I slide my arm over the other side of the bed. It's empty. *What the hell?* You're not supposed to ditch the chick you screwed in your own house. I hear shuffling coming from the front of the house, and search for my clothes. Fuck, they are scattered throughout the house. I don't want to walk out there with a sheet wrapped around my body.

Opening his closet door, I grab the first shirt I see. I pull it over my head and walk out of his room. Johnny is pacing back and forth in the kitchen, running his fingers through his hair over and over again. Does he not want me here? "If you wanted me to leave this morning, you could have woken me up."

He turns around and his eyes go wide, trailing his gaze up and down my body. "You look fucking amazing in my work shirt."

I look down, and realize a Small Town Automotive patch sewn above the pocket. My cheeks warm, and I groan. "Sorry. I'll go find my clothes."

I turn to leave the kitchen, but he grabs my arm and pulls me toward him. "Don't be ridiculous. The only place it would look better is on the floor." He places a kiss on my neck, then my jawbone, and works his way to my earlobe. "Hell, maybe you can leave it on until we're done."

I suck in a breath at his words, and relish the feel of his lips on my body.

Then I remember his pacing when I walked in. "Why were you walking a hole through the floor?"

That snaps him out of his sexy talk, and he runs his hand through his hair again. He pulls back and hurries to the refrigerator. "Are you hungry? I can whip us up something to eat."

Leaning against the wall, I tap my foot, and cross my arms over my chest. His shirt rises, and his eyes shoot to where the hem of it ends. "What aren't you telling me?"

"I don't know what you're talking about."

"You're acting like a kid who has done something wrong and doesn't want to fess up to his parents."

He leans against the fridge, and hits the back of his head on the door. "There may be a teensy tiny problem with your car."

"Is it going to cost more than you thought? It's not a big deal if it is."

"Yes, but I don't need you to pay for it because it's my fault."

I whip my head back. His fault? He's supposed to be fixing it. "What did you do?" I'm trying really hard to not accuse him of anything, but he's acting cagey and I need to know why.

"Well," he shuffles to his right until he has a clear path out of the kitchen. "There may have been an incident."

"What kind of incident?"

"Well, you know how you had a back bumper?" He waits for me to nod. "You're getting a brand new one."

"Did you back into something?"

"Not exactly." One shoulder rises until it's almost touching his head. "When I was working on the front bumper, and headlight, I had it lifted up a bit. And well, apparently, I forgot to shift the car from neutral to park, and when I leaned on it…it rolled out of the garage and into the fence."

"What?" I shriek. I should have had him tow it to a dealer to get it looked at, but he was so earnest about fixing it. "How bad is it?"

He shrugs. "It's not horrible, but it's not pretty."

"Show me." I storm to the front door, not caring that I'm still wearing only his shirt and no shoes. I march onto the porch, and I'm about to take a step off when he tugs me back.

"Don't you think you should put on some pants?" He's looking toward the road, determining if anyone can see me.

"Not until you show me my baby."

"Fine," he huffs. He leads me to the garage walking on the side that faces the road, and then behind me when we turn toward the garage.

The dying grass digs into my feet, and I wish for a second that I would have at least put on some damn shoes. My tender feet can't handle this nonsense, and I wince with every step I take.

Right before we get to the garage door, Johnny stops me in my tracks. "Promise you won't freak out."

"I'm not a hundred percent sure I can promise that."

"Okay," he sighs. "I'll open the door for you, and I won't come in until I know you won't chop my balls off."

Smart man. He opens the side door, and lets me pass in front of him. True to his word, he doesn't follow. My baby is sitting next to an old rusted car, and I almost cry at the sight of her. I'm grateful to Johnny's mom for letting me use her extra car, but there's nothing like driving your own.

I stare at the front of the car and take stock of the work he was doing on the front end. That part looks almost finished. It will only take a few more hours to be back to the condition it was in when I drove it off the lot. The back is the problem he mentioned, though. I take a deep breath, run my fingers along the side of my car, and walk to the backend. Holy shit. He wasn't lying. The bumper is completely gone. The plus side…the metal thingy it attaches to is still there, but the bumper lies, discarded, on the floor.

"Is it okay for me to come in?" He calls from outside. "If not, I completely understand, and I'll get someone to tow your car to a lot."

Honestly, it's not as bad as I envisioned. The way he was acting in the kitchen made it seem like he totaled the thing. "Yeah, it's safe. I'm not going to rip you to shreds for hurting my baby."

Rather than coming all the way in, he pokes his head into the spacious room. "Are you sure?"

"Yes, I'm sure," I sigh. Men can be such babies when they think they've royally fucked up. "It's not terrible, just a small hiccup in getting it put back together again."

I run my fingers across the trunk, and Johnny's arms wrap around me. "Kind of like Humpty Dumpty."

"No. Not like him. The rhyme says he couldn't be put back together." I turn until I'm facing him, my arms going around his neck. "And you'll get her all fixed up and pretty again…or else."

He bends down, placing small kisses along my cheek. "Or else what? It's not like you're big enough to actually hurt me or anything."

A small smirk crosses my lips. "You remember what happened last night?" He nods and grins. "Yeah, that won't happen as frequently."

"Now you're playing dirty." His hand slides down my side until his fingers trace the bottom of my shirt. Well, his shirt. He lifts it, slowly, gliding his fingers across the bare skin of my legs. A part of me wants him to keep going. To pull the shirt off completely, and bend me over the car. But one look at said car shuts that feeling down pretty quickly. I miss my baby, and I need to be behind the wheel again.

"Nice try, Johnny." I back away from him, trying to get my breathing under control. "How about you work on my car, and I'll organize some work stuff while you do it." He scrunches up his nose, clearly not in favor of my suggestion. "I'll even sit out here with you."

"There are about a million other things I'd rather be doing," he mutters under his breath.

Yeah, me too, buddy. Me too.

I don't why I thought I would get any work done sitting out here watching him fix my car. This asshat decided he was going to take off his shirt. It's almost as if he is punishing me for making him do it. He's the one who backed into a damn fence.

He stands up from under my hood, and I stare down at my phone so he doesn't think I have been ogling him this whole time. "Hey, are you hungry?"

"I could eat." In my rush to see what the hell was wrong with my car, I totally spaced on eating breakfast.

"I guess we better get dressed then." He grabs a black stained rag off one of the work tables, and wipes his hands off. It doesn't do much good because there are still streaks of what I'm assuming is oil covering his hands.

"Why?"

"Because, I told Angie we'd stop in the bar today."

I vaguely recall him talking to her before we left the bonfire. I was too focused on the unannounced guest that crashed the party to fully listen. "Oh, okay. Can we run by my house so I can get some clothes?" I don't want anyone to see me in the same smoke smelling clothes I wore last night.

"Sure." His strides are long as he walks toward me. "Why don't you run to your house, and I'll take a shower to get all this grease off of me. Then I'll pick you up, and we can head into town."

"Sounds like a plan." Truth be told, I feel like I need a shower, and it will be nice to be in clothes that are mine. Johnny found a t-shirt and some sweatpants for me to wear. The pants are baggy even after tightening them all the way and double knotting the string. I hop down from the table I'm sitting on, and Johnny steps back. I'm not taking any chances of him getting his hands on me. If that happens, there's almost zero chance we'll actually go get food, and my stomach is growling. "See you at my house in twenty?"

He groans and slides his hands over his face, leaving black streaks on his cheek. "Yeah, I'll see you then." I wasn't playing when I said that I wanted my car fixed. Although, I'm not sure how long I can resist him. At least not after last night. I had a taste of what it feels like to be with him and I am hooked.

Chapter Twenty-Three

AFTER A RIDICULOUSLY LONG drive we finally pull into Out of the Ashes. Okay, maybe I'm exaggerating just a bit, but when there's nothing to look at except cows and fields during the twenty-minute drive…it seems endless. If I go anywhere in Austin it can take just as long to get there, but there are so many other things going on that I don't even notice the time passing by. Unless, of course, I hit traffic. The only traffic people out here have are tractors going slow on the main road. It's weird, and something I never thought would happen to me, but I've gotten stuck behind those huge ass vehicles twice in the past week that I've been here.

"Are you going to sit there and stare out the window the whole time?"

"Huh?" I shake my head.

"Are you ready to go in or do you want to go back to my place?" He laughs.

Rolling my eyes, I reach for the door handle. "Someone is a little sure of themselves."

"What can I say?" He shrugs and opens his door. "For all I know you were over there thinking about all the ways I can make you feel good, and want to head back home. How many times was it you said my name last night?"

"Whatever. Let's go eat, I'm starving."

The bar is relatively quiet considering its lunch time on a Saturday. I figured the place would be filled to the brim with college football playing on the few TV screens they have around the bar. I really need to set aside some time to talk to Angie, even if it means parking my ass in the bar stool while she works.

"Hey guys," Angie waves at us as we approach the bar. "Do y'all want to sit at a table or the bar? As you can see, you have your pick."

"Is the bar good with you?" Johnny whispers in my ear, sending shivers down my spine. Does he have to put his mouth so close to my skin? He knows what that does to me.

"Yep," I nod. "There's no use making her run around all over the place. We should make it easy for her."

"The bar is good, Ang."

He grabs my hand and pulls me toward the stools in the corner, as far away from the door as possible. "Why are we sitting way over here?"

"I don't like my back toward the door."

"That doesn't even make sense. Do you think some hitman is going to come in and take you out?"

His head whips back, and he stares at me for a few moments. "Your mind works in weird ways, Stella. I just like being able to see who's coming in and out."

"So, what you're saying is you're just as weird as me?"

"I guess."

"Do y'all want your usual?" Angie is wiping the counter down in front of us.

"Yep. Except can I have one of those beers you gave me last night?"

"I'm good with the same. Thanks, Angie."

"No problem. I'll go let the cook know what y'all want."

"You're the best," Johnny smiles.

Angie turns toward the kitchen and disappears behind the swinging door. "What were you working on this morning while I was killing myself getting your car put back together?" He still hasn't let go of my hand, and I'm not mad about it. It feels nice. Like our hands were meant to be intertwined.

Groaning, I lean my head against his shoulder. "The stuff for the Job Fair. I have no idea how I'm going to get it all done and set up by myself."

"You know it's okay to ask for help, right?"

"Yeah," I sigh. "I'm just not used to being the one that asks. Mr. Granger usually piles all of his work on me, and I'm the one that has to deal with it all while he takes credit for it."

"That sucks, and it's one of the reasons why I don't think I'll ever be able to work for a corporate company."

"I don't blame you. I love my job, I do, but sometimes I wonder if I'd be happier doing something else."

"Have you ever done anything else?"

"Nope," I pop the *p*. "I was hired by Mr. Hart as soon as I graduated from college. I worked my way up from grunt to assistant for one of the project managers. If I can get this center up and running without any problems, I'll be promoted to project manager myself."

He squeezes my hand, and the small action lets me know he's actually listening. "That's pretty impressive. Not many people stay at one job for very long."

I look up at him, his strong jawline in my view. I'm not sure that I've ever noticed another guy's jawline. "How long have you been a mechanic?"

"All my life," he smiles. "My grandpa taught me how to work on cars, and when my uncle needed someone in the shop full time after I graduated from high school, I went there."

"So, you've been there a while." It's a question, but not really. It's obvious it's the only place he's worked.

"Yep. The customers can be a pain in the ass sometimes, but I love what I do." He glances down at me, "It makes me happy."

He's so content with his life working at the shop. I don't think I've ever met anyone that is perfectly happy with their position and doesn't want more. It's refreshing. "I can tell. If only your happiness could lead you to finish fixing my car."

Johnny presses his lips together to hide a smile. "Truth be told, I've been taking my sweet time on your car. I could have had it fixed within two days."

"What?" I shriek.

Angie pokes her head through the door. "Is everything okay?"

"Yeah, sorry. I didn't mean to scare you."

"Calm down, Stella." He pulls my hand into his lap. "It's not because I'm lazy, or anything. I just knew that if I finished your car fast, then I'd never see you again."

"This town is tiny. There's no way we wouldn't have run into each other." The smell of our wings coming from the kitchen makes me sit up taller. We should have come sooner because right now I'm so hungry I might eat my napkin.

"True enough. But, I'm not sure that you would have agreed to go on a date with me."

"You knew the second you cornered me in the kitchen that I was going to say yes. I don't know what it is about you, but I don't think I could deny you anything."

His lips curl up. "Oh yeah. So, you wouldn't say no if I said we should get out of here and go back to my place."

"Well maybe not anything," I snort. "I'm on the edges of hangry and if I don't get food soon…it won't be pretty."

"Okay, okay." He holds up his hands in surrender. "So, what do you need help with for this Job Fair?"

It's more like what do I not need help with. "Honestly, everything. I have the tables, chairs, and snack trays ordered. I just don't know how I'm going to set it up and man everything on my own."

"Just give me the date and I'll help you."

His generosity has no bounds. "And what do you expect in return?"

"Nothing…" he shrugs. "Though, I wouldn't say no to a repeat of last night." There goes that devilish grin again.

Men. I roll my eyes, but I can't deny I am considering it. The people in this community know him, and trust him. "We'll talk about it. Your help would actually be great. It's during the week. Will you be able to get off work?"

"I have plenty of vacation time banked. Besides, my uncle wouldn't say no to me helping you."

"Then consider it a deal." His offer to help eases so much stress from my shoulders, and I visibly relax. That is until Angie comes out of the kitchen with our food. The plate has barely hit the bar top, and I'm picking up one of the wings to shove into my mouth. It must have just come off because it's so hot that it slips from my fingers, and slams back on the plate.

"Slow down and give it a second to cool off," Johnny laughs. "It's not going to go anywhere."

"Yeah, yeah. I'm not used to going this long without eating. I'm pretty sure my body is pissed at me right now."

"Suit yourself." He takes a sip of his beer and lets his food cool down while I dig in without abandon. It's a good thing I'm not one of those girls that will only eat a salad to appeal to men. What's better is that it doesn't seem to faze him how I am devouring these wings. Some of the guys I dated back in Austin would try to order for me. They obviously didn't know what to do with women that actually do things for themselves.

The grocery store selection in Asheville isn't very big. There are two chain stores and one local store. Even though I primarily eat fast food, I need to grab things I can snack on when I don't have time to go get something. Or, when I'm lying on the couch bored, and binge-watching TV shows. Of course, Johnny drives us to the smaller grocery store. Hopefully they have the type of stuff that I like. It's not like I'm difficult to please or anything. Just point me in the direction of all the crap food and we should be good to go.

"What do you want for dinner?" Johnny asks as he grabs a cart from beside the door.

"We literally just ate. How can you already be thinking of food again?"

The store is on the small side, but the multiple aisles of food eases some of my worry. I shouldn't have a problem finding the snacks I like. Newspaper clippings and photos of the high school football team plaster the walls when you walk in. It's a nice touch, and I can understand why Johnny brought me here instead of one of the bigger stores. This town thrives on community and the pictures show how much pride they have.

"Because I'm pretty sure we are going to have to eat again at some point today." He pushes the cart down the first aisle, searching for something.

"Good point." A box of fruit snacks catches my eye, and I grab it before throwing it in the cart. "The only problem is I don't cook. If it's not frozen, or take out, I don't eat it."

"You know that shit is bad for you, right?" Dammit, is he one of those people who get all judgy about others' food choice. Because if that's the case, this isn't going to work out. I don't need a man dictating what I can and can't do. The only person I allow to do that is Mr. Granger, and that's because he's one of the people responsible for my paycheck.

Shrugging my shoulders, I continue scanning the snacks that are on the shelf. Some of these I haven't had since I was a kid. Into the cart the boxes go. I have exactly zero cares to give what other people think about what I eat. "Yeah, I know that. But I also know that I can't cook, and that poses a problem when making healthier foods."

"It can't be that bad." He stares at me before he turns down the next aisle. "Haven't you ever made macaroni and cheese, or boiled eggs?"

"Yep, and they both turned out inedible." I glance away so he can't see my face. "I, um, let the water boil so long there was nothing left inside the pan."

"Well, today is your lucky day. I'm going to teach you how to cook."

"That really isn't necessary." I spy a bag of hot Cheetos and throw it into the cart. If anybody saw the contents of the cart, they'd think a college kid was buying food for their dorm. "I can always run into town and pick us up some food."

We turn down yet another aisle, and he stops in front of jars of pasta sauce. "Nope. Spaghetti is easy enough. It's almost impossible to screw it up."

"You've clearly never met me before," I mutter under my breath.

"What was that?"

"Oh, nothing. Spaghetti sounds great." Little does he know that I have zero plans on helping him. I'm going to sit back and watch. A man that can cook is beyond sexy.

We're almost done getting everything we need for dinner tonight. The last stop is the produce area to pick up a few things for a salad. Johnny is too busy inspecting lettuce to see the woman making her way toward us. This shit seriously cannot be happening. Does she have some kind of homing beacon on him?

"Hi, Johnny." Sarah's voice is sugary sweet, but the daggers her eyes are shooting my way are anything but.

Johnny's back stiffens at the sound of her voice. He takes his time placing the lettuce in the cart before facing her. "Um, hi, Sarah." His voice is tight, and he reaches for my hand for moral support. "You remember Stella?" Nice subject change, buddy. Too bad it's as obvious as a two by four to the head.

Sarah scrunches up her nose in disgust. "Yes, how are you?"

Funny how she saw me and didn't acknowledge me, but one little question from Johnny and suddenly I appeared to her. "I'm fine." I refuse to ask her how she's doing. Call it bad manners, I don't care. She walked over here with an agenda to make me feel like shit, and I just can't let that stand. "We were actually just about to head out." The only way to get this woman to understand that she can't push me around is to put a stop to the conversation, and make an abrupt exit. Some may say that I'm being a coward, and I'm okay with that. These two have a history together and she still makes him uncomfortable after all of these years. Even though I have no idea exactly what we are to each other, I don't share. I'm not letting her worm her way back into Johnny's head. Tiffany would be so proud of me for standing up for what I want. I just wish I knew where all of these overprotective feelings have come from. I don't attach myself to others easily, and no other guy I have dated has pulled this sort of emotion out of me.

"Can I speak with you for moment, Johnny?" Geez, this girl does not get a hint. If he wanted to talk to her, he would.

"Actually, now isn't a good time." Johnny grabs the cart and starts walking away pulling me along with him since he still has a hold on my hand. "We have things we need to do."

"What are we doing?" I whisper to Johnny once were a few feet away. If he thinks I'm doing anything strenuous, he's out of his mind. Though, there are a few things I still need to iron out with the Job Fair. And since he offered to help, it'll work out perfectly.

"Nothing. We're going to go to your house, relax, have an amazing dinner, and just hang out."

That actually sounds like a really fun night, and I push anything that has to do with the Job Fair out of my mind. Removing my hand from his, I wrap my arm around his waist. Walking side by side like this is awkward, but I'm doing it so Sarah can see that she's not going to wreck whatever it is that we have going on between us. I glance back, making sure she sees us. Her mouth is hanging open and her eyes are wide. If I'm not mistaken, her cheeks look pinker than they did before. Mission accomplished. I hope Sarah has this image burned into her head for the rest of the day.

Chapter Twenty-Four

The past few weeks with Johnny have been amazing. We've spent more time together than we've spent apart. I'm either at his house or he's at mine. I've almost forgotten what it feels like to sleep alone. He makes me feel better than I've ever felt before. And the help he's given me with this Job Fair has been more than I could ask for.

He's unloading tables, while I grab all the paperwork I'll need for every station. Each one will cover a different job, and I hope we get a lot of applicants. I need every position filled before I can leave this town and go home. The thought sends a pang through my chest. What's supposed to happen when I leave? Will we continue the long-distance thing? Or, go our separate ways? We still haven't made anything official, but I can't stop these feelings from growing every moment we spend together.

I know that I shouldn't be hanging out with him as much as I have been, but I can't fight this pull I have toward him. I can leave work with all kinds of stress and pressure weighing on my shoulders, and the minute he wraps his arms around me all of the negativity melts away.

The guy who brought the tables is pulling out of the parking lot, and Johnny comes in to the small office. "How do you want these tables set up?"

"I have no idea. I feel like if we put them in rows potential employees will undoubtedly miss some of them." I tap my finger against my chin trying to figure out the best setup. "Maybe a U-shaped layout would be best. Then they can just hit one table after the other to see if they're interested in the position and fill out whatever paperwork I have on the table."

"That's a good idea." Johnny looks at the stack of vegetable trays on my desk. "What are we going to do with that stuff?"

"Just leave one table open in the middle and we will set it on there."

"You're the boss," he gives me mock salute and walks out into the warehouse area. He is such a smart ass. It's a good thing he's hot as hell. It's almost time to get this thing going.

I breathe a sigh of relief. So far there has been a steady flow of people. I was worried that nobody was going to show up, but Johnny assured me that there are a lot of people in this town willing to work. They just needed an opportunity to open up for them. Even though I dreaded relocating here, it really has turned out for the best.

There is only twenty minutes left of the Job Fair, and my feet are hating me. I should have worn flats, or anything besides these heels. I'm not used to actually standing in them. Almost everybody has left and I start cleaning up the abandoned tables. The boxes holding their personal information need to be sorted through, and I stack them all up on one table.

"Oh no, did I miss the fair?" And just like that, my happiness over the success of the event diminishes. What is she doing here?

Forcing a smile on my face, I turn around. "Hi, Sarah. We are just wrapping things up. How can I help you?"

"If you're already cleaning up, I can just submit my resume to your company directly." Excuse me, what? Did she just say what I think she said?

"Oh, I didn't realize you were in the market for a job." Please let this be a joke. I cannot be the person who has to interview this woman, let alone work with her.

She looks around the warehouse, squinting at the room. "I wasn't, but I've decided I'm going to stay here for a while."

My heart clenches, and I can't fathom a reason for her to stay in Asheville aside from Johnny. She'll be there to swoop in as soon as I'm gone. "Wh—what type of job are you looking for?"

"Something in management. No offense, but I'm not cut out to do grunt work." I hate that she refers to manual labor as grunt work. Everything about this woman rubs me the wrong way.

"Yeah I have those forms right over here." The table isn't very far away, but I don't want to turn my back to her. I have this feeling like she's up to something. However, we are both grown women, and our bitchiness toward each other is beyond childish. We don't have to like each other. Turning toward the table that has the management applications, I quickly walk to it and pick one up. "Here you go."

"Thank you. Do you have somewhere I can sit to fill this out?"

There's only one place she can have privacy to do it, and I'm not leaving her in the small office alone. "Let me grab you a chair, and you can sit at one of these tables to fill it out." She huffs as I rush to my temporary office to get her something to sit on. If there were other people here, I'd make her stand with a clipboard like everyone else did. But I just want her out of here as fast as possible.

Sarah is quietly filling out the application while I continue clearing the tables. The only sound coming from the cavernous room is the sound the pens make as they hit each other in a box. I jump when I hear a deep voice from somewhere behind me. "What are you doing here?" Johnny's voice is gruff.

"Applying for a job, silly." Sarah's voice is high and flirty, and I grit my teeth to keep from saying anything. The familiarity she has with him makes me crazy, and sad. I've never had that with anyone other than my cousins.

"I didn't realize you were here to stay."

"I haven't fully made my decision, but it's nice to have a plan if I decide to." That little liar. That is not the story she gave me before asking to fill out an application.

"And this is where you decided to apply?" Watching them speak to each other is like watching a ping-pong match and trying to figure out which side is going to win. I don't miss the skepticism in his voice, though. He fully believes she had ulterior motives coming here today, and that makes me feel a little less crazy about the whole thing.

"Well, I can't put all my eggs in one basket. This isn't the only place I'm applying."

I can't help but roll my eyes. This lady spouts off so much bullshit, and believes everyone is going to take her word for it. I know what attention seeking looks like. Tiffany could give a master class. Either way, I feel like I need to save Johnny right now. "Are you almost done filling out your application? I need to finish getting these tables taken down in time for the guys to come pick them up."

"Here you go." She places the application on the table I'm next to, gathers her things and walks toward the door. "Hopefully I hear from your company soon."

"Thanks." Hopefully that one word didn't come off too bitchy, but everything about her drives me insane. Not to mention she's trying really hard to get Johnny back, and that's just not going to happen. At least I hope not. She's turning this into a competition and I'm too old to be playing games like this. Johnny doesn't seem like he's falling for her crap, though.

Once Sarah is out of the building Johnny grabs my hand. "You aren't seriously going to turn the application in, are you?"

"Of course, I am." I pull my hand from his. How could he even think I wouldn't? "It would be unethical of me not to. My whole promotion at the company rides on this warehouse opening up without a hitch. If word got out that I didn't turn something in because I didn't like a person, it would be career suicide."

"Yeah. I get that. I'm sorry for even suggesting it." Johnny takes a step toward me and grabs my hand again. "I just know that everything she wrote on it is probably a lie, and she's doing all of this to get under your skin. I don't want her to hurt you."

"I appreciate your knight in shining armor routine, but I'm a big girl. I can handle myself. You don't get as far as I have in my industry without having thick skin and a backbone. Besides, if she lied on any part of the application, the people in HR will figure it out."

He pulls me into him, chest to chest. "I have no doubt that you'll get the promotion. And I know you can take care of yourself. I know how she is, though. She's vindictive as hell and will do anything to get what she wants."

"You realize that will only work if that's what you want too, right?" Fear creeps up my spine at what he might say to that. We haven't established what we are, and whether I continue to date him or not hinges on what he says next.

"I don't want her. I haven't in a long time." I breathe a sigh of relief. "*You* are the only person I want." He runs his hand through my hair. "I want to be more than casual with you. God. I feel like a dumbass teenager even asking this, but what do you say to being my girlfriend?"

Holy shit. He wants to be a legit couple. Does that change anything? I mean, we're already doing things that couples do. This just makes it official.

"Stella? I'm not sure if I should take your silence as a yes or no."

"Yes," I scream and throw my arms around his neck. A little dramatic, maybe. But this man sets my soul on fire, and makes me feel like I can have it all. The career and the relationship.

Chapter Twenty-Five

"WHAT IS THAT NOISE?" Johnny groans from the other side of my bed.

"I don't hear anything. Go back to sleep." He must've been dreaming about something because there's not a single sound coming from my room.

"I swear I'm not going crazy. It sounded like something was vibrating." He pulls me closer to him and nuzzles my neck. "You aren't hiding any toys, are you?"

I push him away and laugh. "No, you perv." Actually, I do have some hidden away, but there has been no use for them. He gets the job done just fine. A buzzing sound comes from my dresser, and I sigh. It's early, and the only person who would be calling is my boss.

"Told you I wasn't crazy," Johnny mumbles. The phone stops vibrating, but whoever is calling is adamant because it starts right back up. "Would you answer it already? They obviously aren't going to stop calling, and that means we don't get to sleep in."

He has a point, but I'm not going to tell him that. "Fine," I huff. Reaching toward the nightstand, I grab my phone and answer it without looking at the screen. "Hello?"

"It's about damn time you answer your phone." Tiffany's voice startles me. Something has to be wrong because she never calls this early. "I thought we were going to have to send out a search party."

"I'm fine," I say. "Is everything okay over there?"

"Yup. We just haven't talked much, and I was worried something had happened." That's not normal for Tiffany. She usually checks in whenever she feels like it, or when she wants something. "How's the job going?"

Why is she acting so weird? "It's fine. I put on the Job Fair a couple of days ago, and we got a lot of applicants. Where's Audrey?"

"I'm here." It's good to know they still have each other even though I'm hours away. Not being with them stings, though. Normally we'd be seeing what trouble we could get into for the day. Now they are living their lives, and I'm settling into a routine without them.

I glance over at Johnny and grimace. Covering the phone receiver, I whisper, "This may take a while."

"I'll run into town and grab us some breakfast." He gives me a quick peck on the cheek. "Tacos sound good?" When I nod, he grabs his clothes and gets dressed. "I'll be right back."

"Was that the hot mechanic?" Now I've gotten Tiffany's attention. "Is it as good as you imagined?"

"Tiffany," I hear Audrey admonish her, then a dull thwack. Holy shit, I think Audrey just hit Tiffany. "You don't ask people things like that?"

"She's not people," Tiffany grumbles. "She's our Stella."

If I don't jump in, these two will argue for the next thirty minutes. "First off, he has a name. It's Johnny."

"Okay, then is Johnny better than you imagined?"

This girl will be the death of me. I roll my eyes, and answered her question anyway. "Not that it's any of your business, but yes." I can't stop the stupid smile that takes over my face. "He's amazing in so many ways."

"Uh oh," Tiffany sings songs. "It sounds like somebody's catching feelings."

"That's insane," Audrey butts in. "Stella isn't stupid enough to start something with a guy when she knows she's leaving soon. Right, Stella?"

"Well," I begin. But Audrey cuts me off.

"You're in a relationship with him?" She screeches. "That's probably one of the most irresponsible things you have ever done. What were you thinking?"

Geez, maybe she'll tell me how she really feels. Tiffany comes to my defense. "Hey, lay off of her. She sounds happy. Happier than she's sounded in a really long time, actually." It's odd that Tiff is the one that has my back. It's usually her against the two of us, but this time I'm grateful she's in my corner.

"Thanks, Tiff." I grab the pillow Johnny was using this morning and prop it up to block some of the sunlight. "I am happy. He makes the hard days seem better, and we have fun when we're together."

"What are you going to do when you come home?" Tiffany whispers, unknowingly breaking any joy that I'm feeling. She just had to ask the hard question.

"I'm not sure. I guess we'll see when it happens."

"Who is this girl that takes things day by day, and what did she do with my workaholic cousin?" Tiffany laughs. "Just think of all the fun times we could have had with this version of you."

"Shut up," I groan. "I'm still the same me. Just a slightly less stressed version. Now I know what all the love sick girls in the RomComs we used to watch feel like."

"Has it gone that far?" Audrey questions.

"Gone that far for what?"

"You said love sick," she says. "Do you think it could be love?"

"I don't know," I whisper. It's something I haven't considered. I'm not even sure what love feels like since I've never been in love before. "What does it feel like?"

"Don't ask me," Tiffany snorts. "I've never once in my life claimed to love anyone. I keep them around until they are no longer fun."

"I wasn't asking you smartass. Audrey?" She has to be able to tell me. She was in a serious relationship when she was in high school. Though, she never said why it didn't work out.

"It kind of sounds like it," she finally answers. "If you can't imagine what it would be like without him, I'd say that's a pretty good indicator."

"Well, shit." It looks like I'm screwed when I leave because I'll be leaving my heart here. Maybe Audrey was right, and I've done something I shouldn't have. She *did* try to warn me before she headed back to Austin.

A door slams outside, and I sit up. Weird, I didn't hear Johnny's truck coming down the driveway. "Hey, I think Johnny may be back with food. I'll call y'all later."

"You better," Tiffany demands. "I have roommate drama I need to fill you in on."

"See," I laugh. "That's what you should have led with. Love y'all."

"Love you, too," they both scream in unison.

I hang up the phone and set it back on the nightstand. Johnny hasn't come inside, yet. At least not that I know of since the front door didn't make its usual creaking noise. I don't know who else would be coming by, though. I still don't know very many people here. Getting out of bed, I grab the robe I left on the floor last night. Hopefully it's someone that doesn't mind the just rolled out of bed look.

The stairs are cool against my bare feet as I make my way down to the kitchen. There's a bag from one of the mexican restaurants in town sitting on the counter, so he has to be back. Why didn't he come upstairs and get me? A better question is why didn't I hear him come in? "Johnny?" I call out. "Are you here?"

No answer. I'll just take a quick peek out the front door. If his truck isn't sitting in my driveway, then I'll freak out. I grab a knife from the drawer, in case something crazy is about to happen, and tiptoe toward the door. Cracking it open, I look in the driveway. Johnny's truck is nowhere in sight. As I close the door, something catches my eye.

No fucking way. *My car* is parked where his mom's car should be. I throw the door open, and run onto the porch. "Sweet baby Jesus," I scream into the quiet morning. "I've missed you so much." I drop the knife and almost trip down the stairs to get to my baby.

I'm so busy checking every nook and cranny on my car that I don't realize Johnny is actually here until he wraps his arms around me. "Are you surprised?"

"By the car, or you sneaking up on me?" I turn until I'm facing him. "She's really ready?"

"I wouldn't have brought it over here if it wasn't." He gives me a peck on the tip of my nose. "I was trying to get back before you saw it."

"First off, my car is not an 'it'." I notice his truck is back in the driveway. "Second, I didn't even hear your behemoth truck."

"How did you not hear it?"

"I was too enamored by this beautiful piece of machinery." I lean against my car. "Until recently, she's never let me down. Not that it was her fault." Stupid animal running me into a ditch.

"I won't let you down, either." That may be the cheesiest thing I've ever heard, but from him it's adorable. "Have you eaten yet?"

"Nope. I thought I heard something outside and came to investigate." There's one thing that doesn't make any sense. "How did you get here so fast after I heard the noise? There wasn't enough time for you to go all the way home and come back."

He shrugs and grins. "My mom was waiting at the end of the driveway with my truck. We switched vehicles and she went home."

Holy shit. His mom was here? "Why didn't you invite her to come in so I could meet her?" That's something most guys would do, right? Unless, of course, he doesn't want to introduce us.

"Honestly, I thought you would still be in bed, or on the phone with your cousins. Besides, there's plenty of time for you to meet her." That time is slowly dwindling, though. Now that the applications are turned in, I won't be here much longer.

"Yeah, I guess you're right." Those are both solid reasons, but I would have gotten up for the woman who loaned me her car without knowing who I was. It is plain to see that Johnny gets his giving soul from her. He wouldn't let me pay for anything on the car. "Let's go eat. I'm starving."

He picks me up, waiting until my legs are wrapped around him before walking toward the house. "I know something I'm hungry for." He winks at me. We're halfway across the porch when he comes to a stop. "Why is there a knife out here?"

"My protection."

"From me?"

"I didn't know it was you at the time. Your truck was gone, and I heard noises. It's better to be prepared." I tighten my grip around his neck as he bends down to pick up the knife.

"I thought you were laying off the scary movies. You know, because this house is the perfect setup for one."

"It's a hard habit to break when I've watched them my entire life with my cousins. It helps me feel more connected to them when I miss them and they aren't answering their phones."

"If you say so." He opens the door with his partially free hand. He bypasses the kitchen and my stomach rumbles. He wasn't kidding about wanting me. "Don't worry. You can eat after."

"After what?" I bat my eyelashes, feigning innocence.

"Don't be a smartass." He walks into my room and plops me on the bed. I could definitely get used to this whole alpha male thing.

His fingers go to the sash holding my robe together, working furiously to get it untied so he can see all of me. He's almost got it done when my phone rings. "Ignore it," he grunts.

I do, but it rings almost as soon as it has stopped. "I swear I'm going to murder my cousins." They seem to only call at the most inconvenient time.

Johnny glances at my still ringing phone, and his brows furrow in confusion. "Who is Satan?"

Shit this can't be good. "It's my boss."

"He's calling on a Saturday?"

"Only when something is fucked up."

"Apparently nobody wants me to get laid this morning," he mutters. Poor guy. First, my cousins wake us up. Now this?

I scramble across the bed and snatch the phone from the nightstand. "Hello?"

"Stella, you have a huge problem." Mr. Granger's voice is hard and gruff. Dammit, what could have possibly gone wrong in such a short amount of time?

Chapter Twenty-Six

My stomach drops. This can't be happening. There's so much I have to do now. I've almost completely tuned Mr. Granger out, but the words he says before hanging up destroy my hopes. "Get it fixed now, or you're fired."

Can he even do that? I know Mr. Granger is still my direct boss, but I assumed if there were any problems, or concerns, they'd come from Mr. Hart. I move the now silent phone away from my ear, and drop it onto the bed. I will not let this snafu be the end of my career. To be the end of everything I've busted my ass for.

Johnny is now in my line of sight, crouching down until his eyes meet mine. "Is everything okay?"

Wet, tears slide down my face. "No, everything is going up in smoke."

"What happened?" He grabs my hand and pulls me off the bed until I'm on the floor next to him. Wrapping his arms around me, he brings me in closer. "Whatever it is, I'll help you in any way I can."

"Thanks," I sniff. "But I have to do it on my own. Apparently, the forms I sent in weren't the correct ones. And one of the bay doors isn't working."

"How is the door your fault?" I don't miss that he mentions nothing about the applications. That is one hundred percent my fault. I should have made sure I had the updated ones.

"No idea." I wipe my nose on my robe, and curl into Johnny. "I need to find the contact number for the company that installed it. That's the easy part. It'll be much harder wrangling everyone together to fill out the applications again."

"I can help you with it."

"No, you can't. It's confidential information, and I would get my ass handed to me if I let someone else handle it."

He's silent for a few moments, unsure of how he can help alleviate my stress. This is what I get for spending so much time with him. I should have been focusing on getting this new center started off with a bang. Instead, I'm drowning in my own pit of failure. This is what I get. Audrey was right. I need to execute my plans instead of getting sidetracked by a man. He may be a man who makes me feel like I can do anything, but I need to back off a bit. Hopefully he understands. I have my job to save.

Johnny's voice breaks into my thoughts. "Well, I'll take care of the door repair. If the company can't get out here quickly, I'll do it myself."

"Do you even know what you're doing when it comes to those things?"

He whips his head back, hurt from my question. "Of course. We have the same type of doors at the garage, and I'm the one who does the repairs there."

"Sorry," I grimace. "I didn't realize you had actual experience with things like that." I feel like a bitch for questioning his knowledge. He works on cars for goodness sake. "I'll run up to the building tomorrow to get all the information."

I start to stand, but Johnny touches my arm, stopping me. "Stella, it's Saturday, and you haven't eaten yet. Let's go chow down on those tacos I brought, and we'll figure out what to do tomorrow."

"You don't understand. I need to get this taken care of now." I stand up all the way, and tie my robe closed. "If I don't, I'll be fired. That means no promotion. No job. All my hard work…"

Johnny gets off the floor and sits on the bed. "It's not a good idea to go rushing off. You need to figure out how to get everyone to come in and refill everything out. Otherwise you'll be running around like a chicken with your head cut off."

He has a point. I won't be able to get anything done if I don't have a clear and concise plan. I can't afford to lose this job. Austin isn't exactly the cheapest place to live, and I'm not about to room with either one of my nosy cousins. "You're right," I sigh. "Let's eat. Maybe food will help me think better."

I'm so close to being done with Operation Save My Ass. Johnny called the company that installed the door, and they came out right away. I guess it's a good thing I have a boyfriend that knows all the local companies. I'm not so sure they would have made fixing the door a priority if I would have called them. Maybe they would have, who knows. I'm just glad it's done.

Almost everyone who originally filled out applications have come by to do the correct ones. They were more than understanding, and told me it wasn't a big deal. I'm only waiting on a few more, including Sarah. Maybe she really is going to stick around. She called me back and said she'd come in this afternoon sometime. My stomach has been in knots since I got off the phone with her.

The silence surrounding me is pure bliss. It's going to be odd hearing other people in the building when the new hires come in to train. That's okay, though. It's one step closer to being able to go home. And, leaving Johnny. I'm not so sure that's what I want anymore. He's become a staple in my life, and I'm terrified to rip it out.

I'm typing up the potential employees and putting them into the system myself. I want to make sure it's all properly done this time around. I'm not a hundred percent sure, but I think Mr. Granger had something to do with sending me the wrong forms.

My phone rings and I hit enter before I mean to. Ugh, I'm going to have to go in and correct that one. "Dammit," I mutter. "Whoever this is, it better be important."

A picture of Tiffany from one of the music festivals we went to flashes across my screen. I really need to put my phone on do not disturb when I'm working, or with Johnny for that matter. My cousins have the worst timing. If I don't answer, she'll blow up my phone until I do. "Yes, dear cousin. How may I assist you today?"

"Have you always been such a smart ass?"

"Since the day you were born. What's up?"

"You never called me back over the weekend, and I still need to fill you in on the roommate drama."

Crap. I knew I was forgetting to do something. "I'm so sorry, Tiff. Shit hit the fan over here and I've been in panic mode."

"Did something happen with you and Johnny?" She's actually concerned with what's going on in my life. I can't tell if it's genuine, or if it's to keep her mind off her own problems.

"No. It's work crap. But I got it handled for the most part, with Johnny's help."

"That's good." She pauses for a few seconds and I'm worried the call has been disconnected. "I meant what I said the other day. You seem happier. I don't know if it's him, or the small-town life, but it agrees with you."

I can tell she's sincere. For once she isn't only thinking of herself. Maybe my little cousin is finally growing up. "Thanks, Tiff. That means a lot. I have no clue what I'm going to do when it's time for me to leave." That date will be getting closer and closer after we officially hire some people. "So, what's up with your roommate situation?"

"Besides the fact that I should put you and Audrey in charge of finding me one? Everything. This guy needed a temporary place to stay, and I felt a good vibe about him. There wasn't anything giving me any weird signals. But he was a total creep. He'd wait outside the bathroom door when I was showering, and was always hovering around."

"Tiffany, please tell me he's not still there. And if he is, take your ass to my apartment and call the cops." This girl is going to end up on the news one day if she doesn't start making smarter choices.

"He's not. After the second day I told him to get his shit and get out. I also told the security guy downstairs not to let him back up."

Thank God for that. "You've got to be more careful."

She cuts me off before I say anything else. "I know. I've got a bunch of interested people in my email for the open room. I'm going to forward them to you and Audrey. Y'all are going to make the decision for me. Just remember, I need someone who isn't going to be all in my personal space or get on my nerves."

"So, anyone who isn't female and won't take any attention away from you?"

"Exactly."

"I'll get to it as soon as I can." A knock on the outside of the office door pulls my attention away from Tiffany. Sarah is standing in the doorway. I wish she would have given me a specific time so I could have prepared for her arrival. "Hey, Tiff. I'll call you back later."

"Okay. Talk to you soon. Love you." She hangs up as soon as the words are out of her mouth.

"Hi, Sarah. Thanks for coming in on such short notice. I'm sorry for the inconvenience." I point to the chair in front of my desk. "Have a seat, and I'll grab the correct application."

"No rush," she waves the comment away. "I got out of my appointment earlier than expected.

She really doesn't have to share her schedule with me. I don't care. But I can't tell her that in a professional capacity. I pull the application from a tray and hand it to her across the desk. "Here you go."

She grabs a pen out of the cup on my desk and begins filling it out. "How much longer are you here?"

Why? So, you can swoop in and make Johnny feel better when I'm gone? That's not what I say, though. "Probably a few more weeks. Corporate should be making hiring decisions by the end of the week. Then it'll be a couple of weeks for training. After that, we'll have the grand opening." I don't know why I just told her all of that information except for the fact that she makes me nervous, even when she shouldn't. This is my domain, damn it.

"Are you and Johnny going to do the long-distance thing?" She glances at me and her eyes brighten as she waits for my answer.

"I don't think that's appropriate to discuss in this setting." That's it, Stella. Take the classy way out. Don't let her make you feel like shit.

"He's not going to pick up and move to the city with you. He's a small-town guy through and through. There is no way a woman he barely knows will make him change his mind." She sets the pen and application on my desk and leaves without another word. She's done what she came here to do, and it had nothing to do with the job she applied for.

What did I do to make her dislike me so much? She doesn't even know me, and she's been gunning for me since that night at Johnny's bonfire. She only wants what she obviously can't have, and instead of dealing with whatever emotions she has, she's made me the target.

I shouldn't let her get under my skin, I know that, but it doesn't stop me from texting Johnny.

Stella: What do you think about Austin?

A few minutes pass by with me staring at my phone, waiting for those three little dots to show up.

Johnny: I wouldn't mind visiting there.

Visiting, not going there to see you, or possibly moving there. He *knows* that's where I'm from. Without even realizing it, he's already sealed our fate.

Chapter Twenty-Seven

I'M NOT CUT out to train other people. The past two weeks have been brutal. It wouldn't be so hard if I actually knew how to do all the jobs' I'm showing these people. I've been relying on videos and printed material Rosie is sending me.

The biggest victory for me…Mr. Hart didn't do anything with Sarah's application. I debated even turning it in, but didn't want to stoop to her level. Maybe I'm a masochist, but I'm not one of those women that will keep another woman from excelling just because she's a thorn in my side. Now I only have to worry about her interfering in my life outside of work hours. If the cards are on my side, it won't be an issue even then.

An email from Mr. Hart comes through on my phone listing out the details of what is going to happen next. Apparently, he wants me to come back to the office for a couple of days next week to plan the ribbon cutting. It will be my first time going back home since I came to Asheville, and I'm nervous.

My phone pings with a message, and I close out of my email.

Johnny: Want to meet at Angie's place for dinner?

I only have a couple of days until I have to head to Austin. Going to dinner at a crowded bar isn't exactly how I want to spend time with him. But I can't be mad at him for suggesting it. He doesn't know about the travel plans that just got thrown at me. I mean, I assumed I'd have to go back before finishing things up here, but I didn't think it'd be so last minute.

**Stella: That's fine. I can meet you there as soon as I make sure everyone else
is out of the building. And, I have to head to Austin on Sunday.**
Johnny: For good?
**Stella: Not yet. They need me there to go over the details of the grand
opening.**
Johnny: Then I guess we better make tonight extra special.

Even though I don't want to go to Out of the Ashes, I'm excited to see
Johnny. With me training, and him busy at work, we haven't seen each other as
much as we were. And I'm not going to lie, I've been putting a little bit of
distance between us since that text message. I probably should have talked to
him about it when I got home that night, but I didn't want him to think that I
let Sarah get into my head. All I know is that it's going to suck sleeping alone
while I'm gone. Having him beside me at night is one of my favorite parts of
the day. I'm so screwed.

The last few people in the warehouse finally walk out the door. Today is one of
those days that feels like it's never going to end. I'm not sure if that's because
it's Friday, or because I would much rather be wrapped up in Johnny's arms.
Either way, I'm happy I can finally leave.

I lock up the building, and walk to my car. The weather is cooling off, and I
wish I had brought a light jacket with me to work. It's crazy to me that I've
been here for a season change. It feels like it hasn't been very long at all.

Unlocking my car, I slide into the driver's seat and pull out my phone.

Stella: I'm on my way.
Johnny: See you in a bit.

Out of the Ashes isn't very far from work which is why we meet there so
often. The amazing wings are a bonus. Angie is at the bar training a new
bartender when I walk in. "Hey Angie," I wave to her. "Have you seen
Johnny?"

She nods her head toward the adjoining room. "He's at the table you
usually sit at."

"Thanks. And, good luck." I point toward her trainee.

She rolls her eyes and then grabs a towel to clean up the mess her new
bartender has just made.

I round the corner to the next room and stop in my tracks. Johnny is there
all right. But Sarah has her arms around him. I can't believe what I'm seeing.
He knew I was coming. Why in the hell would he let her hang all over him like

that? Much less let her do it in public when we've made it known that we're an item.

Everything she said two weeks ago floats through my head, and I can't stop the tears from sliding down my face. She was right. I've been falling in love with him, and he's just been using me. That's what I get for starting out on this journey with him. I should have kept it light and fun, or said no to begin with.

He still hasn't seen me. If I leave now, I can text him and say I'm not feeling well and decided to go home instead. That's a totally plausible excuse to not show up. Now to see if he buys it.

Pulling out my phone, I debate whether to send the text now or once I'm safely in my car, and away from the scene. It's probably best if I wait. I shove the phone into my pocket, take a step back, and turn to go right back out the front door. My only miscalculation is the waiter with a tray full of food in his hand. The tray clatters to the floor, and the chatter in the bar dies. This may be the only time I've heard the bar this quiet. So much for my quick escape.

Johnny's head pops up and his eyes meet mine. I can see the regret pouring out of his stare willing me to give him a chance. Sarah, however, is beaming. This is exactly what she wanted. For all I know she planned this little stunt, and was biding her time until she knew I would be here. My head says it's the most logical answer. But my heart only sees betrayal and pain. Johnny pushes her away and tries to stand up to get around her.

I don't wait to see what happens next. I rush through the front of the bar and out the door. My name from Johnny's lips is the last thing I hear before I'm enveloped by the chilly autumn air. I take a deep breath, and almost choke from the temperature change. The sobs trying to break free. I'm such a fucking idiot. I should have known better.

It's a good thing my car is parked close. My vision is blurry from the tears, and there's no way I would be able to find my car in the back of the lot before he caught up to me. I get in and pull out of the parking spot. Looking in my rearview mirror, I see Johnny run out of the bar. I can take a right and go home. Or, I can take a left and hit the highway.

He's running toward my car now, but I can't face him. Not tonight. I need to get away from all these emotions. Away from Asheville. And, away from *him*.

I turn left. To my real home where the only things that matter are my cousins and my job.

My eyes are red and swollen by the time I pull into the parking garage at Audrey's apartment building. I could have gone to my own place. I should have. But I don't want to be alone. Not tonight. If I had my way, I'd undo everything that happened tonight and tell Johnny I'd rather stay in and cook dinner. Anything to keep *her* hands off of him.

There's a spot open next to Audrey's car, and I pull in. The drive here was exhausting. I didn't even stop to go to the bathroom. My cousins would be so proud of me. Maybe I'll just stay in the car. The thought of getting out and walking up fifteen million stairs to her apartment is already exhausting me. At least I'll get my cardio in.

The TV is loud as hell when I let myself in. She's about to regret giving me a key. I never show up unannounced. Hell, I didn't even call to let them know I was coming tonight. It was a split-second decision, and I fought back tears the entire drive here. A scream from the surround sound penetrates the otherwise quiet apartment. Shit, I hope I'm not interrupting a date. Talk about awkward.

I tiptoe into the living room to scope it out. Despite my own heartache, I don't want to interrupt whatever my cousin has going on. I prepare myself to see Audrey cuddled up with some hunky guy, but stop in my tracks when I see *both* of my cousins partially hiding behind a blanket watching one of my favorite horror movies. "You, assholes are watching *Halloween* without me?"

They scream and jump off the couch. "What the hell? You scared the shit out of us." Audrey bends down and picks up the popcorn that flew all over the floor when she jumped.

"Why didn't you tell us you were coming?" Tiffany asks. "We would have waited until you got here."

"I didn't mean to scare the pants off y'all." I drop my purse on the end table and help Audrey pick up the popcorn. "It was kind of last minute."

"How is kind of last minute an explanation? You live four hours away." Tiffany pulls the blanket they were sharing around her, and taps her foot. Waiting for me to answer her. Do I lie, or tell them the truth? I'm not in the mood for "I told you so."

"I was planning on coming home Sunday because they need me in the office on Monday, but…" I'm such a coward. I can't even finish the damn sentence. I stop my efforts in cleaning up the mess, and sprawl out on the floor.

Both of them look at me then search around for my bags. When they don't see any, Tiffany rushes to my side, wrapping her arms around me. "What happened?"

The tears I held back for over four hours run freely down my cheeks. I can't stop them. As if the dam I had built up has broken. "His ex-girlfriend happened."

"Wait," Audrey holds her hand up. "He has an ex-girlfriend."

"Yes."

"And she's been giving you trouble?"

"I wouldn't say trouble, but she definitely hasn't been making my relationship with Johnny easy."

"Why didn't you tell us?" Tiffany pulls back. "We could have made a trip for moral support."

"Because," I sigh. "I'm a big girl, and I was handling it."

"What did she do to make you drive so far to get away from them?"

Rehashing the events that took place is frustrating, and I feel like a dumbass after I've told them everything. From the bonfire to the grocery store run in. And end with her applying for a job at the distribution center and what I witnessed before running to my car and driving here.

"That is such a classic bitch move," Tiffany wrinkles her nose in disgust. "I would know, I've done it."

"Um, Tiff," Audrey nudges her shoulder. "I don't think that's going to win you any favors right now."

"It's fine. I'm the idiot that let her get under my skin." I grab my purse off the table, and rummage through it for my phone. It's dead, of course. Charging it didn't even cross my mind when I got on the highway.

"You're not an idiot," Audrey rubs my back, and takes my phone out of my hand. "I'll charge it and give it back to you in the morning. Texting him right now isn't very smart."

"You're right." I grab the blanket from around Tiffany, and climb up onto the sofa. "I think I'm going to try to get some sleep now."

Audrey and Tiffany wait until I'm lying down and tuck me in the way our moms used to do when we were kids and stayed with each other over the holidays. It's the little things that make you appreciate those in your life. "I love you guys," I mumble into the pillow.

"We love you, too." They turn the TV off and walk toward the kitchen whispering to each other just low enough so I can't make out what they are saying. It probably has to do with what a mess I've let myself become over a man. That's a turn of events I never saw coming.

Just before I fall into a deep sleep, I hear Tiffany talking. "She's asleep right now. Audrey and I are going to try to talk some sense into her over the weekend." I'll have to ask her about it tomorrow. Right now, I need to pass out so my brain will stop trying to overthink everything.

Chapter Twenty-Eight

"OKAY, STELLA," Audrey pulls the blanket off of me. "I love you, but you haven't moved from the sofa unless it was to use the bathroom since you got here Friday night. You have to go to work tomorrow, and you smell like death."

"No, I don't," I argue. Raising my arm, I take a sniff and scrunch up my nose. Maybe she's right about that. "Besides, it's not like I'm trying to impress anyone at work."

"Wrong," she points a finger in my face. "You still have to impress your bosses. You don't have that precious promotion yet."

Of course. She has to throw logic in my face like it's fucking confetti. I don't want any of it. I want to sit here and mope about Johnny. "Can I have my phone back?" They said they were going to give it back yesterday, but haven't done it. I don't understand why they are keeping it from me.

"Nope." Next she grabs the pillow I stole off her bed. The pretty ones on the sofa look comfortable but they are hard as hell, and my neck was not amused with me. "You are going to get your ass up, take a shower, and put on some of my clothes."

"Why?"

"Because it's Sunday, dummy."

"And?"

"We're having brunch. Tiffany should be here soon." Seriously…my love life is in turmoil and all they can think about is our weekly ritual.

"I'd rather sleep."

"Too. Damn. Bad." Audrey grabs my arm and pulls me off the couch. "Get up and get in the shower. Don't make me call your mom."

What the actual hell? "That's probably the most childish thing you've ever said."

"Well, you're acting like one." She starts walking to her bedroom. "If you aren't in the shower by the time I finish my makeup, I'm coming back with a cup of ice cold water."

This is the problem with being so close to my cousins. They know everything I dislike and they aren't afraid to piss me off. Why couldn't I have normal friends that won't give me the tough love treatment? Instead I'm stuck with these two crazies. Who am I kidding? I wouldn't have it any other way.

The apartment is silent as I walk out of the bathroom. Audrey was right, I *was* starting to smell. It's amazing what a shower will do for your attitude. The water washes the sadness away, leaving me feeling better. Not that I'm completely happy all of a sudden, but I feel fresh. Like I can tackle this hurdle and still come out on top. Maybe?

"Audrey?" These two better not have left me here after making a big deal about getting off the sofa. She's not in the kitchen or living room. I open her bedroom door, and she's applying her lipstick. "Where's Tiffany?"

"She's going to meet us there." She rubs her pale pink lips together and glances at me. "We're taking your car, though."

This is weird. We always Uber to brunch, and we almost always go together. Something is going on, and I need to find out what it is. "Fine. But you're driving." I grab a hair tie off her dresser and put my hair up into a messy bun without bothering to brush it first. They'll take me how I am, or they can kiss my ass. "Are you ready?"

Eyeing me up and down, she nods. She grabs something out of one of her drawers then sweeps by me without a word. Is that my cell phone? I try to make a grab for it, but she drops it in her purse as she picks up my keys. "Let's go. With any luck Tiffany will already have a table for us by the time we get there."

The drive to the restaurant is boring. Audrey puts the radio on some talk radio station and doesn't say a word to me. I watch the cars pass by, and stare at the tall buildings as we drive through downtown. This used to be my normal, but now it doesn't hold the same feeling it once did. I can't help but long for the small town I've come to like. The nonexistent traffic in Asheville is pretty nice, too. It takes me less time to get from my house there to town than it takes us to get five miles from Audrey's apartment. Being here today is a good thing. I can acclimate to my world once again, and get back in the groove of things.

Tiffany is sitting at one of the front tables when we walk in. Instead of her customary bloody mary in front of her, there's a glass of water. Audrey takes the chair next to Tiff, leaving me to sit opposite of them. "What is this? An intervention?"

"Sort of," Tiffany shrugs. "We need to talk about your priorities."

"Are you sure you should be leading this discussion?" Tiffany winces but doesn't show any sign of backing down. I'm already on edge, and I don't need these two trying to parent me. "I'm fine, guys. I'll be back here for good in a week, two tops."

"We don't think you should come back." Tiff's voice is barely above a whisper as she sneaks a look at Audrey.

"Wh-what?" She's kidding, right? There's no way I heard her correctly. "What do you mean I shouldn't come back?" The chatter of the restaurant seems louder than it was only seconds ago. Going from minor background noise to a constant buzzing. "Are y'all done with me, too?"

"Don't be stupid," Audrey scolds. "We'll never be done with you."

"Then why?"

"Because," Tiff raises her voice causing the couple at the table next to us to stare at her. "When you were in Asheville, you focused on you and what made you happy. It wasn't all about the job. You even met a great guy."

I can't believe this. "You agree with her?" I point at Audrey. "You thought dating Johnny was a mistake from the very beginning."

"Would you believe me if I said I had a change of heart?"

"No," I yell, not caring if I make a scene. "You don't get to stay on my ass about it then change your damn mind." I stand up and the chair falls to the floor. "After all the whining y'all did about me moving for my job, and you want me to *stay* there. Knowing damn well I don't have a reason to stay anymore."

I need to get out of here. Dozens of eyes are focused on me, and I stiffen. I'm making an ass of myself in one of my favorite places in Austin. I can't believe this. These two are something else. They are supposed to have my back. I was falling for Johnny. I can't go back there and see him all cuddled up next to Sarah. The pain would be too much.

Nope. I can't do this. Not right now when the pain is still too fresh. I grab my keys from the table where Audrey laid them down. "Y'all can have your weekly brunch. I'm out of here."

This feels like deja vu. Running out of yet another one of my favorite places to eat and away from the people I love. I can't believe they have the audacity to lecture me on my life. Even if they have a point, I can't tell them that. I've spent so much of my time and energy on trying to make it to the next ladder rung and I'll be damned if letting a man into my heart....

Tears blur my vision as I make my way toward the back of the parking lot. I look over my shoulder but my cousins aren't following me. Maybe they really are done with me. Finally, I get in my car, turn it on and start driving. The only place left for me to go is home, and I don't really want to be alone. I have work tomorrow, though, and I need to be ready for whatever they need me to do.

Once I'm safely inside my apartment building, I dig through my small bag for my phone. Shit. Audrey still has it. I hope to God that nobody from the office is trying to call me. It'll be the first time in a long time that I'll be unavailable.

The elevator is taking forever. I don't have time for this crap. I need to see what I have in my closet that I can wear, and figure out what I'm doing with my life. I slide the key into the doorknob of my apartment, twist it, and throw the door open. I'm back to a space in my life that is normal. This should be able to perk me back up, if not, I'm completely screwed.

With the door closed and locked behind me, I realize that I'm not alone. Audrey and Tiffany couldn't have beat me here. I slowly turn around and see *him*. "What are you doing here?"

I'm going to murder my cousins for this little stunt.

Chapter Twenty-Nine

Johnny doesn't say anything. He holds up his hands in surrender. This wasn't what I was expecting when I walked through my apartment door. "Seriously, why are you here?"

"You didn't give me a chance to explain before you ran out of the bar."

What the hell? Today is full of confrontations that I am not ready, nor am I equipped to handle. "I can't do this right now."

I turn back toward the door and lift my hand to the lock. "Dammit, Stella." Not once has he ever raised his voice at me. A part of me wants to walk right out the door and not look back. The other part, the one full of feelings and hope, thinks maybe I should listen to him. "Just, let me tell you what happened. Then, if you never want to see me again, I will walk out of your life and never bother you again."

Holy crap. He is being sincere. Normally he wraps his kindness in innuendo and dirty jokes, but I've never heard him this heartfelt.

I step away from the door, and walk to the living room, giving him a wide berth before I sit down on my sofa. God, I've missed this thing. It's much more comfortable than the crappy one Audrey has. I should have just come home Friday night instead of storming my cousins' apartment. I would have slept better at least. "I'll listen, but first you have to tell me how you even got in here." I have an idea; I only need confirmation.

He runs his hand through his hair and his cheeks redden. It's hard to stay mad at him when he looks so adorably uncomfortable, but I'm not going to let him off that easily. There's no reason Sarah should have been anywhere near him Friday night. "Your cousin may have let me in."

"I'm going to assume you're talking about Tiffany. When did you get here?"

"Yup. However, it also came with a threat to my manhood should I piss you off even more." He takes a step closer to me and stops when I hold up my hand. "I got here late last night. I couldn't leave my uncle hanging, so I worked all day. Then I got in my truck, and drove here. I needed to see you."

A man guilty of cheating wouldn't drive four hours to make his case, right? I've never had a serious relationship. Hell, I've barely had any one-night stands. There's no bar for me to measure this against. I have no idea what to think. This is where I need my cousins, even though I'm pissed at them. Maybe I imagined what I saw. Except all I keep seeing in my head is Johnny staring down at his phone, and Sarah pressed up against him. I shake the image away, "Now would be a good time to explain." Before I get mad all over again and start crying.

"First off, I don't blame you for running." Johnny takes a deep breath and slowly lets it out. "And it wasn't at all what it looked like. I was sitting at the table checking my phone, and waiting for you to get there."

"So, how does Sarah fit into all this?" I interrupt him.

"If you would give me a second, I'm getting there." He watches me, waiting to see if I'm going to say anything else. When I don't, he continues. "I heard you talking to Angie, and I was about to send you a text letting you know where I was. Sarah, who I didn't even know was there, came out of nowhere and threw her arms around me at the same time you walked around the corner."

Although his explanation could be true, it seems a little convenient. "Why didn't you push her off of you as soon as she was touching you?" I'm not a jealous person, and I never have been. But, I'm not a fan of other people touching my things.

"I don't know. Because I'm not an asshole." He throws his hands in the air, exasperated. "I didn't want to have to physically put my hands on her. She can be vindictive when she doesn't get her way, as you might've noticed." Obviously. "I was trying to be civil since we were in public. But when I heard the tray hit the floor, and saw you standing there mortified, I had no other choice than to physically remove her from beside me."

He takes one, two, three steps toward me and crouches down until my eyes meet his. "Do you want to know why I would risk the possibility of her calling the cops on me for some bullshit reason?"

I can't say anything. It's like my brain forgot how to make words, and I shake my head waiting for him to continue. "Because of you. I don't give a shit about her, and I haven't for a long time. *You* are the one I want. You are the one I'm falling in love with. Hell, I think I partially fell in love with you the first night I met you and you accused me of being a serial killer."

I can't help the snort of laughter that bubbles from me. Only he would find my serial killer comments endearing. "Really?" It's a stupid question. I know it is as soon as it leaves my mouth. No guy in their right mind would drive this far for a girl they don't care about.

"Yes, really. I wouldn't have said it if I didn't mean it." That's one thing I've always been able to count on with him. He may be playful most of the time, but he doesn't sugarcoat anything. "Why would you think for one second that I was interested in Sarah?" I don't say anything. "I thought I made it pretty damn clear that I want nothing to do with her since the day she came back to town."

Because I'm a dumbass, that's why. "She may have made a few comments when she came to fill out the application again."

"What did she say?" He climbs up on the sofa next to me, and turns me until I'm facing him.

"Basically, that we'd never work once I moved back here." He looks like he's about to interrupt so I rush on. "And that you'd never pick up and move for someone you barely know."

He taps his finger on my leg, thinking. "Is that what the vague text asking what I thought about Austin was for?"

"Yeah," I squeak. I should have talked to him about it. But no, I let fear and her words dig into me so far that I couldn't let them go.

"That's not true. You know that, right?" I shrug because I don't. We never talked about the logistics of how we would work so far away from each other. "We can do the long-distance thing until we're ready to move forward. It wouldn't be hard for me to find a job here."

I don't want him to have to move for me, though. I'm not even sure I want to live here anymore. The noise and crowded streets aren't comforting the way they used to be. I miss the quiet of my house in the country. "I'm not going to ask you to do that."

"Just know that I would. The past two nights have been brutal not knowing what is going to happen to us." He leans forward and kisses me on the forehead before pulling me to him.

This feels right. It feels like home. "I'm sorry I ran away instead of talking to you. If I stayed, all of this could have been avoided."

"We're good now, aren't we?" I nod into his chest and his hold on me tightens. "Any chance your cousins are still at the restaurant? I'm starving and you have no food in the fridge."

"Yeah." I scoot back and scrunch my nose. "How did you know we were at a restaurant?"

"They texted me and told me where you'd be. They also said you'd probably get pissed and storm off." He pokes me in my side. "Is that something I'm going to have to get used to? You running off anytime I piss you off?"

I straighten my back. "Not unless it's something I really care about."

"It's nice to know you think I'm important," he winks at me, and tries to pull me toward him.

I resist. I may forgive him, but he's not going to goad me into giving him compliments. "Whatever. Let's go back to the restaurant." My stomach growls driving that point home. I haven't eaten actual food since Friday at lunch. It's a wonder my body hasn't gone into shock from all the ice cream and chips.

Johnny glances down the hall toward my bedroom and raises his eyebrows. "Do we have to go right this second?"

Smacking his arm, I stand up. "Yes, unless you want me to starve. There will be plenty of time for that later."

"I guess." He pouts.

"There will be." I grab his hand and pull him toward the door. "Until then, let me show you a little bit of my city."

At least it will be for now.

Chapter Thirty

WAKING up next to Johnny is the best I've felt since before my freak-out on Friday. I silence the alarm on my phone before it blares through the room. Apparently, it's annoying to him, or that is what I am guessing because he keeps hinting for me to change it to something less jarring.

As much as it pains me, I have to go into the office today. I have no idea what is going to happen once I get there. I've worked so hard to get this promotion, but it's not what I really want anymore. In a few short months, I have fallen in love with a man who changed everything. It's still weird admitting that I love him because I never saw myself settling down with someone, at least not for a few more years. But life is funny that way and takes you completely by surprise.

Lifting the comforter off of me, I attempt to slide out of the bed, but a muscular arm wraps around my waist and pulls me back. "Don't leave yet."

"Technically, I'm not actually leaving," I laugh. "I have to get ready." I untangle myself from his embrace and hurry out of the bed before he lures me back in. "Will you be here when I get back?"

"Probably," he mumbles into the pillow. "I don't plan on leaving until tomorrow at the latest. I already cleared it with my uncle."

"Good." I bend down and give him a quick kiss. I haven't told him that I plan on leaving with him. I just came to the conclusion myself. The only thing I know for sure is that being alone in this apartment is not what I want for my future, and I can't ask him to move away from everything he knows. He belongs in the country with me by his side.

My legs are shaky as I walk into the building. This was supposed to be a final planning meeting to sure up the distribution center and tell me my future within the company. Now, it's going to be a lot more than that. Hopefully, they will accept what I have to offer, but if not, I have a plan, thanks to Angie.

The elevator doors are almost closed when an arm coming through the crack forces them to open again. *He* is not the first person I wanted to see this morning. "Good morning, Stella. Are you ready for today?"

"Hi, Mr. Granger." I paste a fake smile on my face. Being in his presence grates on my nerves, but hopefully I won't have to deal with him for much longer. "Yes. I'm already."

"Good, good." He smooths his suit jacket and presses the button for our floor. I don't trust his smug smile. He's up to something, and even though I want to know what it is, I'm not going to bother trying to pry it out of him.

The elevator doors open and Mr. Granger turns right to go to his office. *Good riddance.* Instead of going to my office, I walk to the back of the room and turn for Rosie's desk. She's sitting in her chair painting her fingernails. She's such a rockstar and gives no fucks what others think. It's a good thing Mr. Hart likes her, or she would have been fired long ago. "Good morning, Rosie. How are you this fine morning?"

"Hi, Stella," she beams. "I'm good. Are you looking for Mr. Hart?"

"Yes, ma'am."

"He's in his office." She points a shiny red nail toward his office.

"Thank you." I take a deep breath and put one foot in front of the other. Each step taking me closer to either the biggest mistake I've ever made, or the beginning of a new adventure.

I knock three times in quick succession. "Come in," Mr. Hart calls through the thick wood. He's not at his usual place behind the desk. He's standing next to the tall window, staring out at the city.

"Good morning, Mr. Hart." He jumps at the sound of my voice, even though he told me to come in. "Sorry, I didn't mean to startle you."

"You're fine, Stella. How are you?"

"I'm great." And for the first time, in a long time, I mean it. Happiness fills every part of my soul, and I realize now that all I felt before was content. I was okay with only having work to fill my days, and it filled my nights a lot of the time, too. Now, I spend my time with a great guy and new friends.

"That's good." He walks around the desk and sits in one of the chairs in front of it instead of the big, leather one behind it. "You're here awfully early. Is there something you wanted to discuss before the meeting?"

It's remarkable how perceptive he is. I guess that's why most of his employees are happy and we don't have a ton of turnover when it comes to staffing. "Actually, yes."

"Why do I get the feeling that I won't like what you have to say?"

I don't beat around the bush; I jump right in with what I have to say. "Is the manager position at the distribution center set in stone?"

"Yes. Why?"

"Are there any other positions I could apply for?"

He sighs, "You know better than anyone that there aren't. *You* were the one in charge of training after we filled all the positions."

"That's what I figured." Deep breath in, long exhale out. Just say it. Don't hold back. I reach into my bag and pull out the letter I secretly typed up this morning. "I'd like to hand in my resignation notice."

His eyes widen. He wasn't expecting that. "Is there anything I can do to change your mind? Or, is there something we did as a company to push you away?"

"No, sir," I smile. "It's been amazing working here. It's just time for me to move on to something, and somewhere, else."

I hear a gasp come from the door I didn't shut all the way. Rosie is so nosy, and I can't stop my laugh. Mr. Hart glances at the door and rolls his eyes. "You might as well come all the way in, Rosie. There's no use hovering outside."

She claps her hands together without letting her fingers touch. That polish still has to dry after all. "You met someone, didn't you?"

Nodding my head, I look out the window at the city I'm going to leave behind. Not for good. I still have to come back and see my cousins, after all. "Not that it's any of your concern, but yes."

"Oh sweetie, I'm happy you finally found someone you're willing to stop working nonstop for."

"That's kind of mean. I dated."

"Not enough." She laughs at my scowl. "Don't think I didn't notice all of those late nights you spent up here. A young woman your age should be out enjoying life, not shutting herself up inside four walls."

She has a point. I didn't realize how much I was working until I was given the chance to slow things down. I'm not telling her that, though. She loves being right, and I won't give her the satisfaction. Instead, I change the subject. "I'll stay on until the grand opening, and however long you need me until you find a replacement. But I won't be able to come into the office as much."

"As much as it pains me to lose such an amazing employee, I'm fine with you staying until the opening." He stands up, and I do the same. "I'm not happy about this turn of events, but as long as you're doing what you think is best for you, I'll accept it." He holds his hand out, waiting for me to shake his. After I place my hand in his, he squeezes it slightly. From anyone else it would weird me out, but he's more of a grandpa figure in the office. "You're still getting that bonus, though. You've done an excellent job in handling everything with this new operation. You are going to make someone else a great employee."

"Thank you, sir." As much as I fight it, tears well up in my eyes. It's a bittersweet ending my journey with the company, but it's for the best. It's time to move on to bigger and better things.

Johnny is sitting on the couch scrolling through my saved Netflix shows when I get home. It's a total mix-up of different genres, and he's probably worried about the kind of girl he's dating. It's too late now. He's stuck with me. "How was work?" He pauses his scrolling, and pats the space next to him on the sofa.

"It was…good." I grin from ear to ear. Mr. Granger tried his best to prove what an inept person I am, and why I don't deserve the promotion. It was satisfying watching his face fall when I announced my resignation. He's only mad because he wasn't the one that pushed me out the door.

"When is the grand opening?"

"Next week. There isn't much left for me to do to finish up the project. The PR team is getting the local paper to write a piece about the opening and get some pictures. All I have to do is show up and cut a ribbon."

"Oh," his face falls. "I guess that means you'll be here permanently after that."

I shrug my shoulders, making him wait for my news. It's cruel, but he'll be happy about it in the end. "Are you ready to go home?"

"Damn, you're already kicking me out?" He laughs in an attempt to disguise the hurt.

"No, weirdo," I shake my head. "With me."

"You're already home." He stares at me in disbelief.

"To Asheville." It's like I have to spell it out for him. It's still not registering. "Home is where you are."

"Does that mean what I think it means?" His eyes brighten and he pulls me into his lap.

"Yes, it does." I kiss him on both cheeks and grab his face between my hands. "I'm moving to Asheville…permanently."

"That's the best damn news I've heard all day." He looks around the apartment. "You've got a nice set up here, but it's nothing like the fresh country air."

"How about we say goodbye to my apartment properly before we leave in the morning?" I climb off his lap, grab his hand and pull him off the sofa.

"I lied," he grins. "That's the best news I've heard." He sweeps me in his arms and carries me to my bed.

I never thought I'd find a reason to leave the city. But here he is. He helped me see there's more to just working day in and day out. I am ready for the next chapter in my life, and I think the slow and steady pace of Asheville suits me just fine.

Epilogue

Food covers the counters of my kitchen. Johnny's friends from work, Angie, and my cousins are in the living room while we try to figure out the best placement for everything. Friendsgiving is something I've always done with Audrey and Tiffany before we'd get together with our entire family.

"Where do you want the turkey?" Johnny asks from behind me.

There's literally nowhere to put it. "On top of the stove, I guess."

"How's everyone doing out there?"

Laughter, and easy conversation comes from the other room. "It sounds like it's going great. I think Tiffany and Audrey are feeling Angie out. Making sure she'll be a suitable friend for me."

"The three of you are so freaking weird."

I shrug my shoulders, "Would you have me any other way?"

"Oh, I can think of a few ways I'd like to have you," he wraps his arms around me.

I grab a spoon out of the drawer and smack him with it before adding it to one of the dishes Angie brought. It's nice having all of my things here with me. I've really made the space my own. I'll stay here as long as I can afford it. I put most of my bonus from Mr. Hart in savings. It's a nice cushion for when things are slow at Out of the Ashes. Angie has been amazing to work with, and she likes having the breaks she gets since I've come on as assistant manager. All of the social media marketing I've put in place has helped bring more people into the bar. She's flourishing and I love being a part of that.

"Is the food ready, yet?" Tiffany stomps into the kitchen. "I'm wasting away over here."

"I swear you care more about food than you do anything else."

"I do when I haven't eaten all day," she pouts.

"You better watch it," Johnny steps away from me. "You put her in charge of finding you a roommate. She'll pick someone horrible if you aren't nice to her."

"I'm more worried about whatever food she cooked," Tiffany ducks out of the way of the towel I throw at her head. "What? It's true. Your cooking is shit."

"Don't worry, I didn't make anything." I step around the counter and walk into the living. "Everything is ready."

Our friends start filing into the kitchen. Reaf, his wife and their daughter at the front of the line. Tiffany is right behind them with Audrey and Angie bringing up the back.

Seeing all of our friends in one place warms my heart. I've grown so much since moving here, and feel lucky to have relationships outside of my bond with my cousins. They'll always be my best friends, but it's nice having other people I can talk to. Ones that are a hell of a lot closer than four hours away.

Once everyone has their plates filled to the brim, they take a seat at the table. Johnny and I are last. Being a hostess is a completely new thing to me, and I'll have to do it again when we get together with our families for Thanksgiving. Hopefully none of them are expecting me to cook anything. I'll find the nearest place that caters to avoid embarrassing myself.

"I'd like to make a toast," Johnny announces to the room. Everyone pauses in their eating, except for Layla, Reaf's cutie of a daughter. She's eating with gusto. "Thank you all for being here tonight. We hope to have more get togethers, like this in the future. Stella, you literally crashed into my life, and have made it better every single day." I blush at his words. "Thank you for not killing me when I messed up your car worse than it was. You truly are the best thing in my life."

"Ditto," I agree.

"And because I know you won't cuss me out in front of a room full of people, or a toddler, I want to ask you a question." Oh shit, he's not about to propose is he. I can't handle that shit right now. It's way too soon for that. "Will you move in with me?"

I breathe a sigh of relief. That I can handle. "That depends. Is that stupid hole in the floor fixed?" That earns some chuckles from our guests.

"It will be if you say yes."

"Will you promise to keep all creepy crawly things out of the house? Oh, and not to turn into a serial killer?" That last question didn't earn as many laughs as the first two.

"Yes. I'll do my best to keep snakes out of the bathroom." He looks around the room. "As for becoming a serial killer…I have no plans on that happening. I'll let you know if it changes, though."

"Then yes. I'll move in with you." He pulls me into his arms, and slams his mouth into mine. Everyone hoots and hollers, celebrating with us. Even Layla can be heard over everyone else.

"You've just made me the happiest man in the room."

"Good. I'll make you even happier later." I whisper in his hear. "Let's hang out with our friends before we run them out of the house."

"I'm not opposed to that."

"Shut up and eat."

Tiffany claps her hands together, silencing everyone. "That's enough PDA for the evening. I'm going to lose my appetite."

"Fine," I laugh. "Let's eat."

Life can't get more perfect than it is right now.

Gone Steady

ONE

Tiffany

THE BASS IS THRUMMING through my body as people press against each other.
The music flows through the crowd. This is my happy place. The only thing
that would make this better is if Audrey and Stella were here tonight. Stella, of
course, couldn't make it because she had to get into a committed relationship.
Don't get me wrong, she deserves all the happiness in the world and I am truly
happy for her. But, did she have to fall for a guy four hours away? She can't
join me on my spur of the moment adventures anymore. Audrey, on the other
hand, bailed on me and is lame. I get this isn't her scene, so I don't blame her
completely.

I just need them here to keep my crazy ass in line. Hopefully, they're busy
finding a roommate. The last few they've picked have been complete duds.
They need to stop thinking about what their likes and dislikes are and start
thinking about what works for me. It is too bad I can't be trusted to pick my
own damn roommate. My bullshit radar is on the fritz, and the last few people
I've moved into my apartment have been horrible choices.

The band on stage plays a cover of "The Imperial March," and as much as I
don't care for Star Wars, I can't deny that the rock edge they put on it is amazing. It's enough to have me acting like a damn fool jumping up and down. This
is what I live for. Getting lost in the music and giving up any worry I have over
living up to the same expectations as my cousins. If my mom or dad mentions
how proud they are of my cousins one more time, I will lose my shit. As the
band switches to a cover of Nirvana, I sing at the top of my lungs. Putting all
my frustration at being the family screwup into every single word.

Being serious is overrated. I love my life. I only need to live up to my own expectations and flutter wherever the wind takes me. It may have caused me to make a few bad decisions along the way, but I don't regret any of them. Who needs a steady nine-to-five job? Not me. I won't be happy in that environment. And if I had that job, my ass wouldn't be at a concert on a weeknight, having an incredible time.

Someone bumps into me from behind causing me to fall to the ground. Suddenly all my doom and gloom thoughts are gone and I am pissed.

A man looms over me, his lips moving, but I can't hear what he's saying.

"What?" I scream above the roaring crowd.

He bends closer, his eyes hidden behind square black frames, brows furrowed. "Are you hurt?" He holds his hand out to help me up, taking me by surprise.

"I—I don't think so," I reach for his hand and allow him to pull me up. "You kind of came out of nowhere."

"I'm so sorry," he brings me closer to him so he doesn't have to yell. "I didn't mean to plow you over. The assholes back there are being kinda pushy."

Most girls would be uncomfortable so close to someone they don't know. Not me. All I want to do is get to know him a little better. The way his plain white t-shirt molds to his body is perfection. "It's okay." He opens his mouth to protest, but I cut him off. "We are in the pit. The likelihood of me getting jostled around is pretty high." I stare at him for emphasis.

"Jostled and getting your ass knocked to the ground are two very different things." His dark brown eyes study me. *What is he looking for?*

"Seriously, I'm good." I turn back toward the stage, ready to rock out. This guy is cute and all but he can't give me the high music gives me. Not yet, anyway. After a few more drinks, that may change.

Tap. Tap. Tap. A finger raps on my shoulder. "Are you sure?" I'm not even fully facing him before the words are out of his mouth.

Do I blow him off? This is the big question of the night. He's not too shabby to look at, and he's kind, if not a little too kind. "If you really want to make it up to me, you can buy me a drink." I'm not above getting free drinks.

"I can definitely do that." He walks toward the bar area, and stops. "Want to come with me?"

Not really. I love this band, and I don't want to miss any part of their set. But he was nice enough to help me up after knocking me over. Not to mention the fact that I've seen this band almost ten times, prompts me to hook my arm into his. "Sure."

We push our way through the crowd, trying to keep from getting jostled around. It shouldn't be this hard to get out of the pit. It never has been before. The fans are amped up, though. It'll be almost impossible for us to get back in the area we just left.

"What's your name?" My new, bespectacled friend asks. His mouth is near my ear to be heard over the crowd, and a shiver runs down my spine. I'd be lying if I said that's never happened before. I'm no stranger to lust, and this guy fits the bill.

"Tiffany," I yell, unsure if he can hear me over the roar of the crowd.

Finally, we get to the exit. Once we leave the main concert area, the noise is down and everything feels muted. It's crazy how one thick wall can change the sound of everything, even in an open air venue. "What's your name?" My voice is louder than necessary, still adjusting the quieter atmosphere.

He chuckles and removes his arm from mine. Nobody has ever done that before, and the rejection stings. "It's Spencer."

"Do you live in Austin?"

"Yeah," he leads us toward the closest vendor. "I've lived here all my life." The woman behind the counter asks for our ID's. "What do you want to drink?"

"I'm not picky, you choose." Neither one of my cousins could do that. They typically drink the same thing no matter where they go. However, Stella has been broadening her horizons since she started working at that bar in Asheville. It is hilarious because she's acting like these drinks are new just because she's never had them before.

"You're pretty brave," he grins. "I could pick out something horrible for you to drink and you wouldn't even know it."

I shrug my shoulders and lean against the sticky counter. "I guess it's a good thing I know what most of these beers taste like."

"Very clever," he taps me on the nose and orders our drinks. "Back to our earlier conversation."

Shit, what were we talking about.
"Do you live in the area?"
Oh, right. We were talking about living in Austin.

The band starts a new song and a part of me is itching to go back to the pit, but this guy is nice. It wouldn't be a horrible decision to see where tonight may lead. I'm not getting any bad vibes off of him, so all is good. "Yep. I've lived here for a few years."

"What made you pick Austin?"

"My cousins." It's as simple as that. Stella was already here, but when Audrey moved, it just made sense. I didn't want to be stuck in our small town by myself, and moving to a big city seemed like a good thing to do. The adventures I could have here were endless.

"Most people try to get away from their families, not run to them," he laughs.

"They're my best friends. Being around them and seeing them all the time is fun. Until they get all judge-y and get on my nerves. Even then, I love them and can't imagine being away from them. Now, it's kind of boring since my oldest cousin moved away. Audrey doesn't like to go to these things unless Stella is with us."

"That's a shame." He shakes his head and looks toward the crowd we were just in. "If you ever need someone to join you for live music, I'm available."

Whoah. Wait a hot damn minute. Is he trying to ask me on future dates, or is he just making small talk to make me feel better? I'm not that type of girl. I don't do multiple dates, at least not for long. I know that one statement shouldn't shake me up this much, but my good sense is being distracted by his looks and how easy he is to talk to.

"We'll see." I shrug, hoping the answer is as noncommittal as possible. I wouldn't be opposed to seeing him again, but I plan for concerts months in advance. Hell, I had tickets for my cousins for this one since before Stella moved to nowheresville. Then, Stella couldn't make it because she was busy with her new job in Asheville, and Audrey bailed last minute, naturally.

We grab our beers and instead of returning to the pit, we find an open spot on the lawn. It's easier to talk up here while enjoying the music. "So, what do you do for a living?"

"I'm a waitress at a restaurant downtown." I wait for the look of horror to cross his face, or for him to decide that I don't have any aspirations. You'd be surprised how many times I'm asked when I will get a real job. For me, this is a real job. I enjoy what I do, and I don't think I should make apologies for it.

To my surprise, he doesn't say one bad thing. "How do you not get tired standing in the pit after you've been on your feet all day?"

"It's an entirely different energy when I'm at a concert."

"That makes sense," he nods. We watch the rest of the show in silence, soaking up the music and enjoying the night air. Once the band is finishes their encore song, we stay seated while everyone gets up in droves to walk to their cars. "Did you drive here?"

"No, I took an Uber. I don't want to drive if there's a chance I'll be drinking." I grab my phone to let Audrey know the show is over. She may not be here, but I at least like to let her know I'm safe.

"Any chance you want to grab something to eat with me?" His eyes are on the ground while he asks, unsure of what I'll say.

"Sure," I say. "How do pancakes sound?"

We get up and walk to the exit of the venue. "I'll get us a ride."

"Thanks." Phone still in hand, I send a group text to Audrey and Stella.

Tiffany: Concert is done. Having dinner with a fellow concert goer.
Stella: Is he hot?
Tiffany: Who said it was a "he"?

Audrey: Because when isn't it a he?
Tiffany: You have a point.
Audrey: Turn on your location sharing so I know you're safe.
Tiffany: Yes, Mom.
Stella: Have fun. Don't do anything I wouldn't do.
Tiffany: Do you know who you're talking to? Besides, it's not like I'll ever see him again.
Audrey: I'm not kidding. TURN IT ON!
Stella: You better do it. Call me tomorrow with all the details. Also, I put out another ad on a roommate for you.
Tiffany: You got it.

I turn on the location sharing on my phone. If I don't Audrey will bug the hell out of me until I do. I can't have her cramping my style tonight. I have every intention of going home with this guy.

The Uber he requested pulls up to the curb. "After you," he opens the door and I slide into the backseat. He sits beside me instead of the front seat, and I know he's definitely interested. "Want to get those pancakes to go?"

TWO

Spencer

Holy crap. How do I answer that? This is new territory for me. I don't do hookups. Hell, I don't date. Nobody likes the nerdy guy. Not that I think I'm hideous or anything, but usually as soon as comic or movie facts burst out of my mouth, they run away. Plus, if they ever saw my apartment, they'd never come back. I'll blame talking to her on liquid courage. There is *no way* I would have been able to talk to a force of nature like her without it.

I can just tell she lives life fearlessly and does whatever she wants. In all the concerts I've been to with my friends, I've never seen a woman hang out in the pit by herself. Let alone, feel confident that she'll be okay.

"Spencer?" Her voices breaks into my thoughts.

"Huh?"

"The pancakes? Are you good with getting them to go?"

Oh, right. I forgot I'm the one who initiated this whole eating thing. Even worse, where are we supposed to go after we pick up the food? She didn't offer her place, so I guess it is my apartment then. "Sure."

"Look guys," the Uber driver speaks up. "I just need to know where you want me to go."

"Actually pancakes would be a horrible idea," Tiffany sits up straighter. "Run us through the nearest drive through, please. Then, Spencer can decide where to go from there."

"I can do that," the driver says and puts the vehicle in drive.

The car is deadly silent aside from the low music coming from the speakers. A stark contrast from the loud concert we just left. Fear courses through me. She's going to realize just how awkward I am, and bail. Not that I'd blame her.

Tiffany is looking out the window, taking in the city she lives in. "You look at your surroundings like you've never seen them before."

She shrugs her shoulders, and keeps staring. "I've lived here for a few years, but it seems like there is always something new to see. A new adventure that opens up." She glances at me no doubt seeing my confusion. "It's just a lot different in the town I grew up in."

"You're very spirited in the way you describe things."

"Try living in a place where you have expectations to do things a certain way, and everything closes before ten at night." She turns to me. "You start taking chances and doing what makes you happy."

There's a lot more to this woman than I thought. Maybe she isn't just a party girl. She could be the one who doesn't laugh at my obsession over comic books.

The driver pulls into *Whataburger*. "I'll pull up to the speaker where your window is."

"Sounds good," Tiffany beams, still somehow full of energy.

As soon as we're at the speaker, I roll down the backseat window, and turn to Tiffany. "What do you want?"

She taps her finger against her chin. "Um, a large fry and chocolate shake."

I nod my head and turn toward the static voice coming through. "I need two large french fries, a regular chocolate shake, and large Dr. Pepper."

The person working the drive thru gives me the total and we pull forward. "Can you ask for spicy ketchup when we get up there?"

"Sure," I shrug. "It really is the best ketchup out there. They just never give enough."

"Maybe you should ask for a specific amount."

"Good idea."

The Uber driver stops with the back window in front of the drive thru window, and I hand my card over to pay despite Tiffany's objections while she digs through her small bag. "You can stop looking. I already paid."

"Thanks," she breathes and relief washes over her face.

Our food now taking up the small space between us, the driver asks where we're heading next. I rattle off my address, and don't miss the way Tiffany's shoulders sag. I'm not sure if it's from disappointment or relief, but I'm not going to question it. The car is already following the path on GPS , and I don't want to annoy our driver more than we already have.

He pulls up to the house, and Tiffany gasps. "This is your house," she almost yells as she gets out of the car.

"Thanks, Man," I tell the driver as I grab the bag contenting our food and shut the door. "No. My place is the apartment above the garage. But we have to be quiet I don't want to wake the landlords." I'm not going to mention they are also my parents. As soon as I graduated from college, I came back home. Not willing to live in the house, I asked if I could move into the small apartment over the garage. She doesn't need to know all that, though. Not unless she actually sticks around.

"Oh," she covers her mouth. "Sorry. I didn't realize."

"It's okay." Grabbing her hand, I start walking toward the stairs that lead to the apartment. She doesn't pull away. I wasn't sure if she'd balk at me grabbing her, but I'm going off of what I've seen in movies. The few girlfriends I've had were like me, and awkward as hell. I should have grabbed another drink before they stopped serving it at the concert. I'm losing my buzz…and my bravado. *Come on alcohol. Stick with me just a little longer.*

"Can you hold onto these for a second? The door can be a little tricky." She nods, and I hand off the bag holding our food and my drink. Pulling the key out of my pocket, I insert it into the door knob. Nothing happens when I turn it, and it's going to be one of those nights. I really should replace this door. The only plus side is my parents haven't figure out how to get it unstuck, and I don't want to get rid of that small piece of privacy.

With my hand still on the key, I use the other one to pull the door toward me and lift up. Turning the key quickly, the lock release and the door swings open. Hopefully there isn't a mess in there.

Grabbing the bag and cup from her hand, I gesture for her to go in ahead of me. I flip the light switch on as soon as she's through the door, and follow her. "Wow," she turns in a circle, taking in the small space. "You have quite the obsession."

Is that a good thing, or bad thing? I can't tell from her expression. But she comes toward, taking the food and drink from me and sets them on the small table in the middle of the room. My eyes widen and I blurt out, "Aren't we going to eat?"

"Later." She clearly has one thing on her mind, and I may be awkward as hell, but I'm not stupid. Tiffany is actually interested in me, despite seeing the posters all over my walls. And I'm more than interested in her. She's funny, energetic, and everything I could possibly want in a woman. Who cares if I just met her.

She wraps her arms around my neck, leans forward and presses small kisses along my throat. Then my jawline until her lips reach my mouth. Her tongue sweeps across the seam of my lips, and I grant her entrance. *Stay calm. You've had sex before. This isn't anything new. Don't freak out.*

Her hands slide down my chest and stop at the edge of my shirt, her mouth never leaving mine. She wasn't lying when she said she goes after what she wants. I wish I could be more like her. But even now, with her doing all the work, I'm barely holding onto my sanity. She lifts my shirt up, breaking the kiss long enough to pull it over my head, and grabs the hem of her shirt tossing it near mine.

I ignore my hammering heart, and pull her toward me. I can't let her think I'm a complete loser. Even though, deep inside, that's what I feel like. I still live on my parent's property for crying out loud. Tiffany left her small town and moved hours away to a city she didn't know much about.

Crashing my mouth down on hers, I reach around her, fumbling with her bra. Shit, they make these things impossible to take off even if you're looking directly at it. Her fingers unlatch the button of my jeans and begins shoving them down. I help by moving my feet bringing them down faster. But, this stupid bra is giving me hell.

Tiffany pulls back and grins. "Need some help?" She reaches her arms behind her and the bra is unclasped in less than two seconds.

"How in the world did you do that?" I can't keep the awe out of my voice. Women must have magical super powers.

"I've had to wear a bra since I was like twelve," she laughs. "It's pretty much second nature. Now, less talking and more kissing." She leads me to the couch along the wall by the door and pushes me down.

She undoes the button on her own pants, and slides them off, taking her panties with them. She is fucking glorious and I can't look away. Stalking toward me as if I'm her prey, she sits on my lap. Legs straddling either side of me. My breath hitches and I can't believe this gorgeous woman is interested in *me*. "Do you want to keep going?"

I nod my head vigorously. Who in their right mind would turn this woman down? Nobody, that's who.

"Good," she smiles and kisses me once again. Even though I didn't hide my interest in her when I was drinking, now I feel like that lonely virgin nerd I was in high school. Dumbfounded when someone showed any sort of interest in me. Not overthinking things any longer, I place my hands on her face and deepen the kiss.

She needs to know that I can actually be more than what I appear. That I won't be content letting her do all the work. But one thing is for sure, this couch is not big enough to do much of anything. Moving one hand down to the small of her back, I pull her closer to me, and stand up. Her arms grip my neck tighter, and her mouth works against my jawline and nibbles on my ear as I make my way toward the room and my bed.

I almost drop her at the new sensation. Nobody has ever done that before. Well, not the way she does it with her tongue sliding against my earlobe before gently biting down. My dick grows harder, and son of a bitch, ears should not be this sensitive.

Finally in my room, I lower her to my bed. Her fiery red hair spread out like a halo on my dark sheets. She may look like an angel, but the way she's biting on her bottom lip and looking at me is a sign of just how much of a temptress she really is. She brings out a reaction in me that nobody has before, and I don't want this night to end.

Shucking off my boxers, I hover over her before she pulls me down on top of her. She wraps her legs around me, and twists, forcing me to roll over until she is on top. Bending down she whispers, "Do you have a condom?"

I nod and point toward the nightstand beside my bed. "In there."

Her body leaves mine for a minute and I take deep breaths, trying to regain some sort of control. If I don't relax, I'm not going to last more than a few minutes.

I hear Tiffany rip open the condom wrapper, and seconds later her hands are sliding it over my erection. My body jerks and she climbs on top of me once again.

The way she's approached me since we arrived at my place seems like she's done this before…a lot. However, the thought floats away as she slides onto my dick, and I can't think of anything else but making sure she comes before I completely blow it.

The sun shines through the small crack in my curtains, and I want to staple the stupid thing shut. Then, I remember the gorgeous redhead in my bed. As I slide my arm over searching for her body, all I feel is the empty space.

What the hell? Where could she have gone? Stumbling out of bed, I search for my boxers, finding them on the other side of the room. I slide them on and bask in the thoughts of what happened between me and Tiffany. Last night was a whirlwind of sex. When we finally ate our food from *Whataburger*, the fries were cold and her shake was a melted mess. We ended up tossing most of it before climbing back in bed for another round of the most amazing sex I think I've ever had.

The bedroom door is open, and I could have sworn I closed it last night. There's a small possibility it slipped my mind, but not likely. I peek around the door, looking for the woman who blew my mind, but I don't see her. The only closed off area of the space is my bedroom and bathroom, but I know she isn't in either one of those places. She left. Just like that. No goodbye or anything. We didn't even exchange phone numbers.

I search the apartment for a note, something to let me know that last night wasn't a dream. That the girl who is unapologetically herself actually exists. The only evidence I have is our bag of food sitting on top of the full trashcan, and her lacy bra halfway under the couch. I can't believe she left without saying anything. I thought we had a connection while we were at the concert. I thought she felt a zing, too.

Looking around my apartment, I sigh. It was all the comic posters. They drove her away just like I knew they would. Or maybe it's the fact that I live above the garage? I'm not sure what the deal is, but I can't help feeling like shit. I have to do something to get out of this place and on my own. Maybe I will look for a roommate, because I'm not sure I'm capable of living fully on my own just yet.

Sighing, I grab my laptop off of the counter. The only way I'm going to get any woman to take me seriously is if I grow up, and stop acting like a nerdy child. I can do my programming work from anywhere. I just need to find a place to live that isn't my parents' backyard.

I plop onto the couch and open up my laptop. Once everything is loaded, I search for apartments here in the city. I like being close to everything, and I don't want to give that up.

A listing that was posted just yesterday catches my eye. I'd have my own room, and it says that males are preferred. This better not be some cougar trying to get a younger guy to live with her. If it is, it will be a hard no for me. But another requirement makes me pause. *Must agree not to touch food that isn't theirs.* Relief floods through me. Only a dude would be that particular about a roommate.

One last look around the room, and I sigh. I'll apply for this apartment. How bad could it really be?

THREE

Tiffany

My fifth alarm is going off, and I want to press the snooze button one more time, but I'm supposed to meet Stella, Johnny and Audrey in twenty minutes. I don't even have time for a proper shower. I turn the alarm off and roll out of bed. It's a good thing I keep a large supply of dry shampoo for these occasions.

My phone pings before I make it to my closet, and I check the message. It's the one between me and my cousins the other night.

Audrey: Are you up?
Tiffany: Yep. Getting dressed now.
Stella: You just rolled out of bed, didn't you?
Tiffany: I've been up for hours.
Audrey: Liar. You're probably shacked up at some guy's house.
Tiffany: Nope. I woke up in my own bed. Thank you very much.
Stella: Speaking of guys... What happened with the dude from the concert.

Do I really want to tell them? I've never kept my conquests a secret from them, but there's just something about Spencer, and I want to keep him all to myself. A part of me wishes I had left a note with my number. I actually got along with him, and wouldn't be too disappointed if we hung out again. I guess I'll never know since I crept out of his apartment before the sun even came up.

Tiffany: We had amazing sex.
Stella: Go girl.

Audrey: Don't encourage her. I hope your safe when you meet these guys.
Tiffany: I'm not a moron.
Audrey: I wasn't implying that you are.
Tiffany: If you say so.
Stella: Not going down this road today. Have you left yet, Tiff? We're almost there.
Tiffany: Yep. See you in a few.

They don't need to know that I'm not even dressed. I'll get there soon after they do. I'm the closest to the restaurant, and they don't realize my ninja skills at getting ready quickly.

"You know this talk didn't require a visit, right?" My cousins and Johnny are sitting across from me while we eat brunch. It's taken a while getting used to Johnny being around. For so long it's been just the three of us and it's weird having him as a staple when we get together. Though, he makes Stella happy, and that's all I care about.

"I know," Stella grabs her Bloody Mary and takes a sip. "It's just that I know how you react, and as much as we love Audrey," she gives her a pointed look. "We all know that she can't deal with your freak-outs on her own."

"I'm not that bad. I mean, seriously. I'm not some petulant child. So what, if I enjoy going from job to job, roommate to roommate, and guy to guy. Surely whoever you picked can't be that horrible, or you wouldn't have picked them. But it's time for the important question… Do they know not to mess with my food? I can't have another fiasco like that last steady roommate I had. She totally threw out all my takeout leftovers, and they were still slightly edible."

Audrey rolls her eyes. "Yes, we made sure he understood that. God forbid anyone throw out something that is at the point of growing stuff on top of it."

See, that's where she doesn't understand what happened. They threw out everything without even asking if any of it was still good. That's the issue I had. And let's not mention how long she'd take in the bathroom when she knew I had to get ready for work. Honestly, I never should have let her sign the lease. She was a thorn in my side from day one.

"Will y'all be there when the person you picked out comes?"

"If you want us to be," Stella shrugs. "It's one hundred percent up to you. But, the applicant is a guy. We figured that was the best option. We know how well you get along with other women… besides us."

That's interesting. It's not surprising, though. I've never gotten along with any girls, except my cousins. Maybe it's because I've grown up with them. I don't know. I just know that most women get on my nerves. Every single one

I've lived with has been high maintenance, bossy, or downright awful. Like, no thank you, I already have parents. I don't need someone else telling me how to live my life. Living with a guy brings on a whole new set of issues, though. It means he's completely off limits for any kind of sexual, or romantic relationship. "Since the last guy I let stay there for a few days was a creeper, I'm totally okay with y'all being there. Especially Johnny. He can serve as intimidation."

Audrey's mouth drops open. "Wow. She's being very agreeable this morning. Who is this new version of Tiffany, and what have you done with the original?"

"Maybe we have a changeling on our hands," Johnny laughs.

It's the first thing he's said since we started this conversation, and I'm not sure how I feel about that. Is my attitude really so bad that the new guy in the family has noticed? It's not like I try to be a pain. I'm just tired of all the questions my parents pepper me with. When are you going to settle down? When are you going to have kids? It immediately gets turned to background noise because it's nobody's business but my own. I'm perfectly fine not settling down. It could happen one day, but for now, I'm good. And, I'm pretty set against having kids. Not that I don't like them, or anything like that. But I don't see myself as a mothering type. I'm too selfish and focused on me.

"Hilarious, guys," I stick my tongue out at them. "When is he supposed to come by the apartment?"

"In a couple of hours," Audrey says, matter of fact.

"What?" I screech. "My apartment is a disaster area. You could have warned me he was coming today."

"When else were we supposed to do it?" Stella shrugs. "Johnny and I are literally only here for twenty-four hours. We have to head back to Asheville first thing in the morning."

Ugh, I keep forgetting they have to account for travel time when they visit. "I think I liked it better when you lived here and didn't have to adult."

"Tiff," she rolls her eyes. "All I've ever done is adult, especially when it comes to making sure you're making smart decisions." She glances at Audrey and then back at me. "And, let's face it. You don't exactly have a great track record of doing that."

Ugh. She doesn't have to throw it in my face. She acts like it's a crime to live a life without a to-do list or massive goals to reach. I'm perfectly happy just the way I am. At least, I think I am. Lately, I've been feeling lost. With the trio disbanded, I don't know what to do with my life now. Stella was always there to stay on my ass.

"Do we need to come help you clean up?" Audrey asks before taking a bite of her food.

"No," I sigh. "I'll head home in a few to at least get the laundry off the sofa and coffee table. I mean, I don't want to him to get the wrong impression and think I'm this neat freak when I'm not."

Stella laughs, "Because God forbid, you put your best features forward."

"Don't be all uppity, Stella. Not everyone is an over-achiever." I hate when she gets like this. She doesn't mean anything by it, or anything. It's just who she is. I remember trying to be like her when I was younger because I idolized her. Then, right around the time I hit my teens, I realized that I needed to figure out who I was while still looking up to Stella.

"I'm not trying to be bitchy," Stella sighs. "This roommate isn't a done deal yet, and I *know* you need help to cover the rent."

She's not wrong, but I will not admit that to her. It will just be more salt in the wound. I can't imagine what my parents think every time I have to call them to borrow money. It's not like I do it on purpose, but Austin isn't exactly a cheap place to live, especially on the measly check I bring home.

"Fine," I pout. "I'll clean the place up some. It's not like I have anything better to do with my weekend."

"If it makes you feel any better, our house would be a mess if it wasn't for your cousin." Johnny comes to my defense. It's sweet how much he cares about Stella and relies on her to keep him in line. "Hell, the first night she saw the inside of my place, she fell through the floor."

"Yeah, my apartment isn't quite that bad." I reach across the table and pat his arm. "Nice try, though."

The chatter in the restaurant is getting louder. More people have come in, and that's my cue to leave. Even though it's not too early in the day, it's still early enough that I don't want to hear a million conversations. "I'm going to head out. I guess I'll see y'all in a couple of hours. Preferably before the possible roommate shows up." I throw a twenty on the table and scoot my chair out.

Rather than wait for them to say anything else, I turn and walk out of the restaurant. It may be a bratty thing to do, but I loathe cleaning, and it's the first full weekend I've had off in months. It's not how I envisioned spending my day.

People that like to clean are insane. I've been working on the spaces my possible new roommate will see since I got home. None of this is fun. Maybe I should have taken Audrey and Tiffany's offer to help me. I honestly didn't think it was this bad, but apparently I was wrong.

There's only one thing that could make this better. I grab my phone and the small Bluetooth speaker off the kitchen counter. Connecting the speaker to my phone, I pick a random playlist on *Spotify* and set both on the coffee table in the tiny living room. Music makes everything better.

I'm belting out a Taylor Swift song and shaking my ass while dusting the entertainment center when a deep laugh breaks through. "What the hell?"

Standing in my small entranceway is Johnny and my cousins. And that asshole is holding up his phone... In. My. Direction.

"Sorry, Tiff." He brings the phone down and shoves it in his pocket. "That was too great an opportunity to pass up."

I throw the dust smeared rag at him, and glare. "I swear to God, Johnny. If that video ends up on the internet or anywhere else, I will *murder* you."

Stella squeezes by her boyfriend and stands in front of him like she's going to protect him from me. Good luck, lady. "In our defense, we knocked and you didn't answer."

"So, you just barge in?" I throw my hands on my hips. "I'm not playing, Stella. If that video winds up on anyone else's phone, I will be pissed." If it had been any other song, or singer, I wouldn't have an issue with it. But nobody can know that I'm a closet *Swiftie*. I'll never live it down. It's bad enough my cousins hold it over my head. Not that I'm too grunge and metal to like other music. I like to think of myself as eclectic. I'll listen to whatever moves me. But for them to now have video proof of me jamming to it, that's just not acceptable.

I hold my hand out toward Johnny. "Let me see your phone."

"Nice try," he laughs. "There's no way I'm giving it to you. Think of it as a bargaining chip should I ever need you to do something for me."

That's not what I was expecting him to say. What in the world could he need me to do for him that he needs something to bribe me with? That's a question for another time. "Since y'all are here, want to help me?"

"With what?" Audrey asks from behind Johnny. At least she didn't see me shaking my ass, even though I'm sure she heard my off key singing. "It looks like you've gotten most of it done."

That would a huge negative. "Why don't you come and see for yourself?"

Johnny moves out of the way so Audrey can get around him. Her and Stella approach the living room and gasp when they see the huge piles of crap on the sofa. "Where the hell did all this stuff come from?"

"My living room, obviously." I widen my arms to signify the whole room. "This is all crap I've been meaning to put away, but between work, concerts and my weekly brunch with Audrey, I haven't had time."

"You could always skip on the concerts," Audrey mutters under her breath but still loud enough for me to hear.

"Just because you don't enjoy listening to any sort of rock isn't my problem." I glare at her. "It's the only way I have to chill out now that I don't have you two to go out with me anymore."

"Last time I checked, I'm the only one who moved away," Stella pipes up.

"I'm not talking about you." I point toward Audrey and don't miss the guilty look she gives Stella. "Since you've left, Audrey does nothing with me anymore except brunch."

Stella turns toward our cousin and is about to say something but Johnny stops her. "I don't think we really have time for this. The guy is supposed to be here in ten minutes."

The three of us rush toward the couch, and scoop up armfuls of the random junk I have piled on it. I'm not sure what all I will do with this stuff, but it needs to disappear while the prospective roommate is here. "Where do you want it?" Stella grunts trying to keep it all in her hands.

"Um," I'm struggling with my own load. "Just throw it on my bed." He doesn't need to see that for any reason. This will be a roommate free zone. Hell, if I could afford it, my whole apartment would be roommate free. Alas, I need one. I should have moved in with Audrey when I came to Austin, but I wanted a space of my own.

I grab the dirty clothes basket and empty the contents on the floor. Screw trying to get it all in our arms. Picking up the trail of things we've dropped, I make my way toward the living room. "This should make things go faster."

I toss the basket on the couch, and we throw everything else in it. Knock. Knock. Knock. All of us stare at the door. There's no way it's been ten minutes. "Looks like he's here early," Johnny shrugs his shoulders. "Want me to let him in?"

"No," we yell in unison. "Let us get this out of here, and then you can answer the door." We scramble over each other trying to get all the random crap inside the basket. Most of this stuff can probably be thrown out, but I have a problem with letting things go.

Audrey and Stella straighten the blanket and pillows that decorate the sofa, and I rush down the hallway into my bedroom. Setting the basket on my bed, then sit down next to it. There has never been a point in my life that I've been nervous about meeting a potential roommate. Maybe it's because I didn't meet them beforehand, or didn't pick from the applications myself, but I feel on edge. What if they are horrible? What if this guy puts on a nice front in front of my family, but as soon as they sign the lease become a raging asshole? I can be an asshole, too, if needed. I'd rather not go down that road, though.

I hear voices coming from the living room and know that Johnny has let my soon to be roommate in. Deep breath in, and out. *You've got this. It's no different from any other roommate you've had. You still have veto power if you don't like him.* With that in mind, I gather my resolve and stand up. I *need* this to work out. If not, I'll have to see if Audrey will have mercy on me and let me live with her. Even though that's disaster waiting to happen.

A quick glance in the mirror has me reeling back. My clothes have dust all over them, and my red hair is sticking out in all directions after falling from the bun. Oh well, if this guy will be living here, he'll have to get used to seeing me as the hot mess I am. Not that it matters, roommates are *off limits.*

I step into the hallway and listen to my cousins firing off question after question. Geez, I thought they had this part taken care of when I they told him to come look at the apartment.

The potential roommate is standing with his back to me when I enter the living room. "Oh, look, there she is now," Stella waves me over. "Tiff, this is Spencer, the guy who wants to move in."

FOUR

Spencer

THIS IS REALLY WEIRD. I'm not a hundred percent positive, but I don't think most roommate interviews include a cavalry. When the guy, Johnny, opened the door, I thought he might be my roommate, but then a tall blonde came up to him and wove her arm through his before extending me her hand and introducing herself as Stella.

There's no way I'm going to live with a couple. That's beyond weird. I was about to apologize for wasting their time and leave, but she said, "Why don't you come in and wait for our cousin?"

These two weren't the ones looking for someone to live with them. *Thank God*. I can't even describe how relieved I am.

Stella, says "Tiff." I can't help but think of the Tiffany that infiltrated my brain a few weeks ago. It would be too much of a coincidence for this to be the same person, and awkward.

I turn around and my eyes widen. It is her. *Holy shit*. What sort of gods are smiling down on me today? Except, I don't know where to go from here. She bailed without a single fucking word. "Tiffany? You're the one that needs a roommate?"

"Wait," Johnny steps between us, cutting off any eye contact I had with the girl that ran. "You know each other."

"Yes," I lean around Johnny and grin. This is too surreal. Normally I'm not so emboldened, but today is obviously not a normal day. I'm now looking at the red haired temptress that blew my mind. The one that didn't bother trying to get to know me even though I *know* we both felt a spark that night. "We met at a concert not too long ago."

Stella, and the brunette girl gasp at the exact same time. "No," Stella whispers. "That's him." She points at me not acknowledging that I can in fact hear her loud whisper.

I watch Tiffany nod without saying another word. So, she told her cousins about me. That's interesting, and unexpected. Why would she say anything about me if I was just some conquest?

The room is quiet and I swear you could hear a pin drop. Everyone is looking between us, but mine and Tiffany's focus is on each other. "This isn't a good idea," someone finally says. I think it may have been the brunette girl. Another one of Tiffany's cousins, I assume. What was her name? Oh yeah, Audrey.

Tiffany opens her mouth, about to say something, but I cut her off. "It's perfect. I kind of know her so it's not like we're strangers. She needs a roommate, and I need out of my current situation."

Now her eyes widen in shock. "Why are you looking for a roommate?" That's not a completely uncalled for question.

I cross my arms over my chest, and keep my eyes on her. "I'm tired of living with my parents. It's time for me to branch out and get off their property."

"So that was why you wanted me to be quiet?" She slides one hand to her hip. "You didn't want to wake up your parents." She tilts her head from side to side, then says, "It makes sense, I guess." Then she points at her cousins and crooks her finger, telling them to come here. "I need to talk to y'all really quick."

They follow her into a room and I hear the door close behind them. "This must be pretty damn awkward," Johnny says before walking into the tiny kitchen. He opens the fridge and comes back with two beers.

"I thought the application said not to touch her food." He hands me one of them, and motions for me to sit on the couch with him. I'm reluctant to open it, worried I'll anger Tiffany. I'm not entirely certain how she's reacting about any of this.

"Yeah, that would be important if it wasn't my beer." He nods his head toward me. "It's okay to open it. She won't bite your head off. At least, not about this. Touch whatever takeout she brings home, and that's a different story entirely."

"Is she as unstable as her cousins are making her seem?" Maybe her cousin is right. This isn't a good idea. I can find another roommate. Or, I can continue living over the garage. I haven't actually told my family that I'm looking for another place to live. They will freak out. I'm their only child, and they want me as close as possible. They have this overwhelming need to always take care of me. Hell, they've barged through my door in the middle of the night asking if I was hungry because they saw a light on. No, it's definitely time for me to branch out. If it doesn't work here, then somewhere else. It's time for me to grow up.

"Naw," he shakes his head. "I think they worry about her more because she's the baby out of the three of them. Also, she's not exactly as put together as they are. She has a habit of doing whatever she wants and damn the repercussions."

That much I know about her. Hell, she left me in the wee hours of the morning without a word. Her bra the only proof that she was actually there. It's my own fault for getting myself in that situation in the first place. I'm the one that asked her if she wanted to get some food. Drunk Spencer tends to be a dumbass. He'll be in retirement if I end up living here.

The door opens and they file out until finally Tiffany is standing right in front of me. "As long as you're okay living here, then I'm okay with it."

Wow, could she say that with any enthusiasm at all?

Her cousins and the guy left. Two of them needing to get back to whatever town they live in and the other going to her own place. The stink eye the brunette gave me before walking out the door, proves how much she doesn't like me being Tiffany's roommate. For my preservation, or for her cousin, I'll never know.

I'm sitting on the couch taking the living room in. Now that the shock has worn off, I can finally *see* where I'll be living. There are a lot of dreamcatchers and astrological designs hanging on the walls. It's not over the top, but it's also not what I expected after seeing what she was like when I took her home. I figured the colors would be bright and bold with abstract designs filling the space. Looks like someone is trying to reach their inner zen no matter how much she fights it.

Instead of joining me on the couch, Tiffany sits down on the floor, opposite me. Is she that unnerved by me being here? She could have told me that she didn't want me living with her and that would have been fine. I mean, I hardly know her. "So," she says, eyes hitting every space except for the couch. "What do you do for a living? It's only fair that I ask since you already know what I do."

"I'm a programmer."

"What does that even mean? Do you make video games or something?"

"Sometimes," I shrug, leaning my elbows on my knees to see her better. My glasses slide down my nose and I lift a hand to push them back up.

"Like for *Playstation*?"

"No," I laugh. "The games I help develop are mostly apps for your phone, but I do a lot of work on websites and email systems."

Her brows furrow in confusion. "Where were all your computers when I came to your place? If you're a programmer, shouldn't you be able to afford living on your own?"

Wow, she comes out and says whatever is on her mind. "My computers are in the garage, so you wouldn't have been able to see them. But I do most of my work on two computers. The laptop and desktop I have in the corner of my room." She waves her hand, motioning for me to continue. She's persistent, that's for sure. "And, I do okay. I've never truly lived on my own before and figured I should try a roommate situation before branching out that far."

Traffic noise from outside filters into the room, and she's still not looking at me. It's doing absolutely nothing for my ego. *Was the sex that bad?*

"We're going to need some ground rules."

"Ground rules?" I move over on the couch so she has to meet my eyes, and she starts picking the polish off of her nails. Playing the shy card now that I'm questioning her.

"Yeah, rules," she points toward the kitchen. "I assume you know not to touch my food. My cousins said they mentioned it to all the applicants."

So I wasn't the only person who applied. I wonder what made her cousins pick me. "Yeah, it was written on the application, and you had to agree to it before the form would submit. What's that all about?"

"An incident with a previous roommate last year." She waves her hands in the brushing the comment away. "It doesn't matter, just don't touch my food."

"What other rules are there?"

She takes a deep breath and lets it out. "In no way, shape, or form are we to have sex while we're roommates."

I laugh but rein it in as soon as I notice she's not joking. The thought may have crossed my mind, but I'm not going to act on it. "What? Are you scared I'm too much of a temptation?" I don't know what it is about her, but she brings out a side of me I never knew existed. Verbally sparring with her is something I'm going to try to do every single day. Not like it matters, she's clearly not as into me as I thought she was that night.

"No," she snaps. "I just have a no sleeping with roommates policy."

"How many male roommates have you had?" I'm curious who hurt her so badly that she feels she has to voice this.

"That doesn't matter," she lifts her head high. "From what I've seen, it all leads to ruin and heartbreak, and I'm not okay with either of those scenarios."

"Fine," I agree, even if I don't want to. "Anything else?"

"Nope. I think we covered it with the food and sex talk." She stands up, signaling the end of our chat. "Oh, and don't hang out by the bathroom door while I'm in the shower."

"Do I even want to know?" It's such an odd comment to make. What kind of weirdos has she let live with her?

"Probably not. When do you want to sign the lease and move in?"

"Is tomorrow too soon?" I'm anxious to get away from my parents. Even if I can't have anything more than platonic friendship with her, it'll be nice being around her.

She grabs her phone off the coffee table and taps the screen a few times. "I get off work tomorrow at three. Be here around four-thirty so we can catch the superintendent before he leaves for the day."

"Sounds good." I stand and make my way toward the door. "I'll do my best to keep to myself." It's not what I want to do, but she's letting me live with her. The least I can do is respect her wishes.

"Good," she nods and brushes past me. She opens the door and leans against the wall. "I'll see you tomorrow."

I lean in for a hug, but sense that maybe it's not a good idea. I straighten and put my hands in my pockets. "Tomorrow it is." I turn and walk out of her apartment. I mean *our* apartment.

FIVE

Tiffany

"Tiffany, your order is up." Dennis calls from the kitchen. "You better get it out there before our customers become angry."

I snort. "This restaurant caters to hipsters, they don't get angry."

"Whatever you say, kid."

Rolling my eyes, I grab the plates of food off the counter and place them on the tray. One day people will stop calling me "kid." I'm twenty-two and no longer a child. Now is not the time to dwell on it, though. There are people waiting on their food.

With the tray balanced on one hand, a skill that took me *forever* to learn, I weave around the tables. My phone vibrates in my back pocket, and I almost drop the tray of food. Who in the hell is calling me right now? Both Audrey and Stella should be at work, and they know I can't answer my phone while I'm working. We don't have many rules here at The Dreamcatcher, but no phones while working is a hard and fast one. They say it gives an off-putting impression. I don't blame them. My cousins and I have been to restaurants where almost all the employees have been on their phones at one point or another, and the service has always been shitty.

Finally, at the table I'm supposed to be serving, I slap a wide smile on my face. "How are y'all this afternoon?"

"We're great," one of the two women sitting at the table replies.

I pick up the plate closest to me on the tray. "Who had the grilled chicken salad?"

The woman who spoke raises her hand, and I place the plate in front of her.

"And that means you have the chicken tortilla soup. Is there anything else I can get you?"

They both look at their glasses of tea and shake their heads. "We're good, thank you."

"I'll be back to check on y'all, but if you need anything, let me know."

The Dreamcatcher is slow today so I only have the one table. I'm hoping it picks up before I leave for the day. The tip money would be great so I can buy a few groceries. I make my way toward the kitchen to drop off my tray. Dennis pokes his head about the food counter. "How mad were they?"

Rolling my eyes, I set the tray on the rack. "Not at all. They were the picture of Southern politeness. I told you they wouldn't be upset."

"Yeah, yeah," he laughs. "One of these days you're going to get someone in your section that will give you a hard time."

"If you say so." I glance back toward the almost empty dining area making sure nobody else has come in. "Since it's slow can I take my break?"

"Sure thing. I'll come get you if anyone needs anything."

"Thanks." Pulling my phone from my pocket, I walk through the kitchen to the door that leads to the alley. It's not an ideal place to take my break, but I need to see who called me. I tap the screen and groan. Of course it'd be Mom that calls while I'm at work. It should relieve me she didn't blow up my phone after I didn't answer the first time.

I tap the icon and call her back. The phone rings twice before she picks up. "Hi, Mom," I blurt out before she's even said anything.

"You know you're supposed to let me say hello first, right?"

"I don't have much time. I'm on my break."

"Are you still working at that restaurant?" In the past, she's never once questioned any of the choices I've made in my entire life. She and Dad have always let me do whatever I want, and that might be why I'm in the roommate predicament I'm in now. It's a little late to start actually parenting me now.

"Yes."

"I guess I should be happy you still have a job," she sighs. "This is the longest you've ever worked in one place."

Wow, thanks for making me feel like a failure. "I like it here. The hours are great, and we're normally busy since we're downtown. The tips aren't bad, either." Why am I defending myself?

"You have enough for rent, right? Don't forget, your dad and I will not be helping you out anymore." Like I could forget. It's the only reason I *have* to find a roommate. Maybe Dennis was right to call me "kid." I definitely haven't done anything to make people think otherwise. I float from job to job and relationship to relationship, constantly combatting my parents wishes for me.

"I know. You don't have to worry about it, I've got it covered." At least, I think

I do. Letting Spencer move in is not something I'm too keen on. I've never lived with someone I've slept with. It implies things will go further, and I'm not the type to give up my freedom to be with someone. No matter how hot the sex was.

"That's good, Dear." She's silent for a few moments and I know a lecture is about to happen. "I just wish you would settle down. Maybe find a nice boy to date."

"Mom, I don't want to *date* anyone. And I'm doing okay. Or, at least I will be soon."

"I am proud of you for moving off and finding your own way in the world." There's a *but* coming, I just know it. "But, there are times I wish you were more like your cousins. They have steady jobs with incomes that don't fluctuate. And Stella…"

I cut her off. "I don't want to be like them, Mom. My whole life you've given me space to make my own decisions, even though you'd compare me to them. I've appreciated that more than you'll ever know. But, their life isn't mine. I'm perfectly happy with my job and not being in a relationship with someone. I'm fine on my own."

"Tiffany," she sighs. "That's not what I—"

"You literally just asked why I wasn't more like my cousins. So, you can't say that's not what you meant. How else am I supposed to take it?" The silence on the other end of the line is deafening. I don't have time to keep going over the same old arguments. "Look, I'm doing the best that I can. And I'm doing what I need to do for me."

"I know that, sweetheart. I just want you to be happy and be able to take care of yourself."

Because clearly I haven't been doing that for the majority of my time away from home. So what if I had to get help from them a few times? It's not like I'm destitute on the street. "My break's almost up, Mom. I'll call you later. I love you, bye." Ending the call, I sag against the wall. I'm doing the smart thing by getting a roommate, but it seems like no matter what I do, I will never be enough. Things would be so much easier if they would stop treating me like a child and recognize my accomplishments. For instance, I didn't throw the phone against the wall when I hung up with my mother. That is a huge win for today.

The door to the alley opens slowly, and Dennis steps out beside me. "Your table looks like they are almost done, are you good to come back in?"

I stand up taller and push myself off the wall. "Yeah, just parental drama."

He nods in understanding. "I know I'm most likely your parents' age, but if you need anyone to vent to, the door is always open."

"Thanks, Dennis."

There's another win for today. I could have pouted, spilled my guts to Dennis, or texted my cousins complaining. But, I'm not going to. Opening the door, I walk right back into the kitchen and then out into the dining area. This is me being an adult and taking care of my responsibilities. I have customers to take care of, and more people to seat.

This afternoon will be another step in adulting when Spencer comes to sign the lease. I only hope it won't be a huge mistake.

SIX

Spencer

My car is full of boxes. I stayed up late last night packing up the essential stuff I'll need. Anything else I need after that, I can come back and get. I have to meet Tiffany in two hours. I still need to tell my parents I'm moving out.

I could have told them last night, but I didn't want my mom over here all day today badgering me about staying. She would try to guilt me in so many ways, and I don't have the energy to deal with it.

One more trip upstairs and I'll have everything I need. Surprisingly, Mom and Dad haven't noticed anything amiss yet. I hope to keep it that way for at least thirty more minutes. Then, I can go talk to them.

I have the last two boxes in my arms when I see Mom standing beside my car, peering through the windows. She hasn't seen me yet, and jumps when I set the boxes on the hood of my car. "Hi, Mom."

"Spencer, what's all this?" She waves her hand toward my car. "Are you finally getting rid of your comic collection and donating it? Your dad will be happy to have that chunk of the garage back."

Geez, even my parents have a problem with my nerdiness. It's not that I didn't know this already, but Mom has never come out and said anything outright. "Is Dad home?" I know he is. His car is in the garage, but I need something to say to her to get her focus off of my car.

"Yes, he's in the house."

"Want to come inside with me. I have something I want to tell you."

She claps her hands together and squeals. "You met a girl, didn't you? I can't wait to meet her."

That's not exactly a lie, but it's also not the truth. "Just come on crazy woman."

Mom rolls her eyes. "I'm not crazy." She can be though. She always makes a huge deal out of every little thing. I honestly blame my parents for the way I turned out.

We walk in the patio door that leads to the kitchen. Dad is standing in front of the refrigerator, door wide open, most likely looking for something to eat. "Dear," Mom announces our presence because obviously the door opening didn't. "Come to the table. Spencer has something he'd like to tell us."

My dad closes the door and turns toward the table. "What's her name?"

Jesus. Why do they think it's because of a girl? "Nobody, Dad. There isn't anyone I want to tell you about."

"Then what is it?" Mom asks while she pulls out a chair to sit in.

"I'm moving out." Mom gasps, and Dad nods his head as if he knew I'd eventually tell them this. "It's nothing against y'all. I'm just ready to be on my own. I appreciate everything you've done for me, but it's time."

"Who on earth will cook for you? Or do your laundry? How am I going to make sure you're staying healthy and not cooped up in your room on your computer all the time?"

"Mom," I sigh, rubbing my temples. "I'm not moving that far away. Also, I've been doing my laundry for a long time. I'm also perfectly capable of cooking for myself as well as making sure I take breaks."

"This is because of some girl isn't it?" Gee, two seconds ago she was over the moon that I might have met someone. Now the imaginary girl is the reason I'm leaving the nest.

"No. This is something I should have done a long time ago."

"When are you moving?" Dad cuts in before Mom has another chance to go on another tirade.

"Today, actually." It doesn't put them in a bind because they refused to let me pay rent. And if I gave them a date in the future, I know Mom would try to find some way to sabotage my plan.

"That's good. Do you need help with anything?"

I shake my head. "Not unless you know someone with a truck and trailer to get my bed and dresser. Otherwise, I'll rent a moving truck to grab it and a few of my computers from the garage."

Mom's face is bright red and looks like she's about to explode. Dad sets his hand on her arm, and sadness fills her eyes. Her baby boy is going out into the big bad world alone. She doesn't count the college years because I was still in the city. "Don't worry about doing that. Just send me the address and we'll bring it over."

Cringing, I shake my head. "It's okay. I'm probably not getting anything tonight. I packed the air mattress, some blankets and a pillow. I'll come get it tomorrow."

Dad gives me a knowing look. "Just make sure you bring someone to help you. It'll be a pain getting that stuff down those stairs on your own."

"I can help him," Mom pipes in. More like lock me inside the apartment and bolting it shut so I can't leave.

"We have those lunch plans tomorrow, Tamra. The reservations are already set, and we can't cancel them."

I seriously doubt that. He'll probably call while she's not paying attention to keep her out of my hair. Mom scoots out of her chair and wraps her arms around me, squeezing me tightly against her. I mouth "thank you" over her head to Dad, and he smiles. "I'm going to miss you so much. Promise you'll call."

"I'm literally less than twenty minutes away. You can't get rid of me that easily." Though, I'm not going to visit all the time. We all need to learn boundaries, and I need to know that I can make it on my own without my parents constantly interfering with my life.

I pull away from her. "I need to go. I want to make it before the office closes, and I can sign the lease."

"Fine," my mom pouts and stands next to my dad. "Call me when you get there."

Grabbing an apple from the table, I take a bite. "I will." As soon as I'm settled and probably not until later tonight. "Love you."

"We love you too, son." She comes at me again and wraps me in another fierce hug. "You take care of yourself."

"Always, Mom." I back away from her again and hurry out of the door. If I keep talking to her, I'll hit traffic and miss the timeframe Tiffany and I agreed on.

It's four-thirty and Tiffany isn't here. We're going to miss office hours and I'll have to go back to the apartment over the garage. I really wish I would have gotten her number yesterday. That would make this whole situation so much easier.

I feel like a creeper pacing in front of the apartment door. It won't be long until her neighbors call the cops about a strange man in the hallway making everyone uncomfortable. Rather than staying and waiting to see how long until someone reports me, I go back downstairs to the lobby area. Maybe I'll be able to catch her before she goes upstairs. While I still have a place I can stay, I'd rather not go back after giving my I need to spread my wings speech. Mom would never let me live it down.

Pulling my phone out of my pocket, I check the time. Fifteen minutes until five, Tiffany needs to get here soon. My thumb hovers over the mail app. The only other way I know to get ahold of her is through her cousin. I'm almost certain it was Stella who set up the meeting. She's not here yet, and I need to make sure she's all right. Even if I don't get to sign the lease today. She got off work over two hours ago, and anything could have happened.

Just as I scroll through my email messages the door slams open and Tiffany comes running through it. She sees me and skids to a stop. "I'm so sorry I'm late," she pants. "The new waitress didn't show up for her shift, and I didn't want to leave Dennis in a bind."

"It's okay. It's not five yet, we still have time." She rushes past me and waves at me to follow. "Who is Dennis?" Yes, she said no sex, but she didn't say that anything about a possible future relationship when we aren't roommates. I need to make sure I don't have any competition.

"He's my boss." She skids to a stop in front of a door. "Thank God. It looks like the Super is still here." She knocks and lets herself in before I hear anything from the other side.

"Hi, Mr. Sosa. I need to add someone to my lease."

Behind the desk sits an older Hispanic man, and he groans as soon as he hears Tiffany's request. "Again," he sighs. "I'm going to start charging you a double fee if this becomes a habit."

"It's not. This one will be on the lease until the end of the term and we can revisit after that."

Mr. Sosa looks at me. "Are you sure? The fee to be taken off is pretty high."

"Absolutely, sir." I need to make this guy like me so I can sign the lease and get on with the rest of my day. There are a lot of boxes that need to be brought in. "You won't have any problems out of me."

"It's not you I'm worried about," he mutters. "You realize it's ten minutes until five?" This time he's staring straight at Tiffany. "I need to find your file and get it all together for your new roommate to sign."

"Mr. Sosa," she grins. "You know darn well that my file is somewhere close by. We've been through this before."

"Yes, Tiffany, I know. Make sure this is the last time. I'd like to actually file this thing." He reaches into a drawer and pulls out a manila file folder. Tiffany wasn't kidding about it being close by.

"Mr…" Sosa says waiting for me to supply my name.

"Oh, sorry." I hold out my hand. "I'm Spencer Cain."

"Mr. Cain, as long as you're okay with being on the lease, I just need a copy of your driver's license, the make and model of your car along with the license plate number." He grabs a pen from his desk and hands it to me. "The only other thing I need is your signature."

Taking the pen, I bend over and scribble my name on the line Mr. Sosa is pointing at. Next up is my driver's license and I hand it over for him to make a copy while I fill out the information about my car. "Here you go," I slide the pen across his desk and he hands my ID back to me.

"Thank you." He walks to a cabinet on the other side of the room and pulls out a key. "Here's your key to the apartment. There's a fee if you lose it. Just ask her." He hikes his thumb toward Tiffany. "I can't count how many keys I've replaced for her."

"Hey," she throws her hands on her hips. "I still pay the fee for being a pain, don't I?"

"That you do." He glances at his watch and shakes his head. "It's after five. The two of you get out of here so I can go home to my family."

"Thanks Mr. Sosa, you're the best." As soon as we're out of the office, Tiffany's bubbly exterior deflates. "I really am sorry about being late. It's been one of those days."

"It's all good. Now that I have a key, I'll go grab some boxes out of my car."

"I can help you." This sudden helpfulness is odd. Yesterday she made it seem like me moving in would be horrible, and now she wants to help me. She must really need me to move in. That's the only reason for the attitude shift.

"You go and rest. I can move my own crap in."

"Are you sure?"

"Yes. Now go before I change my mind." I still want her, and if she spends more time than necessary with me, I'm not sure I'll be able to stick to her rules.

SEVEN

Tiffany

"Where the hell is that robe?" I mutter under my breath. It's not hanging up in my closet. Pushing my shoes out of the way on the floor, I dig in the piles of clothes and random shit I've been collecting over the years. It's been months since I've *needed* the stupid thing. I usually walk from the bathroom to my room in nothing but my towel. That all ends now that Spencer is living right across the hallway from me.

It's weird having someone in my space again. Add in the fact that I've slept with him, and it's so much more awkward. So far, he is doing his best to stay out of my way, or, at least, that's what it seems like. I don't think I've ever seen anyone stay in their room as much as he does. It makes me wonder what exactly he's doing in there.

My phone rings and I stand up too fast, misjudging everything. My head hits the bar my clothes are hanging on, and I flail backwards into the wall, clothes slipping off hangers and landing on top of me. "Son of a bitch," I yell.

"Tiffany," Spencer's voice is not as far away as it should be. "Are you okay?"

Shit. He can't be in here. I don't have any clothes on. "Yes, I'm fine." Reaching out, I try to cover myself with as many of the fallen clothes as possible. Hopefully, he'll turn around and go back to his room.

"Are you sure? I heard a loud crash." He's definitely closer.

"Yep." Please go back to your room. I will sacrifice a night out on the town if he'll go away.

No such luck. A tall shadow fills the closet doorway. Damn it. Why can't he mind his own business?

"Oh, yeah. You look fine." He laughs until he looks down and his eyes widen. "You aren't wearing any clothes?" He acts like he hasn't seen me in all my naked glory before. I don't know if I should be offended, or not, that he's so stricken.

There's no way to make this situation any better. "Technically, I'm wearing part of my closet." I wave my arms in front of me, showing off all the clothes covering *only* the top half of my body.

His cheeks redden, and he forces his gaze up until he meets my eyes. "I'm just going to, uh, go." My bedroom door slams shortly after. Why does he have to be so gentlemanly? This could have been avoided if he would have minded his own business like he has been. Although, it is kind of sweet, I guess. *No, Tiffany. You cannot have those thoughts about your roommate.*

Shoving the pile aside, I scramble off of the floor, no longer worrying about the towel that was once wrapped around me. There's no chance of him coming back in here.

Stomping to my dresser, I grab a pair of panties, yoga pants, and a t-shirt. Buying a robe is now at the top of my list. This is why I don't do well with roommates. I can't do whatever I want whenever I want. And I have to be modest. It's even worse when it's someone I've had sex with.

I grab my phone off my bed, checking to see whose call caused that whole embarrassment. I guess I should be happy the bar didn't come down on top of me. Kudos to whoever built this place.

Stella's name shows up on my screen. I tap the missed call and wait for her to pick up the phone. It rings three times before going to voicemail. *Oh no, sister.* You will answer my call after what I just went through. I tap her name again and wait somewhat patiently for her to answer.

Finally, she does. "Hello."

"Is there a reason you called?" I flop on my bed, causing my purse to fall and all the contents to spill onto the floor. Today just keeps getting better and better.

"Wow," she huffs. "Someone woke up on the bitchy side of the bed today."

"You cannot imagine how horrible this day has started out."

"I take it things aren't going well with Spencer living there."

I throw my arm over my face, covering my eyes. Maybe if they are closed, I can pretend it was all a bad dream and I'll wake up. "Until about five minutes ago it's been manageable."

"Uh-oh," she giggles. "Did he try to make a move on you? You know, pick up where things left off when you scurried from his bed while he was still sleeping?"

"Hey," I protest. "I never said anything about leaving before he was awake."

"Sweetie," Stella sighs. "It's kind of your M.O. You don't do overnights.

And when you do, you make every excuse possible to leave as soon as you can."

She has a point. "I don't do relationships. Especially, not with someone who is living with me."

The line is quiet and I worry we've been disconnected. It's not uncommon considering where she lives. I still cannot believe she managed to find a town smaller than the one I grew up in to make herself a home. "So, what made this day so horrible for you?"

I give her the rundown on the events that just took place and the only thing I can hear on the other side of the receiver is laughter. Not just her's, though. There's a deep chuckle, and I groan. "Please tell me you don't have me on speaker."

"Okay, I don't have you on speaker."

"Hi Tiff," Johnny's deep voice reaches my ears. "Sorry about your bad luck this morning."

"I hate you both."

"Actually, you love us." Stella laughs. "Imagine if you told Audrey. What do you think she would say?"

"Well, it wouldn't be funny to her." Not that it is to me, either. In fact, it might be the most mortifying thing that's ever happened to me, and I don't get embarrassed by much. "She'd probably lecture me on locking the bedroom door. Or, telling me how she was right about it being a bad idea."

"That's accurate," Stella laughs again. "At least she loves us enough to worry about us all the time. You remember the grief she gave me about getting involved with Johnny."

"Hey," Johnny pipes up. "Audrey loves me."

"Yeah, now," I snort. "But in the beginning she was firmly *anti-Johnny*. I, on the other hand, pushed my lovely cousin toward you."

"Well, thanks for that." I hear a noise that sounds an awful lot like kissing on the other end of the line. I swear if they start making out while I'm on the phone, I will puke.

This is getting awkward. Stella giggles, and that's where I draw the line. "And that's my cue to get off the phone. Bye, guys." At least, I wasn't video calling her. That would have been horrible. The time on the clock pulls my attention away from my phone. Shit. I need to get dressed and get to work.

"I heard you have a new roommate," Janie bumps into me while we're picking up orders for our tables.

I swear this girl drives me crazy. She always acts like we're best friends, but she's kind of annoying and known for being a gossip. "Oh yeah. Where did you hear that from?"

"Your cousin. She came in a day or two ago grumbling about your new roommate situation." I seriously doubt Audrey told her anything. She probably overheard her on the phone with either Stella, her parents, or my parents. Janie is only needling me for information because she wanted to be my roommate. But, if I can't stand working with her for a couple of hours every day, there is no way in hell I could live with this woman. She would want to do pedicures and all that other stuff that I typically do with my cousins. Not that it's a bad thing. I just don't mesh well with her. I haven't since they hired her. I also learned the hard way not to tell her anything that I didn't want others to know.

Now, how much do I want to tell her? "Well, for your information, I have a new roommate and things are going great." This is a total crock of bullshit and seriously overstating how *well* things are going, but the truth is none of her business.

"That's good." She nods her head up and down as if I asked her a question. "If that ever changes, and you need a new roommate, you know where to find me." And that's why I never told her I was looking for one.

First thing I'm going to do when I go on my break is make sure I only have shifts opposite of hers. People like her are the reason I don't do well with female roommates. Too much drama and trying to one-up everyone else.

My shift is over and I am so ready to leave this place. Most days, I don't mind working here, but today has been non-stop running around to different tables, even some that weren't mine. Mix that with Janie constantly peppering me with questions about my new roommate, and I'm ready to throw in the towel. The only thing keeping me from going home is Spencer.

"It's time to get out of here, Tif." I jump at the sound of Dennis's voice, completely forgetting that he was still here.

"Dammit Dennis, you can't sneak up on me like that."

He shrugs and chuckles. "Scaring you provides me with more entertainment than it should, so I think I might keep doing it." Dennis moves around the table until we're facing each other. The soft lights giving everything in the room a spooky shadow.

I'm filling the last of the shakers on the tables. It can be a messy job, but for some reason, I enjoy doing it. "I'm happy to know that I'm here merely for your entertainment and not to keep your lovely patrons happy."

"It's time for you to go home now. There is literally nothing left that you can do to occupy your time," he repeats as he stares at me knowingly. "Is there a reason you don't want to go home?"

Normally, there wouldn't be a reason, and I'd be out of here as soon as my shift was over. Now… There is one reason I don't want to go home. And he happens to be about a foot taller than me, wears glasses, and is hotter than anybody has a right to be. "Not at all. Just doing a couple of things that needed to be done."

"And most of those things are items I can usually never get you to do." He rests a hand on my shoulder, "Go home. And if you ever need to talk about the reason behind you picking up more shifts and staying late, you can come talk to me."

"I guess I'll get out of your hair. I'm sure your wife and kiddos are missing you." Maybe I will go to a bar. It would be more preferable than going home and having to see Spencer. I make my way to the break room beside the kitchen, but pause and turn to face Dennis again. "Also, can you make sure I'm not working with Janie?"

"You got it. I'll send the new schedule to you in the morning."

"Thanks." I continue toward the break room and grab my things. If I have any luck on my side, Spencer will be asleep by the time I get home or I will be too drunk to notice.

EIGHT

Spencer

HOLY SHIT. I can't believe I saw her naked…again. That's not how I envisioned the week starting out. Even if I I clung to the fantasy of her maybe bending her rules and seeing where things might go between us, I never thought I'd see her gorgeous body again so soon.

For the past week, I've been holed up in my room trying to avoid her. This whole living situation is awkward as hell, and it's not too far from how I lived when I was above the garage. At least the rent was free there, and I'd occasionally get home-cooked meals. Now I'm paying rent to not leave my room. It's ridiculous.

Moving in here was obviously a bad idea. I should have bowed out when her cousin gave me the option. Instead, I was hard-headed and signed the lease. Maybe things will get better as time goes on. It's not like I can just move out. My name is on the lease for the next six months.

The only plus side is I don't have constant interruptions while I'm trying to work. A series of letters and numbers fill my computer screen, and my eyes are glazing over. This project is almost done and I couldn't be happier. The client I'm working for has been nothing but a huge pain in my ass. Every time I send him what I hope is the final product, he comes back with changes he wants to make. Or, he's changed his mind about a certain function. I love coding and creating programs that people will use, but clients like him make me want to quit and find some boring corporate job that sucks the life out of me.

I highlight a section of code to fix his latest change when the door slams shut. I jump and my fingers hit the keyboard deleting a bunch of stuff that I didn't want gone. *Son of a bitch*. Thank God this is a copy of the original or I'd be pissed. It's a lesson I learned after the fourth change he wanted.

Glancing at the clock, I do a double take. It's after one in the morning. I've been working for the past three hours without stopping. I wonder why Tiffany is coming home so late. Even when she works late at the restaurant, she's always home well before midnight. But, it's none of my business. She made it home safely and is most likely getting ready for bed, which means I can leave my room and get something to eat. You can only live on beef jerky for so long before you have to get actual food in your system.

My chair glides along the carpet as I scoot back, and I'm thankful the floors aren't wood or some other material. I don't want Tiffany to hear me moving around. Walking to the door, I open it wide enough to peek through the crack. All the lights are off, and I take that as a clear sign that she's down for the night.

Tip-toeing down the hall, I make my way toward the kitchen. *Be stealthy like a ninja.* I'm accomplishing that goal until my foot catches on something and I go tumbling to the ground. So much for being silent. "What the hell was that?" Tiffany screeches from her bedroom door. "Spencer, is that you?"

Groaning, I sit up. "Yeah," I huff. "It's me."

Slowly standing up, I reach for the wall and flip the light switch up. If this woman does not stop leaving shit on the floor, I'm going to end up breaking something. The culprit of my graceful fall is none other than Tiffany's massive bag. I pick it up by the strap and dangle it in front of me. "Does this belong to you?"

She steps out of her room, and holy shit. In nothing but a tight fitting shirt and shorts that can hardly be classified as such, she walks down the hallway toward me. "You know damn well that's mine."

I clear my throat, tamping down my lust. This girl will be the death of me. There's no way in hell I'm going to make it the entire six months with my sanity still intact. "Is there any way you can leave it somewhere else besides the floor?"

She taps her finger against her chin before reaching out and grabbing the purse out of my grasp. "I'll think about it." I open my mouth to argue, but she holds her hand up. "In my defense, I thought you were asleep, and I just dropped it on the way to my room. Old habits die hard."

"Maybe this is a habit you could try to work on before I end up breaking my neck?"

"And my cousins say I'm dramatic." She doesn't say anything else. She turns and walks back to her room. All I can do is stare. Her ass is barely covered by the tiny piece of fabric, and I don't think she realizes what kind of torture she's putting me through. I now fully understand the saying: "I hate to see her leave, but I love to watch her walk away." Because that sight, right there, will haunt my dreams for nights on end.

"How are things going with your roommate?" Mom asks. She finally called me once she realized I wouldn't be the first one to give in. It's not that I don't love my mom, I do. She just has a tendency to overstep boundaries. Even when she promises she'll be more considerate and respect my wishes, she can't seem to follow through. She would show up at my dorm unannounced all the time when I was in college. It drove me insane, and it's precisely why I haven't given her my address. I don't need her here stirring up trouble with Tiffany. Things on that front are shaky at best.

"Great," I force a smile. She can't see me, but I'm positive it makes the word sound more believable. "I'm finally settled in and getting used to living with someone."

"That's good." She's quiet for a moment. "I had extra food leftover from the casserole I made last night. I can drop it by while I'm running errands." And there it is. I knew it wouldn't be long before she tried getting the information out of me. Not. Going. To. Happen.

"How about I come over for dinner?" Maybe the offer will get her off my case, at least for a bit. "I'm all caught up with work, so I have plenty of time to come hang out with you and Dad tonight. What do ya say?" Okay, so that might have been overkill, but I can't have her showing up at all hours of the day over here. She would freak out at the state Tiffany leaves most of the apartment in. She's not exactly the best at putting shit away. Not to mention, Mom would read way too much into the fact that I live with a woman. A woman I have absolutely no relationship with.

"Really?" Her voice raises in pitch, and I pull the phone away from my ear as I start to sit up on my bed. Mom woke me up when she called because I had another late night. I've got to stop staying up to make sure Tiffany gets home okay. She's not my responsibility but I feel this need to take care of her. "What do you want me to make? You name it, and I'll cook it."

She must really miss me if she's willing to make anything I want. She only does that for special occasions and birthdays. "Hmmm," I mutter trying to figure out the most complex thing I can tell her to make so it will take her all day. If she's busy, she can't call and bug about my apartment and roommate. "Any chance you'll make lasagna?"

Most people would buy the frozen kind and call it good. Not my mom, though. She'll get all the ingredients and make it from scratch. Nothing, not even restaurants, compares to her lasagna. "Absolutely. Maybe a salad and garlic bread to go with it?"

"That sounds delicious, Mom." See, now I've given her something to do besides obsess over what I'm doing and how I'm living my life. "What time do you want me to come over?"

"I should have everything ready by six, and then maybe we can play a card game or two before you have to leave."

The last part of her statement sounds like she's unsure of what I'll say, but if it makes her happy, I'll do it. "You bet."

"Is there anything else you want me to make? Dessert? Some of your favorite dishes that I can send home with you?" So many questions all at once. She acts like I live hours away instead of twenty minutes.

"I'm running out to grab some lunch, do you want anything?" Tiffany's voice is muffled through the door, but Mom undoubtedly hears it.

"Do you have a girl over there?" Her voice accusatory.

"No, Mom. It's the TV." Hopefully Tiffany will take my silence as a refusal. It's weird enough that she's even asking. She usually goes out of her way to avoid talking to me. I wonder what changed her mind.

"Spencer?" Dammit, Tiffany. Just go. Do whatever you have planned for the day.

"There is no way you're watching a show about another person named Spencer. Are you living with a woman?" She demands an answer but I don't have the energy to give it to her.

"I have to go, Mom. I'll see you for dinner tonight." I hang up the phone before she has a chance to argue. The stupid phone rings in my hand before I have a chance to set it down. Silencing it, I throw it to the other side of the bed, and get up.

When I open my bedroom door, Tiffany is standing on the other side. Her mouth hanging wide open. "Di—" She clears her throat. "Did you want me to grab you something while I'm out?"

What the hell is she staring at? I'm not naked or anything. Not like the way I found her the other day. The only thing I'm missing is a shirt. It's much more PG than what I saw. And it's not like she hasn't seen me without a shirt before. That night she was trying her best to get it off of me as fast as possible. *Shut that shit down, Spencer. She's already made it perfectly clear that there will not be any sort of relationship with you.* Her long red hair is pulled into a messy bun on top of her head and she's wearing yoga pants with a tank top. She looks like she is ready to work out or just finished one, but I haven't seen her do any type of exercise since I've been here. Maybe she's gotten a gym membership? "No, I'm good. Thank you, though."

"No problem. Just thought I'd ask since you've been holed up in your room so much." Her eyes travel down to the waistband of my sweats and then back up to meet my gaze. Her cheeks redden and she shakes her head. "I'll just go now."

I wonder if one of her cousins said something to her. Maybe they told her to be nicer considering I'm not a huge pain in the ass. At least, I hope I'm not. It would be damn near impossible since I don't make a habit of leaving my room unless I know she's gone. She is temptation on a stick, and I don't have the willpower to constantly fight it. I close the door as soon as she turns around because I can't watch her ass walking away in those tight-fitting pants again without doing something I will regret. The only way I can resist the pull toward her is by keeping four walls and a shut door between us.

After the stress of dealing with my mom and whatever is going on with Tiffany, it's time to go back to bed. I have a few hours before I need to be at my parents' house, and I can't think of a better way to spend my time. Setting the alarm on my phone, I put it down beside my pillow and pull my comforter over my head. It doesn't take long for sleep to pull me under its spell.

Well, that went about as well as I thought it would. My mom lost her shit when I confessed that my roommate is female. I don't understand why she's so up in arms about it. It's not like I'm sleeping with her, much to my dismay. Tiffany stays in her lane, and I stay in mine. We have privacy and I've managed to get more work than I thought possible done while living here. For once, I don't have a huge backlog of clients sending me messages wondering when their project will be completed. The apartment is dark as I walk in, and I breathe a sigh of relief. I don't have to dance around my attraction to her and can watch a movie. She wasn't home when I woke up from my nap either, though. I hope everything is okay.

I grab a beer out of the refrigerator and head to my room. Shucking off my clothes and putting some sweatpants on, I turn on the TV and wait for it to connect to the WiFi. It's been a while since I've binge watched a show and waiting up to make sure Tiffany makes it home sounds like a good excuse to start one. I search *Netflix* for *Supernatural* and settle in to watch these two brothers kick some demon ass.

I've made it five episodes into the first season and she's still not home. Part of me itches to pick up my phone and text her to make sure everything is okay. We traded numbers when I moved in just in case there was an emergency. This seems like one to me, but maybe she's hanging out with Audrey. Yeah, that's it. She'll be home soon enough, and I'll be waiting to hear the door close as soon as she comes in.

It's nearing three in the morning, and still nothing. I send her a quick text.

Spencer: Is everything okay?

Fifteen minutes later and there's still no response. There's only one reason she wouldn't come home, and it doesn't sit well with me. All it does is give proof that the night we spent together meant absolutely nothing to her. Why am I concerning myself with her well-being if she can't even answer a simple text? No more. Staying up late ends now.

NINE

Tiffany

I TIP-TOE THROUGH THE APARTMENT, hoping Spencer is still asleep. I'm not sure why, but I don't want him to know I was out all night. My night out wasn't intentional, at all. Audrey asked if I wanted to come over to watch a movie, and since I didn't have anything else going on, I said okay. It's been a while since I've hung out with her, and I needed a break from being around Spencer so much. The additional shifts at work are doing nothing to squash my attraction to him.

Now here I am, sneaking into my own house so I don't have to explain myself to a guy I'm not even dating. He thinks I don't know that he waits up for me to get home, but I see the blue light from his laptop shut off as soon as I walk into the hallway. If I'm honest, it's sweet. And, if I did relationships, he would be the *perfect* guy for me. When did my life become so complicated? Oh, that's right… The day I agreed to let a man I've slept with move in with me. A guy that I'm still attracted to. I'm obviously a glutton for punishment.

Just a few more steps and I'll be in the safety of my own personal space. I twist the doorknob and take a step into the room, but my foot doesn't hit the floor. Whatever I just stepped on slides and I fall to the side. My elbow hits the door before I manage to grab the knob and use it to steady myself.

"Damn it," I mutter a smidge too loud. This hurts so freaking bad. I'll never understand why someone coined the elbow as the "funny bone." There's nothing funny about the pain shooting through my arm. At least this time, I didn't fall on my ass while naked. I'm choosing to look on the bright side. Though, I wish I knew where this sudden bout of clumsiness is coming from. Stella is the one always tripping over her own feet, not me. It doesn't escape my notice that both times I've fallen, it's happen happened while I'm thinking about Spencer.

I search the floor for the culprit of my almost fall, and my gaze settles on my hairbrush. How did it end up on the floor? I could have sworn I tossed it on the bed before I left yesterday. It must have slipped off the bed when I threw it. That's the only possible way the brush could have ended up on the floor. I reach out with the arm not currently throbbing and pick it up before setting it on my bed.

Turning around, I half expect to see Spencer standing in the hallway checking to see if I'm okay. But he's not there and silence fills the apartment. My shoulders sag, and a tinge of disappointment fills me. It's a good thing, though. If he cared, he would have rushed in to make sure all was well... right? While this realization should make me happy, a pang of sadness hits me in the gut.

Spencer hasn't come out of his room since I've been home. At least, not that I can tell. I haven't left my room much either. Not because I'm scared of some sort of confrontation, but because I really need to clean my room. I am twenty-three years old, and do not need to have my room looking like a twelve year old girl lives here. Audrey and Stella would be proud of me. My messiness is one of their pet peeves. Actually, most of the things that I do fall on their list of pet peeves. This small thing would make them happy, and maybe I'd look like an adult in their eyes. I love them both more than anything, but sometimes they try to parent me too much. I have parents, and I don't need them treating me like I'm their child. Even if I act like it sometimes.

Cleaning my room should not take hours. Hell, it shouldn't take me that long to clean my whole apartment, yet it does. However, finally, everything is in its place. There are no longer hairbrushes littering the floor daring to trip me once again. I think I'm going to use having a roommate as a new beginning. A chance to get my shit together and grow up.

I mean, that's what my parents have been pushing me to do for the last couple of years. It's what Audrey and Stella want. And, maybe a small part of me wants that too. To finally stop being treated like the little kid pretending to be at the grown-ups table.

With a clean room and new determination, I think I've earned a snack. My steps are slow and deliberate as I walk past his room. I'm not trying to be creepy or anything, but I want Spencer to hear me. If anything, just to give me a chance to explain. Sadly, the door stays firmly shut and I continue to the refrigerator trying to mask my disappointment.

I open the refrigerator door, looking for a package of cookie dough. The jury is out on if I will actually bake the cookies or eat the dough right out of the package. I push things around, careful not to mess with any of Spencer's food. It's only fair for me to have the same rule about food that I gave him. Damn, there is no cookie dough.

Next up is the freezer. There's bound to be something in there. It hasn't been that long since I've gotten groceries. Who am I kidding? I never actually get groceries. I normally grab a bunch of stuff that looks good when I'm walking through the store, and most of it is frozen. There's no use in me buying a whole bunch of food when I can get a meal from work.

Peering into the freezer, I spot a small pint of cookie dough ice cream. That's even better than actual cookie dough. I pull it out of the freezer and pry the lid off. Tiny crystals of frost covered the top, and I debate whether it's still good or not. If it were Audrey, she would throw it out because in her eyes, it's not fresh. But, since I'm kind of in a bad mood, I ignore it and grab a spoon out of the drawer. I don't even bother putting it into a bowl and dig right in, sighing when that first delicious bite hits my tongue. I swear, I could live off of ice cream. It might be the best dessert in the universe. It holds the magical ability to take away all of your worries and it's exactly what I need right now.

I don't really want to go back to my room. Even though it's clean now, there's nothing to do in there since there's no TV. I walk the short distance to the living room, and sit on the couch after grabbing the remote. Along with my ice cream, I think I deserve a little binge-watching session.

As soon as Netflix loads, I begin scrolling through their suggestions. The only problem is nothing sounds good. They are all love stories, comedies or look flat out ridiculous. A banner with two guys catches my attention. What is this show? It's apparently been on for a long time, and it's about two brothers fighting demons. I love anything that has monsters in it, and this sounds like the perfect fit for my mood today. I press play and get lost in the story.

I'm not even sure how long I've been watching this show because I didn't expect to get sucked into it. Any other time I've started a new show, or even with some of the ones I'm already a fan of, I tend to lose interest halfway into one episode. This one though… It's keeping me engaged. I've even had to press yes on the judgmental "are you still watching" question. Because yes. Yes, I am still watching. I don't see me not watching anytime in the near future. I have been up for a while, and it's a good thing I have another day off from work. Otherwise, I'd be screwed waiting on my customers.

"I see you're watching my favorite show," Spencer's deep voice is louder than the Winchester brothers arguing.

"Holy crap. You scared the hell out of me." I pause the TV and turn around to glare at him. Instead, my gaze meets his bare chest. That's twice in as many days that I've been caught off guard by him shirtless.

"You're drooling," he laughs.

"Shut up." Grabbing a pillow, I toss it at his head. "Why did you sneak up on me like that?"

"Why did you sneak through the house when you got home this morning?"

So he was awake. "I wasn't sneaking," I huff. "I was respecting your boundaries by being quiet so as not to wake you."

"Except, I was already awake." He rolls his eyes and heads toward the kitchen. "And I'm not sneaking either. I'm hungry and have to pass through the living room to get to the kitchen."

"Maybe, I should put a bell on you."

He turns around and lifts an eyebrow in question. Waiting for me to continue.

"You know, so I can hear when you're coming?"

Spencer snorts and grabs a plastic bowl out of the refrigerator. Grabbing a paper towel, he places it over the bowl and puts it in the microwave. The low hum fills the space and I'm antsy to hear what he's going to say next. "It's not my fault you walk through here and sound like a herd of cows. I feel bad for your downstairs neighbors."

"I do *not* sound like a cow." *What a jackass*. Who the hell says that to someone?

"Maybe not, but you're not exactly stealthy either."

The microwave dings and he pulls his food out. He is facing me, and I can't help admiring the defined muscles in his shoulders. Muscles that had zero problems picking me up and carrying me to his bedroom. *Don't go there, Tiffany.*

"Mind if I watch a couple of episodes with you?"

"Huh?" I shake my head, clearing all the indecent thoughts I'm having about him.

"The show? Can I watch it with you?" He scoops up the pillow on his way to the living room and sits down on the opposite end of the sofa. "It's pretty dumb for us to be watching the same thing in two different rooms."

"I didn't realize we were watching the same thing." Or that you would intrude on my binge-watching spree and be all shirtless. The shirtless thing is going to be a problem. I can already tell. "But I guess you can watch it with me since you're already sitting down."

"You can press play now," he nods toward the TV.

I do as he's requested and pull one of the other pillows over my lap. I have no idea why except that it provides a small sense of security. The brothers on the screen are kicking ass and taking names, and I'm over here sneaking peeks at the man next to me. I'm not entirely sure what's going on in the show anymore. He's distracting me... Yet again. Pausing the show, I turn to his confused face. "Okay, we need to add another rule."

"And what would that be?" He sets his bowl on the coffee table. I'm not sure what he's eating, but it smells delicious. Like home and love, if those things had a scent.

"You," I twirl my finger in his direction. "Need to wear a shirt when you're in the main areas of the apartment."

"Why?" He shrugs and turns back to the TV, waiting for my to press play. "It's not like I'm doing anything indecent. Lots of guys walk around without a shirt."

He has a point, and normally it wouldn't affect me, but he's another story. He gave me a night of amazing sex and then ended up living here. I can't think straight when he's clothed, much less when he's not. "It makes me uncomfortable." There. That sounds like a good enough reason.

"If you say so," he stands up.

"Where are you going?"

"To put on a shirt, like you asked." He jogs to his room. His steps are so light that I can't even hear them.

"Oh," I call into the space he left. "Thank you."

He comes back in, sitting in the same spot he was in before. "Can you turn the show back on?"

"Sure."

"One more thing," he holds up his hand. "The rule also applies to you. No more skimpy clothes when you're in here." He waves his hands up and down in my direction. "It's distracting."

Maybe he does think of me as more than just his roommate. "That's fair." I nod my head, point the remote toward the TV and press play.

We watch a few more episodes, but my mind isn't solely on the images filling up the TV screen. I'm still glancing at him, longing for him to scoot closer. To pull me onto his lap. Hell, to touch me tenderly, the way he did before. But, he doesn't do any of that. His eyes are glued to *Supernatural*, acting as if I'm not there. As if he can't feel the tension building between us.

I can't take it anymore. I throw the pillow covering my legs to the side and stand up. There's no way in hell I'm the only one feeling this way. He looks up at me. "Where are you going?"

I toss the remote on the sofa next to him and turn to walk around the couch. "I'm going to bed." It's a lie. I'm not going to bed. At least, not yet. I'm going to take a cold ass shower so I can wipe all lustful thoughts of Spencer out of my mind. "Just turn the TV off when you're done."

It's a statement and there's no room for argument, even if he looks like he wants to. I stomp to my room, grab the robe I bought from the rack beside my door and march straight into the bathroom. There's only one way to squash these insane feelings. I *need* to go on a date. To see another male besides Spencer. There's a guy I know that is totally okay with casual dates and doesn't always want to hook up. Maybe I'll give him a call.

TEN

Spencer

THE CASSEROLE my mom sent home with me yesterday smells amazing. She still doesn't think I should live with a woman, but she's not giving me hell about it anymore. Small victories always feel like major ones when it comes to her. I'm hoping the homemade dinner will be an olive branch for Tiffany after the way she stormed out of the living room the other night.

I didn't even do anything that I know of. Though, I am sure the blame will somehow be placed on me. Besides, there's only one reason she would come up with the new rule. She's attracted to me and is fighting it. Of course, I don't want her to feel uncomfortable, so I obliged. But it threw my resolve to be done with her right out of the window. I'm still wondering where she was that night she didn't come home, except it's not really my place to question it. It's not like we are a couple. We're barely even friends. Watching TV together was the most time we've spent in the same space since I've moved in. It was nice, and even better that she was into a show I love. I've been watching it since it first started airing and watched it many times since then. Walking in on her so absorbed in the show and seeing Sam on the screen with his research and general "good guy" vibe gives me hope that there is someone out there for me. That I can be totally badass and have a sweet side. I just need Tiffany to realize that. To throw whatever fears she has out the window and take a chance on me.

The timer on the oven beeps and I pull out the casserole. If this doesn't make her open up, I don't know what will. She seems to like food, and there's nothing better than homemade. It'll be a wonder if I don't eat it all myself. The only downside to not living above the garage anymore is no more daily meals from my mom. Even if she drove me nuts always coming into my tiny apartment without knocking, she makes the best food.

Footsteps come down the hallway, and I can't help but wonder if it's because Tiffany smelled dinner. I've noticed she rarely cooks anything that's not frozen. I'm not much better, but I do occasionally cook actual food with nutrients. "Hey, Tiffany," I call out while putting the towels back in the drawer. "I've got plenty of food if you—" Tiffany is standing at the edge of the kitchen in a short black dress, and heels that make her almost as tall as me. "Where are you going?"

"Not that it's any of your business, but I'm going out."

"With your cousin?" Please be going out with Audrey. It's a long shot hoping for that. I can tell by the look on her face, she's determined to go out tonight despite how badly I want her to stay in.

"Nooo," she draws out. "With a *friend*." I don't like how she said a friend, implying that it's someone who is most definitely more than that.

"Oh," I work to keep the rejection out of my voice. "I was going to see if you wanted to eat dinner with me."

"Sorry," she winces. "Maybe we can raincheck for lunch tomorrow? I work from two until close, so I am available."

"Sure," I sigh. This is what I get for trying to be nice. Trying to at least be friends with the woman I want more than friendship with. I grab a spoon and scoop a small portion into a bowl. "That works."

"Okay," she pauses to see if I'm going to say anything else to her. "I'm going to head out."

"Have fun on your date," I call to her retreating form.

She doesn't respond and seconds later I hear the door open then close. Looking at my bowl, I decide I'm no longer hungry. Jealousy curls throughout my body and I want nothing more than to throw the bowl across the room for letting her get into my head. I'm so stupid thinking she's interested in me. She may play coy and awkward around me, but that's not at all what she's proving to be tonight. I feel like I am back to being the kid that wasn't asked to dance at a party.

A distraction is what I need. I could go out and see if one of my friends wants to get together, but they all have lives and girlfriends. I'm lacking both. *Netflix* will have to do. I refuse to hide away in my room, though. I live here too, and I will watch TV in the living room like a sane person.

I grab the remote off the table, and lie down on the couch, my feet almost hanging over the edge. I don't think this thing is full size, and I pull my knees up until my feet hit the bottom of the armrest. The TV comes to life and I scroll through the apps until I land on the red square.

Suggestions for her account pop up, and I groan. Rom-Com. Chick flick. Horror. Well, that last one is a surprise. I didn't picture her as a slasher movie fan. I keep scrolling through all the shows and movies that come up, but nothing is catching my attention. And, I'm sure as hell not watching anything related to love or clandestine events. Tonight was supposed to be what spurred a blooming relationship, or at least provided a stepping stone toward that, with Tiffany. The plan blew up in my face like everything else.

The only thing that might pull me out of this ridiculous funk is Sam and Dean Winchester. If they can't do it, then there is no hope for me.

Twenty minutes into this episode and I can't focus. My mind keeps wandering to Tiffany and her *date*. Is he touching her? Running his fingertips over her smooth legs. Pulling the tiny straps of her dress down. *Fuck*. I shouldn't let my thoughts drift in that direction. All it will do is piss me off. But I can't help it. She would rather enjoy the company of some guy, I'm sure she just met, than me. We live together and can't seem to spend more than ten minutes in the same room without arguing.

Pulling my phone out of my pocket, I hold it up, almost dropping it on my face. I know we exchanged numbers for emergency use only, but I think this qualifies as one. Even if it's only for my sanity and to keep my jealousy in check. It is better than what I really want to do, which is pop into every restaurant and bar she might go to until I find her. I don't know how to deal with these feelings. I've never been so enthralled with a woman that they occupy most of my waking thoughts. Hell, she's even found her way into my dreams.

My finger hovers over her name, debating whether I should text her. I don't have any right to do it, we're nothing to each other…besides roommates. I can't stop myself though. I click her name and my fingertips fly over the small keyboard.

Spencer: Are you having fun?

No response even though I can see that she read it. If she's taking the time out to look at her phone, she must be bored. Or maybe she only opened it because she thought it was an actual emergency and not me trying to pester her.

Spencer: Where did he take you? What did you order?
Spencer: Is he at least a good conversationalist?

Still nothing. What will it take for her to respond? I take a deep breath and let it out. This is ridiculous and the type of crap that teenagers pull when envy gets the best of them. A part of me is ashamed that I'm blowing up her phone. It's not enough to keep me from sending another text.

Spencer: Is he holding your hand?

Tiffany: Spencer, please stop.
Spencer: Are you coming home tonight? Or are you going home with him?

There's no response. *Damn it.* I went too far. I take my glasses off and groan into my hands. I'm a fucking idiot. I should have never text her. I'm sure I've ruined her date, not that I care that much, but she's going to be *pissed* when she gets home. There's no doubt in my mind that she's going to go talk to the leasing office to see what she can do to get me out of the apartment. I can't let that happen. Living here has been torture with her right across the hall, but I don't want to go back to living in the tiny space above my parents's garage. How lame is it that a guy in his mid-twenties can't seem to get his shit together?

Maybe there's a way I can play it off as a joke. I don't see how, but I need to figure something out. I can't have the woman I'm living with angry at me and making the whole situation worse. The show is still playing in the background, except the only thing I can focus on is the phone sitting on my stomach. Willing it to ring or alert me with a new text. Anything to show what sort of mood she's in right now. I need to be prepared for when she gets home. *If* she comes home.

I'm not sure how much time has gone by, but the front door slams open. I push my glasses back onto my face and stand up. I should have stayed silent on the couch.

Tiffany is staring at me and has fire in her eyes. "Who the hell do you think you are?" When I don't answer she continues, "Seriously, what is your problem? You said you would be okay living here knowing that the night we spent together was just that. One. Night."

She's stalking toward me. A predator about to pounce on her prey. I've seriously screwed up. "I'm sorry. I didn't mean—"

Tiffany cuts me off, "You didn't mean what? To ruin my date? To pry information that's none of your damn business?"

I have no escape. She's blocking the way to both the front door and my bedroom. "You're right. I shouldn't have asked."

She's within a foot of me, and she pokes her finger into my chest. "You have no right to question what I'm doing. Or whom I'm doing it with. We are roommates, nothing more. Yes, we slept together, one time, but that doesn't mean you can question me like I'm some sort of criminal." Another poke. "There are boundaries that you should never cross. Things you shouldn't ask—"

I close the distance between us, pull her to me, and crash my mouth into hers. It may get me slapped, but I don't care. This is either the smartest or dumbest idea I've ever had. I guess I'll find out soon enough.

ELEVEN

Tiffany

<hr>

Is this actually happening? This fool thinks kissing me will lessen how pissed I am. I pull back from him and step out of his arms. "Are you insane?"

He doesn't say anything. At. All. A boyish grin lifts his lips and his cheeks are a bright red. I guess he wasn't planning that after all. My fingertips brush across my lips. I can't believe he did that. He has the audacity to kiss me after the stunt he just pulled while I was out on a freaking date. Seriously, who *does* that? He takes a step toward me and I take a step back. Warmth floods my body. Even though I'm not happy with how he acted tonight, I can't deny the way he makes me feel. There is a pull I feel toward this man who is still practically a stranger even after living with me for a few weeks. He reaches a hand out toward me, waiting to see what I will do. I could turn around and go to my room, end this dumpster fire before it begins. Or… I can give in to the lust, to the thought of his hands all over me once again. He is an itch I can't scratch, and he's provided the perfect opportunity to soothe the feeling. One more chance to be with him and get him out of my system.

There is so much hope in his eyes I'll let that one wall down and let him in. I have no choice but to let him have me after dancing around each other all this time. Not when he makes his insecurities fall away and shows me exactly what he wants from me. Instead of turning toward safety, the smart decision. I close the gap, wrap my arms around his neck and stand on my tiptoes until my lips meet his.

My body heats as his tongue intertwines with mine. His hands trailing down my sides until they wrap around me, grabbing my ass and bringing my body even closer to his. The only thing separating us is our clothes. Well, his clothes since my dress is so short it covers less than my pajamas.

He pulls back for a second and mutters, "Thank God" before kissing my neck. It's a good thing I wore my hair up. The feel of his lips working their way up my neck to my earlobe has me trembling with anticipation. He shouldn't be allowed to do the same thing to me. To make me feel pleasure with that one tiny nibble.

I back up toward the hallway, and he pulls away. "Where are we going?" He whispers, afraid to break the mood.

"My room." This is new territory for me. I don't bring guys home. *Ever.* It's a little more awkward considering he lives with me, but my room has always been off limits to everyone except me. Call it self-preservation. I don't care. It helps to keep those looking for more than what I can offer away from me. Hell, most of the guys I have been with rarely know where I live.

He nods and lifts me up enough that my feet are no longer touching the ground. His mouth is trailing every inch of bare skin as he walks me backward to my room, being careful to keep us from running into any walls.

Reaching my hand behind me, I feel for the doorknob when we get to my room and we fall into the room. Even though I just cleaned it yesterday, my bed is riddled with clothes from tonight's date. He peers over my shoulder at the mess and laughs. "Maybe my room would have been a better choice."

"Shut up." I turn and gather as many clothes as I can and toss them on the floor. He grabs another pile and sets them on the dresser, taking more care of my belongings than I am. I take advantage and start to pull my dress over my head, but he stops me.

I fully expect him to pounce on me in the same hurried, frantic motions that just took place. But, he doesn't. He takes a step back from me, eyes trailing my body. "I didn't get to say this before because it wasn't for me, but you are fucking beautiful tonight."

My heart warms and heat pools at my center. Never has a man called me beautiful. Hot, yes. I was even called bangable by one of douchebags I've crawled into bed with. I didn't mind then because I was after one thing, a night with zero strings and full of fun times. With Spencer, it's different. It's *more.*

"Thank you." It sounds stupid as it comes out of my mouth, but I can't take the words back now.

Even though I see desire written all over his face, his eyes don't leave mine. "I'm serious. You. Are. Beautiful." I rush toward him, eager to speed up whatever he's trying to accomplish and lure him into my bed. But, he holds his hand out. "Let me just enjoy the view for a minute."

This man will ruin me. Never has anyone slowed things down so they can admire me. I mean, I don't think I'm hideous or anything. I'm just not used to the care and tenderness that Spencer is doling out like its candy.

"Um, okay." I feel awkward just standing here. What am I supposed to do with my hands? Cross them in front of me? Wrap them around my waist? This is uncharted territory for me. By this time, I'm usually between the sheets with my date. His intense gaze would be creepy if I didn't see the adoration on his face. He is in awe, and I wish I knew what it is about me that makes him think I'm something special. I'm still fully clothed, and nobody has ever looked at me like that unless I'm as naked as the day I came into this world.

The only thing I've done is push him away any chance I can. But this, tonight, will change everything, whether or not I want it to.

Spencer stalks toward me, done with his appraisal. I step back on instinct. A game of cat and mouse, and I'm wondering when I became the prey instead of the predator.

My legs hit the edge of my bed, and I'm out of room to run. Not that I would, it's kind of nice being the one who is pursued, even if it's also scary as hell. I'm not equipped to handle anything serious. Shit, what did I get myself into when I kissed him back?

"Are you sure this is okay?" Spencer whispers into my year. Can he sense my reservations? "We can stop and it's totally fine."

Now is my chance to back down and listen to the voice saying this is *not* a good idea. That's not what happens, though. I snort, then cover my face with my hands. "Like that isn't something I've heard before, only to get the cold shoulder when I back out."

"Maybe," he kisses my jawline before continuing. "You've been with assholes before, and I'm not one. I will one hundred percent respect your wishes."

This man is a hard puzzle to figure out. How can he be so sweet, reassuring, and reserved all the time while dominating me in the bedroom? It makes me wonder how many women have seen this side of him. The thought makes me uncomfortable, and while unlikely, I hope that I'm the only one.

"Yes," I breathe out. "I want to keep going." I will make damn sure he forgets every woman before me. I want to be seared into his mind just as he has been in mine.

His fingers trail up my arms until they reach the tiny straps of my dress, pulling them down until the dress falls to the floor. I feel exposed even though I'm still wearing a bra and panties. My breath hitches as he runs his finger over my nipple. The lace of my bra providing the perfect friction.

I reach my hands behind me to take the stupid bra off so we can touch, skin to skin, but he stops me. Hands brushing against my ribcage, they wrap around me until I feel his fingers at the clasp. Within seconds my bra is undone, and he's pulling it off of me. "You know, I don't think I've ever managed to get my bra off that fast."

"What can I say? I'm a fast learner." His voice is gruff, as if he can barely contain his lust. I sit on the edge of the bed before lying back, scooting myself toward the center until my feet are hanging over the edge, watching as he strips each piece of clothing he has on, until he's as naked as I am. "I guess that's a good thing. Want to show me just how good?"

He doesn't answer me, and before long my panties are being pulled down my legs and tossed over his shoulders. I reach down to pull my heels off, and he stops me, once again. "Leave them on." This shy guy that has kept to himself since he's moved in is giving me orders, and a thrill hums through my body. Who knew this man could shut me up with one simple sentence. The last time I was in a bed with him, I took control. Tonight… I want him to lead. To show me how much he wants me with no input from me.

He parts my legs and kisses his way up my calf all the way to my thigh before his mouth closes over my clit. My body jerks, relishing the way his tongue moves, bringing me closer and closer to an orgasm. This is going too fast. I'm going to come before he's even had a chance to be inside of me. I try to pull away from him and ease some of the sweet torture. But he grips my thighs, bringing me even closer. He doesn't let go until a moan escapes my lips and I come. Riding the waves of ecstasy, before he pulls away and climbs over me. I don't hesitate. I pull him on top of me, wanting to fill me up in the best way possible, but he leans back and jumps off the bed. He grabs the sweatpants he had on and groans in frustration. "Is something wrong?"

"I, um," he scratches the back of his head, "don't have a condom."

Rolling over, I reach to open the nightstand drawer and pull one out. Just because he's the first man I've ever brought to my bed doesn't mean I'm not prepared. "Here," I toss it to the end of the bed.

He wastes no time opening the packet and slipping it on. My eyes widen at how hard he is, proof of how much he wants me. Before I can say anything, he's over me again. Lowering himself and sliding in. Filling me to my core. He rocks into me slowly, building up the momentum and savoring every second. He's not rushing it the way I did that first night we were together. He's taking his time, kissing along my neck with each thrust.

I lean up and crash my mouth to his, tasting myself on his tongue and it turns me on even more. Spencer picks up speed, and soon he's coming. Each pulse sending me further over the edge, until I follow him. He falls onto his elbows and rests his forehead on my chest.

"That was…"

"Amazing," I finish for him. And it was. I've never felt that connected to someone during sex in my life. I've never even kissed a man after he's gone down on me. Spencer brings out something inside of me I have been terrified to set free.

He looks up and holds one of his hands in the air. "High five."

Wait, what? "High five?"

"Yep," he pops the *p*. "I mean, it was pretty awesome and most people high five after they do something they are satisfied with."

"You are so weird." I don't argue though. I'm more than satisfied, and if he wants my to slap his hand, I'll do it. My hand hits his, and he clasps it instead of letting it go. He kisses my knuckles and slides out of me.

"I'll be right back." He walks out of the room and into the bathroom, I think.

I slap my hand to my forehead and exhale. What happens now? Will he go to his room and act like nothing happened tomorrow? Pulling the comforter and sheets down, I slide between them, waiting to see if he'll come back. My eyes close, and sleep is just out of reach when I feel the bed dip behind me. He wraps an arm around me and pulls me to him, my head nestled right beneath his.

I'm relieved that he came back but also scared of what this might lead to. What does this mean for our living arrangement? That's something I can worry about tomorrow. For now, I snuggle into him and let go of the worries, at least for tonight.

TWELVE

Spencer

THE LIGHT COMING in from the window wakes me up, and I squint my eyes to adjust to the sudden brightness. Looking around, I see the clothes scattered all around the room and remember I'm not in my bed.

A grin overtakes my face as I remember last night. The way Tiffany looked up into my eyes and opened up to me. The look on her face when I kissed her to shut her up and when she kissed me back. I thought for sure she would slap me, but she surprised me instead.

I roll over, wanting to glimpse her before I go to my room to get dressed. Except… She's not there. Damn it, not this again. Just when I think she's going to let me in. Let me see beneath her snarky comments and "don't need anyone" attitude, she does this, *again*. Am I really that bad in bed that she has to sneak off? She wasn't complaining last night when I made her moan my name. Maybe I was too caught up in the moment to notice that she wasn't feeling it the way I was.

The only difference between now and last time is that I'm in *her* bed, and we live in the same damn apartment. She won't be able to hide by running away. Tiffany will have to face me at some point. I shouldn't leave it up to her though. Hell, I'll be lucky if she hasn't already run off to her cousin's place to keep from seeing me. It's not a far stretch. The apartment is still and silent. It doesn't sound like anyone else is here, and my heart drops. One day, I'll stop being stupid and realize that she wants nothing more from me.

No, Spencer. No more wallowing in pity. I slide out from beneath the sheets and search for my boxers on the opposite side of the room to put them on before walking into the hallway. I have two options. I can go to my room and act like last night didn't happen. Act as if I don't have actual feelings for this woman. Or, I can walk my ass into the living room and see if she's there. Hiding behind my bedroom door is cowardly. I moved in here so I could grow up and learn how to handle things on my own. That includes figuring out what the hell is going on with me and Tiffany. It's time to find out how she feels about me once and for all. No more of this hot and cold business.

I'm so focused on my thoughts when I round the corner at the end of the hall I run straight into Tiffany. Hot liquid splashes out of the cups she was apparently holding and hits my legs. "Damn it," I yell and hop around thinking that will actually do anything to help.

"I'm so sorry." Tiffany sets the cups on the floor and turns back toward the kitchen, grabbing one of the few hand towels. "I was just bringing us some coffee. I was trying to make it back to the room before you woke up."

Well, that makes me feel marginally better. She wasn't running this time. Then guilt slams into me for thinking the worst of her. I should have known better. Not because she's given me any reason to trust her reactions, but because this is technically her place and I'd be the one that would have to find a new place to stay.

"Um, thanks." I hold out my hand expecting her to give me the towel so I can wipe the coffee off my legs, but she doesn't. Tiffany gets on her knees and pats my legs with the cloth, cleaning up the mess we've both made. "You don't have to do that," I bend down and pull the towel from her hands. "I'm perfectly capable of cleaning myself up."

"I know, but I feel bad." She grabs both mugs and carries them back to the kitchen. "I was trying to do something sweet and screwed it up." She looks at me over her shoulder and shakes her head. "You'd think I didn't carry multiple things in my hands on a day-to-day basis while at work."

"In your defense, you weren't expecting me to bowl you over while you were carrying them."

"Thanks," she sweeps her hair out of her face. "I'm so out of my comfort zone here. I've never stayed the night with anyone. Definitely not in my own bed."

"Never?" I find that hard to believe. She was out all night just a couple of weeks ago. "What about the other night?"

"Nope. I was at Audrey's. I passed out on her couch while watching movies." Well, that makes me feel so much better. I thought for sure she was out with some guy. Not that it would have been any of my business. It's still not, but I'm hoping that changes now. She scrunches her eyebrows together. "Why?"

Shit. She wasn't supposed to pick up on the fact that I noticed. "I was just wondering. I didn't hear you come in before I went to bed."

"I see," she rolls her eyes. She's definitely not convinced. Oh well, there's no use poking the bear, especially not this early in the morning.

"I'll make us new cups of coffee," I grab the mugs off the counter and pour the remnants in the sink. "You go back to bed."

"I can do it. Besides," she waves her hands up and down my body. "You are breaking one of the rules."

"I didn't think that one would apply after last night."

Tiffany sighs, "I guess you're right. But at least put some pants on while the coffee is brewing. You don't want to have another mishap and the coffee splash you anywhere important."

"Like where?" I'm loving her playful banter. I usually get attitude, or pretend disinterest, from her. I could get used to this new side of her.

"I think you know the answer to that." She turns and walks toward the hallway.

"But I want to hear you say it," I call to her retreating form.

"Put some pants on." She doesn't look back and continues down the hall to her room.

I'm not even sure who I am anymore. Never in a million years would I have thought I'd be making slightly dirty jokes. Hell, I had to be almost drunk to even talk to her the night I knocked her down at the concert. But here I am, owning my confidence and not letting my brain get in the way. She's right though, I need to put on some pants. Knowing my luck so far today, I'd spill coffee all over my junk and end up in the emergency room. We can't have that. Not when I fully intend on seeing what we are after last night. Where *she* stands on us. I'm sure she knows my feelings by now, but I need her to be honest with herself about her own emotions.

"What do you want to watch?" We're on the couch and Tiffany is leaning against my chest. This feels *right*. Like she was meant to be in my arms. I just need to make sure she stays there and doesn't freak out about being more than roommates. I'd like it to be an actual relationship, but I know she needs to figure herself out before she makes that commitment. And I'll respect that. Some people need baby steps and don't jump in one hundred percent like me. Not that I've had a ton of experience in this realm. There aren't many girls ready to jump into something serious with a guy that until recently still had comic posters covering his wall.

"I don't care," Tiffany says. "Anything besides romance. Those are reserved for when I hang out with Audrey."

"Why do you only watch them with her?" I thought most girls like chick flicks, but apparently, I've been wrong my entire life. Or, I've just spent way too much time with my mom watching them. I've probably seen more than Tiffany has.

"Because it's my payment for when she has horror movie marathons with me." She nestles further into me. "She doesn't like them, and Stella and I love them. She sits through them with a blanket over her face for most of the movie."

"You sound like you do a lot with your cousins." This is entirely new for me, my parents were only children, and I'm an only child. Though hearing about big families is kind of weird, it is also fascinating because I have always wanted one.

"We're best friends. And they make sure my ass stays in line no matter how much I fight them on it." She grabs the remote out of my hands and finds some obscure horror film that I've never heard of. If I'm being honest, I'm not a huge fan of all the blood and guts. *Supernatural* is the only show other than super-hero ones that I've been able to get into. They may fight monsters, but there is so much humor mixed in with it.

"I'm guessing you're the baby of the family."

"You'd be correct," she sighs. "It's a blessing and a curse. I get away with so much stuff, but they also have a tendency to parent me when they think I'm doing something wrong. It's annoying, but I know they mean well."

"It must be nice."

"You don't have any siblings?"

"Nope. I'm an only child of two only children. I had no one to play with growing up besides the few kids from school that I hung out with."

"That sounds boring." She sits up and faces me. "My cousins and I did everything we could together. Even though most of the time I felt like was just following them around."

"Well, I'm glad you had them." I pull her back toward me, keeping my arms wrapped around her. If she had any fears about things being weird between us after having sex, they were unwarranted. This is the longest we've gotten along since I've lived here. Now may not be the best time to ask, but I'm going to do it, anyway. "So, what happens now?"

She pauses the movie, "What do you mean?"

"With us. Are you going to say this is a fluke and will never work?" I tighten my hold on her to prevent her from avoiding the conversation. There's no way she's getting out of this. We *need* to have this discussion.

"I don't know," Tiffany squirms in my arms. "I don't exactly have the best track record with relationships."

"Have you ever actually tried to have one?"

"No, and I never planned on it." She gives up trying to fight her way out of my arms and crosses her arms against her chest.

"Does that mean there's no chance for anything past this with us?" Her adamant refusal against relationship is a punch to the gut.

She silent for so long that I don't think she'll answer. She takes a deep breath and lets it out slowly. "I wouldn't be opposed to it, if it's with you." Bending her head back she looks at me. "You're different than anyone I've ever been with. I'm not just a piece of ass with you."

Well, that's good to know. I'm not sure what it says about me that I'm ranked right above douchebags she's gone out with. "Soooo, you're saying you'll give us a shot." I don't form it as a question on purpose.

Her head falls back on my chest. "Yes, I'll see where things go. But I'm not making any promises."

"I'm not asking you for any."

"And if things get too heavy, or begin being more than I can handle, I think we should put the brakes on the whole thing." She waves her hand around the apartment. "If things go South, we still have to live together. I'd like to do that as friends rather than enemies."

"Because we've been so cordial to each other this whole time."

She smacks my arm. "Shut up. It could be worse. We could be at each other's throats like I was with my last roommate."

"Yeah, let's be happy for that." She snuggles further into me, and presses play on the movie. I don't even care that we're watching a shitty horror movie. I've succeeded and have the girl. I only hope it stays that way.

THIRTEEN

Tiffany

WAKING up next to Spencer is strange and satisfying. I'm not even sure how that makes sense, but it does. He makes me feel better than I do on my own. Not because I feel like I need a man. I think the way I've handled relationships prior to this is a testament to that. It is that he's comfortable to talk to and doesn't judge me or scold me. I have enough of that with Stella and Audrey. For now, we'll see how this goes. I've never been with one person more than a couple of weeks, and even then I wasn't exclusive.

"Where are you going?" Spencer mumbles into the pillow as I slide out of bed.

"This little thing I like to call a job," I laugh. "Not all of us are lucky enough to work from home."

"Or, you can call in sick and stay in bed with me all day." He reaches out for me, trying to grab the bottom of my shirt and pull be back into his arms.

I twist to avoid his grasping hands. "I also have to pay rent. Unless, you're offering to pay my half."

"I could."

Yeah, we're not going down that route. We've barely started this whole relationship thing, and there's no way in hell I will rely on him to pay my bills. I may do it with my parents but they birthed me. It's in the rules to call them for help from time to time.

"I'm good," I search through my closet for my shirt and pants. "Besides, I enjoy working there. I get to meet new people every day and it's almost always busy." I shrug my shoulders as I pull out my clothes, "Time flies and I make good tips."

"If you say so," he tosses my pillow at me and misses.

I pick it up and throw it back at him, hitting him right in the face. "Clearly, you never played sports when you were younger."

"I preferred to mess with computers and play video games."

"I can tell," I wink at him and rush to the bathroom before he can throw another pillow at me.

My shower is quick since I woke up later than I usually do when I have to work. Spencer is waiting outside the bathroom door when I open it. "That's another rule you're breaking, Mister."

He lifts one shoulder not caring. "I'm more upset that you're fully clothed. What happened to the whole robe thing?"

"I didn't want to give you any ideas, and I'm already running late." I scoot by him, careful not to touch him. "I will not be tempted by you this morning. Besides, the rule still stands," I call back as I walk into my room.

"Seriously," he pouts and follows me. "That's a dumb rule now that you're my girlfriend."

"Not really," I shake my head, which is hard to do while trying to brush it at the same time. "It's still kind of creepy to have someone hanging around outside the bathroom door while you're showering."

"I literally just walked up to the door right as you opened it." He points his hand at the hallway. "My room is directly across the hall."

"If you say so," I smirk. "I guess I should consider it a win you're at least following my *wear clothes in the main parts of the apartment rule.*"

He nods his head up and down. "Yes, because I thought really hard about walking out here in my boxers, or even nothing at all."

"Jackass," I mutter under my breath. This man is so full of himself this morning. I kind of miss the shy, quiet guy from two days ago. That guy wouldn't have argued with me.

"What was that?" He walks closer to me, and I can't let him corner me. His reflection in the mirror showing how much distance he's covering. Stalking me and getting ready to pounce.

"Nothing," I sing-song and turn toward him. "I've gotta go." I give him a quick peck on the cheek, grab my bag, and rush out of the apartment. Is that what girlfriends do when they have to leave? I don't even know, I'm not usually around long enough for that part. We did this whole thing ass backwards since we lived together before we decided to see where things go. God, I hope this doesn't blow up in my face. I cannot afford to ruin things with yet another roommate, even if I am sleeping with this one.

I should have taken Spencer up on his offer to stay in bed all day. Janie is working this shift, and I completely forgot. I need to mentally prepare for the days we are stuck together. Oh well, it's too late to do anything about it now. Maybe I'll be lucky and she won't try to talk my ear off between tables and getting our orders.

That was too much to hope for. She's talking nonstop as I wait for the fries to be done for my table. I don't know what she's saying. I tuned her out after two words. "Are things still going well with your roommate?"

"Huh?" Shit, she will know I wasn't listening, now.

Janie just laughs and repeats the question. "Your roommate? Are things still okay in that area?"

"It's going really well, actually." She doesn't need to know that it only started going great about forty-eight hours ago.

"That's great." She nods her head toward the food counter, "Looks like your fries are ready."

"Thanks." I pick them up and add them to the tray of food in front of me. I feel kind of bad that she's so hung up on me not asking her to be my roomie. At the same time, I did just tune her out for a couple of minutes, and I just can't live with a person who needs to talk constantly.

I deliver the order to one of the small garden tables on the patio. It's a beautiful day to eat outside, and I'm slightly envious that this couple gets to enjoy lunch together. My mind needs to put brakes on those thoughts. It is *way* too early to be fantasizing about day dates with Spencer. *Ugh.* This is why I don't do relationships, especially with guys that I actually like. I will not end up like Audrey.

After returning the tray, I clean off the tables in my section. It's been a steady day, and the small break brings me some relief. That is until Janie comes to stand beside me. "Wow. Look at that hottie that just walked through the door."

I didn't realize people still said "hottie." It's something I haven't heard, or said, since I was in junior high. It doesn't stop me from glancing toward the door. It's okay to appreciate a good-looking man even if I'm seeing someone, right? My eyes widen at the sight of Spencer standing in the doorway, searching the room. "What is he doing here?"

"I take it you know him," Janie says. "Is he one of the guys you've dated?"

Geez, does she think I'm some floozy that flits guy to guy? She's not wrong, but did she have to say it like that? "He's my roommate." I feel no need to elaborate. What I do within my own walls is my business alone.

Janie's mouth drops open, and for once in all the time we've worked together she's speechless. I may have to drop bombs like this on her all the time. The work environment would be a hell of a lot better.

Spencer spots me and makes his way toward the table I'm clearing. "There you are." He gives me a peck on the cheek and wraps me in his arms.

"What are you doing here?" I whisper louder than I intend.

Janie grins and mutters, "I'd keep him as a roommate, too," before she walks off to take care of her own tables. I roll my eyes at her back and focus on Spencer again.

"I wanted to see where you worked, and I was getting hungry." He looks around the restaurant and then back at me. "Is that okay?"

And now I feel like shit for questioning him. I suck at *this*. "Yeah, it's fine." The worst girlfriend award should definitely go to me. "Sorry, Janie drives me insane."

"No worries." He sits at the table I finished cleaning as he walked in the door. "Is it cool if I sit here, or are there people ahead of me?"

"You're fine. You came in during one of our slow times." I look around my section to see if any of my tables need immediate help, but none do. I'm not sure what to do in this situation. None of the other guys I've *dated* have ever come to The Dreamcatcher before. "What do you want to eat? I can get your order in pretty quick."

He looks at me when I mention food. "Do you have a break coming up? I need to ask you something."

Oh crap. I have no idea what he's about to ask me, but I'm terrified. We literally became a thing yesterday. What the hell could he have to ask me. "Sure. Let me ask Janie if she'll watch my table."

She's waiting for me by the food counter like a lion ready to pounce. "Oh my gosh! He's your roommate and your boyfriend." She's bouncing up and down on her toes. "No wonder things are going great."

"Yes," I draw out. "Can you watch my tables while I take my break?"

"Absolutely." She looks over at the table he's sitting in. "I'll bring y'all some drinks and fries, too."

"Thanks." Maybe she's not as horrible as I've made her out to be.

I rush back to the table, and slide into the chair opposite him. "What's up?"

"What are you doing next weekend?"

"No idea," I shrug my shoulders. "I haven't gotten my work schedule, yet."

He taps his knuckles against the table, nerves getting the best of him. I wish he would come right out and ask whatever it is he's wanting an answer to. "If your boss hasn't made the schedule, can you ask for next weekend off?"

"Why?" He seems nervous to even ask me, and I'm ninety percent sure it has to do with the fact that we are a baby couple. We haven't yet found our legs, and probably won't for a while.

He grimaces. "Here's the thing. I have tickets to Comic Con next weekend.

A buddy of mine was supposed to go with me, but something came up. He's out. I really don't want to sell my tickets, but I don't want to go alone, either." He takes a deep breath. "That's where you come in. If you want to," he waves his hands toward me. "No pressure or anything. I understand if it's not something you're in to."

I bust out laughing. I can't help it. *That's* what he was so nervous to ask me? "Seriously?" Spencer's face falls, and he moves his hands from the tabletop to his lap. And now I feel like the biggest bitch that's ever lived. "Sorry. I'm not making fun of you, I swear. It's just that I was expecting some life changing question, but I definitely wasn't expecting that."

He perks up a bit at that. "Does that mean you'll go with me?"

I feel so bad that he's ashamed to like the things he does. Everyone has something they enjoy and they shouldn't have to hide it. I knew what I was getting into that first night I met him and saw the posters on his wall. I will not make him feel like shit about geeking out over comics. "Of course, I'll go. Getting off shouldn't be a problem since I work most weekends. That just means I'll have to work all week."

His shoulders sag in relief, and I hate that people have made him feel like crap because of his hobbies. I've always been a big believer in doing what you want. "He'll let you off just like that?"

"Perks of working here for a while." I lean in closer and beckon him to come closer. "Don't tell anyone, but I'm his favorite employee." I whisper. Smacking my hand on the table, "Besides, with all the extra shifts I've picked up, I deserve a weekend long break out of town. Just let me know the exact days, and I'll ask."

Janie brings over an order of fries and two sweet teas before winking at me and walking away. I'm sure I will get a million questions when Spencer leaves. He grabs a fry and dips it in ketchup. "I'm honestly surprised you said yes. I didn't think it would be something you're interested in." He pops the fry in his mouth and waits for me to say something.

"I've never been to anything like it, but I'm always up for trying new things."

"Good to know."

Now that I'm no longer freaking out over his big question, I can finish up my break and get back to work. I'm going to have to research what one wears to comic con so I can be fully prepared next weekend.

FOURTEEN

Spencer

We may be in the same city, but driving to the event venue is a pain. Traffic clogs the streets in every direction and it might have been faster walking here from the apartment. I'm just happy I got a hotel room next to the event, and Tiffany had no issues with staying there for the weekend.

"Wow," she says as she looks out the passenger side window. "You weren't playing when you said people dress up for this thing."

"It's fun for them." I spot a few people dressed up as various movie or comic characters walking down the sidewalk to the event. "A chance for them to be someone else for a day, or show their love for their favorite characters."

Tiffany turns toward me and raises her eyebrows. "Why aren't you dressed up? I know you have a couple of different characters that you love."

My cheeks redden. I've never brought a girl I was dating to one of these things. Most of them would outright laugh in my face, which is what I thought Tiffany was doing when I asked her. But, she didn't. How could she possibly understand how hard it was for me to ask her to take part in this part of my fandoms.

"I didn't want to scare you off. Most girls that aren't into comics and super-heroes are put off by this sort of thing." I reach across the console and grab her hand. "I don't want to ruin things before we've even had a chance to see what happens."

"Dude," she laughs. "You've seen, or heard, how badly I fight my cousins on conforming to their idea of life. I'm a huge advocate of people doing what makes them happy. I would never belittle you for wanting to have fun doing something you love."

"Thanks." Her reassurance dulls some anxiety I had about bringing her. Knowing that she won't make fun of me, the other fans, or cosplayers will make today much easier. We pull into the valet of the hotel we're staying at and grab our bags before they take off with the car. The event is right across the street, and I'm not trying to fight to get into their parking garage. "Let's get checked in and then we can head over."

As soon as we're in our room, I put away my suitcase and get our weekend passes. "Why are there two beds instead of one?"

It's a reasonable question, but I can't help laughing inside that it's her first question. "Because I was originally sharing the room with a friend, and I'm not a huge fan of cuddling with him. You, however," I sweep her into my arms, "are a different story. I'm good with whichever bed you want to sleep in."

"We'll see how today goes," she winks at me before breaking my hold. "Let's get this show on the road. I'm ready for a new adventure."

Her love of life and living with no rules no matter how things turn out is what drew me to her in the first place. One day, I hope I can be like this red-headed beauty, and not care what others think of me.

"Holy shit," Tiffany's eyes widen when she sees the line we have to get in. "I was *not* expecting so many people."

"This is nothing," I grin. "There will be more as the day goes on. Everyone in this line is a diehard fan and love going to Cons."

She's eyeing everyone and pointing out a few people with elaborate costumes. "Can we get pictures with the people dressed up? Please, say yes. I would love to get a shot with some of them to show Audrey and Stella."

Nodding my head, I pull her closer to me. "Yep. You just have to ask them first." I try to look at the event from her eyes, someone who has never been, or even realized this world exists. "The best part is when little kids come for the first time and see their favorite superheroes in real life. It's like Christmas morning for them."

"All I'm saying is if there is a hunky Thor, it might be hard to pull me away."

"I didn't know you liked Thor." In all the time I've spent watching shows on her *Netflix* account, I've never seen a superhero movie in any of the suggestions.

"It's more that I like Chris Hemsworth dressed up as Thor, but I've seen the movies plenty of times."

"That's good to know." I'm not as muscular as Thor, but I'm sure I could find something and wear it for her. I mean, it could be fun. Or it could blow up in my face and she'll dump me on the spot. Really, it might go either way. "Are you sure you're ready for this?"

"Absolutely," she grins and looks up at me. "It's a new experience. Let's do this thing."

The doors open and the line finally speeds up. When we get to the entrance, they check our badges and bags. I learned a long time ago to bring a backpack for any purchases I make. Let's be honest. I will buy a lot of stuff I don't really need, but I have to have it because it's part of one of my fandoms. "What do you want to do first?"

Tiffany is looking at the surrounding chaos. People dressed up, posters, and lines going in every direction. "I'm not even sure what there is." She glances at a board that has the events for today listed. "It's a little overwhelming. Even the big music festivals I've been to haven't been this… much."

"We can start off with a panel until you get your bearings." The market-place sign is to my left, and I wonder if she'd rather do that. "Or we can walk around the market hall and check out what the different shops have."

"There's shopping here?" She shrieks and jumps up and down. "Let's do that. Shopping is my other hobby besides going to concerts."

We turn into the room and run into cosplayers left and right. "Do you want to get a picture with any of them before we go any further?"

"I don't know who any of these people are supposed to be."

"It's okay. I'll explain which characters they are portraying when we get back to the room."

"Can you ask them?"

I walk over to the group and ask them if Tiffany can get a picture with them. Naturally, they all agree and she keeps talking to them after I've snapped the photos. I stand back and watch her take in this part of my life like a champ. She's asking them about the makeup and how long it takes to get ready. I love that she's not faking her excitement or interest.

"Where to next?" She loops her arm into mine and drags me toward the shop booths.

"Wherever you lead me," I laugh. I think I've lured her in. Hook, line and sinker. Hopefully, even if things don't work out between us, she'll continue to attend cons like this. She has the same sort of excitement I felt at the first one I went to.

We stop by a few booths. She's buying all sorts of fandom soaps and I have no idea how she's going to use them all. An art booth catches her eye and she pulls me to a stop. "I'm going to need a few of these for the living room. What do you think?"

The artist steps in front of us after overhearing her question. "If you like fantasy, I don't think you can go wrong with any of these. How long have you been together?"

"Two weeks," I say as I smile down at the woman who has captured my attention, and try to tamp down the fear of losing her that keeps bubbling up at unexpected times.

"Wow, and you already live together?" I feel like she's being a little judgy. Who is she to tell us how to do things? We could have known each other for years and just realized that we're perfect for each other.

"It's a long story," Tiffany laughs. "If I buy the ones I want now, can we leave them here until the end of the day?" She glances around the massive room. "I don't really want to carry around everywhere and risk damaging it."

"Absolutely," the woman beams at her. Of course she's all smiles now when she knows she's going to make a sale. Where are all your judgemental questions now?

"Thank you." Tiffany points out the ones she wants and hands the artist her card. "Spencer, can you make a note of which booth this is on your little map thingy? I don't want to forget when we come back for the art."

"You've got it," I pull the map out of my pocket and swing my backpack around to grab a pen. After the location has been marked, we continue on our way.

We're almost to the end of the marketplace area when Tiffany gasps. "Are they really doing tattoos here?"

I look around for the area she's talking about and notice the "Tattoo Zone". "Looks like it. Why?"

"I want to get one." She's steering me toward the line of tattoo artists, checking out their work, and trying to decide where she wants to get ink.

"Are you sure?" I don't have any tattoos. The thought of needles going into my skin repeatedly weirds me out.

"Yep." She stops in front of a booth with a sign that says *Life in Ink*. "And this is the artist I want to get it from."

A man with tattoos covering his arms walks up to us. "Hi, I'm Adrian. Are you looking to get some ink today?"

"Not me." I point to Tiffany, "her."

"Yes," she screams. "I've always wanted one, and what better time than during my first time at Comic Con."

"I couldn't think of a better reason to get one." Adrian smiles at her, and I don't like it. "Soph, can you bring the schedule for the rest of the day to see when we can fit…"

"Tiffany," my girlfriend supplies.

"Tiffany in." Adrian motions for a brunette girl to come over.

"Absolutely." The brunette comes over with a piece of paper and examines it like it's a test. "It looks like we have an opening in about two hours." She looks at Tiffany, "Will y'all still be around then?"

Tiffany turns her excited gaze to me, "Will we?"

"We're here all day, weirdo." She wraps an arm around my waist and I love that she is willingly letting this tattoo artist know that she's taken.

"Alright," Soph says and writes something on the form. "My *boyfriend* here is one of the best tattoo artists in Dallas. You won't be disappointed. Just have an idea of what you want him to do when you come back."

My heart lifts when she says the word boyfriend, and I know she did it for my benefit. Somehow she saw just how uncomfortable I was with Adrian smiling at Tiffany. I have got to get this jealousy bug under control. It's bad enough that I'm awkward in my own skin. I don't need to let that overflow into my relationship.

"Awesome," Tiffany gives Soph a high five. See, people do that when they are happy about something. I'm not going to bring that up here, though. "I want to check out whatever panel is going on right now. Preferably horror themed."

Who am I to deny this woman anything?

We're about to walk into one of the large meeting rooms when she stops. "By the way, we're going to have to go by a store tonight."

"Why is that?" The hotel we're staying in has room service and almost anything we could possibly want.

"Because you and I," she points back and forth between us. "Are going as Sam and Rowena from *Supernatural*. It's a perfect fit. You're tall, nerdy, and hot as hell. And I'm the red-headed, smart ass, witch."

"Works for me." I open the door and motion for her to go ahead of me. If she didn't have me falling for her before, she does now. Never in a million years did I think I would find my match. Someone to binge watch TV shows with, go to cons, and cosplay. I feel like I've just hit the damn jackpot.

FIFTEEN

Tiffany

I CAN'T BELIEVE I got a tattoo over the weekend. Audrey is going to lose her shit when she sees it. The whole weekend was amazing, and not even Janie's mindless chatter can bring me down.

"How was your weekend?" she asks while closing up the restaurant.

I'm not even sure how to describe it. "I went to Comic Con with Spencer."

"I feel bad for you, then." She sweeps her section and bends down to push the dirt into the dustpan. "One of my ex-boyfriends thought it would be a fun date, but I would have rather watched paint dry."

That seems a little harsh. "It couldn't have been all that bad." I can't imagine anyone going and not having the time of their lives.

"It wasn't great either." She tosses what she collected in the dustpan in the trash. "I was bored out of my mind. There is nothing fun about hanging out with grown ass people playing dress up."

Whatever brownie points she had with me are going right out the window. "Don't you do the same thing on Halloween?"

"Yeah, but that's different. These people do it all the time. Whereas, I might do it once a year."

I'm choosing not to comment on that. Why does she care what they do with their time? They aren't forcing her to hang out with them, or dress up. I was impressed with the amount of work the cosplayers put into their costumes. Everything was so detailed and looked like it belonged in a movie. I felt like a phony when Spencer and I dressed up on the second day. "Well, I think I will head out if we're done." This conversation is going downhill and I don't want to hear anymore from her.

"Yep," she heads to the kitchen. "That was the last bit that needed to be cleaned up."

"Alrighty, I'll see you on our next shift together." I walk to the break room to gather my things and let Dennis know I'm leaving. He's been doing his best to keep Janie and I off the same shifts, but it's not always possible. It will be a lot easier when we find another waitress to balance out the workload. The problem is he can't find anyone dependable. They show up for a couple of days then disappear when they realize this job isn't easy.

"I'm out of here, Dennis."

"Be careful on your way home. Do you still want extra shifts?"

A couple of weeks ago, the answer would have been a resounding yes, but now I'm enjoying my free time with Spencer. "Not really." He says nothing and I add, "unless you need me. Then I'll be here."

"You're fine. I just wanted to make sure." He straightens the stack of papers in his hands. "I'm glad everything is working out. Tell Janie to head out when you leave. I just need to finish up this paperwork and I'll be going home."

"Will do." I wave before turning toward the main area. "See you later. Don't work too hard."

"Never," he laughs. "That's what I have y'all for."

"Whatever, Old Man." I hurry down the hall to go back to the dining area. "Janie."

"Yeah," she calls from the kitchen.

"Dennis said it's time to get out of here." Despite her pissing me off with her comments about the cosplayers, I'm not a total bitch. "Have a great rest of the night."

"You too," she hollers on her way to the break room.

The sky outside the front windows is pitch black, and although the tips are better when I work evenings, I hate having to get home in the dark. I let myself out of the door, locking it once I'm outside. Janie will have to go out the back since she hasn't been here long enough to be given a key to open or close on her own.

The key is being a pain, and I don't realize that someone has come up behind me until they wrap their arms around me and I scream. Pulling the key out of the lock, I whip around to face my attacker, ready to stab. But they pull back, hands in the air. "Calm down. It's just me."

"You gave me a mini heart attack, Spencer." I slap him with the hand not holding the keys. "Don't you know you're supposed to announce yourself before you sneak up on someone?"

"That would negate the sneaking part, I think." He laughs and dodges my next hit. "Next time I'll remember to cough loudly so you know I'm here."

Dennis comes running around the corner, and skids to a stop in front of the door. Wow, for a man his age, he sure can move. He unlocks the door and throws it open. "Is everything okay? I heard screaming." I'm actually a little surprised with all the street traffic. Being downtown brings in background noise at all hours of the day.

"Yes," I sigh. "I'm fine. My bonehead boyfriend is the cause."

Spencer winces when the words leave my mouth. "Hi," he extends a hand toward Dennis. "I'm Spencer, the bonehead boyfriend."

"So you're the reason she's been more chipper than usual." Dennis grasps Spencer's outstretched hand and shakes it. "It's nice to meet you, I'm Dennis."

"And you're the reason she avoided the apartment so much when I first moved in."

Dennis holds his hands up in surrender. "I only did what I was asked. She wanted more hours, and I gave them to her."

"Understandable." Spencer puts his hands in his pockets and takes a step back. "I just came to pick her up."

"I'm happy someone is looking out for her," Dennis nods toward the guy who is slowly capturing my heart. "Someone needs to. This girl worries me sometimes."

"Hello," I wave my hands up and down. "That girl is standing right here and is perfectly capable of doing things." Frustration that they are talking about me like I'm a child fills me. This is something Stella and Audrey would do. Well, old Stella. She's mellowed out a lot since she's starting dating Johnny.

"I know you are," Dennis concedes. "I only wish you'd think things through a little more."

"Noted." Now he sounds like my parents and I'm not sure how I feel about that. "Are you ready to get out of here?" I grab Spencer's hand and pull him down the sidewalk. "I'll see you later, Dennis."

"I'll text the new schedule to you in the morning. Have a great night," he calls to our retreating backs.

Spencer bends down and whispers in my ear, "I parked in the other direction."

"Just go with it," I bite back. "We'll wait a few minutes and then turn around."

"Are you okay?"

"Yeah," I sigh. "Just annoyed with my boss. He's never once said anything like what he did to you. I know he cares, but there's a better way to go about voicing it than what he just did."

Spencer glances behind us before pulling me into his arms. "I think we're good to go. But, before we do, I want you to know that I think you're fully capable of taking care of yourself. We all make mistakes, but it's a chance for us to learn from them."

"Thanks," I mutter. "I needed to hear that."

His lips graze my forehead and everything he said feels true. I mean, I did what I thought was best when I let my cousins pick my roommate. So far that is working out better than I thought it would. We turn around, passing The Dreamcatcher once again, and get into his car parked at the end of the block.

"Let's get out of here," he grabs my hand after putting the car in drive. He merges into the traffic easily, but he misses the turn we need to take to go home.

"Where are we going?" I'm not sure I have the energy to do anything else today and my tattoo is itching. I dig through my purse for the lotion I threw in there this morning.

His gaze meets mine for the briefest moment before he focuses on the road again and smiles. "It's a surprise."

Instead of complaining about being tired, I sit back and enjoy the ride. The red taillights blurring by as we get on the highway on our way to an unknown destination. Dennis's worries still wiggle in the back of my head, but I will not focus on them. I'll talk to him when I go back into work. It's not worth ruining my mood for the rest of the night even though I wish we were heading home to snuggle up on the couch while binge watching TV.

I must have fallen asleep because I open them when the car comes to a stop and Spencer puts it into park. "Rise and shine, Sleepyhead."

"Sorry," I mutter. "I didn't realize I was that tired. Was I asleep long?"

"Nope," he shakes his head. "Only about ten minutes. We're still in Austin."

"Good to know." I'm not prepared to go anywhere else. Loud music accompanies the sound of cars driving up and down the street, and my interest is piqued. "Are we at a bar?" It's been a while since I've been out. Audrey doesn't like going, and from the look of the grungy walls, this isn't a place I would normally frequent.

"Yep." He turns the car off and rushes around to open the door for me. Ever the gentleman, this one. "There is a local band playing here tonight similar to what you like. I thought since you went to Comic Con with me, I would treat you to a night of music."

"It's like you know how to read me or something." I grab his hand, letting him pull me out of the car.

"I like to think I do," he shuts the door behind me. "And it looks like you might need it today."

He has no idea. Between the crap with Janie, then Dennis's comments… I need to decompress. The only thing that has ever worked besides a night out with my cousins is music. There's a short line at the door, but we bypass it completely. "Are you special or something?"

"I know the owner," Spencer grins. "I designed the website for this bar."

"Wow, look at you," I laugh. "Any other bars you've done tech work for? It would be awesome to get out of some of those lines."

"Doubt it," he gives me a knowing look. "But I can always check." It's nice to have a boyfriend with connections. I mean, if things work out between us.

If I thought the music outside was loud, it's deafening in this small bar. The outside looks bigger than the inside, and while it would put most people off, I feel at home here. The band on stage isn't all that bad either.

The atmosphere is chaotic but cozy at the same time as if I'm on the same musical high as the band playing. These are my people. I wrap my arms around Spencer and wonder how I found a guy that gets me so completely. More than even my cousins have and I've known them my entire life.

SIXTEEN

Spencer

SEEING Tiffany completely let go of all her stresses at the concert the other night was exactly what I hoped for her. I don't know what prompted me to take her. It was just a gut feeling that she needed a pick me up. Apparently, I was right. She never told me what put her in a bad mood, but I don't think it was just her boss's comments. We're working on her opening up more. I want to break down all the walls she has put up.

A quick glance at the clock tells me I have roughly three hours to finish up this project before Tiffany gets back. The great part about working from home is I can sync my schedule with hers. Normally, I'm a night owl and do everything then. But, I've noticed I get much quicker responses when I work during the day like normal people. This should have occurred to me before, but I'm stubborn and don't like changing my routine unless I have a good reason to do it. And Tiffany is definitely a good reason.

My phone rings, and I'm hoping it's Tiffany calling during her break. Sadly, it's not. Mr. Harrison, also known as my pain in the ass client, is who shows up on the screen.

"Hello," I answer on the third ring, not wanting him to think I'm making myself too available. He'll take advantage of it.

"Spencer," he yells into the phone. "I'm glad I caught you."

"Is there something you wanted to discuss? I'm putting the finishing touches on the app you wanted for your customers." Please, don't let this be a call to change things.

"About that." Here we go. I really need to put a limit on how many changes can be made before they are charged more. "Can you change the colors again? Also, some of my employees tested out the app and they said the buttons aren't linking to the correct inventory."

I pull up the notes app on my laptop and start typing in his requests, even though I'm sure he will change his mind… again. "I can change the colors, no problem. Is the color scheme on the website changing as well? It's easier if they branded in the same style."

"Yes," he replies. "Our tech department is working on that now. What about the buttons not linking?" His voice is panicked and I'm not sure if I want to scream or sigh.

"As long as you send me the color codes, I can get those switched out." I take a deep breath and tell him the same thing I've told him time and time again. "The buttons aren't linking through because it's not live yet. When you send the information on the inventory set up, I can put those into the app and everything will work seamlessly."

"Thank goodness," he breathes right into the phone. "I was starting to worry since the launch date for the app is looming."

This, ladies and gentlemen, is why you don't promise customers something by a certain date. When changes are made this late in the game, it's almost never going to be ready in time. "If you get me the information in the next couple of days, I'll make the changes and have it over to you for approval by the end of next week."

"You are a lifesaver, Spencer." He says something to somebody else and then continues to the conversation he is having with me. "I'll get the new information sent over as soon as possible." Then he hangs up. No goodbye, or thank you, just silence on the other end of the line. I swear Mr. Harrison is going to drive me to drink.

Now that I'm stuck waiting on his crap, I need to see what else is in the queue. There's nothing pressing though. Most of my other clients have their shit together before they even contact me. They know what they want and send it over in a nice checklist format. I wish Mr. Harrison was more like that. It would make my job a hell of a lot easier.

I'm about to close my computer down when an email pops up. It's not from the form on my website, but I recognize the name of the email. It's the band that played the other night.

Spencer,

Well, I hope this is the right Spencer. Rob showed us the website you created for him, and we would like for you to create ours. We've been using social media, but if we want to have a presence, we know we need to up our game. Hit me up with your rates and we'll talk.

-Dale

It's good to know that Rob was so impressed with my work that he referred me Crooked Halo. Now I need to figure out if I will work with Dale, or not. They are a newbie band and I'm sure they don't have what I charge for complete website builds. On the other hand, I've never created a site for a band, and it could be fun. I'll ask Tiffany what she thinks when she gets home. She can sense whether something is a good idea, and her opinion matters to me.

❧

"What's that delicious smell?" Tiffany calls out. I've been in my room playing video games and ignoring all work responsibilities. I'll get it done. Mr. Harrison's app is the most pressing one, and he still hasn't gotten the information back to me.

I walk out of the room and down the hallway, wearing clothes per *her* rules. You'd think she'd lay off them, but nope, she's stubborn as hell. "Some casserole my mom sent home with me."

She throws her bag on the counter and wraps her arms around me. "Has your mom made all the meals you've been cooking?"

"I swear you never look in the freaking freezer." I walk her backward until I'm in front of the refrigerator and open the freezer door. "Any time I visit her she sends food with me. I can't cook for shit."

"At least you're honest about it," she laughs. "Most guys would have taken all the credit. Then one day their girlfriend, or wife, will find them unloading casserole dishes from their car and hiding them behind the ice cream."

"You realize not everyone eats ice cream, right? Some people actually use their freezers for real food."

She pulls away from me. "Last time I checked ice cream has dairy in it. And, dairy is a food group. Therefore… Ice cream is real food."

"Is this an argument I can win?"

She scrunches up her nose, looking adorable. "Probably not. Better cut your losses while you can." She looks around me at the stove. "How long until it's ready?"

"About thirty-ish minutes. Why?"

"Good, I want to get cleaned up." She pulls her shirt away from her and groans. "One of the cooks called in sick and I offered to help in the kitchen. It reminded me why I prefer giving people their food instead of cooking it. I burned at least ten things today."

"All I'm hearing is that you can't cook, either."

"Why do you think I have so much ice cream and frozen pizza? If I tried to cook something, there's a big likelihood that I would catch the whole building on fire."

"Noted." I push her toward the hallway. "Go take a shower. I'll get the plates and stuff out. It should be ready when you get out."

"Or, you could join me…" She lets the statement trail off, waiting for my response.

"Then we'd both starve. There's plenty of time for that later." I shoo her away. "Besides, I have some news, and I want to get your opinion on it."

She crosses her arms across her chest, and all it does it amplify how well-endowed she is. "You realize I have zero patience, and need to know now, right?"

"You'll have to wait."

"Ugh," she stomps her foot. Is it weird that I'm attracted to her even when she's trying to throw a tantrum? "You sound just like Stella and Audrey."

"I've been called worse. Go take a shower."

She doesn't say anything else and stomps toward the bathroom. The door slamming shut to show how much I've annoyed her.

Our food is separated onto plates and sitting on the coffee table when Tiffany gets out of the shower. I would advocate for a kitchen table, except there's no room for one in this tiny apartment.

"So are you going to tell me the news?" She sits down and looks at the plate. "What is that?" Revulsion. It's written all over her face. "How can something that smells so good come out of the oven looking like something a cat threw up?"

"It's chicken spaghetti. It's supposed to look like that." I see what she means, but it tastes better than it looks. "You've never had it?"

"Uh, no," she shakes her head back and forth. "And I'm not sure I want to try it now."

"Just take a bite, you big baby." I twirl some noodles onto my fork and fly it through the air like an airplane. Her mouth is tightly sealed. "If you try it, I'll tell you the news."

Tiffany glares at me, but she finally opens her mouth. Her eyes close, and she makes a *mmm* sound. "Okay, so it's not that bad." She swallows and picks up her own plate and fork, digging in like she didn't insult it moments ago. "Now, tell me the news."

"Remember that band we saw the other night, Crooked Halo?" She nods while shoveling food in her mouth. It's like she hasn't eaten all day, and I wonder when they will hire more people so she's not juggling so much. "Well, they sent me an email today and want me to build them a website."

"That's fantastic," she bounces up and down on the couch, spaghetti noodles sliding to the edge of her plate. She scoops them back toward the middle and sets the plate down before another near spill happens. "You're going to do it, right?"

"I wanted to get your opinion on it before I answered."

"Hell yes! You should do it. They were fantastic and big things are coming for them. Mark my words."

"Are you sure?" I pause while she nods emphatically. "It will definitely push my boundaries. I've only ever taken on corporations, and this will be a whole new ballgame."

"Absolutely." She picks up her plate to eat again. "First thing in the morning, you better send them a response." Grabbing the remote, she pulls up the show we've been binge-watching. "But now, we watch. I need to know what happens next." I've already seen this entire series multiple times, but seeing her get into it makes me happy. We're on the episode where some heavy stuff goes down with a relationship and the character decides it's best to leave the woman he loves to protect her. I wonder if I can wedge in a question without her guard going up.

I'm about to ask her why she's so jaded, but she talks first. "That must have been so hard for him." She sighs and leans into me. "He was the happiest he's ever been, and to just leave like that. It's terrible."

"Agreed," I nod against the top of her head. "Speaking of…"

"Why do I get the feeling we're about to have an uncomfortable conversation?"

"Because we are, sort of." She moves until she's sitting in front of me. "You don't have to answer, but what happened that made you rebel against relationships? Who hurt you so badly?"

She pulls one of the throw pillows into her lap and groans. This isn't a conversation she wants to have. "You know how I told you that my cousins and I have always been close?"

"Yeah, but I don't see what that has to do with anything."

"Well, Stella has always lived in Austin, but Audrey and I lived in this super tiny town up by the Oklahoma border. I idolized Audrey and in my eyes she could do no wrong. I wanted to be just like her… Until I didn't."

"Okay," I draw out.

"She had a boyfriend, and he seemed like the perfect guy. He always let me tag along with them because he knew I was part of the package with Audrey. Where she went, I went. Well, right before the second semester of their senior year started he dumped her and it *destroyed* her. She wouldn't get out of bed and I had to force her to eat. It was bad."

Tiffany takes a deep breath and continues her story. "The two of them were so involved with each other. They literally did everything together, and there wasn't any room for them to breathe. I was fourteen at the time and all I saw was the pain my cousin went through."

"That had to have been confusing at such a young age. To see someone you love hurting so much."

"It was. But it also showed me not to give all of myself to someone. I knew that if I ever did that, I would open myself up to the heartbreak Audrey went through." She pulls the pillow close to her chest. "That is why I've never gotten into a serious relationship. There's less pain that way. As long as the other person knows that things won't go further than a fun time, then we're good."

Damn. Something she saw when she was a teenager has shaped her whole view of relationships. "Did the guy give her a reason for breaking up with her?"

"Nope. And that was the hardest part for her. A few weeks later she saw him at a party with another girl, and it sent her into a spiral once again."

"So where does that leave us?" I don't want to ask, but I feel like I need to after hearing her story. After finding out just how against relationships she is. "Are we just having a good time, or can you see something more with me?"

She shrugs her shoulders and looks everywhere but at me. "I don't know. I like being with you. You're fun and get me on a level even my cousins and most people in my life don't. All I can say is I'm willing to see where things go with us. I can't make any promises, though."

I guess that's better than hearing her say I'm disposable. "That's good enough for me. At least for right now. We can see what the future holds for us one day at a time." I'm not lying when I say it even though it pains me to utter those words. I pull her back to me and press play on the show. I'll just make damn sure she has no reason to get rid of me.

SEVENTEEN

Tiffany

THE PAST FEW weeks with Spencer have been amazing. Even though I told him I can't make any promises, he's choosing to stick around. All while I'm still trying to wrap my head around why. There's nothing that stands out. I'm a party girl and have been since I moved out of my parent's house. Though recently, I've been going out less and less because I haven't really felt the urge to. I'm enjoying the dinners and TV marathons with Spencer. We may have done this thing backwards, but it might have been what I needed to make me see there's more to relationships. When Justin broke up with Audrey, it made me lose any hope I had of finding someone for me.

"Tiffany," Dennis calls my name making me jump.

My hand hits my water bottle, knocking it down as water spills all over the table. "Shit," I mutter, rushing for the paper towels to clean it up before someone comes in here and falls.

"I didn't mean to scare you."

I roll my eyes, "Sure you didn't."

"It wasn't my intention, I promise." He grabs the roll of paper towels and tears off a few sheets to help me. "Your break is over."

"Sorry," I wince. I've never been so lost in thought at work that time flew by so quickly. "I didn't realize it was up. I'll finish getting this cleaned up and head back out there."

"Is everything okay?"

"Yeah," grabbing the towels out of Dennis's hand, I wad them up with my own and throw them in the trash. "Just trying to figure out what makes me girlfriend material."

He places a hand on my shoulder and waits until I look up at him. "I'm sure there are a ton of reasons besides the fact that you are intelligent and kind."

"You're just saying that because you're my boss."

"No, I'm saying it because you're the most dependable employee I have and you've grown leaps and bounds since I hired you." He removes his hand and nods toward the door. "Don't second guess yourself. Y'all are a cute couple."

"Thanks." It's time for me to get out there and do my job. I'll ponder my misgivings later when I'm not at work, which is easier said than done. Why do I keep trying to find ways to sabotage this relationship? It has barely lifted off the ground.

It doesn't help that I got a text from Spencer asking if I wanted to have dinner with his parents. Are we even at that stage yet? This is new territory, and I'm unsure how to navigate it. There's only one person I know actually in a relationship and I need her advice now more than ever.

Come on. Pick up the phone. The Dreamcatcher is empty, and it's the only time I can call Stella without worrying about Spencer overhearing me. Or letting him know just how much I'm letting my mind mess with me.

"Wow, long time no talk." She finally answers the phone. "I was wondering if you forgot about me."

"No, I didn't forget about you," I wipe down the table in front of me before putting the chairs upside down on top of it. "I've just been preoccupied."

"I take it things are going well with Spencer?"

"Yeah," I hesitate, wondering if I should even tell her we've started dating. But, I did call her to ask for advice, so I might as well get it all out there. "We're actually dating."

She laughs, and I realize how much I've missed her. I've been so wrapped up in hanging out with Spencer that I haven't made the time to call her like I used to. I can't even remember that last time Audrey and I did Sunday brunch. "I was wondering how long it would be before y'all hooked up."

"It's kind of hard to resist a guy when you've already seen him naked."

"That's very true." I can hear the knowing smile in her voice and I'm happy that she's found her person. "I mean, Johnny was half naked when he came to rescue me from that stupid snake."

I could let her keep talking and put off what I want to talk to her about, but I'm not one to hold my thoughts in. I never have been. "How long were you and Johnny dating before you met his parents?"

She's silent, and I worry she's not going to answer me. "A couple of months, I think. Why?"

"Spencer asked if I wanted to have dinner with his, and I don't know how to respond."

"How long have the two of you been officially dating?"

Ugh, I have no idea. He's been living with me almost three months. "A little over a month?"

"Before I get into that," I can imagine her ticking off the finger with her palm up. "First of all, you better never wait that long to call me again. It's like you get a boyfriend and forget all about me." She takes a deep breath. "Second, if you think it's too soon, then don't agree to it. There's no right, or wrong way to be in a relationship. You just do what your gut says."

"My gut feelings have a tendency to get me in trouble," I argue. "That's the whole reason y'all had to find me a roommate."

"I know. But you're a smart cookie, you'll make the right choice no matter what it is."

"And…" I trail off, not wanting to admit my insecurities. "I'm not even sure what he sees in me. I'm not good girlfriend material. I'm barely friend material."

"Nope," she interrupts me. "Do *not* go down that train of thought. You are amazing. At least, once you get past the temper tantrums and *it's all about me* attitude."

"I'm not that bad." I move on to the next table and clear it off. I don't normally like being here by myself, but tonight I relish it. Spencer and I have been spending so much time together, and work is the only place I've been able to be alone. He hasn't pushed me about committing to more than right now, but I know he wants to.

"Do I need to remind you of the fit you threw when I told you I was *temporarily* moving?"

"In my defense, you did eventually move there permanently. So, you can't throw that in my face." Lifting these chairs is a pain to do with one hand, but I'm not ready to get off the phone with Stella.

"I'll give you that," she sighs. "Just take it day by day. And maybe don't tell Audrey about y'all dating. There's no telling how she'll react since she was so against him living there when she found out you slept with him."

Hiding things from Audrey doesn't sit well with me, but Stella has a point. She's sure to give me a lecture. Telling me how reckless I'm being and that I should end it now. "Okay. I won't tell her. I think if I really want to give this whole relationship thing a shot, I need to do things most couples do. Even if it means an uncomfortable dinner with his parents."

"Why does it have to be uncomfortable?"

"Because what if they know he was meant to be a one-night stand?"

"Oh Tiffany," she laughs. "I'm almost a hundred percent sure he didn't tell them that. If he did, run as fast as you can. That's a definite over share of information to his parents."

"Good point," I concede. "I'll call you and tell you how the dinner goes. I need to finish getting the restaurant cleaned up so I can go home."

There's a knock at the front door, and Spencer is standing outside with a light jacket on. "Okay, Tiff. You better call me more often. I miss you and love you."

"Love you, too." I hang up and go to the door to let Spencer in. "Hey, you." Did I really just say that? If there's anything that will give away he was the topic of conversation, it's that oddly high-pitched statement.

He doesn't comment on it, though. He comes in and sweeps me in his arms. "I wasn't sure what time you'd be done, so I came early."

I laugh and pull away from him. "You know you don't have to pick me up, right? I've been getting home on my own for some time now."

He rolls his eyes and grins. "I'm perfectly aware of that. But when you work late, I'm not a huge fan of you taking public transportation. So many things could go wrong."

I finish wiping down the tables, and he puts the chairs on top. "Now you sound like Audrey." Sweeping and mopping are the last things on the to-do list and I can go home. The only time my brain doesn't worry over being with Spencer is when I'm actually with him. "I just have a couple of things to finish up and we can leave."

"Anything I can help with?"

"Not unless you've figured out a way to sweep and mop at the same time."

He taps his finger against his chin. "Maybe I'll come up with a program that does just that."

"You'd be a millionaire," I giggle. "Now move out of the way so I can get this done."

Thirty minutes later and I'm locking up the door. It's almost ten-thirty, but people are still driving around the city. I used to be one of those people. Before Spencer, I would head straight to a club, or concert, as soon as I left work. Now, though… I just want to go home and spend time with him. Flashes of Justin and Audrey constantly being together enter my mind, but I do my best to shake them away. This is different. I know my boundaries. At least, I think I do.

Spencer grabs my hand and we walk to his car. "So, did you give any more thought to eating dinner with my parents?"

"Yes," I answer, slowly. "I'm game. I've never actually done the whole meet the parents' thing so I'm a little nervous."

"You shouldn't be," he gives my hand a reassuring squeeze. "They will love you."

I sure as hell hope so. If they don't, I'm not sure what I'll do. He seems to be close to them, and I don't want to cause a rift. Rather than focus on that on the way home, I think about how nice it will be snuggled up against Spencer, throwing all my self-doubt out of the window. He's been in my bed more often than his own these days, and I'm oddly enough, perfectly okay with it.

EIGHTEEN

Spencer

THE DRIVE to my parents is silent. Tiffany keeps her gaze focused on the window and her knee bouncing nonstop. It's weird seeing someone nervous to meet my parents. They are the most non-threatening people I know. Any past girlfriends I've brought over were eager to meet them. She looks like she wants to hurl herself out of the car while I'm still driving.

I turn the music down and rest a hand on her knee. She stops moving it and looks over at me. "It's going to be okay. You know that, right?"

"No," she shakes her head. "I don't. I'm not sure I can do this." Placing a hand on top of mine, she grips it so hard I'm not sure I'll have blood coursing through it by the time we get there. "I thought I could, but I've never done this before."

"Do you want to go back home?" She doesn't answer me, and I continue, "I can make up a reason we have to cancel. I'm not going to force you to do something you're not ready to do."

Her grip on my hand loosens, and her shoulders relax. "No, I don't want to go back home. This is normal, I think. Meeting your parents shouldn't be this terrifying."

"You have nothing to worry about." I hope she can hear the sincerity in my voice. "My mom might try to pepper you with questions, but Dad and I will do our best to keep that from happening."

"That doesn't make me feel any better." She groans and drops her head into her free hand.

"You've got this, Tiffany." I give her knee a gentle squeeze. "We'll come up with a code word, and if you feel uncomfortable work it into the conversation and we'll say our goodbyes."

She turns her head, hair hanging in her face, and stares at me. "What did I do to find such an amazing person? I'm not even sure what you see in me."

"I see everything in you." I take the exit to my parents' house, pull into a gas station and put the car in park. "You represent everything I'm too scared to do unless I'm dressed up like my favorite character. You're energetic and live life day to day, never apologizing for enjoying whatever you take on." I sweep the hair out of her eyes, my thumb brushing against her jawline.

"Too bad most of the decisions I make end up making my life, and sometimes other's lives, difficult." She leans into my hand and let's me soothe away her fear.

"Nobody is perfect," I slide my hand under her chin and lift her face until her eyes meet mine. "Well, except for maybe me."

"You are so full of shit," she rolls her eyes and tries to swat my hand away.

Instead of arguing with her, I lean in until my mouth touches hers. She opens up for me, wrapping her arms around my neck, pulling me closer. Well, as close as possible considering the console between us. This feels right. Regardless of whatever fears she has about us or what happened to Audrey, there was a reason I ran into her at that concert then answered that roommate ad.

My phone dings bringing us back to reality. "That's probably my mom wondering where we are."

"I guess," she sighs. "But you can't just kiss me stupid anytime you want to win an argument."

"Is that another rule?"

"Yes," she nods. "Yes, it is. Rule number five, or is it six? Hell, I don't remember anymore. No more kissing if it's to keep me from arguing."

"That goes for you, too."

"Why do you always turn my own rules against me?" She mutters under her breath, but I still hear it. I put the car in drive and continue to my childhood home.

Tiffany stands frozen between the passenger door and car. "You know you have to move to shut it, right?"

She nods and stares at my parents' house. "I know that. I'm trying to psych myself up. It's the only way I'll be able to get through dinner." Shaking my head, I grab her hand and pull her away from the car. "What code word do you want to use?"

"Huh," her eyes widen. "What are you talking about?"

"We discussed having a word to bail. Just tell me which word you want to use, and when you say it, we'll go."

"Oh yeah," she taps her finger against her chin. "Let's go with banana."

"Banana?" That's a strange word. How in the hell is she going to work that into a sentence without it sounding off?

"Yep," she nods her head, and bumps the door with her hip. It slams shut and she jumps. "Sorry, still nervous."

"Don't be." Neighborhood kids are playing in the street. It's a form of hockey and I think about all the times I wanted to join in when I was a kid, but was never invited. Nobody likes the person they assume is a know-it-all because they make good grades. They'd rather exclude that person. I shake the thoughts from my head and bring Tiffany to my side. "They will love you."

She grips my hand so hard my knuckles turn white and takes unsteady steps up the porch stairs. A shadow crosses in front of the living room window, and I know Mom has been watching, waiting for us to decide when we're going to come in. At least she gave us that small bit of privacy. Normally, she'd come out and ask what's taking so long. I send a silent thank you into the air and knock on the door.

"Spencer," Mom says before she completely opens it. "You know good and well that you don't have to knock."

I shrug my shoulders and lean in for a hug. "It's the polite thing to do when I bring a guest."

"You must be Tiffany," Mom reaches around me and grabs Tiffany's free hand. "I've heard so much about you."

"Uh, hi Mrs. Warren," she shakes her hand but Mom hasn't let go and she's becoming uncomfortable. "Spencer has been feeding me all the food you've sent home with him."

"Oh," Mom's eyebrows raise. "I didn't realize both of you were eating them. How did you like them?"

"They were delicious," Tiffany smiles and pries her hand out my mom's grip. "It's been a while since I've had a home-cooked meal."

"That's a shame." She glances at the kids playing in the street and shakes her head. "What a terrible hostess I'm being. Come on in. I'm putting the finishing touches on dinner, but you can hang out in the living room with Dad. He's watching some show about ancient civilizations on *History Channel*."

We step inside, and I close the door behind us, prepared to lead Tiffany into the living room and hoping mom didn't pull out the baby albums. But Tiffany stops. "Do you need any help?" Considering how terrified she was to come inside, I'm surprised she offered. I glance between her and my mom, waiting for the answer.

"That's so kind of you," Mom finally says. "But, you're a guest. Take some time to relax. There isn't much left to do."

Tiffany's entire body sags in relief. Once Mom is heading back toward the kitchen and I whisper in her ear. "Why did you offer to help?"

"I wanted to give a good impression," she mutters back. "I told you, I have no idea what I'm doing. Offering to help always works in the movies, and I thought it might win me some brownie points."

Bumping into her shoulder, I smile. "She already likes you. You don't have to do anything you're not comfortable with." She sidles closer to me and I wrap an arm around her waist as I lead her into the living room. "Now, it's time to meet my dad."

He's sitting in his favorite recliner, despite how much Mom hates it, she doesn't get rid of it. The chair is leaned back, and an excited voice is talking about ruins at such a loud volume, I cringe. "Dad." He doesn't hear me, and I lean closer. The old man is asleep and I can't stop the laugh from leaving my mouth.

"What's so funny?" Tiffany asks from behind me.

I lean back, and point toward my father's prone figure lying in the chair. "Apparently waiting for us tired him out." I run my hand through my hair. "Or, Mom put him to work this morning, and he's exhausted. One of my favorite things about not living here anymore. No chores."

"And here I thought, I was your favorite part of moving out." She pulls her hand out of mine and crosses her arms over her chest, bottom lip sticking out. Pouting will get her nowhere. "I didn't even know it was you I might be moving in with." I roll my eyes and bend down to my dad again. "Dad," I whisper. "Dad," a little louder this time. I swear this man could sleep through a tornado. This time I grab hold of his arm and shake. "Dad, wake up."

"I'm up, I'm up." He jumps up and almost hits me in the face with his flailing arms. "What did I miss?" He's looking around the room and his eyes widen when he registers that I'm standing in front him. "When did you get here?"

"About five minutes ago," I laugh. "How long have you been asleep?"

Dad runs his hand over his balding head and grunts. "I was only resting my eyes."

"Sure you were." I gesture for Tiffany to step up. "Dad, this is Tiffany," I wave my hand toward her. "Tiffany, this is my dad."

"It's nice to meet you, Mr. Warren." She holds out her hand waiting for him to shake it.

He doesn't, though. He lifts the lever on his recliner until it's back into a sitting position and stands up. "We hug around here." He pulls her into a warm embrace and her eyes go wide. It would comical if I didn't see panic written all over her face. "It's good to meet you, Tiffany."

She untangles herself from his arms and takes two steps back, peeking over at the TV. "What are you watching?"

"Before my eyes closed," he gives me a pointed look. "It was a show on the Mayan ruins. Interesting stuff." Yeah, so *interesting* he passed smooth out while he was watching.

She doesn't say anything right away, instead waiting for the commercial to come to an end. Once the show's title comes up, she leans closer to my dad and whispers, "It looks like the same show is still on. I don't think you were asleep for very long."

That small reassurance means a lot to my dad, and he beams. "We'll keep my small nap a secret. Just between us or his mom will have my butt."

I snort, "I thought you were just resting your eyes."

"Exactly," he winks at Tiffany before telling us to make ourselves at home. I think he forgets that I'm not the guest, but I'm also not going to correct him. Some of the tension Tiffany held while meeting my mom has diminished, and I know she's going to get along great with Dad. Mom can be a little difficult sometimes, especially when things don't go the way she expects them to.

Dad sits back in his recliner and we sit on the couch, our attention on the TV. Tiffany is completely relaxed now that the attention is off of her. She can be in the zone without a single worry. The TV has her full attention, and I didn't realize she liked documentaries. Nothing on her *Netflix* account has suggested that she would. I'm not going to question it, though. It will ruin the moment. Instead, I place my arm behind her head on the back of the couch, basking in this moment where she's not freaking out and wondering if she's good enough to be a part of my life.

Mom calls from the kitchen, "Dinner's ready." She may try to act like she's little miss hostess, but she's not really. Someone hung up on that title would have walked in here and told us. Not Mom, though. She yells it through the house and expects us to congregate at the dining room table. Dad stands and looks from us to the kitchen. "We better get in there or she'll physically push us to the table."

"We'll be right there," I nod toward my dad. "Can you give us a second?"

"Absolutely," he grins. "I'll help your mother set the table and whatever else she asks me to do."

"Thanks." When he's gone, I turn toward Tiffany. Our knees a mere inch from touching. "Are you ready for this?"

She gulps, and I can see her throat working, wishing it was working for another reason than nerves. "Not really."

"We've got this," I glance toward the hallway that leads to the kitchen. "Remember, our code word is banana. You only need to say it once and I'll sweep you out of here like the damsel in distress you are."

"Pfft." She smacks my arm. "I'm not in distress... yet." Mom's voice is coming from the dining room, and I know we have seconds until she comes looking for us.

"Let's get in there," I reach for her hand to pull her off the couch at the same time I stand up. "The plus side is you get a free home-cooked meal out of this whole ordeal."

As soon as she's standing, Tiffany pulls her hand out of mine, and straightens her shoulders. "The worst that could happen is your mother hates me, and I'll never be able to look her in the eye again."

She follows me into the kitchen and takes a seat on the side of the table. Mom is at one end and Dad is on the other. I can sit across from Tiffany or beside her. Mom already set my plate on the other side of the table, but I feel like I sit over there I will betray Tiffany's trust in me. However, if I move the plate, Mom might make some snide comments when I come over some other time. Not that I blame her, it's the same seat I've sat in since I was a kid.

In the end I take the seat across from Tiffany. I want to read her facial expressions during dinner. She may not realize it, but her face speaks louder than her words ever could. She raises her eyebrows at me in question, but I grin at her, hoping she knows all is well. This is the best position to read the situation.

Mom passes each dish around, making sure Tiffany gets the first helping. It's her way of making Tiffany feel welcome, but I can see my girl struggling with how much is appropriate to spoon on her plate. She has a pretty healthy appetite, at least from what I've seen. There are times she's eaten more than me.

"What do you do for a living?" Mom asks as she digs into the mashed potatoes on her plate.

"I'm a waitress at The Dreamcatcher, downtown." Her mouth is in a wide smile and I know how much joy that job brings her.

"I see," Mom says, and Tiffany's smile drops. "What do you see yourself doing in the future?" Tiffany's eyes widen, and I can tell she's about to freak out. She wasn't prepared to deal with my mom's nosiness. She doesn't mean anything by it, I don't think. I open my mouth to answer for her, but Tiffany speaks first. "I'm not sure," she shrugs her shoulders. "I haven't thought that far ahead."

"Don't you think—" Mom begins, but Dad cuts her off.

"Honey, they aren't here so you can interrogate the woman who's captured our son's attention. They are here for dinner and so you can get to know Tiffany better."

"That's what I'm trying to do."

Dad only shakes his head and does his best to steer the conversation in a different direction. Focusing all of his attention on me. I glance over at Tiffany, and she's sitting rigid. She smiles when appropriate and nods her head at the right times. She hasn't said the code word yet, but I'm tempted to pull the plug and whisk her away to safety. Somewhere my mom can't reach her. I've never held any resentment toward Mom, but tonight is a new low for her. She's always been pushy and intrusive, except it was always only directed at me. However, I grew up knowing how to handle her when she was in those moods. Tiffany shouldn't have to deal with this crap.

When I make a move to stand, Tiffany subtly shakes her head. She doesn't want to let my mom get to her, but I know she is.

The rest of dinner is relatively quiet. Small talk about the weather and what sports teams we're rooting for this year. It's awkward between these walls, and something I haven't felt before. Not here, anyway.

Tiffany helps me gather the dishes while Mom puts the leftovers into containers for us to take home. She doesn't say anything while we load the dishwasher, just dutifully puts the dishes into the dishwasher, fitting everything in like a puzzle.

Once we're back at the table, Mom puts the pies she made on the table. As much as I would love some of her homemade pie I can't let Tiffany endure the energy my mom is throwing out there. "We should probably get going." I pat Mom's shoulder and lean in for a hug.

"It's still early, and I'd love to get to know Tiffany better." Mom argues.

"She needs to make some *banana* bread for one of her cousins."

"Well, drat." Mom looks toward Tiffany. "Maybe next time."

We say our goodbyes and are at the door, a bag full of food in my hands. "It was nice to meet you Mr. and Mrs. Warren."

"You too," Mom beams. Dad leans over and whispers something in her ear, a small grin takes over and she nods in agreement.

"Thank you for dinner and welcoming me into your home."

"Come back anytime." What's with Mom's change in attitude? She was grilling her moments ago, but all that has dissipated into nothing. I'll have to call her later and ask her what her deal was.

"I will," Tiffany replies and walks toward the car. Her steps are fast and she almost drops her bag of leftovers as she walks down the stairs. This will be a long drive home.

NINETEEN

Tiffany

———

THE DRIVE HOME IS SILENT, and I feel horrible. The whole thing was exhausting. I know I put on a tough bravado when I was interacting with Spencer's parents. Inside though… I was a bundle of nerves. Forcing each word out without sticking my foot in my mouth and doing it all with a smile on my face. I don't like how his mom was questioning my work choice. I may not have my whole life planned out but at least I'm happy. For the most part, anyway.

Spencer pulls into the parking garage, puts the car in park and comes around to my side to open the door. I want nothing more than to fall into my bed. He waits until I'm out of the car before grabbing my hand, giving it a gentle squeeze. It is terrifying how well he can read me. My cousins would be finding ways to correct me or give advice, but he gives me silent strength.

As soon as we're in the apartment, he pulls me into his arms. "I'm sorry about my mom," he whispers into my hair. "She's a little overprotective of me."

"It's fine," I say into his shirt. "It went better than I expected. I just wasn't ready for her to question my choices."

"Is there anything I can do?" He leans back until his eyes meet mine. At least he's not mad at me. He shouldn't be since I didn't respond to his mom, but I can't help but feel like a disappointment.

Most people my age already have their shit together, and I'm only now figuring out how to adult without my parents' help. "I just want to go to bed. I have an early shift tomorrow."

"I'll go get the bed ready," he starts down the hallway but my voice stops him.

"I kind of want to sleep alone tonight."

His face falls, and he tries to recover with a small grin. "Okay. I'll, uh, just get it ready for you, then."

"You don't have to do that." I feel like the worlds biggest bitch for wanting sleep on my own, but I need the space. I rely on him way too much to pick me up when I'm having a bad day. It's not healthy for either of us.

"I want to," he says and continues down the hallway toward my room.

I set my bag on the counter and take stock of what my life has become. It's not bad at all, but I can't help feeling like maybe I rushed into things with Spencer. He's amazing and everything a woman could want. And... I know I'll screw it up.

Spencer hasn't come out of my room yet, and I'm wondering what exactly he's doing. My steps are slow as I make my way down the hallway. When I get to my door, Spencer is stacking the last of the pretty pillows from my bed in a neat pile on my dresser. The comforter is pulled back and my jammies, which consists of a t-shirt and shorts, are on my bed. "Thank you," I whisper.

"Get changed, and I'll bring you some water." How is this man still so incredibly sweet while I know he must be disappointed? If the roles were reversed, I'm sure I'd be pestering him about something and demanding to know why he wants to sleep alone. Further proof I'm not on the same maturity level as him.

I change into my jammies and climb into bed. It's still early, but I just can't bring myself to care about that. Spencer comes back with my water and sets it on the nightstand before pulling the blanket on top of me, tucking me in the way my mom did when I was a kid. "Get some rest."

With that, he walks out of the room, closing the door gently behind him. I pull the pillow he sleeps on toward me and I squeeze it to my chest. It smells like him, and I can't help thinking I've made a huge mistake in asking him to sleep in his own bed. But I ignore that feeling, and snuggle closer to the pillow, hoping for sleep to find me soon.

Spencer doesn't wake up before I leave for work. It's that moment I realize I've truly hurt him. I should have sucked it up and let him sleep in the same bed as me, but I needed time alone. Meeting his parents was *not* one of my most favorite things, even if his dad is cool. He stepped in to stop Spencer's mom from badgering me. He'll never know how grateful I am for that kindness.

I open the door to The Dreamcatcher and the smell of fried breakfast meets my nose. This must be what Heaven smells like. "You're cooking early, Dennis," I call out as I pass the kitchen for the break room.

When I walk out, my boss is setting two plates on a table and motions for me to sit. "That's because I'm making my most valuable employee some breakfast."

"Does this mean I get a raise?" I take a seat and stare down the greasy food in front of me. I'm not sure how Dennis knew that I might need a pick me up this morning, but he did. This is one reason he's the best boss ever. Not that I've had many bosses for longer than a few weeks, but he's a large part of the reason I love working here. He fills my parent's role since they are so far away.

"Funny," he deadpans. "But… I might have an opportunity coming up for you soon."

I can't tell if that's good or bad, so I don't respond. "Thank you for breakfast. I definitely needed it."

"Is everything okay?" When I don't respond, he continues, "Are you and Spencer good?"

"I think so." It's the only answer I can give him. "I met his parents over dinner and it didn't go all that well." It wasn't horrible either. I was expecting it to be so much worse.

"Did you say something embarrassing?"

"Not exactly, but his mom is…" What would be the best way to describe her? She's not mean by any stretch, and I can tell she loves her son more than anything. "Abrasive." It's still not the right word, but it's the best I can come up with.

"Ah," he laughs. "I take it you didn't hit if off with her."

"I don't think she likes me very much."

He taps his knuckles on the table and stands up. "Don't worry. She'll come around." With that bit of so-called wisdom, he walks off with his plate in his hand.

I didn't realize I was the type of person others would have to "come around" to, and it makes me feel kind of shitty. There's no time to dwell on it, though. The diner opens in twenty minutes. I need to scarf down this food and get ready to open the doors.

It's almost time for my break. I just need to get this credit card back to the table, and I'll be free for fifteen blissful minutes. The plus side to being busy is not having time to overthink things. I haven't had time to worry over every single second I spent at Spencer's childhood home, wondering if I made an ass of myself, or if his mom likes me.

I'm on my way back to the table when I see Audrey walk through the door. The little bell overhead jingling happily. Too bad the sound doesn't match her expression. She has a tight smile, but when her eyes meet mine, it's with laser focus. *Oh shit*. Did Stella tell her about me and Spencer?

A part of me wants to take the next customer that walks through the door so I don't have to find out why my cousin is here. The other part tells me to shut the hell up. My feet hurt and I need this break. Maybe I can sneak out to the alley and take my break there? Audrey is already coming toward me, and I know avoiding her will be impossible.

"Here's your card," I set the small portfolio holding the card and receipt on the table. "Y'all have a great day." I smile, hoping it doesn't look as manic as I feel.

Audrey follows me to the break room, completely ignoring the employees only sign hanging on the wall next to the door. "Where the hell have you been? You haven't called me in weeks," she barely keeps from yelling.

"I've been busy." I shrug my shoulders, pull out a chair and plop into it.

"You've been busy before, but that's never stopped you from coming over, or at least calling me." Geez, she sounds like my mom when I don't call her back right away. "How are things going with Spencer living there? He's not giving you any trouble, right?" She pulls out the chair next to me and sits down more gracefully than I did. "I just want to make sure Stella and I didn't make a horrible decision about him moving in there after your history with him."

I know Stella told me not to say anything to her, and that it's a bad idea to do it. Except… I can't keep secrets from her. It felt gross when Stella suggested it and feels icky even now. "We're kind of, um, dating each other." I look down at my hands resting in my lap. Like a child terrified of getting in trouble for doing something wrong.

"I'm sorry," Audrey crosses her arms. "Did you say you are *dating* him?"

Her waiting silence is brutal. I don't do well when my cousins are mad at me, but I don't think I can handle the disappointment that is no doubt pouring from her.

"Yes," I say, barely above a whisper. She stands so quickly the chair screeches across the floor, and I know it has to be loud enough for the diners to hear. My shoulders tense at the sound, and I prepare myself for the lecture I know is about to come.

Seconds later, she's pacing back and forth across the small room. "Of all the idiotic things you have done, this might be the icing on the cake. What will happen when you decide you're bored with him and want to move on to someone else?" She pauses, and waits for me to look up before adding, "He is on the lease, Tiffany. It's not like you can just force him to move out because you decided things were getting too real."

"We've already talked about that," I argue. "If things get too heavy, then we'll break it off. Being amicable to each other is better than hating each other's guts."

"By the time things get *heavy*, it's too late to go back to friendship. You realize that, right?" When I don't answer she shakes her head. "Of course you don't. You've never been in an actual relationship. Is he why you haven't made time to talk to me, or come over?"

Her relationship comment is a punch in the gut, and as badly as I want to lash out, I don't. "This right here is why I didn't tell you sooner." My hands are now balled in my lap. Fingernails digging into my skin. "You overreact about everything. It's bad enough that I have my own doubts and fears about dating him. I don't need your negativity adding to it." It's like high school all over again.

Audrey's eyes softened, and she takes small, cautious steps toward me. "I'm not trying to make you feel bad, Tiff." She stops directly in front of me and puts her hands on my shoulders. "I just… don't want to see you get hurt. I don't want you to go through the same heartache I did."

I step back, out of her grasp. "Seeing what you went through in high school is the entire reason I've never let myself get close to someone. I didn't want love to break me." She looks like she's about to interrupt, but I continue full steam ahead. "I'm not saying that I love Spencer because it is way too damn early for that, but I like him… A lot. I can see where you're coming from, and believe me, that thought is stuck on repeat in the back of my head. For now, though, I want to see where this might lead."

Tears filled her eyes, but she doesn't let them fall. "Just, be careful. Don't let yourself become too attached too early. It might come back to bite you in the butt."

With that wisdom, she's gone. All the fight left her when I brought up the way Justin dumped her. Now, I not only have my own fears when it comes to being with Spencer, but also the knowledge that I've hurt my cousin's feelings. Today is shaping up to be fan-fucking-tastic.

TWENTY

Spencer

FINALLY. I'm finished working with the client from Hell. I'm almost certain that man has given me gray hair with all the changes he requested. The app is exactly how he wants it. For now, anyway. I hope I don't hear from him in six months wanting to change the design, again. I can now safely tuck these files away on my external hard drive and move on to another project. There's nothing due for a few weeks, and I'm still waiting to hear back from Dale. I'll lowball my fee if I have to, or figure out some even exchange. Working with Crooked Halo would not only stretch my creativity, but I really want to work with them. Maybe I should I have contacted Dale when Tiffany told me to, but I decided to wait a couple of days. Not wanting to seem too eager.

I glance at the clock. It's almost six, and Tiffany will be home soon. Dinner at a nice restaurant seems like a perfect reward for finishing Mr. Harrison's project, and I know she'll be happy to no longer hear me bitch about him. I'm also hoping a nice night out will go toward mending whatever has broken between us. Things haven't been the same since we had dinner with my parents and I worry they've scared her off. I shouldn't have pushed her to meet them before she was ready. I don't sleep in her room as much as I was, and when I bring my parents up, she tenses up and changes the subject.

The door to our apartment opens and closes, and I run out of my room to greet her. Damn, I'm like an excited puppy, happy their person is finally home. And that's what she is… *My person*. Now, if only I could get her to see that. To show her she's it for me without scaring her off.

She looks exhausted. Her hair is a mess with flyaways coming out of her ponytail. Her usual chipper attitude is nowhere in sight. I grab her bag off her shoulder and set it on the kitchen counter. I'm almost afraid to ask, but I do anyway. "How was your day?"

"Long," she sighs. "Dennis is training me for a new position."

"Oh, yeah?" She didn't mention anything about it before, and the realization sucks. "What is he training you for?"

Tiffany scrunches up her nose. "He hasn't really told me. He just keeps showing me things that he normally does." She shakes her head, "Well, except for the cooking. We all know I'm a lost cause when it comes to trying to feed people."

"It sounds like he wants you to take on a management type of position."

"That's my guess, too." She drags her feet to the living room and falls, ungracefully, onto the couch. "I don't want that kind of responsibility. It's too much, and I don't know if I can handle it."

I sit on the floor next to the couch and take off her shoes. "You can."

"How do you know that?" She doesn't look at me when she asks. Her eyes are fixed on the ceiling.

"Because," I scoot closer to where her head is, and wait for her to turn toward me. Anything to show she does still care. "I see how much work and effort you put into The Dreamcatcher. You know the inner workings more than anyone else aside from Dennis." She finally turns her head toward me, and her gaze meets mine. "He sees that in you, too."

"You have a point," she nods. "I know damn well that Janie wouldn't be able to handle half the things I do. She definitely doesn't care about the job like me." Leaning forward, her lips touch my forehead. A peck before leaning back on the couch. "Thank you for the reminder. I needed it today."

"That's kind of what I'm here for as your boyfriend," I poke her arm. "To pick you up when you're down and make you feel better."

"You're doing a damn fine job of it," she smiles. "How was your day?"

I lean back against the coffee table, and it scoots out from behind me. I fall backward, but throw my arms out to catch myself. She really needs something sturdier in here. Maybe I'll buy her a new one when Dennis tells her she's being promoted. "It's been pretty good, actually." I reposition my arms to even out the weight of my body. "Do you remember that pain in the ass client I'm working with?"

"How could I forget?" I feel her eye roll more than I see it. She's back to staring at the ceiling, and I swear her eyelids are closing then fluttering back open. "You only complain about him every other day. Sometimes multiple times if he's bugging you nonstop."

"There's no need to be a smart ass," I groan.

"You wouldn't have me any other way." The corner of her mouth lifts, but the words are slow and lazy. She's right, though I wouldn't. She challenges me more than anyone else I know, and I always look forward to our random conversations.

"True," I laugh. "Anyway, his project is officially done."

She sits up, holding herself up with her elbows. "That's amazing," she yells. "Now you don't have to worry about his five million fickle decisions. I swear, he changes his mind more than Stella buys shoes."

"I take it she buys a lot of them?"

"Yep," Tiffany pops the *p*. "Though, I don't know what use she's getting out of all those heels since she lives in the country now." She pauses waiting for me to say something. "So, are we going to celebrate or something? I'm sure you've had bigger clients you've worked with, but this one in particular feels like a real victory."

"I was actually going to ask you if you wanted to have a nice dinner when you got home." I lean forward and run my fingertips through the red strands of hair in her ponytail. "But you look like you want to fall into your bed. We can go some other time."

"No way," she plasters on a smile. I can't tell if this one is real or fake, and it's bugging me. "This is a huge deal. No more phone calls from the indecisive guy, and it gives you time to reach out to Crooked Halo. We're going out tonight."

"I've actually already emailed Dale. I'm just waiting to hear from him." I lay my head down on the couch next to her arm. "And we really don't have to go tonight. Only if you want to."

"Let me take a quick shower and get the smell of diner food off of me." She hops up from the couch, suddenly full of energy. "I'll be ready before you know it." Without a backward glance, she races down the hallway.

Tiffany wanted steak for dinner, so we sit at a steakhouse not too far from the apartment. This wasn't exactly what I was thinking when I said a nice restaurant, but if this is what she wants, I'll do it with a smile. Anything to see her light up again. Things almost feel normal tonight. *Almost* being the keyword. I wish we could go back in time to dinner at my parents' house and I could tell Mom not to look down on Tiffany's job. Especially since she loves it so much. She should never feel ashamed of what she does for a living, and I have a feeling that's what shut her down. It's been almost two weeks, and I'm only now seeing some of her sparkle come back. Why does my mom have to insert herself into every aspect of my life? I'm her son not her friend, even if she wishes I would confide in her more. I'm an adult now, and perfectly capable of making my own choices. Good, bad, or whatever else is in between. Being with Tiffany is *my* choice, and hopefully the two of them can get along one day.

It would make things less awkward, but if it doesn't happen, mom will have to get used to it.

"Can you pass the butter?" Tiffany points her knife toward the tiny bowl on my side of the table. The best thing about this place is the bread. It's crispy on the outside, and warm and soft on the inside.

I scoot the butter closer to her, and place my elbows on the edge of the table. We came in late so there isn't much chatter. "When do you think Dennis will officially promote you?"

She shrugs her shoulders. "I don't know." She takes a big bite out of the piece of bread in her hand and moans. The sound kills me. Not sleeping in the same bed as her is my own personal hell. It's not because of the lack of sex, though I miss that too. It's that I enjoy holding her in my arms. Being the one she leans into when she's most vulnerable. Correction. The one she used to lean into before my mom screwed it all up. It's my fault for letting her be so involved in my life. I should have drawn a line in the sand ages ago. I didn't because I was too damn worried I would hurt her feelings. Now she's possibly ruined the best thing that's ever happened to me. "When do you think you'll hear from Crooked Halo?"

I'm so lost in my thoughts that the question takes me by surprise. "I'm not sure."

"How long have you been waiting on a response?"

Crap. I wasn't expecting her to ask this. I wonder how mad she will be when I answer. "A couple of days."

"What?" She shrieks and a couple a few tables down looks in our direction. "They emailed you two weeks ago, and you waited to respond?" She whispers loudly.

"I was scared," I shrug. If anyone will understand my fear of the unknown, it's her. I mean, she didn't date anyone seriously out of fear. I'm not going to voice that, though. It's a sure-fire way to piss her off and watch her stomp right out of this restaurant.

"You have no reason to be scared." She reaches her hand out to place on mine, but thinks better of it and pulls it back. "Your work is amazing, and assuming they haven't found someone else, they'll get back to you soon."

Her actions tonight are confusing. One minute she's attentive and the next she's reserved. Acting like the Tiffany I moved in with. The back and forth will drive me insane, and I hope this isn't the beginning of the end. I'm too far gone to be friends at this point. I'm falling in love with her, and she doesn't even realize it. At least, I don't think she does. For all I know, our relationship became too much the moment I asked her to meet my parents. I'd ask her what she's feeling, but I don't think she would tell me. She's too busy building up her defenses, once again.

"Let's hope they email me back soon, then." I force a smile and the look on her face is the same as mine. Trying to be happy even though we're both feeling the strain of something we can't identify.

"Give it a few more days." She grabs another piece of bread, slathering it with butter. "They are probably busy writing music or whatever it is bands do when they aren't performing."

The rest of our meal comes and we eat in silence, mostly. The tension isn't something I'm used to with her. Hell, even when we were fighting after I moved in, at least there was emotion behind it. Now there's only a shell of the woman I met that night at the concert. There's no way dinner that night messed her up this much. My bet is someone said something to her, and she's trying to find an easy way out. One that doesn't hurt either of us.

A night that was supposed to be celebratory has turned into something else altogether. I feel nothing but fear. Fear of her shutting down all of her emotions. Fear of losing her before we've even given each other a real shot. Lucky for me, I don't plan on going down without a fight.

TWENTY-ONE

Tiffany

<hr>

SINCE DINNER THE OTHER NIGHT, Spencer has been relentless about spending time together. It's as if he's made it his mission to fix whatever it is he thinks is broken. I only wish he'd realize that right now. *He* is part of the problem. This is all too much, especially after talking to Audrey the other day. I can't allow myself to be consumed by him. It will only hurt in the end. At the same time, I'm not ready to end things with him. Not ready to say goodbye to the one good thing in my life.

"Order up," One of the cooks Dennis hired calls out. Honestly, I need to stop getting inside my head when I'm at work. It's starting to affect my tips.

I grab the plates and set them on my tray before balancing it on my hand. "Thanks," I say over my shoulder. The food on the tray makes my mouth water. I haven't eaten all day because we've been so busy. I didn't even get to take my full break earlier. Hopefully, the kitchen staff can whip something together for me to take home. I glance at the big clock on the wall on the way to the table. Only an hour left, and I get to leave for the day. The extra shifts are definitely padding my bank account, just in case the inevitable happens and I'm left without a roommate again. I need to prepare for the worst. I don't want to be a mess like Audrey was and calling my parents for money is *not* an option.

A young couple and their toddler son are seated at the table, and I take my time setting the plates down in front of each of them. "And these yummy chicken tenders are for you." The little boy is so excited and clapping his hands as I place the plate in front of him. "Be careful, though. The plate is a little warm." He beams at me and grabs one of the tenders and dips it in the gravy.

"Adam," his mother admonishes. "What do you say?"

He pauses, chicken almost to his mouth, "Thank you, ma'am." Wow, this kid speaks so clearly. Maybe he's a little older than I first thought. Either way, his thanks makes me feel better.

"You're very welcome," I smile at him. "Let me know if y'all need anything else."

"We will, thank you." It's customers like these that make me love my job. Sliding the tray under my arm, I head back toward the food counter.

Janie is there, putting an order in for one of her tables. "Hey, Tiffany. How is everything?"

"Good," I drawl.

"That's good." She turns until she's facing me. "I was just wondering because you've been here a lot again."

"Just trying to save some extra money," I say, voice tight. Not that it's any of her business. "The way things are going with my cousin and her boyfriend, I'm sure I'll be buying wedding attire soon enough." It's not a complete lie. I have a feeling Johnny will pop the question sooner rather than later. Those two are definitely meant for each other.

"Wow. I didn't realize it was that serious for them." She tightens her ponytail. "It's a good reason to save money, though."

"The fact that he drove all the way down here to win her back, and she moved to where he is, I'd say it's always been that serious for them." I take a deep breath. "I guess when you know you've found the one, you'll do anything for that person."

"Is it like that with you and the hottie that came in here?" She's not trying to be malicious or anything. It's an honest question and I don't know how to answer it.

"Not really," I finally say. "We're just having fun and seeing where things go." And this is the biggest lie I'll tell myself all day. I feel more for him and it's terrifying. I'm saved from having to say more when the hostess seats another table in my section. "I better get back to work."

"Alright," she gives me a small wave. "I'll catch up with you later."

Not if I can help it. She's making me think about things I'm not ready to face. And that's how the rest of my shift goes. Staying busy and avoiding Janie.

～

Spencer is on the sofa watching TV when I come through the door, and I can't stop myself from admiring the way he looks so comfortable in my life. That is until the fear bubbles up, and takes over my brain. "Hey," I call out, in case he didn't hear the door open.

He jumps up, and rushes into the entryway, wrapping me in his arms. "How was your day?"

It wasn't horrible, but I don't want to let him know just how much I've been trying to distance myself from him. So, I pull myself away from him and hold up the bag of food in my hand. "I brought dinner."

"Fantastic," he says, grabbing the bag from my hand. "I'll get some plates and silverware. Sit down and relax."

"Thanks." I walk to the living room and notice everything is put away. All the little odds and ends I've left out and haven't put up. The stray clothes I've left in my wake when folding laundry. All of it is gone. "It's really clean in here." I want to feel like I'm contributing, but anyone who *knows* me, knows that I hate cleaning. If I could afford it, I would hire someone to come in and hit the big things that I put off.

"Yeah," his voice is hesitant. "I needed something to do while waiting for a response from Dale. I finished working with another client and got tired of sitting at my computer hitting refresh on my email."

Now for the important question. "Did you touch any of my food in the refrigerator?" Please say no. He knows I don't like anyone messing with my food.

"No," he rushes out. "Everything is still in there." Good. I'm glad he didn't throw anything out. "You don't have much in there except snacks since we've been eating stuff my mom has sent over."

"I'll go through the freezer this weekend. I'm pretty sure some of that ice cream isn't any good."

"Sounds good. I know better than to touch your beloved *Ben & Jerry's*," he laughs.

I toss my bag on the floor beside the coffee table, dirtying up the tidy space. Maybe I'll install some kind of hook by the entryway to put my bag when I get home so it isn't just lying wherever I chuck it. It feels nice to sit down. My feet are aching and I wonder if I should get some new shoes. It's the one thing about waitressing that I despise. The need to buy new shoes whenever my feet hurt. "You still haven't heard from Dale?"

"No," he sighs. "I sent a follow up email, though. Hoping maybe the first one got lost in cyberspace."

"He'll get back to you," I lean back and close my eyes. I kind of don't want to go into work tomorrow. "He wouldn't have reached out to you in the first place if he didn't want to work with you."

"I hope you're right." His voice is closer and I open my eyes. "Here's your dinner. What do you want to watch?"

"I'm good with anything." I yawn and scoot into the corner of the sofa until I find the perfect level of comfort. "I can't guarantee I'll make it through the whole movie."

"You need to take some days off," he says, sheepishly. Hinting at what I already know I'm doing. Avoiding alone time with him as much as possible. I swear avoidance is my middle name. He picks up the remote and presses play on the movie he was watching. It's one I've seen, so I don't make a big deal about starting something from the beginning. "I hope this is okay."

"It's fine." I dig into my dinner. I really need to stop skipping meals because I'm going through this plate of food way too fast, and I have no doubt I'll feel like crap after I'm done.

The TV is booming with spaceships flying through the galaxy, and I set my plate on the coffee table before getting comfortable in my corner of the sofa again. My legs are tucked under me, with my feet poking out. Normally, I would be curled up next to Spencer, with his arms wrapped around me. Tonight, though, I just can't bring myself to pretend like I'm okay. Like I'm not freaking out with each day that he's pushing to get closer. He seems to sense this and stays on his side of sofa, but he reaches out and places a hand on my foot. "So," he breaks the silence between us. "They've announced the date for Austin City Limits Festival. One of my clients reached out to ask me if I wanted some of the tickets he has for the whole festival. I just need to let him know soon."

That wakes me up. I've wanted to go to ACL for a long time, but my ass has always been too broke to even consider buying tickets. At the same time, the event is months away, and I don't even know if I'll be with Spencer when the time comes. Hell, I don't know if we'll be together for the rest of the month. "Let me check with Dennis and see if I can get off that weekend. We're usually slammed during festival weekends and he wants as many of us there as possible."

His face falls. I hate that I've disappointed him, but he's talking *long-term relationship*. I'm barely cut out for whatever it is we have going on now. "Just let me know as soon as you can so he doesn't offer them to someone else."

"I will." I need to let Audrey's hurt get out of my head. Just because she was destroyed after being so wrapped up in a guy doesn't mean I will. The fear is still there, though. Until working at The Dreamcatcher, I never even held down a steady job because I can't commit to anything. We watch the rest of the movie in silence. It's weird having this chasm between us and not knowing what to do to close it. Before the movie is over my eyes close and I fall into a fitful sleep.

TWENTY-TWO

Spencer

I'M TRYING HARD NOT to let Tiffany's actions hurt me. She's scared, and I get that. Hell, I am too. Never has a woman stuck around this long. She doesn't make fun of my comic collection or the fact that I like cosplay. She seems to *really* get me. If only she could get over the hurt her cousin felt all those years ago. It's crazy to me she's carried this view on relationships her entire life. This fear is so ingrained in her she won't even give us a fair chance.

I am doing my best to think about something else, but it isn't working. Scrolling through color options for my client is doing nothing to quell my frustration. Hell, I'm not even sure what time she'll be home since she's working a double.

Any hope that I was showing her relationships aren't all that bad are dying a slow, miserable death. Nothing I've done has helped. If anything, she's pulling back with each day that passes, and I don't know how to fix it. If I keep pushing, I'll lose her forever. I know that, and I still can't stop trying to spend all my free time with her. This has always been my problem when it comes to women. I put more effort into relationships than they want or are ready for. Then I end up with a broken heart and a lot of time wasted.

My computer dings with an email, and I minimize the window open on my computer. It's also ridiculous that I'm waiting next to my computer for an email like a teenager waiting on a phone call from their crush. All I know is that I want to work with Dale, and Crooked Halo, more than anything right now. I've worked for some high profile companies, and it's this small band that has me anxious.

I open my email and nearly fall out of my chair in excitement seeing Dale's name on the unopened email. *Calm down, Spencer. You don't even know if you have the job yet.* I move my mouse over the email. The small arrow hovering until finally, I click it.

Hey Spencer,

Sorry I haven't answered sooner. We were recording some music. We're definitely on board for you to design our website. Could you also tie everything in with our social media, too? We were approached by someone wanting to sign us, but we need to have a consistent "brand," whatever that is. Can you help us out? We'll be happy to pay your fee and throw in admission to some of our shows.

-Dale

Tiffany was right. They were just busy. I jump out of my desk chair and throw my hand in the air. Victory is mine! Before I reply to Dale, I want to let Tiffany know. I could wait and tell her when she finally makes it home, but it's too exciting not to share now.

Spencer: Guess who's designing a site for Crooked Halo?

I'm not sure when she'll reply. She usually texts me on her breaks, or when she has a free moment. It all depends on how busy they are. So, I'm surprised when my phone dings a minute later.

Tiffany: I told you. Congrats!
Spencer: Want to go out to eat to celebrate?
Tiffany: Actually, a couple of the girls asked if I wanted to grab a drink after work. Raincheck?
Spencer: Sure.

What else am I supposed to say? I didn't even realize she hung out with anyone from work. She hasn't done that in the time we've been together. If it had been Audrey asking her out, I wouldn't think twice about it. But she's never once mentioned going out with any of the girls at The Dreamcatcher. I wonder if Janie is also going because from my understanding Tiffany doesn't get along with her. I could press for more information, but I don't want to freak her out more than I have already. Or, at least I assumed I have. There's no time to stress over it though. I need to email Dale again.

Dale,

Absolutely. I can do anything you need me to do. As far as branding, that's the overall look you want to portray. If you have time, my evening is wide open. We can meet and go over everything y'all want. Just let me know.

-Spencer

His reply comes back.

Sure. Meet at Rob's around 7.

The lack of a greeting bugs me, but I don't want to ask them to change who they are because I like things a certain way. I need to get over it. I have the opportunity to help lift an up-and-coming band to a larger audience. I'd be crazy not to take it up. I wonder if I should let Tiffany know. A part of me wants to leave her wondering where I am in retaliation of the way she's been with me, but I can't do that. It's not who I am.

Spencer: I'm meeting with Crooked Halo tonight. I'm not sure when I'll be home, but it shouldn't be too late.
Tiffany: Have fun.

That's it. Two little words, and nothing else. Instead of dwelling on that, I pull up *Photoshop* and start pulling colors and images into a blank document to show the band. It won't be set in stone, just a general idea how things they might like that relates to them.

Dale and the rest of Crooked Halo are sitting in one of the few booths at Rob's bar. I used to wonder why he would give up that precious space that could be used for additional standing room at shows. When I asked him one day, he said it's for those people that love coming to see live shows but don't want to be a part of the crowd.

He basically described me. Hell, the only reason I was in the pit the night I met Tiffany is because my friend needed someone to go with him. We aren't even that close. He just didn't want the ticket to go to waste. He's also the one that bailed on me for Comic Con. Not that I'm mad about any of it. It led me to Tiffany.

There's a band warming up on the stage as I walk toward the booth. The crowd is almost non-existent. I don't know if it's because it's a weeknight, or because nobody wants to take a chance on them. Who knows? I do feel kind of bad for them, but they aren't who I'm here to see.

I pull out the chair at the end of the booth. "Hey guys, thanks for meeting me."

"Anytime," Dale says. "What do you have for us?"

I pull my laptop from the bag I carried with me. Opening it up, I turn it to face them. "This is the color scheme I came up with."

"What is the yellow? I'm not sure how I feel about that."

"It's just an accent color to keep it from looking so dark. And it really ties the blue and gray together." Oh shit. I'm losing them. I thought the yellow would work. Maybe they want to stick to the stereotypical grunge look. I really need to sell them on this color. "I've listened to y'all play, and I've seen you perform. We can take the yellow out and you'll have the same branding look as every other band out there. Or… You can keep it and set yourselves apart. It's your call, but this fits your playing style. You aren't heavy, but you're also not timid. These color choices fit you perfectly."

They sit quietly, looking from my laptop screen then at each other. There isn't a word uttered between them, and the only sound is the band warming up. They all turn toward Dale and nod. "Are you sure you aren't a salesman?"

"Yeah," I look at the band, confused. "Why?"

"Because you've just sold us on using yellow in the branding. What else do you need from us?"

Yes. That's exactly want I wanted to hear. "Do you already have a logo for the band?"

"Not really," Dale answers. "We tried drawing something up a few times, but none of them stuck. We've just been saying who we are since we don't have any merchandise at the moment."

"Is creating a logo for you something you'd like me to do as well?"

"Actually, that would be great," Dale sighs in relief. "It is better if we can keep everything with one person who will make it all cohesive. Thank you so much, man. Shoot me an email with the total, and I've got you."

"I'm excited to be working with y'all." I'm turning into a fanboy and I have no clue why. This isn't some character I love in a movie, or comic character. Being able to do something that broadens my creativity has me all giddy. "If we don't need to talk about anything else, I'm going to head out. Hopefully, my girl is home by the time I get there so I can share the news with her."

Dale grins knowingly. "Is that the redhead that was here with you that night we played?" He shakes his head. "She's one of those music lovers that really gets it. She feels the words as they are being performed. She's the fan all bands want to have. Get home to her."

"Thanks, man," I reach my hand out and shake his. "I'll send you all the details and the mockups as soon as I'm done." It is nice hearing someone else talk about Tiffany like that. Her passion is why I fall for Tiffany more and more every day. It's those qualities that make her worth fighting for.

Damn. She's not here yet. I'm not sure if I should text her or not. I don't want to seem like I'm forcing her to check in with me, but she hasn't gone out since we've been together. Well, other than the night when she was at Audrey's place and then when she went out with that one dude. Luckily, it didn't end well for him since she left their date and ended up in bed with me.

The apartment is quiet without her here. Although, lately, it's been that way even if we are in the same room. Whatever is breaking down between us needs to fix itself. Or she needs to tell me what I'm doing wrong. I've been in relationships before, but they've always been short-lived. Tiffany thinks she is the only one freaking out about us being an item. Being with someone who gets me is new to me. I have just as much reason to be worried about a broken heart as she does.

Spencer: Just wanted to let you know I'm home. Hope you're having fun.

There. That isn't too intrusive. I keep expecting my phone to ding. Any second now. But it doesn't. It's silent in my hand. I can't sit here and watch my phone until she decides she's going to answer me. For all I know she can't hear it over the music. Instead, I'm going to get to work on the logo for Crooked Halo. It should keep my mind off things, at least for a bit.

I turn my computer on, and wait for it to load. Rather than sit in my room and feel suffocated by the tiny room, I'll set up shop in the living room. I'll be able to hear Tiffany come in, and the space is more open. I can spread out across the coffee table and turn the TV on in the background. It resembles the setup I had when I lived in the apartment above the garage. For whatever reason, I think better when I'm like this. The laptop and a notepad are on the coffee table, side by side. My Dr. Pepper is next to it, and I'm sitting on the floor. The computer is still lower than my vision, and I have to look down, but I'm okay with that. I grab the remote and turn on the first thing that pops up under Tiffany's recommendations. It's some rom-com, and I laugh at the suggestion because that is so not the girl I know. She only watches them at Audrey's. I wonder if Audrey forgot to switch profiles when she last watched. Oh well, I'm not actually going to watch it. I have work to do.

Hours have passed and I still haven't heard from Tiffany. I'm getting worried now. It's after midnight and she hasn't answered my text. A part of me wonders if I should text her cousins. They may be able to get ahold of her before I can, but I don't want to be a bother. Hell, I'm not entirely certain they even know we're dating. She hasn't mentioned them much lately. My fingers hover over the keyboard on my phone. It's not absurd if I text her now, right? I mean, it's not like I've been blowing up her phone while she's hanging out with her friends. I don't want to be that guy that makes his girl lose her friendships, but I'm genuinely concerned. What the hell. The most that will happen is Tiffany will be pissed off. I can handle that. It's preferable to any other alternative.

Spencer: Just checking in. I haven't heard from you and wanted to make sure you're good.

I hope she answers me soon. I'm not sure I could go to sleep without at least knowing that she's okay. I save my work on the progress I've made for Dale. There are five different logos I've created for them to choose from. I could send them over to him now, but I'll wait until tomorrow. Right now, all of my concern is focused on Tiffany.

Another hour goes by and there's been no response. I have no other choice than to text one of her cousins. I'm happy I have both phone numbers saved from when I answered the ad for the apartment. Now to decide on which cousin to ask. Audrey acted like she didn't like me much, and I'm better Stella is a safer bet.

Spencer: Hi Stella, I'm not sure if you saved my number, but it's Spencer. Have you heard from Tiffany?

My phone rings in my hand immediately after the text delivers. "Hello," I answer cautiously.

"Spencer," Stella's voice is panicked. "What's happening with Tiff?"

I didn't realize she would call me back. I didn't intend to alarm her, and I'm ninety percent sure I've done just that. "I'm not sure," my voice cracks. "She told me earlier that she was going out with friends from work, but I haven't heard from her since. I figured she would be home by now. She hasn't answered either of the messages I sent her."

Stella groans on the other end of the line. "Damn it," she mutters. I don't think I was supposed to hear that, even though I did. "When is the last time you sent her a message?"

"About an hour ago, I think."

"Fingers crossed she just can't hear her phone. Or, that she's still with her friends." She signs and mumbles something to someone. I'm assuming it's the guy she was with before I moved in. "I wish I could say this is out of the ordinary for her, but it's not. She has a habit of not answering anyone when she goes out. It drives Audrey crazy because her mind always goes to the worst scenario."

"You aren't exactly making me feel better." In fact, she's making me worry more than I was before. I want to go to every bar in the area and search for her. That would most likely freak her out, though.

"Sorry." She pauses for a second. "Let me try to get ahold of her and I'll call you back. If I can't, then Audrey may know what's going on since she lives closer."

"I don't know about that. She hasn't hung out with Audrey much since we've become a couple." Shit. Does she know? "I didn't mean to say that."

"It's okay," Stella laughs. "I already knew. I'm happy she has someone looking out for her, though."

"Thanks." I check the hallway to see if she might have come in while I've been on the phone, but no such luck. "I'll let you know if I hear from her."

"Same. I'll touch base with you later." She doesn't say goodbye, just hangs up. Even though it's a pet peeve of mine, I'm not upset about it. She wants to figure out what's going on as much as I do.

The night grows later, and there's still no word. Stella is doing what she can from Asheville. It's mostly just calling her repeatedly. Even Audrey is trying to get ahold of her to no avail. Her cousins mentioned that she was careless over the night, but I don't want to believe that. I don't want to acknowledge that she didn't have the forethought or need to let me know what's going on. Instead, I'm pacing the apartment waiting for the door to open. Waiting for her to come in with some explanation.

The early morning light is coming in through the windows and my blood is boiling. I've done my best to let her know what's going on with me. If I'm going to be late, I tell her. If something comes up, I give her a heads up. But I've never not communicated with her

Finally, the door opens. I grab my phone and send a text to Stella.

Spencer: She just walked in.

I'd love to know what kind of excuse she has for me right now.

TWENTY-THREE

Tiffany

Son of a bitch. **Spencer is awake, and he does *not* look happy.**

"Where the hell have you been? I've been worried sick all night thinking something horrible had happened to you."

"I'm sorry," I say just above a whisper. "My phone died, and I passed out when we got back to Janie's place."

"And she didn't have a charger you could use?" He runs his hands through his hair and pushes his glasses up his nose. "Or you couldn't text me from her phone? Something to let me know that you were okay. I've been on and off the phone with your cousins all night trying to figure out where you were."

Hold up. Did I hear him correctly? "You called my cousins?" Anger rushes through me. "You had no right to get them involved."

"What else did you expect me to do?" He throws his hands up in the air. "You weren't answering me, and it was after midnight. I figured if anyone knew what was going on with you, it was them. You told me y'all were close."

"We are, but in case you haven't noticed, I haven't been spending much time with either of them." The reason doesn't need to be said aloud. We both know it's because of him I haven't made time to talk to either of them. I drop my bag in the middle of the floor. I'm tired, feel like crap, and I still smell like the food cooked at The Dreamcatcher. "You shouldn't have called them. I'm a big girl and can take care of myself. I've been doing it for years."

"Yeah? And where has that gotten you?" He motions to himself. "I've done nothing but try to show you how special you are. To break down your walls and hope you realize that not all relationships are doomed to fail. But you don't seem to care. You'd rather go out all night, with a girl you can barely stand, rather than spend any time with me. I never asked you to give up every-thing you did for fun when we started dating."

I stomp toward him and poke my finger at his chest. "You didn't give me much choice either. You wanted to spend every moment we could together. Not once thinking I might need room to breathe." My voice is becoming loud and shrill. "I used to go out all the time. I did whatever I wanted without feeling like I needed to check in with someone like they were my parent."

Spencer backs away and waves his hands between us. "I can't," he stops for a second and shakes his head. "I can't do this right now. Not until I've calmed down." He walks down the hallway and into his room. Moments later he comes back out with his keys and wallet in his hands. "I'll be back later."

He doesn't say anything else. Just walks out the door, slamming it behind him. I grab my keys out of my pocket and hurl them at the door. Does it solve anything? No. But I don't know what else to do. My emotions are all over the place.

How did this become my life? This exact moment is what I've worked so hard to avoid my entire adult life. I lean against the wall and slide down until my ass hits the ground. The apartment is so quiet now that *he's* not here. I don't know what to do with myself. A tear slides down my cheek and I wipe it away. Another one follows and soon they are flowing with no end in sight. I give up trying to wipe the wetness away.

This is why I don't get involved with men. I never thought I'd get so attached to Spencer. That he'd be the one to ground me in ways my cousins have failed at year after year.

Sitting on the floor crying isn't going to solve anything, though. I got what I wanted. He is most definitely backing off. The crappy part is he may never come back. When I told myself I wanted space, this isn't exactly what I had in mind.

I wipe the tears from my cheeks and stand up. I feel gross. Not to mention the fact that the bottom of my shoes are sticky from the floor at the bar. I need to wash off last night, and now this morning, away. Maybe a shower will make the day a smidge better. I doubt it, though.

Standing up, I grab my bag off the floor and trudge to my room. The first order of business is charging my phone. If he really called Stella and Audrey, I'm sure I have a shit ton of messages from them. And I'm a hundred percent sure none of them are warm and cuddly. There's no way in hell I'm waiting around for the phone to charge so I can read them. A shower is much more important.

Grabbing some towels from the linen closet, I walk to the bathroom. The bright light is hurting my eyes and I can't remember drinking ever causing me to feel the way I do right now. Achy, tired, and a headache from Hell. It just proves that my tolerance has gone down since I started dating Spencer. All those nights that I used to hit the bars were spent binge watching TV, talking about nothing important, or in my bed. I miss him and the fact that he's not likely coming back hits me like a ton of bricks.

I turn on the bathtub faucet and wait for the water to get warm. Peeling off a layer of clothing with each passing second is like stripping off all the bad decisions I made last night. The first was agreeing to go out with Janie. I've only hung out with her a few times, but she parties more than I ever did. She's the only person I've ever met that can out drink me. If I were responsible, I would have left the bar after two drinks. But, no. I'm the dumbass that ran from their problems and drank way more than I should have. I'm just happy that Janie let me sleep off the hangover on her couch instead of pushing me into an Uber when I couldn't even think straight. Even if it cost me a relationship. One that I'm no longer certain I want out of.

Steam fills the bathroom, and I adjust the temperature. Being scalded on top of everything else would make this day so much worse. I lift the little knob that turns the shower on and step in, pulling the curtain closed behind me. The water pouring down on me feels amazing, and it almost erases everything from my mind, except the way Spencer looked when we were fighting. The resolve on his face when he walked out the front door. And here I go again. It doesn't count as crying if the tears mix in with the water… Right?

My phone is ringing when I turn off the blow dryer. I already know who it is when I pick it up and swipe it open. "Where the hell have you been?" Audrey's voice screeches over the phone.

"Do we have to do this right now? It's already been a shitty morning." I flop onto my bed, waiting for whatever tongue lashing she's about to give me. It's not going to be pretty, and loathe as I am to admit it, I deserve it.

"Yes, Tiffany." Her words are biting and I flinch. "We absolutely have to do this right now. We were up all night worried about you. I tried calling every bar you frequent to see if you were there. With every *no*, I freaked out even more. Wondering if you were in a ditch somewhere, or if someone had taken you."

I'm going to regret putting my two cents in, but I can't help it. "You realize I'm not a child, right? You don't need to parent me on stranger danger."

She keeps going. As if she didn't hear a word I said. "And poor Spencer. I can't imagine how angry he is. After that big show you put on about how important he is, and you stay out all night without letting him know anything."

Audrey is still yelling at me as I press the red circle ending the call. She'll get to flog me in person soon enough. I pull random clothes from drawers and throw them in a pile on the bed. There's no way in hell I'm staying here until I figure shit out. The thought of running into him packing up his stuff is too painful. I never meant for *this* to happen. We had a good thing going, and I let my fears screw with my head. Janie was just an excuse for me to run from my problems yet again.

Searching under my bed for a bag, my hand clamped around something soft and I pull it toward me. It's one of Spencer's shirts. In all honesty, I should go put it on his bed. I mean, it is his and I'm sure he'll want it back when he inevitably comes to pack up all of his belongings. But… I'm not that strong. I need the shirt as a reminder of the one time I've ever let myself fall for someone. Who cares if I totally screwed it up and let him slip right through my fingers because I'm immature and don't know how to deal with my feelings?

Using my other hand I reach back under my bed and finally find the strap to my duffel bag. I yank it out before standing up and putting my clothes into it. Hopefully, this is enough to get me through at least a couple of days. I can get anything else I might need from Audrey. The zipper is halfway closed when I lay my eyes on Spencer's shirt once again. Lifting it up to my nose, I inhale his scent. It smells woodsy and clean and my heart breaks because I'll never get to smell that again. At least not with him.

With my bag packed, I grab my purse and head toward the living room. A part of me wants to leave him a note and apologize profusely. Telling him he may have been one of the best things that's ever happened to me and that I was falling for him. But I'm not going to. This is what happens in all those romance movies Audrey forces me to watch, and they are not real life. If I am being honest, he's most likely better off without me in his life. He doesn't need someone who can barely take care of themselves.

With one final glance around the apartment, I walk out the front door. Locking it behind me while a tear escapes down my cheek. Hopefully Audrey isn't so pissed off at me she won't let me stay with her. At least for a bit.

I knock on Audrey's door and it swings open so hard that the knob hits the wall. I'll be surprised if there isn't a hole in it after that.

"Are you kidding me right now?" She stands in front of me with her arms crossed over her chest, barring my entrance. "You honestly think I'm going to let you come here and stay after you hung up on me in the middle of my rant?"

I shrug my shoulders and nod. "I was kind of hoping that you would overlook that and be happy to yell at me in person." My fingers are crossed that she'll let me in. Give me sanctuary from my own dumbass mistakes.

Audrey's foot is tapping, and normally that isn't a good sign, but finally she gestures for me to come in. "Fine. Don't think I'm through with you, though. I have a lot of words that need to penetrate your thick skull."

I step over the threshold and push my way past her. "Can it wait until I get settled in? The past twenty-four hours have been a complete shit show." Throwing my bag on the floor next to the sofa, I turn toward my cousin. "Please tell me you have something with alcohol."

"Yeah, that's what got you in the mess you're in. I'm not giving you any." She picks up my bag and begins carrying it toward the spare room. "I'll give you a small reprieve, but that's only because Stella should be here soon."

Son of a bitch. This isn't going to be good. Maybe staying here isn't a good idea. Too bad it's my only option.

TWENTY-FOUR

Spencer

SHE DIDN'T EVEN TRY to defend herself. Not that I gave her much of a chance to do that, but it would have been nice if she would have fought me on it at least. Mom has been hovering at the door of the garage apartment. If I'm being honest, some of the problems between me and Tiffany started with her. Not that it's at all her fault Tiffany went out last night and didn't come home. Tiffany is the one who didn't send a simple text message, or call me, to let me know what was going on. Instead, I got to spend my night on the phone with her cousins and worrying something had happened to her. I never believed she was as irresponsible as she claimed until I saw her walk through the door this morning.

"Spencer?" There's a knock on my door and my mom doesn't wait for me to allow her entrance. She barges right in without a care in the world. Not that she needs my permission since I don't technically live here anymore and it is her property. "Are you okay? Is there anything you need?"

That is the million-dollar question. What I need is for Tiffany to grow up and realize what is right in front of her. I need her to understand that there isn't anything to be afraid of, and even if she is, I'm not going anywhere. Well, I guess I actually did kind of go somewhere. But, I didn't want to say anything that I couldn't take back. "No, just let me wallow in peace." I've never been one to drown in misery with alcohol, but right now I could really use a twelve pack or two.

Apparently my mother does not know the definition of peace, or has the capability to allow me space. She sits down beside me on the old ratty couch and wraps her arm around my shoulders, pulling me close to her like she did when I was a child. Back then it was comforting. Now, it's annoying. "Whatever it is, the two of you can work it out. I know I wasn't the kindest when I was peppering her with questions but I like her. She's unapologetic, and I could tell that she cares about you a lot. I just needed to know that she was right for my baby boy. It's difficult entrusting someone else with your happiness."

"Well," I sigh. "She sure has a funny way of showing it." And it's nice to hear that Mom didn't actually have anything against Tiffany. If only she would have gone about it differently.

"She'll come around. She looks at you the same way I looked at your father when we were young. I know love when I see it."

Groaning, I slide away from my mother. "That's the thing, Mom. I don't think she loves me. She's so terrified of relationships. After we had dinner with you and Dad, she put up wall after wall." I didn't mean to say that last part, but I also want her to know that she's part of the reason Tiffany freaked out.

"That was a couple of months ago. Surely that wasn't what scared her away now." She taps her fingers against her chin. "Did you do something differently? Or maybe something she didn't like?"

"Not that I know of." I stand up and pace around the tiny room. "Everything was okay. She was a little skittish after dinner since y'all were the first parents she has ever met. But I thought things were going great. Until she started picking up extra shifts again and then last night happened. I don't know what the hell I did."

"Wow," Mom gasps. "You weren't kidding when you said she doesn't do relationships." She shakes her head still astonished about Tiffany's lack of boyfriends, when she smiles. "Why don't you give me her phone number, and I'll call her. Maybe I can get to the bottom of it and figure out what's going on. I hate seeing you like this."

I throw my hands up in the air. "Not. Going. To. Happen." Shaking my head, I continue pacing. "That would overstep your boundaries. Hell, that would be leaping over them and would probably freak her out even more." I take a deep breath and run my fingers through my already disheveled hair. "I'm going to give her some time and let her figure out what it is she wants." In the end I hope it's me.

"I was just trying to help," she huffs. Without another word she stands and leaves the apartment. I swear that woman might be more impossible than Tiffany. Now to figure out how much time to give her. First, I will need clothes in case this is more than temporary.

～

Our apartment is dark and quiet. The hum of the refrigerator my only soundtrack. She isn't here and my heart sinks. I had all of my hopes pinned on her still being here when I showed up. But that was obviously too much to hope for.

Should I stay and see if she comes home? Or, do I let her have some space? The questions bounce around in my head, and I don't know what to do. I head toward the living room, seconds from sitting down on the couch when I stop. No, I told my mom I would give her room to think, but damn, it's hard. I know what I want. I know *who* I want. I just need her to realize she wants the same thing. Maybe I'm hoping for something that will never happen.

The fact that she isn't here speaks volumes. I search every room for a note or some sign that she's coming back. But, I leave each area of the apartment empty-handed. It's not like she's never going to come back since she is the main signer on this place. The question is when she'll come back. Either way, my heart hurts knowing that she left. She didn't even bother to stay and fight for me...for us. I guess, she got what she wanted. And now I'm left to mend my battered heart.

I go to my room and pack a few days' worth of clothes. There's no way I can stay here. Or, live with her. Not now. Not when she can't be mine. I'm not going to screw her over though. There are still a few months left with me on the lease, and even though her actions are breaking my heart, I will pay my part of the rent, whether or not I live here. Despite everything that has happened, I can't leave her struggling to make ends meet on her own.

Glancing around the room, I take stock of everything I will have to move out. It's not a lot, but the emotional baggage I'm taking with me will make it seem that much harder. I still have her work schedule for the rest of the week, and I'm going to come back when I know she won't be here. Hopefully, my dad will be available to help me. Loathe as I am to move back into the apartment above the garage, it is probably what is best for now. At least, until I can get over Tiffany.

She didn't leave me a note, and though I want to let her know that I'll be okay, I don't leave her one either. She's made her decision. Allowing herself to have the freedom she thinks she needs. Instead, I walk out of the apartment and close the door quietly on this chapter of my life. Too bad this isn't like my favorite comic books, and I won't get the girl in the end.

TWENTY-FIVE

Tiffany

Stella stands in front of me, finger pointing in my face as she goes on and on about all the ways I've royally fucked up. As if I didn't already know that. I regretted not saying anything the second he walked out the door.

"You're being a coward," she finishes her diatribe. That catches my attention.

"Excuse me?" I can't believe those words just came out of her mouth. "You ran over four hours away rather than talk to Johnny when you thought he had a thing for his ex."

"That's different," she scoffs and flips her hair over her shoulder. "I wasn't there permanently."

"No, Stella," I stand and she stumbles back. She should have known I wasn't going to sit there and let her call me a coward. "It's the same damn thing. The only difference is, I know I screwed up while you moped around on the sofa for a week."

"So you aren't here hiding out?"

She has me there, but that's not the full reason I'm here. "A tiny part is."

"And what is the other part?" Geez, I don't remember being this hard on her when she did the same thing.

"Regrouping," I nod, trying to convince myself as much as I am her. "I have to figure out what my next step needs to be."

"Does this mean you're going to fight for him?" Audrey finally joins the conversation. She's been sitting on the other end of the sofa letting Stella berate me. I wish I could say it wasn't normal, but it is. She doesn't do conflict and never has.

"Yes." And I'm going to. I don't have a choice. Spending my evenings with him rather than at a bar have been the highlights of my days. Being able to celebrate the little things and venting to him when I get home from work are what I look forward to most. Even his obsession with comics isn't enough to deter me from wanting him, no matter how hard I tried to fight it. All it did was make me like him more. Well, like may be an understatement. I fell for him. As much as my brain tried to fight it, my heart knew all along.

"That's it," Stella rolls her eyes. "The only answer you're going to give us is a *yes*. You don't have any plan?"

"Not yet," I reply. "But I'll figure something out." I have to, and it needs to be something big.

"Are you sure this is a good idea right now?" Audrey asks when she notices the direction our Uber is heading. This plan calls for food and alcohol. Not a lot since that's why I'm in this mess. Well, that was the catalyst anyway.

"Yes," I answer, watching the buildings as we speed past them. "I'm sure."

"Shouldn't we be at home plotting your next move?" Stella pipes in, needing to add her two cents.

The driver stops in front of our favorite restaurant, and we all get out. The doors slamming closed one after the other. "That's what we're doing."

"That's funny because it looks like we're at our usual spot. Which is pointless." Audrey points to all the people standing outside, no doubt waiting for a table to open up. "There's no way we will get in there soon."

I laugh and reach for the handle on the door. "Don't worry. I've got that covered." The restaurant is packed and loud. Conversations blending together until I can't pick one out from the others. Leaving them behind, I walk to the hostess stand. "There should be a group of people waiting on me."

I'm happy to know that she doesn't have to ask my name despite me not coming in for a while. She glances around the dining area and nods her head. Pointing toward the back corner. "They are right back there. Let me grab you some menus and I'll lead you back."

I look over my shoulder to my cousins. They are patiently waiting by the door, but look at me like I'm wasting my time. The line behind me has doubled within the few moments I've been standing here. "Don't worry about that. I know my way through the place, and we can share menus with my friends. You look like you have your hands full."

She sighs in relief. "Thank you. Let me know if y'all need anything."

"Will do." I tap my hand on the stand twice before waving Audrey and Stella over.

When they are near me Stella whispers, "Is this some perk for being long-time customers?"

We weave between tables and people leaving until we come to a stop. "Nope," I beam, sweeping my hands in front of me at the table of new friends. "I've brought in reinforcements."

"Who are these people?" Audrey asks, her voice barely audible.

"Cosplayers, these are my cousins," I motion to my two best friends, and partners in crime. "Cousins, these are my friends from Comic-Con."

"When did you go to that?" Stella scrunches up her nose.

"Don't' worry about it. Right now… They are going to help me get my man back."

"Are you sure this will fit me?" I stare at the latex costume doubting my entire plan. If I can't get that thing on, everything will fall apart. Audrey went by the apartment after we ate, and it didn't look like he'd even been there. I should have gone but I don't think I could have faced him on the off chance he was there.

"That girl, Rachel, said y'all were about the same size when I ran by her house to pick it up." Stella holds it up, inspecting the fabric. "It looks like an oversized condom to me."

"You are so ridiculous," I snatch it out of her hands. "It's not even see through."

"Maybe not, but it doesn't leave very much to the imagination." Audrey shakes her head. "Are you sure you want to leave the building in that?"

She has a point. I may not dress conservatively, but I've never worn something in public that could show off every single flaw that I have. Nerves over my plan take hold, and I sit down on the sofa. "I don't think I can do this."

"Oh no," Stella bends down in front of me. "You are not backing out. If you love him, and I'm pretty sure you do, you'll do whatever you need to get him back."

"I do lo—" the word gets caught in my throat. I've never uttered that word to anyone besides the people in my family. I take a deep breath then let it out. "I love him. He grounds me in a way that you two jerks never have."

"Hey," Stella yells. "We're the ones that usually bail your ass out of trouble."

She has a point. They've saved my ass more times than I can count. I'm just happy to have them by my side as I go to make a complete ass of myself. Hopefully Spencer will think it's endearing and take pity on me.

"Okay. Let's do this before I chicken out," my voice is confident, at least I hope it is. I look at the outfit dangling from Stella's hands and shake my head. I can't believe I'm going to do this. "Please tell me you have a robe for me to wear out of here."

TWENTY-SIX

Spencer

I PICK my phone up then set it back down. It's what I've been doing for the past twenty minutes. Totally normal, right? Maybe if I stare at the stupid thing long enough, it will ring or ding with a text message. *Something.* I half-hoped Tiffany would have called me by now. I could call her. Mom has told me more than once today to get over my pride and take the first step. I didn't do anything, though. Why is it my fault she can't accept my love?

No, my dumb ass would rather sit in a dark room and whine about her not freaking calling me. I should have left a note when I stopped by the apartment. She'd at least know I cared. I will need to text her eventually to let her know my part of the rent is taken care of until the lease is up. Even if it's not what I want.

"Honey," my mom comes into my room. "I love you, but can't you be gloomy in the garage apartment?"

Did I forget to mention that I'm in my childhood room? If that's not sad, I don't know what else is. I couldn't bring myself to stay in the space I lived in before Tiffany. That is where everything began between us. "Seriously? You're rejecting me now, too?"

"No, sweetheart," she sighs before turning on the light. "It's just that this isn't healthy. You obviously want to be with her."

"How do you know that?"

"You're sitting alone in the dark. In the room you grew up in." She pats my head like I'm a puppy that needs reassurance. "There's no better proof than that."

"What should I do?" I've always been able to think through problems logically and do what needed to be done. But I can't be logical when it comes to Tiffany.

"Well," Mom clears her throat. "If you love her, or want to make things work with her, then you need to go after her."

"What if she rejects me, again?" I'm not sure my heart can take it. Being with her has been like a game of tug of war. A constant push and pull but never knowing who will come out hurt. Not to mention I feel like a total loser coming to my mom for advice about my love life. How pathetic is it I don't have any close friends to talk about this shit with?

"It's something you'll have to accept. If you think she's worth fighting for, then go wait for her. She'll show up at your place, eventually."

I guess I need to go grab my bag. Tiffany is more than worth it, even if she drives me insane sometimes. "Thanks, Mom. That was what I needed to hear."

"Good luck," she calls to my retreating back.

I rush out of the house, flying right by Dad's confused stare. *Sorry, old man. I don't have time to stop and talk. I need to get my girl.* My feet pound up the stairs of the garage apartment, and I charge through the door. My bag is sitting on the sofa, still zipped closed. At least, I don't have to search for anything, except my keys. Where did I put those damn things?

I lift my laptop, shuffle around some papers, and then look around the room. They have to be here somewhere. No such luck. The sheets from the blow up mattress are thrown on the floor and the keys aren't on any of the flat surfaces. Oh well, looks like I will have to get an Uber to take me over there. In the main room, I lift my bag. Something shiny catches my eye, and my keys are right there. I guess I threw them down before I set the bag down when I came in. It doesn't surprise me. I was in a foul mood when I came in, and I didn't think I'd be able to get out of it. Thanks to my mom, I'm willing to put my heart on the line once again.

Grabbing the keys, I run out of the apartment and almost miss the second step on the stairs. Breaking my neck wouldn't help me convince Tiffany to stay with me. Though, it could help me in the sympathy department, but I don't want that to be the reason she sticks around.

With my keys in hand, I hit the fob to unlock the car doors, but head-lights swing into the driveway. I lift my hands up to shield some of the brightness, trying to see who is walking toward me. "Spencer?" My heart lifts at the sound of her voice, and it takes everything in me not to rush to her and wrap her in my arms. She sought me out. This has to mean *something.*

"What are you doing here?" My words stop her in her tracks. I'm not sure if my tone was desperate or accusatory, but I want her to keep walking toward me. The car behind her turns the headlights off, but the orange parking lights are still glowing. Whoever brought her isn't leaving, and I have a sneaking suspicion it's one of her cousins.

"I, um," she pauses her words for a second and starts walking toward me again. A shadow coming into the light from the garage. "I wanted to talk to you."

Finally, I can see her. And holy shit. She's every nerd boy's wet dream. She's in a tight yellow and green suit. A black belt with an "X" in the middle wraps around her waist. She has a few strands of white hair clipped into her fiery mane. "You look…" I swallow hard. "Amazing. Is there a cosplay event happening somewhere I didn't know about?" Please don't say that you're coming here to break up with me then heading to an event I would love to go to.

"No," she smiles. That one gesture kills any doubt I have about her wanting to end things with me. There's no way she would smile if she was here to destroy my heart for a second time. "I asked Rachel if she had anything I could borrow that you would like. This is what she came up with. It's not complete since it was so last minute, but do you like it?"

"Like is an understatement." In reality, I want to haul ass up the steps to the apartment, and have my way with her on the blow up mattress.

"I just wanted to show you I lo—love you. I was a dumbass for pulling the shit I did. I was just scared."

"There are other ways to handle that fear. You know that, right?" She's still a couple of feet in front of me, and I need her to take those last few steps. To be within touching distance.

"Yes, I know that. But giving my heart to you had me questioning every-thing. I don't want to end up like Audrey. I love her to death, but she can be bitter when it comes to relationships. And well, if I give into you completely, I open myself up to that same hurt." She wraps her arms around herself. The one and only time I've ever seen her self-conscious of herself.

Rather than wait for her to come to me, I close the distance between us. Placing my hands on either side of her face and lifting her head until her eyes meet mine. "You don't have to be scared of that. I told you, I'm yours. I think I was yours that first night I met you at the concert. I'm not going anywhere. I just needed you to figure out what you wanted."

"I want you. Comics, cosplay and all. *You* make me happy. You make me feel more alive than bars or one-night stands ever could."

I laugh. I can't help it. "It's nice to know I rank above booze and sex." She's opening her mouth to argue her point but I crash mine down to hers. Not letting her say anything else. She had me when she said she loved me. Even more, when she said, I make her happy. Our tongues dance around each other, and this feels *right*. Like everything I've done my whole life has led me to this moment. To my happiness. "I'm here. For as long as you'll have me."

"What do you say we head home and *talk* more?" She winks at me and pulls me toward my car.

"That depends. How long do you get to keep the costume?"

Tiffany scrunches up her nose. "I have to get it back to Rachel, in perfect condition, tomorrow." She points at me and wags her finger, "So no funny business."

"I can't make any promises," a devilish grin sweeps across my face. I'm going to take full advantage of her dressed up as my favorite character. "But, yes, let's go home."

I walk around to the passenger side of the car and open the door for her. She slides into the seat, trying her best to get comfortable in the skin-tight costume. I see my mom's shadow standing in the doorway and she waves. I wave back, grateful to know that she doesn't dislike my girlfriend. I throw my bag in the backseat and get in behind the wheel. "Are you sure about this?"

"There's nothing I've ever been more sure of." She grabs my hand on the gearshift, and squeezes it. That's all the confirmation I need. I'm ready to see where life takes me. Between the new design contract with Crooked Halo, and Tiffany back on my side, I feel like I've conquered the world.

Epilogue

THIS MAY BE the best concert I've ever been to in my life. I could kiss Spencer for getting tickets to ACL from his client. Let's be real, I probably will… repeatedly. For now, we'll sit at the back of the crowd and listen to the music roll over us. Normally I'd be in the thick of things at the front of the stage, but that's not where Spencer wants to be. This is better in every way possible. I may not be in the action, but I'm beside the one person who means the most to me.

Three months have passed since that night I showed up to his parent's house in costume, and I haven't looked back once. Am I still terrified of our future? You bet your ass, but I will not let my fear of getting hurt dictate my relationships anymore.

"I'm going to go get us some drinks," Spencer leans in to tell me. Even though we're nowhere near the stage, it's still loud as hell back here. "I don't want to miss them when they come on stage. Do you want anything?"

"Whatever you're having," I wink at him, remembering the night I met him. It feels like ages ago, now. "Hurry back, though. You know how these people are when someone vacates a spot."

"I'll be right back." He gives me a loud, smacking kiss on the cheek and heads to the nearest beer stand.

I pull out my phone to see if I have any signal. Two little bars show on the strength and I sigh in relief.

Tiffany: Are you coming? We have a spot saved for you.

I've laid my backpack and blanket out on the ground just in case she shows up. The next band had an extra pass, and I knew I needed to drag her out of the house.

Audrey: Traffic is insane. I don't think I will be able to make it. Y'all have fun.
Tiffany: That's bullshit. You're in walking distance from us.
Audrey: I don't want to be the third wheel.
Tiffany: You won't be. You're my cousin!
Audrey: It's fine. I have some things I need to take care of, anyway.
Tiffany: Suit yourself. But don't say I didn't invite you to anything.
Audrey: Haha. Have fun and stay safe.
Tiffany: Will do.

I hate that she's holed herself away since Spencer and I have gotten more serious. It's like she's turned into me, except she's avoiding people in relationships entirely. It's not healthy. Oh, this is rich coming from me, the queen of one-night stands… Well, the former queen. I'm just happy to have found my person.

"Why are you frowning?" Spencer hands me a cup and sits down next to me. "That band wasn't so bad."

"Audrey."

"She's not coming, is she?" He scoots closer to me even though the fall air is still hot. "She'll get over whatever funk she's in."

"I know," I sigh. "I just wish she wouldn't keep blowing off plans when it's the both of us."

"You should go on more girl's nights with her. Just the two of you."

"I guess." The crowd ahead of us yells, and I know the big moment is finally upon us. I stand up with Spencer, trying to see over everyone's head. Geez, I hate being short. Finally, someone moves and I can see the logo Spencer created. He did an amazing job, and I can't wait to see the doors that open up to him now that he's designing for bands and companies.

Crooked Halo comes on stage and the crowd goes wild. Some of these people have never heard of them, but they've grown quite a following in the few months they've been performing. They got this gig because they are an up and coming local band. I'm just happy to know that I was one of their original fans.

The guitar and drums begin a rhythm and Dale is crooning about a guy and a girl who meet by chance. I like to think the song is about me and Spencer, but Dale will never confess it.

Gone Inn

Chapter One

Stella

"Are you sure this is a good idea?" Johnny is pulling our suitcases behind him. The airport is bustling with families rushing here and there. People coming home from visiting family, or heading off on adventures. The only thing I'm over is the noise. When I lived in Austin it wasn't an issue because I loved the loudness, but after living in the middle of nowhere for so long, I'm not used to it anymore.

"Why wouldn't it be?" I stop to grab one of the suitcases from him. He looks like he's struggling to pull mine. I may have packed too much. You can never be over-prepared, though. I have an outfit for anything that could possibly come up, and I regret nothing.

He's grumbling while weaving between people. "Our entire family. In a cabin. Together. For a week." He's being way more dramatic that he should be. It's not going to be that bad.

The doors to leave are up ahead, and a line of cabs sits in front, waiting to pick up passengers. Fingers crossed they won't all be gone by the time we get outside. There are clusters of people blocking the door, and I'm sure they are waiting until they can go out together to avoid the cold.

I wait for him to catch up to keep from yelling over my shoulder. "Your parents won't be there for a couple of days, and my aunts and uncles will only be there for the weekend." There's no use trying to force our way through the crowd. We'll get to the cabin soon enough. "You're getting worked up over nothing. My family is used to taking trips with each other." I pause for a second. "It's usually to a beach, but it's been a while since I've been skiing."

He stands next to me and wraps an arm around my shoulder. I lean into him and put my arm around his waist. There's something bulky in his pocket, and I move my hand to see what it is, but he quickly slips out of my grasp. I guess our momentary embrace is over now. That's odd. "I've never been skiing. We also don't do many family vacations. At least, not ones that include my cousins."

There's a small break in the crowd, and I move forward. "You'll have the time of your life. Just wait and see."

"At least Spencer will be there," he mutters before following me to the exit. He sounds anxious, and I wish I knew why. He's also been confidant no matter the situation. It's not like he's just now meeting the family. We've seen everyone dozens of times since we became a couple.

"If you keep grumbling about everything, I'll start thinking you have something against my family." The doors slide open and a gust of cold air hits me square in the face. This is a whole different level of cold than we have in Texas. I can't tell if I prefer this or back home. The plus side is there is actual snow here and not that damn ice we get back home.

"It's not that," he sighs and pulls me into him. This time I'm on the opposite side of him, and I can't help but think he did that on purpose. "I just...I wish it was just going to be us on this trip. It would be romantic, and all that." He waves his hand in the air as if he's brushing off the last comment as no big deal.

"We can have romance any day of the week," I laugh. "We don't have any kids, and we're both home at a decent time. That leaves all the time in the world for romance."

"I guess," he pouts. "What time are we supposed to be at the cabin? Do we need to check in or anything?"

People are clamoring to get into the cabs and out of the cold. There are a couple of cars pulling forward, and if we don't grab one soon, we'll be stuck in the cold. Don't get me wrong, I love the snow. I just don't like being stuck in it with my traveling clothes. They aren't as warm as what I wear on the ski slopes. "Whenever we get there. Mom and Dad already got keys for us and all that jazz. The only thing we have to do before anything else is stop and grab some coffee."

"Can it wait until we get to the cabin? I'm almost certain your parents grabbed some of your favorite blends."

"Do you want a bitchy girlfriend? The plane ride was bleh, and I didn't get any of the sleep I was hoping to catch up on, and I'm exhausted. I need a small pick me up."

"Okay. I'll run into whatever coffee shop we find on the way to grab your favorite drink." I don't know what I would do without this guy. He lets go of me and rushes to the cab that pulls up directly in front of us. "Let's go before we're stuck standing out here all day."

"That may be the best thing you've said all day." I feel a little bad that he feels like we won't have any alone time, but I wouldn't do that to him. I have plans for just the two of us when we get to the resort. I love our families, but this is the first time Johnny and I have gone out of state together. We need to make our own memories while we're here. I'm not going to tell him that, though. Not yet, anyway. I want to surprise him. Well, try to. He always figures out what I'm going to do before I actually do it, and it's kind of annoying.

This week is either going to be amazing, or a disaster. When I'm with my cousins, it could honestly go either way. I just hope Johnny doesn't freak out at exactly how much time my family likes to spend together. My fingers are crossed that he likes late night card games, and is competitive. It's a side of him I've never seen, and if anyone can bring it out...it's my family.

Chapter Two

Johnny

THIS WEEK IS EITHER GOING to be awesome, or it's going to go up in flames.
There is no in between. Even though Stella and her cousins have been planning
this since spring, I was hoping it would fall through before then. Apparently, I
have a lot to learn when it comes to the determination of those three.

I had grand plans for Stella and I on New Year's Eve. I mean, I know it will
be more special because her entire family is around, but I kind of wanted to do
this just me and her. It doesn't matter now, though. I am at the mercy of her
family.

"Have you ever been skiing before?" Stella scoots closer to me and the backseat of the Cab. I swear this tribe is taking forever.

"Do you want the truth, or do you want me to lie to you?"

"Truth. Always the truth." She grabs my hand and lifts it up to her lips,
placing a gentle kiss on my knuckles. When I don't answer her right away, she
grins mischievously. "You haven't, have you?"

It's no secret that I don't like the cold. I never have, and I probably never
will. Skiing or snowboarding have not once crossed my mind as fun things to
do. I've done a lot of dumb shit in my years, but gliding down a slick as hell
mountain on a toothpick is not one of them. "Nope. Any vacations we took
growing up were within driving distance. My parents aren't much for flying."

Stella takes a moment to look out the window and waved her hand
showing off the scenery. "Technically." I really hate when she starts off a

sentence with technically. It always ends in an argument that she wins. "This is drivable since we all are, in fact, driving up a mountain…in a car."

"You know what I mean, smart ass," I grumble and pull my hand out of hers. Maybe I don't want to carry out the plan I have for the weekend, after all.

She bends her shoulder into mine, and takes hold of my hand again. "Don't be so moody. It will be fun, and we can start off on the bunny trail. It's where everyone starts."

I can't tell if she's making fun of me, or trying to reassure me. Either way, this sentiment makes me feel slightly better. "Only if you go with me."

"Like I would let you go alone? There's a good chance you would hurt yourself if I weren't there on that and I kind of like having you around." So much for reassurance.

"You're starting to make this baby trail sound more like a gauntlet than anything else."

She squeezes my hand and her laughter fills the car. "They aren't baby trails. They are *bunny* trails, and you will be just fine. Look," she points out the window and starts bouncing in her seat. "We're almost there."

A massive resort looms in the short distance, and I'm really not prepared for this. Log cabins pepper the snow, and my mouth drops open. These shouldn't be considered log cabins that would mean they are small and quaint. No, these houses rival mansion like ones I've seen on TV. "With how big those are, are we even going to see your family at all?"

"Probably," she giggles. "They plan on us playing cards tonight as soon as my cousins get here."

"Who is they?"

"My parents."

I groan. My parents are awesome and they like to play games, I've seen Stella, Audrey, and Tiffany play spoons…and that is the most dangerous shit I have ever seen. "Hopefully you don't mind if my parents don't stay up all that late."

"No worries. You don't have to stay up and play, but it's going to be fun."

Her definition of fun and mine are definitely not the same.

Stella's parents are sitting on the porch when our cab pulls up to the cabin. Not a coat on either one of them. I don't understand. It's freezing out here and the only thing they are wearing are long sleeve shirts with a puffy vest over it. How does that protect anyone from the cold?

Her dad comes down the steps to meet us at the car. "We're glad you finally made it." He gives Stella a quick hug and sticks his hand out for me to shake. I place my hand in his and he pulls me in for a hug. "Let me help you get these bags unloaded so the both of you can get settled in."

"Thanks, Sir." I pull away from him. It's always been so odd how open her family is. It's not something I'm used to. Don't get me wrong. I hug my mom and dad, but Stella's family...everyone gets a hug. They are also so open about almost everything. I've been scarred for life because of some of the things they discuss. The only one who seems to hold back is Audrey. I see *a lot* of alcohol in my future. At least for the week while we're here.

He grabs Stella's suitcase out of the trunk, and I grab mine, plus the suitcase holding Stella's accessories. She never travels light, and even if it drives me nuts, I love that she has all of her favorite things with her. If it makes her happy, it makes me happy. I follow her dad up the stairs, and her mom almost tackles me when I reach the landing. My foot slides on the small sheen of ice under the snow, and her mom pulls me closer to keep me from falling. "It's so good to see you," she squeals.

I literally saw them last weekend. We probably would have flown in with them, but I had to work a couple of days while Reaf is out of town. The shop isn't usually too busy this time of year, but he asked for the time off before I did. "You, too." I breathe a sigh of relief when she lets go of me. I wonder if she's always been this way or if the rest of the family rubbed off on her when she married into it. Is this a glimpse of future me?

"You are on the second floor. Do you need me to grab anything?"

"No, thank you. I think we got it." I trudge to the door, and notice Stella has pulled her suitcase from her father's grasp.

She follows me inside, then quickly gets in front of me. "This is the cabin we usually rent, and I always get the same room."

"Lead the way." She starts up the stairs and I take a couple of moments admiring the way her jeans hug her ass as she climbs them. I can't wait until we get a moment alone. I rush to catch up to her, but she stops fairly close to the staircase. "Is this our room?"

"Yep." She pushes the door open. It's wall to wall windows with a stunning view of the mountains. I see the appeal of taking vacations here. Who knows maybe I'll whisk her away for a romantic getaway, just the two of us, one day.

"Who is next door to us?"

"My parents." She's so nonchalant about it.

"What do you mean, your parents? How are we going to have any privacy with them right next door?" My voice is getting louder, but I can't help it. I'm going to be terrified doing anything with her since her parents are in the next room.

"Don't freak out," she throws over her shoulder as she puts her clothes away. "We all sleep next to our parents. Tiffany and Spencer will be close to hers as well." She stops taking clothes out of her suitcase, and comes to wrap her arms around me. "It will be just fine. I have other plans for us."

"If you say so." I'm not feeling confident, but I'll have to trust that she's worked some kind of magic. I definitely should have asked more questions before coming on this trip.

Chapter Three

Stella

"ARE YOU ALL READY FOR AN ALL-NIGHTER?" Tiffany is bouncing in her seat and about to knock over her glass of wine. I think Spencer is starting to question what he got himself into.

"Calm down, Tiff." I scooped her glass of wine away from the edge of the table. I am in my favorite pair of sweats, and I don't want them stained red. Johnny scoots further away from me, and I can't tell if it's to get out of the spill zone or, because he's scared, she's going to knock me into him. "Nobody is going to want to play with you if you're acting like one of those Animaniacs cartoon characters."

"What's wrong with them?" She pauses her bouncing and picks up the deck of cards to shuffle them.

Johnny takes this moment to scoot back from the table, "I am going to go gather the spoons." I know this isn't his favorite game. He has seen just how serious my cousins and I get when it comes to spoons.

I turn my attention back to Tiffany. "Nothing is wrong with them. But it's been a long day for all of us, and I'm not certain everyone is ready for an all-nighter."

"You're such a party pooper." Tiffany finishes shuffling the cards, and slams the deck in front of me. "Cut them please."

As I'm cutting the cards, Spencer mouths "thank you" over Tiffany's shoulder. He is probably the only one who hasn't had the pleasure of watching my cousins fight it out over the last spoon. "Mom, Dad, are you all playing?"

"No." Mom grabs one of the bottles of wine from the counter and walks toward the living room. "I think we're going to hang out with Johnny's parents." Just before she disappears from my view, she calls back, "You kids have fun."

"We're not kids anymore," Tiffany grumbles under her breath.

"Are y'all ready to play?" Johnny sets way more spoons on the table than what we need.

"Where's Audrey?" She went upstairs to take a shower, but I haven't seen her since. "Maybe we should wait on her."

"Nope," Tiffany shakes her head. "She can join in on the next round. She should have showered faster." She deals out the cards, and promptly begins the game, not caring that I should be the first person to draw. It's fine, though. I don't feel like arguing with her. If I do, the fight for a spoon will be that much worse. She plays dirty when she's trying to win. For such a free spirit, she's competitive as hell.

Spencer's hand glides across the table for a spoon, and both Tiffany and I snatch one up as fast as possible.

"I didn't stand a chance," Johnny groans. "Do I need to ref the rest of the game?"

"What does that mean?" Spencer's eyes are wide, and he looks terrified.

"You'll see." Johnny doesn't give him any more information. He will just have to wait and see. When we were younger, I pulled her across the table to take the spoon from her. We got in trouble, but my victory was worth it.

After six rounds, Audrey still hasn't joined us. Tiffany and I are tied, but Johnny is yawning. I feel bad keeping him up. At the same time...I want to claim victory. He lays his head down on the table, closing his eyes, and I know that we'll have to rematch another day. "You ready to head to bed?"

"You can keep playing, I'll be fine." His words are lazy and slow. He's exhausted and worth more than this game.

"Let's go." I scoot the chair back and stand. "We'll rematch tomorrow, Tiffany."

"What?" She screeches. "He said he was fine. It's just one more round."

Spencer leans over and whispers something in her ear. She sits back in her chair, crosses her arms over her chest, and pouts. "Fine. But this isn't over."

Rolling my eyes at her, I touch Johnny's arm for him to get up. He follows me through the living room and up the stairs. Our parents are still sitting by the fire chatting so we will have privacy for a little bit. Not that it will do much good with him practically falling asleep on his feet. "Hang tight and I'll get our jammies out of the dresser."

He sits on the edge of the bed, and I turn to grab our things out of the dresser. I love my family, but a little bit of alone time with Johnny on our first night here is much needed. Especially after Tiffany's crazy ass tried yanking a spoon out of my hand. I'm pretty sure my body moved like they do in The Matrix and I'll be hurting tomorrow. Who knew all those other muscles existed?

With our pajamas in hand, I turn back toward the bed. So much for alone time. My back was to him a whole two minutes max, and he's already lying down with his eyes closed. A tiny part of me wants to wake him up. To demand his attention. He's already lightly snoring, though and I don't want to be that person. The trip here must have taken more out of him than I realized, and I feel like crap for forcing him to play card games with us. I should have let him relax with our parents, or at least, told him to take a nap.

Worst girlfriend of the year award goes to me. I'll just have to make it up to him tomorrow. The appointment is ready for our skiing session, and I have a few more surprises up my sleeve. Hopefully tomorrow he'll be well rested and not as moody as he's been today.

I throw his pajama bottoms back on the dresser. He's obviously not going to need them. After changing into my own, I lift up the comforter and slide in next to him. I pull more of the blanket out from under him to wrap around me, and he doesn't budge. He's definitely out for the night.

Chapter Four

Johnny

WHY IS it so bright in here? I cover my eyes and turn over. The blankets aren't covering me, and I vaguely remember coming to bed. I wasn't drunk or anything. Exhaustion hit me like a ton of bricks. It takes a lot of energy to be around Stella and her cousins. Not to mention playing spoons with them. It's…a lot.

Cracking my eyes open, I peer at the space Stella should be occupying, but she isn't there. Did I sleep late or something? The alarm clock, on her side of the bed, is glowing red with the numbers seven thirty-four. I definitely did not sleep late. I listen for any sounds coming from the other rooms and it sounds like everyone else is still asleep. That means one of two things, Stella is being extra quiet, or my snoring was so bad she went to Audrey's room or the couch.

Looks like I need to find out where she is. We're supposed to go skiing today, and I have no idea what time that's supposed to happen. Stella has everything scheduled out in her phone, and when I tried to take a peek, she closed the app. She's up to something. I only hope it doesn't interfere with what I'm trying to do.

"Johnny," her voice comes from the now open door. "Are you up?" She's wearing a pink plaid pajama set that hugs her curves in all the right places. I want nothing more than for her to close the door behind her and climb into bed with me.

"Yeah," I grunt. "I'm awake. Why are you up so early?"

She actually closes the door, but she sits on the edge of the bed instead of lying down next to me. "I went downstairs to get the coffee started and make sure everything was ready to go for us."

"You sure it didn't have anything to do with my snoring?"

She grins. "Well, there was that, too. But mostly the other stuff. The snores didn't get bad until about an hour ago."

At least I didn't run her off. "What's on the agenda for today?" I debate rolling out of bed, but I don't want to get up yet. Between the late night and flying into another time zone, I'm still wiped.

"You need to get up soon. We have an appointment with a ski instructor."

Wait. What? I lift up on one elbow. "I thought you knew how to ski?"

"I do," she huffs. "But it's been a while, and a refresher never hurt anyone. Besides, you didn't think I'd make you do the ski lessons on your own, did you?"

Actually, I kind of did. "You shouldn't have to spend your time waiting until I learn how to do it without killing myself."

"It's not that bad, and this is our first trip here together. There's no way in hell I'd miss being a part of the ski lessons."

"But what about all the stuff about spending time with the whole family?" Did I imagine that conversation? Or maybe I just freaked out for no damn reason. Big gatherings make me nervous, even when it's people that I've been around multiple times. Even though Stella and I have been together for a while, her family is still intimidating with how close they are.

"We are here for a whole week," she rolls her eyes. "We don't need to be with them every second of the day. Besides, we all get on each other's nerves before it's time to leave. If we make ourselves absent for part of it that means we won't be on anyone's shit list."

As crazy as she sounds, it makes a certain sort of sense. And…I'll be able to do what I want to without an audience. "What time do we have to be there?"

"An hour." She stands up and digs through the closet for the snow gear she bought me. "We'll eat breakfast then head over."

I'm happy it'll be both of us at the ski lesson. I'm sure I'll make a total ass of myself, but at least I'll have her there to cheer me on.

Stella's giggles are muffled. I'm going to blame it on the hat I'm wearing. This is the fifth time I've busted my ass in the last thirty minutes. "I'm sorry. It's not funny. I mean, it kind of is."

"You're not helping," I grumble while trying to stand up and catch my balance.

"It's just cute, Johnny." She steps out of her skis and makes her way toward me. "You're like a baby deer trying to find its footing."

I point to a group of kids that's been here the same amount of time I have. "They are younger than me, and are catching on just fine." I won't pretend it's not a punch to the gut. This shouldn't be that hard. I mean if a bunch of kids that can't be older than ten seem to get it, I should be able to as well.

"Kids are easier to teach." Wrapping an arm around my waist she leans into my chest. "They are more fearless and up for most challenges thrown their way."

She may be right. I pride myself on being able to take on any challenge that comes my way. Hell, it's how I managed to get the woman of my dreams. You wouldn't think this would be so hard. I'm sure the bruises on my ass would beg to differ. "How much longer do I need to subject myself to this embarrassment?"

She lets go of me and goes back to her skis. "Give it another thirty minutes. If you haven't improved by then, we'll stop for the day and grab some hot chocolate instead."

Is that disappointment I hear in her voice? Come on Johnny. Get it together. You just have to balance on toothpicks down a slippery hill. You've got this.

Chapter Five

Stella

JOHNNY IS GETTING frustrated and I feel awful for making him try to do this. It's not for everyone, and I wish I would have gotten his input before I booked the lesson. This is way outside of his comfort zone. Hell, I don't think he's ever even been around this much snow before. Texas doesn't usually get a lot unless we have a freak winter storm in January or February.

I'm so lost in my thoughts that it takes me a moment to hear the clapping and cheering. Johnny is skiing down the tiny bunny hill by himself. The kids in the class are giving him the momentum he needs to get to the bottom. He finally got the hang of it.

He's nearing the bottom, and I'm worried he won't have time to stop, but he twists his hips and stops like he's been doing it all his life. I unstrap my books from the skis and run down the hill to him. "You did it," I yell, louder than the kids will ever be.

"I did," he grins back at me. "I couldn't let a bunch of kids show me up. Not in front of you."

I smack him on the chest and laugh. "You don't have to prove anything to me. I would have been proud of you just for trying." It's true, too. Him doing something he normally wouldn't is a huge turn on. That he mastered it to impress me? It makes him even hotter than before.

"Yeah, well," he sniffles. Hopefully he doesn't get sick being in the cold. I made sure to pack him clothes that would keep him warm. "I think I'm ready for a break. I'm sure my ass is black and blue from all the times I fell before finally getting it."

"Let's head to the lodge and grab some hot chocolate while we rest. Maybe we can try one of the easier trails this afternoon." He unstraps his boots and steps out of them. Grabbing the skis and poles he begins walking back up the hill and bends to pick mine up. "I can carry my own. It's not like I really did anything this morning."

"It's okay. I've got them." He walks a few paces ahead of me. "But maybe we can try the other trails tomorrow. I think I need to give my body a bit of time to recoup."

That's not a bad idea. Maybe everyone will be out of the house and we can get some alone time. Or I can see if the small cabin I rented is available early. "We can do that. It's not like we don't have plenty of time. Let's get warmed up first."

He looks over his shoulder at me with a smirk. "I can think of about a thousand other ways besides hot chocolate that can warm us up."

"I swear," I laugh. "That's all men think about."

Shaking his head, he continues toward the lodge. "Not all the time." He pauses for a few seconds, and continues. "Just most of the time. It's hard not to when you look like that."

Rolling my eyes, I rush to get ahead of him. You can't even see my figure in this outfit. It's big, bulky, and leaves everything to the imagination. This definitely wouldn't be my first choice in outfits if I were trying to seduce him. "If you say so."

"I do, and that's all that matters." He catches up and tries to bump me with his hip, but the skis are in the way and he almost falls trying to get around them.

"Let me take my skis." I take them out of his hand and wrap my arm around them. "You look like you're having a hard time controlling yourself." He doesn't argue. Thank goodness. He's always arguing trying to do the gentlemanly thing, but I'm able to do things on my own with or without his help. It's good to see him now picking his battles. It's taken forever, but I think he finally realizes I'm not a damsel in distress.

The lodge is hot with all these clothes on. We unzip the top of our suits and let them hang down behind us. I swear, ski resorts are the only places where nineties fashion never goes out of style. You can always find someone with their suit hanging down or their jacket wrapped around their waist.

Johnny heads to the counter to buy our hot chocolates and I try to find a table for the both of us that's not in the center of the room. Yes, we get tons of privacy at home, but I want the same here. I just need to find an empty table settled in one of the nooks in this place. Glancing around the room I see a waitress cleaning off a table right beside a window. There aren't any other tables around it, and I rush toward it.

Another couple has the same idea, and I slide into the seat before they get a chance. Only, it's Tiffany and Spencer I was racing. "Damn it, Stella. I've been waiting for the last couple to leave for the past fifteen minutes."

"You should have been faster," I grin up at her. "Besides, we just came in from the cold."

"Where is Johnny?" Spencer looks around the area beside me.

"He's grabbing our drinks. We just finished ski lessons."

"How did he do?" Tiffany's eyes are wide with excitement. "Is he ready to take on the rest of the trails?"

"He progressed. We aren't hitting any more trails today. Johnny has a few bumps and bruises. We may hang out at the cabin and watch movies."

"You can do that at home. Y'all should do something adventurous." Tiffany bends down next to the table. "Live a little."

"We have a whole week, Tiff. I don't want to throw everything at him all at once." I pat her hand. "Not everyone is as free-spirited as you."

"More people need to be," she pouts. "Anyway, we'll let y'all get back to it. I think we're going to give snowboarding a try." With that she grabs Spencer's hand and pulls him out the door. I guess she didn't want this table all that bad after all.

"Where did they leave off in such a hurry to?" Johnny sets a steaming cup in front of me before taking a seat.

"Snowboarding." I roll my eyes. "She's going to drive that boy crazy with all her antics."

Johnny grins. "I wouldn't worry too much about them. Spencer seems to be okay with it. As long as they make each other happy, that's all that matters."

"You're right," I sigh. "To each their own." We clink our mugs together and take a sip. "Let's go back to the cabin after this. I could use a nap."

"I really hope you're not being literal."

Winking at him, I take another drink from my mug. "I guess you'll just have to find out."

Chapter Six

Johnny

She's actually taking a damn nap. Would it be horrible if I attempted waking her up? I'm about to wrap my arm around her and bring her closer to me, but she starts snoring. I'd be an asshole if I woke her from a deep sleep, no matter how much I want to. Since my snoring is what kept her up, I'll leave her be. We'll have other opportunities for extracurricular activities this week. Especially if she's right about having made sure we have alone time.

I slide off the bed as gently as possible. Surely someone is downstairs by now. Maybe I'll run into Audrey. I haven't seen her since we all came in. Crossing the room and closing the door behind me, I make my way down the stairs, and almost slip on the last one. Spencer and Tiffany are on the couch making out, and that's a sight I could go without ever seeing again.

"I thought y'all were out causing trouble," I try to shield my eyes while making my way across the living room to the kitchen.

"Oh shit," Spencer yells. He pulls away from Tiffany like he just got caught by their parents. "Sorry. We thought everyone was gone."

"Nope. Stella and I were upstairs but she's napping." My feet lead me straight to the refrigerator and I pull a beer off the shelf. "I thought I'd find Audrey out here instead of that."

I can hear Tiffany laughing from the living room and I shake my head. Spencer joins me in the kitchen and his face is bright red. "Sorry, man. We really didn't think anyone was here."

"It's all good." I grab another beer and hand it to him. "I'm kind of glad someone else is here. This place is too big to be alone. Where are my parents?"

"Oh, they went off sight-seeing. Something about treating this like a second honeymoon."

Ugh, that's not what I wanted to hear. I'm all for them having a good time as long as it's rated PG. I do not in any way, shape, or form want to think about my parents having sex. A shiver runs down my spine. "Good to know." I twist the cap off the bottle and toss it in the trash before sitting at the table. "Any chance you found somewhere beautiful and secluded while you were on the trails today?"

"I wasn't really paying attention, but I'm sure there are tons of spaces off the beaten path." He eyes me cautiously. "Why?"

Tiffany skips over to us, and wraps her arms around Spencer. "What are y'all talking about?"

"Nothing," I shake my head.

"Liar."

"He actually isn't," Spencer bumps into her. "He was about to tell me, but then you came over here and interrupted."

"I just don't want anything getting back to Stella." Leaning back in my chair, I wait for Tiffany to have something to say. She has a tendency to put her two cents in even when nobody wants it.

"It better not be anything bad. Stella is the sweetest person in the universe and if you hurt her, I'll cut you." And there she goes. Without even knowing what I have or haven't done, she's threatening me.

I hear the door slam and I worry we've woken up Stella, but Audrey's voice fills the space. "Who are we cutting?"

"Johnny," Tiffany points at me and raises one eyebrow. "If he does anything to hurt our cousin."

"You're so dramatic," Audrey rolls her eyes as she enters the kitchen. "You know good and well that he would never do anything to make her upset."

"Yeah," I grin. "I thought we were past all that now."

"We were," Tiffany crosses her arms over her chest. "Until you started whispering with Spencer."

"Secrets don't make friends," Audrey adds. I miss the days when she was quiet and didn't say much. Not because that's how she should be. But she didn't seem to team up on me quite so much then.

They are never going to leave me alone unless I give them something. And it might as well be the whole thing. Otherwise, they'll slip up and let Stella in on what I have planned. "I'm going to ask Stella to marry me." There. It's out in the open and I hope like hell she's still in the room.

"Oh my gosh." Tiffany and Audrey scream in unison.

"Keep it down. I don't want to ruin it."

"Sorry," Tiff mock whispers. "When are you going to do it?"

"I'm not sure. I want to find somewhere secluded but that's also romantic." That should be easy considering the resort we're at, but I don't know this place like her family does. "Do y'all have any suggestions?"

"Why don't you do it somewhere in the lodge?" Audrey asks.

"I kind of want to do it outside." I shrug and set my beer on the table. "This is my first time in snow that's more than a couple of inches deep and I want it to be something she always remembers."

Tiffany snorts. "A proposal isn't exactly something a girl forgets."

"We are literally in the mountains," Spencer chimes in. "You could take her anywhere and it'll be secluded."

"True, but I'd like to be able to find my way back."

"You won't have to worry about that," Audrey says as she pulls a seat out at the table. "Stella knows these woods like that back of her hand. Or, at least, she used to."

"Isn't there a fire ring not too far from here?" Tiffany asks. "That would be a perfect spot. We could go get a fire started before you do it and take pictures."

"No offense," I shake my head. "But I want to do it alone. I'm happy everyone will be here to celebrate afterward, but I don't want an audience."

"Fine," Tiff stomps her foot. "We can at least set it up for you. The hike isn't too bad and we can circle around so we won't run into you."

Audrey grabs her phone from I'm assuming her back pocket, and opens it up. "Now, I just need a list of everything you'll need. I'll get it together."

Even though Tiffany was driving me nuts last night, I am grateful for her help now. If anyone can help me pull this off, it's her cousins.

Chapter Seven

Stella

Last night was fantastic. Even Audrey seemed like her normal self while we were playing games. It has to be hard for her to be around other couples. It's the only thing I can think of that would have her out of sorts. That doesn't matter, though. For the first time in years it felt like we were teenagers again. Johnny and Spencer didn't interfere with any of our fun either. Most of their time was spent arguing over the right way to play *Uno*. We have, and always will, play the way we want to.

I drag my finger down on my phone and wait for it to refresh. Johnny is whispering about something with Tiffany and I want to know what it is. I can't investigate because I'm waiting for the email to come through about the cabin I rented for the two of us.

"Secrets don't make friends," I call back to the two of them. It shouldn't take this long for the email to come through. They said it would be available first thing this morning.

"Neither do nosey people who don't mind their own business," Tiffany sing-songs.

She's such a smart ass. Instead of letting her get under my skin, I put my full attention on my phone. Maybe if I will the email into existence it will show up.

Hands settle only my shoulder and Johnny bends down to kiss the top of my head. "Why are you staring at your phone like it holds all the answers to the universe?"

Do I tell him about the cabin or keep it a surprise? "I'm waiting for something to come through." Hopefully he won't badger me about what it is.

"Oh," he runs his hand through his hair. "Okay. If you need me to help with anything, just let me know." He doesn't say anything else before walking back to the kitchen.

I'm not sure if it's just me, but Johnny has been acting weird since yesterday. He was his normal self when we were skiing, and it's like a flip switch after I woke up from my nap. My cousins even seem to be in a much better mood than normal as well. They are up to something, and as much as I want to investigate what it is, I have to figure out what is going on with this cabin.

Getting up off the sofa I rushed upstairs to the room I'm sharing with Johnny. This should give me some privacy while I call the front desk. I pull up the phone number on the reservation, hit the call button, and wait for someone to answer.

In less than a minute a cheery voice picks up. "Good afternoon, thank you for calling Snowy Inn. This is Hollis, what can I do to help you?" She sounds entirely to chipper for how I feel right now. It shouldn't annoy me, but it does.

"Hi, Hollis." I do my best to not let the tone of my voice show the mood I'm in. "I had a reservation for a cabin for the next couple of nights. They said I'd get an email this morning with the information I need for the key."

"Let me see what I can find out. Can I have your name?" I give it to her and hear her fingers click clack on the keyboard. Hopefully there's a good reason for not having the information sent earlier. Another minute passes by and I'm beginning to wonder if she forgot about me. I know they must be busy, but I haven't heard her say one word. I can still hear her typing, though. Finally, she says, "Stella, I think I know what happened."

"Okay," I let out a sigh. Remember, keep your cool. It's not her fault.

"The email was put in without the dot com at the end." She pauses. "But you're all set and can come pick up the key at any time. We'll even throw in a bottle of wine for the inconvenience." I imagine Hollis staring at the computer with a bright white smile not letting my screw up affect her.

I feel like shit now. I should have paid attention when I didn't get an email to begin with. I was in vacation planning mode and didn't even realize it. "That's not necessary. Thank you for your help. I'll be there in twenty minutes."

"It's not a problem at all. I'll have it all ready when you get here. If you need anything else, feel free to ask for me and I'll get whatever you need handled."

"Thank you so much, Hollis." This woman is a godsend. "I'll see you soon."

"You're very welcome." I press end on the call and breathe a sigh of relief. I need to remember to double check my information before I submit anything. I feel like a moron for not doing that in the first place. That's a Tiffany mistake and not one I usually make.

I'll go ahead and pack while I'm up here then let him know that he needs to pack for a few nights when I go get the key. I want it to be a complete surprise. We were supposed to go skiing on one of the bigger hills today, but a few romantic nights in a cabin with him sounds much better.

The lingerie is hidden under my comfy pajamas in the drawer, and I grab them before throwing them in the small bag I brought along for this reason. A few more clothes go on top when the door to the room opens. Shit.

"Why are you packing?" Johnny's eyes are wide and he sucks in a breath. "Did I do something to make you want to leave?"

Weird. He's not usually this vulnerable. "No. But, I need you to pack for a couple of nights."

"Why?"

Sighing, I shake my head. I don't want to tell him why yet. "It's a surprise. Please, humor me."

Is he panicking? What the hell is going on. "Um, okay." He grabs a few clothes from the closet, and walks toward the bed. "Anything in particular I need to bring?"

If I have my way, we won't be wearing actual clothes the whole time we're in the cabin. "Not really. Just think comfort clothes." I round the bed and wrap my arms around his waist. "It's nothing bad. I'll be right back, though."

"Be careful," he gives me a quick squeeze and releases me. There's something going on with him, but I don't have time to figure it out right now. I have a plan that needs to be set in motion.

Chapter Eight

Johnny

Fᴜᴄᴋ. What if she doesn't come back? When she's out of the room, I peer into her bag, but all I see are oversized shirts and leggings. She wasn't kidding about packing for comfort. What in the hell is she up to?

I throw a few more clothes into the bag and rush downstairs. After peering around to make sure Stella isn't here, I head to the kitchen. Tiffany and Spencer are making sandwiches and hot chocolate. That doesn't sound like a good mix, but who am I to judge. "We have a problem."

"That sounds foreboding." Spencer grabs his sandwich and takes a bite. "What happened?"

Lifting my hand, I run it through my hair, trying to make sense of anything that is going on right now. "I'm not sure. Stella told me to pack for a few days but didn't give me any other details. I have no idea what she has planned, but we won't be able to set up for the perfect proposal."

"I don't get what the big deal is," Tiffany chimes in. "We'll just push it back to whenever you get back from whatever she has planned for the two of you."

"You mean you don't know what she's doing?" I find that hard to believe. Stella, Tiffany, and Audrey share pretty much everything. I don't think I've ever seen them keep many secrets from each other.

"Believe it, or not, but we don't tell each other every little detail of our lives." She rolls her eyes and picks up her mug. "I'm sure she's got some corny adventure for the two of you to go on. Or some museum type thing. Who knows? Just calm down. You'll know when the time is right."

Will I, though? I've been carrying this ring around for months. I'll think it's the perfect moment then chicken out. What if she says no? I mean, we've been together for a bit and I know without a doubt that she's it for me. I think I knew it when I rescued her from the side of the road. Some women like to date for a long time before a proposal and I'm not sure if she's one of them. The old her definitely would have waited until she crossed every milestone she could, but the new…I'm not so sure.

"Dude," Spencer breaks into my thoughts. "You look like you're about to pass out." It is kind of warm in here.

Before I can say anything, Tiffany jumps in. "Make sure you take the ring with you. The moment may jump out at you when you least expect it."

"You're right. Good thinking." I pat my pants pocket as if I actually have it on me. It's hidden in our room, and I hope Stella hasn't found it.

"What is Tiff right about?" Speak of the devil.

"That sandwiches and hot chocolate are a horrible combination," Spencer grins as he takes another bite of his sandwich.

That was probably the most ridiculous thing he could have said. "I'll go grab our bags." It's the only way I can make sure to grab the ring and keep it hidden from her.

"Sounds good," she beams. "I'll just hang out down here and question the life choices of my cousin and her boyfriend."

"I happen to think my life choices are amazing," Tiffany snarks as I walk away. It's a wonder they are as close as they are and haven't killed each other yet.

∼

"Where are we going?" We're in the car her parents rented for the week, and we're headed away from the lodge. Maybe Tiffany was right and she has some sort of excursion planned.

"To get groceries." That's it. No other explanation.

"Okay," I drawl out. "But why are we getting groceries?"

She shrugs as she pulls into the parking lot of a small, family owned store. "You'll have to wait and find out."

"Do I get a say in what food we get?"

"Nope," she opens the car door. "You are going to stay here and I'll be back in ten. It won't take me long, I promise." She gets out, closes the door behind her, and runs into the store.

Way to leave me in suspense. A part of me wishes she would have left her phone so I could snoop to find out what's going on. But she took it in with her. I'm sure it has her list of what to get. That thing is how she manages her entire life. She even has a separate calendar thing on there for Out of the Ashes. If it isn't on her phone it's not getting done. I swear she has a list of things I need to fix and I refuse to look at it when she shows me because that means I'll have to do it.

It hasn't even been ten minutes and she's back with a few grocery bags in each hand. I rush out of the car to open the back door for her. This is why I wanted to go in with her. Okay, maybe part of it was to see what all she was getting for us to eat, but it's also because I knew she wouldn't be able to open the car door with her hands full. That's what I'm around for. To help her when she doesn't even realize she needs it.

She throws the bags in the seat, closes the door with her hip, and gets in behind the wheel. "You ready to hit the road again."

We're back on the resort grounds and confused doesn't begin to cover what I'm feeling. When she said let's hit the road, I thought we might be going to a nearby town. Boy, was I wrong. We aren't around the cabin we've been staying in with the family. If I were to guess we're on the opposite side as far away from everyone as we can be.

She parks in front of a small cabin tucked into a wooded space. It's more secluded than any of the other dwellings I've seen while we've been here. "Are you ready?" She smiles at me, and I would do anything to keep her smiling like that.

"Sure." I get out of the car and go around to open her door. She gets out and heads to the cabin door with a key in her hand. I grab our bags and the groceries before hurrying to catch up to the woman who never ceases to amaze me. Once inside, I scope out the studio setup to the cabin. There's a king size bed in one part of the room and a small kitchen on the other side. A small door leads to what I can only assume is the bathroom. "I'll put these away then you can explain what exactly is happening here."

It doesn't take me long to put up the groceries, or figure out what dinner is going to be. Spaghetti, just like our first date because it was the only thing she knew how to cook. I turn back toward the main part of the room and my mouth drops open.

Stella is standing in front of the bed in nothing but her bra and panties. "Welcome to our private getaway. I told you we'd get time away from our family."

"This is probably the best thing you have ever done since I met you."

Chapter Nine

Stella

It doesn't take Johnny long to get to me. "This is what all the weirdness today has been about?" He places soft kisses along my collar bone and shoulder.

"Mhmm." It's the only thing I can manage. It feels like we haven't truly been alone in ages, even though it's only been a couple of days. I want to question him about his odd behavior but I don't want to ruin the moment. I wrap my arms around his neck, bringing us closer together. "I'd say it was worth it." I manage to eek out as his finger traces a line down my spine. A shiver runs down my body and it's almost enough to make me come undone "The only problem I have now is that you have way too many clothes on."

"I can fix that," he whispers in my ear. The scruff on his face is the perfect friction against my cheek, sending another shiver through me. He takes a step back and makes good on his word. Removing every piece of clothing he was wearing. "Now, you're wearing too many clothes."

"That I am," I raise an eyebrow, "any chance you want to help me with that?"

Instead of replying, Johnny runs his hands over my sides and up my back to undo the clasp on my bra. When it hits the floor, his hands trail down to the top of my panties. Hooking his thumbs in the material he slides them down. His entire body following the same path until he's on his knees in front of me.

"I'll help you with anything if it means I get these moments with you." He leans forward. His mouth brushes against my inner thigh, and my knees buckle.

Holy shit. He has to say something like that and make me damn near fall off my feet. How is that even fair? From the moment I met this man he's always been able to take me by surprise. From his unexpected sweetness for such a gruff looking guy to the way he knows how to work my body like an instrument. "I think I need to lie down."

"Okay." Another kiss. "I've got you." That is one thing I know without a shadow of doubt. He always has me.

My entire body is relaxed. I didn't realize how stressed and tense I was until Johnny worked all those kinks out in the best way possible. My stomach growls and he chuckles. He must have super hearing because even though this cabin has an open floor plan, he's in the kitchen, cooking. "Dinner will be ready in just a few. I'm not used to cooking on an electric stove and it feels like it's taking forever."

"At least you're smart enough to not allow me near the kitchen." I pull the heavy comforter around me tighter. It's cold when you're naked and the only source of warmth is fire. I think the heater is on, but I'm not sure. Even with the soft whirring sound coming from the vent it doesn't seem to be doing anything. Johnny doesn't seem to notice, though. He's wearing nothing but gray sweatpants. It's hard for me not to stare any time he turns around. I have zero intentions of leaving this bed without a damn good reason. Hopefully he feels the same. Well, except for when we have to eat. We'll have to get up for that.

"Hey," he turns toward me with a spoon in his hand, and damn I kind of want to practice making babies with him right now. "You aren't as bad at cooking as you were when we first started dating. You've made progress."

"If you say so," I mutter low enough he can't hear me. He faces the stove again and continues cooking. "Is it almost ready, yet? I think my stomach is trying to eat itself."

"Yes," he sighs dramatically. "It's done. Let me get this on some plates and I'll be right there, Princess."

A part of me thinks the princess remark is a dig. He doesn't mean anything by it, though. I was very much a city princess when we first met. I like to think I've come a long way since then. I've even embraced small town life and have a hard time adjusting to the city when we visit my parents in Austin.

"Here you go," Johnny sets a plate piled high with spaghetti in front of me. "Do you want me to get you a shirt?"

"Why?" I pick up the fork and twirl the noodles around the tines before taking a bit.

"So, you don't get sauce all over you?" He eyes me as if that should have been my first though. "And it's a little distracting watching you eat topless."

I didn't even realize that the blanket fell when I sat up. My only motivation is to get the food in my belly. "Well, it was distracting watching you cook in sweatpants and no shirt. I think we're even."

"You better be happy you're starving, otherwise I'd take the food away and show you just how distracting I can be...again."

"I'm not that hungry after all." I lift the plate and move to set it aside. My stomach chooses then to growl once more.

"I think your hormones and your stomach are in disagreement." He grins and scoots closer to me. "Keep eating and I'll be right back."

I'm not going to argue because I was lying when I tried to push away my food. He goes into the bathroom for a few moments before walking out again. Except he's holding something. Something that looks a lot like a jewelry box. "Are you going to do what I think you're going to do?" And now I sound like a bumbling idiot.

He doesn't answer me. He strides to the side of the bed I'm situated on, and gets down on one knee. "Stella, I was going to do this today regardless of the place. Your cousins, and Spencer, were helping me get it all set up. It was going to be romantic and picturesque. I've spent the past few weeks fretting over making this proposal perfect. And I just now realized that it doesn't have to be perfect. As long as we're together we'll find our moments of perfection in the everyday things. In the small moments. You are the only woman I can see myself growing old with. Having children with. And building a future with. Will you, in all your naked glory, do me the honor of being my wife?"

Chapter Ten

Johnny

Now is the time she should be screaming yes. Not staring at me with her mouth wide open like she can't believe what I just asked her. Damn it. I should have gone with the original plan. Popping the question now is probably the worst thing I could have done. She's for sure going to say no. Or, she'll laugh when she comes to her senses.

When it becomes apparent that I'm not going to get the answer I was hoping for, I begin to stand. My knee is killing me and I feel like a dumbass. Before I have a chance to get all the way up, Stella lunges at me. "Of course, I'll marry you." Her arms are around my neck and her skin is warm against mine. She kisses every available piece of flesh she can find.

"Are you positive?" I have to make sure because I don't plan on ever doing this again. She's one hundred percent it for me. I don't want her saying yes unless she's has zero doubts.

"Why wouldn't I be?" She leans back until our eyes meet. "I love you more than I've loved anyone else. Even more than my cousins and that's saying a lot."

"But you hesitated." I should leave it alone and accept the answer before she decides I'm not worth it.

"That's because I was a little shocked that you chose now to do it." She runs a hand along my cheek and maybe I'm all up in my feels, but I lean into her touch. Lean into the comfort she's giving me now. "All of those things you want? I want them too. I want you to be the one I go through all of my obstacles with."

"Good." I pull her down to me and kiss her as if she's the last person on earth. For me, she is. She's my universe.

She shifts until I'm lying down and she's on top of me. Glass shattering jolts her away from me and has us both searching the room for the culprit. Red sauce is splattered on the comforter and the floor. A spaghetti death scene if I ever saw one. "Crap," she mutters and moves to get off me. "Hopefully they'll charge it to the room."

"We'll clean it up later." I lift her off me and roll her to the other side of the bed. I follow and shove the entire comforter off the bed in case there is glass in it. I'm not about to let a small mishap ruin the moment. I grab the ring box off the floor. It must have fallen when she threw herself at me. I hover over her as I open the box. "I think you should put this on."

"Oh, you do, do you?" She lifts her hand between us and wiggles her finger.

"Yep. I want to make love to my fiancé." I take the ring out of the box. The fire from the fireplace reflects on the white gold. I could have gone more traditional with gold, but that isn't Stella's style at all. Sliding it on her finger, I let my hand linger for a few moments.

She takes a moment to study her now adorned hand. Her eyes are shining with unshed tears. "It's beautiful," she whispers. "I always thought about marriage in the abstract. Like it might happen for me one day after I accomplished everything I wanted, but look at me. Engaged to an amazing man who I didn't count on crashing into my life." She sits up enough to give me a quick peck before lying back down and admiring her ring.

"Technically, you crashed into my life if I remember correctly," I smirk

"Shut up and have your way with me already," she pulls me down to her. "It's getting cold in here without the blanket and I need you to warm me up."

She's so damn bossy, and I wouldn't have her any other way. Now to make good on her demands.

Those two nights away was exactly what we needed. We called up to the resort and requested a new comforter and ordered room service for the rest of the time we were there. It was just easier than messing with cooking. And it allowed us more time together. Stella's aunts and uncles are coming in today and I'm sure we have a full packed schedule of skiing and games. They are huge on family time. I'm not quite so bothered by it now, though. The little bit of a break we had rejuvenated me and Tiffany is going down in spoons tonight.

I'm grabbing our bags from the car when said cousin shows up in my line of sight. "So," she draws out. "How was your mini getaway?"

"It was good." I reply and swing the bags over my shoulder. The key here is to downplay it and really get under her skin. It will annoy her to no end. She's like a kid sister to me and ribbing her has been one of my favorite things to do since I met her.

Audrey sidles up beside her. "Just good. Nothing exciting happened?"

A smile is my only response. If they want details, they can hound Stella. I close the car door and make my way up the slippery stairs.

Stella went inside before me. She said something about being presentable before the rest of the family comes in. Whatever that means. I'm sure they've seen her at her worst. Except, she's standing in the living room when I walk in. Our parents are gathered around her with tears and wide grins. I guess she told them the news.

Tiffany and Audrey bump into me in their rush to get inside and gasp at the commotion in front of them. "What's going on?" Tiffany speeds around me to her cousin. "Are you okay?" She's silent as she checks Stella over and her eyes go wide. "Is that what I think it is?"

Audrey joins them and they all start squealing and jumping around. "You're getting married," Audrey yells into the house as if we aren't all gathered.

Spencer pokes his head out of the kitchen. "Congrats, man. I'm sure the entire resort heard them. I'll grab some champagne for a toast."

"Good idea," Stella's dad chimes in.

We all make our way to the kitchen so Spencer doesn't have to try to carry out a ton of glasses. He's pouring the bubbly into glasses and Stella comes to my side, throwing one arm around my waist. "They act like they're surprised."

"I don't think they thought I'd do it while we were gone."

"I guess you proved them wrong," she winks up at me.

Spencer hands out the glasses while Stella's dad lifts his glass in the air. "We've gotten to know Johnny pretty well since him and Stella started dating. I couldn't have picked a better man for my baby girl. Congratulations to the both of you, and welcome to the family, Johnny."

We all raise our glasses, and I'm taking a drink when Tiffany calls out. "I can't wait until y'all start having adorable babies." That sends the champagne down the wrong pipe and I choke.

Stella laughs beside me and pats my back. "Calm down, Tiff. One thing at a time."

Thank God she's on my side. When I clearly react on emotion, she's the one who stays calm. Don't get me wrong, I can't wait to have babies with this woman...but I want to focus on us for a little longer.

Gone Again

Chapter One

Audrey

I COULD BE DOING SO many other things tonight. For instance, I could catch up on *Project Runway*. Or, I might even get caught up on my laundry. Hell, I could be washing my hair. But no. Instead, I'm sitting in a restaurant with these lovey-dovey couples planning Stella's wedding.

Don't get me wrong, I'm happy for my cousin. She finally let go of her weird obsession with work and started enjoying the little things in life. She's happier than she's ever been. I only wish it could have been us girls only.

Of course, wherever Tiffany goes, Spencer follows. That wild child found someone that keeps her leveled out. I never thought I'd see that day come. He's good for her, though.

While it fills me with joy to see my cousins so ridiculously in love, it makes me feel like the third wheel. I've been avoiding both of them for months. It's just hard seeing them glow because of their relationships when I can't seem to find anyone who completes me. Gah, could I sound any more like a sappy love movie? I haven't been truly happy since the day Justin dumped me our senior year of high school. I've gone on dates just to see if there is some sort of spark with anyone else, but they are all dull in comparison to him.

It's stupid to never move on, I know that. But I moved to this city in the hopes that maybe I'd run into him. Maybe with us being older and away from his dad, we could give things another go. My cousins thought it was because I wanted to be closer to them, and that's partly true. It's not the whole truth, though. I knew Justin was going to Hilltown University. I was supposed to go with him. We had our whole future planned out. It hurt too much then to go to the same college. I couldn't be in the same vicinity of the boy who destroyed my faith in relationships.

I hoped it would give me the space I needed to heal. To get over my high school sweetheart. It didn't. When Stella asked me if I wanted to be her roommate until we both got our feet beneath us, I jumped at the chance. I needed to get out of my town and all the memories I shared with Justin. The only way to do that was to start over completely.

Tiffany nudges me in the ribs with her elbow.

"What the hell is that for?" I whisper loud enough only for her to hear.

"Stella is talking about dresses. Get out of your head and pay attention."

Geez. When did she become so serious? I know this is important for both Johnny and Stella. I just don't understand why the planning has to be such a big production. Yes, it's important, but this could have been done at one of our apartments. Or, with just us girls. I'm really hoping there's more of that in the future. Not that I don't love Johnny and Spencer, but they are distracting from things that need to be done. And maybe I'm being a baby because I don't have anyone to cozy up to. This is all just too much.

It's a reminder of what could have been. What would have been if someone's parent wouldn't have gotten in the way. It pisses me off that his dad got married not long after Justin went off to college. He seemed lighter when I saw him around town. Where was all that understanding when his son was dating me? Why was I not good enough for his son to be with? Nope, my mind can't go there. Not tonight. I won't let.

"What do you think about burnt orange for your dresses?" Stella asks.

I haven't been listening, but that color definitely caught my attention. "Please don't make us be a college cliche," I whine. "If it's what you really want, I'll wear it, though." The color would look awful with Tiffany's hair. It makes sense that she would choose it since she wants a fall wedding. I hope she looks at other colors.

"I'll go ahead and mark it out. Y'all don't seem too excited about it," she sighs. "If you wouldn't have said anything, Tiff's face did."

The cousin in question bursts into laughter. "Who would have thought it'd be sweet Audrey that would object to that horrific color. She usually goes along with whatever." She's not wrong. I'm very go with the flow...to an extent. I don't like surprises, and tend to stick to myself. Okay so I'm nothing like Tiffany. Maybe that's what's wrong with me.

Nope. Not going down that road again. It's not a good headspace to be in. Why the hell does Justin keep popping into my thoughts? Is it because Stella is getting what I should have already had? My fairytale, happily ever after. I need to get out of this mood. If I don't, I won't be any help to her or anyone else.

Even though I'm alone and not completely happy, I can't help but feel excited for Stella. This is something I never thought I'd see with her. At least, not for a very long time. Men weren't even on her radar until she met Johnny. But I need a break from the stolen kisses and planning. "I'll be right back."

I walk toward the back of the restaurant so they know I'm not leaving. The restroom is the closest escape I can think of. The chatter from the patrons is barely audible as I close the restroom door. Finally, peace and quiet. I know Tiffany means well, but she didn't have to call me out like that in front of Stella. I refuse to be the third wheel. The realization that most people take dates to weddings finally dawns on me. Crap, I'm going to have to find a date. Maybe I can ask someone in accounting to come as my plus one. It's not ideal but I don't see myself finding my soulmate between now and Stella's wedding.

My reflection in the mirror is pale, and I look exhausted. I've basically turned into Stella. Well, the Stella that existed before she went to Asheville. I've thrown myself into work and doing things around my apartment. Anything to keep me occupied and not have to go out with Tiffany and Spencer.

Minutes pass by and I'm still not ready to go back out there. If I don't, someone will come barging in looking for me. Tiffany and Stella have zero patience, especially if they think I'm acting weird. I step back through the door. My gaze on my feet as I walk through the restaurant to the table.

Someone blocks my path and I slam into them. Liquid splashes all over me, the person, and the floor. Shit, and now I've knocked someone's drink out of their hand. "I'm so sorry," I say before I look up. My eyes meet warm brown eyes I could never forget, and I gasp. No way. There's no way in hell I would run into him...here. But here he is. The guy who broke my heart all those years ago and who I still see in my dreams to this day. It's as if my thoughts conjured him.

"Audrey?" My name spills from his lips and all I can think about is the way we used to lie on the hood of his car and stare at the stars. Talking about our futures.

I can't do this. Not tonight. Not ever. I thought he moved to Dallas for fuck's sake. He's not supposed to be here anymore. I don't bother going back to the table. I'm running through the restaurant and out the front door. Stella and Tiffany calling my name before the door cuts off their voices.

Chapter Two

Justin

THERE'S ABSOLUTELY nothing that could have prepared me for that. To run into the girl, no woman, I loved all those years ago. My shirt is drenched, the sticky alcohol seeping through, and my mouth wide open as the only person I've ever truly cared about flees from the restaurant.

I didn't know she lived in this area and I've done my share of social media stalking under the guise of making sure she ended up happy. She must have everything on tight lockdown or I might have sought her out. I've lived here since I graduated from college and haven't run into her once. Austin is big, but it's not *that* big.

"Excuse me." A guy wearing an apron steps in front of me. "Is there any way you can move over? I need to get this cleaned up before someone falls and hurts themselves."

How long has he been trying to get my attention? It doesn't matter because my feet start in the direction of the door Audrey just flew out of. I need to make sure she's okay. "Sorry, man."

He waves me off. "It's not the first time and it won't be the last."

I'm almost to the hostess stand. The lights from outside fill the window next to the door. I'm so close, but a hand grabs my arm and I stop in my tracks. "What the hell are you doing here?"

A redhead in her twenties is glaring at me. Hatred coming through loud and clear. I have no clue who this woman is, but something wiggles in the back of my brain telling me I'm wrong. "I'm not sure what you mean." Glancing around the restaurant, I pull my arm from her grasp. "Last time I checked, I'm free to dine wherever I wish."

"Maybe," she shrugs her shoulders. "What did you say to her?"

"Say to who?" I'm honestly confused. I haven't said anything to anyone… except for Audrey before she ran out.

A tall blonde, who I do recognize rushes toward us. "Tiffany," she spits. "Stop being rude."

No way. This can't be happening. I know exactly who this is. She's not so little anymore, and it seems like her temper has gotten worse over the years rather than better. "Holy shit. You grew up," I laugh, not able to hold it in. I should have known it was her when Stella walked up. That's one thing I remember from my time dating Audrey. When Stella was in town, all three of them went everywhere together. I see not much has changed since then.

"Seriously, that's what you have to say to me?" She raises a finger and pokes me in the chest. "You. Broke. My. Cousin's. Heart." Each word is driven home with a jab.

Stella looks confused. "What do you mean? Audrey told me it was mutual."

Tiffany gives her cousin a pointed look. "That's because she was too sad and didn't want you to worry." She shifts her gaze to me again. "I'm going to go look for her. You," she points her finger at me again, "Stay away from her."

I don't really have a choice in that matter since I couldn't get ahold of her if I wanted to. Audrey became a ghost when I left for college. I wanted to see her when I went home to see my family, but she wasn't there. My dumb ass assumed she'd gotten over us and was off living her own adventures. Apparently breaking up with her messed her up pretty bad. It's not something I'm proud of. Hell, I didn't even want to do it. But I didn't have much of a choice. Things my dad said made sense…in a weird twisted way.

Tiffany runs out of the restaurant. A tall guy with glasses walks over and shakes his head. "I'll go after them, Stella." He leans in and hugs her. I'm not sure who this guy is. Is he here with Tiffany, or Audrey? I hope like hell it's the former. They are standing pretty close to me and I hear him whisper, "Congrats on the engagement. Don't worry about the bill. I paid it when I saw Tiffany stomp over here." He steps back. "With the fury in her eyes, I kind of figured the night was over."

"Thanks, Spencer." Stella gives him a small wave. "Text me when you find them and I'll come over."

"Will do," he salutes. "Johnny should be over here in a bit." He looks over at me, but I can't decipher what it means. It's like understanding hits him, and before I can question it, he leaves.

Stella faces me once again. "Want to fill me in on what just happened? One minute Audrey is fine and the next she goes to the restroom before running out of the restaurant like the hounds of hell are on her feet. What did you do to her?"

Why do they all think I did something to her? I was minding my own business, walking back to the bar when she ran into me. How am I the one to blame? "I didn't do anything. She ran into me when she came out of the restroom, I guess. The only thing I said was her name and she took off."

"So, you didn't say anything else to her?" She crosses her arm and taps her foot. Geez. This is one thing I did not miss about the three of them being together. When one of them gets pissed off, all of them have to throw in their two cents. You'd think they'd get tired of fighting each other's battles.

"No," I deadpan. "I didn't say anything. She didn't give me a chance."

"Did you know she was here?"

I guess the interrogation isn't over yet. "No. I haven't seen her since I left town. I didn't even know she was living here until about five minutes ago when she ran into me...literally."

"So, what happened way back then? Clearly, that is what caused her reaction."

A man comes up behind her, I'm assuming Johnny, and wraps his arm around her. "Stop questioning him," he rolls his eyes. "That's kind of private."

"There are no secrets between me and my cousins." But the fact that she doesn't know what really went down is proof that there are.

I can't deal with this right now. Not when Audrey is somewhere out there, so distraught she couldn't even handle me saying her name. "Look, you'll have to ask her. In the meantime," I pull my wallet out of my back pocket and grab a business card. "Can you call me when you find her so I know she's okay."

"Why do you care? You didn't bother trying to see her after things went south with y'all." She crosses her arms over her chest, waiting for my reply. What does she want me to say? I haven't seen any of them in close to ten years.

I open my mouth, even though I have no idea how I'm going to answer, but Johnny intervenes. "Drop it, Stella." He reaches for my hand holding the business card and pulls it from my fingers. "Audrey is a big girl and can handle herself. Just because you're the oldest doesn't mean you need to come charging over here like a mama bear protecting her cub." He gently pushes her toward the exit, and nods at me, "I'll give you a call when I know what's going on."

"No, he won't," Stella grumbles under her breath, but I hear her anyway. They don't say anything else to me and leave.

I'm still trying to process what exactly happened tonight. And what was Tiffany going on about? Audrey acted fine when we went back to school. I mean we avoided each other, sure. But she didn't seem to upset about our break up after the first couple of weeks.

Nobody knows, but she's the one I let go of when I shouldn't have. Despite what I wanted, I listened to the one person that was supposed to have my best interests at heart. Seeing her tonight brings back all those memories from when we were younger, and I'm kicking myself for not trying harder to find her.

There's nothing I can do tonight, though. I have no way to contact her and I have no guarantee that Stella's fiancé will actually call me. I can only hope that he's a man of his word. I turn back toward the bar area, pay my tab, and tell the bartender to give the waiter who cleaned up my mess part of the tip. Someone should have a good night, at least.

Me? I'll be heading to my house…alone. It's not that unusual, but after seeing Audrey, I can't help wishing I had someone to go home to. I'm still not sure if that first guy is her boyfriend, but I'm hoping like hell he isn't. I wouldn't mind getting to know the woman she has turned into.

Chapter Three

Audrey

I. Can't. Breathe. It's not only because I bumped into Justin, though he's a big part of the reason. But, holy crap, I haven't ran in way too long. Why do people enjoy this? It's pure torture. My legs are on fire, and I'm going to go ahead and say this is my work-out for the week.

"Dammit, Audrey," Tiffany gasps from behind me. "Would you slow down? It's almost impossible to run in these heels."

I slow my pace until I come to a stop and look over my shoulder. Tiffany is doing this weird wobble run, and to people looking in, she probably appears drunk. Well, she is a little tipsy. She started drinking before we even made it to the restaurant. She justified it by saying she was "pre-gaming." Spencer settled her down, but not so much that she doesn't still imbibe more than she should during celebrations.

She's within feet of me, and I take a deep breath. "It's about," I gasp trying to get the words out, "time you." Another gasp. Seriously, I need to up my cardio. I know I've only gone a few blocks, but I shouldn't be this out of breath. It's ridiculous. "Caught up," I finally finish the sentence.

Tiff smacks my arm and rolls her eyes. "I would have a long time ago if I was in regular shoes." She taps her heel against the concrete and it's annoying. "Besides, I had to stop and tell off a certain someone."

I groan. "What did you say?"

A car speeds by and we both take an involuntary step back. The speed limit isn't very fast downtown, but if the roads are empty…not many people follow it. I'm not okay with either of us being roadkill because some jackass isn't paying attention and winds up on the sidewalk. Tiffany shrugs her shoulders, "That he better not talk to you."

"And that was it?" I really hope Stella didn't hear any of it. She doesn't know the extent of what our breakup did to me. She was away at college and I didn't want to bother her with my stupid high school drama. My cousin looks down at the ground, and that's all the answer I need to know that she said way more than she should have.

"I, um," she begins before she clears her throat. "I may have told him just how much he hurt you when he dumped you. And Stella may have told me that I needed to stop being rude."

"Ugh." Freaking Tiffany and her big mouth. "Why did you have to say anything? I was handling it."

The bubble of laughter that comes out of her mouth takes me by surprise. "You call running five blocks away from the restaurant handling it? I think we have different definitions of those words." I have no comeback prepared. She has left me speechless. "Be honest with yourself, cuz. You were running away like a scared little girl."

"No, I wasn't. I avoided a situation that could have gotten out of hand." Who am I lying to? If there's anyone who knows me better than I know myself, it's Tiffany. That's only because we grew up in the same town, right down the road from each other.

"You totally ran," a deep voice says from the darkness and I jump, almost falling backward. How in the world is he so freaking sneaky?

"You know it's not very nice to scare the hell out of people, right?"

Spencer wraps his arms around Tiffany from behind and leans his chin over her shoulder. Gah, seeing them being all couple-like makes me want to puke. Especially after the shit show back at the restaurant. "I wasn't exactly quiet. How is it my fault you weren't paying attention?"

"Whatever," I roll my eyes. "I'm going to assume the other two are right behind you."

"Maybe not right behind me," he bats away a strand of Tiffany's hair that gets in his face. "But it's a good bet that they'll find us soon enough."

"Stella is going to be pissed," I say to nobody in particular. "I can't believe I managed to ruin the night. That's totally your job, Tiff."

"There's no need to be an asshole," Tiffany huffs while leaning further into Spencer. "It's not my fault you don't know how to deal with guys."

She's wrong. I know how to deal with men. Just not this man. "I think I'm going to go home now."

Stella comes into view. "You're crazy if you think we're going to let you go home to mope by yourself. We are coming with you."

Tiffany turns toward Stella, "We are?" One chastising look from our oldest cousin and she knows it was the wrong thing to say. "I mean, yep, we are. I just need to run by our apartment first."

"For what?" Spencer looks dumbfounded, but he ought to know how this works by now.

"Alcohol, of course." She grins up at him, and I swear I just threw up a little in my mouth. "Little Miss Goody Two-Shoes over here," she hikes her thumb in my direction. "Never keeps a steady amount of booze at her place."

"Not all of us need a drink to have fun."

"Maybe not, but you need one to get over the shit storm that took place tonight. And you're going to drink until I think you'll have a hangover in the morning."

I shrug my shoulders. She has a point. I don't know if she has enough alcohol to wipe the night from my memory, but we can sure as hell try. "Are we ready to go to my place, then? As much as I like this city, I'm not a huge fan of having serious discussions on the side of the road."

"I'll go grab my truck and bring it around," Johnny announces before kissing Stella on the cheek and jogging off.

She definitely found the perfect guy. And I can't believe she's getting her happily ever after. The way Johnny looks at her makes me long for a relationship like that. One where you know you're the most important person to them. I used to have that…once upon a time. Then he dumped me without rhyme or reason. A few weeks later Justin was with someone else and I realized he didn't care about me as much as I did him. A tear escapes my eye and slides down my cheek. The old hurt coming back with a vengeance. Why did I have to bump into him tonight of all nights? It just had to be the one night that my cousins were here to witness it all. At least she'll have a funny or sad story to tell her future kids.

Stella comes closer to me and pulls me into her arms. "You obviously need to fill me in on a few details."

"Yeah, probably." I twist out of her hold, not wanting to feel like a child that can't handle heartache. "But it might not be tonight."

"That's fine. I'm here for you whenever you're ready."

"Do y'all want us to hang out here until Johnny pulls around?" Tiffany asks, bouncing on her toes. "If not, we're going to run by the apartment to grab the alcohol and meet you at your place."

"Go ahead," I nod toward the street. "We'll be fine." A kid whizzes past us on a skateboard. "It looks like we'll have a bunch of teens to keep up safe."

"Are you sure?"

"Yep. It won't take him long to get over here."

Tiffany is already walking backward, the way they came. She waves and smiles. "Love you and I'll see y'all in a few."

Not long after they've left, Johnny pulls up. Rather than sit in the front seat with her fiancé, Stella climbs in the backseat with me. I'm not sure why. It's not like I can do anything stupid with her in the same truck. Not that I would. Honestly, I think I'm still in shock. After all these years I never expected to run into him away from home. Hell, I didn't realize he was still in this area. I figured he moved off to whatever big shot job he was following.

Now, I need to figure out how to adjust to knowing he's in the same city as me. To know that I could potentially run into him again. I can't let those thoughts take root, though. He may be here, but it took years for me to run into him. What are the chances I'll run into him again?

Chapter Four

WALKING INTO A DARK, empty house has never bothered me before. Tonight, though, I want something more. Bumping into Audrey is completely throwing me off my game. She's making me question everything and not one single word passed between us. Well, except when I uttered her name. A part of me wonders if the guy Stella was with will actually call me once they find her.

I flip on every light switch I pass by on the way to my room. I've got to get out of these clothes. They are dry now, but I can feel the sticky residue from the whiskey. I still can't believe I ran into her. In this city of all places. Tonight was supposed to be low-key. A way to unwind after the meetings I've been in all day. The firm I work for is merging with another one. Normally I wouldn't have to attend any of the meetings, but with a promotion they came with the territory. My only hope is the transition will go smoothly. That's not likely to happen if I can't get Audrey out of my head.

I didn't even get a chance to eat anything. I peel off my shirt and pants, throwing them into the hamper. My stomach growls at the thought of food. I was going to take a quick shower but that will have to wait. Opening my dresser drawer, I pull out a pair of sweats and shove my legs into them. I'm not a hundred percent sure I even have groceries. Hopefully, there's something I can throw together, or at least have some cereal.

I walk out of my bedroom, but stop in my tracks. My phone is still in the pants I just took off. I need that in case that guy calls me. Hurrying back to the room, I pull the pants out of the hamper and grab my phone out of the pocket.

The likelihood that he'll call is slim. I won't let that kill my hope, though. Sleep isn't going to come easily tonight if I don't hear that Audrey is home and safe. With my phone in hand, I can finally look for food.

I set down my phone before I pull open the pantry door and grab the first box of cereal I can find. It's not my favorite, but it will do. My stomach grumbles as I get a bowl and pour the cereal into it. Note to self…don't go almost all day without eating. It was entirely my fault, but that doesn't matter. I could have easily called for something to be delivered. The day just got away from me and when it was time to leave, I still hadn't eaten anything.

The air from the refrigerator is cool as I open it. It's almost bare, and I need to get some groceries. Taking my lunch will be imperative if this merger will be taking up most of my day. I doubt I'll have any downtime when we're moved into the new offices. My eyes land on the milk, and I open it, about to pour it into my cereal when a pungent smell hits me.

"Son of a bitch," I yell. Holding the jug of milk up to my face, there are small chunks formed in what should be liquid. I can't believe I almost poured that in my bowl. I gag as I look at the date. This shit went bad almost two weeks ago. Looks like I'll be eating my cereal dry. It's just another punch to the gut on this shitty day. Setting the milk back in the fridge to deal with another day, I close the door and grab my bowl. It's not as satisfying, but it's better than nothing.

My phone vibrates against the countertop and I almost drop the bowl in my rush to answer it. I don't bother seeing who it is before I swipe it open to answer the call. "Hello."

"Why do you sound like you've been running?" Ugh, it's just my stepsister, Corrine. Dad finally found someone to put up with his grumpy ass and she came with a daughter that was older than me.

"Don't worry about it," I snap. I swear she drives me nuts. She may be older than me, but she acts like a little sibling way more than I do.

"Gah, who pissed in your cereal?" She just had to say that. I don't even want my cereal now. I'll call for delivery as soon as I get her off the phone.

"Nobody." It's a lie. She doesn't need to know that, though. "It's just been a weird day."

"Is this my chance to make it weirder?"

"I'm sensing there's a reason you're calling so late at night." Please don't let it be another call asking for money. It wouldn't be so bad, except that I just helped her with the down payment on her studio a few months ago. I have no problem helping her with her business ventures as long as she's turning a profit, and she has been. I would know. It was the one condition I had to helping her. I am the one that goes over her books. Who would have thought the small town we live in would be the bulk of her photography clients?

"Actually," she drawls, trying her best to build suspense behind whatever she wants. "How would you feel about me staying with you for a week or two?"

The laugh bursts from my lips before I have a chance to rein it in. "You can't be serious. Aren't we a little old for sleepovers?"

Corinne clears her throat, "Under normal circumstances, yes I would say we are. But this is for a good reason."

"And what's that?" I reach my hand up to rub my temples and realize I'm still holding the bowl of cereal. I set it down and wait for her answer.

"Do you remember that guy I was dating?"

"How could I forget? He was kind of a dick."

"That's the problem. We broke up and he can't move out of my house for another week or so."

"He is living with you?" It shouldn't surprise me, but it does. I thought she was smarter than that. I can't even count how many times I've told her not to jump into being serious with someone, and she does this.

"Look," she huffs. "I know I'm a dumbass for letting him move in with me. There's no need to yell at me for it. He's leaving, and I need to be away from him."

"Why don't you go to our parent's house? They live in the same town as you." It's the logical choice. Hell, they took her in after her divorce until she was able to get back on her feet.

"You know damn well why I won't." I'm ninety percent sure she's crossing her arms over her chest. It's something she's always done when she's mad. After a long pause, she continues, "Never mind. I'll just stay here at the studio. I'm sure someone will lend me a cot for a couple of weeks."

Dammit. I hate when she does things like this because she knows damn well I'm not going to let her stay there. It's not a bad place, but there isn't a shower or an easy way to cook things unless it's in the microwave. "No, don't do that. You can stay here."

"Thank you," she yells into the phone, and I pull mine away from my ear. She's so freaking loud. "You won't even know I'm there."

"Yeah right," I mutter.

"What was that?"

I lean against the counter, resigned to the fact that it's late and I'm not in the mood to wait for food. I grab one of the small sugared flakes from the bowl and pop it in my mouth, crunching loudly. I'm the little brother, I'm allowed to be immature at times. "Nothing. When will you be here?"

"Probably tomorrow. I don't have any clients coming in for portraits so it won't interfere with that." She sighs and I know even though she doesn't completely have all her shit together, she didn't want to call me. "Thank you, Justin. Going to Mom and your dad wouldn't be such a huge deal, but he made it pretty damn clear that he doesn't approve of my career choice. I'm sure he's waiting for me to fail."

"No, he's not," I argue. "He only wants what's best for you."

"Oh, you mean like when he basically forced you to dump that girl in high school because you were too young to be in a committed relationship before leaving for college?" I sucked in a breath and hate that she brought up Audrey, especially tonight of all nights. "I guess I hit a nerve. You still think about her, don't you?"

All the damn time. She sneaks into my thoughts without me even realizing it. "It's funny that you mention her. I ran into her tonight…literally. Well, she ran into me."

"You're joking."

"I wish I was." I hear her take a breath, ready to launch into a thousand questions, but I don't give her a chance. "I don't want to get into it tonight. Maybe not ever. It's not like I'm ever going to see her again."

"You never know. This could be Fate's way of bringing you back together. Y'all were such a cute couple when you were in high school. At least, it looked that way from the photos." When did she even see those? I hid them in a box in the back of the storage. Forever burying the memories.

"This isn't high school anymore," I argue. "She probably hates my guts for breaking her heart."

"Or maybe she'll see what a fine young man you've become and she'll be willing to give you another chance."

"I'm not going to take your bait. I'm tired and ready to go to bed." Food, or no food. Talking to Corinne is exhausting sometimes.

Luckily, she doesn't push me for more. "I'll see you tomorrow. Goodnight, Baby Brother."

I hate when she calls me that. She isn't even my real sister. Though we are as close as blood relatives. It makes me feel like I'm twelve years old. "Goodnight. Text me when you're heading this way."

"Will do." With those parting words she ends the call, and I'm left wondering what could happen between me and Audrey.

I leave the bowl of cereal on the counter and go back to my room. I wasn't playing when I said I was tired. Pulling back the sheets on my bed, I climb in and plug my phone into the charge. As I close my eyes, my phone vibrates.

Unknown number: Audrey is home safe and sound.
Justin: Thank you.

• • •

That's one less thing I have to worry about. The memory of her running out of the restaurant at the sight of me will haunt me for a while. I must have really messed her up all those years ago. With that last thought, I roll over, pull the covers over me and drift to sleep. Everything that weighed me down today will be waiting for me tomorrow morning.

Chapter Five

THE DRIVE to the apartment is quiet. Johnny navigates the streets while Stella sits beside me, forever my rock. It reminds of when we were kids and she was always standing up for me. She has a tendency to act more like an older sister than my cousin. I'm not complaining since it was just me. We're all only children, and I think the closeness we share is exactly like what siblings must feel. At least, that's what I think. I don't really know anyone that has close family. She wraps her arms around my shoulder and gives me a light squeeze.

"You doing okay?" She whispers in my ear. It feels loud in the silence and I don't know how Johnny didn't hear it from the front seat.

I can only nod my head. I'm not like my cousins. I don't go for those things that they do. I can't take charge the way they can. That could be why dating has never worked for me. For whatever reason, I don't have that drive to want to put myself out there…emotional scars and all. That clearly bit me in the ass when I was in high school. I didn't fight hard enough for my relationship with Justin. It's why he walked away so easily without looking back.

Within minutes we're in front of my apartment building. The streets are empty and Johnny has no problem finding a parking spot in front. He moves to get out of the truck, but Stella places her free hand on his shoulder and shakes her head the tiniest bit to tell him to stay. "I'll call you in the morning to pick me up, or I'll get a car to take me to the hotel."

I'm not sure why they stay in a hotel. I have a guest bedroom. Tiffany does too since Spencer is no longer just her roommate. I get it, though. They want some privacy. It makes me feel like a bitch that I'm actually happy they made that choice. As much as I love them, I don't know that I could handle all the kisses. I'm content with my life. Well, maybe not as content as I should be, but I'm fine as long as I don't have to witness all the stolen kisses and cuddling. If I become a spinster, I think I'd be okay with it. You don't worry about your heart being ripped out of your chest if you're alone. It might be time for me to look into getting a pet. Maybe that will cure the loneliness.

Stella drags me out of the truck and we head to my apartment. As much as upstairs neighbors can be a pain, I love living on the first floor. I open the door and Stella closes it behind us once we're inside. She points to the sofa and says, "Sit."

I know better than to argue with her. There's a reason she made it to the top of the project management team in her previous job. She knows how to go after what she wants and be stern with those that need it. Apparently, I'm the one that needs that tone of voice right now. She disappears into my kitchen and comes back out with the only bottle of wine I have and two glasses. "Now, tell me what happened."

"I told you," I shrug. "I ran into him."

She raises an eyebrow and gives me the same look my mom does when she thinks I'm being mean to Tiffany. "You know that's not what I'm talking about. What happened back then?"

Sighing, I grab the glass of wine she poured me, and lean back into the corner of the sofa. Running into him tonight brought back all that old pain and anger. Pain that after almost three years of dating, he could dump me without a care in the world. Anger that he did it. That he listened to whatever bullshit his father fed him, and decided I was no longer worth fighting for. Then resignation that I wasn't enough. Not for his father, and obviously, not for him.

I tell her everything that happened. How I thought things were great, and he was going to get his own place if his dad kept being a douche. He dumped me right before Christmas with no warning. He just came by my house and told me things weren't working out and left. And then I tell her about how he had his arm around the most popular girl's shoulder two weeks after we went back to school. "That is what really gutted me, Stell. It made me question my entire relationship with him. If he could move on that easily…how important was I to him when we were together?"

"Well, that was kind of a dick move on his part." Stella lifts her glass and takes a drink. I am already on my second glass and Tiffany still isn't here yet. She knows the full story, though. She was there with me drying my tears for more weeks than I care to remember. "And don't ever question your importance. If he was too stupid to see it, that's his problem. Not yours."

I nod in agreement. "You're telling me. I thought we had our entire future planned out, and it all went in flames." It was more than that, though. It was as if my entire world exploded in the blink of an eye.

She sits up and gasps. "Is that why you didn't go to Hilltown when you graduated? I had everything set for you to join me up here and was floored when you said you were going to a local college. I thought I did something to piss you off."

"Yep, that is why. I couldn't stand to even be in the same school as him. And, we would have had a lot of the same classes since we were on the same business track. It was easiest to stay as far away from him as I could."

"It all makes sense now." She leans back into the sofa and pours more wine into her glass. "Now I feel shitty for being so angry at your sudden change of mind."

"Don't be," I sigh. "It wasn't your fault. I was the one who kept things pretty quiet after he dumped me. I didn't want you to feel like you had to come back and take care of me."

"It still sucks though. And you handled Christmas like nothing was wrong. I did find it odd that he wasn't around considering he did as much as he could with the family."

Before I get the chance to respond my front door flies open and Tiffany stumbles through. "Have no fear, the party is here." She's carrying two grocery bags and they are so full they are almost bursting.

I shake my now empty wine glass in the air. "It's too late for that, little cousin. Stella and I almost finished an entire bottle."

Tiffany laughs as she sets the bags on the floor "Oh Audrey, it's cute you think that's all you're drinking tonight." She picks up a bottle of vodka and a bottle of bloody Mary mix. "This is just a pregame. We literally have the entire night to ourselves no boys, no jobs, and no drama."

That's easy for her to say. Both her and Stella have significant others. They can finish getting me drunk and go home to somebody. I don't get that luxury. Even after they leave, I'll be here. Alone. With only my thoughts to keep me company. "You aren't going home tonight, are you?" I just want to make sure that I have them until morning, and it will be like the old times.

"No, silly." She goes to the kitchen and fills a few glasses with ice to form bringing them back out to the living room. "You get to put up with my sparkling personality all night long. It'll be just like old times."

That is what I need more than anything right now, something to feel normal and ground me. "So, should we make drunken wedding decisions?" I need to change the subject. Think about something else for a bit.

"Absolutely," Tiffany screams. "This is going to be amazing."

"I'm beginning to regret this decision," Stella sighs into her bloody Mary. "Just know that whatever y'all pick tonight, I will make you wear. So, if I were you, I wouldn't decide on anything ridiculous."

I look at Tiffany and shrug my shoulders. "She's not serious. She wouldn't make us wear something hideous." My two best friends are exactly what I want tonight. It gets my mind off of running into Justin, and gives me a tiny smidge of normalcy.

It's not long before were giggling and looking at off-the-wall wedding pictures online. This is what I needed. They take the loneliness away and give me something to look forward to.

Chapter Six

Justin

I JOLT UPRIGHT. What was that sound? Something bangs around in the kitchen, and even though I'm confident in my ass-kicking skills, I'm not sure I want to face down someone breaking into my house. I push the comforter aside and slide out of bed as quietly as possible. In all of my years living here, I've never had to deal with an intruder. I'm not going to rush out of my room like a crazy person, though. Whoever is out could be armed, and quite frankly, I don't want to get hurt. Especially after finding Audrey is here.

Tip-toeing to my closet, I open the door and grab the baseball bat. Thank God I never got rid of it after my one stint in the softball league. Now, that I have a weapon, I can confront the person in my house. As quiet as possible, I open my bedroom door, hoping it doesn't squeak. It doesn't, and I slip through.

My feet are silent as I make my way down the hall, bat raised above my shoulder like I'm about to swing at a pitch. I round the corner and my fridge slams shut. The person in my house turns around and my bat falls to the ground. "What the hell Corinne? I thought someone was breaking in."

"And you think a bat was going to save you?" She rolls her eyes before opening the freezer. "I think you have bigger problems."

Damn it. She messed up my day of sleeping in and woke me up from my dream about Audrey. It was getting good, too. We were back home and doing the things we normally did when we were in high school except, we were adults. "You were supposed to call me before you came in. What time is it anyway?"

She closes the freezer door, and faces me with her hands on her hips. "I didn't want to wake you up. I had to get out of there because he was being annoying. I didn't realize by not calling I'd be welcomed by my brother with a bat." I like that she's never bothered with adding "step" in front of brother. As far as we're concerned, we're siblings, even if we didn't become family until we were adults. "And it's like 7:30, or something."

"Damn, Rin," I groan and rub my hand over my face. "It's too early to be awake. Did you even sleep last night after we got off the phone?" I did, but it wasn't that great deep sleep you're supposed to get into. Dreams of Audrey kept me tossing and turning. Until the one I was in the middle of before waking up, all of them were a loop of what happened at the restaurant last night. Except sometimes I'd run after her, but I'd always wake up before knowing what happened. I should have gone after her. It's too late now, though.

"Not really," she shrugs. "I packed some stuff, tried to fall asleep, and when I couldn't…I hit the road." She scrunches her nose at me and waves her hand in my direction. "You need to get dressed."

I look down. I have on a t-shirt and basketball shorts. There's nothing wrong with what I'm wearing. "Why?" This is the problem with her being an entire year older than me, she thinks she can tell me what to do. I have a love/hate feeling toward having a sibling most days. I think it'd be different if we had grown up together, but we didn't. Today…it's closer to the latter.

"You don't have any food, and I'm hungry."

"How is that my problem? You could have gotten food before you started rummaging through my fridge. I think you should take a nap, and we'll figure food out at a reasonable hour." She's crazy if she thinks she's going to try to boss me around in my own house. That's not how this works. I'm offering her a place to stay until her latest ex gets out of her house. I'm doing this so that she doesn't have to deal with our parents giving her a hard time about her life choices.

She taps her foot against the tile floor. It's the same thing her mom does when she's about to blow up about something. Usually something Corinne has done. I'm the golden child, at least, to her I am. "Nope. You are going to get dressed," she points to my room. "I'm going to get unpacked. Then we're getting something to eat." She shakes her head as she grabs her suitcases. "I don't see how you survive with no food in the house."

"Like everyone else."

"Which is?" She's heading down the hallway to the guest bedroom.

"Takeout. I don't have a ton of time to cook with work, and I'll have even less time for the next few weeks. It's easier to grab something on the way home."

"That's not going to fly while I'm here. Now, go get ready. We're leaving in thirty minutes."

For someone who is as flighty as she can be, she's sure as hell bossy. I'll do it, though, because now my stomach is growling. I forgot I didn't even get a chance to eat last night.

When Corinne said we were going to get food, I thought she meant we were going to a restaurant. I didn't think she'd drag me to the damn grocery store. She can do this kind of shopping while I'm at work. There's absolutely zero reason for me to be with her. Cooking has never been my strong point. "Why can't we just go somewhere and get food?"

"Because," Corinne shakes her head. "You need actual food in your house. If you keep eating takeout, you're going to get pudgy."

"No, I won't." We're walking into the store and I'm already feeling overwhelmed. Don't get me wrong, I've gone into the store for a few things here and there. Milk, cereal, ramen, and frozen dinners. You know, the basics. But I've rarely come in to get stuff for actual meals.

She continues as if I haven't said a word. "And if you get fat, you won't be able to win Audrey's heart."

That stops me in my tracks, and Corinne runs into my back. "Who said anything about that? I'm not trying to get back with her."

She moves until she's standing by my side instead of behind me. "Your pissy tone since last night says otherwise. Now walk, you're holding up traffic to get into the store."

I move forward and wait for my sister to get a shopping cart. "I'm serious. I didn't even know she was in the area until last night. Besides, I don't have time to try to start, or restart, a relationship. I work long hours and the merger my company is a part of happens this week."

Corinne shakes her head and pushes the cart into the produce section. "I don't see how that's a problem. The fact that you're protesting so much means you still harbor feelings for her. You can have a career and a girlfriend. People do it every single day."

"I don't think you're the most qualified person to give relationship advice." She winces and drops the orange she just picked up. "Sorry, Rin. I didn't mean it like that."

"Yes, you did." She huffs and continues picking out fruits. "I may not have the best track record when it comes to guys, but I'm not scared to follow my heart."

It's my turn to wince. She knows how to go for the jugular. We turn down the next section and she's now putting vegetables in the cart. I'm not scared. Well, not completely, anyway. I didn't end things well with Audrey. If Tiffany is to be believed, I destroyed her heart, and I'm not sure if that's something she can come back from. "Still out of the question. She probably has a boyfriend, and I don't have a way to get a hold of her. Besides, I still don't have time to commit to anything."

"If you say so, Baby Brother." Now we're going down the aisles of food and I watch her throw things into the cart. I don't know what half of it is. Hopefully she plans on cooking. There's no way in hell I know what to do with any of the food. "So, tell me about this merger."

Thank God she's changing the subject, and knows when to do it. This is something I could talk about for hours. I love my job and what I do. I only wish we had a chance to meet all of the employees at the company we're merging with. The short turnaround made it hard to do, though. Tomorrow will definitely be interesting, and I hope it all goes well.

Chapter Seven

THE SMELL of bacon wakes me up. It makes me miss home. Mom used to make it every weekend. Tiffany and I would always fight over the last piece of bacon. My stomach rumbles as I open my eyes. I'm not sure if it's because I'm hungry or hungover. Most likely the latter. Drums are pounding a steady rhythm in my head, and I could murder my cousins for pumping all that alcohol into my system last night.

I roll out of bed and grab my robe off the back of the door. As I make my way to the kitchen, I start a mental list of everything I need to get done today. Well, assuming my cousins leave at a decent time that is. Otherwise, I'll be digging through the back of my closet trying to find something to wear. The company merger takes place tomorrow and I don't really want to make a bad impression with the new bosses.

Stella and Tiff are sitting at the table when I walk into the kitchen. Johnny is at the stove cooking. "Good morning, Sunshine," they yell in unison.

The sound reverberates in my skull, and I lift a hand to smooth it away. "Can you bring it down a notch?" My voice is barely above a whisper, and even that is too loud. "How did you get talked into cooking?"

Johnny doesn't turn to answer me, completely focused on his task. "I was going to pick y'all up for brunch, but Stella said you were still passed out. So, I asked her what you had in the fridge and bought some things on my way over." He pauses his stirring to shoot a glance my way. "Besides, with these two, you likely wouldn't have had an edible meal."

He's not lying. Neither one of them can cook to save their lives. Tiffany's mom didn't teach her since she was always eating at my house. And Stella, I don't know what her excuse is. My uncle is a great cook. She can bake, but actual food...she burns to a crisp. "Hey," Stella gasps. "That's not fair. We would have bought something and had it delivered. We're not monsters."

Pulling out an empty chair, I plop into it. I fold my arms on the table and lay my head on top. "How are you feeling?" Tiff's mouth feels like it's right next to my ear. She doesn't need to be this close.

"Like death," I groan, trying, and failing at keeping my voice at a reasonable level. "I drank so much last night." I lift my head about an inch and glare at the two of them. "How are y'all functioning already?" If I hadn't smelled food, my ass would still be in bed, hiding under my blankets.

Tiffany snorts. "You realize I drink a lot, right? Every time Spence and I see Crooked Halo, we end up drinking. It's part of what we do." She takes a drink of her coffee and sets the cup on the table.

Stella shrugs her shoulders. "I work in a bar most days. Angie is always getting me to try new drinks."

"Who would have thought you would be adventurous," I joke with Stella. "You used to drink around the same amount as me."

Our older cousin scoffs. "I don't think that's true at all. My weakness has always been wine." She waves away the current conversation. "Do you at least feel better emotionally?"

As much as I want to say yes, it wouldn't be the truth. As shitty as I feel right now, I'm grateful my cousins were there for me last night and gave me a chance to drown my sorrows. But...it doesn't stop thoughts of Justin from creeping in. Stella will go back to Asheville and Tiff be will wrapped up in Spencer, leaving me alone with my memories of the boy I used to love. I don't want to give them a reason to worry, though. "Yeah, I'm better. Well," I laugh, "aside from feeling like I'm dying." I push back from the table and sneak to the counter where Johnny is putting the cooked bacon. "I just hope I don't run into him anytime soon." Or, at all. I snatch a piece of bacon from the plate. Johnny tries to sway my hand away, but he's too slow.

"I don't think you'll have to worry about that," Johnny says while flipping the bacon.

My eyes go wide and Stella slowly turns around in her chair until she's facing her fiancé. "How do you know that?" When he doesn't answer, she leaves her chair and marches toward him like a woman on a mission. "What did you do?"

He has the good sense to back away from the stove. Not that Stella would do anything rash, but she can be terrifying when she's pissed off. I grab the tongs out of his hand before he gets too far. There's no reason to let the bacon burn. I'll probably need it after whatever bomb he's about to drop.

He's almost to the living room when he finally speaks, hand raised in the air in surrender. "I text him last night after I dropped y'all off."

"You did *what*," Tiff screeches. "You are not allowed to talk to the enemy." The chair almost topples to the floor as she stands. "How do you even have his number?"

My hand is frozen mid-air. The sizzling bacon in the pan momentarily forgotten. I need to know the answer to this, but I'm terrified to turn around. I don't want anyone to see the panic that must be etched onto my face. I'm almost certain Stella has her hands on her hips with a scowl on her face. If he actually somehow knows Just, I will be mortified.

"Calm down, Tiffany," Johnny sighs. "I don't know him. He gave his number after all of you hightailed it out of the restaurant."

"And you called him?" I can hear the accusation in Stella's voice and her foot tapping a steady, irritated rhythm on the floor. If there is one thing my cousins are, it's loyal. If someone gets on one of our shit lists, they are on all of ours.

I turn off the stove and pull the last of the bacon out of the pan. It's crispy and almost black. Johnny will be getting those pieces. I need to see his response now. If only to put my own mind at ease.

"No, I sent him a text." He throws his hands in the air. "What was I supposed to do? He asked me to let him know that Audrey was okay." He nods toward me and sags his shoulders under his soon to be wife's stare. "He seemed sincere."

"Easy," Tiffany slaps her hand on the table. "You tell him to fuck off and go on about your night. He lost his right to know anything over a decade ago."

"How can you say that?" Johnny argues. "Y'all helped me when I screwed up with Stella." He has a point, loathe as I am to admit it. I swear watching the three of them argue is like watching a ping pong match. And even more frustrating, they are talking about me like I'm not even in the same room.

"That was different," Tiff starts her argument.

I cut her off. "You didn't give him my number or anything, did you?" That's the only thing I need to know. Not that I haven't wondered about him over the years, but thinking about him, and him having a way to contact me are two different things.

"No," he scoffs. "I'm not an asshole. Y'all act like he did something horrible." He pauses for a second. "He didn't, did he? If he ever laid a finger on you, I'll text him again and then kick his ass."

"No," my laugh is soft and sad. "Nothing like that. He was my first love and heartbreak. It's just hard seeing him after all these years."

"Good," Johnny nods. "I didn't want to end up in jail." I love that he's protective over all of us. He's the big brother we never had, and I'm happy he'll officially be part of the family soon.

"Please," Stella scoffs. "You act like you would actually fight him. If anything, you would have a heavily worded conversation with him and be done with it."

"I mean," he shrugs. "If that's all it takes then it's not a bad thing."

I roll my eyes and rush toward Johnny, wrapping my arms around him. "Thank you for looking out for me." Stepping away, I look at the three most important people in my life, aside from my parents. "Seriously, I appreciate y'all being defensive on my behalf, but I'll be okay. I just hope to never see him again."

"That shouldn't be too hard," Tiffany says as she walks to the cabinet to get a plate. "It took you over five years for it to happen this time. Maybe it won't happen for another five."

"You realize you just jinxed me, right?" I grab my own plate and fill it up before sitting at the table. "I don't have time to focus on it, though. Tomorrow is a big day and I need to get everything ready to go so I have a decent start to the week."

"Johnny, why don't you come back in a few hours to pick me up." Stella says as she takes a bite of bacon. She doesn't phrase it as a question. She's demanding it and if he knows better, he'll say okay and go on about his business.

"Why?" He cocks his head to the side like a confused puppy. "Our hotel is on the opposite side of the city. It doesn't make sense to go there, then come back here, only to go back to the hotel to get our things."

"Well, you can get our things in the truck before you pick me up." She nods toward the bottles of wine and liquor in the living room. "Tiffany and I are going to stay and help Audrey clean up. It's not fair for us to make a mess then leave her to pick up after us."

"Um," Tiff raises her hand. "I didn't sign up for this. I don't even like cleaning."

"Too bad," Stella gives her a stern look that stops her from arguing. "Just because we're grown doesn't mean we stop doing the things our parents instilled in us."

"I guess." Tiffany crosses her arms and pouts. "But," she perks up. "Only if we can help her choose her outfit for tomorrow. We have to make sure she wows the new bosses."

Oh God, no. Anything but that. Tiffany will have me showing off all kinds of skin that is anything except professional. "I don't know." Seriously, cleaning the apartment from top to bottom on my own is preferable to letting my younger cousin dress me.

Stella laughs. "It'll be fine. It's not like I'll let her pick something you aren't comfortable wearing. While we want you to capture their attention, that won't happen if you have clothes you hate."

They aren't going to let it go. They are like a dog with a bone, and it would be in my best interest to let them do their worst. Besides, how will they know if I decide to wear something else. I can always change after whatever picture they demand. It means I'll have to get up earlier, but so be it. I'll allow them to do their little makeover. Their chatter might just be the only thing to keep my mind off Justin. I fear the more I think about him, the more likely I'll run into him. Not that I believe in all that woo woo stuff with thinking things into existence. But I don't want to take my chances. "Fine. Just know that I'm putting the two of you to work. There's a lot I want to get done before tomorrow. I'm not sure if I'll be able to get to anything else for the rest of the week. Who knows what the new bosses are going to throw at us."

Both Stella and Tiffany rub their hands together like they are evil geniuses. Maybe I should be scared after all.

Chapter Eight

Justin

"ARE YOU LEAVING WITHOUT BREAKFAST?" Corinne asks.

Shit. I didn't even see her there. She's such a weirdo. Who the hell sits that quietly in a dimly lit kitchen at six in the morning? "Um, I'll grab something on the way." Maybe that will get her off my back. At least, for today. It's something I know she won't let me get away with for long. Not if the amount of groceries she made me buy yesterday says anything.

"Sit down," she points to the chair across from her. "I already started some biscuits in the oven. I'll cook up some sausage and eggs to make a couple of sandwiches for you."

I take a couple of steps toward the door, hoping she won't see me. It's nothing against her. I only want to get to the office as soon as I can. It's a new building and I need to time the commute. Plus, I need to pump myself up for whatever today is going to bring. It's always a toss-up with how you're going to connect with new co-workers. Or, in my case, employees.

My step sister doesn't miss a beat. "I said sit. You need to start making time for eating something before you leave. It's not healthy to constantly be eating on the go."

"And eating fatty, greasy food at home is better?" I point to the frying pan she pulls out of the cabinet. I honestly don't remember the last time I even used that thing.

"It's better than worrying about getting some sort of food on that expensive ass suit you're wearing. Now take off your jacket, grab a glass of orange juice and sit down."

"When did you become so bossy?" I do what she says, though. There's no way she'll let me out of this house if I don't eat whatever she's cooking. She doesn't care if I'm late or not.

"When I started dating men that didn't know how to be an adult." Her voice is filled with frustration and I want to tell her it's her own fault, but that will start a fight.

I grab a glass out of the cabinet and the orange juice out of the refrigerator. As much as I loathe her ordering me around, I might actually eat a bit healthier. Maybe her visit won't be so bad. I only hope it doesn't turn into a permanent one. I love her, I do. But if she's meddling in my diet, there's no telling what else she will push herself into. I know it's killing her that I'm not doing anything about the whole Audrey situation. I could have sent that guy a text asking for a way to get a hold of her. Hell, I almost did. But that's creepy and I'm not about to do that. Not to her. She deserves so much more than that after the way I treated her.

While I wait for her to finish cooking, I take a seat at the table and pull out my phone. The calendar is going to be my best friend today. There is meeting after meeting scheduled. It's how the higher ups decided to introduce us to the different departments. I think it's ridiculous. We should have met them before the merger even took place. I don't get to make those calls, though. One day, I will. And I'll do things drastically different.

I'm so lost in my thoughts on company domination that I don't notice Corinne has set a plate down in front of me until she starts talking. "Are you nervous about today?"

How could she even know that? I do my best to keep any sort of emotion hidden and tucked away. Emotions portray weakness. It's something I finally learned dealing with my dad. If I acted like his bitching didn't affect me, then he'd stop...eventually. "Not really," I shrug. If I don't let on that I'm okay, she'll badger me about it until I leave. "It's just another day at the office."

"But it's a new office." She lifts her sausage biscuit to her mouth. "New things are typically terrifying."

"It's not that big of a deal. The only difference is there will be new faces. All I have to focus on is learning their names." I take a bite of my food and wait for the next question she has.

"You mean you take the time to learn everyone's name? Is that normal?"

"I like to think so. Not everyone does it, though. They'll get the name of the few people that they'll work with directly and not bother with anyone else."

"That seems very impersonal." Her mouth twists in disgust. Knowing people on a personal level is why she's grown so much as a photographer. People spill their stories to her without a second thought. I think that's why we get along so well. We don't stick to one group of people. We like to get to know everyone. It's also why I never had many enemies when I was in school.

"It is. You can't build trust with your fellow employees if you don't even know their names." I glance at my phone, noting the time. If I don't get going soon, I won't be able to do the car pep talk I started years ago.

"So true." She checks out my plate to make sure I'm eating. "Do you mind if I keep the extra key while I'm here? I kind of want to get out and explore the city, maybe take some photos."

"You plan on being the best photographer in all of Texas?"

She laughs. It's loud and boisterous. Something that isn't heard often in this house unless some of my co-workers are over for a night of football. "How else am I supposed to dominate the photography game?"

Finishing my breakfast, I grab my phone and stand up. "While I'd love to see you take over the world, I need to get to work. I'm pushing it on timing how long it takes to get there on a normal day." I stop where she sits and give her a quick hug. "I'll be home at some point today. I'm not sure when since our last meeting starts at four thirty."

"Have a good sort of first day," she grins, and if I didn't know any better, she's hiding something. It's the way the corner of her mouth lifts up slightly higher than the other. What isn't she telling me? "I'll have dinner set aside for you whenever you get here."

I swear she's trying to fatten me up. I'm going to end up rocking a dad bod and I don't even have any kids. The only thing I can do is shake my head. When she goes back home, I'll be hitting the gym a lot more than I do now. "See you later, Sis."

My car is already warming up in the bright summer sun. The way it beats down on me makes me wish I could dress casual for my job. I need to be in my new office in fifteen minutes. You can do this. It's just like any other job. Technically, it's still the same job, just in a different building. The people you'll be managing won't hate you. Put one foot in front of the other and learn their names. That's all you have to do.

Now that my talk is out of the way, I turn off the car and open the door. It's even warmer out here thanks to a lack of air conditioning. Normally, I'd park in the garage attached to the building, but I don't have a parking badge yet, so the open parking lot a block down will have to be good enough. I grab my jacket off the passenger seat and close the door behind me before pressing the lock button. One foot in front of the other, I walk to the building I'll now be spending so much time at.

Cold air blasts as I enter the lobby and the man at the desk looks up when my shadow passes over him. "Hi, how can I help you?"

"Hello, today is actually my first day in this building. I'm part of the merger with TK. I still need to get my badge."

"I can get that started for you right now. I just need your ID." I pull it out of my wallet and hand it over to him. He scans it into his computer and hands it back. "Now, if you'll step around here, I can get your photo."

It's the same thing we did at the other office. We had part of one of the buildings and I'm no stranger to this song and dance. I stand against the wall and he takes a couple of pictures. "I'll have this ready for you around lunch."

"Thank you," I wave at him as I make my way to the elevator. "I'll see you then."

It feels like forever until an elevator door opens up and I step inside. The door is about to close when someone rushes in yelling, "Wait."

Hold on, I know that voice. I look down and none other than Audrey is standing in front of me wide-eyed. "What are you doing here?"

"You have got to be fucking kidding me," she backs out of the elevator and starts running back through the lobby. Something about Tiffany being a bitch. She's not wrong there at times.

Why does this woman continue to run away from me? This time I'm not going to stand here in stunned silence. I chase after her.

Chapter Nine

Audrey

THESE HEELS ARE impossible to run in. Is Justin stalking me? I can't think of another reason he'd be here…in my building. "I'm going to murder Tiffany," I mutter. This never would have happened if she wouldn't have said anything. She wished this into existence.

"Audrey, wait." Shit, he's following me. I'm not sure what to do. I could duck into one of the other buildings, or stores, but I know he'd come in right behind me. I'll round the block and make my way back to the car. Calling in sick is my best option until I figure out why he's here.

I round the corner, and keep going as far as my feet can take me. If this is going to become a habit, I'm really going to have to start working out. This is becoming ridiculous. I should not have to run this much in such a short period of time. One day I'll understand why people think it's fun. Today is not that day.

I'm so lost in my thoughts that I don't hear Justin close the distance between us. A hand grabs my arms and pulls me to a stop. "Why," he gasps. "Are you." Another gasp. "Always running from me?" He lets go of me only to put his hands on his knees and bend over, trying to catch his breath.

I could run again, but let's be real, I'm just as out of breath as he is. Never in a million years will I show it, though. Instead of answering him right away, I stand up straight and take a few deep breaths. Anything to make it easier not to gasp while I'm talking to him. It seems like that's the only way I'm going to put an end to running into him. "Why were you at my job?"

There. Answer a question with a question. Stella would be so proud. He doesn't have to know that underneath my false bravado, I'm quaking. Terrified of how he'll answer. That he's purposefully seeking me out and this isn't a coincidence. I'm not sure how I'll react either way. On the one hand, it'll mean he still does care. Or, at least wants to see how I'm doing after all these years. On the other…I can't believe that's it. If Tiffany were here, she would say its Fate's way of pushing us together, even though she hates his guts. She'll probably feel differently if that's the case in the end. Please, don't let it be.

That gets his attention, though. He's still breathing hard. His chest moving up and down, his shirt damp from sweating while trying to catch up with me. He's much more defined now than he was when we were eighteen. Shouldn't that mean he's in shape and can handle the running? "Wait, you work there?"

Oh snap. He didn't know I work there. What other reason can he have for being there. I don't remember anyone saying anything about there being new employees with the merger. Unless… "Please tell me you aren't with the company joining us?"

Justin stands ramrod straight. "If I say yes, are you going to run again?"

I take a few steps back, the instinct to run higher than ever before. I'll never be able to escape his presence now. Should I run? Yes, undoubtedly. Will I? No. There is no energy left to do any sort of physical activity. "No, I won't run. But how did you not know that I worked there?"

His shoulders sag. My promise not to jet visibly relaxes him. "There wasn't much time to do anything. And they didn't give us the list of employees already here."

"That's kind of stupid." I want to reel the words back in as soon as I've said them. He could have been one of those people that made the decision.

"I agree." He surprises me by the answer and even seems a little pissed that he didn't get a list. "I wanted to meet as many people as possible before today. It helps with morale and doesn't feel like a complete takeover."

"But that's essentially what you're doing right?" I tap my foot against the concrete waiting for his response. "Y'all were all brought on as management. You may even be my boss. Wouldn't that be a conflict of interest?"

He shrugs his shoulders. "Maybe? But that's beside the point. We came on to make the company you work for better. They weren't exactly in great shape and came to us to help fix it. Though, don't tell anyone that. I don't think y'all know exactly how bad off y'all were before we stepped in."

They didn't. I assumed everything was fine and we were joining to help another company. Obviously, I was wrong. So much for transparency in the work place. I mean, I understand why. People would have freaked out, but some sort of communication would have been nice. "Well, I guess the only thing to do now is go back to the office and see where we end up."

"Why did you run the other day?" His question is completely out of left field and takes me by surprise...again.

"You, Justin. You seem to be the only reason I revert to cardio on sight." It's hard for me to admit that, and I can't believe I just did. He seems to bring out the best and worst in me.

He takes a step closer, his hands up as if he's placating a scared animal. He's not totally off. "That doesn't answer why."

It doesn't and I'm one hundred percent okay with that. "I think I should probably get back to the office. I'm sure my boss is wondering where I am."

Without giving him a chance to argue, I brush past him and head toward the building. I don't look back to see if he's following. That point is moot now that I know he's not stalking me, and is working with me. Hell, I may even be under his supervision. I wonder if it's too late to consider a career change. Or, maybe even a new job.

I haven't seen, or heard from, Justin since I came back to the building. Good. I don't have the mental capacity to deal with him right now. The only thing I need to know is if he will be one of my direct bosses. If so...that will suck. Looking for a new job will suck even more. I love working here, and even though my emotional wounds from him are old, they still hurt. I don't want to deal with him on a day-to-day basis.

My phone vibrates with a message just as my computer dings with an alert. I check the work notification first. Looks like we have a meeting in a few hours. Too bad it isn't voluntary. I'm pretty sure I know what we'll be going over. Now time for my phone. It's the group text with my cousins.

Tiff: So how did the new bosses like your outfit?

Me: I'm going to kill you.

Stella: They hated it that much.

Tiff: I don't see how. It was perfect.

Me: Never mind about the damn outfit. You wished me seeing Justin into existence.

Tiff: No, I didn't. I said I hope you don't run into him again.

Me: Which one hundred percent jinxed me. He's part of the merger.

Stella: Oh shit.

Tiff: Maybe it won't be so bad. He may be over one of the other departments.

Me: You better hope so.

Stella: There's nothing you can do about it now. Finish out your work day and let us know when you find out more. We'll figure it out.

Stella is right. It doesn't make it less frustrating, though. I'll just power through my tasks until the meeting. We're bound to find out more. I'm just crossing my fingers he's not directly over me. How embarrassing will it be having to report to the man who broke your heart?

Chapter Ten

Justin

THERE AREN'T VERY many meetings left for the day. I've yet to see Audrey in any of the ones from this morning, which means there's a higher chance that she'll be one of the employees under my supervision. I don't want that to be the case. I'd be lying if I said I wasn't nervous about seeing her, or the fact that seeing me causes her to run like her life depends on it. I'm shuffling through their merger information for the fifth time. I know these words like the back of my hand. Right now, though, I can't remember them for the life of me. The words blur together and I shake my head in an attempt to clear my vision.

"Is everything okay?" Carter asks. He sits down next to me at the long conference table. He's the only person that I can count on. We were hired on at Bolder & Barnes around the same time and have been buddies ever since.

I run a finger between the collar of my shirt and neck. The closer it gets to the next meeting, the harder it is to breathe. "Yeah, I'm fine," I clear my throat and reach for my bottle of water.

He laughs, and I wince the tiniest bit. "You can't bullshit a bullshitter. You've been tense all day, but I didn't want to say anything. Now, you're sweating and I know something is up." I open my mouth to speak, and he shakes his head. "Aside from new employee nerves. This is something else."

Should I tell him about Audrey working here? I gave him a few details yesterday, but didn't say much. Not enough for him to know that there's a history between the two of us. One that goes back over a decade. "You know how I was telling you about that girl?" He nods his head, and motions his hand for me to continue. Fuck. I feel like a teenager defending my choices to my father all over again. "Well, I dated her in high school. More like I broke her heart."

"Okay, and what does that have to do with how you're acting right now?"

"Well," I clear my throat again. This time it has nothing to do with being thirsty. "She also works here."

"Like in the building?" He waves his hand. "Do you realize how many companies are in this place?"

"No, she works in this company. The one we're here to fix and keep an eye on." I pause waiting for his reaction. I'm usually the levelheaded one in this duo, but now is obviously not that time.

"Damn, man." He lets that sink in for a few moments. The chatter outside the conference room is the only background noise. "You aren't trying to pursue her, are you?"

A chuckle escapes from me. "Dude, she hates my guts. Even if I really wanted to, she'd shut that shit down pretty quickly." I mean what I'm saying, but she's already gotten under my skin again. Corinne was right. Running into Audrey and chasing after her this morning is proof of that. If I didn't care, I would have headed straight to work. But no, I had to run after her. I really wish she would have been honest about why she ran from me. But she didn't give me an answer. Not really.

"Then you have nothing to worry about," Carter shrugs and leans back in his chair. "Want to grab a drink when we're done for the day?"

I weigh my options. On one hand, I'd love to go out for drinks after this stressful day. On the other…Corinne would kill me if I stayed out even later after she made dinner. "I probably shouldn't. Corinne is making dinner."

"Your sister is in town?" He grins and I don't like it at all. "We can always have drinks at your place. I know you keep it pretty well stocked." He's not wrong. I have a full bar set up, but I rarely touch it. If I want a drink, I go out with him.

"You are not going to try anything with my sister. She's coming out of yet another shit relationship, and doesn't need you trying to jump in her bed."

"Since when do you have a sister?" The sound of her voice makes me straighten my spine. Is it already time for the next meeting? I check my phone and we still have another ten minutes before people are supposed to come in.

Before I can say anything, Carter vacates his seat, rounds the table and holds out his hand. "You must be the one who hates his guts." He points his thumb in my direction. "I'm Carter."

Audrey's cheeks blush a dark pink. It's nice to see some things never change. She's never been great at handling attention. She takes a deep breath and places her hand in Carter's, "I'm Audrey. I guess you're one of the new guys on the block."

"Yep," he nods. "And if you're here for the next meeting, I'm one of your new bosses."

"I guess that means he is my other one." She nods toward me and I don't miss the disdain she adds to "he".

"Sort of?" Carter phrases it like a question. "He's more like my supervisor. So, I report to him if there are any problems."

Audrey takes a seat as far from me as possible. "So how does this work? Y'all move in and kick out our current management?"

"Actually," I begin, but she cuts me off.

"Sorry, Justin. I was actually speaking to Carter since he's the one I'll be sending reports to." Damn. When did she get so sassy? I think Tiffany and Stella are starting to rub off on her. Or she's trying to make me feel stupid. That's not who she is, though. At least, that's not who she used to be.

Carter mutters "damn" and shakes his head. He's getting a kick out of this. Asshole. He doesn't pay me any mind, though. "I'll be working with your current boss." Carter sits down next to Audrey, and it kills me that she's allowing him to be so close to her and she just met him. I don't care if it's work related. Why won't she let me tell her how it all plays out. "We're not trying to replace anyone. The whole point of us being here is helping the company you work for survive and thrive. We," he waves his hand between me and him, "are the best of the best in the area. We have multi-million-dollar accounts that we bring with us."

Audrey snorts, and Carter stops in his tracks. "Sorry," she laughs again. "It's just that your clout," she adds finger quotes to the words. "Doesn't mean anything to me. I'm here to do my job. As long as I know my job is safe, and I have little to no interaction with him, then I'm good."

"I think we're good, then." Carter leans back in his chair. "Have you ever thought about management? I like how straightforward you are. You cut straight through the bs."

"Nope. That's more my cousin's expertise." She's blushing again. Not only does attention make her uncomfortable, so does compliments. It's the one thing I made sure to give her every day when we were teens. I wanted her to know that even though she was sometimes overshadowed by her cousins, she was strong and deserved to be seen as well.

"Is your cousin as feisty as you?" Carter asks.

Okay, I have to step in now before he makes an ass of himself. "Calm down, Romeo. From what I saw the other night Stella is one hundred percent taken."

Audrey glances at me before turning her attention back to Carter. "She's actually engaged."

"Congrats to her," Carter says. "You should come have drinks with us after work."

I never agreed to have drinks especially since he has his eyes on my sister. Luckily, I don't have to shut that shit down because Audrey answers, "Sorry, I have plans."

Nobody has a chance to say anything else because the rest of her department shows up for the meeting and take their seats around the table. I stand to give someone my seat. I do my best talking when I'm on my feet. Audrey is glaring at me while I wait for everyone to be seated. All that does is make me want to know the reason. I mean, I know, but I want her to tell me. I want her to show me the spunk she just showed Carter. Even if it makes her uncomfortable.

Chapter Eleven

Audrey

WHY DOES he have to stand at the front of the conference room looking hot while I'm sitting here pissed because he is in my space once again. That last half of Senior year was miserable. It was impossible not to run into him because our graduating class was less than a hundred. It seems I can't escape him now, either. And why am I finding him attractive? I mean, I have eyes, but remember the way he dropped me and moved on like I meant nothing still stings. He was my forever. At least, I thought he was.

"Audrey," Luke, my coworker, nudges my arm with his elbow. "The meeting is over."

"Sorry, I guess I zoned out." Or maybe I was stuck in my head and couldn't snap out of it long enough to realize the meeting was over.

He laughs and shakes his head. "Must have been some daydream." He scoots out of his chair and offers his hand to help me out of mine. I don't take it, but he's used to that and doesn't get offended. He likes to be a gentleman. "Want to grab drinks after work? Or is your cousin dragging you off to another show?"

"No," I sigh. "Thank God. It seems Crooked Halo is playing out of state right now so I have a reprieve." I push out of the chair and make sure my phone is in my pocket. "I'm good with drinks. But I don't want to stay out too late. Stella is supposed to video chat with us about our bridesmaid dresses."

"Sounds good." He heads toward the door and waves. "I'll catch ya at quittin' time."

I'm about to follow Luke out of the room when I hear Justin call my name. "Audrey." Luke had me distracted long enough that I completely forgot him and Carter are still in the room. "Can I talk to you for a second?"

I'm not sure I have much of a choice since he's part of management now. "Sure, what do you need?" Carter shrugs his shoulders and leaves the room as fast as he can.

"I thought you said you have plans tonight?" He crosses his arms over his chest, and I don't miss the way his biceps fill out the button up shirt he has on. He was tall and lanky when we were in high school. But now…he's the man I always envisioned him to be with bigger muscles. And, if I'm not mistaken, jealousy crosses his face. He's not even looking directly at me. He's staring at the door where Luke passed through minutes ago. This is going to be fun.

"I do," I motion toward the door. "With Luke."

"Yeah, but you literally just made those plans. You couldn't have known he was going to ask you out before the meeting started." His eyes meet mine, and they're asking a question that's quite frankly none of his business.

"It's a normal thing. We go have drinks at least once a week. Why are you so concerned?" I lean against the table and wait for his response. Wanting him to come right out with the question. It's the only way he's going to get an answer from me. Not that he deserves one. What I do is none of his business.

"Are you…," he begins then changes course completely. Coward. "Are we going to be able to work together without any issues? I can try to transfer to payables if it's going to be a problem."

My head snaps back at the offer. Who knew he would attempt something so considerate it? Maybe he's changed after all this time, and stopped letting his dad run his life. "When did you get a sister?"

He taps his fingers against his arms, and for a second I don't think he's going to answer me. After all, I didn't confirm that working together was going to be a problem. "Not long after I left for college. Dad met someone and they got married a few years later. Corinne is barely older than me, but she's pretty awesome."

Wow. His dad got remarried. You would think I'd know that considering I was still in town when all that went down. Or that my parents would have told me since I avoided him at all costs. If I went to a store and he was there, I'd enter a different aisle or leave the store altogether. "That's good. I'm glad y'all are one happy family."

Not going to lie, it sucks that his dad was so quick to judge me and get me as far from him as possible, but he jumped into a marriage fairly quick if you ask me. "Don't be like that, Audrey." He reaches one hand toward me and I step back, leaving it hanging in mid-air.

"It's fine." I start toward the door, ready to leave this conference room behind. "As long as we don't have to interact on a daily basis, I think we'll be able to work together just fine." I'm out of the door before he can say anything else. Everything will be okay. It has to be. As much as I don't want to work with Justin, I have no desire to look for another job. I like the people I work with for the most part. I'm not going to let him run me out of my job.

Sports are on every television in the bar. It's a hole in the wall place a couple of blocks from the office. It's close enough to walk to when we get off. A lot of my coworkers come here after a long day of dealing with clients. The few tables here are taken, and it's too warm to sit on the patio. At least in this outfit. My legs would be chafing before we got our drink order if we sat out there.

A trio leaves the bar and we take advantage. Luke sits on the barstool to my right. We're regulars and the bartender doesn't even ask us what we want. She knows, and I appreciate that. Even though I don't drink much, today definitely calls for it. I looked over my shoulder constantly to make sure Justin wasn't looking for me or watching me. Yeah, that makes him sound creepy. He's not, but I wouldn't put it past him to try to find out if Luke and I are dating.

Hannah sets our drinks down in front of us and I take a long drink before placing it on the bar top. Luke turns toward me. "Tell me if this is too personal, but I have a gut feeling you know that Justin guy."

My head falls back and I groan. "Yeah, I know him. Well, I used to." I take another drink.

"I'm sensing there's a story there." When I say nothing, he leans forward the tiniest bit. "Are you going to spill? Or, am I going to have to make up scenarios?"

He's as bad as my cousins. But aside from them, he's one of my closest friends. We tried the dating thing once and it was weird. He's like a sibling to me, and if I don't tell him, he's going to bug the hell out of me.

"Wow." He takes a long pull of his beer and rests an elbow on the sticky bar. "He just dumped you with a bullshit excuse. That's harsh."

"Tell me about it." I let out a breath. "At eighteen, I thought it was the end of the world. He was my first love. Time should have made that feeling go away, right? It almost hurts as much now as it did then."

"There's two possible reasons for that." I roll my eyes at him. Here we go. He's a lot like me. He likes to solve problems, but never his own. I think that's why we get along so well. We offer the other a different perspective. "Just hear me out." He waits for Hannah to give us another drink before he begins. "One, you don't have closure. He dumped you out of the blue and you never really recovered. Two…you still love him."

"I really dislike you right now." There may be a bit of truth to both of them. Hell, I haven't seriously dated a guy since him. When he left for college, I would fantasize about him coming back to me. Without his father watching his every move, I just knew he'd come sweep me off my feet. The longer it didn't happen, the more I realized I didn't mean much to him. It didn't stop me from carrying a torch for the asshole, though. I've measured every man to the guy I loved with my whole heart and they've all been lacking.

"Because I'm telling you what you don't want to admit?" He nudges me with his shoulder. "I'm one hundred percent fine with that. We need to see if he still has a thing for you. You never know. He may not be the same douchebag he was the night he broke up with you. It's been a decade; he might have changed."

"That's a horrible idea." Luke starts to argue, but I cut him off. "He's our boss for crying out loud. I can't go down that hole. I'm sure there's something in our employee handbook about that sort of relationship."

A grin takes over his face. "I'm going to look through it to double check. Then…it's on."

"Ugh, it's a horrible idea." My phone rings and I grab it out of my bag. "Oh shit. I lost track of time." Swiping my phone, I answer the video call. Stella and Tiffany are squinting at me trying to figure out where I am. "Hey, guys."

"Are you in a bar? How the hell are we supposed to look at the horrible dresses the two of you picked out when you're around a bunch of people." Stella whines.

I mute the phone. "Sorry, Luke. I need to go."

"No worries," he waves his hand before throwing some bills on the bar, "I'll drive you home while you talk to your cousins then get a ride back to my car."

"You don't have to do that."

"It's fine." I reach in my bag for my wallet. "Put that away. Tonight, was my treat. You had one fucked up day."

He's not lying. It was the most stressed out I've been in years. "Thanks." I unmute my phone and we walk out of the bar. I'm sure once I'm alone my cousins will bombard me with questions about how the rest of my day went. But I needed this tonight with Luke. I'm also interested in what the handbook says about dating. Not that I'm going to pursue anything with Justin. The only thing I'll find down that path is heartache.

Chapter Twelve

Justin

"YOU KNOW you look like a stalker, right?" Carter claps me on the back and leans on the door of my office.

"I don't know what you're talking about." I do, but I'm going to play dumb. I thought it would be easy working with her. Guess I'm a moron for letting that into my head. We don't interact with each other. It's been three weeks and she comes in to drop reports off on my desk before hightailing it out of my office.

"How many times have you gone out there to make copies?" I answer with a shrug. "There's no way you need that many copies of a report that you can print off your computer." He points toward the corner of the table along the back wall. "On the printer that is right here in your office. You have it bad."

I lay my head down on my desk. Why is this so damn hard? I thought about her over the years, but it wasn't anything like it is now. I feel consumed by her...the same way I felt when we were in high school and she was my universe. "I know. I don't know how to make it stop, though." When I lift my head, he's staring out the door.

"That's easy, friend." He walks back to my desk and points at me. "That's easy. You get off your ass and go talk to her." Carter shakes his hand and tries to pull me up from my seat. "Seriously, dude, it's the only way you're going to solve anything. As far as you know, she's having the same thoughts as you."

I pull away from him. "I doubt it. She's all buddy, buddy with that Luke guy." My stomach churns at the thought of him touching her. For fucks sake. I don't get jealous. Especially when I'm not even with the girl. How is that even possible?

"Have you asked her if she's dating him? That would go a long way in dealing with this macho man bullshit you have going on."

I haven't. I was hoping that day after the meeting she would tell me. Hell, I begged her with my eyes. A look that worked so many times when we were younger. She didn't, though. Instead, she changed the subject and wanted me to feel that pang of hurt that she might have moved on. "No. It's not really my business. Not only because I'm her boss, but also because I don't have that right. Not after the way I ended things when we were in high school."

Now that he's given up on trying to force me to talk to the woman I let get away, he sits on the edge of my desk. "How did all that go down? I mean, I'm not trying to start a gab session, but you've never really said exactly what happened."

Rubbing a hand over my face, I exhale. "It's a long story. But the highlights...my dad pretty much hounded me until I did it. At the time his reasoning made sense. Now, though, I think it was one of the biggest mistakes I've ever made."

"Okay, I'm going to need you to spill more than that. That's nothing but a tease. What exactly was your dad's reasoning? Was she a troublemaker in school? Cheated? What? Because from where I'm standing, she's a pretty amazing woman."

Why does it sound like he's fawning over her? Honestly, I think if I didn't have a past with her, he'd be doing everything he could to go on a date with her. "She's so much more amazing than she was in high school. Back then, she'd let people push her around and I, along with one of her cousins, would always stand up for her. It's good to see she has a backbone now." I'm more than likely the reason for that. Or she just grew into the woman she was meant to be.

"And your dad?" Damn, he's really not letting this go. I mean I guess that's what best friends are for. I don't think Corinne even bugged me this much. I need to find out when she's going home. She's driving me as crazy as Carter is with all the Audrey questions.

"He didn't think it was a good idea to go off to college with a girlfriend."

"That's not that uncommon. There's something you're not telling me."

I don't think my stepmom even knows the real reason. I told Corinne not to tell anyone when she finally nagged me enough to tell her. "So, my dad and mom were high school sweethearts. They both went off to college together. Their last year before they graduated, they got pregnant with me. The only problem is...after I was born, Mom decided she didn't want to have the mom life. She met someone else ran away with him as fast as she could leaving me and my dad behind."

Carter whistles and stands. "Damn. But why does he think that would happen to you? He knows not everyone is the same right? I mean he did get remarried."

"I have no freaking clue. I think a lot of it is we reminded him of them. We were inseparable and did everything together. I can count on two hands how many days I went without seeing her when we were teens." And it's true. I spent every moment I could with her outside of school and work. "It was almost obsessive. As much as it broke both of us, maybe it was the right decision. I don't think either of us will ever really know. It's not like we can go back in time."

"Does she know any of this?" He nods to the main area.

"No. I dumped her pretty fast and after a couple of weeks dated a few other people to keep my mind off her. It just made sense because the two of us were intense together. We had our whole future planned out." I'm at a place now where I can appreciate that, but then...it scared me shitless.

"And that is why she dislikes you so much."

"Why?"

"Because you moved on, Man. Do you not watch any movies? She thought she didn't mean anything to you."

Looking back, I did act like a dick. "It wasn't that bad."

"If you say so." He glances out the window to the farm of cubicles again. Laughing he looks back at me before heading to the door. "Now is your chance to talk to her. She's coming this way." Then he leaves. Asshole.

"Here's the report you asked for," Audrey says as she plops the folder on my desk. "Is there anything else you're going to need? I do actually have other work to do besides answering your five thousand questions. I'm not your personal secretary."

Damn, she's got some fire in her veins today. And here I am, emotionally spent from spilling my guts to Carter. If I didn't know better, I'd say he did this on purpose. He wanted me vulnerable so I'd actually do something about this mess with Audrey. "I'm sorry. I don't mean to take up all your time. I only want to know where the company stands so we can see what needs to happen to make it better."

She throws her hands on her hips and it's shocking how much she looks like her mom when she does it. I remember being on the receiving end of that scowl when were teens. Her mom wasn't mad at us often, but she was a stickler for curfew. As long as Audrey was home, I could stay as long as I wanted. I even fell asleep on their couch once and they didn't have any issue with it since Audrey was in her own bed. Her voice pulls me from the memory of much better times. "Well, is that all you need? Like I said, I have stuff to do, clients to call and billings I need to get out."

I wonder if she'd talk to any other boss that way. I'm guessing no because she doesn't like confrontation. Hell, I'm surprised she's confronting me the way she has. It seems like a bad time to ask her about Luke, but I need to know. Maybe it'll stop me from making an ass of myself. "Sort of. I, um, need to ask."

"Ask me what, Justin?" Her hands are no longer on her hips. They've moved down to the edge of her blouse, playing with the ends. It's something she did when she was nervous. At least I know that I'm not the only feeling some sort of way.

"Is there something going on with you and Luke?" There. It's out there and we'll see if she answers me.

She chews on her bottom lip, looking everywhere in the office except at me. Everything in my body is telling me to get up, shut the blinds on my windows and replace her teeth with my lips. She's not out of my system, and never was. Every other woman was a poor replacement for the one person I've wanted since the day I dumped her. Finally, she lets go of her lip, takes a deep breath, and looks me square in the eye. "We're just friends. We have been since we started working here." My shoulders sag and I can feel that weight lifted from me. "Why?"

Okay, I wasn't prepared for that. "I'd rather not get into that on company time. Maybe we can grab a bite to eat after work. Or, just go somewhere to talk?" It's a long shot and I hope she accepts.

"I can't tonight."

"For real, or are you making an excuse?" I need to know if she's just avoiding me

"No, I really can't. Stella scheduled a dress fitting for me and Tiffany. Apparently, she doesn't trust us to do it ourselves." She looks toward the window that shows parts of the city. "Even though I'm the most responsible one," she mutters under her breath.

It breaks my heart all over again. She's amazing and her cousins have never given her the credit she deserves because she usually goes along with whatever they want with no fuss. "Oh, okay. Just let me know when you're free. I guess you're pretty busy with Stella's wedding."

"Yeah," she scrunches her nose, annoyed. "Actually, Friday night I'm going to see Crooked Halo with Tiffany. She wouldn't take no for an answer and I have to go. They're pretty decent. I think Tiffany is trying to persuade them to play at Stella's wedding."

"Sounds good." I stand but she backs up toward the door. "I'll, um, meet you after work on Friday."

"I better get back to work." She runs into the chair in front of my desk and stumbles before hurrying out the door.

We have a plan. This is it. I have my chance to explain and to see if she wants to give this another go. Despite how much I've told Carter and Corinne that I don't want her, I can't lie to myself. Working with her is too much. I need her in my life outside the office.

396

Chapter Thirteen

Audrey

"TELL me again why you invited him?" Tiffany leans against the bar next to me while Spencer is explaining how he got involved with Crooked Halo. She's one hundred percent against this idea. It's why I didn't inform her of my plan. And it's why I didn't let them pick me up like they normally do. Him meeting me here was always an option. But the only way I'm going to find out what he has to say is if he's here. If I came with him, he wouldn't be able to back out.

"He said he wanted to talk about stuff but we couldn't do it at the office." I've already told her this five times since we've been here. She hasn't even had anything to drink so I know that's not the reason. "Besides, maybe it'll bring me closure. Do you know how hard it is working with him?"

"Does he treat you badly at work?" Tiffany turns her glare toward the man in question.

"No, not at all. It's just...I don't know. It's weird seeing him every day. I think most days he's going out of his way to be around me. There's no way he needs all the reports he says he does." For others that might be off putting, but for me, it shows me that he does at least care. In some weird sort of way, anyway. It's those little things. My annoyance is only somewhat of an act. I really do have better things to do. I like it on some masochistic level, though. I get to see him and know that he's as affected as I am. He's not bad to look at, either.

I glance at him now. He's still taller than me and carries himself confidently. I thought he looked amazing in a pair of slacks, but the jeans he changed into before we came to the bar hug him in all the right places. "Stop looking at him like you're going to jump his bones. It's gross." Tiffany pulls my gaze away from him.

"I don't know what you're talking about." He looks good enough to eat. Would it be such a bad thing if we did have sex? It wouldn't be the first time. We weren't exactly innocent when we were teens. It'd be interesting to see what each of us has learned since we've grown up. Not that I have a ton of experience. Dating definitely wasn't a priority when I moved here no matter how much my cousins pushed me to do it. I'm not like Tiff, though. I need to have real, tangible feelings for someone before I hop into bed with them.

"Mhmm." Tiff takes a drink of her whiskey. "You're looking at him the same way I look at Spencer. I know that look well."

I fake gag. "I did not need to know that Tiffany." A shiver runs down my spine. I swear she has no filters. She says whatever she thinks, and I'm rethinking having Justin here. There's no telling what she'll say to him, especially if it's been bottled up all these years.

"Do you not like your drink?" Justin says from behind me, and I jump. "I can get you a water or something else."

"No," I shake my head. "I'm good. I tolerate alcohol much better than I did back in high school."

Tiffany snorts. "You don't have to lie to him. You barely drink unless I'm forcing it on you."

I glare at my cousin and shake my head trying to tell her to shut up. He doesn't need to know that I only drink when I'm upset or nervous. It helps numb whatever is bothering me or lets me speak more than I normally would. "Really, Justin, it's fine. I typically go for the fruity drinks and not the stout ones."

"Give me two seconds," Justin holds up two fingers. "I'll fix that for you."

As soon as he leaves, Tiff raises her eyebrows. "Wow, he's sucking up big time. Whatever he wants to talk to you about is either going to destroy you or land you in his bed."

From where I'm standing, both options suck. Admitting that he still has the power to destroy me is like a slap in the face. And even though ending up in his bed wouldn't necessarily be horrible, it's definitely not something I'm looking forward to since we're just reconnecting. Hell, I don't even have a reason about why he got me all those years ago and then went on with his life as if I never existed. "I'm not gonna let him do either of those things. I won't allow him to have that sort of power over me anymore."

Tiffany almost spit her drink all over me as she laughed. "That is the most full of shit statement I have ever heard. If he no longer had power over your emotions, you wouldn't run every time you see him."

"I work with him, Tiffany. I can't exactly run from him anymore."

"Whatever you say Audrey." She rolls her eyes and strolls away from me just as Justin comes up beside me.

"What was all that about?" He hands me a bright pink drink, and I hope I like this one much better than the last he gave me.

I sigh and shrug at the same time. "It's just Tiffany being Tiffany. You know how that goes."

"Yeah," he chuckles. "She really hasn't changed much after all these years. I figured if anything her temper would've calmed down some."

"Oh no, it's still there. Now it just takes a little bit longer to piss her off," I looked him up and down, "unless you're already on her bad side. Then she's just going to shoot flames at you as much as she can."

"About that," he begins. "I wanted to explain what happened then."

I've already decided I'm going to give him that chance. Now, I need to figure out if I'm going to allow him to do it without me giving him any crap about it. "Oh, you mean when you dropped me like I meant nothing and started dating half the senior class? You mean what happened then?" Yeah, I'm definitely going to give him crap. He turned the last half of my senior year into my own personal hell.

"Dammit, Carter was right," he mutters under his breath.

"Right about what?" The band that is playing before Crooked Halo is beginning to warm up and we are going to lose the chance to hash this out.

He runs a hand on his face and groans. "About how you felt. You would think I would've put two and two together, but apparently, I'm an idiot. Please, don't tell him he was right. I'll never hear the end of it."

But I'm definitely telling him he was right. I knew I liked Carter for a reason. "Let's see how the rest of the evening goes, then I'll decide whether or not I'll keep your secret. So, how about you tell me what happened because from where I was standing everything was perfect and we are ready to set off on our lives together."

"You may want to sit down for this."

Luckily for me, the bar owner always has a table ready for Tiffany and Spencer whenever Crooked Halo plays here. I don't know why, because they never actually sit at it, but it's there just in case. "Follow me."

The instinct to grab his hand and pull him along like I used to when we were teenagers is strong, but my resolve is stronger. I weave between bar patrons until I find the table tucked away in a corner. It's not so far back that you can't see the stage clearly, but it's its own little private paradise for when you need a breather at a concert.

We take our seats and he places his hands on the small circular table. "First off, I want to apologize for how I handle things in high school. I was 18, dumb, scared, and believed my dad had my best interests at heart."

I was right. His dad definitely had something to do with him breaking up with me. Realistically, I know most relationships from high school don't last when you go to college, but I think what Justin and I had was different. Or, at least I thought it was. "Okay," I drawled out. "What exactly did he have to do with our break up?"

"Well, you already know he wasn't a big fan of us being together when we went off to college. He didn't exactly make that a secret. What you don't know is his reason for being that way."

"Which was?" I wish he would get on with it already. It'll help me decide whether to stay here and listen to what he has to say, or go find my cousin and act like the beginning of this evening never happened.

He gives me a sob story about how Justin and I reminded him of himself and Justin's mother. About how she ran off with somebody right before graduation and left his dad to care for the child. "His heart was in the right place, and at the time I thought it made sense."

He has got to be kidding me. That is probably the most ridiculous thing I've ever heard. "You're telling me that you dumped me because of your father's fears. After everything and all of our plans, that made sense to you? Justin, you are going to get your own apartment while we were still in high school just so we could be together and you would be out from under your dad's thumb. But you let that pull you away from me?"

"Audrey, I was 18 and terrified I would lose you to someone better off or smarter than I was. That's essentially what happened with my parents."

I cut him off. "And when did that fear actually come into place for you?" I get it, I do. At the same time, it makes absolutely no sense to me. "Was it before after your dad told you what happened with them?"

He staring at me with panic written all over his face. The answer to this question is going to determine how the rest of the night plays out. "Honestly, before." This is a surprise to me because he never let on that he questioned the relationship at all. Or, maybe that was just me viewing my love for him through rose colored glasses. "You were in all the honors classes, and busy with volunteer and after school activities. While I did good to make good grades while also working. We were already starting to spend less time together, and I felt like it wasn't going to work once we left high school. What if you joined a sorority or were too busy for me? I wasn't ready to set myself up for that kind of heartbreak after hearing what happened to dad."

This is all news to me. Even though we didn't see each other daily like we did before senior year, I always still went on dates frequently enough. "Instead, you made me go through it."

"If it makes you feel any better, I think it's probably one of the biggest mistakes I've ever made. Every time I would go home during school breaks, I would look for you while I was out running errands. I even drove by your house, but the lights were always off, and I was scared you would hate me."

His voice trembles a little at that admission, and for a split second I feel awful for him.

"You would've been right," I say. Not to make him feel bad, but to let him know just how deeply he hurt me. "I changed all of my plans after you dumped me. It was hard enough going to school with you the last half of senior year, and I didn't think I could handle running into you while on campus."

"I'm so sorry, Audrey. If I could go back and do it all over again, there's so many things I would have changed. Not breaking up with you is one of them."

I believe him as crazy as it sounds. I've always had a knack for knowing when he's being sincere, and he is. And as much as it hurt then and hurt when I saw him again, I'm not sure I would have changed any of it. "Honestly, I think it turned out for the best." His shoulders sag and he's no longer looking at me. "It made me realize who I could be, and that I'm perfectly capable of standing on my own 2 feet despite what my cousins think."

"They always were pretty protective of you. And judging how Tiffany yelled at me that night at the restaurant, they still are."

"Yeah, it's a little ridiculous, but they aren't so bad. At least I know they'll always be on my side." I take a drink, and gag. The drink would still be good if it wasn't watered down. As I push it toward the middle of the table and my hand brushes his.

"Well, that's all I came here to say. I think I should probably go now." He moves to stand and I place my hand on his arm.

"No, stay. While your reasoning doesn't make a lot of sense to me, I get it. I let the break up affect me way longer than I should have, and it took a long time for me to realize that." And if I'm being honest, I don't want him to go. It takes a lot of guts for someone to admit they were wrong, and he really isn't all that bad. Plus-side, I have somebody to sit at the table with me and I will be by myself while Tiffany and Spencer join the throng of people next to the stage.

"Are you sure?"

I nod, "As long as you get me something else to drink because I can't drink this. It's watered-down, and gross. Maybe a Margarita? They should have my name on a notepad up there, just tell them to put it on my tab."

"I got you." Well, I wish he would have said those words back then, I'm happy he's saying them now even if it's not the way I thought he would. And who knows, the night is still young.

Chapter Fourteen

I'M WAITING on the bartender to pour another drink for Audrey. The counter has people lined up, shoulder to shoulder. I don't think I've ever been to a bar to see a band play. Not that I've gone to many shows. I've been one hundred percent focused on my future and my job. I'm actually surprised Audrey comes to them. She was never one to go out like this when we were in high school. Tiffany was usually dragging her to parties she had no interest in attending. I'm almost certain it's the same thing here. This isn't her scene, or it wasn't. Things can definitely change in ten years.

The bartender slides the margarita toward me. "This is the most I've ever seen her drink." I don't tell him that she didn't actually drink the other two I got her. He might take offense about his bartending skills, and everything he's made is fine.

"Does she come here a lot?" I don't know why I ask. I only want to know more about her, get a feel for the woman she is today.

He gives me a look like he doesn't know if he should say anything. Something must signal him in that I'm not horrible because eventually he does, "Only with Tiffany and Spencer. She doesn't usually come by herself."

"That's not surprising." I was right. And if I know Tiffany, she's doing it so Audrey won't spend too much time alone even though that's how she's always preferred to spend her nights. Cuddled up with a blanket and watching a movie.

"If any of you want anything else, just let me know. I'll be here all night." He grins at the woman standing next to me and grabs her drink order.

At least now I know she comes here often enough the bartender knows she doesn't drink much. She took my confession pretty well considering she also pretty much called me a coward. She has every right to think of me like that. I was a coward. I finally let my dad's words get into my head and boost the fears I had even more. I just can't believe she thought she meant nothing to me. She was my entire world, and if I play my cards right...she might be again.

I fight my way through the crowd until I see Audrey staring at her phone in disgust. After setting the drinks on the table, I try to spot Tiffany. It'll let me know if the look she's giving is because they are talking about me. But she has the same look on her face. So, not about me. "Did your phone do something to piss you off?"

"Look at this monstrosity." Audrey shoves the phone in my face. "Stella is nuts if she thinks I'm going to wear that. No single man will want to dance with me at her wedding if I'm wearing it." Well, that was a kick to the gut. I'm not sure when the wedding is, but I do know that she one hundred percent plans on being alone for it.

"It's not that bad," I smile, trying to play off the hurt. "I'd still dance with you. I'd dance with you if you were wearing a potato sack." It would also give me a chance to get her on a dance floor period. Because I'm a dumbass we didn't get that dance at senior prom. We didn't experience our lasts together the way we both assumed we would. Well, you know what they say about assumptions. Especially when the problem is one you created yourself.

"Yeah," she rolls her eyes. "Okay. This is worst that the dresses we picked out when we were drunk." That had to have been recently. Maybe she's changed more than I thought.

"Why were you drunk and picking out dresses? That sounds like a horrible idea."

Her cheeks blush in the dim light of the bar. Leaning back in her chair she puts her phone on the table and lifts her drink to her lips. "That's the night I ran into you."

Damn, she knows how to pack the punches. This is the third time she's had drinks in less than a week, by my count at least, and it's all because of me. Not only do I make her run away, but it seems I cause her to get drunk as well. The information is doing wonders for my self-esteem.

"Sorry I made you drink." I've never been the cause of someone's bad choices. "Was it really that bad seeing me?"

"Justin," she laughs. "I literally ran out in the middle of dinner. How did you think I was going to handle it? It sucked, for sure. But as long as we can be civil around each other then I don't see why we have to avoid each other." She takes another drink of her margarita waiting for me to respond. I have no clue how I'm going to do that without sounding like a dick.

"If it makes you feel any better, I really do wish I could go back and change everything." I would in a heartbeat. Even if things didn't turn out the way they have for each of us, I feel like I missed out on years we'll never be able to get back.

"Seriously, it's okay. I've had time to adjust to seeing you. It's not bad at all anymore. Luke told me I was being ridiculous." She bites her bottom lip again and I can't help wondering if she wants to try a relationship again. Though, I could have gone without her mentioning her coworker. Knowing that he's part of the reason she's back to feeling okay makes my blood boil. Too bad I don't deserve to have that feeling. Not when I was the cause.

"So, there's another reason I wanted to talk to you tonight. I have another question." I'm almost yelling to be heard over the music. "I was thinking, maybe we-"

I'm not able to finish the sentence. Audrey grabs my arm while setting her drink on the table and pulls me toward the crowd of people outside the roped off section. "Let's find Tiff and Spence." It's nowhere close to what I want to do, but she seems to need the distraction and I'll follow her anywhere. By the end of the night, I'm asking her for another chance whether she wants to hear it or not.

Audrey and I are leaning against a wall with Tiffany while Spencer does his thing at the merchandise booth with the band. His branding is the best I've seen, and I wonder why he doesn't try to get in contact with more bands.

"How did you like the show?" Audrey bumps into my shoulder. For the first time since I've known her, she actually looks comfortable in a crowded space.

"They are actually really great. I was surprised."

"Why?" Tiffany scoffs. "They are amazing. And when they are playing on every radio station, I'm going to run around to everyone and tell them I told you so."

"This normally isn't my thing. That's all." I give Audrey a knowing look. This didn't used to be her thing either. "But I can see the appeal in coming to see them. It was the perfect way to blow off steam after a day at the office."

"That's the only reason Audrey comes," Tiffany points at her cousin. "I drag her out here knowing she'll have a good time before she does."

"You realize that if I *really* didn't want to come, I wouldn't, right? I like the band, and a night out every once in a while, isn't going to kill anyone." She argues. "Unless it's a work night. I typically bail on those. I like my sleep more than I like live music. Getting up early for work after a late night is the worst."

"So true," I agree. "The only morning person I know is Corinne, and she drives me crazy with her early breakfasts on the weekends. She also insists on making me a *balanced* meal before heading into the office. I love her, but I can't wait for her to go back home."

"I feel like I would get along great with your step-sister." Audrey beams.

"Who knows," I shrug. "Maybe that can be arranged before she drives me insane."

The crowd in the bar is thinning out as fans finish up their purchases. The band is signing items and Spencer takes that opportunity to come talk to us. "We should be done here in a few. We can take you home if you want, Audrey."

"I can take her." There's no way I'm letting anything else get in the way of me trying for another chance with her. "Her car is still at the office."

"Cuz?" Tiffany asks Audrey and lifts an eyebrow. She really is not a fan of me. I may have to win her approval first. It's the only way I can see any of this working without her being on my ass all the time.

"It's fine, Tiff." She reaches around me and gives her cousin a brief hug. "I'll call you the minute I get home."

"You better." Tiffany pulls out her phone and points to it. "Don't make me use our tracking system on you."

"You know good and well we haven't used that thing since you settled down." Audrey waves at her cousin and grabs me by the arm. "Let's get out of here before Tiff says anything else embarrassing."

She'll get no arguments from me.

Chapter Fifteen

THE DRIVE back to the office is just like old times. Justin must have something on his mind. He has both hands on the steering wheel and leather squeaks the tiniest bit from here he's wringing it. The music on the radio is so quiet you can barely tell it's playing. It's an exact replay of how he acted when him and his dad got into arguments over a decade ago.

The urge to reach out and put my hand on his arm the way I did when we were teens is strong. Even after all this time it's second nature and I have to force myself to keep my hands in my lap. He glances over at me and I turn until all I can see are the brake lights in front of us.

This is weird and awkward. Like when you're on a first date with someone but you don't know what to say. The only difference is we have years of history behind us. As much as I want to, I'm not sure how to move past it. For now, I'm giving him the chance to gather whatever thoughts he has while I process what he told me at the bar.

I knew deep in my gut his dad had something to do with it. I just didn't think he'd stoop so low to create an emotional rift between me and Justin. The news that Justin had his own fears about us was new to me as well. I guess when you really love someone you look past all that, and clearly, he didn't love me enough. Not that I blame him. We *were* young. Neither of us knew anything about the big wide world we'd be stepping into. I wasn't lying when I told him it was probably for the best. That's something ten years of distance can give you...perspective. We may have ended up exactly where we are now. Or, we may have been so codependent on each other we would have held ourselves back and never flourished the way we were meant to.

Justin is still driving like he has a purpose, and I want to know what's in that skull of his. Tiffany was right when she said whatever he tells me could destroy me or make me want him. The conversation in the bar wasn't enough for either. Whatever he has to say when we get to the parking garage will be what does it. It'll be what gives me hope, or lets me know that there will never be anything between us again. Luke wasn't wrong when he said I still have feelings for him. In all honesty, they never went away. I wonder if that's true for all first loves or if it's singular to me because he was my world back then.

The silence is getting to me. I'm used to car rides listening to music as loud as I can stand it or the chattering of my cousins on speaker phone. Even at home I have something going so I don't feel quite so alone. One of us needs to break the silence before I get stuck in my head more than I already am. It's obvious he's not going to be the first one to do it. "Did you really like the show tonight? Crooked Halo is quickly becoming one of my favorite bands."

"Yeah," His eyes never leave the road in front of him. Not one single glance my way. That shred of hope I had before, is withering away. "They were decent. Not what I usually listen to, but I can definitely see the appeal."

"They grow on you." I smile at the memory of Tiffany dragging me to one of their shows. I didn't think it was my speed either, but sometimes that grungy, rock is exactly what I need to get through the day. "If you stick around, you'll get to know the band. They are probably the most down to earth musicians I've ever met." Shit. I didn't mean to say that. Word vomit is the worst, and I practically threw out the words without thinking.

"Have you met a lot of musicians?" Now he looks at me, and from what I can tell, his eyebrow is raised a fraction. As if he can't believe I would ever be in that position to meet famous people. And why the hell can everyone I know do that eyebrow thing except me? From Stella it's disapproving and when Tiffany does it, you know she's about to wreak havoc on the world. Maybe I should practice more.

I shake the random thought away. "When Tiffany drags you to shows, and magically gets backstage and after the party passes, it's kind of hard not to."

"Wow." Is that...condescension coming from him? What was I supposed to do when I realized he wasn't coming back to confess his undying love for me? Sit around and be boring. I mean yeah, I'm pretty boring compared to my cousins, but seriously?

"Why is that so hard to believe?"

"I don't know," he shrugs, focusing on the road once again. The corner of his mouth tilts up the tiniest bit. Maybe he isn't looking down on me. Ugh, it's so hard to read him now after all these years. "I just didn't think going to concerts was something you would be into. You've changed a lot since we were teens."

Could he give any more mixed messages? One minute he seems intrigued, the next it's like he misses the old me. The one that went along with every little thing and stayed in the shadows to stay away from attention. Not that much has changed. I *still* don't like the spotlight. But I do know how to go out and have a good time. It's not completely outside of my comfort zone any more. I've finally gotten to a point where I'm happy in my own skin. Sure, it's lonely because no other man has ever lived up to my idea of *him*, but the back and forth is getting old.

"It's not like I'm out there crowd surfing. I like live music. I just don't like the drunken idiots I usually encounter. It's also why I never go alone. I'm always with Tiffany and Spencer because they know my boundaries and back me up should an issue arise."

"Have there been any problems?"

"There was one time a guy wouldn't stop asking me out, but we handled it."

"How?" And now he's interested again. I'm getting whiplash.

"Tiffany threw his beer in his face. That ended things pretty fast. When I go, we don't go to the pit, we hang on the outskirts." Exactly where I like it.

"Now that I can totally picture," he laughs. "She really hasn't changed all that much since high school."

"No, she hasn't." She's fiery, passionate, and takes no shit. I admire her for all the qualities I don't possess. I should tell her that one day and let her know how much she means to me.

Finally, we pull up to the parking garage. He enters and parks next to my car. He takes his hands off the steering wheel and turns until he's facing me completely. The air is charged and it feels like possibility and heartbreak. Maybe a mixture of the two. "It may not seem like it, but I did have fun tonight. It was nice seeing you let down your hair and live in the moment. It's all I've ever wanted for you. Even in high school."

"Thanks, I think?" There's no way to respond to that. "I had fun, too. It's nice to not be the third wheel. I always feel like I'm cramping their style and bow out of most outings."

"That's too bad. You look like you fit in. But I'll be around if you need someone with you." He slides his hand over the console, creeping closer to mine in my lap. Is he saying what I think he's saying? There's no way, right? He's been so wishy washy all night.

"What do you mean?" I need him to come right out and say it. No more of these stupid games. Luke tells me it makes the chase that much sweeter, but damn it. I don't want there to be a chase. I need to know point blank what his intentions are for me. What he wants out of whatever this weird thing is. The mental ping pong is getting old. I knew I'd forgive him and fall head over heels again the night Luke pointed out my feelings about Justin. Hopefully my heart doesn't suffer a repeat.

He scoots as close to me as he can while still in his own seat. "I mean, Audrey, I was an idiot at eighteen. Hell, I think most people are. But…I want to see if we can give this another go. To see where we might end up this time. Teenager me didn't know what he was doing. I let an irrational fear get in my head, and ruin what could have been the best thing for me. Would you consider dating me again? To see if we're still as compatible as we used to be."

My heart is beating double time in my chest. Everything I had hoped to hear so long ago just fell from his lips. "What about work? Won't people talk?"

"Let them. It's not against the rules. I checked the employee handbook." I don't bother telling him I know that. Luke sent me an email with the page highlight in bright yellow. I needed to know whether that would stop him. It may be immature, but after he let his dad add to the rift he was feeling, I want reassurance he won't let it happen again.

I lean toward him until my lips are against his ear. "Let's see where this goes."

He pulls back just enough for our eyes to meet. Without a word, he thrusts his fingers into my hair and slams his lips against mine. In so many ways it's just like back then, but we're older and have experience we didn't at eighteen. His tongue teases my lips open and I moan at the contact. I'm not sure if it's because of him or the fact I haven't been intimate in so long. Either way, I'm not complaining.

When he breaks the kiss, both of us are panting. My hair feels like it's all over the place and I rest my back against the door. "I've wanted to do that since the day you ran out of the elevator."

"Don't worry," I laugh. "You'll be able to do again."

"I hope so." He opens his door and comes around to my side to open mine. "Will you come to dinner at my place tomorrow?"

Stepping out of the car, I nod. "Sure. Want me to bring anything?"

"Just yourself." He waits until I'm safely tucked away in my car before he backs up to his own. "Goodnight, Audrey."

"Goodnight." The night could have ended a completely different way, and I'm so happy it looks like things are finally going my way in the relationship department.

Chapter Sixteen

Justin

NOTHING CAN BRING me down right now. I feel like that scene in Rocky where Stallone is standing on top of the stairs with his fists raised in victory. Asking Audrey to date me again was terrifying and this is one hundred percent that moment for me. It took me back to the very first time I asked her out. There weren't sweaty palms this time, but the nerves were probably worse. She could have shot me down and I wouldn't have blamed her. It's not like I've been a joy to be around.

The living room light is on as I walk up the sidewalk to the front door. Hopefully Corinne is asleep, and I won't have to deal with her and her million questions tonight. I open and close the door as quietly as I can. My feet are silent as I make my way across the rug.

"Are you whistling?" Corinne's head pops up over the couch. Fuck. I was so worried about a creaky floorboard and door that I forgot I was actually still making noise.

"So, what if I am?" I know I'm not ready for her interrogation. I'm tired and still have to figure out what exactly I'll attempt to cook for Audrey tomorrow night.

She doesn't say anything and I think I'm off the hook. I take a few more steps toward the hall. "I guess tonight went well?"

And...we're doing this. "Not that it's any of your business, but yes, it did."

"Good," she nods her head in approval. "When do I get to meet her?"

My dear, sweet, annoying sister has been bugging me to meet her since I mentioned working with her. Hell, she's been pushing me to ask Audrey out since she showed up in my kitchen. "Soon. She's coming over for dinner tomorrow night, but I need you to make yourself scarce."

"And miss my opportunity? Not a chance in hell."

"If you'd go back home, I wouldn't have to worry about having you leave." I feel like shit for even saying it. I'm the one person who has never judged her, and I'm being a dick right now because it's inconvenient for me. "Sorry, I didn't mean that. I do like having you here, but I want our second first date to be less of a community affair."

She shrugs away the hurt and that makes her a much better person than me. "I get it. I would be the same way. What am I supposed to do while you are occupied?"

"I'm sure there are more places you can photograph. Or, maybe you can hang out with Carter."

Her laugh is loud and echoes in the room. "I thought you didn't want me around him. Scared he's going to try to date me."

Maybe I should take Audrey out to eat instead. Corinne's right. I don't particularly want her around my best friend. Not because he isn't a good guy, he's just overly curious about her. And I don't want either of them to end up hurt if they dated. Not only will it suck seeing two of the most important people in my life in pain, but it puts me in the middle. I'd have to choose between family and friends. "You're right, I'll figure out something else."

"Don't be ridiculous. I'm perfectly capable of taking care of myself and pushing off any unwanted advances. This isn't the regency era. I have a voice." She stands and points her finger at me. "You need to have your date and catch up. There's a decade worth of learning to do between the two of you."

I laugh and take a step back. "I know you can handle yourself. It's him I'm worried about."

"Well, don't." She folds her arms across her chest. "What are you cooking for her? Do you need me to do anything?"

That's a great question because I still have no fucking clue. "Do you have any ideas on something easy?" She opens her mouth, but I cut her off. "I mean very easy. Something that even I can't screw up."

"Everything I know of is pretty boring. I could always cook before I head out."

It's a good idea. Her food is much more appetizing than whatever I would come up with. But no. I want the food to be prepared by me. And, if I can't come up with something, I'll order something and have it delivered before she gets here. "Boring is fine. I'm certain she's not expecting anything amazing. It's no secret that I lived off ramen and fast food our senior year of high school."

"Thank God you aren't trying to fix her ramen. That's definitely not going to wow her." She shakes her head, disgusted.

"Hey," I step back, hand on my chest in mock offense. "I found plenty of ways to jazz up some ramen. Don't knock it until you try it." I glance at the clock on the wall and my eyes widen. How the hell did it get so late? "I'm going to go to bed. It's been a long night. I'll make spaghetti or something. It's hard to screw that up, right?"

"It's relatively easy. I'll run to the store in the morning and get everything you need. Just leave your debit card on the counter."

Rolling my eyes, I pull my wallet out of my pocket. "Here," I grunt. "Can you bring back breakfast tacos, too?"

"Yep. Now get some sleep. We want you at your best tomorrow. You're gonna have to impress the hell out of her to keep her around forever."

What the fu—? Now, I'm nervous. I don't know that we'll end up as forever, but has she changed so much that I'll need to do some insane thing to keep her attention? I don't have the energy to worry about it. I walk down the hall toward my room. "Night, Sis." Nerves are a problem for tomorrow.

I feel like I need a checklist to make sure I have everything just right. I think Audrey might also like that idea. She's definitely way more organized than I've ever been. I did send her my address earlier, so at least that is out of the way, and now it's time for me to freak out even more. She should be here any minute.

The food is done and sitting inside the fancy bowls Corinne bought when she did the grocery run. Apparently, I can't just serve it out of the pans. I don't know why? All it's going to do is give me dishes to clean up after she leaves. I swear my sister is over the top extra and is doing more to make sure this date goes well than I am. There's just this fear that she's going to see all this work Corinne helped me do and realize that I'm a huge fake. That I'm not capable of this all the time.

Glancing at my phone, I check the time and see if I have any missed messages from Audrey. I'm good on that front, but I'm running out of the former. I grab the plates out of the cabinet and set them on the table, along with a bowl for the salad, and two forks. Should I put them next to each other with a plate on either side of the corner? Or, should I put them on either side of the table so we can be face to face over the food? Why the hell is this so hard? I place them in each spot at least five times before I decide on setting them next to each other. I don't want to be on the opposite side of the table from her.

Headlights coming down the road capture my attention from the kitchen window. Shit, shit, shit. That has to be her. I'm not ready. The last thing I need to do is light the candles. The car is driving slow and it will give me some time. I turn from the table and head toward the counter. Flinging the junk drawer open I rummage around for matches. A lighter. Something. I don't see them anywhere. I could have sworn I bought more the last time I did a run for emergency supplies. Apparently, I didn't.

The car that was creeping toward my house pulls into the driveway and the engine turns off. Time is up. I'll just brighten the lights a smidge and call it good. The candles can be decorative. I'm surprised Corinne didn't have the forethought to grab some when she was getting everything else. I'm almost terrified to look at my bank account. It will all be worth it if Audrey loves it, though.

I hear a car door close and pull some wine glasses from the hutch they are in and set them on the table. I rush back to the cabinets and pull down two glasses in case she'd rather have water. Going out to eat would have been so much easier than all of this.

As I set the glasses on the table, there's a knock on the door. Okay, Justin. You can do this. It's not like you're total strangers. Just be your normal charming self. That might be part of the problem. With a deep breath, I make my way to the front door. One more breath as I put my hand on the door knob and turn. Please let her like this.

I don't think I've ever been this insecure about a damn date. Time to see if it pays off. I pull the door open and my mouth drops open.

Chapter Seventeen

Audrey

WHY IS he looking at me like that? Do I have something on me? I take a moment to glance over my outfit. I don't see any stains. Surely Tiff would have said something if there was something wrong with the dress. Despite her feelings about Justin, she came over and helped me get ready. She even brought some of her clothes for me to wear, but I'm a bit bustier than her. I also wouldn't have felt comfortable in clothes that weren't mine. I'm trying to do everything in my power to make sure this date goes well.

When I look up, he's still wide-eyed with his mouth hanging open. I shift on my feet. "Is, um, everything okay?" Geez, that didn't come out strong and confident at all. I sound like a girl who's unsure of herself and needs approval. Probably because I am. Dating isn't new territory for me, but dating an ex who broke up with me…that is one hundred percent new.

His mouth snaps closed and he shakes his head. "Not at all." Opening the door wider, he motions me inside. "You look amazing."

That's a relief. Tiffany found this black dress in the back of my closet. I don't even remember the last time I wore it. Honestly, I didn't even think it would still fit. It's low cut and shows just enough cleavage to tease, but not so much that I'm falling out of it. And it stops mid-thigh with a skater skirt. It's cute, comfortable, and I feel amazing in it. I swear my cousins know me better than myself sometimes when it comes to my clothes. "Thank you."

He waits for me to walk through the door and closes it behind me. "You can set your bag here or in the living room." He points toward the entryway table and I slide my small purse off my shoulder and set it down. "The kitchen, and more importantly dinner, is right through here."

He walks closer to me as he leads me to the kitchen. His hand so close it brushes mine. As immature as it might seem, butterflies erupt in my stomach at the small contact. A part of me wishes he would grab my hand already and pull me toward him. Maybe it's been too long since I've been touched by a man, or the fact that it's him, but after our kiss last night, all I can think about is his hands all over me. Focus, Audrey. You have to see what's even going to happen before you try ending up in bed with him.

The kitchen is dimly lit and pretty bowls are lined up in the middle of the table. It's not so dark that you can't see, but it helps the mood for the night. At least I'm not the only one trying to set the tone for the evening.

"Did you cook all this?" I lean over the table and see pasta, sauce and meatballs in each of the dishes. A gigantic salad sits in a bowl to the side. When did he learn how to cook? He was never that great at it when we were in high school and burnt more than food than I can recall. "It smells amazing."

"Thanks." His cheeks redden and I find it funny that I'm the one causing him to blush. It's always been the other way around. "Corinne left me very detailed instructions on how to not fuck it up."

I almost forgot his step-sister has been here. "Where is she anyway? Did she go back home?" I want to meet her. Not only because he obviously cares for her like they've been siblings all their lives, but also so I can try to pry stories out of her. She's known him for the time I've been away from him. It'll give me a deeper look into who he is now from another perspective.

"No, she's still here." At my expression he waves his hands in the air. "Not like right now. She went to hang out with Carter and take pictures or something. She's out of our hair for the night so we can have a proper date without her asking you a million questions."

So, she knows Carter. I guess he's been friends with him for a long time if his sister feels comfortable going out on the town. "Are they together?"

"They better never be," Justin growls and I can't stop the laugh that bubbles out of me. There's the protective man I know. "What's so funny?"

"Nothing." I'm still giggling and do my best to rein it in. "It's just been so long since I've seen you like this. I remember you'd get that way when some jockhole we went to school with would pick on me."

"Well," he throws his arm over my shoulder and I relish the touch. He pulls me closer to him. "Nobody messes with my girl." For a whole two seconds I think he's going to bend down and meld his lips to mine, but he clears his throat and points to the chairs with plates in front of them. "Are you ready to eat?"

He has to be just as nervous as I am. He's never gone through this much work to impress me. Don't get me wrong, he set up an amazing backyard picnic with the help of my cousins the summer before senior year, but nothing like this for a run of the mill date. I take a seat and wait until he's sitting before asking, "What happened to Corinne to make you so protective?"

"She hasn't exactly had the best track record with dating. Most guys treat her like shit or they use her until she doesn't have anything else to offer before they split. It's only ever been her and her mom until me and Dad. It felt right to do what I could to help be a big brother even though she's slightly older than me." He points at the table, "Let's eat before the food gets cold."

It's good to know that even after all this time nothing has really changed with him. He's still down to earth from what I can see and takes care of those he feels are important to him. Sitting here with him now feels like it's been forever and also like no time has passed since we were those lovestruck teenagers.

I pile my plate with food, take a bite, and moan. "This is really good. It may even be better than most Italian restaurants."

"Yeah," he croaks. "I'm going to need you to stop making that sound."

"Well, you shouldn't cook really good food. I can't help how my body reacts." Now that the words are out of my mouth, I can't help agonizing over them. Did it sound bitchy? I was going for flirting, but I've never been great at it. It's one of the things I wished my cousins would teach me because they are pros. I'm awkward to put it mildly.

Justin mumbles something under his breath before shoving a forkful of spaghetti into his mouth.

"What was that?" All I heard was something about showing me how my body reacts.

He sets his fork on the plate and pins me with a stare. He looks like he'd rather have me for dinner. "I said, I can help show your body how to react." His voice is much deeper than it was even seconds before and his jaw is tight.

Be flirty, Audrey. It's not that hard. "Wine me, dine me, and then maybe you can show me."

The rest of dinner was very anticlimactic. We talked about what we've been doing the past ten years. Me working in my cubicle, minding my own business, and him working his way up the ladder at the accounting firm that's now merged with ours. Basically, we're both boring. Though, I think I've lived it up a little more than he has thanks to Tiffany. She drags me to shows any chance she gets and any time I say yes.

I rinse off my plate and put it in the dishwasher despite his protests. It's ingrained in me. Mom always made us clean up after ourselves when we were kids. He knows that, and I don't know why he's acting surprised. I don't realize he's standing right behind me until he asks, "Do you have room for dessert?"

"What kind?" That's the important question. Does it mean actual food? Or, me and him having each other? This new highly sexual Audrey is a shock. I feel like Tiffany would be proud of me for putting myself out there. For hinting at what I want. Justin is the only person I can think of that I'm remotely comfortable being like this around. Even though we've only just reconnected, I've known him my entire life. He was all of my firsts. He's the only one that can pull out this side of me.

"That depends," he leans on the counter next me and winks, "I have tiramisu in the fridge, but if you have other things in mind, I wouldn't mind."

"Well, when you put it like that…" I turn toward the fridge and open the door. There is a massive pan with what I can only imagine holds the delicious coffee cake. I pull it out of the fridge and set it on the counter. "Did you make this too?"

He snorts, "Please, I could barely pull off the spaghetti. I do not have the talent to make a cake like that."

Instead of looking for a plate, I search the drawers until I find a fork. I dip it into the cake and pull out a forkful, lifting it to Justin's mouth, waiting for him to take the bite. He doesn't disappoint. The way his mouth moves over the fork is slow and seductive. Who knew eating could be such a turn on? "Is it good?"

He nods and pulls the fork from my hand. "See for yourself." He scoops some out and feeds me in the same exact way. I try to do what he did but I feel like a moron.

Another moan escapes my lips as I close my eyes and savor the moment. The way I feel with him feeding me, and how delicious the cake is. "Can I take some of that home with me?"

"You can have whatever you want." A tiny smirk lifts up the corner of his mouth. "You've got something right—." He doesn't finish the sentence. Leaning in he lifts his hand as if to wipe away whatever piece of cake is on my face, but at the last second, he drops it around my waist and pulls me flush to him. His lips are on my mouth in seconds, and I know right now all bets are off. The likelihood of me going home tonight is zero.

Chapter Eighteen

Justin

AUDREY MOANS into my mouth at the contact. She has to know I did it on purpose. I didn't even try to play it off too much. The icing on her mouth? Total cliche, but it was worth it. I purposefully slid the fork into her mouth at an angle. I wanted an excuse to get my lips on hers. Ever since she made that damn comment during dinner, it's all I've ever been able to think about.

She throws her arms around my neck and deepens the kiss. This woman manages to steal my heart over and over again. It doesn't seem to matter what age we are. Now, it's my turn to groan. Her lips are soft and full. I move to kiss her cheek then her neck. She's so damn short that I have to bend over. Without warning, I pick her up to sit on the counter. She spreads her legs wide enough for me to nestle between them. Her breathing is ragged as I continue kissing her skin.

Dragging my lips up her neck once again, I stop when I get to her ear. Nibbling her lobe until her legs wrap around my waist and she pulls me closer to her. "Please, don't stop."

"I don't plan on it." I pause for a second before I continue worshipping her skin.

She leans back, resting her weight on her hands, giving me access to the rest of her body. She's definitely more open now than she was back then, and I'm not complaining one bit. My lips follow the line of her shirt and the cleavage on full display. Trailing my fingers from her waist to her breast, I softly squeeze until she's moaning again. "Justin, I need you to—."

"Need me to what?" I hope like hell she was going to finish that with fuck me, but I don't know that she'd ever say that in a million years.

"I don't know," she pants. "Something."

Instead of replying, I slide my hand down her breast with just enough pressure to cause friction. We both may be fully clothed, but it doesn't matter. My hand follows the path down her stomach before lifting her skirt and rubbing along her inner thigh. "Tell me what you want."

Her breath hitches. "I want you to make me feel good."

"That I can do." I press my lips to hers as I let my finger slip beneath her panties into her wet pussy. Jesus, she feels good. My tongue dances with hers, and I rub her clit with my thumb. She takes the weight off one arm and grabs my shirt, yanking me closer. She shifts her hips until she's grinding my hand, and fuck, I'm going to come before I'm ready.

She's buzzing with pent up energy, and I want to taste her before she comes undone. Breaking the kiss, I feverishly kiss down her body as I pull her panties down and get on my knees before her. "You deserve to be fucking worshipped." I don't wait for a response. My lips meet her sweet folds and I groan. "You taste so good," I mumble against her.

Her fingers are in my hair and she's pulling me closer. Riding my mouth to get closer to that sweet release. My tongue swirls around her clit and her legs shake. "I'm so close, Justin."

I slide a finger into her and pump until her body goes tight and she's all but screaming my name. That won't be the last time my name falls from her lips in pleasure tonight.

"What the hell? Tell me you're not doing what I think you are on the counter where I prepare food." Oh shit. No, no, no. What the fuck is she doing here?

"Get out, Corinne," I bark.

"Oh my God." Audrey pulls away from me and jumps down from the counter. I barely stop myself from falling backward at the force of her landing. "This is so embarrassing." She pulls her panties up and her face is bright red. "I think I should go."

"No," I reach out to grab her hand. "Don't. I'll find out why she's back already. You can go hang out in my room if you don't want to stay out here." She starts to argue, but I pull her down to my level. "It's not the end of the world, I promise. I'll smooth things over with my sister. I want you to stay."

She bites her lip and glances toward the entryway. I can see the indecision warring in her eyes. Finally, she sighs, "Okay, I'll stay. Which way is your room? I'm not leaving this spot until you have your sister distracted."

"Thank you," I whisper and give her a quick peck on the cheek. "Give me a couple of seconds. Just follow the hallway. My room is the one at the end of it.

If you look through my drawers, I should have some t-shirts and sweats you can wear."

She snorts. "Who said I was staying the night?"

At least I can make her laugh past her mortification. "Um, me. Besides we have plans then I intend to order breakfast to be delivered. How do you feel about breakfast tacos?"

She rolls her eyes and shoos me away. "We'll talk about that later."

"Fine." I stand up and smile down at her. "I'm glad you're here." Before going to the living room, I make a quick stop at the table, grab a napkin, and wipe my face. I plan on doing more of that later.

Corinne is standing by the front window when I walk in. "Why are you already back? You weren't supposed to come home until a lot later than now." My voice is strained and I'm trying to keep my cool. She did me a huge favor by leaving for a majority of the night, but she could have called.

"I'm sorry, Little Brother." She put emphasis on the little. "I forgot my extra battery and Carter stopped by here so we could grab it before going downtown. I thought y'all would still be eating dinner, or watching a movie. I didn't expect to walk into, well, that. How was I supposed to know y'all would be getting down and dirty on the kitchen counter?" She crosses her arms and glares at me. "You're going to sanitize the counter, right? I love you, but I don't know if I can cook in the kitchen again until I know it's clean."

"You are impossible." I rub my hand over my face. "Of course, I'm going to clean. I'm not an idiot." I take a few seconds to think about what she just said. "Wait. Carter is in the driveaway?"

"Yeah," she shrugs. "I was supposed to be in and out, not scarred for the rest of my life. I don't think I'll ever unsee that."

"You better not utter a word to him." She likes to talk, and I have a feeling, despite my warning he's going to find out anyway. "I mean it, Rinne. He'll give me hell for days."

"I won't tell him. Do you honestly think I want to relive that?" I'm hoping by keeping her attention on me, Audrey has already slipped off to my room. "But I expect to properly meet her soon."

"You will after she's gotten over her embarrassment." She'll most likely meet her in the morning. "Are you coming home tonight?"

"Duh," she spits out. "I like Carter and all, but I'm not staying at his place. Have you seen it? It's messier than anything I've ever encountered. That includes the deadbeats I've dated."

"Well, that's good to know." Honestly, I think she protests too much and too quickly. "I guess I'll see you in the morning, then." I don't wait for a response. I need to make sure Audrey has calmed down. She's most likely freaking out that she's made a bad first impression.

When I open the door, Audrey is sitting on the edge of my bed wearing one of my old t-shirts. It's reminiscent of when she used to wear my hoodies to school. It's like a status saying she's mine, and I'm happy she had no qualms about putting it on. "Are you okay?"

She turns and looks at me, her long brown curls hanging over her shoulder. "Is your sister gone?"

"She will be soon. Apparently, she forgot to take her extra camera battery. She won't be back until later tonight." I sit next to her and wrap an arm around her waist, pulling her toward me.

She leans her head on my shoulder. "That wasn't how I planned on meeting her you know? Hopefully she doesn't think I'm an awful person."

I laugh and kiss the top of her head. "She doesn't. She was just taken off guard. Besides, she doesn't get the right to judge you, or me. This is my house."

"Yeah," she sighs. "But she's a guest and you should have some sort of respect for that."

"Eh, I do. But the same goes for her. She tends to have boundary issues and needs to know everything. It's kind of annoying."

"Most siblings are from what I've seen." She leans back. "Though, I guess I have some experience since my cousins are almost like my siblings." She laughs for a second. "Can you imagine the trouble any of our parents would have had if we were sisters and lived under the same roof all the time? We would have driven them crazy."

"That's no lie. The three of you together are a handful. But I was always a little jealous of the bond you had. I never had that close of a relationship with anyone outside of y'all. Now that I have it, I totally get why your bond was so strong." I lean back until I'm lying on the bed, dragging Audrey back with me. "Having that means a lot, and we have each other's back when shit goes down. Which is why she's here. And it's also why she has no room for judgement. She's made plenty of bad decisions."

"Are you saying that was a bad choice?" Audrey smiles up at me. "Because from where I'm standing, it was the best one I've made in a really long time."

"There was no mistake in what happened in the kitchen," I wink at her. "Maybe we should continue where we left off."

I'm waggling my eyebrows at her and she snorts before hitting lightly on the chest. "Maybe later, I'm still pretty mortified. Hell, I don't even know how I'm going to look her in the eye without thinking about how she saw us."

"Well, what do you want to do?"

She taps her chin, deep in thought. "Let's watch a movie. You have popcorn, right?"

"Yes, but it's not going to be one of those cheesy romances you used to make me watch when we were in school is it? I don't know if I have the mental energy to watch that."

"Fine," she sighs. "You can pick the movie, but just know there's a possibility I'll pass out during an action movie."

"Chick flick it is." I pull both of us up and peek out of the door to make sure Corinne is really gone. If I play my cards right, I'll have Audrey in my bed before the movie is even over.

Chapter Nineteen

THE HOUSE IS quiet when I wake up. Justin is lying next to me, shirtless, and I want more than anything to run my fingers along his chest. Wake him up and spend hours making love to each other the way we did last night. He's a lot more experienced now, and I have a feeling we've barely tapped the surface of what we can make each other feel.

I need to get out of here, though. Not because of anything he did, but because I don't want to run into Corinne. That will be an awkward conversation and I'm not ready to have it. Hopefully, Justin isn't to upset with me when he wakes up.

I slide out of the covers and bed, and when my feet meet the floor, I check behind me to see if he's stirred. All I can hear is light snoring coming from his side of the bed. The sweats he found for me are on the floor and I move to put them on. The thought to change and put my dress back on enters my mind, but I brush it off just as quickly. It will only add time to my departure and I'm trying to creep out of here like a thief in the night. How the hell did Tiffany do this all the time before she met Spencer? It feels so cruel to leave someone in bed while you scamper off.

The bedroom door is open a fraction and I pull it wider, listening for any creak or noise that might give me away. That would look way worse than him waking up to me gone. Catching me leaving…I think that would be a slap in the face.

Tiptoeing down the hall, I'm at the entryway table bag and keys in hand when his voice stops me in my tracks. "Going somewhere?"

Damn it. Busted. There are two ways to play this cute and dumb, or give him the truth. The only problem is he'll see straight through the former. Guess honesty wins. Not that I'm upset about it, I just don't know if I'm ready for meet the family. I've had issues with his Dad, and the thought of meeting his sister has me going back to eighteen-year old me when I was doing my best to get his dad to love me. Hell, I would have been grateful if he even liked me. "I was, uh, going to go home."

"This early?" He raises an eyebrow in question.

"I have things to do before work tomorrow?" Ugh, that was pathetic. Who the hell answers with a question?

"You can stop bullshitting me, Audrey. I know you have your laundry done well in advance, and your place is probably spotless." Well, shit. He has me all figured out. He crosses his arms and his muscles flex. I know exactly what he can do with his arms. And if I'm being honest with myself, I want to be wrapped up in them.

"I just…doesn't this seem really fast? Last night was our first date and I've already ended up in your bed. Then there's the pressure of meeting Corinne, and I'm not sure I can handle that." My eyes roam the room, looking anywhere but at him. Anything to keep my focus off him. To keep me from jumping in his arms without a moment's notice. "I mean you saw how well received I've been by family members before."

"First of all, Corinne isn't like that. You'll love each other." He takes slow, cautious steps toward me, as if I'll skitter away. "And believe it or not, my dad has changed quite a bit. There's no reason for you to go home. Not yet."

Luckily, I don't have to see his dad anytime soon. All that excitement I had about meeting his sister is waning after what she walked in on last night. I don't understand how he's so cool with it. The way he acts as if it wasn't a big deal. Or, maybe it is, and he's doing everything he can to keep me calm. "Promise she won't make it weird." That's ridiculous though. I'm more likely to make it awkward as hell. These are the times I wish I was more like Tiffany. She would have laughed the incident off and gone about her day. Me? No, I have to sit there and dwell on it. I stopped thinking about it last night because out of sight, out of mind and all that. But this morning is a different story. She's in one of the bedrooms off the hallway.

"She won't." He finally reaches me and grabs my hand. "Come back to bed and in a couple of hours I'll order breakfast. After that, if you're still feeling skittish, I'll tell Corinne that you'll meet her some other time. Deal?"

I'm not good with making decisions for myself. When anyone else comes to me with a problem, I can think of a million solutions. At this moment, I'm having a hard time deciding. If I leave, Justin will be disappointed. If I don't,

I'm opening myself up to be hurt by yet another one of his family members. I'm about to say no. It's on the tip of my tongue, but I can't. I promised this man I'd give us a fresh start. I can't do that if I'm holding on to the fear of his family not liking me. It's time to put my big girl panties on and give this thing an actual chance. "Deal."

I allow him to lead me back to his room. "So, you were just going to take off in my clothes? What if those were my favorite ones?"

"You would have been out of luck." I grin up at him. And just like that we fall right back into teasing banter. He's always been the one that can calm me down, and he hasn't lost the touch.

We enter his room and he closes then locks the door behind us. Within seconds we're in his bed and he's pulling my shirt off. I can do this. I can be with him and not worry about my likability.

What feels like half a day later, but in reality, it's only a couple of hours, Justin leans on his elbow and stares down at me. "Are you ready to meet Rinne? Or, do you want to duck out? Before you overthink yourself to death, just know that I'm fine with either decision."

Of course, he is. He'll always do whatever he can to ease my fears and make sure I'm comfortable. Even if that means not doing the one thing, he wants me to. It's one of the reasons I love him. Wait. Loved. It's one of the reasons I *loved* him. We may have past ties, but there's no way I can just pick up where we left off. Not completely. We're both drastically different than we were all those years ago.

"Audrey?" He tilts his head like a confused puppy and I can't help smiling. Oh yeah, he asked a question.

"Sure. I mean as nervous as I am, I should probably go ahead and get it over with." That is definitely the best option. It's better to find out if she'll hate me now rather than later. I have to protect my own mental health.

"Well, let's do this then." He climbs out of bed and puts his clothes on. I watch every muscle in his arm as he lifts the shirt over his head and pulls it down. "Just put my shirts and sweats back on. I'm not even sure where you put your dress."

"It's folded on the dresser," I say.

He waits for me to get dressed and holds his hand out for mine. "You ready?"

I nod. It's the only answer I can give. I don't know if I'm ready or not, but there isn't much choice now.

His sister is in the kitchen making breakfast tacos. "I thought you were going to have some delivered?"

He rolls his eyes and nods toward her. "I was, but Corinne over here is an overachiever and thinks I should eat less fast food. She prefers to cook breakfast while she's here."

"And lunch and dinner," she sing songs.

"Those too." He pulls me closer to the stove. "Corinne, this is Audrey. Audrey, my pain in the ass sister, Corinne."

"It's nice to meet you," she beams at me.

"You too." Good she's not going to say anything about last night. Everything might end up okay. "How long are you in town?"

"Until my ex-boyfriend gets his shit out of my place." She pushes the scrambled eggs around the pan. "I may have to get a few friends involved. I never intended to stay this long, and I'm eventually going to have to get back to work. I have appointments coming up."

"What do you do?" I know Justin mentioned she forgot her camera battery, but I don't want to assume anything.

"I'm a photographer. Mostly family portraits, but a few weddings here and there." She shrugs her shoulders as if it's no big deal.

"That's amazing." I want to take a look at her work. "My cousin is actually getting married in the Fall. Maybe I can hook you two up."

"That would be awesome," she smiles. "I'll get you one of my cards to give her. I'll go pretty much anywhere. I'm always up for an adventure."

Justin gives me a huge grin that says I told you so. "Now that girl bonding time is over, is breakfast almost ready? I'm starving."

"I'm sure," Corinne rolls her eyes. "Go set the table. I only need to heat up the tortillas."

"Aye, aye, Captain." He pulls me toward the table. "You sit. I've got this."

I watch the two of them interact and it's like watching me with my cousins. Justin was right. There was no reason for me to worry. I can already tell I'm going to get along with Corinne fabulously.

Chapter Twenty

Justin

AUDREY IS STEPPING onto the elevator, and I rush behind her and grab her around the waist. "I've missed you so much."

She's been busy helping Stella get things ready for the wedding. While I'm happy for Stella, I'm not so happy that my time with Audrey is being cut short. I'm just happy they finally decided on a dress, and Audrey can stop complaining about the horrible choices Stella sends her.

"I thought we said no PDA while at work," Audrey screeches. The fact that she's leaning into me and smiling tells me she's not all that mad. "People are going to start talking."

I place a quick peck on her neck and whisper in her ear, "People are already talking." I mean, she couldn't expect it to stay quiet. Not when one of her best friends is Luke and he has a habit of saying anything that enters his mind. Although, all those questions he was asking me before Audrey agreed to date me all over again are beginning to make sense now. He was her scout, and he was digging for information. If I was half as smart as he is, I would have had Carter doing my dirty work for me. Except, Carter already knew somehow, and I was too stupid to realize it.

"No, they're not." She slaps my shoulder and then stands on her tiptoes to kiss me. "They are probably just wondering why I'm in such a good mood."

"I don't think you were ever in a bad mood before the merge, but definitely think they can tell something is up. Especially with how often you come to my office, and how many times we go to lunch together." The elevator doors open, and another person gets on. "Besides," I whisper. "You're acting like they can't think for themselves, and we haven't exactly been discrete."

Her only response is a shrug. She knows she's being naïve about our coworkers, but I'll go with it. She can live in the fantasy world as long as she wants.

"So, are you coming to dinner with me, Tiffany, and Spencer?" Her eyes are wide and she reminds me of a sad puppy. There's absolutely zero way I can say no to that. Even if Tiffany scares the hell out of me. She's not quite as forgiving as Audrey, and she makes a point of letting me exactly how much she dislikes me any time I see her. And Spencer, intelligent man that he is, doesn't interfere. I feel like he sympathizes with me, though.

"I could have sworn I already told you I was. Besides, I'm planning on riding with you because Corinne has my car."

"Why?" The door opens again on our floor, and both of us step out of the same time.

"Her car is making some kind of noise, and she's freaking out. Instead of getting a new car, she's throwing an insane amount of money at this one. With as much driving as she does, she'd be better off getting another one and writing it off on her taxes." I already know how Audrey is going to argue this point. She will be firmly on Corinne's side. Hell, the car she's driving is at least a decade old, but she refuses to upgrade because it's still perfectly drivable.

"You know, you have to let her make her own decisions. As someone who is constantly being pushed around by my oldest and youngest cousin, I get where she's coming from. She'll figure out what's best for her, or be stuck on the side of the road needing you to come rescue her." She glances up at me. "When is she going home anyway? There's no way her ex is still slumming it at her place. Hasn't it been like two months?"

I've been asking myself the same thing. Not that I don't love her, but she's starting to get on my nerves. Whenever Audrey and I want to hang out, we usually have to go to her place because Corinne invites herself to stay and hang out with us. How can you properly date someone when you're never alone? "It has. I plan on asking her about it soon. Honestly I think she's starting to love it here."

"It's hard not to. Even with a city this size there are so many things to do. I don't think I've uncovered half of Austin's secrets and I've been here for what feels like forever." As much as she doesn't care for being in crowds, she has a wanderer's heart. She likes to explore and see what she can find no matter where she is.

"True, but it'd be nice if she fell in love and explored from her own place, not mine."

"Yeah, it does put a damper on things sometimes and my place isn't very big. The walls are also really thin." She winks at me before stepping away. "See you at lunch?"

"Absolutely." She heads to her cubicle and I go to my office. It's almost the end of the month…again. The one time that we're all insanely busy. Some of us even work longer hours just to make sure everything gets closed out.

I'm booting up my computer and getting my desk ready for the day when Carter walks in. He pulls one of the chairs right next to my desk and plops into it. "So, it looks like your love life is panning out pretty well."

"I guess," I shrug and continue signing into my computer. "It's only been a month since we started dating. She doesn't want to rush things and I'm respecting that boundary."

"Dude, y'all are all over each other. Don't think the rest of us haven't noticed the frequent trips to the copy room." He grins and slaps his hand on the desk. "I'm pretty sure y'all are it for each other."

"There's no pretty sure. I knew at sixteen she was it for me. I just had an idiotic streak when I was eighteen."

"At least you're correcting it now. That's better than nothing, and she seems to be on board. At least from where I'm sitting." Here he is stating the obvious once again. As if I need help seeing what's right in front of me.

"What have you been up to? I haven't seen you in a bit." There are already twenty emails needing my attention, and I know it's going to be a long day.

"Well, you've been preoccupied with a certain brunette," he laughs. "But not much. Trying to figure out why Corinne is dodging me. She asked if I could show her some spots to take photos and then bailed on me."

"Man, I don't know. She's been acting off, but she's probably figuring out her stuff for work. I think she has actual appointments coming up." I click the first message and make notes of everything that needs to be done before I respond. "I can ask her if you want."

"It's all good. What are you doing this weekend?" He glances around to see if anyone needs him. "Want to grab drinks? It's been a while."

"Sure. I think Audrey is visiting Stella so they can see the dress she wants in person." He's being weird. Well, weirder than normal.

He stands and pushes the chair back to where it was. "Cool. I'll get out of your hair. I need to check on a few reports. I swear if I see one more worksheet I'm going to scream. I'm just ready for the weekend."

"Me too. Let me know if you need any help with the worksheets." I see his outline leave the room and I dig into my work. It's going to be a long, busy day. Sadly, I think my lunch date is going to have to be postponed.

❀

"Shouldn't you be getting ready?" Audrey throws one of my shirts at me. I've already started leaving clothes here for moments just like this. As much as I can pull off a suit, I don't want to wear it after work hours. It gives off a stuffy vibe.

"Probably," I shrug. "It's kind of hard when you're walking around the apartment half naked."

"That's because I'm actually getting ready." She steps into her closet and slides hangers to the right. I don't even know what she's looking for. It's not like it's a formal dinner or anything. We're meeting at the diner where Tiffany works.

I don't even understand how Spencer and I got roped into going. We literally have zero purpose for being there. They are planning Stella's bachelorette party and I'm certain I don't want any of those details. I only hope it doesn't involve a strip club. Just the idea of some random dude grinding on my girl has me wanting to fight.

Instead of arguing with her, I walk slowly to her and put my arms around her waist. "You act like we have to be there at a certain time. You know your cousin is always late."

"That doesn't mean we have to be." Her words are breathy. That could be because I'm sliding my hand over her stomach and continuing on south. Before I have a chance to slip my hand beneath her panties, she spins away from me. "Oh, no. You aren't distracting me this time."

"I don't know what you're talking about." Damn, I was really hoping that was going to work.

"You know exactly what I'm talking about." She jabs her finger into my chest. "You are not allowed to use your magical fingers, or tongue, until we get back. Tiffany and I have a lot to get planned. Stella's wedding is creeping up on us, and we're not prepared for anything, except the photographer, food and DJ."

"Fine," I pout. "Though you know most of the night will be spent with Tiffany glaring at me, right? Is she ever going to like me and welcome me back into the circle again?"

"I don't know," She tosses the words over her shoulder as she pulls out a dress. It has flowers and a low-cut top. She's trying to fucking kill me, I swear. "You know how she is. Holding grudges will always be something she does until she sees a reason to let it go."

"Yeah, but that was over a decade ago. Who the hell holds a decade long grudge?" It's infuriating.

"It's like you've never met my cousin. She still doesn't like some of her classmates from kindergarten." She thinks for a moment before slipping the dress over her head. "Actually, she ignores one kid completely, even now. All because he left her outside during one of mom's Halloween parties, and that was well over twenty years ago. Never underestimate my cousin's temper."

That's way too long to dislike someone over something so trivial. I'm sure the other kid doesn't even remember. "Fine. I'll play nice, but don't think I won't grill Spencer on what I can do to make her at least tolerate me."

"Good luck," she giggles. "She's got that man wrapped around her finger."

"Huh," I grunt. "Sounds familiar."

"Oh please, if anything it's you always wanting time together. I don't even remember the last time I slept alone." Wow, way to make a man feel wanted. She sees my expression as she turns, modeling the dress. "I didn't mean it like that. We're almost seamlessly falling into our old patterns. What if we lose ourselves in the process?"

This sounds like second thoughts about us, and I don't like it. "If it makes you feel any better, I actually have plans with Carter while you're with your cousins."

She nods. "Good. We didn't have any friends outside of us back then. I don't want that to happen again."

"Me either." I think back to how my dad described his relationship with Mom, and I can't help but wonder if Audrey and I are bound to the same fate. Minus the college classes, of course. Speaking of, I have a question I've never asked her. "Why didn't you go to Hilltown like you planned?" It's something that always bothered me.

That stops her in her tracks. Maybe I shouldn't have said anything. "I couldn't," she pauses. "Not with you there. We were on the same course track. Running into you would have been inevitable, and at the time my heart couldn't bear it."

Damn it. That's exactly what I didn't want to hear. "I feel like I robbed you of your college experience. I hope you know that was never my intention."

"I know." She closes the distance between us. "I didn't get it at the time, and it took a while. But I ended up okay." When I begin to speak, she places a finger over my mouth. "We ended up okay. We're never going to be able to move forward if we dwell on the past."

I tip her chin up until her mouth is aligned with mine. I know she won't let me kiss her senseless, so I settle for brushing my lips over hers one, two, three times. "You're right. Are you almost ready?"

"Yep. I just need to grab my bag and we can head out." She places her lips to mine once again. "I'll talk to Tiffany. Even if she doesn't understand, she can at least be nice."

I've never been so happy that she isn't like her younger cousin. Hell, if she was, she never would have given me, us, a second chance.

Chapter Twenty-One

Audrey

WE PRETTY MUCH HAVE THE diner to ourselves, so we can be as loud as we want. Because I have a feeling, they will be some screaming matches between me and Tiffany tonight. There's a good chance she's not going to agree with some of the things I think we should do for the bachelorette party, and she's going to want to go all out, but I know Stella better than that. She likes to go out, but this is the night about her, not what Tiffany wants to drag us around town doing.

"Do you want anything else to drink?" Justin leans over and whispers in my ear. He's sitting as far away from Tiffany as he can. I don't blame him. She's done nothing but shoot him icy glares since we came in.

"No, I'm good." I tap Tiffany on the arm to get her attention. "Come with me to the ladies room?"

She scoffs, "I am pretty sure you're perfectly capable of going to the restroom by yourself."

"Now, Tiffany." She is going to have to get used to Justin being around without being a pain. If I have to force her to act like an adult, I will.

"Fine." She stands and follows me to the restroom and slams the door shut behind us. "What do you want?"

I point to the counter. "Sit." Of course, being the baby that she is, she drags her feet to sit on top of the counter. "Look, I know you don't like Justin, but that doesn't mean you have to be such a bitch to him." She opens her mouth to argue but I cut her off, "I'm not playing Tiffany. He's here, we are dating, and there's nothing you can do about it. It would make things a hell of a lot easier if you would just be nice to him for once."

"Are you seriously chastising me like I'm a child?"

"Yeah. If you're going to act like one, I'm going to treat you like one."

She sighs and shakes her head. "I can't make any promises, but I'll try. I know things seem to be going great right now, but I worry about what happens if he dumps you again."

"I'm a big girl, Tiffany. I'll be able to handle it if it comes to that."

She hops off the counter and throws her arms around me. "I hope so because you were a mess the last time it happened. I'm just trying to look out for you."

"Isn't it supposed to be the other way around," I laugh. "Don't worry about me. I can handle myself now."

"It's about time." She squeezes me to her one more time before letting go. "Well let's go hash out this bachelorette weekend party."

Spencer and Justin are sitting next to each other at the table talking quietly when we get back. Tiffany sits down on the other side of Spencer, and Justin stands to move. "Sit back down," she mumbles. He falters for a second. "Seriously, sit down. I'm going to do my best to not be an asshole to you."

Justin eyes her warily, "This isn't some sort of trick is it?"

"No," she sighs. "No trick. I'm trying to be a grown-up."

Spencer Snickers, and Tiffany elbows him in the ribs. "What happened to being an adult?"

"Don't press your luck, Babe. You still have to go home with me."

This time I laugh, and she shoots me a glare. "Calm down, Tiff." I pull a notebook out of my bag and set it on the table in front of me. "We have a ton of planning to do."

"Why do we have to be here for this?" Spencer complains as he dips a french fry into a pile of ketchup. "We aren't the ones getting married. Besides, Johnny doesn't have us doing all kinds of stuff."

"Because I said." And that's it. That is Tiffany's entire explanation on why they have to be here. Spencer must realize he's not going to get anything else because he continues eating his fries and shuts up. I'm almost certain they will do something low-key like a bonfire, or something. That seems to be all Stella attends these days.

"I think that went pretty well," Justin guides me to the car and opens the passenger side door for me. I could drive, but I'm grateful he does it. Arguing with my cousin wears me out. She's so stubborn. He's right, though, it could have been so much worse. I was prepared for outright tantrums because she wasn't getting her way. Maybe she really is growing up.

"Yeah, I just need to call and make reservations." I watch him round the car and get behind the steering wheel. He reaches under the seat to scoot it back. It's not a problem I have since I'm short, but his knees were touching the wheel and that had to be uncomfortable. "Thanks for coming tonight, by the way. I know it probably wasn't the highlight of your night, or what you really wanted to be doing."

He starts the car and puts it in reverse. "It's all good. I think I know why the both of y'all insisted on me and Spencer being there. You could have told me I was going to have to play referee between the two of you."

"He's used to doing it. I didn't want to scare you off." I stare out the window. "Are we going to your place or mine?" I'm honestly fine with either option, but I'm tired of being in my apartment all the time. Everything feels so cramped.

"Yours then mine?" He flips on the blinker to head back to my building. "Nothing against your bed or anything, but mine is much bigger. My feet hang off the end of yours."

"You won't see me complaining. But I'm glad we're going to my place first. I need to grab a few things."

"Like what?"

"Clothes, for one. But I need to get the rest of my wedding prep stuff. I know there is still time to plan for it, but I want to make sure Stella has everything she needs for her big day. She shouldn't have to worry about any of the small crap that can go wrong."

He pulls onto the road in front of my place. "Why doesn't Tiffany help with any of that? She sounded pretty capable at the diner."

I can't help the laugh that bursts from my lips. "Are you serious? Stella and I had to pick her last roommate. She kept letting flaky, and even questionable, people move in, and we couldn't let her throw safety out the window anymore." He raises his eyebrows at my admission. "Seriously, I love her to death. She's one of my best friends, but she has zero organization skills. It's just not one of her strong suits. Mingling and throwing killer parties are more her scene. She'll compliment the areas that I lack. It's a win-win situation."

"You have this all figured out, don't you?"

"I wouldn't say that," I pull my hair into a side ponytail. "I just know how to use my strengths and those of others. Why make the work harder on myself in areas I know nothing about? It's why I put Tiffany in charge of the reception."

"Is there going to be a DJ at the wedding?" It's like he has no clue what happens at these events. Didn't his dad have another wedding when he married Corinne's mom?

"Yes, but even better…Tiffany talked Crooked Halo into playing, too. How awesome is that?" It really is. I knew she was going to try, but I assumed they would shoot her down. I know their schedule has got to be busy. They are rising to the top of the genre at such a quick pace, it's a wonder they still play at the hole in the wall bars my cousin frequents.

"That's the band we heard right before our first date, right?" He glances over to see my nod. "I think they'll be great. And it'll give me an excuse to get you out on the dance floor."

"Not in front of a bunch of strangers." I reach over the console and grab his hand. "Besides, I haven't even officially invited you to the wedding."

"Oh, I'm going. So, you better go ahead and add the plus on to your little RSVP list I'm sure you have." He gives my hand a quick squeeze before pulling into the parking garage. "I'll also be there for all the pre-wedding events. You aren't going to shake me so easily."

"We'll see about that." I quietly unbuckle my seat belt. As soon as he has the car in park, I open the door and take off at a sprint toward the elevator. Childish, maybe. But we used to do this all the time in high school. The only difference is back then we were surrounded by trees and now it's concrete.

I glance back to see him climbing out of the car. "There you go again," he calls out. "Always running from me. Just know that I'll never be far behind." He presses the lock button on the key fob and jogs after me. I know he can run faster than that. I mean, he did it in a suit. He likes this little game of cat and mouse, I think.

He's catching up and I press the button for the elevator over and over again. Why is this thing so damn slow? I definitely need to make a complaint to the owners about this. What if I was in actual danger?

The doors finally open and before I step on foot inside, Justin's arms are around my waist, and his mouth is next to my ear. "Told you I wouldn't be far behind."

"That's really not a fair assessment. It's not like this garage is huge." I lean into him and let him lead me into the elevator. "A toddler could have caught up to me."

"Talk about unfair. I don't think the comparison is, either." He lets go of me long enough to glance around the elevator to make sure we're alone and backs me up to the wall. "I caught you."

"You did," I smirk. "What are you going to do about it?" I still can't get over how different I feel when I'm with him. I feel empowered. Like I can ask for anything and he won't laugh.

"I can think of a few things." I don't have time to think about what he's going to do. His mouth slams onto mine and his hand dips beneath my dress.

I break away for a second. "What if someone gets on the elevator?"

"I guess I'll just have to hurry."

I don't know if it's because we could get caught or his fingers are moving at a furious pace, but I'm so close I can barely hold in my moans. He sucks on my ear lobe and slips another finger inside of me. "Fuck," I pant. That one word spurs him on. His thumb moves over my clit and right before we reach my floor, I fall apart. "I guess this means we're not going to your place tonight."

"Not a fucking chance," he groans. "The only place we're going is your bed." That's a plan I can get on board with.

Chapter Twenty-Two

W AKING up next to Audrey is how I want to spend my forever. You'd think we'd get tired of seeing each other, but we don't. Aside from lunch and accidental run-ins, we rarely see each other at work. She's busy doing her job and I'm doing mine. She probably interacts with Carter more than she does me since he's her direct boss.

"What time is it?" A yawn escapes at the end of the question. Her hair is splayed out on the pillow. She looks beautiful and ethereal. I was a dumbass all those years ago. I could have had this perfection for the last decade and I blew it.

"I don't know. Do we have somewhere we need to be?" I run a finger along her jaw and she nuzzles closer to me. It's a little warm in here, but I don't want her to move. This, right here, is where we both belong.

"Sort of." Another yawn. "I need to talk to your sister about the wedding and see if she can take bridal pictures. I know she said she had some jobs coming up and I want to get Stella on her calendar before it fills up."

"It's not like she's leaving any time soon," I mutter under my breath.

Audrey pulls away from me the tiniest fraction. "I know her staying with you is putting a slight constraint on us, but I like her. Who knows, maybe she's going to move here."

"She probably will. At least, after she finishes up with some clients back home. I didn't know parents get so many pictures of their kids taken. It's like every tiny milestone warrants a celebration."

"Things are a lot different than when we were growing up, that's for sure." She tries to get up, and I hold her tight. "Justin, we need to get ready." She places a soft kiss on my forehead. "It won't be so hectic once Stella and Johnny are married."

"That's what you think. Next thing you know Spencer will propose to Tiffany." Then we'll never be alone because she'll take it upon herself to make sure it is flawless.

She laughs loud and long. "I think Tiffany will propose to him before he gets the nerve to do it."

"Why do you say that?"

"Because she's the assertive one in the relationship. Once she stopped fighting her attraction to him, she was all in. Even when she screwed up, she dressed up in cosplay and went after him." That is something I can actually imagine. Tiffany has never been one to do things half-assed.

"That makes sense." I let her get out of bed and watch her walk across the room to get her robe. Her body is magnificent in the early morning light. "What else do you need to do today?"

Sliding the robe on she turns as she ties it. "The bridal shop got my dress in so I need to go try it on. Stella wants pictures to make sure it looks okay. I think she may be as controlling as I am."

That isn't a lie. She's always been the take charge cousin. She gets shit done. Audrey does, too, but at a much quieter level. She doesn't bark orders or anything like that. She does the work in the background when she doesn't have any attention on her. "Do you want me to go with you?"

"No, I think I can try on a dress by myself." My smile turns down a fraction. "Don't give me that look. You'll be fine. I need to run errands. I'll be in Asheville with Stella next weekend and I want to grab some stuff to run by her for decorations. Luckily stores have already started putting out fall products."

That sounds like a boring day. I'll definitely let her do that alone. "Yeah, I'll pass on that. Maybe I'll see if Carter wants to do something. Or hint to Corinne that she needs to get her own place."

"First," she comes back to the bad and crawls over me until she's in my lap. "We need to figure out what we're going to do for breakfast. Maybe we can pick something up on the way to your house and feed your sister for a change."

I smirk. "I know exactly what I want for breakfast and it doesn't involve food." My fingers glide up her thigh, until I reach the knot she's tied in her robe, and I slowly pull it.

"If you keep that up, we'll never leave this bed."

"That's the plan." I untie the robe completely, grab her by the waist, and flip her over until she's underneath me. "If I had my way, we'd stay here all day and night."

"But—."

"Did you give the shop a time you'd be there?" She shakes her head. "Okay, then. Problem solved. My sister, errands, it can all wait a couple more hours."

She rolls her eyes. "I guess there could be worse ways to pass the time."

"Oh, we're doing more than passing the time. We're practicing for when we can be in a bigger space." I wink and trail my hands up and down her body. Before long she'll forget about all the plans she made for the day.

Unfortunately, she didn't forget. She gave me the few hours I asked for, at least. Now, we're sitting in a drive through line. "Is your sister going to want fried chicken?"

"Why wouldn't she?"

"I don't know," Audrey shrugs. "She seems to prefer food cooked fresh at home. I guess this just seems like the complete opposite of that."

I shake my head and chuckle. "Don't let her fool you. She loves to cook from scratch, but she's never been one to turn down fried food. She'll indulge if we bring it." It's the one thing we both love. When I visit my parents, we usually grab some chicken and head down to the lake to decompress from being around them. They aren't horrible or anything, they both like to pry. It's why Corinne came to me for a place to stay instead of going to them. I get it. I would have done the same thing in her situation.

"Are you sure?"

"Yes," I sigh. "I'm sure. We just have to make sure we grab honey for the biscuits. According to her there's no other way to eat them."

"If you say so," she scrunches her nose in disgust. "The only thing I can think of that absolutely needs honey are sopapillas. Specifically, the ones at the restaurant I go to with my cousins when Stella is town."

It's finally our turn at the window and I place our order. "Can you grab my wallet out of the glove box?"

"When did you put it in there? I didn't see you do it." She pulls it out of the compartment and hands it to me.

"Last night before you made me chase you to the elevator." I flash her a devilish grin and her cheeks grow pink. When it comes to sex, she's definitely more open now than she has ever been.

"You probably shouldn't leave your wallet in the car overnight. This isn't like back home where we didn't have to worry about people breaking into our vehicles." She tucks her hair behind her ear.

"Believe me, that was the last thing on my mind. You were my number one priority." I grab my card out and pull up to the window.

Within minutes we have our food and are about to exit the parking area. "Crap. They didn't put in honey in the bag." She looks at the line of cars behind us and grimaces. "We should go back and ask for some. I don't want to disappoint your sister and have her eat less than stellar biscuits."

That's my girl…always thinking of other people. Sometimes to her own detriment. As much as we've both changed, some things still stay the same. "It'll be fine. I think I have some in the pantry." I grab her hand and pull it to my lips, kissing each knuckle. "You know you don't need her approval, right? She loves you and I don't think you could do any wrong in her eyes." What I want to say is I love you, but I don't think she's ready to hear it. Especially with what she said before we met Tiff and Spencer last night. It's hard to date at her pace when we have all this history behind us, but I'll do it because it's what she wants.

"If you don't, I can always run to the store."

A car behind us honks and I roll my eyes. These people are so impatient. It's not like they aren't going to get stuck at the next light. And that lasts a hell of a lot longer than what I'm doing. "Rinne will survive either way. Don't give it a second thought."

She shifts in her seat until she can lay her head on my shoulder. "I'll do my best, but I'm not making any promises."

"That's all I ask." I pull out of the lot before any other rude drivers start their nonsense. I really hope we get lucky and hit this light just right. If not, it's going to take us another twenty minutes to get to my house.

A car I don't recognize is parked behind my car. Maybe Corinne got a rental while her car is in the shop. That's the only possible reason. Otherwise, that would mean she has someone over and I'm not okay with that. "Who is that?" Audrey points to the car.

"I have no idea, but we're about to find out." I turn off the car and hand Audrey her keys. I don't want to misplace them before she has to leave. It'd be a good way to get her to stay, though. As much as I think I could be that devious, I can't. I know she needs to get wedding stuff done today and I don't want Stella's anger raining down on me. I've seen her pissed and I'm not a fan.

I grab the bag holding the chicken and sides from the backseat. Audrey tries to take it out of my hand, but I don't let her. "Can you grab the drinks?"

"Sure," she nods. She opens the door then puts one of the drinks in the crook of her elbow, and grabs the drink box holding the other two. You'd think they'd upgrade to something that carries at least four drinks. "Need me to get the door for you?"

"I've got it. It's only two bags." Once she's out of the car she bumps the door closed with her hip. Normally, she'd walk right into the house. But I think after Corinne walked in on us, the thought of going inside and seeing something she can't unsee is keeping her glued to the sidewalk until I join her.

I push the door open and see Corinne pacing in the hallway. "I hope you're hungry, we brought chicken."

"Mom and your dad are here," she frantically whispers. I go to the kitchen and set the bags on the counter. What the hell? Why are they just dropping in? It's not like it's a short drive. They didn't even tell me they were planning to come this way. And whose car are they driving? That's not the same one they had the last time I visited over Christmas.

"Why didn't you warn me? I don't want to deal with them today."

"There wasn't time." She's fidgeting with her hair and I have a feeling they are here because of her.

I hear Audrey close the door behind her and I hurry to intercept her before she walks into what I'm sure will be madness in a few minutes. Not just because of whatever Corinne has to do with it, but because I've been keeping her my own little secret.

Within steps of the entryway, I hear dad's voice. Fuck, I'm too late. "Audrey, what are you doing here?"

My feet skid to a stop behind Dad and I can see the look on her face. Her eyes are as big as saucers and her mouth is wide open. She moves her lips to talk but nothing comes out. "Dad," I admonish.

"What?"

"You're being rude." I'm hoping by getting on to him, Audrey will find her words and the shock will pass by. It doesn't. She sets the drinks on the table, opens the door, and runs out of the house. "Audrey, wait."

I start for her and don't make it far. My dad grabs my arm. "We need to talk. It looks like both you and your sister have been hiding things from us."

"Last time I checked, we're both adults and don't need you butting into our lives." I yank my arm out of his hold and rush to the door. The engine turns over and by the time I make it to the driveway, she's gone. Fuck.

Chapter Twenty-Three

Audrey

I can't believe I froze like that. What the hell is wrong with me? I didn't even give Justin a chance to explain. For all I know he didn't even know his dad was going to be in town. That's something he would have mentioned. At least, I hope he would.

I pull over at a gas station down the road from Justin's house and grab my phone out of my bag. I tap the last number I dialed. The phone rings three times before she picks up. "Tiffany, are you home? I need to come over."

"Slow down, what's going on?" She sounds out of breath and I don't want to know what she was doing. At least she answered.

"I'll tell you when I get there."

"Audrey, right now isn't exactly a good time," she sighs. I hear her hand cover the receiver and she mumbles something to someone I can only assume is Spencer. "Okay, come over. How far out are you?"

"Maybe fifteen minutes."

"Okay, I'll be ready." She hangs up before I can say anything else.

Tears blur my eyes. I don't even know why I'm crying. It's not like his dad even said anything mean to me. At least to anyone looking it wouldn't be. I've just spent so much of my life wondering why that man hated me so much. Him asking why I was there sounded accusatory, and as if I didn't belong.

My phone starts dinging with messages and I turn it off before getting back on the road. It's a good thing I'm not going home. That would be the first place he checks. He also doesn't have Tiffany's number so he can't call her. Right

now, I need to be away. I need to wrap my head around how things are going to work with Justin when his dad obviously doesn't want me around.

Twenty minutes later thanks to the stupid red light I hate, I'm standing in front of Tiffany's door. I knock three times and Spencer answers the door. "She's in the living room."

"Thanks," I mutter. I'm probably overreacting. I hope I am. Even though I haven't said it yet, I love Justin. I always have and I always will. I've only been asking him to take things slow just in case he breaks my heart again. I didn't want to get too close and then have it all ripped away...again.

The door closes behind me as I make my way to the sofa. It looks so different in here with Spencer's touch. There are comic posters on the side of the wall and he's added his DVD collection to the shelf under the TV. It's mundane and perfect. They balance each other out and have small pieces of both of them peppered through the apartment.

"You're here. What took so long?" Tiffany pats the space beside her. "I took the precaution and poured you a glass of wine."

"Red light." I take the glass of wine she offers me and down it in one go. It's a decent wine and I wonder if it's from the winery by Stella. It definitely tastes like it.

"Wow. She downed that thing like a shot." It's only then that I notice the computer sitting on the coffee table and Stella's face filling the screen. Her eyebrows are furrowed and she looks concerned.

"You called her? She has other stuff to do, she doesn't need to worry about me."

Tiffany shrugs. "It sounded like boy problems and you know we only ever hash that out together." She doesn't add the I told you so even though I know she wants to.

Spencer grabs my glass and goes to refill it. Stella on the other hand has her eyes on me. "What happened?"

I tell them about Justin's dad being there when we walked in, and they gasp. They know my history with him and aren't as surprised as I am about my own reaction. "I just ran. It's apparently the only thing I know how to do when I'm confronted with my past."

"Did he sound mad?" Tiffany asks. She motions for Spencer to get her a glass of wine and I hand her mine. I don't want it. I just needed something in the moment.

"I couldn't really tell. I sort of freaked out." I pause replaying the scene in my mind. "But he said something about Justin and Corinne keeping secrets from him."

"He never told his dad y'all were back together?" Tiffany shrieks. "That's absolutely insane. It's been a couple of months."

That's what has me second guessing everything. "In Justin's defense, he doesn't really talk to his dad much anymore. He visits for holidays and that's pretty much it."

"Don't defend him," Tiffany scoffs.

"Tiff," Stella admonishes her. "Chill. Audrey, why did you run?"

"Because I spent most of high school trying to get that man to like me. Wanting him to approve of my relationship with Justin." I take a deep breath. This is where I lay all of my insecurities out on the line for my cousins. "Both of you know why Justin broke up with me then and I thought today would end up as a replay of that night. I love him and I don't see how a relationship between us is going to prosper if his dad sticks his nose in our business and is dead set against it."

"So, basically you want his dad's approval?" Stella asks.

Do I? I take a few moments to let that sink in. I guess so. Or, at least a reason why he doesn't like me. Anything at this point. "That seems to be the root of the issue. I've loved Justin since I was sixteen and I never stopped. I don't even know if Justin said anything to him after I left, or if he tried to come after me."

Stella sighs over the screen. "He did. He's been blowing up Johnny's phone wondering if we've heard from you."

"What did you tell him?"

"That you're fine and you'll go over there when you're ready." I can hear her tapping her finger against her laptop. "Do you think you'll ever be okay with his dad not liking, or approving, your dating?"

"I honestly don't know." I pull a strand of my hair in front me and start braiding the ends. "I'd like to say yes, but I'm not sure I can handle any animosity from his dad if we are around him."

Tiffany turns until she's facing me completely. "I can't believe I'm saying this," she mutters. "If you love him as much as you say you do and he feels the same way, you're going to have to confront his dad. Stand your ground and let him know the two of you aren't going to let him push you around."

"I'm not good at that. I just want him to like me. To think I'm good enough for his son."

"No," Tiffany butts in. "That's not what matters. Your only focus should be Justin regardless of what his dad says or feels. You'll just have to get used to not being liked by everyone. Look at me, I don't give a rat's ass what people think of me. As long as I'm happy, they can live in their own little world."

She has a point, and as much as I don't want to admit it…she's giving me solid advice. "When did you become so wise?"

"I have two pretty amazing cousins who taught me everything I know."

She pulls me into her arms. "So, are you doing this thing? Or, are you going to give up again and let his dad dictate what happens between the two of you?"

"No," I yell, a little too loud. "My happiness will not be held in the palm of his dad's hand. I'm going to stand up for myself."

"That's my girl," Stella claps. "Tiff, go with her in case she freaks again and needs an escape. Spencer, stay on standby."

"Why?" He scratches his head in confusion.

"Because if everything goes the way we want it, you'll need to pick up Tiffany." She claps her hands together like she's coaching a team. "Now, get a move on. First, Audrey, you need to go get cleaned up. You look like a mess."

"Gee, thanks," I mumble. Without any more prompting I get up and head to Tiffany's room. She'll have whatever I need in there. I can do this. Be strong and fight for what you want.

"Do you need me to go up to the door with you?" Tiffany asks from the passenger seat. We're parked on the street across from Justin's driveway. His dad is still there and I can feel my throat closing up.

I won't let his dad scare me into not being with the person I love. "No." I put the car in drive and park next to what I can only assume is the car his dad and step-mom drove in with. Turning the car off I get out of the car. "Here's the keys just in case."

"Go get your man. You've got this." Tiff throws her fist in the air, cheering me on.

My steps are slow and steady as I make my way to the door. The curtains are closed and nobody can see me approach. I take three deep breaths and raise my hand. There are raised voices coming from the house, but I don't care. I have to do this. Not only for me, but for Justin. He needs to know I'm strong enough to stand up for myself. I ignore the doubt bubbling up in my stomach and knock.

Chapter Twenty-Four

Justin

DAMN IT. She ran without even looking back to see if I'd follow. I know she is leery about my dad since he wasn't exactly the kindest person to her, but I didn't realize it went so deep. I pull out my phone and try to call her. It rings once then goes to voicemail. I press her number again and it goes straight to voicemail. She turned her phone off. I hope she realizes I didn't purposefully spring this on her. I had no clue my dad was going to surprise us with a visit today. He usually gives me a heads up, at least.

Rushing back into the house, I find Corinne staring at the window. She can't see anything outside because the curtains are still covering them. "Where are the keys to my car?"

That pulls her attention away from wherever her thoughts took her. "They're on the key hook I installed last week. I'll go get them."

"You can't go running off, Son. I didn't come here for my own—." My dad starts to say, but I glare at him

"You don't get to tell me what to do in my own house." I grab the keys off the hook and throw the door open. "Stay, or go, I don't really care. Just know that if you stay you will treat me *and* Audrey with respect. Corinne, are you coming or staying?"

She doesn't have to be asked twice. She grabs her wallet off the table and hightails it out of the house in front of me. Once we're tucked into my car, she finally speaks up. "I would have warned you if I had time. They were jumping my ass right before you pulled in."

That's news to me. "Why would they be mad at you?" I mean, sure, she's been here longer than I was prepared for, but she's an adult and can do whatever she wants.

"Because my ex has been out of my place for a month?" Her voice pitches higher at the end. Scared I'm going to bitch her out. That's not my style. It would have been nice if she was upfront with me, but I get it. After years of growing up with a father that questions your every fucking move, I do my best to not pry.

"Okay, but that can't be all there is." I pull out of the driveway and head toward downtown. Toward Audrey.

"I may have also put my house and studio on the market." Ah, so that's what they are pissed about. She's fleeing the nest and they worry they won't be able to dictate what she does. Not that they've done it to the extent Dad has me, but still.

"So, that's why you've been here so long." I don't phrase it as a question. It's not. "You know you could have told me, right? I wouldn't have run off to them to tattle."

"I know that." She rolls down the window a bit to get some fresh air. All it does is let the heat roll into the car. "I wanted to do it on my own, though. I *should* be able to, anyway. It's a lot harder to find what I'm looking for in this area. I need a space big enough for me, but also to have an in-house studio. I don't want to rent a ridiculously over-priced space I barely use."

Audrey was right. My sister fell in love with the city. "We'll get you set up. Assuming I can get Audrey to talk to me again, maybe you can take over the lease in her apartment until you find something. You still have jobs lined up, right?"

"Yeah. I've been updating my website and have quite a few inquiries. At this rate, I'm actually going to have to use my calendar." She shudders. She's always been able to keep up with the small-town people wanting photos. The way of life is slower-paced. But here? It's another world. And there are so many more potential clients. I'm honestly shocked she didn't try to make the move sooner.

"That's good. First up, we find Audrey. After that, we'll have a talk with our parents." It's past time they started living their own lives and stopped worrying about what we're doing with ours.

Less than thirty minutes later I'm in front of Audrey's door. I didn't see her car in her usual spot, and she's probably not here, but I need to make sure. My knuckles tap the door harder than I expect and I jump at the loudness of it. "Audrey," I call out in case she's in her bedroom. No answer. I go through this three more times and admit defeat.

On the way back to my car, I pull out my phone to see if Stella's fiancé has texted me back. I just want to know that she's good. That is what's most important more than anything else. I open the car door and sigh as I slide behind the steering wheel. "No luck?" Corinne is peeking around me, hoping to see my girl following.

"Nope," I grunt. "My guess is she's at Tiffany's but I don't have her number or address." There's not much left to do other than go home and wait for Audrey to get in touch. "Will you keep an eye on my phone?"

"Sure," she grabs it out of my hand. "Why?"

"I'm waiting on a message from her soon-to-be cousin-in-law." Fingers crossed he has enough empathy for me to respond. I don't see why he wouldn't, especially since he texted me that first night I ran into Audrey to let me know she was okay.

Corinne is scanning through the radio stations as I drive and while normally that would annoy me, it's keeping my mind off the thought of losing Audrey once again because of my old man. We're almost home when my phone beeps with a message. "Who is it?"

Corinne holds the phone to my face to unlock it. "It's an unknown number, but it says she's fine. Just give her a bit."

"Thank God." I breathe a sigh of relief. At least I know she's okay. Now, I need to take care of the next mess. How does one prepare to tell your dad to accept who you love or shove it?

∼

Well, they didn't leave. I nudge Corinne with my elbow. "Are you ready for this?"

"Not even a little bit," she shakes her head. "But it has to be done. At some point, they have to let go. We aren't their puppets to control."

"I think my dad has been controlling me much longer than your mom has you." I open the door and get out of the car.

"Let's not turn this into who has the crappiest parent." She gets out and comes to stand beside me. "They are both awesome and suck to a certain extent. We just have to roll with the bunches and hope they understand."

Walking into the house, it looks like they haven't moved the entire time we've been gone. I fully expected them to make themselves at home. I guess me blowing up at Dad freaked them out a bit. I've never done that before. Not even when I was a teenager. I would halfway listen then go to my room to blow off steam. I don't have the energy to do that anymore.

"You're finally back," Dad stands up from the couch. "It sounds like we all need to have a talk."

"If you are going to spend this time to bitch us out for the choices we make, then you can leave. This is my home and we're adults. As long as you're here, you'll respect that." I feel like Stella and Tiffany would be proud of me for standing up to him. Maybe, even Audrey would be, too.

"How long have you and Audrey been dating, and where did you reconnect?" He crosses his arms over his chest in an act of intimidation. Sadly, that doesn't work with me anymore. I've been taller than him for years.

"Not that it's any of your business," I begin. He may want to prove that he's the bigger man, but I don't care. The only thing that will piss him off more is if I show that *he* doesn't bother me. I sit down on the chair closest to the couch. "We ran into each other when the company merged. I found out she was an employee of the other company."

"Jesus, Son." Dad runs a hand down his face. "Are you out of your mind? First you stick to her like glue as a teenager, then you work with her and you decide it's a good time to date? Do you have any idea what that could do to your career?"

"Oh, did I mention I'm one of her bosses?" That will be the icing on the freaking cake.

"Are you serious?" He roars. "You are making a huge mistake once again. I don't know what it is about that girl that makes you lose all common sense, but it needs to end. What is it this time? Some kind of office fetish between the two of you? When your bosses find out..." He's standing over me and that was the last line I'll allow him to cross.

I get up from the chair and he has to take a step back. "They will do nothing." My teeth are clenched and I'm barely holding in my rage. "There's nothing against it in the handbook. I checked. And that's the last time you will *ever* say anything bad about the woman I love. If you can't find it in your heart to accept her, then you can stop talking to me. End of discussion. I won't continue to allow you to make her feel like shit."

Just then I hear a voice in the entryway. "You love me?" My mouth drops open at the sight of her.

Corinne rolls her eyes. "I tried to get your attention, but you were too busy telling your dad off. Bravo, by the way."

"Corinne," her mother spits.

"Nope, you and I can have this conversation outside," she points at her mom. "If you'll follow me." I'm happy she's standing up for herself, too. They never really approved of her career choice but didn't say much about it because she takes care of herself. The two of them leave without a backward glance.

"That wasn't exactly how I wanted to tell you," I shrug. "But yes, I do."

"I love you, too." She launches herself at me. Arms around my neck, clinging to me like I'm the most important thing in her life. She's right where she belongs and I feel a sense of relief that we might just be okay.

"Give me a break," Dad mutters. And the relief is gone.

"Look, Mr. Petersen, I don't know what I did to make you hate me, but I'm done letting you make me feel like crap. I've done nothing but love your son since we were sixteen. I never stopped." She stands tall next to me and I beam with pride. There's that fire she's always kept hidden. "You'll either respect me, or you won't. That's your choice, but I don't have to allow it."

"I can't believe how ridiculous you two are. Nothing has changed. It's like watching you in high school all over again," he grunts.

"Well, until you can accept it, you can leave." I lead Audrey to the kitchen. "Stay right here, I'll be back." She nods and I go back to the living room. "I wasn't playing, Dad. If you can't act like the adult you claim you are, go home. When you're done with whatever it is that's made you dislike her from such a young age, then you can call me. Until then...don't bother."

Dad's mouth opens wide and he stomps past me. He doesn't say another word. I watch him walk out the door, pausing long enough to tell his wife to come on, and they get in the car. Just like that he's gone.

I don't know Audrey is right behind me until she wraps her arms around my waist. "I'm sorry."

I turn until my eyes meet hers. "Don't be. That man has more hate in his heart than anyone I've ever met. You will always be worth it."

"I didn't want to cause a rift between the two of you." She pulls me tighter. "He's the reason I ran earlier. Not you, never you again. I'm back where I was always meant to be."

"Audrey, you're my home." I bend down until my lips touch and I could get lost in them for hours. Corinne clears her throat behind me. "First, we have to find her a place to live. I'm certain both of us have been disowned."

"I'm betting probably so," Audrey laughs. "We'll find you a place."

"Thanks, sis." Corinne rushes and throws her arms around the both of us. "Welcome to the family...again."

Yeah, she definitely needs her own place. She's cramping my style. How am I supposed to knock Audrey's socks off if my sister is here?

Epilogue

Audrey

"I THOUGHT you said Johnny was easy going?" We're at our favorite Mexican restaurant, going over last-minute wedding preparations. "He has Spencer running around trying to find these obscure snacks his brother likes."

All I can do is laugh. The only time I've ever seen him this keyed up is when he was getting ready to pop the question at the ski resort. "He has a weird relationship with his sibling. Just go with it."

"If you say so." He takes a chip from the middle of the table and dips it into the salsa. "I can promise you I won't be like that when we get married."

I turn my head in his direction so fast, I could be that little girl in The Exorcist. "Excuse me?" This better not be the way he decided to ask me to marry him. I just might murder him.

"When, and if, we decide to get married, I'm leaving all of this to you." He sees the look on my face and backtracks. "I mean, I'll do whatever you tell me to do." That's better.

"You say that, now," I grin. I steal the chip he's about to put in his mouth. "Will you be upset if your dad is still not on speaking terms with you when that day comes?"

He stares at me, the chip, and his now empty hand. Seriously, that's what he thinks is the most important part? He grabs another chip with the hand furthest from me. "Honestly, I don't know. But if he's going to be disrespectful, I don't want him there anyway. He'd do his best to make the day miserable for us." He grabs my hand and kisses my open palm. "That's not what I want when it's our turn. It will be special, magical, and everything you deserve."

And I think my panties melted off of their own accord. Back then he put me above all else as much as he could under his dad's roof, and we had to deal with it. Now, though, we can make our own rules and write our own story. "I love you."

He opens his mouth, but Tiffany yells across the table. "If y'all don't start paying attention, I'm going to split you up."

Justin pulls me so close, I'm almost in his lap. "You can try."

"Do you really want to go that route?" She lifts an eyebrow.

"On second thought," Justin clears his throat. "What were you saying?"

I don't miss Spencer laughing at the way he backs down to my baby cousin. He's known her most of her life, though. He knows *exactly* how ruthless Tiffany can be.

I snuggle further into him, and relish the feel of his arms around me. I thought running into him after a decade would be the worst thing that could happen to me. Turns out, I found love again.

Gone to the Chapel

Chapter One

Stella

I SWEAR, if my cousins don't come through that door in the next hour, I'm going to turn into a bridezilla. It will be a fit worse than Tiffany has ever had. They said they were going to leave Austin this morning. They should have been here by lunch, at the latest. My texts have gone unanswered and I'm pacing back and forth in the kitchen. What if something happened to them? Surely, they would have let me know. Or my aunts and uncles would have.

"What's wrong with you?" Johnny asks as he strides to the refrigerator. Not a single care in the world, even though our wedding is in five days. How in the hell is he so calm and collected? There are still a million and one things to do.

"Have you heard from Tiff or Audrey?" I whirl around on him. "Please say yes."

He shakes his head and my shoulders sag. "Sorry." He twists the lid off the bottle of water. "I can call them."

"Don't bother. I've been texting all day and I haven't gotten a response." I lean against the counter and let my head fall back until all I can see is the ceiling. "It's like they are trying to give me a heart attack. This isn't something Audrey would typically do."

Arms wrap around my waist and I'm sinking into Johnny's embrace. "I'm sure there is a logical reason they haven't contacted you. Give them another few hours and if they aren't here, I'll drive up and down the highway until I find them."

This is one of the many reasons I love this man. He always goes out of his way to help others. Especially when it affects me. "You're too good to me," I mumble into his chest.

He bends down until his eyes are directly in front of mine. "I would do anything for you. Even go on a wild hunt for your cousins." Rising up again, he kisses me on the forehead. "Just let me know what I need to do. I've told you from the beginning that I'll do whatever you need, all you have to do is ask."

"Thank you." I lift to my tiptoes and capture his mouth with mine. I could get lost in him for hours. I have on many occasions. But right now, it's pure gratitude for letting me have my freak-out moments and not running away. Wrapping my arms around his neck, I pull him closer to me, deepening the kiss. Showing him just how amazing he truly is. His fingers brush along the waist of my jeans, slowly inching their way toward the button. It's exactly the distraction I need.

With one hand he undoes the button and the zipper being pulled down is loud in the quiet kitchen. The front door slams into the wall and he yanks his hands away from my waistband. Like his mother just walked in on us or some-thing. Now they show up? Talk about shitty timing on their part. "We're here," Tiffany yells from the entryway.

"I'm pretty sure the entire town knows you're here," Johnny grumbles under his breath. "I guess this means I don't have to search for them."

"I guess not," I sigh. "To be continued?"

"You bet your ass," he winks before reaching toward me to button my pants up again.

Tiffany rounds the corner into the kitchen and sets a big bag on the table. "Where do you want me to put the wine?"

"Seriously?" I throw my hands on my hips and glare at her. The audacity she has thinking she didn't fuck up big time.

"What did I do?" She glances at me, then Johnny, before pulling the bottles out of the bag. Each thunk of glass hitting the table annoys me more and more.

"Where the hell have y'all been? You said you were leaving this morning and then I didn't hear from either one of you all day. I was worried sick." I throw my hands in the air and take a deep breath. "Never mind. You're here now and that's all that matters."

With one bottle in hand, she turns to face me. "I'm so sorry." Nothing good ever comes after that. I wonder what catastrophic event led to the radio silence. "I completely shattered my phone and I didn't think I'd have time to get another one."

"Is Audrey's phone broken, too?" She's the responsible one. Hell, she makes us turn on location services if we're in an area we aren't familiar with. For her to not text, or call, something must have happened.

"No." Audrey walks into the kitchen and lets five bags fall from her hands and shoulders. "Thanks for the help, by the way." She shoots Tiff an annoyed glare. "My phone died and she doesn't have a charger in her car for some ungodly reason. Since we got a late start, she didn't want to stop at a gas station so I could buy one."

"Why did you get a late start?" Audrey is punctual and always early.

Tiffany's eyes light up and she bounces on her toes. "Because she was too busy banging her hot boss." Ugh, I did not need that visual.

"Why do you have to say it like that?" Audrey groans. "You've known him your entire life. It sounds weird when you don't call him by his name." She pauses long enough to make her way toward me and gives me a quick hug. "Justin doesn't like it either."

"Awesome," Tiffany snorts. "I get to annoy two people with one comment."

Audrey shakes her head and sighs. "She's never going to grow up. And here I thought being with Spencer would tame her."

Tiffany laughs and grabs another bottle of wine before taking them to the refrigerator. "It's funny y'all think I can be tamed. Admit it," she grins. "Your lives would be boring without me in it."

"It'd be a lot less stressful." I mumble under my breath.

Tiffany cups a hand behind her ear. "I'm sorry, could you repeat that? I didn't quite get the bitchiness way over here."

"She's not wrong," Audrey comes to my defense.

Johnny groans, "Can y'all not today? I really don't want to play referee between the three of you...again."

Tiff skips over to him. "Good. Because you are banished from the house until you get married."

"But I live here."

"No," she grins. "You technically live in the other house. You just spend most of your time over here."

Johnny turns toward me. "Is she serious?"

All I can do is nod. I knew she was going to pull some sort of stunt like this. It's almost as if she's determined to be a pain in my ass. Maybe I should have gotten the last few things done by myself. It would save me this headache. "Plus side, you don't get roped into doing anything you don't want to do."

"I guess," he mutters. "If you need me to take care of anything that's not decorating, let me know." He closes the distance between us and whispers in my ear. "She didn't say anything about outside the house."

"Love you," I whisper back and give him a quick kiss on the cheek. Tiffany thinks she's being a smartass, but I plan on putting her to work until the big day.

Chapter Two

Johnny

I CAN'T BELIEVE that little punk made me leave. Actually, no, scratch that. I can one hundred percent believe it. She's used to getting her way. I guess it's the byproduct of being the baby in the family.

I pull into the parking lot of Out of the Ashes. There's a reason I've been staying with Stella. Since she came into my life, I can't seem to stay away from her. Probably a good thing since we're getting hitched. Tonight, I need to be around people. Maybe I'll call Reaf and see if he's free to hang out with me. How sad is it that one of my closest friends is almost a decade younger than me?

The lot is full, and this has turned into the place to be. Even if it is the beginning of the week. Before I get out of the truck, I shoot off a text to Reaf. I hope like hell he can come have a few drinks with me. If not, I'm sure I'll look like a miserable lonely fool. Maybe I am. I've gotten so used to doing everything with Stella, it's weird not having her around.

I shove my hands in my jacket pocket and stride to the entrance. There's no line tonight. It could be because it's a weeknight, but I'm counting my lucky stars I can walk right in. Not that I'd have to wait if there was a line. Angie always has space for me. She's told all of her staff to make sure I get in as well. Someone walks out and I rush to grab the door before it closes. I'm still in awe over how Stella has helped Angie turn this place from a hole in the wall bar to one of the best places to grab food and drinks after a long day at work.

There's a young woman standing by the host stand and I can't remember her name. She's been here for a while and beams when she sees me. "Where's Stella?" Of course, that would be the first thing she asks. Not how are you tonight? She's so used to seeing the both of us together that the thought never crossed her mind that we may come separately.

"She's at home." I squint trying to read her name tag, but it's too dark. "Her cousins came in to help with final wedding preparations."

She claps her hands and jumps up and down. "I can't wait to see what she comes up with. If it's anything like the Pinterest boards she's shown me, it's going to be epic."

The what boards? I'm going to have to ask Stella about that. She hasn't shown me anything except screenshots on her phone. "Are you going to the wedding?" At this point I've lost track of the guest list. It's not going to be massive, but Stella knows a lot of people.

"Technically," she shrugs her shoulders. "I'm helping with the catering set up. I think it's awesome that y'all are serving bar foods at the wedding instead of something formal."

A wide grin takes over my face. "That would be my doing. There's no way I could pass up having the wings served at the wedding. It's what Stella and I had on our first date."

"Well, you have good taste. It's our number one seller on the menu." She glances around the crowded dining area. "It looks like there's space at the bar. Or I can check for a table in the back."

"The bar is fine, thanks." I take a step toward the one space in the newly redesigned bar that has sports playing. It'll give me something to do while I kill time. I really don't want to go home. Not yet, anyway. I can't even remember the last time I was there without Stella. Or, with her, for that matter. We usually stay at her place since it's in much better shape than my place. "Reaf may be coming in a bit. If you see him, send him my way, please."

"You got it," she salutes. I'll never understand why people do that. It's not like I was giving her an order. The only time Stella does it toward me is when she's being a smartass.

"Thank you." I weave through people standing around the bar having conversations. There are a few guys shifting from foot to foot, no doubt on their first date with someone. Honestly, Angie should work that somewhere into her slogan. I'm almost certain a lot of new relationships have started in this place.

There's an empty barstool at the very end next to the wall and I quicken my pace to snatch it up before anyone else does. At least there's a football game to keep my attention. Pulling my phone out of my pocket I check to see if Reaf has texted me back. No such luck. He must be busy with the family. I know it's not a book club night. Stella usually goes to those while I help Reaf keep Layla out of everything. I used to want kids, but after a few nights watching her, I'm not so sure. Maybe Stella and I will get lucky with a chill kid.

A glass slides in front of me and I jump. Where the hell did that come from? I haven't even seen the bartender yet. Looking up, Angie is smirking at me. "I'm guessing Stella is doing wedding stuff?"

"How did you know?" I pick up the glass and take a long drink. This is exactly what I needed after being pushed around by Tiffany. It's a good thing that woman uses her forces for good and not evil.

"Stella mentioned her cousins were coming in when she stopped by yesterday to finalize the menu and headcount." She leans against the bar. "My cooks are going to be making a lot of wings."

"I would say I'm sorry, but I'm not. I plan on taking whatever is left home with us." Rubbing the sweat off the glass, I search for her other bartenders. "Why are you working tonight? It's rare that I see you during the week."

"One of my new staff was a no show. The other two back here have a handle on it, but I didn't want them to get overwhelmed."

"That sucks. I hope it's nothing serious."

"We'll see when they come in tomorrow. I hired a few of the kids from the high school to work your wedding so my normal staff can stay here and make sure everything is under control."

It makes sense. I just hope none of the kids try to swipe any of the alcohol. "What about the girl by the door? She said she was helping."

"Oh, Lisa," she nods toward the entrance. That's her name. I should put that down in my phone so I don't feel like a dumbass the next time I see her. "She'll be there in a sort of managerial position. She's there to keep it all running smoothly since you said I'm a guest."

"You are." She's crazy to think otherwise. We've always been thick as thieves. There's no way in hell I'd let her work at my wedding.

"I have to have someone to keep everyone in line. She may look like a pushover, but she can handle herself."

"That's good to know." Our day is in capable hands. Not that I had any doubt, but it's nice to have reassurance.

"You need another drink?" She nods toward my half empty glass.

"Naw, but I'll take an order of wings to go."

I reach for my wallet, but she waves me away. "Tonight, it's on the house. I've seen the havoc Stella's cousin can cause," she pauses for a moment, "well, Tiffany in particular. Consider it part of your wedding gift."

"Thanks, Ang." I sip on my beer while I wait and watch the game. I have no idea who is playing, and I don't really care. I'm just anxious to see my soon-to-be wife. Tiffany thinks she's going to keep me away from her, but I'm crafty when I need to be.

Thirty minutes later and I'm pulling into my driveway. The porch light is the only indication someone might live here. It's so bright it lights up the entire driveway thanks to Stella. She said the dim one gave off a creepy vibe. There's only one thing to do after dinner. It's time for the floor to be fixed. We agreed I'd move in with her completely, and I don't want this house sitting here collecting dust. There are a ton of memories to be made and renting it out seems like the perfect option. I wonder how shocked Stella will be when she realizes I finally fixed the damn thing.

Chapter Three

Stella

THIS GIRL IS crazy if she thinks I'm going to let her sleep in this morning. Especially after making Johnny leave last night. Never mind that we were in the middle of something since they were late and rudely interrupted us. My feet are silent as I stalk toward Tiffany's bed. I did my homework on this house since I've moved in. I know exactly which boards creak.

My cousin looks sweet and innocent when she's sleeping. It's about the only time that's actually true. For the most part she creates chaos wherever she can. She hasn't moved a muscle since I came into her room. My fingers curl around the bottom of the bedspread and I yank them off of her.

She bolts upright in the bed. At least I know she reacts to something. "What the hell?" She yells into the quiet house. Her gaze travels around the room until they finally settle on me. "Are you kidding me right now?"

I can hear Audrey's footsteps as she rushes into the room, almost barreling over me. "What's wrong? Did someone break in?" Of course, that's her first reaction. Not surprising, though. She always worries over every little thing. It's not a bad thing, but it can go over the top sometimes.

"Nope," I grin. "Just a little payback to our dear baby cousin." Tiffany reaches toward the blanket to pull it back over her, and I snatch the other edge before she gets another chance. "It's time to wake up. We have a lot to do today." Turning around, I march out of the room, blanket and all.

Not even a minute has passed before Tiffany storms after me. "You could have woken me up like a normal person. And why didn't you give Audrey the

"

same treatment? She was with me when we got here late, and she was the reason. It's not fair to single me out."

"Eh," I shrug my shoulders. "You forced my soon to be husband to leave when we were in the middle of something."

"Come on," Tiffany throws her hands up. "It's not like y'all were going to get it on with us in the room. That's just tacky."

"You're one to talk," I argue. "At least from what I've heard from Audrey."

"That was ONE time. And we were only making out." She grabs one of the ends of the blanket and yanks it out of my hands before wrapping it around her. "It's bad luck to see your fiancé before the wedding."

Audrey clears her throat behind Tiffany. "That's the day of the wedding. We're," she ticks off the count on her fingers. "Four days out. She can see him before then."

"How was I supposed to know? I've never done this whole wedding thing before. It's not like I've had any practice." She taps her foot before sighing. "Fine," Tiff pouts. "He can come back over. But I fully expect him to get crafty with us. If I'm being forced to work, then he is, too."

I seriously doubt he'll be doing anything crafty, unless I have him build something. Otherwise, he'll be in charge of booze and food. "Okay. Now get ready, we need to go to the bridal shop for a fitting." I take two steps toward my room and stop. "You did bring your dresses, right?"

"Yep," Audrey answers. "I've held onto Tiffany's just in case. They are in a dress bag in her car."

She is a lifesaver. I just knew Tiff would forget it if someone isn't in charge of it. She's become more responsible since she started dating Spencer, but she still has her moments. "Okay, I'll meet y'all downstairs. I'm going to take a quick shower and start the coffee."

Twenty minutes later I'm in the kitchen with my fingers wrapped around a warm mug of liquid energy. Tiffany had the coffee ready to go for me. She knows when she's screwed up, no matter how small or big. She may not come outright and apologize, but she'll go out of her way to make things easier to show it.

I take a quick sip, letting it fuel me before setting the cup on the counter. "Okay, so we have our appointment at the shop in less than an hour. We also need to stop by the craft store and get a few more pumpkins for the decor."

"Why aren't you using real pumpkins?" Tiffany opens my freezer to see what food I have inside. "It'd be more authentic."

"Because I don't want to mess with what to do with them after the wedding." I thought about it because it would be prettier, but I really don't want the hassle. "And the fake ones, I can store to use every year when I decorate." Audrey laughs, and I can't figure out what is so funny. "What?"

"You're totally going to turn into one of those people that decorates for every season, aren't you?" She grabs the box of frozen breakfast sandwiches out of Tiffany's hand and heads toward the microwave.

"I don't see why that's a bad thing," I huff. "I have this big beautiful house, why not make it pretty?"

"You should decorate a Christmas tree and decorate it for every single holiday," Tiffany joins the conversation. "I saw this woman doing it on social media. I think she's an author, or something, and her trees always look really cute."

"That seems like a lot of work," Audrey says.

It does, but it's not a bad idea. We could put it in the corner of the living room where it's out of the way. I'll have to wait and see what all Johnny brings with him when he officially moves in. There may not be any room for it. I grab my mug and take another drink. "We're way off topic. Let's get to the dress shop and store before we have lunch. Year-round decorations are a conversation we can have after the wedding."

"You should add it as a board on Pinterest for ideas when you can finally get to it." Audrey grabs the sandwiches out of the microwave and places them on plates for all of us.

"I'll do that." I take a bite, completely forgetting it's still hot, and almost spit it out. "Let's get this party on the road. I've got wine in the fridge for later tonight."

"That's a perfect reward," Tiffany claps. "I'm just excited to see us all decked out in our dresses together. It's going to be amazing."

I hope so. I had to be careful with dress colors so it wouldn't clash with Tiffany's hair. They threw out a lot of options before finally agreeing to one. Now I guess we'll see what kind of alterations these dresses are going to need.

Chapter Four

Johnny

I swear if this damn nut doesn't come off this tire, I'm going to break it off. Who put this thing on here? Metal clanking around the shop doesn't do anything to put me in a better mood.

Seconds away from throwing the tire iron across the garage, it's plucked from my hands. "You know we have tools to make that faster, right?" Reaf's shit eating grin only annoys me more.

"I needed to work off some frustration," I grunt. Replacing the floor last night didn't go as planned. The plywood was warped then I cut my finger on the tape measure. I should have stayed at the bar. I may have been lonely, but I wouldn't have this huge cut on my hand making my job even harder.

"Damn, man." Reaf shakes his head. "If I would have known you were going to be in a mood about me not hanging out last night, I would've taken Layla to my mom's. Besides, you're getting married this weekend, you should be excited."

I laugh, which is probably what he intended when he focused my mood around him. "Shut up. I know you have a family and it was last minute." Wincing as my hand grabs my tool, I take it away from my friend. "It's just sometimes Stella's cousins drive me nuts."

"Better get used to it. They are with you for life." He picks up the impact and takes the lug nuts off in less than a minute. It takes everything in me not to roll my eyes. "It's probable the wedding stuff that has them all out of sorts."

I snort. "Have you met Tiffany? She's always out of sorts. She made me leave Stella's house last night because she said it's bad luck for me to be around."

"Yeah, that's only on the wedding day. I'm sure Stella will set her straight."

"I hope so." I roll the new tire to the car. "I want to help as much as I can. Especially since we're having it at her place. There are a few things I want to take care of in the yard."

"If you need any help, let me know." He pulls the bad tire off the car. "What are we doing for your bachelor party? I know I'm supposed to be planning it, but you haven't given me much information."

Oh shit. I totally forgot about that. "Bonfire in the field?"

"I'll get with Spencer and see what we need to get." He steps away so I can put the new tire on. "I didn't want to assume you wanted one, but figured if you did, it would be lowkey. I'll be sure to check with our parents to babysit. I'm certain Tonya is meeting up with Stella."

"Sounds good. Feel free to invite your friends. I'm sure they could use a night out."

"Probably." He turns toward the office and stops. "Is it okay if my sister comes to the wedding to help with Layla? She was going to go to Jake's, but Charleigh has been having a hell of time with the pregnancy and they should be having the baby any day now."

"You didn't even have to ask. Where is your nephew going to be? You can bring him, too."

"My mom is taking him to a classmate's birthday party."

I can only nod in understanding. It seems like having kids will cause busy schedules. I hope we're ready for that in the future. My mom is already bugging me about grandchildren. "Can you grab my phone while you're in there? I haven't heard from Stella and I need to make sure her and Tiffany haven't killed each other."

"Sure." He puts his hands up, "but I'm not going to listen to your uncle's wrath about phones in the garage."

"Don't worry about it," I laugh. My uncle is definitely a hard ass about that. "I'm almost done and I'll check it then." I don't want him to get in trouble because I'm impatient.

My uncle is at the counter when I enter the store front from the garage. Setting the keys for the car I just finished next to him, I reach under the counter for my phone.

"Hey," he slaps my hand away. "You know the rules."

"Calm down, Old Man." I use my other hand and grab the phone. "I'm getting married in a few days. I need to make sure there aren't any fires I need to put out."

Shaking his head, he holds his hand out. "I didn't make any exceptions for Reaf. Why would I for you?"

"Because I'm your favorite nephew?"

"Nice try, kid." He motions his fingers for me to deposit my phone in his hand. "You can check your phone during your next break."

"I don't think you understand the havoc Tiffany can cause. She's like a bomb ready to explode." And that's on a good day. There's no telling what her mood is like today.

"Fine," he rolls his eyes. "You have two minutes then you need to get back in the garage. These cars aren't going to fix themselves."

"Thank you." I swear sometimes getting chastised by Uncle Rick is worse than getting yelled at by my parents. He has a way of making me feel like the awkward teen I used to be. Always seeking his approval.

When I open my phone, there's a text, but it's not from Stella.

Tiffany: I'm sorry about last night. I obviously didn't know the bride and groom rules.

Tiffany: Anyway, to make it up to you, your presence is required this afternoon. There will be food and beer. Unless I consume it all before you get here.

Stella: Ignore my bratty cousin. There is plenty of both.

The texts came through about an hour ago. I'm assuming Stella was reading Tiffany's messages over her shoulder. I fire off two texts.

Johnny: Thanks, Tiff. I'll be there.

And to Stella: I love you and can't wait to see you. This has been the LONGEST day.

Before I have a chance to put my phone up, it vibrates in my hand.

Tiffany: Y'all are gross. Stop.

I can't help the chuckle that leaves my mouth. I imagine she'll be the same way if Spencer ever gets the balls to ask her to marry him.

With those messages my day has suddenly become better. Maybe the tools will work for me now, too.

All the lights are on when I pull up to the house. Music is blasting and I can see three shadows moving in front of the window. I'm unsure of what awaits me inside, but now is as good a time as any to check it out.

I step out of my truck and head toward the house. The closer I get to the door I see one shadow chasing another. This can't be good. Rushing to the door, I push it open and my mouth drops open. Stella is chasing Tiffany around the dining room and it looks like a glitter bomb exploded.

Chapter Five

Stella

Johnny grabs me by the waist as I try to zoom past him. "Woah, what's going on?"

"Go look and see what she did to my pumpkin." I shriek. "She's ruined the decorations. I don't know if I can get another one ready in such short notice."

"It's ONE pumpkin," Tiffany yells from across the room. "The store had plenty. It's not even one of the main ones. It's a pumpkin the glitter didn't even stick to."

"I still planned on using it."

He glances toward Audrey. She shrugs, "it's nothing less than we'd expect Tiff to do."

"Can you keep Stella over here while I check out the damage?" As soon as he lets go of me, I start toward Tiffany. "Audrey, come get her now, please. Tiffany...outside." He points toward the door.

Tiffany stomps her foot but listens. The rage in my face must speak for itself. Audrey rushes over and grabs my hand before pulling me into the living room. Apparently, he's trying to put as much space between us as he can. I'm not sure how I feel about that.

He takes a deep breath and walks to the dining room table. I know as soon as his eyes land on the monstrosity my baby cousin created. A laugh bursts from his lips and I'm marching his way. Audrey tries to grab my arm again, but turn to stay out of her grasp. "It's not funny."

"It kind of is."

"She drew a penis into the side of the pumpkin. How in the hell is that funny? If she was a teenager, it'd be hilarious, but she's a grown ass woman." With the humor of a teenage boy, I don't say that, but it's implied.

Tiffany's voice comes from the front door. "A funny one." I didn't even see her when I came into the dining room. She had to have ducked back when she saw me.

"Not that funny," I mutter under my breath. We were having such a good day, too. There wasn't any drama. She text Johnny and told him to come over. Then she pulls this crap? It's almost as if she's doing all she can to piss me off and she's barely been here twenty-four hours.

"Life must be boring without a sense of humor," Tiffany sing songs. "It was a joke, Stella. I thought you were going to laugh about it."

I can't do this with her right now. If I stay inside this house, I'm going to say something I can't take back. A part of me understands. She's young and maybe she's just as scared as I am. Johnny and I have been together for a while, but now it's permanent. What if she's lashing out because she thinks he's going to take me away from her and Audrey?

It's too much to think about. Too much to try to dissect. "I'll be back." I turn toward the front door, push past Tiff, and walk down the steps into the darkness. It's pitch black and being outside at night still gives me the creeps. But it's better than being in there and attempting to not murder my cousin while also figuring out if I can salvage the penis pumpkin.

I'm barely halfway down the driveway when I hear Johnny calling my name. I still can't believe he laughed. He's supposed to have my back. Or, maybe I've truly turned into one of those crazy brides that has to have everything perfect. I pick up my pace not wanting to be around anyone right now. Am I pouting? Yep. Do I care? Not even a little bit. The wedding is in a few days and it feels like it will be impossible to finish everything I want.

"Stella, wait up," Johnny's voice is closer. He must have been booking it. "Geez, why are you walking so fast, woman?"

Instead of responding, I stop in my tracks and look up at the sky. There are times I miss living in Austin, but this isn't one of them. You can see the stars. Each one a bright pinprick in a dark canvas.

Johnny comes up behind me and wraps his arms around my waist. "Are you okay?"

His embrace, along with the tranquility of the night, are exactly what I need. My shoulders relax and I lean into his chest. "Yes."

A light breeze blows through the open yard and I shiver. "Are you sure?"

"Mhmm." I turn until I'm facing him and my arms go around him instinctively. "I'm sorry for acting like a brat. Tiffany's antics usually don't get to me as much as they have since last night. I don't know what's wrong with me."

"That's easy," Johnny laughs. "Stress. I know how much you want everything to be picture perfect. But it's okay if it's not. Having a pumpkin with a penis carved into it isn't the end of the world. I bet most of our family and friends will think it's hilarious."

My head rears back and I glare at him. "I may have calmed down, but there's no way in hell we're putting that pumpkin out during the wedding." He doesn't say anything, but pulls me back into his capable arms.

After a few seconds, he pulls one arm from around me tilting my head until our eyes meet. "Honestly, we could be wearing shorts and t-shirts. It doesn't matter to me what everything else looks like, as long as I get to be your husband by the end of the day."

I lift up on my toes and press my lips to his. It was supposed to be sweet and innocent. He trails his fingers down my side before pulling me closer and getting his fingers tangled in the ends of my hair. For all the ways he's incredibly sweet, he sure knows how to take control of a situation. It's a nice change of pace. Not because he's a pushover but I know my tendencies to control every little detail. It's why I'm so stressed out.

Johnny breaks the kiss and releases me. That cool breeze comes back with a vengeance. It bothers me more now than it did earlier, and I miss the warmth of his embrace. "Is there a reason you stopped?"

He grins and reaches for my hand. "If I didn't, we wouldn't be walking back into the house for a while."

"I'm completely okay with that."

He doesn't even try to hide his chuckle. "You're also full of shit. I know you're wondering what other chaos your cousin is constructing. And, you're in the middle of a project. You never leave those unattended for long."

I hate when he's right, but I'll never admit it. "It could have waited." I'm trying to be nonchalant.

"Okay," he drawls, disbelief evident in his tone. He ushers me back toward the house. "The sooner we get all the arts and crafts done, the sooner you'll be able to rest. And the less you'll have to worry about Tiffany's antics."

"You have a point." Our steps are slow as we approach the door. "Then we can focus on the outside. I mean, what could she possibly screw up out here?"

"Just," Johnny rubs his forehead with his free hand, "don't let her touch the lawnmower while I'm at work. I'd like for it to be in one piece when I get home."

"I thought you were off the rest of the week?" This is going to be a tight schedule to get everything picture perfect.

"I did, but Uncle Rick forgot about a doctor appointment he had in the morning. I'm only there long enough to cover for him then I'm heading back over here. Reaf is going to come by when he gets off work to help out."

"He doesn't have to do that." It's very sweet of him, but I don't want him to go out of his way when he has a family waiting for him at home.

"Don't turn down my free help. He offered." Johnny pushes the door open, and motions for me to walk ahead of him. I'm not sure that's the smartest idea if Tiff decides to run her mouth. "Make a list of everything you want, and need done, we'll get it taken care of."

"Are you sure you want me to make that list?"

He shudders remembering the list I made when I moved up here from Austin. "Try to keep it doable, please."

I snort, "I'll do my best. Let's find my cousins and try to get some of these arrangements done." I think I hear a bottle of wine calling my name in order to get through everything.

Chapter Six

Johnny

WHAT THE HELL? Uncle Rick's truck is in the lot as I pull into the shop. He's not supposed to be here until around lunch. Did he get his days mixed up? I better get inside and see what's going on. I put my truck in park, and get out. I swear this man never gets his dates and times right.

The sun is bright and it's warm despite it being Fall. Gotta love the Texas weather. I just hope there isn't any rain for this weekend. Even though the guest list is small, I don't think we can fit everyone in her house. Well, soon to be our house.

Pulling open the glass door, I stop in my tracks. Reaf is yelling at my uncle, and it sounds heated. I slowly let the door close behind me, doing my best to keep them from knowing they are no longer alone. Normally, I'd rush to see what the problem is, but it takes a lot to make Reaf mad. Whatever it is, it has to be important.

"You aren't supposed to be here right now, Old Man. There's still time for you to go." I can imagine Reaf pointing his finger at my uncle like a scorned child.

"No. I can't do that to Johnny. I wasn't paying attention to the date when I made the doctor appointment." There's a pause. "I can go sometime next week."

"Why are you so stubborn? If you don't get checked out regularly, you'll never know if there's anything else you need to do. Your arthritis is only getting worse. How long until you won't be able to work on cars anymore?"

Damn. I hadn't noticed anything amiss with Rick. Have I been so wrapped up in Stella that I've been shrugging off how my family is feeling?

"I'll pass the shop over to Johnny…and you. That's been the plan all along."

Okay, I can't listen to this anymore. I barge into the closed office door. "Unc, go to the doctor."

"Shit." He shakes his head. "I meant to call you and tell you not to come."

"Too late, I'm already here. Now," I move until I'm behind him and nudge him toward the door, "go. We can't have you falling apart on us now. Who are we going to get to boss us around if you retire over something that could be managed?"

"But you have to get ready for the wedding."

"I will. Reaf is going to help me when he gets off work. And you'll be back in the shop by lunch. There's plenty of time."

"Yeah," Reaf adds, crossing his arms. "No get going old man."

"I don't know when I started letting the two of you, boss me around," he grumbles. But he doesn't argue with us. He grabs his keys off the desk and slowly makes his way out of the shop.

"He's more stubborn than a mule," Reaf sighs.

"You're preaching to the choir, Man." I grab the appointment book to see what we have to do today. I'm hoping he didn't schedule a bunch of hard shit. I can feel Reaf's eyes on me and when I look up, he's grinning. "What's so funny?"

"Are you secretly a vampire?"

What the actual fuck? "Excuse me?" That question was random as hell.

"You're sparkling," he shrugs. "That's what vampires do in one of the books Tonya reads."

"One," I hold up a finger, "vampires do not sparkle. And two, I'm not sparkling."

He reaches forward and plucks something out of my hair. "Actually, you are." He holds his finger out to me and some shimmers in the low light. "Why do you have glitter all over you? Decide to hit up the strip club instead of a bonfire for your bachelor party?"

I'm going to murder those women. "Ugh, I was helping Stella and the girls with crafting. Some of the decorations have glitter on them."

"Did nobody tell you glitter is like an STD? Once you come into contact, you'll never get rid of it."

"No," I grunt. "They failed to mention that." No wonder they had me handling it last night while they stood back with a gleam in their eyes. They knew and just let me get it all over myself. Better yet, how did I not notice it when I took a shower this morning.

"I feel sorry for you, dude. You'll be finding it everywhere for weeks. Tonya doesn't allow it in our house. Anytime Layla gets something with glitter it goes straight to Grandma's house."

"Any chance I can send three grown ass women over there?"

He laughs, "Honestly, Lucia would most likely take them in with open arms. She doesn't turn anyone away."

"Good to know." Not that I'd actually banish them from the house, but it's nice to know it's an option. "Let's get the shop ready for the first customers. You know they'll be banging on the door before we even get the open sign turned on."

"It's like nobody in this town has anything better to do." He leaves the office ahead of me and opens the door that leads to the garage. "Speaking of, what all do we have to do at Stella's today?"

"I have no idea. I'm sure she'll have a list a mile long."

"That's what I was afraid of," he grins. "We'll get it knocked out in no time, though." I wish I could share his enthusiasm. We'll most likely spend a majority of the time keeping them out of our hair.

One day I'll stop being surprised when I pull into Stella's driveway. Today is obviously not that day. There are stacks of tables and chairs sitting next to the porch. I mean, I know Stella likes to be prepared, but I don't think we need those just yet. We still have a couple of days before we're even at that point.

"Johnny," Stella screeches and she runs down the porch steps. "What are we going to do with all these tables?"

"I was going to ask you the same thing. I thought they weren't being delivered until Friday morning."

She throws her hands on her hips and taps her foot. "That is when they were supposed to be delivered, but one of Mr. Jones's employees got the dates mixed up and refused to bring them back on the scheduled date."

Her cheeks are bright red, and if I know her, I'm sure the guy got an earful. "We can move them around back once Reaf and I are finished with the yardwork."

"It's supposed to rain tonight. We can't just leave them outside." She looks around as if a storage space will magically appear. "I can move some things around the living room and store them there."

She worries so much about the little things. It'd be adorable if she didn't get worked up about it. I place my hands on her shoulders and bend down until we're eye to eye. "Look at me, babe." She does. "Take a deep breath." She looks like she wants to say something, but she must see the determination in my face for her to listen to me. Two breaths and she seems to have calmed down. "We're not moving them inside. The living room is full of the decorations. And I'll be damned if I go anywhere near the glitter again. I'll ask Reaf if he'll pick up a few tarps and we'll keep them covered."

She eyes me skeptically. "A piece of plastic is going to keep them from being ruined?"

"You'd be amazed at what all you can do with it." I turn her toward the house. "Now, go grab the list so I can get started on the yard."

"Fine," she pouts. "But just so you know, the glitter suits you well."

Before I have a chance to say anything else, she hauls ass inside the house. Laughter on the breeze behind her.

Chapter Seven

Stella

Johnny wasn't kidding about wrapping the tables and chairs. I figured he'd load them up and take them to his or something. I was wrong. It looks like there is a big blue box in my backyard. It's not pretty, but if it keeps them clean, I won't say anything.

The yard looks amazing, thanks to my soon-to-be husband and Reaf. I didn't think they'd get much done since it's so massive. The wedding is in two days and I feel like we won't get everything done. It wouldn't be a huge deal, but there's so much we can't do until the night before and day of the ceremony.

It's a good thing the rest of the help is coming in today. I mean, they are mostly here for Johnny's bachelor party tonight, and to see their girlfriends, but I'm definitely putting them to work. It's going to take all hands on-deck to pull this thing off. I'm really regretting not hiring a wedding coordinator. All of this would be in their hands and I wouldn't be a ball of nerves and anxiety.

"Earth to Stella," Audrey is waving her hand in front of my face.

"Wow, sorry." I shake away the fear that everything is going to be ruined. "What were you saying?"

"Spencer and Justin should be here in about an hour. I just got off the phone with them. Do you want them to head here, or drop their stuff at Johnny's?" She's smiling so I know spacing out didn't offend her. Thank goodness. She's the one I'm going to rely on for all my freak outs the morning of the wedding. Tiffany will only make me freak out even more.

"Um," I tap my finger on the window sill. "Have them come here. They can take their stuff to Johnny's when they go over there tonight for the party."

She nods. "Okie dokie. I'm still surprised Johnny is having one."

I roll my eyes. "You realize it's just a bonfire, right? His idea of party is pretty tame."

A laugh comes from behind and I turn to find Tiffany standing close by. "Yours isn't much better. We're going to a winery for crying out loud. We should be hitting up a strip club, or at least something with music."

Of course. You can tell the differences in our ages. "There will be a band tonight. Besides, a strip club is not my idea of a good time. I don't want some sweaty dude bouncing his junk in my face." A shiver runs through my body without my permission. "Gross."

"She's right," Audrey says. "I'm not sure that I'd be okay with that, either. Can you imagine how Johnny would take it? I mean, I've never seen him jealous, but I have a feeling he'd go all alpha male in that situation."

"Yep. He doesn't like sharing the attention." Which I think is hilarious. Everyone sees him as this laid-back person, but some guy checked me out one time and I swear I heard him growl.

"Y'all are so boring." Tiff whines. "It's a wonder I'm even related to y'all. Do you think maybe I was switched at birth? Maybe I'm a changeling."

"You sound more excited about that than you should," I laugh. "But I'd be lying if I didn't think it a time or two."

"Okay," Tiff sighs. "Enough trying to figure out if I'm really a fae princess. How much longer until we can get ready? We may be going to a lame ass winery, but that doesn't mean I can't be show stopping."

"It's not lame." I hold out my hand and begin ticking off fingers. "There's wine. There's music. And I'll be with the best women I know."

"What about our moms?" Audrey asks.

"I mean, they are amazing, too. Tonight though, I only need my main crew. The gals that know me better than anyone else."

Audrey sniffs and Tiffany grins. "Are you crying?"

"No," Audrey wipes her eyes. "There's something in my eye."

Tiffany claps her hands together and rubs them. "You are going to be a mess when you get hitched. Especially if you're already like this now."

"Shut up," Audrey scoffs. "I can't wait until you get put in your place and tie the knot."

"Not going to happen anytime soon," Tiff sing-songs.

"Okay, you two," I step between them. "We need to get all the decorations moved to one place and the house straightened up before we can get ready."

Audrey pulls a notepad and pen out of nowhere. "Tell me what needs to be done and we'll do it."

"Do you seriously carry that in your pocket?" Tiffany shakes her head.

"No. But I've been carrying it around while we're here so nothing is missed in the preparations."

This is why I can always count on her. She knows how to get shit done. It looks like that paper collection she's been hoarding finally came in handy.

"Why is there a wannabe TARDIS in your backyard?" Spencer says while looking out the back window.

"Um." I'm not sure how to respond to that. Hell, I don't even know what that is.

"Ignore him," Tiff sighs. "He's nerding out again."

"Okay…" I still don't know what it means, but I don't really want to be here for hours while he explains it to me. "We should probably get ready to go to our respective parties."

Johnny strides into the room. "There's no point in us getting ready. We'll be smelling like smoke within an hour."

"Wait," Spencer groans. "We're having an actual fire?"

"You were sheltered as a kid, weren't you?" Justin pats him on the back before sidling up next to Audrey. "It's called a bonfire for a reason."

Spencer rolls his eyes. "I was an only child that lived in the city. We didn't have bonfires."

"Well," I clap my hands. "You get your first experience." I level my gaze on Justin. "Do *not* make him try any of the crazy shit you pulled when I'd visit over the summer."

"It's not like I was the only one that tried to jump over the flames," he mutters. "Tiff was right there with me."

"Which is why it's a good thing she's with me."

"Unless…we crash their party after ours." Tiffany smirks. I don't know what I'm going to do with this woman. Every time I think she's moving a step toward actual adulthood she does things like the penis pumpkin and this.

I don't bother responding. It'll only encourage her. "So, is everyone ready to head out? I want to make sure we get a good table at the winery for all of us. Hopefully we beat Angie and Tonya."

"Yep," Johnny nods. He comes to stand next to me and wraps his arms around my waist. "Promise me you'll call for a ride if you need one."

He's covered in dirt and sweat, but I don't mind and lean my head against his chest. "I promise. Though Tonya said she'll be the DD since she has to work tomorrow."

"Sounds good. I just want to make sure you're safe." He places a kiss on top of my head and releases me. "Tiff, don't get yourselves into trouble."

"Why are you singling me out?"

"Because you're the one most likely to get y'all banned from the winery."

He's not wrong.

"Fine," she pouts. "I'll be on my best behavior."

"Okay, now tell me with your hands in front of you so I know you aren't crossing your fingers."

"You always have to ruin all the fun." She lifts her hands. "I promise I won't do anything to get us banned."

"That's better."

I stand on my tiptoes and press my lips to Johnny's. "Have fun tonight. I'll see you later."

"Later?" He raises an eyebrow.

"Tiff may have had the right idea when she said we might end up over there. The winery does close early, and it'd be nice for all of us to celebrate and hang out together."

"Sounds good to me." He leans down for one more quick kiss. He isn't one for PDA no matter how small the crowd is. It'll be interesting to see how he kisses me at the end of the ceremony. "I love you."

"I love you, too." I break away from him and head toward the front door. "Let's get this show on the road." Tiff and Audrey kiss their other halves and we head to the car. I really hope Tiff keeps her promise about staying in line. I want this night to be low key and enjoyable.

Chapter Eight

"WHY ARE WE STILL HERE?" Justin asks as I pull a few more weeds out of the flower bed. It's still so hot even though it's almost night in the middle of October. How is this even possible?

"Because I want to get these beds done before Stella gets back." I know he's no stranger to this type of work, but right now he's kind of getting on my nerves. "It'd go a lot faster if I had some help." I get it. He was in the car for four hours getting here...but damn, even Spencer is pulling weeds out.

I can almost feel him thinking behind me. "You're right. Tell me what you need me to do."

"Can y'all bring the flowers out of the back of my truck?"

"Does Stella know you're planting new things?" He looks around as if she might materialize out of nowhere. He obviously knows her well.

"Nope. It's a surprise." One I'm hoping she won't kill me over. She's done better about loosening her control over things. Maybe that will work in my favor. Besides, I matched the flowers to the rest of the theme perfectly. Well, the local nursery did when I brought in a sample of the dresses Tiff and Audrey will wear.

"It's your funeral," he mutters before tapping Spencer on the back and heading to the front of the house.

"Yeah, yeah," I call to their backs. She'll like them...I hope.

My phone dings and I wipe my hands on my jeans before swiping to see the message.

. . .

Reaf: When do you want me to head to your house? I'm dropping Layla off at the in-laws in about 30 minutes.

Johnny: I'm finishing up a few things here, but go over there whenever. If I'm not there, you know where the wood is.

Reaf: Gotcha. I'll take care of it. Don't stay over there too long. You won't get to enjoy your night.

Johnny: See you in a few.

He may be younger than me, but he's the best friend a guy could have. It's a wonder nobody scooped him up before Tonya did. He literally ticks off all the boxes in who a person wants to bring home to their parents.

"I know Justin has his doubts, but I think Stella is going to love these." Spencer sets the armful of flowers on the ground. "They are going to complete the aesthetic."

"Who the hell talks like that?" Justin laughs setting down his own set of flowers.

"Someone who works in design," Spencer sniffs. An awkward silence fills the space. "Anyway, we should get these in the ground and head out. I think Tiff was serious about them dropping by the bonfire."

"You're probably right." I point to the areas I want the flowers to go, "y'all get those planted over there and I'll work on this section. With the three of us, it shouldn't take more than thirty minutes."

Justin salutes me and takes his portion of plants while Spencer only nods. As ready as I am for the ceremony, I'll be happy when all the prep work is done. We should have hired people to do this for us so we could enjoy the last days of our engagement. I'm betting she feels the same way.

～

I can already see flames licking the star-studded sky when I pull into the driveway with Spencer. Justin is following behind in his car. Reaf must have gotten here earlier than he said. I need to take a quick shower to get all the dirt off of me. I'm sure Spencer and Justin need to as well.

"Woah," Spencer gasps. He sounds like a kid at a festival. "Is that fire safe?"

I chuckle. I can't help it. This poor guy must have lived such a sheltered life. "Yes, it's safe. We have a really long water hose out there and fire extinguishers just in case."

"Has one ever gotten out of hand?"

Now, do I freak him out and answer that truthfully? There were a few times growing up that I had to haul ass to get water on the field surrounding us. I'm a lot smarter than I was then. "When I was younger. But recently? No."

"Okay." I put the truck in park and both of us get out. Justin's door slams behind us.

There's a note stuck to the front door and I glance around. There's only one person who has left me a note like this and she should be at the winery. It's not from her though. Reaf's scratchy handwriting says to bring the pizza when we head back there.

"I'm going to jump in the shower," I open the door. "There's one in the hallway if y'all need it."

"Thanks," Spencer says.

Justin nods and heads to the kitchen. "Why is there plywood in here?"

"I've finally fixed the hole Stella fell through when we first met. I haven't had a chance to take the wood out."

"I would have loved to see that."

"No," I shake my head. "You wouldn't have. She wasn't exactly happy about it."

"I bet." He grabs the extra piece of plywood. "I'll take this out for you. Spence, you can grab the shower first."

"Thanks, man." I hurry toward my room and the bathroom. I'm ready to be out of these nasty clothes and by the fire with a beer in my hand.

Both Spencer and Justin are in the living room wearing hoodies when I come out. "Y'all ready?"

Both of them nod. "I'll grab the pizza," Justin offers and he walks out of the house. When we get to the truck, he walks around and lets down the tailgate.

"What are you doing?" I'm pretty sure we're wowing Spencer with how things are done in a small town.

"It's easier for us to just ride back here. But you can get in the cab if you want."

He shakes his head and awkwardly climbs into the bed. Within minutes we're parked next to Reaf and he's pulling beers out the ice chest for us. "Sorry I got started a little early. Tonya's parents got home earlier than expected and demanded to see their granddaughter." He rolls his eyes. "As if they don't see her all the time. I'm not one to complain about a kid free night, though."

Having kids isn't something Stella and I have really talked about. I mean, we're open to the possibility of it, but haven't said anything concrete. "Do you think you'll have another kid?"

Reaf shrugs, "maybe one day. We aren't really in a rush right now. Layla is a handful and I swear that kid rules our house most of the time. What about you and Stella?"

"No idea." It's the only answer I can give him. "It's something we'll need to discuss sooner than later. It's not like we're getting any younger." We stare at the fire crackling and soak in the soundtrack of a still country night. "I feel like I'm not going to know what to do after this weekend."

"You're getting nervous," Reaf laughs. "That's hysterical. You'll do the same thing you're doing now, dummy. The only difference is you'll be married and all official and shit."

"Oh no," Justin groans. "We aren't going to talk about feelings, are we?" He glances at each of us. "This is your bachelor party. We are going to drink, eat, and listen to some tunes. All while celebrating one of the biggest days in your life."

"Remind me not to let him give a toast," I mutter to Reaf.

We grab some chairs out of my truck and do exactly what Justin suggested. He's right. So is Reaf. Tonight, is about hanging out with these guys I've gotten close to. Everything will work itself out.

"So, this is what you do for fun in a small town?" Spencer lifts his beer to his lips and takes a drink.

There's nothing we can do except laugh. There's so much more we could do, but it'd land us in trouble or jail. Not exactly how I want to spend the night, or explain to Stella.

Chapter Nine

Stella

"Are you nervous?" Tiffany is pouring me another glass of wine. Her question catches me off guard.

She hands me the glass and I take a sip. Taking the moment to collect my thoughts. "Well," I clear my throat. "I wasn't until you said something."

Tiffany jumps and yelps as something shifts the table. I'm going to assume Audrey kicked her. "I didn't mean in a way that will turn you into a runaway bride. It's just that everything is going to change."

My cousin's eyes are glittery. I can't tell if it's from emotion or the wine. God, I hope she doesn't start crying. I'm not sure I'm equipped to handle that right now. "How?" Her feelings are important, and I need to know what they are. She loves Johnny like a brother so I know he's not the reason for this freak out.

"I don't know. You'll eventually have a family and won't be able to do anything on a whim like we do now."

Ah, there it is. She's not used to being the last choice. Audrey and I have always had her back, going to her whenever she needed us. I feel for her, I do, but it's time for my baby cousin to grow up a bit more. "That's not too different from what it's like now. We're all growing up, Tiff."

"Even though some of us are fighting it more than others," Audrey whispers. Though it's loud enough to be heard by everyone at the table.

"Tiffany," Tonya speaks up before I can say anything. "Everything will be okay. Some things may be a harder, but even with a husband and kid, I still make time for my friendships and family." She reaches across the table to pat Tiffany's hand.

My cousin opens her mouth, but I cut her off. "You don't have anything to worry about. Our engagement didn't change the closeness between us, and marriage won't either."

"Promise?"

That one question reminds me of the little girl who used to follow me around. There's a reason the three of us are cousins and not sisters. I don't think any of our parents could have handled that. "I promise. Besides, life would be entirely too boring without you around. Or, without you causing some sort of drama."

"I'm not that bad," she scoffs.

Angie laughs, the first input she's had since she's gotten here. "You can be. But it's nothing too horrible."

"That's what you think," Audrey winks. "You didn't grow up with her."

Tiffany folds her arms across her chest. "Why are y'all picking on me? This night is supposed to be about Stella, in case y'all forgot."

I can see Audrey itching to say something. I need to put a stop to this before things get ugly. Even though we're best friends, we can fight like sisters. The band is still playing and will give the perfect distraction. "Exactly, it's my night." Gah, even I can't believe I'm getting married in two. Freaking. Days. I set my glass down and stand. "Let's go dance."

Luckily, there isn't an argument from anyone. They all set their glasses down, except Tiffany, and follow me to the makeshift dance floor. The guitarists picks off the first few notes of "Oklahoma Breakdown" and the five of us squeal. It's an older song, but definitely a good one. We dance around in a circle and then grab a dancing partner, two stepping. Being the center of attention has never bothered me, and tonight I really don't care. I have my friends around me and we're having the time of our lives.

Tiffany grabs my arms and spins me around. "We should head to Johnny's in a bit."

"Why?" I'm not opposed to it. Ending up there was always going to be part of the plan.

"Because it feels wrong celebrating this huge milestone apart from the people we love." And that's what I love about my baby cousin. For all the emotion she has about everything, she loves hard. She knows where we need to be.

"You're right." I laugh, as I spin her. "But not yet." For now, I want to hang out with my girls. Have fun with them like we're still teenagers finding trouble. Tonight, will be almost as memorable as my wedding day.

❧

The guys are sitting on the tailgate when we pull up. Angie begged off to double check everything is ready for the wedding. She doesn't want it to be a hot mess and turn me into a frenzied bride. After the pumpkin debacle with Tiff, I don't think anything could cause me to go off the rails. And if I do, I'm sure my darling youngest cousin will have something to do with it.

"Wow," Spencer shakes his head. "Y'all actually came."

Tiffany rushes to her boyfriend and throws her arms around him. "You obviously don't know me as well as you think you do." She gives him a quick kiss before climbing on the truck next to him. "Hey soon-to-be cousin, did you happen to bring a blanket? It's chilly out here."

"You could grab a chair and sit by the fire, Tiff." I roll my eyes, heading toward Johnny. Grabbing his hand, I pull him off the tailgate and to the chairs I mentioned. There's no way in hell all six of us would fit up there. Wait, there should be another person. "Where's Reaf?"

"He headed home right before y'all got here. He didn't say why, but now I'm assuming it's because he knew y'all were done at the winery."

"You can't blame him," I laugh. "They are baby free for the night, I bet they're taking advantage."

He groans and a shiver runs through him. "I did not need that mental image, Stella." Pulling me toward him, he sits down on the chair and pulls me into his lap. His fingers are cold as he runs them under the hem of my shirt. He kisses along my neck. I squirm as his lips hit that spot right below my ear. I swear, he's doing this at the exact wrong time. I mean, we have an audience. I'm not turned off by PDA, but I know exactly where this is going to lead, and I don't need my cousins and their boyfriends to witness it.

"Oh my gosh, y'all get a damn a room." Apparently, Tiffany thinks the same as me. Even though she's the one who's more public with make-out sessions.

I turn to face the group on the tailgate. "We pl—" A tearing sound rips through the night. I don't have time to react before me and Johnny are on the ground, stuck between metals legs and the square that made up the seat of the chair.

"Did anyone catch that on video?" Audrey laughs. "It'd make great footage for the wedding montage."

Justin can hardly breathe while he attempts holding his laughter in. Tiffany and Spencer aren't holding anything back. Tiff is even slapping her leg. "I couldn't even get my phone out fast enough. That was fucking priceless."

"Har, har," I roll my eyes. "Do you think one of you could stop reveling in our embarrassment long enough to do something productive like help us up?" Audrey is the first to slide off the tailgate, but there's a flash before she takes a step in our direction. "Please, tell me you didn't."

"Oh, I did," Audrey grins. "I mean, how could I not get a snapshot. Want to see it?"

"Hell no," I yell. Johnny says "kinda" at the same time. I face him, scowl in place. "Traitor."

"At least it didn't happen at the wedding," when my glare doesn't change, he adds, "don't act like you wouldn't be doing the same thing as your cousins if the situation was reversed. You'd be laughing your ass off as well."

"You don't have to call out my flaws like that."

Before he can respond, Audrey is standing in front of us. "How do you want me to handle this? It looks like the both of you are packed in there like sardines."

I assess our positions. It's going to hurt no matter what we do. This chair obviously wasn't meant for two people. "Just grab my hand and yank."

She glances at Tiffany. "Are you sure? There's a good chance you'll fall on your face."

The corner of my mouth lifts into a smirk. "No, dear cousin, I won't. You'll be in front of me to break my fall."

Head shaking, she grabs my hand and pulls me toward her. I fly out of the chair, but we don't fall. She digs her heels into the ground and I fall into her. When I look up, I see Justin standing behind her to keep us both from falling. At least I know they still work well together in dubious situations. "See, nobody fell."

"Thanks Justin," I grumble. "And Audrey."

"No problem," they say in unison.

"Now, Johnny is going to be more of a challenge." Justin rubs his chin like some sort of cartoon villain. "Spence, can you come help me."

"I can help," I move toward my soon to be husband.

"We've got it," Justin nudges me out of the way. "Spencer, you grab one hand, and I'll grab the other." He looks at Johnny's legs hanging in midair with his butt planted firmly on the ground between the chair frame. "Actually, Stella, hold on the chair so it doesn't come up with him."

That is something I can do. I know I'm capable of helping pull Johnny up, but let's face it, I'm not nearly as strong as them. "Tiff, Audrey, y'all hold on to the sides and I'll take the back." Tiffany grumbles as she makes her way toward us, but she bends down and grabs the bottom of the chair on one side. Audrey is already on the other, and I squat to hold the back.

"This is so humiliating," Johnny sighs.

Justin calls out, "One, two, three." Him and Spencer pull and us girls hold the chair down. He's wedged in there so tight; we have to double down on our efforts.

The guys stumble back, and Johnny is free of the stupid chair. "Okay, so note to self, make sure we bring actual chairs next time we come out here. I know these camping chairs are supposed to handle it, but they obviously aren't meant for more than one person."

"No shit," Audrey snorts. See this is what happens. One night of drinks and she gets sassy like our younger cousin. How am I going to deal with these two for the rest of the night?

"We could be like normal people and go back to your house to drink." Tiffany leans against Spencer, soaking in his body heat.

I'm already shaking my head no. "We are not chancing messing something up before the wedding."

"Let's go to Johnny's then," Spencer suggests. It's close and we don't have to worry about anything. Me and Tiff will take the couch tonight, and y'all can have the bedrooms."

The unbelievable shock that crosses Tiffany's face is priceless. "Fine. But please tell me there's food."

"There's pizza in the truck," Johnny points in the direction. "And I'm sure we can scrounge something up in the kitchen."

"Sounds like a plan." Hopefully the rest of the night is uneventful. I plan on staying clear of the kitchen. No way in hell am I falling through that damn hole again.

Chapter Ten

Johnny

SHOULD my body be this sore the morning of my wedding? Yesterday was a complete whirlwind. My parents took off to help, and Stella's parents came in. They opted to stay at a hotel in town so the house wouldn't be too crowded. Stella wasn't playing about getting the house dirty before today. I didn't even get to stay as late as I wanted to. Tiffany was shooing me out the door before midnight. According to her, if I was there after it'd be bad luck since it's technically the same day. I kind of see her point, but still. I'm not a huge fan of being bossed around, unless of course, it's by Stella.

"You ready to head over there?" My dad claps me on the back. Spencer and Justin left about an hour to go to help with any last-minute preparations, and muttering something about blankets.

"Yeah," I sigh. "I just hope today goes off without a hitch. I know how much this means to Stella."

"From the looks of things when I left earlier this morning, the both of you have nothing to worry about. Everything looks great." Instead of heading toward the front door, he walks to the kitchen. When he comes back, he has two beers in hand.

"You know she'll kill me if I show up drunk, right?"

"Relax, son. It's one beer. And…you'll brush your teeth before we leave." He twists the cap off one before handing to me. "Besides, I know for a fact the ladies were having mimosas this morning. Red said she needed to calm Stella down and keep her from checking on everything again."

I assume he's talking about Tiffany. "You know how my wife is. A perfectionist on any project she takes on." I can't stop the grin from forming. She's about to be my wife. I feel like I've been waiting ages to be able to call her that, and the day has finally arrived. "Everything is perfect, right?" I have to make sure. This is the only time I'll ever get married and I want it to be what we both dreamed it would.

"Not you, too," Dad groans. "It looks like something out of a movie. I'm happy y'all decided to have it at the house. It's a beautiful way to begin your lives."

"Good." I finish my beer and set it on the coffee table. "I'll be right back." The beer breath has to go before the wedding begins.

Dad is standing by the front door when I get back. "Let's go make your bride proud."

He opens it and a gust of chilly wind blows through. This might put a damper on things. Of course, today would be the day the temperature drops from the mild Fall weather we've been having. "I hope everyone dressed for the weather. We can move the ceremony inside, but it would be a tight fit."

"Don't even worry about it, Johnny. Your uncle, Stella's cousins, and myself have already thought of that."

"What do you mean?" I hope they didn't do something crazy. The last thing I need is for my dad and uncle to have created a horrible eyesore.

"Tiffany and Audrey sent their other halves to pick up blankets for the guests and your uncle brought the outside heaters from the shop." He claps his hands together and points toward the truck. "Problem solved. Now, we need to get over there before we're late to your own wedding."

"Let's get this show on the road." I wait for Dad to walk out and lock up. I can't believe this is the last time I'm leaving this house as an unmarried man. It's the perfect time to close the door on this chapter. Well, not completely. I can't sell my grandpa's house. No, I'll rent it out just in case we need it for something else in the future.

"Dude, where have you been?" Spencer rushes toward me. "Tiff has been on my ass telling me to get her as soon as you show up."

The timing is a little close. There's less than half an hour until the ceremony. "No worries. I'm here now. You can report to the bossy lady." I can't imagine what she needs to see me about before the wedding. If anything, she should be keeping Stella calm and collected. "Before you go, which room am I supposed to be in. Stella never told me." She's most likely in the master bedroom since it's big enough for all of them.

"Oh, just stay in the living room. Tiffany doesn't want any chance of you catching a glimpse of Stella before she's walking down the aisle." With that order, he jogs off to find his girlfriend.

"Red sure does know how to keep people on their toes," Dad says.

All the furniture in the living room has been pushed back, allowing plenty of standing space for the folks to come inside for the reception. I start to sit on the couch, but decide to stand. There's no way I'll be able to sit still. "Yeah, she's used to getting her way. Even if it's not right away."

Dad mentioning her must have conjured her up. She's coming into the living room with Audrey, Spencer, and Justin trailing behind her. "Good, you're finally here." She waits for the other three to catch up to her. Audrey is carrying shot glasses and Justin produces a bottle of whiskey. "We don't have much time, but I wanted to share a shot with you before you are officially a family member. And, before we're in front of a shit ton of people."

"Um, thanks." I'm not sure what I'm supposed to say.

Audrey lines the shot glasses on the coffee table and Justin fills them up behind her. Tiffany doesn't pause a beat. "Everyone grab a glass." She nods toward Dad, "You too." When he does, she lifts her glass into the air and we follow suit. "Think of this as your personal welcome to the family. It's a promise there will never be a dull moment and you're now one of us." We clank our glasses together, but before any of us can drink, she adds, "and if you hurt my cousin in any way, I will hunt you down."

Ignoring my dad's chuckle, I down the shot. "You don't have to worry about that, Tiff. Y'all are stuck with me. This is the second time you've told me that, and I have no intentions of you needing to honor that threat."

"Good." She nods and throws back her whiskey. "Audrey, help me grab the glasses and put them in the dishwasher. You guys need to get outside. The wedding is about to start."

I don't have to be told twice. Audrey and Tiffany rush back upstairs after depositing the glasses, and we head straight for the back door. I can't wait until Stella is by my side.

Stunning. That is the only word that comes to mind as Stella walks down the aisle with her dad. Their steps are slow and measured. I wish they would speed it up. I need Stella in my arms. I need her to be by my side from now until forever.

The guests are seated close together in chairs with plaid blankets draped across their legs for warmth. The outside heaters are lined up along the rows and there's one on the edge of where I'm standing now. I'm not sure if I'm sweating because of the heat it's producing, or because the woman I love is making her way toward me. Toward our future.

Finally, Stella and her dad stop in front of the wedding party. He simply lifts her veil and gives her a quick peck on the cheek before sitting down. We opted out of her father giving her away. In the words of Tiffany, "Nobody owns her." And she's absolutely right. If anyone owns someone it's Stella owning me…heart and soul. I will do literally anything for her.

The preacher from my parents' church clears his throat. "Family and friends, we're gathered here today to celebrate the union—"

I don't know how he finishes because I've completely tuned him out. Leaning forward the tiniest bit, I whisper, "You are breathtaking."

"Thank you," she smiles. Then stops abruptly. "Not that I don't trust my cousins, but I don't have lipstick on my teeth, right?"

The chuckle that escapes my lips can't be helped, and it's loud enough to make the preacher pause. I nod my head for him to continue. "No, but if you did, I would never notice."

"Now, it's time for the rings." Damn, that went by fast. Thank goodness we weren't coming up with our own vows. We wanted the ceremony short and sweet, and it's what we're getting.

Audrey hands Stella a ring, and Reaf hands me the one for Stella. My vision is blurry as I slide the ring over Stella's finger. As soon as it's on her finger, she lifts her hand and wipes wetness away from my cheek. I'm not sure when that started, but I don't care. I wipe a tear from her cheek. The both of us smile at each other as if we're the only people in existence.

Stella slides on my ring and this is it. This is the moment we've promised ourselves to each other. The moment we've become one. The preacher breaks into my thoughts. "You are now husband and wife. You may kiss your bride."

There's no hesitation as I grab Stella by the waist and pull her to me. My other hand rests on the back of her neck and I bend her back as my lips devour hers. Should it be a little less dramatic? Probably. Right now, I don't give a fuck. All that matters is her body pressed to mine. Luckily, she feels the same because she doesn't push me back. Only clinging to me as if I'm the only person that matters.

Tiffany and Audrey interrupt us. I think Audrey groans, but there's denying Tiff's voice. "How many times am I going to have to tell y'all to get a room? You have an audience."

Stella breaks the kiss, but she doesn't leave my side. "And I'm sure the audience doesn't mind." Our family and friends respond with clapping and whistles. Yeah, they know us pretty well.

Tonya leaves her seat and plays the orchestra music for us to walk down the aisle. Our bridesmaids and groomsmen walk ahead of us, but as soon as they are out of the way, we run the rest of the way down the aisle and straight for the house. Once we're inside, I close the door and lock it. Stella pulls the blinds closed and we allow ourselves this small moment of privacy.

Chapter Eleven

With Johnny's hand in mine, I lead him up the stairs and to our bedroom. Before he has a chance to say anything I close the door, lean against it, and pull him to me. "Thank you for making today the best day of my life."

"It's almost amazing because you are in it." From most guys this would be corny, but I know Johnny means it with every word that falls from his lips.

My lips meet his for the second time today, without our family gawking at us. His tongue runs along the seam of my lips and I allow him entrance. This kiss feels frantic. Like we won't survive if we pull apart from each other. His hands are roaming over my hips, trying like hell to lift up my dress. I release my hands from his neck and run them down his chest until I'm fumbling with the belt and button of his dress pants. Should we wait until we're alone? I have no doubt. But it's been a long week, and we have this moment to be alone. With my cousins here, it's been…difficult.

With his pants now loose, I push them and his underwear down. I need him. My dress is bunched around my waist, and he lifts me up until I can wrap my legs around his waist. Within seconds he's inside me, and I cling to him as he thrusts into me. God, I've missed this.

Right now, isn't the time to be gentle, or take our time. We have guests waiting for us. His body tenses and buries his face into my hair. My release follows and I bite down on his shoulder to keep quiet.

We stay like that for a few minutes before we hear a door close downstairs. He slowly pulls out and lowers me to the ground before lowering the skirt of my dress. His laugh is warm on my neck, sending shivers all over my body. "Well, that's a first for me."

I furrow my brows. "What is?"

"I've never had sex with people waiting outside. Do you think they heard?"

Giggling, I push him back. "I don't think so, but I have zero doubts they know exactly what's happening. Especially if they were paying attention to that kiss." I slide out from between him and the door and make my way to the mirror. "I can't believe we just did that." Even though I don't regret it. There's a box of tissue on the nightstand next to the mirror and I grab one fixing my lipstick. "This is something they'd expect from Tiffany, not me."

Johnny is walking toward me while buttoning his pants. He stands behind me and kisses the top of my head. "Who cares? If anything, it'll show how strong our passion is for each other."

I turn and use the same tissue to wipe away the lipstick smudge off him. "True, but now they'll be asking when we're going to have kids."

"It'll happen when it happens." He bends down to pull me into another kiss, but a bang on the door makes us jump away from each other. "Any guesses who that is?"

"I swear if you two don't stop acting like horny teens and get out, I'm going to beat this door down."

"Calm down, Tiff. We're coming." She's not wrong that is how we're acting, but I don't care. When you've got it…you've got it. I don't miss her loud laughter as she walks down the stairs. Who's the teen now?

"We better not keep our guests waiting any longer." Johnny runs his finger along my bottom lip before giving me a chaste kiss. "The sooner they leave, the sooner we can start our honeymoon." He winks and leads me out of the room.

We're sitting down for dinner and everyone is loving the wings. It's definitely a messy meal for a wedding dinner, but there was no way we weren't including it. If it wasn't for that lunch date Johnny and I had, we never would have ended up here. And, let's face it. Angie's wings are amazing.

Both Audrey and Reaf have given their toasts and now Tiffany is speaking. Please don't let her say anything embarrassing. "As you all know, I'm the baby of the family. But one thing I've always done is look up to my cousins. I'm beyond honored to be standing here, celebrating her special day. I hope the two of you have many years of bliss. Who knows, maybe we'll be planning a different party in a few months." She winks at the crowd and they burst into laughter.

They definitely know what we were doing when we disappeared. I'm also sure my face is as red as a tomato. So much for her not being a pain in the ass. She takes a seat next to Audrey and I hope she can feel the death glare I'm sending her way. I whisper to Johnny, "I told you that would be the next assumption."

"I'm not surprised Tiffany is the one who said something first." He wipes his hands and grabs mine. "Now, would you do me the honor of dancing with me?"

A slow song starts playing and I let him lead me to the small dance floor we put down in the yard. "There's nothing I'd love more. Any day of the week."

I can feel eyes on us as we sway back and forth to the ballad coming through the speaker. Before long other couples are joining us. I could have opted for some big fancy wedding, but this, right here, is the perfect way for us to begin our lives together as husband and wife.

Gone Snowbound

Chapter One

Tiffany

THERE MUST BE A FULL MOON, or something. The restaurant has been extra nuts. I can't remember the last time we had to have a wait list, and we aren't prepared for that. We're a small restaurant in a tiny building. What the hell was Dennis thinking making me the manager. I'm not cut out for this. It would be bad if I called him and asked him to come in early and help, right?

I grab the tray of food, remembering those days when waiting tables was what I did all the time, before Dennis gave me a promotion. You've got this Tiff. Pull up your bad bitch panties and deal with it. Not bad as far as pep talks go. Let's hope it gets me through the rest of the shift. Only two hours to go. Dennis is taking over when I leave, and I can take a much-needed break from being on my feet.

With the food in hand, I back out of the kitchen, plaster a wide smile on my face, and act like it's not fake as hell. As much as I want to yell at these people to go home because it's too cold to be outside, all they see is a bubbly redhead ready to serve them.

"How are y'all today?" I ask the table in the corner closest to the window. A group of four women sit at the round top with shopping bags littering the floor around them. "Who had the southwest chicken soup?"

"Right here." The woman in the corner holds up her hand. I reach across the table and place the bowl in front of her. "Thank you." The same routine goes around the table until all the women have their meals.

"Do you need anything else?" I bring the tray down to my side and hold it in the same position you would a cute clutch.

"No, we're good." One of the women shakes her head and picks up her glass of water. "But, thank you."

"You're welcome." I turn and take a step. Except there's something caught on my foot. I fall to the floor, dropping the tray and barely getting my hands in front of me to keep me from hitting my face on the cold tile. A glance back tells me exactly what I suspected. One of their shopping bag handles got caught on the clasp of my boot. I wonder if Dennis will let me put a new shopping bag rule in place. I mean when we're this packed, it's honestly a hazard.

The woman closest to me at the table, slides out of her chair and to my side. "Are you okay?"

A part of me wants to revel in my bitchiness. I mean, I'm on the floor because I tripped over their crap. Of course, I'm not okay. But, I'm the manager and there's a certain decorum I need to maintain. "Yes, I'm fine. It's not the first time I've fallen, and I'm sure it won't be the last." Flipping over until I'm sitting, I reach forward and unhook the bag handle from my boot.

"I'm still so sorry. I told them we should have taken the bags to the car before eating." The woman glares at her friends. "Move those in the corner so nobody else trips over them.

"It's okay. At least I already delivered your food. Otherwise…this would have been a lot messier."

"Thank goodness for that," she smiles and holds out her hand to help me up.

"Thanks." I wipe off my clothes to make sure I don't have anything on me. "If you need anything else, let me know."

"We will," she sits down, "and, again, I'm sorry."

Waving off her apology, I head back to the counter to deposit the tray. Janie is covering her mouth with her hand, and I know the asshole is laughing at me. "Don't even start." I hold up my hand as if that will stop her commentary. It never does. She's grown on me, but that doesn't mean I like her all the time.

"I wish I would have gotten that on video. Dennis would find it hysterical." She's not wrong. He'd be laughing and wouldn't try hiding it.

"I'm sure one of his stupid cameras caught it. He'll get a nice little show when he checks them later." I lift my hand to one of the cameras and discreetly flip it off. There. He can have that parting gift as well. "Let's just get through the rest of this afternoon so we can go home. Your replacement should be here before Dennis shows up."

"Sure thing, Boss." She salutes me and grabs another order. She smirks as she passes by me. What the hell is that about? She only makes that face when she knows something I don't. Please don't let it be Dennis throwing even more obstacles at me.

There aren't many days I regret my life choices, but today is one of them. Had I applied myself, I could be working my own hours like Stella. Or in a cubicle with set days and times, like Audrey. But no, I chose to accept Dennis's offer of manager. It's usually a manageable day. It seems like the closer we get to Christmas, the more insane our foot traffic is. And, this year seems to be worse, even if it is good for business.

I open the door to my apartment that I share with Spencer and kick my shoes off before I close it behind me. It drives him crazy when I leave my shoes here, but I can't find it in me to care. They need to come off. That's the only thing that matters. My plans for the rest of the day include sitting on the sofa with a cup of hot chocolate and binge watching whatever catches my attention. There is absolutely nothing that will move my ass off the sofa.

There's a suitcase sitting outside the hallway before I even make it to the living room. What in the fresh hell is going on here? It feels like a stone is settling in the gut of my stomach, and I don't know if I can handle any other horrible thing happening today.

Instead of going to the sofa where I planned on planting myself and being a potato, I turn down the hall and toward our bedroom. Spencer comes out of the room just as I'm about to enter and I slam into his chest. "Oh, shit." He looks down and leans back until he can see my face. "Are you okay?"

I notice the second suitcase he was pulling behind him. This really doesn't look like it will be a good end to my day. I stiffen and point to the suitcases "I don't know. Is it?" Before he has a chance to say anything, I step away from him. "Were you going to leave without saying anything?" I cross my arms over my chest and wait.

He furrows his brows in confusion. "What are you talking about?" He takes a step toward me and I scoot back again. My back hits the wall and I've run out of space.

"The suitcases, Spencer." I point again to reiterate my point. "Were you hoping I wouldn't be home when you split so you wouldn't have to explain anything." This is why I didn't do relationships. You inevitably end up getting hurt. "This is just the fucking cherry on my shit sundae day."

He moves before I can sidestep him. One hand is braced against the wall beside me, closing off all escape from this nightmare situation. He uses the other hand to gently lift my chin until we are eye to eye. "How could you ever think I'd leave you, Tiff?" He kisses my forehead, and it's the complete opposite of everything currently playing on loop in my brain. "You're it for me. I thought I'd made that pretty damn clear the entire time we've been together."

"But the suitcases," my voice trembles. It pisses me off that I feel so weak at the thought of him no longer being here, and confused as to what's going on.

"That typically means leaving, and you didn't say anything about going out of town. What else am I supposed to think?"

He groans and leans his head against the wall, right beside mine. The memory of how we first got together flashes in my mind. It wasn't so unlike this. I was pissed off then, and we ended up in my bed. His voice close to my ear sends shivers down my spine. "I knew I shouldn't have listened to Dennis."

"Um, what does Dennis have to do with this?"

He moves until he's beside me and leaning against the wall. "I've been working in secret with your boss to get you a few days off so I could whisk you away for a romantic getaway before we are with your entire family for the holidays. I told him I should at least give you a hint, and he convinced me it should be a complete surprise." He glances at me and waves his hands in the air. "Surprise."

Oh, thank God. He's not leaving me. Not that I wouldn't be okay in the long run, but I legit can't imagine him not by my side. "Yeah, probably not the best way to handle things." Grabbing his hand, I lead us to the bedroom. It's the closest place to sit down, and I still need to wrap my head around the past few minutes. "I don't see how I can take off, though. Today was hella insane and I don't see it getting any better the closer we get to Christmas. Everyone wants somewhere warm to eat while taking a break from shopping."

Spencer pulls me into him once again, knocking us both off balance. We're laying on my side of the bed and his arm is wrapped around my waist. "Dennis has run that restaurant for years without you, he'll manage just fine. You need the break. Being manager doesn't mean you have to spend every waking second there."

Now that I think about it, I don't remember the last time I had a day off. I know it's not healthy, but I have to make sure everything is running smoothly. I can't do that if I'm not physically there. He's right, though. I do need a break. "You have a point." I nod toward the suitcase sitting by the door. "I'm assuming you packed for me."

"Yeah," he sighs. "I planned on being at the door with flowers before you got home, but you left earlier than I expected."

"It was a crappy day. We were slammed. I had to wait tables." I tap his stomach with each point I'm making. "And, I fell face first on the floor."

"That's what you should have led with." Spencer runs his fingertips along my arm, causing goosebumps to form. "Are you okay?"

"Mhmm. I was embarrassed, but nothing major." The idea of getting away for a few days is way more appealing than thinking about all the annoying shoppers we've dealt with the past few days. I cuddle into Spencer. "So, where are we going?"

"That will remain a surprise." He lifts up and turns until he is hovering over me. "For now, I think I need to make sure you didn't injure yourself with that fall."

"I like that idea." Though I'm not happy about the location of our vacation being unknown.

Chapter Two

Spencer

Telling Tiff, we were going on a vacation was a mistake. Dennis was right. I should have had the car loaded and whisked her away without any sort of explanation. She has asked me where we're going at least a thousand times.

"Soooo, when are you gonna tell me where we're going?" And that makes one thousand one times. She's loading her suitcase in the trunk of the car. She of course had to make some adjustments to what I packed and it hits the bottom with a loud thud. I swear she added enough clothes and hair products to last her a month. We're literally only going to be gone three days.

"Not until we get there." I wanted to go last night, hoping she would sleep a majority of the way and really be surprised. But that did not happen. She was exhausted from being on her feet all day and then her short burst of emotional turmoil, regardless of how inaccurate it was, I thought it best we wait until bright and early this morning. With the trunk now closed and both of us in our respective seats, it's time to start our adventure.

The sun is barely peaking over the horizon when I pull out of the parking garage. The oranges and yellows picturesque even though they don't seem to fit in with the frigid air. They are colors you'd expect in summer or late fall. Tiffany is staring at the sunrise as if it's the most beautiful thing she's ever seen. She pulls out her phone and snaps a quick picture. Her awe of the world around her is one of the things I'll forever love about this woman. She makes me want to look at our surroundings through her lens.

"You should be driving and not staring at me."

"I'm not—"

"You are. I can feel you." She pulls on her seatbelt making sure it's secured around her body. "Also, that's how people get in wrecks."

"By looking at their hot as hell girlfriends?" Needling her is more fun than it should be, but it takes a lot to really piss her off.

"Exactly by doing that. Now, turn your face toward the road and drive." She grabs a pen and crossword puzzle book out of her bag and opens it up to the next puzzle. "Unless, of course, you want me to tell me where this mysterious getaway is, and I'll handle the driving."

"Absolutely, not." I shake my head and shift my focus to the road in front of me. "Don't worry your pretty head about where we're going."

"As long as it includes a coffee shop and breakfast, then I'll do exactly that." She pauses for a moment, tapping her pen on her book. "But seriously, I need caffeine. I'm not sure how I'm supposed to function this early without it."

She can't. It's something I've learned about her since we started dating all that time ago. She doesn't do mornings, and if she's forced to, she needs a pick me up. Her cousins are the exact same way, and I can't help but wonder how young they were when they were introduced to coffee. If I had to guess it was all Stella's doing.

All I know is I need to get her fed and caffeinated or it's going to be a long drive. I'd like to get to enjoy most of today at the cabin instead of being stuck on the road.

⌁

"Spencer?" Tiffany sounds like she's just woken up, but I know for a fact she hasn't gotten to sleep. "We're getting close to the gas station with the good bathrooms. Any chance we can stop?"

Damn. We've barely been on the road, but I'm not an asshole. "Yeah, we can stop. But in and out. No shopping for knickknacks."

"Fine," she rolls her eyes. "I guess I'll be a good girl. I really do need to pee though. I one hundred percent blame the coffee I guzzled down."

The laugh comes out with zero apologies. "Please tell me I can call Stella and tell her."

"Why would you do that?" I'm not sure why she's so confused about it.

"Because you and Audrey are always giving her crap about having to stop and go to the restroom," I wink at Tiff, "and look who needs to make a potty stop now when we've barely made it an hour on the road."

"If you even think about calling her, I will murder you in your sleep." She crosses her arms over her chest. "This is the one thing I can lord over my cousin and I will do it until the day I die," pointing out the window she adds, "you're about to miss the exit."

Shit. I don't miss the smirk she sends me. As if she just got a one up on me. It's her fault I can't pay attention. She's so damn feisty. It's hard not to interact. Especially when she's really pulled me out of my shell since I moved in with her. I was the quiet guy and didn't have many friends, but now I can give as good as I get.

Luckily, there isn't anyone in the lane beside me as I rush over to take the exit. It's a pain in the ass trying to go to the next exit and backtrack. I would do it in a heartbeat, though. Nice bathrooms are a requirement for her. She mentioned something about stopping at a sketchy gas station with her family as a kid and she made Audrey go in the bathroom with her. She described it as somewhere scary movies begin. I can't really blame her for being picky.

No matter what time of day you come, it's going to be busy. It's worth it. I find a spot close to the doors and put the car in park. Before Tiffany can get out of the car, I grab her arm. "No shopping. In and out."

"I know, Spence." She reaches for the handle. "Can I go pee now?"

"Smart ass." Both of us get out of the car and I lock it. It feels like the temperature has dropped a good ten degrees since we left this morning. I don't remember seeing anything about a cold front, but we rarely watch the news, or weather. We rush inside the store, and the warmth is what we needed after that frigid blast of air. I look at her. "Meet me back here in ten minutes."

"You got it, Boss." She rushes toward the bathroom. I feel like a dick for driving it home so much, but she has squirrel moments and next thing you know we're in this place for hours. I speak from personal experience. When her cousins are with her, all bets are off.

I just want to get to our location. I may have some ulterior motives with our surprise getaway. But I'll never get to reveal them until we get there. First stop for me is another cup of coffee. I feel like I've been going nonstop and the only thing that will keep me going is caffeine. There are a few other things I need to grab for snacks along the way. It's really not that far of a drive. It's actually not a huge distance from Stella and Johnny, but Tiff doesn't need to know that. Some of the snacks we love can only be found here. So, I need to stock up.

As the time to meet back at the register closes, I head that way. Tiffany is already waiting on me. "Jesus Christ." I can't help it. It's the only thing that comes out of my mouth. She has one of the small shopping carts full of things. "Did you grab one of everything the store sells?"

She shrugs and motions for me to add my stuff the cart. "You won't tell me where we're going and I wanted to make sure I'm prepared. Besides, you can never have too many sweets."

"If you say so." There's no use arguing with her. She's going to do what she wants. I watch as she places item after item on the counter. From barbecue sandwiches to fruits and veggies to fudge. She definitely has the all the bases covered. I don't miss the flannel blanket she had hidden underneath everything. I should have known she couldn't resist getting something that wasn't food.

I can hear the people behind us groaning at the amount of stuff we're checking out, but I don't care. As long as my girl is happy, they can wait. Or, go to another line. Tiffany reaches for her card to pay, but I slide mine into the slot before she has a chance. This weekend was my idea, and I'm taking care of all of it. Even if she did get all the food she could manage.

With bags in hand, we rush back to the car. It's definitely getting colder. I hope it stops where it's at because neither one of us are very good at handling the cold. Tiff proved that when the temperature dropped at Stella's wedding. She made sure everyone had blankets to keep warm. I was the lucky guy that had to go pick them up from the store.

I press unlock before we're close to the car and start the car with the key fob. It won't be super warm but at least it won't feel like it does out here. I grab the bags from Tiffany so she can get in the car quickly. After putting everything in the backseat, I slide into the driver side, turn the heat up as high as it will go, and back out of the parking spot. Maybe now we can get this adventure underway without any more hiccups.

Chapter Three

Tiffany

"Are we there, yet?" I know I sound like a petulant child, but I'm so tired of being in this car. And…of not knowing where we're going. It's driving me crazy. I've never been good with secrets. Well, except about what went down between Audrey and Justin in high school. Other than that, I suck at keeping them. Surprise parties are also a no go with me. I sniff them out before they are done planning. It used to annoy the hell out of Audrey and Stella. They quickly gave up on trying to throw them.

"Not quite." He turns the radio up to hear the DJ. "What did he just say about the weather?"

I get out of my own head and long enough to hear them. "Everyone should get what they need and hunker down for the next few days. We're having an unexpected cold front. Well, colder than usual. We're going to get a lot of snow and ice on the roads."

"That sounds ominous," I joke from the passenger seat. They always say there's going to be bad weather. We all freak out and then nothing happens.

"Do you think we should turn around and go back?" Spencer tightens his grip on the wheel. "I mean we still have almost 2 hours to go and we really aren't that far from home when you think about it."

I laugh. "Of course, we aren't going back home. We already made it this far. Besides how bad can it actually get?" I look outside the window to see if there any snowflakes falling from the sky. There are none, big surprise. "They always do this. Over-exaggerate about how bad it's going to be, and then we are left looking like idiots."

"Are you sure?" I don't miss the nervous glance he sends my way. He seems pretty freaked out. But, he freaks out anytime it storms honestly. Especially, when there are tornadoes. As if we could do anything to actually get out of the tornadoes path.

"I'm positive. If it comes to the worst, and were stuck inside for a few days, would that really be so bad? I mean I know we're living alone, but…this is the first time we've gone somewhere that doesn't include my cousins, or our families, and it would be nice for us to do something just for us over the next few days." Leaning over, I place a hand over his and slowly pull it away from the steering wheel, before interlacing our fingers. "Besides, where's your sense of adventure?"

His hand is clammy in mine and he chuckles nervously. "I don't know, maybe with the weather dude who said the roads were going to be covered in ice."

"And if they are, which I doubt they will be, we will stay snuggled wherever we are and find ways to amuse ourselves." I wink at him and he answers with a real smile. "I'm pretty sure we can think of a few ways."

"Oh, no doubt, me too." He gives my hand a gentle squeeze before bringing it to his lips and kissing it. "And they all involve your legs wrapped around me."

The car in front of us slams on their brakes and Spencer has just enough time to switch to another lane and avoid hitting him. I swear, anytime the word ice is even muttered, folks forget how to freaking drive. It's not like the roads have ice over them right now. "So, do you think we'll get to this mysterious place before this supposed cold front comes in?"

"As long as people don't start driving like assholes will make it there in plenty of time." That's reassuring because I am so ready to get out this car.

I know it's only been like thirty minutes since I've asked if we're there yet, but I'm bored out of my mind and ready to be wherever it is we're going. Also, I really need to go to the bathroom again. All the snacks probably wasn't my best idea. I open my mouth to ask once again, but the sign we're passing makes me form another question. "Hey, isn't that the exit we take to go to Stella and Johnny's house?"

"Yes, yes, it is." He looks around as if he might see Johnny or Stella's car as we zoom along on the highway. "Johnny is actually the person who told me about this place I booked for our little getaway."

"And they know nothing about it?" Stella is pretty good at keeping secrets.

Although, she has a habit of letting little hints slip here and there. This is one of these things she definitely would have hinted at.

"No. They don't." He shoots me a satisfied grin. "I knew if I told Johnny, he would tell Stella, and then you would have figured it out. And, I could not let that happen."

"Well, why not? We always meet up with them when we are in the area."

"Because, Tiffany, I want these next few days to be special. I think we both deserve it after the amount of work we both have been doing, and all the preparations we had to do for the wedding." This must be a sore subject for him. He's not usually this defensive, and I'm kind of wondering if he's hiding something. Nothing nefarious, just something.

"Okay, I get that. But…could we maybe see them before we go home?"

He turns on his blinker to take next exit. "For sure. That was one thing I did already plan for because I know you can't go without seeing your best friend when we are this close."

"Yay," I clap. "You, my adorable boyfriend, are the best."

"I have my moments." He squeezes my hand again. "Now, I need to focus on where we turn off this main road. It's a little tricky."

Even though the heater is running on high it feels like it's getting colder. Maybe the weather guy was actually speaking some truth. But that's all this is. A cold snap. Nothing is going to ruin our getaway. Not even Mother Nature.

About ten minutes off the highway, we finally make a left. The road is tiny, barely enough room for one car. It also feels like it's never going to end. The deeper we go into the wooded area, the more unease I feel. "Um, are you sure we aren't going to some house to be slaughtered by a serial killer? This is kind of giving off those vibes."

With the tree lined road, the sun is blotted out. It's dark and creepy. Something directly out of a horror film. "Yes, I'm sure." I can practically feel him rolling his eyes since I can't see them. His complete focus on the road in front of us. "I came out here while we were in town for the wedding. It's why we were late getting here."

"Wow," I nod in surprise. "You've been planning this for a while."

"Well, some of it, yes. But I didn't know the exact date until well, Dennis called me and said I needed to force you to get away. He was tired of seeing you at the restaurant."

Well, that's great. Both of them were conspiring against me. Maybe it's a sign that I have been working too much. That I haven't been giving Spencer the attention and time that he needs. Gah, have I really become that person that puts work over everything else? Look who ended up being more like Stella than anyone thought. I'll never admit it, though.

"Well, geez, tell me how y'all really feel." It's halfhearted after my sudden realization. "I'll get better about not working so much. It's just hard for me to trust that other people will do the job I need them to."

"You know, y'all could hire an assistant manager to handle things when you aren't there." It's not the first time he's mentioned it. Hell, even Dennis has said it. One day I will give in. Most likely when we get back. Even though I'm not sure I'm buying this whole I need a break story. It seems a little to clean. And I do, in fact, need one. It'll be good to rejuvenate the soul.

"Yeah, I kn—." The sentence dies on my lips because we are finally at our mysterious location. It's definitely in the middle of nowhere and absolutely breathtaking.

Chapter Four

Spencer

THE LOOK on Tiffany's face is one hundred percent worth the trip. But this is only the tip of the iceberg. I have so much more planned. Even if this cold weather is actually happening. Nothing will deter me from my objective.

"Do you like it?" Her reaction says she does, but I need to make sure. There aren't any houses around us for miles. I honestly didn't think places like this existed with the amount of development happening all over the state. It's a two-story log cabin with an almost wrap around porch. If it weren't for the satellite dish attached to the side, you'd think you stepped into an old book or tv show.

"It's amazing, Spence." She opens her door and begins to step out, but quickly pulls her foot back in. "Maybe I'll wait until we're parked next to the house. If it's possible, it's gotten even colder."

With that comment, I'm almost regretting the decision to not go back home. Almost. But, it's too late now, and this is something we need. "Okay, I'll park the car and make sure the house is warmed up before you come in." I keep driving forward down the driveway until I'm parked beside the front porch.

Even though I heard Tiff about the cold. I'm not prepared for it as I exit the car. A bad feeling settles in my gut. I don't think is going to be one of those times everyone looks like an idiot for freaking out about the weather. There isn't much I can do about it now. I hurry up the porch steps and look for the small rock the property managers said would be out here. I get why they use these to hide the key in, but do all the rocks have to look the same?

Finally, after picking up the fifth rock on the floral display sitting on a small table, I find it. My hands are shaky as I open it and let the key drop out. The cold makes my grip not quite as strong as normal when I pick the key up from the porch. I just hope they turned the heat on when they stocked the fridge. It's not normal for places to do this, but we were originally supposed to get here late last night and it's a service they offer for an extra fee. I took advantage of that because it would have been even harder to keep the location a secret if Tiff saw all the groceries in the car. I think she was expecting a resort experience. I went the opposite direction with a middle of nowhere vibe.

I slide the key in the lock and turn it before opening the door. Warm air greets me, and I breathe a sigh of relief. Even if we don't pay attention to what's happening with the weather, at least, it seems like the owners do. I leave the door ajar and hurry to Tiffany's side of the car. I pull the handle, opening the door, and stand in front of her to block as much of the wind as possible. "The house is warm. Go ahead and get inside. I'll get our bags."

"Are you sure?" She raises her eyebrows. "My bags are heavy as hell. It's not going to kill me to help you."

"You're practically shaking, Tiff." I reach for her hand. "I'm sure. Now go before I change my mind."

"Okay." She puts her hand in mine and allows me to help her out of the car. She places a quick kiss on my cheek and high tails it inside. I don't miss how she's favoring one leg. I think that fall yesterday may have hurt her more than she realizes. I'll look at her ankle once I'm down unloading.

Pushing the door closed, I pop the trunk and grab as many bags as I can. I don't bother trying to roll the suitcases. The uneven terrain makes it damn near impossible. Setting the bags on the porch, I turn to grab the last of them. It's just easier this way. When closing the trunk, I catch a glimpse of the five million snacks Tiffany got and her blanket. Looks like I'll have to make a third trip.

Tiffany meets me on the porch to grab some of our suitcases and carries them inside. I set what I have on the porch and get the plastic sacks out of the back seat. When I get back to the porch, she's there picking up her suitcase, struggling all the way to the door. I shift the snacks to one hand and grab the last two bags, carrying them inside.

"Your nose is bright red," Tiffany laughs as she pulls the bags of snacks off my arm. "Seriously, you could play the role of Rudolph."

"Gee, thanks." I set the bags on the floor and tap her on the nose. "I guess you haven't looked in a mirror, yet."

"I guess it's a good thing we're the only ones here and I don't have to impress anyone. Though I don't think I'd care much." She pulls out her package of gummy bears, shakes a few into her hand, and pops them in her mouth. "Now, enough talking about appearances. I want to explore the house."

~

The first thing she does is inspect the comfort level of the couch. She sits on each individual cushion until she finds the one she likes best. "I think this one will meld to my body well enough when we watch movies."

"Who said anything about watching movies?" I scratch my head in mock confusion.

"There is a giant television above the fireplace. One bigger than what we have. You can't tell me you don't want to watch some of your sci-fi shows on it." She pats her hand on the seat next to her. "Come sit, and see what you think."

I do as she asks, as if I wouldn't. She could tell me to walk after her off a cliff, and I would probably do it. She has to know just how badly I'm wrapped around her finger. "Okay, I see your point." I grab her hand. "Though we could also use this spot for something a little more intimate," I wiggle my eyebrows. "I mean it's pretty comfy no matter where you sit."

Tiff rolls her eyes and stands up. "You'll just have to wait. I'm not done exploring everything here." Instead of continuing down here, she takes the stairs two at a time. "Oh my gosh, there is an actual library up here."

When I checked the place out last time, I didn't bother going upstairs. The master bedroom is down here, and I didn't see a reason. But now, I might just venture up there. I take my time going up the steps, but come to a stop when I reach the landing. From downstairs it looks like it could be a game room, with a room off to the side. Mostly because the shelves aren't visible. It definitely makes for a nice surprise when you come up, though.

There's a lounge chair sitting in the middle of the room, and one of those chairs that look like a half moon off to the side. The shelves are stained a dark brown to match the walls of the house. Each bookshelf is floor to ceiling on the three walls. I imagine this is what everyone dreams of when they say they want a library. Reading physical books hasn't been at the top of my to-do list in quite some time. When I'm designing, I usually listen to a podcast or audiobook, and I'm kicking myself for that. I used to love the feel of flipping pages in a book. Though, I don't think I've ever seen Tiffany read. She must do it on her phone if she's this excited about it.

"This is impressive." I mutter into the quiet awe. I walk around the space, inspecting the titles. The owners of this house definitely didn't stick to one genre, either. There are romance novels, science fiction, fantasy, and books for teenagers. There are a few non-fictions and biographies, but if I'm looking for entertainment, I prefer to go into fantastical worlds. "Everything is so varied."

"It's pretty amazing," Tiff sighs. "Stella's friend Tonya would die if she knew this house had all these books. They do a monthly book club at the local coffee shop."

"That's actually cool." I run my fingers along the book spines until I'm standing by her side. "Who knows, maybe you can build a library like this one day."

"Eh, I prefer reading on my phone. It's portable and I can sneak in a few paragraphs when we're slow at work."

Well, that doesn't mean I can't get her an e-reader so she has something bigger to read on at home. I think I know what one of my Christmas gifts to her will be. I'll have to order later tonight when she's not looking to make sure it gets here on time. "I think that's a spare room," I point toward the door.

"I didn't even see it when I saw the books." She tugs on my arm and pulls me back toward the staircase. "I want to see what else is downstairs." I follow after her like the love-sick puppy I am.

Chapter Five

Tiffany

THIS PLACE IS like nothing I ever imagined. And, I don't think I've ever stayed in a log cabin. From the outside it looks like something you'd see in books, or even those beautiful shots you see on those home improvement shows. My cousins and I always talked about how we'd love to have log cabins like that, but it's not something you'd see in the city. At the time, none of us were looking to move out of Austin. But with Stella out here, I don't see why she couldn't own one. Although, there's no way in hell I'd give up the house she has right now. It's the epitome of small-town houses.

"Are we allowed to light the fireplace?" Not right now, but later after I'm done looking around the house.

"Yep. Just tell me when," Spencer says from behind me.

I let go of his arm, and make a left toward the only closed door down here. It has to be the master bedroom. I throw the door open and gasp. The bed is massive. It has to be a California king. It's framed by four tall wood posts. But, they aren't solid blocks. They look like pieces of branches that have been sanded down. It's totally not my style, but that doesn't take away from the beauty.

The back wall is floor to ceiling windows with a view of the wilderness beyond the house. The only thing that would make the view better is if there were mountains. Too bad this area of Texas is nothing but small hill and flat lands below that. "Are there any neighbors around here?" Because we're totally leaving those curtains open the entire time we are here.

"Not for miles," he grins. His mind must have gone exactly where mine did. We don't get this kind of freedom at home. If we left our curtains open, there would no doubt be a peeping tom in one of the buildings across the street.

"Good."

There's a sliding door on the wall next to the windows, and I push it open. The first thing I do is rush over to the bathtub sitting in the middle of the bathroom. It's huge and will fit both of us easily. The outside may look like it belongs in a different time, but whoever owns this house did a fantastic job decorating the inside. "Even though, we're way out in the middle of nowhere, this tub is one hundred percent worth it."

"I'm glad you approve." There's another area where I'm sure a shower is, but I don't care about that nearly as much as I do this. "If you want to go put the snacks away and look in the fridge for what you want for dinner tonight, I'll get a nice warm bath started for you. You deserve it after the craziness of yesterday."

This is why I love this man. "That would be amazing." I turn to walk out of the room. "Do you need my help putting the suitcases away?"

"No, I've got them."

I'm almost at the door when I realize what he said about dinner. "Wait. Did you come down here earlier this week without me knowing?"

"Nope. I upgraded the service and they stocked the fridge with items I requested."

I clap my hands in excitement. "A girl could get used to this." I'm not lying either. I loathe getting groceries. Even when we have it delivered, there always seems to be items missing.

He follows me out of the room and stacks the bags on top of the suitcases before wheeling them to our temporary oasis. I head straight to the kitchen. It's an open concept and you can see the rest of the living space from the counter. This would be a perfect place to rent for the holidays with our families if there were more beds.

There's a reason he's the most adult person in our relationship. The fridge truly is stocked. All of the ingredients for some of my favorite foods fill the shelves. I look through the items and settle on spaghetti. It seems like a romantic idea for the first night of our getaway. I check the drawers to see if he got the vegetables for a salad. A smile crosses my face once I find them. This man truly thinks of everything. I want to be the one who cooks dinner tonight. One, because he planned all of this without me guessing. That takes a special kind of person. Two, because spaghetti and salad are one of the few things I can actually make.

The cabinets are well stocked and it doesn't take me long to find a bowl and cutting board. While he's putting the suitcases away and starting a bath, I can get started on the salad. It won't take long and by the time I'm done, the bath tub should be ready. Then we can properly break in this house for our short stay.

I'm sliding the salad bowl into the fridge when Spencer calls me from the other room. My timing is perfect as always. It's most likely the product of working in the food industry for so long. The amount of time it takes to make certain things is something I have down to a science. I grab a paper towel and wipe my hands on it before trashing it and making my way to the room.

The room is dark. The only light coming from the darkening sky outside. Another one of the reasons I loathe winter. There aren't any music festivals and the days are so short. It makes you want to go to bed when you get home rather than do anything productive. There's also light peeking from under the sliding door, but it doesn't look bright enough to be a lightbulb.

My steps are slow and measured as I make my way to the bathroom. Pushing the door aside, my eyes widen. Candles are placed on every countertop, filling the room with a warm ethereal glow. "Spencer, this…this is beautiful."

"Not nearly as beautiful as you." He stands and takes his time getting to me. Wrapping his arms around my waist, he pulls me toward him. "I know this place probably isn't what you were expecting, but I truly wanted these next few days to be special."

I lift up on my tiptoes and put my arms around his neck. Placing a succession of quick kisses along his cheek. "It already is," another kiss, "this house is perfect. I feel like a woodland princess."

He laughs. "You're more like a warrior than a princess, but I get what you mean."

I'm not sure if I should take that as a compliment or be offended. "Or, I could be a warrior princess like Xena."

"I like the way that sounds." He takes a step backward leading me toward the tub. "Any chance I can get you to wear the outfit?"

"Just tell me when," I grin. "There isn't much I wouldn't do for you. Maybe we can go to the next convention dressed as Xena and Hercules."

He backs away from me and looks at himself. "I'm in good shape, but not quite buff enough to cosplay Hercules."

"I don't think that's the point." I reach for the bottom of his sweater and pull it over his head. "Besides, I don't need you to be muscled out." Running a finger down his chest, I place kisses along his collarbone. "You're perfect. Just. The. Way. You. Are." I kiss him with each word so he knows I mean each and every word.

He grabs the hem of my shirt and pulls it over my head before bending down to slip my boots off my feet. His hands run a path up my calves, then my thighs, until his fingers are on the waistband of my leggings. His mouth is warm against my skin as he kisses right below my belly button. I grip his shoulders as he pulls my pants down and I lift one leg then the other until the fabric is in a pile on the floor.

My bra is the only fabric covering my body, and I reach back to take it off. But Spencer is standing now, and stops me. "I want to do it. You know since I've had all this practice now. I want to see if I can take it off with one hand."

"It'll be impressive if you do. I can't even do that." My laugh is real. In all the ways he can be possessive sometimes he's such a dork. Other people would probably mock the way we make jokes when we're having sex, but I don't care. It's one of the things that makes our relationship so special. I can be silly with him in ways I've never been able to with other men.

He holds my hands down between us with one hand and the other traces the outline of my bra until he reaches the small hooks in the back. His fingers fumble to get a grip and I attempt pulling my hands away to help him, but he tightens his grip. "I can do this."

Not a single word comes out in argument. He's determined. His tongue pokes out from between his lips and I know he's concentrating as hard as he can. It's one of his quirks that amuses me way more than it should. Finally, he pinches in just the right spot and the hooks are free of their clasps. My bra straps fall down my arms and he beams at me. "Told you I could do it."

"I never had any doubt." I reach for the button of his jeans but he pushes my hands away. "Um… if I'm naked, you have to be naked, too."

"I will be, but you're going to get in the bathtub first."

"But I want to be the one to undress you." I stomp my foot to punctuate my disappointment. It's childish, I know, but dammit. I always get my way. Especially when it comes to undressing the man I love.

"You'll just have to wait for another time."

"Tease."

His chuckle is low and deep as he helps me into the bath tub. As soon as I'm settled, he reaches for the button but pauses. I swear if this man doesn't get his clothes off in the next ten seconds, I'm going to murder him. Romantic getaway be damned.

Chapter Six

Spencer

THERE'S fire in her eyes and I know she's not happy about my teasing. She does it to me all the time so it's only fair that I repay the favor. Slowly, I unbutton my jeans and slide them down, along with my underwear. She follows the movement every inch of the way down. I take my time pulling my socks and her fingers grip the edge of the tub. She's full-on glaring at me now. I better speed this up, or I'll have to face her wrath. Which, let's be honest, isn't all that bad. It's cute more than anything.

I barely have one foot in the tub, and she pulls me in the rest of the way. Water sloshes over the edge with the movement. "Someone is excited."

"No, someone is losing their patience because you decided to do a strip tease instead of hauling ass to join me." She pushes me to one side of the tub and climbs on top of me, rubbing her pussy against my cock. It has a mind of its own and twitches in response. "I mean, how often do we have access to a bath tub this big. The one at home barely fits me, and while I love shower sex, constantly standing after being on my feet all day tires me out sometimes."

Well damn. I never thought about that. "We could have less shower sex." I run my hands down her back until I'm palming her ass.

"I never said that," she pinches my nipple. She thinks she's punishing me, but it turns me on. "I'm just saying that this, right now, is a luxury for us and one we should take advantage of."

Not that I've asked, but I'm not sure many couples talk like this. At least not while having sex. Or, well, leading up to sex. To show my agreement, I lift her up until she slides over my cock and the tension, she had just moments before is gone. Her head falls to my shoulder and her hands hang over the edge of the tub. I can hear the water dripping off them as I lift her up and down over me.

Before long, her arms wrap around my neck and her hips are rolling over me. She's taken over the pace. Whether or not she wants to admit it, she likes being the person in control. Loves putting my body under her spell, until I lose it. Her movements are faster and my mouth trails along her neck until I get to her ear and kiss the spot she likes right below her lobe.

She's panting and oh so close. I am, too. Moments away from exploding, but I force myself to wait until I know she's ready. She lifts her head the tiniest fraction and I whisper, "let go." She moves quicker than before and I grab her hair pulling her lips to mine, swallowing her screams as she finds her release. I follow after her and lean my head back.

Her arms are still around me and she's leaning against my chest. I drop my hands to her waist and nuzzle into her. "Sorry I ruined what was supposed to be your relaxing bath," I mutter.

"If you apologize for that I'm going to bite you. That was exactly what I needed after being cooped up in the car most of the day." She slides off me and moves to the opposite side of the tub. "Though, I think we killed all the bubbles you had in here."

I can't help but laugh. "Sorry bubbles, I'd kill you a thousand times over. Totally worth it."

She lifts her feet and rests them on the edge of the tub. "Agreed." With a glance toward the window, she shakes her head. "I can't believe how dark it already is outside. If I didn't know any better, I'd think it's midnight."

"Do you want to get out?" I'm hoping she says yes. Not because I'm not enjoying sitting in here with her, but my fingers are getting pruny and that's never a feeling I've liked. It just feels so alien. Weird, I know, coming from someone who loves all things science fiction.

"Sure." Her stomach growls and I know why she wants to get out. "I'm getting hungry and want to get dinner started before it gets too late. I want to eat and cuddle up on the sofa with movies. Tomorrow we can explore." I know better than to get in the way of Tiffany and her food.

I stand and step out of the tub, looking for a towel. Damn, in my rush to get this all set up, I forgot to grab some. My feet slip on the cold tile floor as I hurry to the cabinet to grab a couple of towels. Her giggles are the only thing keeping me from cussing myself for forgetting. After wrapping one towel around my waist, I go back to the tub.

There's a mat for her feet, but it's soaked. I push my sweater next to it so she has something dry to step on. Once she's out I wrap the towel around her and inspect the damage we've done. It's not as bad as I thought it would be, but there's still water everywhere. "Why don't you get dressed? I'll clean this up and throw the towels in the dryer."

"Sounds good. I'll get dinner started, too." She gives me a quick kiss before rushing to the bedroom. "Don't be too long," she calls behind her.

It takes four towels to mop up the water. I'm freezing because of course; I haven't gotten dressed yet. I didn't want to put on clothes only to get drenched in the cleanup process. With the towels piled up by the bathroom door, I pull out my pajamas from the suitcase. I brought them in here, but I didn't unpack anything. My mind was on other things.

Tiffany's clothes are all over the bed, and I roll my eyes. Even when traveling she has the same habits. I scoop them up and deposit them in her suitcase so we have a place to sleep tonight. Otherwise, we'll have to do it later, and I don't want to mess with it. It's a good thing I love this super messy woman.

With my pajama pants and sweatshirt on, I grab the towels from the bathroom and head in Tiffany's direction. I have to cut through the kitchen to get to the small laundry room on the side. Rosemary and basil scents fill the room. It's one of my favorite parts of Italian food. Not only does it taste great, it smells amazing.

Tiffany is at the stove stirring the sauce as I pass by to the laundry room. I throw the towels in the dryer and start it. Hopefully it doesn't take more than one cycle to dry them. The last thing we need is for them to smell sour if we forget about them. Which both of us have done a time or two in the laundry room at the apartment. We set it in there and go eat only to come back hours later. I'll be happy when we can move into a place that has a washer and dryer in the actual space.

"How's dinner coming along?" I stand behind Tiff and wrap my arms around her.

"It's almost done." She smacks my hand when I try to taste the sauce. "Can you make yourself useful and put the garlic bread in the oven? The rest of the food should be ready by the time it's done."

"Sure thing." I move from behind her and grab the pan with the bread, putting it in the oven. This kitchen set up is pretty cool since the oven isn't attached to the stove. It makes it impossible for one cook to get in the way of another. "Where do you want me to set the table?"

There's a big family style table off to the side surrounded by windows. Or, there are barstools set up at the end of this counter. I just need her to direct me. "Actually, I was thinking we could eat in the living room. Maybe watch a movie?"

"Sounds good to me." I search the drawers and cabinets for silverware and plates. I leave the plates on the counter, but take the silverware, some napkins and some wine glasses to the coffee table in front of the couch. The remote is on a side table and I grab it to see what's playing right now on TV. "Oh, hey, The Walking Dead is on. Want to watch that?"

I turn to see her reaction. From the way her face is screwed up, that's a definite no. "I'd rather not. It's gross to watch while we're eating. And, no offense, but I don't exactly want to watch a zombie show when we're in the middle of nowhere. It ratchets up the creepy vibe."

She has a point. "So, what are you in the mood for?"

"Anything that doesn't have death and gore is good with me."

The oven beeps and I hear the door open as she takes out the bread. I'm still scrolling for something that will keep both of our attention. It's close to Christmas so I settle on one of those warm-hearted romance movies. Not exactly what I love, but I know she watches them with her cousins. "Want me to start a fire."

"That would be awesome."

I get to work on getting the fire lit, and by the time I'm done she's setting our plates on the coffee table and a bottle of wine by the glasses. "I could have gotten my own plate."

"Shut up," she laughs, "it's not like I wasn't coming this way." She's not wrong. But I hate that she feels like she has to wait on me after doing it for others when she's at work.

"Let's eat. I know you're starving."

"Yep." She sits down on the floor and leans against the couch. After take a bite, she points the fork toward the TV. "Thanks for choosing something tamer than zombies."

"It's not like I can't watch it whenever I want."

I sit on the floor next to her and we make quick work of dinner. Apparently, I was hungry, too. I've been so focused on making sure everything is perfect that I haven't eaten much all day.

Once we're done, I take the dishes to the sink and pull her up on the couch with me. She lays down in front of me with her eyes focused on the TV. "This weekend is going to be amazing."

"I hope so." I mutter into her hair. We both fall asleep to young couples falling in love over the holidays in their hometown.

Chapter Seven

ONE MINUTE I'm sleeping and the next I'm hitting the floor. "Ugh," I groan. I glance through my hair and see that I've rolled right off the damn sofa. Whose bright idea was it to fall asleep in here? Never again. "Why is it so bright in here?"

Using the sofa and coffee table to help me, I sit up to make sure I didn't spill the bottle of wine during sleep. Thank God it's on the other side of the table. Spencer is snoring, and I can't believe he's sleeping through my falling to the ground. I had to have made some kind of noise. I swear, this fool wouldn't wake up if there was a siren going off beside his ear.

Right now, though. I need to close the blinds because there is way too much light coming through. Groggily, I stand and make my way to the windows by the kitchen table, and my eyes widen. "Holy shit," I yell.

"What? What's happened?" Spencer sits pops up from sleeping like a vampire coming out of their coffin for the night. And of course, my shriek is what wakes him up. Not me falling to the floor right freaking beside him.

"There's snow." The last word is high pitched, and I don't mean for it to be, but we actually got snow. It almost never happens despite what the weather people say.

"Really?" He gets up and makes his way toward me, rubbing sleep from his eyes the entire time. "That's not just a little bit of snow. That's a lot."

"Yeah, it is," I clap my hands in glee. "Please tell me we're going to go play in it. Maybe build a snowman?"

"I don't know," he scratches his head, "neither one of us brought anything to wear for this type of weather." Oh no. He is not bursting my bubble. I open my mouth, but he puts his hand over it. "If you start singing that song from Frozen, I'm going to force you out there in what you're wearing now."

I glance down at my thin long-sleeved shirt and pants. Yeah, that's not happening. "If you come play in the snow, I won't sing it."

He shakes his head, but I can see the tiny grin he's trying to hide. "Fine. But let's go layer up. I also need to make sure there's detergent so we can wash our snow drenched clothes when we're done."

I don't give him a chance to argue. I rush to the room while he checks the laundry room. It takes me less than five minutes to put on multiple layers of clothes, including the fleece onesie I packed. I guess it's a good thing I added more clothes to my suitcase than what Spencer originally put in there. This is working out to my benefit.

Not bothering to wait, I go outside and figure he'll join me as soon as he's ready. It's so cold I gasp for breath. I didn't realize how much the temperature dropped last night. Which, duh, of course it did if we have snow, this morning. But I don't care. Snow days were my favorite as a child even though we barely got an inch. This is way more than that, and I can't wait to make my snowman and send a picture to Audrey and Stella.

What in the world is taking Spencer so long? I know he's not a big fan of outside in general, but come on. It is. Snow. In. December. How often does that actually happen in Texas?

The little angel on one shoulder tells me I should just wait until he comes out here before I go play in the white wonderland surrounding the house. But the devil…she is telling me to hide and get snowballs prepared. Decisions, decisions. It takes me a whole two seconds to decide I'm definitely going with the devil.

I walk as fast as I can down the porch steps without falling, an accomplishment in itself since it's slippery as hell, and hide on the other side of the car. It's a good thing we're on a hill because most of the snow has fallen down here, and it's pretty deep. Enough for my boots to sink to my ankles, and it's still coming down. My sock covered hands are freezing as I roll the snow into tiny balls and set them next to me. The key is easy access. I'd set them on the car, but that would be too obvious. At least it will be if he's paying attention.

There is a pile of about fifteen snowballs when I finally hear the front door open. "Tiffany? Where are you?"

I just need him to take a couple of steps outside the door and I can launch my attack. Too bad he doesn't seem to get the message because he's still standing with his whole body inside the house. I peek over the top of the trunk, and his eyes widened in surprise. "There you are. What are you doing over there?" Damn this bright red hair of mine. I feel like if it was a lighter color, I could've been a bit stealthier here. That's what I like to think anyway. Sneaky is definitely not how I roll most of the time.

"Oh, nothing." Hopefully he doesn't hear the mischief in my voice. The door closes with a thud, and snow crunches under his footsteps across the porch. I scoop up a handful of snowballs and prepare myself for when he gets closer. I mean, I could throw them now, but there's a good chance I wouldn't hit him. My aim isn't all that great. The few times we've gone to play paintball, I lose because I can't hit the broad side of a barn.

It feels like it's taking an eternity for him to make his way across the port. But, his footsteps sound considerably closer now. Counting to three, I pop up from where I'm crouching and launch one, two, three, four snowballs at him. The first two miss, but the third one hits in square in the chest. The fourth one gets him in the shoulder.

"What the hell?" This is the great part about him being so trusting, he never sees my devious ways coming. His mouth is wide open, and he's staring at me like I just took his favorite toy.

I wish I had my phone with me, I would totally take a picture of the face he's making. He is legit surprised that I actually threw snowballs at him. I mean, at this point, he shouldn't be. This is one hundred percent on brand for me. "You were taking too long."

"So, you throw snow at me?" I can't tell if he's really upset or still in shock that I did it.

"You can't tell me you've never had a snowball fight," I roll my eyes and bend down to pick up a few more.

He holds his hand out as if that will stop me. "Not that I can recall. It's not like we get a ton of snow in Austin. You should know that."

He has a point. But gah, what a boring childhood. Aside from the few times we had snow back home, we would always play in it when we'd go on our family ski trips. I take a few steps around the car, closing in on my prey. "Yeah, but it's like a rite of passage."

"Don't you throw another snowball at me." One hand is still up, but he bends to gather a fistful of snow in his other hand. He tries to roll it into a ball as I advance. "Tiffany, this isn't fair. I wasn't prepared."

"Eh, life's a bitch, sweetheart." I pelt him with two balls before he has a chance to stand up. "I'm pretty sure those people you play against in video games feel the same way when you sneak attack them."

"Totally different scenario." He responds. Instead of standing, he barrels toward me and tackles me to the ground. It's a good thing its actual snow covering the ground and not ice. Otherwise, that would hurt. "How did you like that attack?"

I wrap my arms around his neck, laughing. "Not so bad, Spence. Who knew you had it in you to actually tackle me?"

"Sometimes you have to play dirty." He leans over me and kisses the tip of my nose. "So, what all exactly do we do in the snow?" All I can do is raise my eyebrows. This poor sheltered kid. He knows all the things about movies, books, and conventions, but nothing when it comes to playing outside. "I mean, is it pretty much what you see in the movies?"

"Yep." I roll until I'm hovering over him. "Except it's more fun because you have me as your guide." Standing up, I put my hand out to help him up. "We need to see if they have trash can lids or something."

"For what?" He uses my leverage to stand.

"To sled down this amazing hill."

"Oh no," he waves his hands in my direction. "I've seen Christmas Vacation. It didn't end so well for him."

"Quit being a baby," I grab his hand and pull him behind me. "That's a movie and severely over-exaggerated. This hill isn't even that steep."

"What if I choose life?" He tries to pull his hand out of mine, but I tighten my grip.

"You're going to live." I stop and turn to face him. "I'll wait at the bottom of the hill for you if that will make you feel better."

"Not really," he sighs. I can see when he decides he's going to do it. "But, I guess I'll try it."

"There's that adventurous side coming out."

"I think there are trash cans on the side of the house. I'll grab them and meet you at the top."

I watch him go around the house, patting his pockets as if making sure something is still in there. I really hope he didn't have his phone in his pocket. That wouldn't be good if it broke.

Part of me worries that I'm pushing him too hard. That he secretly hates that I want him to try new things. Life isn't worth living if you don't live it to the fullest, though.

Chapter Eight

Spencer

THIS IS SUCH A BAD IDEA. Why do I let this woman talk me into these things? Sure, the hill doesn't look so bad at first, but when you're sitting on a fucking trash can lid about to slide down it. It's terrifying. There's a reason I don't ride rollercoasters and this is it. I don't like not having control over what's about to happen. And let's face it. This could go horribly wrong. Especially when there's no way I'd be able to get the car up this hill with the amount of snow that's accumulated.

Tiffany is already at the bottom of the hill. She went first so she could show me how to do it. Where to place my hands and how to balance my weight. Honestly, I think I'd feel safer if we were using an actual sled, but I don't think people in Texas actually have those. There's no need when we only get snow like this once every decade or so.

She cups her hands over her mouth and yells into the falling snow, "You ready?"

Nope. Not in the slightest. There's no way I'm going to let her know how terrified I am. At least, not more than I already have. "Sure." There. That didn't sound too wobbly, right?

"Come on," she screams, "after this we can build a snowman then go inside for hot chocolate. I promise I won't make you do anything else death defying."

Yeah, because those last two words make me feel any better about this. I crisscross my legs on the lid, and grip one hand to the side. Inhale. Exhale.

Inhale. Exhale. I can do this. I push off the ground with my free hand and then grip the other side of the lid like my life depends on it.

I'm speeding down the hill. The wind is blowing snowflakes into my face and it's hard to keep my eyes open. Bad idea. Bad idea. It's the only thing on repeat as I race to the bottom. Oh shit, I'm going to hit the car. Tiffany forgot to tell me how to stop. I'm going too fast and if I don't do something now, I'm going to crash, face first, into the trunk. I do what's probably the least logical thing and let go of the lid, throwing my body to the side.

The trash can lid flies up with the force of me moving. I have no idea where it goes, but I hit the ground hard. Snow hitting me in the face, and I know I'll be feeling this later. Rolling over, I check my surroundings and all my limbs making sure everything is where it's supposed to be. The lid is about ten feet away from me in the opposite direction. At this point, I should be happy it didn't hit the back windshield of the car. Or take out one of the windows on the house.

Tiffany isn't where I expected her to be. Which is by my side making sure I'm alright. No. She's still in the same exact spot, bent over her knees. Laughing. What the actual hell? Finally, she stands upright and makes her way to me. "What happened?"

"I was heading straight for the car." I point toward the thing in question so she knows how freaked out I am. "What else was I supposed to do?"

She plops down in the snow next to me. "Oh, I don't know. Lean your body to the side to change directions."

"But you didn't tell me that." I shake my head. "How was I supposed to know?"

"I figured you knew. I mean it's not too different from skiing, and you did that when we went to the resort last year." She slides her hand into mine and squeezes.

"And if you recall," I bump her shoulder, "I sucked at that too. I couldn't even make it down the slope little kids ski on."

"True." She leans her head on my shoulder. "Maybe we should stick with less exhilarating tasks from now on."

"Finally, we agree on something." I stand up and pull her up with me. "Want to go build that snowman now?" I've got to do something that makes me feel like less of a failure.

Tiffany tilts her head one direction. Then the other. "Is he leaning?" It's a two-foot snowman so it's entirely possible.

"Probably." My hands are frozen and I'm just ready to go inside. I pat my pocket again to make sure the box is still there. I slipped it in when I was layering up to come outside, but one thing after another keeps happening and I don't think I'll be able to find the right moment while we're outside. Even if it's the perfect backdrop.

She glances at the pocket I reached for moments ago. "Oh well. We'll just have a crooked snowman. Do you have your phone so you can take a picture? Mine's inside, and once I go in, I'm not coming out for a while."

Thank God for that. I'll be happy if we stay inside the rest of the time we're here. But Tiff embraces her inner child every chance she gets, and I'm trying to do the same. So, if she wants to come back out later, I'll follow. "Um yeah." At least the phone is in the same pocket. She must have been watching my actions, and I don't want her guessing the purpose of this vacation. Pulling the phone out, I hand it to her. "Snap away."

After snapping a few pictures, she hands the phone back to me, and starts toward the porch. "Hold on," I reach for her hand. "We have to get a picture with the little guy. It'll mark our first snowy vacation."

"But we had snow at the resort last year," she scrunches her eyebrows in confusion.

"Yeah, but this is unexpected snow, and it's only us here." I pull her toward the snowman, and we sit on either side of it. "It definitely needs to be memorialized."

She smiles up at phone while I take a few selfies. "You better be happy I didn't have my phone when we were sledding down the hill. That is something we should have on record."

"Nope," I shake my head. "It's really not." Talk about mortifying. I can only imagine what her cousins would say. Hell, Johnny and Justin would give me shit for years if they saw me in action. There was absolutely nothing fun about that ride from hell.

"Fine," she giggles. She stands and waits for me to join her. "We should definitely get inside and warm up. I think I lost feeling in my toes."

"I haven't been able to feel my face for a while."

We walk hand in hand to the house. I open the door and let her go inside before I do. Loathe as I am to admit it, despite almost dying on the make shift sled, I did have fun this morning. More than I ever recall having as a kid. Maybe there is something to having adventures with Tiffany. I'm just hoping she'll allow me to have them with her for the rest of our lives.

Tiffany heads to the kitchen and pulls out a pan, filling it with water before setting it on the stove. Once she has the fire going underneath, she goes straight to the room. I follow behind her and she's digging though the clothes in her suitcase. "There they are." She exclaims when she finds yet another pair of pajamas. These are a heavy fleece and she grabs a pair of fuzzy socks before stripping out of the layers she has on.

I pull off my layers and shockingly only the first few are wet. The more I take off, the dryer my clothes are. But they still carry the bite of cold out from outside. I grab my flannel pants and a long sleeve shirt. Rummaging around in my suitcase, I search for another pair of socks, but I think I put them all on to go outside. A ball of pink flies at me. "Here."

"Will these even fit me?"

"They should," she shrugs. "At least, until your feet warm up." She walks by me, stopping to wrap her arms around me. Her fingers are freezing, but I don't move her away. "Thank you."

"For what?"

"For enduring what must be torture for you." Her mouth meets my bare chest and I know of a way we can warm up much faster. Another kiss and she leans back. "I'm going to see if the water is boiling yet. Hot chocolate sounds pretty great right now. And, I'm hungry since we went straight outside." She starts for the door. "Any chance you got bacon when you had them stock this place?"

"As if I could forget." She loves bacon.

"Awesome. Can you start another fire? My body is frigid and I want nothing more than to park my butt in front of it to warm up."

"Yep. Let me get dressed and get our laundry in the dryer then I'll start the fire."

"Thank you." With that she bounces out of the room.

And now I feel like an ass for making a big deal out of nothing when we were outside. And Tiffany's cousins call her dramatic. I think I win on that front today. Tiffany amazes me with how patient she is with me. I didn't have a lot of the experiences she did, and sometimes I freak out with what she throws at me.

I'm going to do my best to make the rest of the trip as complaint free as possible. Especially if I want her to answer a specific question.

Chapter Nine

Tiffany

SPENCER IS LIGHTING the fire and I'm working on the bacon. At least I'm wearing long sleeves. Whatever bacon they bought is popping grease like nobody's business. I can't imagine what it would be like if I was wearing anything but this. Even my legs and feet are protected in warm, comfy clothes.

I pause from bacon flipping to start a batch of fried eggs and put the biscuits in the oven. We'll see how multi-tasking works for me. I mean, the cooks at work do it all the time. How hard can it be? I crack one egg in the pan and wait for that side to cook. Spencer usually handles cooking the eggs so I hope he likes over-medium. It's the only way I know how to cook eggs. "How many do you want?"

"How many what?" He's still trying to get the fire lit. Last night the logs were already in place when we got here and he didn't have to worry about setting it up. Now, though…it looks like the firewood is getting the best of him. I would help, but that's not my area of expertise. Audrey always got our fire pit going when we were younger after I almost set the yard on fire. Our parents decided it just wasn't something I should be concerning myself with. Now, I wish she would have taught me. If we were ever trapped in the wilderness, I'd never survive.

"Eggs." I flip the one in the pan over.

"Three would be great." He glances up at me with a wide grin. "I worked up an appetite during my near-death experience sledding."

I roll my eyes. "It wasn't that bad." My goal before the snow goes away is to get him back out there and video the entire thing.

"If you say so." Finally, the wood in the fireplace catches fire and he high fives himself on a job well done. "Is something burning?"

"Shit," I screech. Apparently, it's really hard for me to do more than one thing at a time. "I'm so sorry." I pull the burnt bacon out of the pan and toss it on a plate. Honestly, I'm jealous of people that can cook multiple things at once. You'd think I'd be able to do it seeing as I manage a restaurant, but alas, that is not one of my super powers. One day, though.

Before I have time to register his presence, Spencer is standing beside me. "Do you need any help?"

I take the egg out of the skillet and put it on a plate before I fuck that up, too. I want us to have some semblance of an edible breakfast. "That would be great." I point the spatula toward the skillet I just emptied, "you want to take over egg duty?"

"Sure," he shrugs. He adds another egg to the pan and I put a few more pieces of bacon in the pan I'm using. "You know, you didn't have to start this by yourself, right? I planned on cooking for you all weekend."

"I know," I sigh. "I just wanted to put in some effort since you planned this entire trip. I feel weird just lazing about."

Laughing he nudges my shoulder. "That's not the way your cousins tell it. According to them, they do everything and you show up when you feel like it."

Ugh, my cousins can be such assholes. "Well, that's their side of the story. Not mine." It's like nothing I do is ever good enough.

"Honestly, I think your cousins still see you as a kid most of the time." He reaches around me for one of the burnt pieces of bacon and takes a bite. To his credit, he doesn't even make a face. I'm not sure how he isn't, but bless him for eating it. "Believe me, I know how that feels."

He's right on that. His mom treats him like he's five most of the time. Refusing to give up her baby. I get it. Spencer is an only child. Hell, my cousins and I are only children, but we had each other. He didn't have anyone. "True, but one day they'll see all of my potential and kick themselves for not giving me the credit I deserve."

"You are absolutely right." He kisses the top of my head and continues making the eggs while I work on the bacon. It's much easier focusing on this one thing. I glance behind me to check the timer for the biscuits. There's still eight minutes left. Looks like our brunch is going to work out splendidly.

"Any chance you got orange juice and vodka?" Breakfast at this time doesn't feel right without a screwdriver.

"Orange juice, yes." A frown mars his beautiful face. "Vodka, no. Sorry."

I stick my bottom lip out and pout. "It's okay. I guess I can drink a virgin screwdriver."

"You mean just orange juice?"

"Yes, if you want to be boring about it."

His only response is a laugh. I'm glad he gets my sense of humor. My cousins would have rolled their eyes and given me crap about it. Since Stella got married, I feel my relationship with them drifting. But not in a bad way. It's different. Like we're all growing up and getting on with our lives even though we'll always be there for one another. I was so scared that I'd lose my friendship with Stella when she got hitched. If anything, I look up to her even more. She has it all. Job, spouse, and beautiful house. Maybe one day I'll have that with Spence.

Spencer plates the last egg and I take the last few pieces of bacon out of the pan. The biscuits are all that is left. The white noise of the dryer suddenly stops and the oven beeps. That's not right. It should be going for at least another two minutes. When I look back at the oven, the display is blank. "Did a breaker blow?"

I walk to the over and pull the door open. At least the biscuits are done enough to be edible. Spencer checks the dryer and punches the button repeatedly to restart it. "I don't think so, but I'll see if I can find the breaker box. It should be here in the laundry room somewhere."

He flicks the light switch up and down. Nothing happens. Oh no. That doesn't look like a good omen. "I'll go see if any of the lights in the other rooms come on."

I hit the switches in the living room…nothing. It's the same in the bathroom and bedroom. As a last resort, I walk back to the living room and try turning on the television. Son of a bitch.

When I said adventure. This isn't what I meant. Hiking through the woods, checking out the local scenery, and maybe finding a place to eat…those are the adventures I want to have. Not sitting in the cold without power.

"Do you think I should call the owners and ask them what we need to do?" Spencer looks worried and defeated at the turn of events. He shouldn't be, though. I'm the one that was like nope, this "snow weather" isn't going to be bad at all. Well, I was fucking wrong. So very wrong. We've been sitting without power for four hours.

"It might be a good idea. At least so we know that it's been reported since they do all that from phone numbers now." I only hope they answer.

Spencer searches through his recent contacts and my phone pinks with a message. Picking it up, I see the group chat with Stella and Audrey.

Audrey: Do you guys have power at your place? Ours just went out.

Stella: We lost it about five hours ago.

I debate if I should respond. I didn't tell either one of them I was out of town and totally forgot to send pictures of our snowman. Hell, I haven't even looked at my phone since we've been here. It's been a nice break from technology. A chance to completely unplug and enjoy the little moments so many of us take for granted. Except this power thing. This is not enjoyable in the least.

If I don't say anything, they'll freak out. Which means Audrey will make Justin get on the roads to come check on me. Or, they'll start blowing up Spencer's phone. And that's something we can't have right now while he tries to get in touch with the owners.

Audrey: Tiffany!!!! ARE YOU OKAY?!?

Tiffany: Yes. I'm fine. I'm actually out of town right now. We haven't had electricity for around four hours.

Instead of another text message, my phone rings and I'm on a group video call with both of my cousins. It's probably a good thing I'm not in Austin right now because if looks could kill, the frustration on Audrey's face would destroy me. "What do you mean you're not in town?"

Standing up I move across the room so I don't disturb Spencer while he's on the phone. We're both hunkered around the fire because the one thing master bedroom doesn't have is its own fireplace. "Spencer surprised me with a mini vacation. We're actually not too far from you, Stella."

"Oh, are you at the cute cabin?" She sighs, "I've been bugging Johnny to book us a weekend there, but we've been so busy with getting settled and his house ready to rent that we haven't had time."

"Stay on topic, Stella," Audrey snaps her fingers. "And y'all thought it was a good idea when they were predicting a massive snow storm?"

"That would be my fault." I raise my hand like I'm confessing something in school. "The snowy weather is never as bad as they say it's going to be. How was I supposed to know that this one actually would be?"

I take that moment to look push the curtain aside and look out the window. The snow is coming down in droves. I've never in my life seen weather like this. Even when we go skiing the weather is mild. I mean, there's still snow on the ground, but it's not blizzard like conditions. "You have really got to start watching the news little cousin."

"Eh, why would I want to? It's almost always doom and gloom."

"Because then you would be informed of stuff like this." I can see Audrey pacing back and forth in the kitchen she shares with Justin. "I've been checking social media and it looks like most of the state is losing power. Some places have started rolling blackouts."

"It'd be great if they roll those blackouts this direction," I mutter. Spencer gives me a thumbs up motion and adds more wood to the fire.

"Are y'all at least staying warm?" Stella turns and I can see the fire lit behind her.

"Yes, there's a fireplace so we've been sitting in front of it." I can't recall if Justin's house has a fireplace. "What about you Audrey?"

"We're managing. Luckily, the stove here is gas so we've got the burners lit and closed off the rest of the house with blankets. We're also layered up."

"If things get too bad, call Dennis. He has a couple of generators and I'm sure he'd lend you one."

"I will." Audrey rubs her forehead. "Just promise me you'll be as safe as possible. I can't have you frozen like a popsicle. Either one of you."

"Yes, ma'am." I mock salute her. "I'm going to go join Spencer by the fire again, if you're done yelling at me."

"I'm done."

Stella finally speaks up. "If things get too bad, call us. We have a four-wheel drive and can probably make it to you."

"Will do. Be safe. Love y'all."

"Love you, too," they say in unison and we end the call.

Spencer pats the floor beside him and motions for me to come over. "I guess we'll just have to hang tight until the state gets their shit together."

"Yep." I'm just hoping it doesn't take too long. Not just for me, but for all those that don't have access to warmth or shelter.

Chapter Ten

Spencer

JUST LIKE THAT, my special romantic getaway has turned into a frozen hellscape. At least we have a fireplace. We would have been freezing our asses off in the apartment had we stayed home.

Tiffany is lying on the floor, wrapped in three blankets we found in one of the closets, reading one of the books from the library upstairs. Her head is in my lap, hair splayed out like a halo. As cold as she must be, she looks relaxed. If anything, this trip made her take a break. Made her not worry so much about work and trying to keep herself afloat. "Are you comfortable?"

"Hmm?" She sets the book on her stomach and stretches her arms. She still hasn't been on her phone much to conserve the battery. But I've been playing games on mine and it's close to dead.

"I asked if you were comfy?"

"Oh, yeah. The only thing that would make it better is if I had a pillow." A quick glance at the decorative ones on the couch tells me all I need to know.

I gather her hair in one hand so I don't step on it when I stand. "Sit up really quick."

"What? No. You don't have to get one for me. I'm perfectly capable."

"It's fine," I laugh. "You keep being a potato. I'm going to grab the blankets and pillows off the bed and bring them in here in case the power stays off and we have to sleep in here."

"Good thinking." She sits up long enough to let me up. Grabbing her book, she rolls over, and turns herself into a human burrito. Leaning on her elbows, she continues reading. I'm not even sure what book she's reading, but I pull my phone out and snap a quick picture. I want it as a reminder that it's okay to slow down when she tries turning into a workaholic again.

Phone now in my pocket I hurry to the bedroom. It's cold without the warmth of the fire. I really hope this doesn't last longer than tomorrow. I didn't get a lot of foods we could cook over the fire. Our saving grace tonight are the snacks Tiffany loaded up on. Words cannot express how grateful I am she decided to splurge on them.

I fold the comforter and up into a tidy square and grab the blanket off the chest at the foot of the bed. Our second night here and we've yet to take advantage of this massive thing. If the power ever comes back on, I plan on rectifying that. Next, I stack the pillows on the blanket pile. These have to be more comfortable than the ones on the couch.

There's only one more thing to get before going back into the living room. I open the drawer of the nightstand and pull out the box. This may not be the most opportune time to ask her, but we're unconventional like that. Hell, our whole relationship started with a one-night stand. When the moment feels right, I'll ask her.

Shoving the box in my other pocket, I grab the pile of blankets and pillows and head out of the room. The items hit the floor with a loud plop, and I hurry to close the bedroom door. I know closing it off when the main space is so open won't do much in containing the heat, but something is better than nothing.

When I turn around Tiffany has set her book aside and is laying the blankets out into a pallet in front of the fire. Not too close. We don't want to burn the place down when we go to sleep, but it's still close enough that we feel the full force of heat from the fireplace.

She notices me watching her and pulls down the edge of the top three blankets. "You have to be freezing after going into that room. Come lay down."

That's one thing I won't argue with. Waiting until she's under the covers, I slide behind her. "I'm sorry this has turned into a shit show."

"It's not your fault, Spence. You don't control Mother Nature," she eyes me skeptically, "unless, you're hiding a super power and you did this so we'd have no distractions."

"If only I was that amazing," I chuckle, "but really, this isn't what I envisioned when I booked this place. Though it doesn't sound as if we would have fared any better at home."

"You're right. We'd be freezing our asses off and wearing every piece of clothing we have." She snuggles closer to me. "We aren't equipped for this kind of weather, and neither is our apartment."

Leaning on one elbow, I use my free hand to comb through her hair, and feel her relax into me. "You're right." I pause for a moment. "Maybe we should look into a new place soon."

"That's not a bad idea." She yawns. That's one thing I've noticed. When there's no power, you constantly feel tired. There's no way to tell what time of day it is without looking at the phone. "Maybe we can find something off the beaten path. Something like this."

"Really?" That's hard to believe. She loves the accessibility of the city.

"Yep," she nods. "Can't you feel the difference out here? There's something so peaceful about the quiet stillness. There's no traffic on the roads. Horns and sirens aren't blaring at all hours of the day. Even when I lived with my parents, the town was just big enough to be annoying at times. Out here…there's nothing. Just you, me, and the beauty of nature around us."

This is why her cousins call her a free spirit. She's finds the good in all situations and goes wherever her heart leads her. Hopefully her heart also leads to forever with me. This is my moment. The perfect time to ask her the one thing I've been wanting to for months.

"Tiff," I shake her shoulder to make sure she's awake. I don't want to disturb her if she's asleep, but I know if I don't take the leap right now, I'll never find the perfect time again.

"Yeah," she rolls over to face me.

I reach into my pocket and pull out the box. "I know this isn't the vacation I planned, or promised, but I wouldn't want to be here with anyone else but you." She opens her mouth to argue, but I don't let her.

I push the blankets off me and kneel in front of her. She follows suit, sensing there's something important I need to say. "I think I fell in love with you the first night we spent together after that concert. I knew I loved you when you came home early from that date, yelling at me for interfering in your life. And the moment you showed up at my parents' house dressed as Rogue, I knew I wanted to spend the rest of my life with you. This isn't the ideal place to ask you this. I had a hundred different scenarios planned. All of them outside, but that is clearly out of the question." I chuckle softly before taking a deep breath. Opening the box, I present it to her. "Will you cosplay with me, and go on a great many adventures with me, for the rest of our lives?"

She doesn't respond right away and I can't help but feel like I've royally fucked this up. That maybe I'm not as adventurous as she needs me to be. Or, maybe I'm too into my fantasy worlds. It takes a few seconds for me to realize tears are rolling down her cheeks. Before I have a chance to plant myself firmly to the floor, she launches herself at me.

We fall to the floor and I'm pretty sure her elbow just went into my ribs. "Of course, I'll spend my forever with you," she cries. The tears are coming down faster and if not for her reaction just now, I'd think she's breaking up with me.

"Are you sure?" Damn, that sounded desperate. But I need to make sure. I saw how freaked out she was when Stella got married, but I don't think that had anything to do with marriage itself. Although, she didn't say much about whatever she talked about with her cousin after the ceremony.

"I've never been surer of anything in my life." She leans down and presses her lips to mine before sitting up. "Even when it feels like nothing can, or will, go right, you're there to brighten my day. Do you seriously think I'd be handling this crazy ass weather as well as I have if I was with my cousins, or alone?" She doesn't let me respond and continues. "No. You are my peace and my calm. I know that no matter what, you'll always be in my corner and I can lean on you when life throws insanity at me."

"You're right, and I'll be there always. Until we're no more for this world."

She laughs, taking the box from my hand and sliding the ring on her finger before cuddling into me. "You sound like one of the guys in those fantasy movies you're always watching. But yes, it'll be us against the world."

Those words have made me the happiest man on earth. I lean up, crashing my mouth into hers. She opens her mouth the tiniest bit allowing me entrance. This really was the magical moment I've been waiting on. Everything dark and silent around us as if we're the only people in the universe.

I tilt forward until I'm able to lay her down on the bed she's made for us. Pulling away from her for the briefest moment, I slide her layers of pants off her legs before taking my own off. All I want to feel for the rest of the night is being wrapped in her embrace. Making this the night we remember for the rest of our lives.

Epilogue

Tiffany

WHY IS it so hot in here? I scoot away from Spencer's body heat and move the hair from my face. Cool metal meets my cheek and I can't help the smile that comes over my face. I'm sure I look insane, but I don't care. Lifting my hand in front of me, I admire the ring on my finger. It's not your run of the mill diamond. It's a polished amethyst stone set on a silver band. He knew exactly what I would like. One of the many reasons he's absolutely perfect for me.

Sitting up, I groan. It's odd falling asleep to utter darkness and then it being so bright when you wake up. Those curtains are blackout curtains, and there shouldn't be any light peeking through them. Wait a minute. I look up and the living room light is on. "Hell yeah," I yell as loud as possible.

Spencer jumps up from his spot beside me. Guess he wasn't sleeping quite so hard. "What is it?"

"We have power, baby." I jump up and dance around the living room. My layers of sweaters coming off with each movement until I'm in my long-sleeve shirt and underwear.

"Seriously," he looks around the room then up at the light. "Thank God. I'll never take electricity for granted again."

"You bet your sweet ass, we won't." I rush to the kitchen and pullout breakfast items. "But I was also serious when I said I want to move out of the city. Who knows…maybe I can talk Dennis into opening up another restaurant in a small town. Then Janie can run the one in Austin."

"I like the way that sounds." The good thing is, it won't affect him at all. He works from home. "I'll even help you bring the subject up with him."

"Nah," I wave his comment away. "I'm a big girl, I can handle it. Thank you, though, for the offer." He truly is the absolute best. I wasn't wrong when I said I knew he'd always be in my corner. That he even offered is why he's so amazing.

I pull a clean pot out of the cabinet and heat some water on the stove. I'm not sure if the water heater has had a chance to warm up and I need to wash the dishes from yesterday so we can cook breakfast. "Do you need some help in there?"

Taking a few seconds to think about it, I almost refuse him, but I don't want another bacon disaster like yesterday. "That would be great. You want to do the bacon today?"

"I guess," he eyes me. "But why?"

"Because," I step around the counter. "I don't have on any pants and I'm not getting grease burns all over my legs."

"Good point." He gets up and joins me in the kitchen. He grabs a dishtowel and dries the pans I've finished washing.

There's a knock at the door and we both freeze. My hands are covered in soap and Spencer is looking around the room as if that will give him some clue as to who could possibly be here. I whisper, "Do you think it's a serial killer?"

"In broad daylight? Naw," he shakes his head. "Besides even serial killers have to be happy there's power again."

"Touché." I glance at all my clothes thrown around the room. "Maybe I should put on some pants after all."

"That's probably a good idea." He sets the pan he was drying on the counter and peeks out the dining room window. Groaning, he turns to me. "Did you have to tell them where we were?"

"Tell who?" I grab the closest pair of pants and pull them up.

"Your cousins." He points toward the window. "Stella and Johnny are on the porch."

"What?" Rushing to the door, I yank it open. Yep, my eldest cousin is standing right there, hand lifted in the air to knock again. "How the hell did you get here?"

She shrugs and pushes her way past me. Johnny follows after her, and I'm staring at the both of them. "I told you Johnny had a four-wheel drive. We parked it up on the street."

"I hope nobody hits it. It's old, but that doesn't mean I'm ready to get rid of it," Johnny grumbles. He sets the bags he has on the kitchen table.

"So, you thought you'd pop in while I'm on vacation?" I should be annoyed, but honestly, I'm glad both of them are okay. It's nice to see their faces after the all the snow.

"Yep." She pops the "p". "You should have known there was a chance we were coming. I had to see for myself that you were okay, and I wasn't sure if y'all got your power back yet."

"That's what phones are for, Stella."

She shrugs. "What kind of cousin would I be if I didn't make the trip in person." Her grin is wide and she starts pulling boxes out of the bags.

"I think you've been living in a smalltown way too long. Next thing I know, I'll find you giving advice to neighbors about how to spruce up their yards."

"Oh," Johnny laughs. "She didn't tell you? She already does that." My cousin glares at her husband.

"We were just about to cook breakfast," Spencer interjects before anyone can say anything else.

"There's no need." Stella waves him off. "We brought breakfast tacos. There's a little bit of everything. Y'all come eat."

Free food? And, I didn't have to cook it? I'm not going to argue with that, I grab some plates from the cabinet and set them on the table. "Thanks, guys."

Reaching into one of the boxes, I grab two tacos for me and two for Spencer. Before I can even reach for the hot sauce, Stella grabs my hand. "What is this?"

"That my dear, soon-to-be cousin in law, is an engagement ring." Spencer reaches for my free hand and gives it a light squeeze.

"Oh. My. Gosh. Congrats you two," she shrieks before rounding the table and throwing her arms around both of us. "It's about damn time."

"Let the insanity begin once again," Johnny laughs from his chair. "I'm happy for y'all."

"Stella," I pat her on the back. "I can't breathe."

"Oh, sorry," she releases us and takes a step back. "Am I the first to know? Please tell me I am."

"Yes, considering you barged in here."

"I cannot wait to tell Audrey that I knew first." She claps her hand and jumps up down. "She's going to be so pissed."

Oh great. I'll have to call her as soon as Stella leaves and tell her. If she hears it from me first, she won't be as upset. Stella goes to the fridge and opens the door. "Yes, you have orange juice." She glances around the counters. "Where's the vodka?"

"Y'all really are related," Spencer mutters to me. "We don't have any."

"Well," she sighs. "We'll have to celebrate with drinks at the house before y'all head back home. As soon as you can get your car out, I expect to see you."

There's no point arguing with her so I nod and take a seat. "She's about to take control of the whole thing, isn't she?" Spencer whispers in my ear.

"Yep." Hopefully we can reign her in. We aren't the traditional wedding sort of couple, and I'm sure she's going to balk at some of our ideas. But I'll let her have her fun…for now.

"We need to get you a wedding binder, and figure out a location." She pulls out her phone and starts listing notes of everything that needs to be done.

Leaning my head on Spencer's shoulder, I take in the scene before us. I was the wild child. The one my family thought would never settle down, much less get married. Spencer wraps his arm around me, cocooning me in his embrace. I can't wait to marry this man.

Also by Katrina Marie

Cousins Gone RomCom Series

Gone Country

Gone Steady

Gone Inn

Gone Before

Gone Again

Out of the Ashes Series

The Taking Chances Series

Cocky Hero Club

Big Baller

Baseball & Broadway

About the Author

Katrina Marie lives in the Dallas area with her husband, two children, and fur babies. She is a lover of all things geeky. When she's not writing you can find her at her children's sporting events, or curled up reading a book.
Visit her online: katrinamarieauthor.com
Sign up for her newsletter http://bit.ly/KatrinaMarieNewsletter

facebook.com/KatrinaMarieAuthor
tiktok.com/@katrinamarieauthor
instagram.com/katrinamarieauthor
twitter.com/katrmarieauthor
bookbub.com/profile/katrina-marie
amazon.com/Katrina-Marie/e/B0749SZVTK/ref=dp_byline_cont_ebooks_1